"Nothing sours the milk of human kindness more than getting pitchforked by a raging relative.

"I gave a beller which shook the acorns out of the oaks and whirled on Esau so quick it jerked the pitchfork out of his hands and left it sticking in my hide. I pulled it out and wrapped the handle around his neck. Then I took him by the ankles and started remodeling the landscape with him.

"I mowed down a sapling thicket with him, and leveled a cactus bed..."

ROBERT E. HOWARD

HEROES
OF
BEAR CREEK

ACE FANTASY BOOKS
NEW YORK

HEROES OF BEAR CREEK

An Ace Fantasy Book/published by arrangement with
the Estate of Robert E. Howard

PRINTING HISTORY
Ace edition/November 1983

ISBN: 0-441-32815-6

Ace Fantasy Books are published by The Berkley Publishing Group,
200 Madison Avenue, New York, New York 10016.
PRINTED IN THE UNITED STATES OF AMERICA

Acknowledgments

Slightly different versions of *Mountain Man, Guns of the Mountains, A Gent From Bear Creek, The Feud Buster, The Road to Bear Creek, The Scalp Hunter, Cupid From Bear Creek, The Haunted Mountain, Educate or Bust* (under the title *Sharp's Gun Serenade*) and *War on Bear Creek* appeared in *Action Stories*, copyright 1934, 1935, 1936 by Fiction House, Inc.

The Riot at Cougar Paw, copyright 1935 by Fiction House, Inc., for *Action Stories*, October 1935.

Pilgrims to the Pecos, copyright 1935 by Fiction House, Inc., for *Action Stories*, February 1936.

High Horse Rampage, copyright 1936 by Fiction House, Inc., for *Action Stories*, August 1936.

The Apache Mountain War, copyright 1935 by Fiction House, Inc., for *Action Stories*, December 1935.

Pistol Politics, copyright 1936 by Fiction House, Inc., for *Action Stories*, April 1936.

The Conquerin' Hero of the Humbolts, copyright 1936 by Fiction House, Inc., for *Action Stories*, October 1936.

A Ringtailed Tornado, copyright 1944 (under title *Texas John Alden*) by Better Publications, Inc., for *Masked Rider Western*, May 1944.

"No Cowherders Wanted," copyright 1936 by Fiction House, Inc., for *Action Stories*, September 1936.

Mayhem and Taxes, copyright 1967 by Mrs. P. M. Kuykendall for *The Summit County Journal*, September 8, 15, 22, 29, 1967.

Evil Deeds at Red Cougar, copyright 1936 by Fiction House, Inc., for *Action Stories*, June 1936.

Sharp's Gun Serenade, copyright 1936 by Fiction House, Inc., for *Action Stories*, January 1937.

Contents

Part One: A Gent From Bear Creek

Part Two: The Pride of Bear Creek

Part Three: Mayhem on Bear Creek

PART ONE:

A Gent From Bear Creek

CHAPTER I

Striped Shirts and Busted Hearts

If Joel Braxton hadn't drawed a knife whilst I was beating his head agen a spruce log, I reckon I wouldn't of had that quarrel with Glory McGraw, and things might of turned out different to what they did. Pap's always said the Braxtons was no-account folks, and I allow he's right. First thing I knowed Jim Garfield hollered: "Look out, Breck, the yaller hound's got a knife!" Then I felt a kind of sting and looked down and seen Joel had cut a big gash in my buckskin shirt and scratched my hide trying to get at my innards.

I let go of his ears and taken the knife away from him and throwed it into a blackjack thicket, and throwed him after it. They warn't no use in him bellyaching like he done just because they happened to be a tree in his way. I dunno how he expects to get throwed into a blackjack thicket without getting some hide knocked off.

But I am a good-natured man, and I was a easygoing youngster, even then. I paid no heed to Joel's bloodthirsty threats whilst his brother and Jim Garfield and the others was pulling him out of the bresh and dousing him in the creek to wash the blood off. I got on to my mule Alexander and headed for Old Man McGraw's cabin where I was started to when I let myself be beguiled into stopping with them idjits.

The McGraws is the only folks on Bear Creek besides the Reynoldses and the Braxtons which ain't no kin to me one way or another, and I'd been sweet on Glory McGraw ever since I was big enough to wear britches. She was the tallest, finest, purtiest

3

gal in the Humbolt Mountains, which is covering considerable territory. They warn't a gal on Bear Creek, not even my own sisters, which could swing a axe like her, or fry a b'ar steak as tasty, or make hominy as good, and they warn't nobody, man nor woman, which could outrun her, less'n it was me.

As I come up the trail that led up to the McGraw cabin, I seen her, just scooping a pail of water out of the creek. The cabin was just out of sight on the other side of a clump of alders. She turned around and seen me, and stood there with the pail dripping in her hand, and her sleeves rolled up, and her arms and throat and bare feet was as white as anything you ever seen, and her eyes was the same colour as the sky, and her hair looked like gold dust when the sun hit it.

I taken off my coonskin cap, and said: "Good mornin', Glory, how're you-all this mornin'?"

"Joe got kicked right severe by pap's sorrel mare yesterday," she says. "Just knocked some hide off, though. Outside of that we're all doin' fine. Air you glued to that mule?"

"No'm," I says, and clumb down, and says: "Lemme tote yore pail, Glory."

She started to hand it to me, and then she frowned and p'inted at my shirt, and says: "You been fightin' agen."

"Nobody but Joel Braxton," I said. "Twarn't nothin'. He said moskeeters in the Injun Territory was bigger'n what they be in Texas."

"What you know about it?" says she. "You ain't never been to Texas."

"Well, he ain't never been to the Injun Territory neither," I said. "'Taint the moskeeters. It's the principle of the thing. My folks all come from Texas, and no Braxton can slander the State around me."

"You fight too much," she said. "Who licked?"

"Why, me, of course," I said. "I always do, don't I?"

This harmless statement seemed to irritate her.

"I reckon you think nobody on Bear Creek can lick you," she sneered.

"Well," I says truthfully, "nobody ain't, up to now—outside of pap."

"You ain't never fit none of my brothers," she snapped.

"That's why," I said. "I've took quite a lot of sass offa them ganglin' mavericks jest because they was yore brothers and I didn't want to hurt 'em."

Gals is funny about some things. She got mad and jerked the

pail out of my hand, and says: "Oh, is that so? Well, lemme tell you right now, Breckinridge Elkins, the littlest one of my brothers can lick you like a balky hoss, and if you ever lay a finger on one of 'em, I'll fix you! And furthermore and besides, they's a gent up to the cabin right now which could pull his shootin' iron and decorate yore whole carcass with lead polka-dots whilst you was fumblin' for yore old cap-and-ball pistol!"

"I don't claim to be no gunfighter," I says mildly. "But I bet he cain't sling iron fast as my cousin Jack Gordon."

"You and yore cousins!" says she plenty scornful. "This feller is sech a gent as you never drempt existed! He's a cowpuncher from the Wild River Country, and he's ridin' through to Chawed Ear and he stopped at our cabin for dinner. If you could see him, you wouldn't never brag no more. You with that old mule and them moccasins and buckskin clothes!"

"Well, gosh, Glory!" I says plumb bewildered. "What's the matter with buckskin? I like it better'n homespun."

"Hah!" sneered she. "You oughta see Mr. Snake River Wilkinson! He ain't wearin' neither buckskins nor homespun. Store-bought clothes! I never seen such elegance. Star top boots, and gold-mounted spurs! And a red neckcloth—he said silk. I dunno. I never seen nothin' like it before. And a shirt all red and green and yaller and beautiful! And a white Stetson hat! And a pearl-handled six shooter! And the finest hoss and riggin's *you* ever seen, you big dummox!"

"Aw, well, gosh!" I said, getting irritated. "If this here Mister Wilkinson is so blame gorgeous, whyn't you marry him?"

I ought not to said it. Her eyes flashed blue sparks.

"I will!" she gritted. "You think a fine gentleman like him wouldn't marry me, hey? I'll show you! I'll marry him right now!"

And impulsively shattering her water bucket over my head she turned and run up the trail.

"Glory, wait!" I hollered, but by the time I got the water out of my eyes and the oak splinters out of my hair she was gone.

Alexander was gone too. He taken off down the creek when Glory started yelling at me, because he was a smart mule in his dumb way, and could tell when thunder-showers was brewing. I run him for a mile before I caught him, and then I got onto him and headed for the McGraw cabin agen. Glory was mad enough to do anything she thought would worry me, and they warn't nothing would worry me more'n for her to marry some dern cowpuncher from the river country. She was plumb wrong when she thought I thought he wouldn't have her. Any man which would pass up a chance to get hitched with Glory McGraw would be a dern fool, I don't care what color his shirt was.

My heart sunk into my moccasins as I approached the alder clump where we'd had our row. I figgered she'd stretched things a little talking about Mr. Wilkinson's elegance, because whoever heard of a shirt with three colours into it, or gold-mounted spurs? Still, he was bound to be rich and wonderful from what she said, and what chance did I have? All the clothes I had was what I had on, and I hadn't never even *seen* a store-bought shirt, much less owned one. I didn't know whether to fall down in the trail and have a good bawl, or go get my rifle-gun and lay for Mr. Wilkinson.

Then, jest as I got back to where I'd saw Glory last, here she come again, running like a scairt deer, with her eyes all wide and her mouth open.

"Breckinridge!" she panted. "Oh, Breckinridge! I've played hell now!"

"What you mean?" I said.

"Well," says she, "that there cowpuncher Mister Wilkinson had been castin' eyes at me ever since he arriv at our cabin, but I hadn't give him no encouragement. But you made me so mad awhile ago, I went back to the cabin, and I marched right up to him, and I says: 'Mister Wilkinson, did you ever think about gittin' married?' He grabbed me by the hand and he says, says he: 'Gal, I been thinkin' about it ever since I seen you choppin' wood outside the cabin as I rode by. Fact is, that's why I stopped here.' I was so plumb flabbergasted I didn't know what to say, and the first thing I knowed, him and pap was makin' arrangements for the weddin'!"

"Aw, gosh!" I said.

She started wringing her hands.

"I don't want to marry Mister Wilkinson!" she hollered. "I don't love him! He turnt my head with his elegant manners and striped shirt! What'll I do? Pap's sot on me marryin' the feller!"

"Well, I'll put a stop to that," I says. "No dern cowcountry dude can come into the Humbolts and steal my gal. Air they all up to the cabin now?"

"They're arguin' about the weddin' gift," says Glory. "Pap thinks Mister Wilkinson oughta give him a hundred dollars. Mister Wilkinson offered him his Winchester instead of cash. Be keerful, Breckinridge! Pap don't like you much, and Mister Wilkinson has got a awful mean eye, and his scabbard-end tied to his laig."

"I'll be plumb diplomatic," I promised, and got onto my mule

Alexander and reched down and lifted Glory on behind me, and
we rode up the path till we come to within maybe a hundred foot
of the cabin door. I seen a fine white hoss tied in front of the
cabin, and the saddle and bridle was the most elegant I ever seen.
The silverwork shone when the sun hit it. We got off and I tied
Alexander, and Glory hid behind a white oak. She warn't scairt
of nobody but her old man, but he shore had her number.

"Be keerful, Breckinridge," she begged. "Don't make pap or
Mister Wilkinson mad. Be tactful and meek."

So I said I would, and went up to the door. I could hear Miz
McGraw and the other gals cooking dinner in the back room, and
I could hear Old Man McGraw talking loud in the front room.

"'Taint enough!" says he. "I oughta have the Winchester and
ten dollars. I tell you, Wilkinson, it's cheap enough for a gal like
Glory! It plumb busts my heart strings to let her go, and nothin'
but greenbacks is goin' to soothe the sting!"

"The Winchester and five bucks," says a hard voice which I
reckoned was Mister Wilkinson. "It's a prime gun, I tell you. Ain't
another'n like it in these mountains."

"Well," begun Old Man McGraw in a covetous voice, and jest
then I come in through the door, ducking my head to keep from
knocking it agen the lintel-log.

Old Man McGraw was setting there, tugging at his black beard,
and them long gangling boys of his'n, Joe and Bill and John, was
there gawking as usual, and there on a bench nigh the empty
fireplace sot Mister Wilkinson in all his glory. I batted my eyes.
I never seen such splendour in all my born days. Glory had told
the truth about everything: the white Stetson with the fancy leather
band, and the boots and gold-mounted spurs, and the shirt. The
shirt nigh knocked my eyes out. I hadn't never dreamed nothing
could be so beautiful—all big broad stripes of red and yaller and
green! I seen his gun, too, a pearlhandled Colt .45 in a black
leather scabbard which was wore plumb smooth and the end tied
down to his laig with a rawhide thong. I could tell he hadn't never
wore a glove on his right hand, neither, by the brownness of it.
He had the hardest, blackest eyes I ever seen. They looked right
through me.

I was very embarrassed, being quite young then, but I pulled
myself together and says very polite: "Howdy, Mister McGraw."

"Who's this young grizzly?" demanded Mister Wilkinson suspiciously.

"Git out of here, Elkins," requested Old Man McGraw angrily.
"We're talkin' over private business. You git!"

"I know what kind of business you-all are talkin' over," I retorted; getting irritated. But I remembered Glory said be diplomatic, so I said: "I come here to tell you the weddin's off! Glory ain't goin' to marry Mister Wilkinson. She's goin' to marry me, and anybody which comes between us had better be able to rassle cougars and whup grizzlies bare-handed!"

"Why, you——" begun Mister Wilkinson in a blood-thirsty voice, as he riz onto his feet like a painter fixing to go into action.

"Git outa here!" bellered Old Man McGraw jumping up and grabbing the iron poker. "What I does with my datter ain't none of yore business! Mister Wilkinson here is makin' me a present of his prime Winchester and five dollars in hard money! What could *you* offer me, you mountain of beef and ignorance?"

"A bust in the snoot, you old tightwad," I replied heatedly, but still remembering to be diplomatic. They warn't no use in offending him, and I was determined to talk quiet and tranquil, in spite of his insults. So I said: "A man which would sell his datter for five dollars and a gun ought to be et alive by the buzzards! You try to marry Glory to Mister Wilkinson and see what happens to you, sudden and onpleasant!"

"Why, you——?" says Old Man McGraw, swinging up his poker. "I'll bust yore fool skull like a egg!"

"Lemme handle him," snarled Mister Wilkinson. "Git outa the way and gimme a clean shot at him. Lissen here, you jack-eared mountain-mule, air you goin' out of here perpendicular, or does you prefer to go horizontal?"

"Open the ball whenever you feels lucky, you stripe-bellied polecat!" I retorted courteously, and he give a snarl and went for his gun, but I got mine out first and shot it out of his hand along with one of his fingers before he could pull his trigger.

He give a howl and staggered back agen the wall, glaring wildly at me, and at the blood dripping off his hand, and I stuck my old cap-and-ball .44 back in the scabbard and said: "You may be accounted a fast gunslinger down in the low country, but yo're tolerable slow on the draw to be foolin' around Bear Creek. You better go on home now, and——"

It was at this moment that Old Man McGraw hit me over the head with his poker. He swung it with both hands as hard as he could, and if I hadn't had on my coonskin cap I bet it would have skint my head some. As it was it knocked me to my knees, me being offguard that way, and his three boys run in and started beating me with chairs and benches and a table laig. Well, I didn't want to hurt none of Glory's kin, but I had bit my tongue when the old man hit me with his poker, and that always did irritate me. Anyway, I seen they warn't no use arguing with them fool boys. They was out for blood—mine, to be exact.

So I riz up and taken Joe by the neck and crotch and throwed him through a winder as gentle as I could, but I forgot about the hickory-wood bars which was nailed across it to keep the bears out. He took 'em along with him, and that was how he got skint up like he did. I heard Glory let out a scream outside, and would have hollered out to let her know I was all right and for her not to worry about me, but just as I opened my mouth to do it, John jammed the butt-end of a table laig into it.

Sech treatment would try the patience of a saint, still and all I didn't really intend to hit John as hard as I did. How was I to know a tap like I give him would knock him through the door and dislocate his jawbone?

Old Man McGraw was dancing around trying to get another whack at me with his bent poker without hitting Bill which was hammering me over the head with a chair, but Mister Wilkinson warn't taking no part in the fray. He was backed up agen a wall with a wild look on his face. I reckon he warn't used to Bear Creek squabbles.

I taken the chair away from Bill and busted it over his head just to kinda cool him off a little, and jest then Old Man McGraw made another swipe at me with his poker, but I ducked and grabbed him, and Bill stooped over to pick up a bowie knife which had fell out of somebody's boot. His back was towards me so I planted my moccasin in the seat of his britches with considerable force and he shot head-first through the door with a despairing howl. Somebody else screamed too, that sounded like Glory. I didn't know at the time that she was running up to the door and was knocked down by Bill as he catapulted into the yard.

I couldn't see what was going on outside, and Old Man McGraw was chawing my thumb and feeling for my eye, so I throwed him after John and Bill, and he's a liar when he said I aimed him at that rain-barrel apurpose. I didn't even know they was one there till I heard the crash as his head went through the staves.

I turned around to have some more words with Mister Wilkinson, but he jumped through the winder I'd throwed Joe through, and when I tried to foller him, I couldn't get my shoulders through. So I run out at the door and Glory met me just as I hit the yard and she give me a slap in the face that sounded like a beaver hitting a mud bank with his tail.

"Why, Glory!" I says, dumbfounded, because her blue eyes

was blazing, and her yaller hair was nigh standing on end. She was so mad she was crying and that's the first time I ever knowed she *could* cry. "What's the matter? What've *I* did?"

"What have you did?" she raged, doing a kind of a war dance on her bare feet. "You outlaw! You murderer! You jack-eared son of a spotted tail skunk! Look what you done!" She p'inted at her old man dazedly pulling his head out of the rooins of the rainbarrel, and her brothers laying around the yard in various positions, bleeding freely and groaning loudly. "You tried to murder my family!" says she, shaking her fists under my nose. "You throwed Bill onto me on purpose!"

"I didn't neither!" I exclaimed, shocked and scandalized. "You know I wouldn't hurt a hair of yore head, Glory! Why, all I done, I done it for you——"

"You didn't have to mutilate my pap and my brothers!" she wept furiously. Ain't that just like a gal? What could I done but what I did? She hollered: "If you really loved me you wouldn't of hurt 'em! You jest done it for meanness! I told you to be ca'm and gentle! Whyn't you do it? Shet up! Don't talk to me! Well, whyn't you say somethin'? Ain't you got no tongue?"

"I handled 'em easy as I could!" I roared, badgered beyond endurance. "It warn't my fault. If they'd had any sense, they wouldn't——"

"Don't you dare slander my folks!" she yelped. "What you done to Mister Wilkinson?"

The aforesaid gent jest then come limping around the corner of the cabin, and started for his hoss, and Glory run to him and grabbed his arm, and said: "If you still want to marry me, stranger, it's a go! I'll ride off with you right now!"

He looked at me and shuddered, and jerked his arm away.

"Do I look like a dern fool?" he inquired with some heat. "I advises you to marry that young grizzly there, for the sake of public safety, if nothin' else! Marry you when *he* wants you? No, thank you! I'm leavin' a valuable finger as a sooverneer of my sojourn, but I figger it's a cheap price! After watchin' that human tornado in action, I calculate a finger ain't nothin' to bother about! *Adios!* If I ever come within a hundred miles of Bear Creek again it'll be because I've gone plumb loco!"

And with that he forked his critter and took off up the trail like the devil was after him.

"Now look what you done!" wept Glory. "Now he won't never marry me!"

"But I thought you didn't want to marry him!" I says, plumb bewildered.

She turned on me like a catamount.

"I didn't!" she shrieked. "I wouldn't marry him if he was the last man on earth! But I demands the right to say yes or no for myself! I don't aim to be bossed around by no hillbilly on a mangy mule!"

"Alexander ain't mangy," I said. "Besides, I warn't tryin' to boss you around, Glory. I war just fixin' it so yore pap wouldn't make you marry Mister Wilkinson. Bein' as we aims to marry ourselves——"

"Who said we aimed to?" she hollered. "Me marry you, after you beat up my pap and my brothers like you done? You think yo're the best man on Bear Creek! Ha! You with yore bucksin britches and old cap-and-ball pistol and coonskin cap! Me marry you? Git on yore mangy mule and git before I takes a shotgun to you!"

"All right!" I roared, getting mad at last. "All right, if that's the way you want to ack! You ain't the only gal in these mountains! They's plenty of gals which would be glad to have me callin' on 'em."

"Who, for a instance?" she sneered.

"Ellen Reynolds, for instance!" I bellered. "That's who!"

"All right!" says she, trembling with rage. "Go and spark that stuck-up hussy on yore mangy mule with yore old moccasins and cap-and-ball gun! See if I care!"

"I aim to!" I assured her bitterly. "And I won't be on no mule, neither. I'll be on the best hoss in the Humbolts, and I'll have me some boots on to my feet, and a silver mounted saddle and bridle, and a pistol that shoots store-bought ca'tridges, too! You wait and see!"

"Where you think you'll get 'em?" she sneered.

"Well, I will!" I bellered, seeing red. "You said I thought I was the best man on Bear Creek! Well, by golly, I am, and I aim to prove it! I'm glad you gimme the gate! If you hadn't I'd of married you and settled down in a cabin up the creek somewheres and never done nothin' nor seen nothin' nor been nothin' but yore husband! Now I'm goin' to plumb bust this State wide open from one end to the other'n, and folks is goin' to know about me all over everywheres!"

"Heh! heh! heh!" she laughed bitterly.

"I'll show you!" I promised her wrathfully, as I forked my

mule, and headed down the trail with her laughter ringing in my ears. I kicked Alexander most vicious in the ribs, and he give a bray of astonishment and lit a shuck for home. A instant later the alder clump hid the McGraw cabin from view and Glory McGraw and my boyhood dreams was out of sight behind me.

CHAPTER II

Mountain Man

"I'll show her!" I promised the world at large, as I rode through the bresh as hard as Alexander could run. "I'll go out into the world and make a name for myself, by golly! She'll see. Whoa, Alexander!"

Because I'd jest seen a bee-tree I'd located the day before. My busted heart needed something to soothe it, and I figgered fame and fortune could wait a little whilst I drowned my woes in honey.

I was up to me ears in this beverage when I heard my old man calling: "Breckinridge! Oh, Breckinridge! Whar air you? I see you now. You don't need to climb that tree. I ain't goin' to larrup you."

He come up and said: "Breckinridge, ain't that a bee settin' on to yore ear?"

I reched up, and sure enough, it was. Come to think about it, I had felt kind of like something was stinging me somewheres.

"I swan, Breckinridge," says pap, "I never seen a hide like yore'n not even amongst the Elkinses. Listen to me now: old Buffalo Rogers jest come through on his way back from Tomahawk, and the postmaster there said they was a letter for me, from Mississippi. He wouldn't give it to nobody but me or some of my folks. I dunno who'd be writin' me from Mississippi; last time I was there was when I was fightin' the Yankees. But anyway, that letter is got to be got. Me and yore maw have decided yo're to go git it."

"Clean to Tomahawk?" I said. "Gee whiz, Pap!"

"Well," he says, combing his beard with his fingers, "yo're

13

growed in size, if not in years. It's time you seen somethin' of the world. You ain't never been more'n thirty miles away from the cabin you was born in. Yore brother Garfield ain't able to go on account of that b'ar he tangled with, and Buckner is busy skinnin' the b'ar. You been to whar the trail goin' to Tomahawk passes. All you got to do is foller it and turn to the right whar it forks. The left goes to Perdition."

"Great!" I says. "This is whar I begins to see the world!" And I added to myself: "This is whar I begins to show Glory McGraw I'm a man of importance, by golly!"

Well, next morning before good daylight I was off, riding my mule Alexander, with a dollar pap gimme stuck in the bottom of my pistol scabbard. Pap rode with me a few miles and give me advice.

"Be keerful how you spend that dollar I give you," he said. "Don't gamble. Drink in reason. Half a gallon of corn juice is enough for any man. Don't be techy—but don't forgit that yore pap was once the rough-and-tumble champeen of Gonzales County, Texas. And whilst yo're feelin' for the other feller's eye, don't be keerless and let him chaw yore ear off. And don't resist no officer."

"What's them, Pap?" I inquired.

"Down in the settlements," he explained, "they has men which their job is to keep the peace. I don't take no stock in law myself, but them city folks is different from us. You do what they says, and if they says give up yore gun, even, why you up and do it!"

I was shocked, and meditated a while, and then says: "How can I tell which is them?"

"They'll have a silver star stuck onto their shirt," he says, so I said I'd do like he told me. He then reined around and went back up the mountains, and I rode on down the path.

Well, I camped late that night where the path come out onto the Tomahawk trail, and the next morning I rode on down the trail, feeling like I was a long way from home. It was purty hot, and I hadn't went far till I passed a stream and decided I'd take a swim. So I tied Alexander to a cottonwood, and hung my buckskins close by, but I taken my gun belt with my cap-and-ball .44 and hung it on a willer limb reching out over the water. They was thick bushes all around the stream.

Well, I div deep, and as I come up, I had a feeling like somebody had hit me over the head with a club. I looked up, and there was a Injun holding on to a limb with one hand and leaning out over the water with a club in the other hand.

He yelled and swung at me again, but I div, and he missed, and I come up right under the limb where my gun was hung. I reched up and grabbed it and let bam at him just as he dived into the bushes, and he let out a squall and grabbed the seat of his pants. Next minute I heard a horse running, and glimpsed him tearing away through the bresh on a pinto mustang, setting his hoss like it was a red-hot stove, and dern him, he had my clothes in one hand! I was so upsot by this that I missed him clean, and jumping out, I charged through the bushes and saplings, but he was already out of sight. I knowed it warn't likely he was with a war-party—just a dern thieving Piute—but what a fix I was in! He'd even stole my moccasins.

I couldn't go home, in that shape, without the letter, and admit I missed a Injun twice. Pap would larrup the tar out of me. And if I went on, what if I met some women, in the valley settlements? I don't reckon they ever was a young'un half as bashful as what I was in them days. Cold sweat busted out all over me. I thought, here I started out to see the world and show Glory McGraw I was a man among men, and here I am with no more clothes than a jackrabbit. At last, in desperation, I buckled on my belt and started down the trail towards Tomahawk. I was about ready to commit murder to get me some pants.

I was glad the Injun didn't steal Alexander, but the going was so rough I had to walk and lead him, because I kept to the thick bresh alongside the trail. He had a tough time getting through the bushes, and the thorns scratched him so he hollered, and ever' now an then I had to lift him over jagged rocks. It was tough on Alexander, but I was too bashful to travel in the open trail without no clothes on.

After I'd gone maybe a mile I heard somebody in the trail ahead of me, and peeking through the bushes, I seen a most pecooliar sight. It was a man on foot, going the same direction as me, and he had on what I instinctly guessed was city clothes. They warn't buckskin nor homespun, nor yet like the duds Mister Wilkinson had on, but they were very beautiful, with big checks and stripes all over 'em. He had on a round hat with a narrer brim, and shoes like I hadn't never seen before, being neither boots nor moccasins. He was dusty, and he cussed considerable as he limped along. Ahead of him I seen the trail made a hoss-shoe bend, so I cut straight across and got ahead of him, and as he come along, I come out of the bresh and throwed down on him with my cap-and-ball.

He throwed up his hands and hollered: "Don't shoot!"

"I don't want to, mister," I said, "but I got to have clothes!"

He shook his head like he couldn't believe I was so, and he said: "You ain't the colour of a Injun, but—what kind of people live in these hills, anyway?"

"Most of 'em's Democrats," I said. "But I ain't got no time to talk politics. You climb out of them riggin's."

"My God!" he wailed. "My horse threw me off and ran away, and I've bin walkin' for hours, expecting to get scalped by Injuns any minute, and now a naked lunatic on a mule demands my clothes! It's too dern much!"

"I cain't argy, mister," I said; "somebody's liable to come up the trail any minute. Hustle!" So saying I shot his hat off to encourage him.

He give a howl and shucked his duds in a hurry.

"My underclothes, too?" he demanded, shivering though it was very hot.

"Is that what them things is?" I demanded, shocked. "I never heard of a man wearin' such womanish things. The country is goin' to the dogs, just like pap says. You better git goin'. Take my mule. When I git to where I can git some regular clothes, we'll swap back."

He clumb on to Alexander kind of dubious, and says to me, despairful: "Will you tell me one thing—how do I get to Tomahawk?"

"Take the next turn to the right," I said, "and——"

Jest then Alexander turned his head and seen them underclothes on his back, and he give a loud and ringing bray and sot sail down the trail at full speed with the stranger hanging on with both hands. Before they was out of sight they come to where the trail forked, and Alexander taken the left branch instead of the right, and vanished amongst the ridges.

I put on the clothes, and they scratched my hide something fierce. I thinks, well, I got store-bought clothes quicker'n I hoped to. But I didn't think much of 'em. The coat split down the back, and the pants was too short, but the shoes was the wust; they pinched all over. I throwed away the socks, having never wore none, but put on what was left of the hat.

I went on down the trail, and taken the right-hand fork, and in a mile or so I come out on a flat, and heard hosses running. The next thing a mob of men on hosses bust into view. One of 'em yelled: "There he is!" and they all come for me full tilt. Instantly I decided that the stranger had got to Tomahawk after all, somehow, and had sot his friends onto me for stealing his clothes.

So I left the trail and took out across the sage grass, and they all charged after me, yelling stop. Well, them dern shoes pinched my feet so bad I couldn't make much speed, so after I had run maybe a quarter of a mile I perceived that the hosses were beginning to gain on me. So I wheeled with my cap-and-ball in my hand, but I was going so fast, when I turned, them dern shoes slipped and I went over backwards into a cactus bed just as I pulled the trigger. So I only knocked the hat off of the first hossman. He yelled and pulled up his hoss, right over me nearly, and as I drawed another bead on him, I see he had a bright shiny star onto his shirt. I dropped my gun and stuck up my hands.

They swarmed around me—cowboys, from their looks. The man with the star got off his hoss and picked up my gun and cussed.

"What did you lead us this chase through this heat and shoot at me for?" he demanded.

"I didn't know you was a officer," I said.

"Hell, McVey," said one of 'em, "you know how jumpy tenderfeet is. Likely he thought we was Santry's outlaws. Where's yore hoss?"

"I ain't got none," I said.

"Got away from you, hey?" said McVey. "Well, climb up behind Kirby here, and let's git goin'."

To my surprise, the sheriff stuck my gun back in the scabbard, and so I clumb up behind Kirby, and away we went. Kirby kept telling me not to fall off, and it made me mad, but I said nothing. After an hour or so we come to a bunch of houses they said was Tomahawk. I got panicky when I see all them houses, and would have jumped down and run for the mountains, only I knowed they'd catch me, with them dern pinchy shoes on.

I hadn't seen such houses before. They was made out of boards, mostly, and some was two stories high. To the northwest and west the hills riz up a few hundred yards from the backs of the houses, and on the other sides there was plains with bresh and timber on them.

"You boys ride into town and tell the folks that the shebang starts soon," said McVey. "Me and Kirby and Richards will take him to the ring."

I could see people milling around in the streets, and I never had no idee they was that many folks in the world. The sheriff and the other two fellers rode around the north end of the town and stopped at a old barn and told me to get off. So I did, and we went in and they had a kind of room fixed up in there with benches and a lot of towels and water buckets, and the sheriff said: "This ain't much of a dressin' room, but it'll have to do. Us boys don't know much about this game, but we'll second you as good as we can. One thing—the other feller ain't got no manager nor seconds neither. How do you feel?"

"Fine," I said, "but I'm kind of hungry."

"Go git him somethin', Richards," said the sheriff.

"I didn't think they et just before a bout," said Richards.

"Aw, I reckon he knows what he's doin'," said McVey. "Gwan."

So Richards pulled out, and the sheriff and Kirby walked around me like I was a prize bull, and felt my muscles, and the sheriff said: "By golly, if size means anything, our dough is as good as in our britches right now!"

I pulled my dollar out of my scabbard and said I would pay for my keep, and they haw-hawed and slapped me on the back and said I was a great joker. Then Richards come back with a platter of grub, with a lot of men wearing boots and guns and whiskers, and they stomped in and gawped at me, and McVey said: "Look him over, boys! Tomahawk stands or falls with him to-day!"

They started walking around me like him and Kirby done, and I was embarrassed and et three or four pounds of beef and a quart of mashed pertaters, and a big hunk of white bread, and drunk about a gallon of water, because I was purty thirsty. Then they all gaped like they was surprised about something, and one of 'em said: "How come he didn't arrive on the stage coach yesterday?"

"Well," said the sheriff, "the driver told me he was so drunk they left him at Bisney, and come on with his luggage, which is over there in the corner. They got a hoss and left it there with instructions for him to ride on to Tomahawk as soon as he sobered up. Me and the boys got nervous today when he didn't show up, so we went out lookin' for him, and met him hoofin' it down the trail."

"I bet them Perdition *hombres* starts somethin'," said Kirby. "Ain't a one of 'em showed up yet. They're settin' over at Perdition soakin' up bad licker and broodin' on their wrongs. They shore wanted this show staged over there. They claimed that since Tomahawk was furnishin' one-half of the attraction, and Gunstock the other half, the razee ought to be throwed at Predition."

"Nothin' to it," said McVey. "It laid between Tomahawk and

Gunstock, and we throwed a coin and won it. If Perdition wants trouble she can git it. Is the boys r'arin' to go?"

"Is they!" says Richards. "Every bar in Tomahawk is crowded with *hombres* full of licker and civic pride. They're bettin' their shirts, and they has been nine fights already. Everybody in Gunstock's here."

"Well, le's git goin'," says McVey, getting nervous. "The quicker it's over, the less blood there's likely to be spilt."

The first thing I knowed, they had laid hold of me and was pulling my clothes off, so it dawned on me that I must be under arrest for stealing that stranger's clothes. Kirby dug into the baggage which was in one corner of the stall, and dragged out a funny looking pair of pants; I know now they was white silk. I put 'em on because I didn't have nothing else to put on, and they fitted me like my skin. Richards tied a American flag around my waist, and they put some spiked shoes onto my feet.

I let 'em do like they wanted to, remembering what pap said about not resisting no officer. Whilst so employed I begun to hear a noise outside, like a lot of people whooping and cheering. Purty soon in come a skinny old gink with whiskers and two guns on, and he hollered: "Lissen here, Mac, dern it, a big shipment of gold is down there waitin' to be took off by the evenin' stage, and the whole blame town is deserted on account of this dern foolishness. Suppose Comanche Santry and his gang gits wind of it?"

"Well," said McVey, "I'll send Kirby here to help you guard it."

"You will like hell," says Kirby. "I'll resign as deputy first. I got every cent of my dough on this scrap, and I aim to see it."

"Well, send somebody!" says the old codger. "I got enough to do runnin' my store, and the stage stand, and the post office, without——"

He left, mumbling in his whiskers, and I said: "Who's that?"

"Aw," said Kirby, "that's old man Brenton that runs the store down at the other end of town, on the east side of the street. The post office is in there, too."

"I got to see him," I says. "There's a letter——"

Just then another man come surging in and hollered: "Hey, is yore man ready? Folks is gittin' impatient!"

"All right," says McVey, throwing over me a thing he called a bathrobe. Him and Kirby and Richards picked up towels and buckets and things, and we went out the oppersite door from what we come in, and they was a big crowd of people there, and they whooped and shot off their pistols. I would have bolted back into the barn, only they grabbed me and said it was all right. We pushed through the crowd, and I never seen so many boots and pistols in my life, and we come to a square corral made out of four posts sot in the ground, and ropes stretched between. They called this a ring and told me to get in. I done so, and they had turf packed down so the ground was level as a floor and hard and solid. They told me to set down on a stool in one corner, and I did, and wrapped my robe around me like a Injun.

Then everybody yelled, and some men, from Gunstock, McVey said, clumb through the ropes on the other side. One of 'em was dressed like I was, and I never seen such a funny-looking human. His ears looked like cabbages, and his nose was plumb flat, and his head was shaved and looked right smart like a bullet. He sot down in a oppersite corner.

Then a feller got up and waved his arms, and hollered: "Gents, you all know the occasion of this here suspicious event. Mister Bat O'Tool, happenin' to be passin' through Gunstock, consented to fight anybody which would meet him. Tomahawk riz to the occasion by sendin' all the way to Denver to procure the services of Mister Bruiser McGoorty, formerly of San Francisco!"

He p'inted at me, and everybody cheered and shot off their pistols, and I was embarrassed and burst out in a cold sweat.

"This fight," said the feller, "will be fit accordin' to London Prize Ring Rules, same as in a champeenship go. Bare fists, round ends when one of 'em's knocked down or throwed down. Fight lasts till one or t'other ain't able to come up to the scratch when time's called. I, Yucca Blaine, have been selected as referee because, bein' from Chawed Ear, I got no prejudices either way. Air you all ready? Time!"

McVey hauled me off my stool and pulled off my bathrobe and pushed me out into the ring. I nearly died with embarrassment, but I seen the feller they called O'Tool didn't have on no more clothes than me. He approached and held out his hand like he wanted to shake hands, so I held out mine. We shook hands, and then without no warning he hit me a awful lick on the jaw with his left. It was like being kicked by a mule. The first part of me which hit the turf was the back of my head. O'Tool stalked back to his corner, and the Gunstock boys was dancing and hugging each other, and the Tomahawk fellers was growling in their whiskers and fumbling with their guns and bowie knives.

McVey and his deperties rushed into the ring before I could

get up and dragged me to my corner and began pouring water on me.

"Air you hurt much?" yelled McVey.

"How can a man's fist hurt anybody?" I ast. "I wouldn't of fell down, only I was caught off-guard. I didn't know he was goin' to hit me. I never played no game like this here'n before."

McVey dropped the towel he was beating me in the face with, and turned pale. "Ain't you Bruiser McGoorty of San Francisco?" he hollered.

"Naw," I said. "I'm Breckinridge Elkins, from up in the Humbolt Mountains. I come here to git a letter for pap."

"But the stage coach driver described them clothes——" he begun wildly.

"A Injun stole my clothes," I explained, "so I taken some off'n a stranger. Maybe that was Mister McGoorty."

"What's the matter?" ast Kirby, coming up with another bucket of water. "Time's about ready to be called."

"We're sunk!" bawled McVey. "This ain't McGoorty! This is a derned hillbilly which murdered McGoorty and stole his clothes!"

"We're rooint!" exclaimed Richards, aghast. "Everybody's bet their dough without even seein' our man, they was that full of trust and civic pride. We cain't call it off now. Tomahawk is rooint! What'll we do?"

"He's goin' to git in there and fight his derndest," said McVey, pulling his gun and jamming it into my back. "We'll hang him after the fight."

"But he cain't box!" wailed Richards.

"No matter," said McVey; "the fair name of our town is at stake; Tomahawk promised to supply a fighter to fight O'Tool, and——"

"Oh!" I said, suddenly seeing light. "This here is a fight then, ain't it?"

McVey give a low moan, and Kirby reched for his gun, but just then the referee hollered time, and I jumped up and run at O'Tool. If a fight was all they wanted, I was satisfied. All that talk about rules, and the yelling of the crowd and all had had me so confused I hadn't knowed what it was all about. I hit at O'Tool and he ducked and hit me in the belly and on the nose and in the eye and on the ear. The blood spurted, and the crowd hollered, and he looked plumb dumbfounded and gritted betwixt his teeth: "Are you human? Why don't you fall?"

I spit out a mouthful of blood and got my hands on him and

started chawing his ear, and he squalled like a catamount. Yucca run in and tried to pull me loose and I give him a slap under the ear and he turned a somersault into the ropes.

"Yore man's fightin' foul!" he squalled, and Kirby said: "Yo're crazy! Do you see this gun? You holler 'foul' just once more, and it'll go off!"

Meanwhile O'Tool had broke loose from me and caved in his knuckles on my jaw, and I come for him again, because I was beginning to lose my temper. He gasped: "If you want to make an alley-fight out of it, all right. I wasn't raised in Five Points for nothing!" He then rammed his knee into my groin, and groped for my eye, but I got his thumb in my teeth and begun masticating it, and the way he howled was a caution.

By this time the crowd was crazy, and I throwed O'Tool and begun to stomp him, when somebody let bang at me from the crowd and the bullet cut my silk belt and my pants started to fall down.

I grabbed 'em with both hands, and O'Tool riz up and rushed at me, bloody and bellering, and I didn't dare let go my pants to defend myself. I whirled and bent over and lashed out backwards with my right heel like a mule, and I caught him under the chin. He done a cartwheel in the air, his head hit the turf, and he bounced on over and landed on his back with his knees hooked over the lower rope. There warn't no question about him being out. The only question was, was he dead?

A roar of "Foul!" went up from the Gunstock men, and guns bristled all around the ring.

The Tomahawk men was cheering and yelling that I'd won fair and square, and the Gunstock men was cussing and threatening me, when somebody hollered: "Leave it to the referee!"

"Sure," said Kirby. "He knows our man won fair, and if he don't say so, I'll blow his head off!"

"That's a lie!" bellered a Gunstock man. "He knows it war a foul, and if he says it warn't, I'll kyarve his gizzard with this here bowie knife!"

At them words Yucca fainted, and then a clatter of hoofs sounded above the din, and out of the timber that hid the trail from the east a gang of hossmen rode at a run. Everybody yelled: "Look out, here comes them Perdition illegitimates!"

Instantly a hundred guns covered 'em, and McVey demanded: "Come ye in peace or in war?"

"We come to unmask a fraud!" roared a big man with a red

bandanner around his neck. "McGoorty, come forth!"

A familiar figger, now dressed in cowboy togs, pushed forward on my mule. "There he is!" this figger yelled, p'inting a accusing finger at me. "That's the desperado that robbed me! Them's my tights he's got on!"

"What is this?" roared the crowd.

"A cussed fake!" bellered the man with the red bandanner. "This here is Bruiser McGoorty!"

"Then who's he?" somebody bawled, p'inting at me.

"I'm Breckinridge Elkins and I can lick any man here!" I roared, getting mad. I brandished my fists in defiance, but my britches started sliding down again, so I had to shut up and grab 'em.

"Aha!" the man with the red bandanner howled like a hyener. "He admits it! I dunno what the idee is, but these Tomahawk polecats has double-crossed somebody! I trusts that you jackasses from Gunstock realizes the blackness and hellishness of their hearts! This man McGoorty rode into Perdition a few hours ago in his unmentionables, astraddle of that there mule, and told us how he'd been held up and robbed and put on the wrong road. You skunks was too proud to stage this fight in Perdition, but we ain't the men to see justice scorned with impunity! We brought McGoorty here to show you that you was bein' gypped by Tomahawk! That man ain't no prize fighter; he's a highway robber!"

"These Tomahawk coyotes has framed us!" squalled a Gunstock man, going for his gun.

"Yo're a liar!" roared Richards, bending a .45 barrel over his head.

The next instant guns was crashing, knives was gleaming, and men was yelling blue murder. The Gunstock braves turned frothing on the Tomahawk warriors, and the men from Perdition, yelping with glee, pulled their guns, and begun fanning the crowd indiscriminately, which give back their fire. McGoorty give a howl and fell down on Alexander's neck, gripping around it with both arms, and Alexander departed in a cloud of dust and gun-smoke.

I grabbed my gunbelt, which McVey had hung over the post in my corner, and I headed for cover, holding onto my britches whilst the bullets hummed around me as thick as bees. I wanted to take to the bresh, but I remembered that blamed letter, so I headed for town. Behind me there riz a roar of banging guns and yelling men. Jest as I got to the backs of the row of buildings which lined the street, I run head on into something soft. It was McGoorty, trying to escape on Alexander. He had hold of jest one rein, and Alexander, evidently having rounded one end of the town, was travelling in a circle and heading back where he started from.

I was going so fast I couldn't stop, and I run right over Alexander and all three of us went down in a heap. I jumped up, afeared Alexander was kilt or crippled, but he scrambled up snorting and trembling, and then McGoorty weaved up, making funny noises. I poked my cap-and-ball into his belly.

"Off with them pants!" I hollered.

"My God!" he screamed. *"Again?* This is getting to be a habit!"

"Hustle!" I bellered. "You can have these scandals I got on now."

He shucked his britches and grabbed them tights and run like he was afeared I'd want his underwear too. I jerked on the pants, forked Alexander and headed for the south end of town. I kept behind the houses, though the town seemed to be deserted, and purty soon I come to the store where Kirby had told me old man Brenton kept the post office. Guns was barking there, and across the street I seen men ducking in and out behind a old shack, and shooting.

I tied Alexander to a corner of the store and went in the back door. Up in the front part I seen old man Brenton kneeling behind some barrels with a .45-90, and he was shooting at the fellers in the shack acrost the street. Every now and then a slug would hum through to door and comb his whiskers, and he would cuss worse'n pap did that time he sot down in a b'ar trap.

I went up to him and tapped him on the shoulder and he give a squall and flopped over and let go *bam!* right in my face and singed off my eyebrows. And the fellers across the street hollered and started shooting at both of us.

I'd grabbed the barrel of his Winchester, and he was cussing and jerking at it with one hand and feeling in his boot for a knife with the other'n, and I said: "Mister Brenton, if you ain't too busy, I wish you'd gimme that there letter which come for pap."

"Don't never come up behind me like that again!" he squalled. "I thought you was one of them dern outlaws! Look out! Duck, you blame fool!"

I let go of his gun, and he taken a shot at a head which was aiming around the corner of the shack, and the head let out a squall and disappeared.

"Who is them fellers?" I ast.

"Comanche Santry and his bunch, from up in the hills," snarled old man Brenton, jerking the lever of his Winchester. "They come after that gold. A hell of a sheriff McVey is; never sent me nobody. And them fools over at the ring are makin' so much noise they'll never hear the shootin' over here. Look out, here they come!"

Six or seven men rushed out from behind the shack and run acrost the street, shooting as they come. I seen I'd never get my letter as long as all this fighting was going on, so I unslung my old cap-and-ball and let bam at them three times, and three of them outlaws fell acrost each other in the street, and the rest turned around and run back behind the shack.

"Good work, boy!" yelled old man Brenton. "If I ever—oh, Judas Iscariot, we're blowed up now!"

Something was pushed around the corner of the shack and come rolling down towards us, the shack being on higher ground than what the store was. It was a keg, with a burning fuse which whirled as the keg revolved and looked like a wheel of fire.

"What's in that there kaig?" I ast.

"Blastin' powder!" screamed old man Brenton, scrambling up. "Run, you dern fool! It's comin' right into the door!"

He was so scairt he forgot all about the fellers acrost the street, and one of 'em caught him in the thigh with a buffalo rifle, and he plunked down again, howling blue murder. I stepped over him to the door—that's when I got the slug in my hip—and the keg hit my laigs and stopped, so I picked it up and heaved it back acrost the street. It hadn't no more'n hit the shack when *bam!* it exploded and the shack went up in smoke. When it stopped raining pieces of wood and metal, they warn't no sign to show any outlaws had ever hid behind where that shack had been.

"I wouldn't believe it if I hadn't saw it myself," old man Brenton moaned faintly.

"Air you hurt bad, Mister Brenton?" I ast.

"I'm dyin'," he groaned.

"Well, before you die, Mister Brenton," I says, "would you mind givin' me that there letter for pap?"

"What's yore pap's name?" he ast.

"Roarin' Bill Elkins, of Bear Creek," I said.

He warn't as bad hurt as he thought. He reched up and got hold of a leather bag and fumbled in it and pulled out a envelope. "I remember tellin' old Buffalo Rogers I had a letter for Bill Elkins," he said, fingering it over. Then he said: "Hey, wait! This ain't for yore pap. My sight is gittin' bad. I read it wrong the first time. This here is for Bill *Elston* that lives between here and Perdition."

I want to spike a rumour which says I tried to murder old man

Brenton and tore down his store for spite. I've done told how he got his laig broke, and the rest was accidental. When I realized that I had went through all that embarrassment for nothing, I was so mad and disgusted I turned and run out of the back door, and I forgot to open the door and that's how it got tore off the hinges.

I then jumped on to Alexander and forgot to ontie him loose from the store. I kicked him in the ribs, and he bolted and tore loose that corner of the building and that's how come the roof to fall in. Old man Brenton inside was scairt and started yelling bloody murder, and about that time a mob of men come up to investigate the explosion which had stopped the three-cornered battle between Perdition, Tomahawk and Gunstock, and they thought I was the cause of everything, and they all started shooting at me as I rode off.

Then was when I got that charge of buckshot in my back.

I went out of Tomahawk and up the hill trail so fast I bet me and Alexander looked like a streak; and I says to myself it looks like making a name for myself in the world is going to be tougher than I thought, because it's evident that civilization is full of snares for a boy which ain't reched his full growth and strength.

CHAPTER III

Meet Cap'n Kidd

I didn't pull up Alexander till I was plumb out of sight of Toma-hawk. Then I slowed down and taken stock of myself, and my spirits was right down in my spiked shoes which still had some of Mister O'Tool's hide stuck onto the spikes. Here I'd started forth into the world to show Glory McGraw what a he-bearcat I was, and now look at me. Here I was without even no clothes but them derned spiked shoes which pinched my feet, and a pair of britches some cow-puncher had wore the seat out and patched with buckskin. I still had my gunbelt and the dollar pap gimme, but no place to spend it. I likewise had a goodly amount of lead under my hide.

"By Golly!" I says, shaking my fists at the universe at large. "I ain't goin' to go back to Bear Creek like this, and have Glory McGraw laughin' at me! I'll head for the Wild River settlements and git me a job punchin' cows till I got money enough to buy me store-bought boots and a hoss!"

I then pulled out my bowie knife which was in a scabbard on my gunbelt, and started digging the slug out of my hip, and the buckshot out of my back. Them buckshot was kinda hard to get to, but I done it. I hadn't never held a job of punching cows, but I'd had plenty experience roping wild bulls up in the Humbolts. Them bulls wanders off the lower ranges into the mountains and grows most amazing big and mean. Me and Alexander had had plenty experience with them, and I had me a lariat which would hold any steer that ever bellered. It was still tied to my saddle, and I was glad none of them cow-punchers hadn't stole it. Maybe they didn't know it was a lariat. I'd made it myself, especial, and used it to rope them bulls and also cougars and grizzlies which infests the Humbolts. It was made out of buffalo hide, ninety foot long and half again as thick and heavy as the average lariat, and the honda was a half-pound chunk of iron beat into shape with a sledge hammer. I reckoned I was qualified for a *vaquero* even if I didn't have no cowboy clothes and was riding a mule.

So I headed acrost the mountains for the cowcountry. They warn't no trail the way I taken, but I knowed the direction Wild River lay in, and that was enough for me. I knowed if I kept going that way I'd hit it after awhile. Meanwhile, they was plenty of grass in the draws and along the creeks to keep Alexander fat and sleek, and plenty of squirrels and rabbits for me to knock over with rocks. I camped that night away up in the high ranges and cooked me nine or ten squirrels over a fire and et 'em, and while that warn't much of a supper for a appertite like mine, still I figgered next day I'd stumble on to a b'ar or maybe a steer which had wandered offa the ranges.

Next morning before sunup I was on Alexander and moving on, without no breakfast, because it looked like they warn't no rabbits nor nothing near abouts, and I rode all morning without sighting nothing. It was a high range, and nothing alive there but a buzzard I seen onst, but late in the afternoon I crossed a backbone and come down into a whopping big plateau about the size of a county, with springs and streams and grass growing stirrup-high along 'em, and clumps of cottonwood, and spruce, and pine thick up on the hillsides. They was canyons and cliffs, and mountains along the rim, and altogether it was as fine a country as I ever seen, but it didn't look like nobody lived there, and for all I know I was the first white man that ever come into it. But they was more soon, as I'll relate.

Well, I noticed something funny as I come down the ridge that separated the bare hills from the plateau. First I met a wildcat. He come lipping along at a right smart clip, and he didn't stop. He just gimme a wicked look sidewise and kept right on up the slope. Next thing I met a lobo wolf, and after that I counted nine more wolves, and they was all heading west, up the slopes. Then Alexander give a snort and started trembling, and a cougar slid out of a blackjack thicket and snarled at us over his shoulder as he went past at a long lope. All them varmints was heading for the dry bare country I'd just left, and I wondered why they was leaving a good range like this one to go into that dern no-account country.

It worried Alexander too, because he smelt of the air and brayed

kind of plaintively. I pulled him up and smelt the air too, because
critters run like that before a forest fire, but I couldn't smell no
smoke, nor see none. So I rode on down the slopes and started
across the flats, and as I went I seen more bobcats, and wolves,
and painters, and they was all heading west, and they warn't
lingering none, neither. They warn't no doubt that them critters
was pulling their freight because they was scairt of something,
and it warn't humans, because they didn't 'pear to be scairt of me
a mite. They jest swerved around me and kept trailing. After I'd
gone a few miles I met a herd of wild hosses, with the stallion
herding 'em. He was a big mean-looking cuss, but he looked scairt
as bad as any of the critters I'd saw.

The sun was getting low, and I was getting awful hungry as I
come into a open spot with a creek on one side running through
clumps of willers and cottonwoods, and on the other side I could
see some big cliffs looming up over the tops of the trees. And
whilst I was hesitating, wondering if I ought to keep looking for
eatable critters, or try to worry along on a wildcat or a wolf, a
big grizzly come lumbering out of a clump of spruces and headed
west. When he seen me and Alexander he stopped and snarled
like he was mad about something, and then the first thing I knowed
he was charging us. So I pulled my .44 and shot him through the
head, and got off and onsaddled Alexander and turnt him loose
in grass stirrup-high, and skun the b'ar. Then I cut me off some
steaks and started a fire and begun reducing my appertite. That
warn't no small job, because I hadn't had nothing to eat since the
night before.

Well, while I was eating I heard hosses and looked up and seen
six men riding towards me from the east. One was as big as me,
but the other ones warn't but about six foot tall apiece. They was
cowpunchers, by their look, and the biggest man was dressed
plumb as elegant as Mister Wilkinson was, only his shirt was jest
only one colour. But he had on fancy boots and a white Stetson
and a ivory-butted Colt, and what looked like the butt of a sawed-
off shotgun jutted out of his saddle-scabbard. He was dark and
had awful mean eyes, and a jaw which it looked like he could bite
the spokes out of a wagon wheel if he wanted to.

He started talking to me in Piute, but before I could say anything, one of the others said: "Aw, that ain't no Injun, Donovan,
his eyes ain't the right colour."

"I see that, now," says Donovan. "But I shore thought he was
a Injun when I first rode up and seen them old ragged britches
and his sunburnt hide. Who the devil air you?"

"I'm Breckinridge Elkins, from Bear Creek," I says, awed by his magnificence.

"Well," says he, "I'm Wild Bill Donovan, which name is heard with fear and tremblin' from Powder River to the Rio Grande. Just now I'm lookin' for a wild stallion. Have you seen sech?"

"I seen a bay stallion headin' west with his herd," I said.

"'Twarn't him," says Donovan. "This here one's a pinto, the biggest, meanest hoss in the world. He come down from the Humbolts when he was a colt, but he's roamed the West from Border to Border. He's so mean he ain't never got him a herd of his own. He takes mares away from other stallions, and then drifts on alone just for pure cussedness. When he comes into a country all other varmints takes to the tall timber."

"You mean the wolves and painters and b'ars I seen headin' for the high ridges was runnin' away from this here stallion?" I says.

"Exactly," says Donovan. "He crossed the eastern ridge sometime durin' the night, and the critters that was wise high-tailed it. We warn't far behind him; we come over the ridge a few hours ago, but we lost his trail somewhere on this side."

"You chasin' him?" I ast.

"Ha!" snarled Donovan with a kind of vicious laugh. "The man don't live what can chase Cap'n Kidd! We're just follerin' him. We been follerin' him for five hundred miles, keepin' outa sight, and hopin' to catch him off guard or somethin'. We got to have some kind of a big advantage before we closes in, or even shows ourselves. We're right fond of life! That devil has kilt more men than any other ten hosses on this continent."

"What you call him?" I says.

"Cap'n Kidd," says Donovan. "Cap'n Kidd was a big pirate long time ago. This here hoss is like him in lots of ways, particularly in regard to morals. But I'll git him, if I have to foller him to the Gulf and back. Wild Bill Donovan always gits what he wants, be it money, woman, or hoss! Now lissen here, you range-country hobo: we're a-siftin' north from here, to see if we cain't pick up Cap'n Kidd's sign. If you see a pinto stallion bigger'n you ever dreamed a hoss could be, or come onto his tracks, you drop whatever yo're doin' and pull out and look for us, and tell me about it. You keep lookin' till you find us, too. If you don't you'll regret it, you hear me?"

"Yessir," I said. "Did you gents come through the Wild River country?"

"Maybe we did and maybe we didn't," he says with haughty

grandeur. "What business is that of yore'n, I'd like to know?"

"Not any," I says. "But I was aimin' to go there and see if I could git me a job punchin' cows."

At that he throwed back his head and laughed long and loud, and all the other fellers laughed too, and I was embarrassed.

"You git a job punchin' cows?" roared Donovan. "With them britches and shoes, and not even no shirt, and that there ignorant-lookin' mule I see gobblin' grass over by the creek? Haw! haw! haw! haw! You better stay up here in the mountains whar you belong and live on roots and nuts and jackrabbits like the other Piutes, red or white! Any self-respectin' rancher would take a shotgun to you if you was to ast him for a job. Haw! haw! haw!" he says, and rode off still laughing.

I was that embarrassed I burst out into a sweat. Alexander was a good mule, but he did look kind of funny in the face. But he was the only critter I'd ever found which could carry my weight very many miles without giving plumb out. He was awful strong and tough, even if he was kind of dumb and pot-bellied. I begun to get kind of mad, but Donovan and his men was already gone, and the stars was beginning to blink out. So I cooked me some more b'ar steaks and et 'em, and the land sounded awful still, not a wolf howling nor a cougar squalling. They was all west of the ridge. This critter Cap'n Kidd sure had the country to hisself, as far as the meat-eating critters was consarned.

I hobbled Alexander close by and fixed me a bed with some boughs and his saddle blanket, and went to sleep. I was woke up shortly after midnight by Alexander trying to get in bed with me.

I sot up in irritation and prepared to bust him in the snoot, when I heard what had scairt him. I never heard such a noise. My hair stood straight up. It was a stallion neighing, but I never heard no hoss critter neigh like that. I bet you could of heard it for fifteen miles. It sounded like a combination of a wild hoss neighing, a rip saw going through a oak log full of knots, and a hungry cougar screeching. I thought it come from somewhere within a mile of the camp, but I warn't sure. Alexander was shivering and whimpering he was that scairt, and stepping all over me as he tried to huddle down amongst the branches and hide his head under my shoulder. I shoved him away, but he insisted on staying as close to me as he could, and when I woke up again next morning he was sleeping with his head on my belly.

But he must of forgot about the neigh he heard, or thought it was jest a bad dream or something, because as soon as I taken the hobbles off of him he started cropping grass and wandered off amongst the thickets in his pudding-head way.

I cooked me some more b'ar steaks, and wondered if I ought to go and try to find Mister Donovan and tell him about hearing the stallion neigh, but I figgered he'd heard it. Anybody that was within a day's ride ought to of heard it. Anyway, I seen no reason why I should run errands for Donovan.

I hadn't got through eating when I heard Alexander give a horrified bray, and he come lickety-split out of a grove of trees and made for the camp, and behind him come the biggest hoss I ever seen in my life. Alexander looked like a pot-bellied bull pup beside of him. He was painted—black and white—and he r'ared up with his long mane flying agen the sunrise, and give a scornful neigh that nigh busted my eardrums, and turned around and sa'ntered back towards the grove, cropping grass as he went, like he thunk so little of Alexander he wouldn't even bother to chase him.

Alexander come blundering into camp, blubbering and hollering, and run over the fire and scattered it every which a way, and then tripped hisself over the saddle which was laying near by, and fell on his neck braying like he figgered his life was in danger.

I catched him and throwed the saddle and bridle on to him, and by the time Cap'n Kidd was out of sight on the other side of the thicket. I onwound my lariat and headed in that direction. I figgered not even Cap'n Kidd could break that lariat. Alexander didn't want to go; he sot back on his haunches and brayed fit to deefen you, but I spoke to him sternly, and it seemed to convince him that he better face the stallion than me, so he moved out, kind of reluctantly.

We went past the grove and seen Cap'n Kid cropping grass in the patch of rolling prairie just beyond, so I rode towards him, swinging my lariat. He looked up and snorted kinda threateningly, and he had the meanest eye I ever seen in man or beast; but he didn't move, just stood there looking contemptuous, so I throwed my rope and piled the loop right around his neck, and Alexander sot back on his haunches.

Well, it was about like roping a roaring hurricane. The instant he felt that rope Cap'n Kidd give a convulsive start, and made one mighty lunge for freedom. The lariat held, but the girths didn't. They held jest long enough for Alexander to get jerked head over heels, and naturally I went along with him. But right in the middle of the somesault we taken, both girths snapped.

Me and the saddle and Alexander landed all in a tangle, but Cap'n Kidd jerked the saddle from amongst us, because I had my rope tied fast to the horn, Texas-style, and Alexander got loose from me by the simple process of kicking me vi'lently in the ear. He also stepped on my face when he jumped up, and the next instant he was high-tailing it through the bresh in the general direction of Bear Creek. As I learned later he didn't stop till he run into pap's cabin and tried to hide under my brother John's bunk.

Meanwhile Cap'n Kidd had throwed the loop offa his head and come for me with his mouth wide open, his ears laid back and his teeth and eyes flashing. I didn't want to shoot him, so I riz up and run for the trees. But he was coming like a tornado, and I seen he was going to run me down before I could get to a tree big enough to climb, so I grabbed me a sapling about as thick as my laig and tore it up by the roots, and turned around and busted him over the head with it, just as he started to r'ar up to come down on me with his front hoofs.

Pieces of roots and bark and wood flew every which a way, and Cap'n Kidd grunted and batted his eyes and went back on to his haunches. It was a right smart lick. If I'd ever hit Alexander that hard it would have busted his skull like a egg—and Alexander had a awful thick skull, even for a mule.

Whilst Cap'n Kidd was shaking the bark and stars out of his eyes, I run to a big oak and clumb it. He comes after me instantly, and chawed chunks out of the tree as big as washtubs, and kicked most of the bark off as high up as he could rech, but it was a good substantial tree, and it held. He then tried to climb it, which amazed me most remarkable, but he didn't do much good at that. So he give up with a snort of disgust and trotted off.

I waited till he was out of sight, and then I clumb down and got my rope and saddle, and started follering him. I knowed there warn't no use trying to catch Alexander with the lead he had. I figgered he'd get back to Bear Creek safe. And Cap'n Kidd was the critter I wanted now. The minute I lammed him with that tree and he didn't fall, I knowed he was the hoss for me—a hoss which could carry my weight all day without giving out, and likewise full of spirit. I says to myself I rides him or the buzzards picks my bones.

I snuck from tree to tree, and presently seen Cap'n Kidd swaggering along and eating grass, and biting the tops off of young sapling, and occasionally tearing down a good sized tree to get the leaves off. Sometimes he'd neigh like a steamboat whistle, and let his heels fly in all directions just out of pure cussedness. When he done this the air was full of flying bark and dirt and rocks till it looked like he was in the middle of a twisting cyclone.

I never seen such a critter in my life. He was as full of pizen and rambunctiousness as a drunk Apache on the warpath.

I thought at first I'd rope him and tie the other end of the rope to a big tree, but I was a-feared he'd chawed the lariat apart. Then I seen something that changed my mind. We was close to the rocky cliffs which jutted up above the trees, and Cap'n Kidd was passing a canyon mouth that looked like a big knife cut. He looked in and snorted, like he hoped they was a mountain lion hiding in there, but they warn't, so he went on. The wind was blowing from him towards me and he didn't smell me.

After he was out of sight amongst the trees I come out of cover and looked into the cleft. It was kinda like a short blind canyon. It warn't but about thirty foot wide at the mouth, but it widened quick till it made a kind of bowl a hundred yards acrost, and then narrowed to a crack again. Rock walls five hundred foot high was on all sides except at the mouth.

"And here," says I to myself, "is a ready-made corral!"

Then I lay to and started to build a wall to close the mouth of the canyon. Later on I heard that a scientific expedition (whatever the hell that might be) was all excited over finding evidences of a ancient race up in the mountains. They said they found a wall that could of been built only by giants. They was crazy; that there was the wall I built for Cap'n Kidd.

I knowed it would have to be high and solid if I didn't want Cap'n Kidd to jump it or knock it down. They was plenty of boulders laying at the foot of the cliffs which had weathered off, and I didn't use a single rock which weighed less'n three hundred pounds, and most of 'em was a lot heavier than that. It taken me most all morning, but when I quit I had me a wall higher'n the average man could reach, and so thick and heavy I knowed it would hold even Cap'n Kidd.

I left a narrer gap in it, and piled some boulders close to it on the outside, ready to shove 'em into the gap. Then I stood outside the wall and squalled like a cougar. They ain't even a cougar hisself can tell the difference when I squalls like one. Purty soon I heard Cap'n Kidd give his war-neigh off yonder, and then they was a thunder of hoofs and a snapping and crackling of bresh, and he come busting into the open with his ears laid back and his teeth bare and his eyes as red as a Comanche's war-paint. He sure hated cougars. But he didn't seem to like me much neither. When he seen me he give a roar of rage, and come for me licketysplit. I run through the gap and hugged the wall inside, and he come thundering after me going so fast he run clean across the bowl

before he checked hisself. Before he could get back to the gap I'd
run outside and was piling rocks in it. I had a good big one about
the size of a fat hawg and I jammed it in the gap first and piled
t'others on top of it.

Cap'n Kidd arriv at the gap all hoofs and teeth and fury, but
it was already filled too high for him to jump and too solid for
him to tear down. He done his best, but all he done was to knock
some chunks offa the rocks with his heels. He sure was mad. He
was the maddest hoss I ever seen, and when I got up on the wall
and he seen me, he nearly busted with rage.

He went tearing around the bowl, kicking up dust and neighing
like a steam boat on the rampage, and then he come back and
tried to kick the wall down again. When he turned to gallop off
I jumped offa the wall and landed square on his back, but before
I could so much as grab his mane he throwed me clean over the
wall and I landed in a cluster of boulders and cactus and skun my
shin. This made me mad so I got the lariat and the saddle and
clumb back on the wall and roped him, but he jerked the rope out
of my hand before I could get any kind of a purchase, and went
bucking and pitching around all over the bowl trying to get shet
of the rope. So purty soon he pitched right into the cliff-wall and
he lammed it so hard with his hind hoofs that a whole section of
overhanging rock was jolted loose and hit him right between the
ears. That was too much even for Cap'n Kidd.

It knocked him down and stunned him, and I jumped down
into the bowl and before he could come to I had my saddle on to
him, and a hackamore I'd fixed out of a piece of my lariat. I'd
also mended the girths with pieces of the lariat, too, before I built
the wall.

Well, when Cap'n Kidd recovered his senses and riz up, snorting and war-like, I was on his back. He stood still for a instant
like he was trying to figger out jest what the hell was the matter,
and then he turned his head and seen me on his back. The next
instant I felt like I was astraddle of a ring-tailed cyclone.

I dunno what all he done. He done so many things all at onst
I couldn't keep track. I clawed leather. The man which could have
stayed onto him without clawing leather ain't born yet, or else
he's a cussed liar. Sometimes my feet was in the stirrups and
sometimes they warn't, and sometimes they was in the wrong
stirrups. I cain't figger out how that could be, but it was so. Part
of the time I was in the saddle and part of the time I was behind
it on his rump, or on his neck in front of it. He kept reching back
trying to snap my laig and onst he got my thigh between his teeth

and would ondoubtedly of tore the muscle out if I hadn't shook him loose by beating him over the head with my fist.

One instant he'd have his head betwixt his feet and I'd be setting on a hump so high in the air I'd get dizzy, and the next thing he'd come down stiff-laiged and I could feel my spine telescoping. He changed ends so fast I got sick at my stummick and he nigh unjointed my neck with his sunfishing. I calls it sunfishing because it was more like that than anything. He occasionally rolled over and over on the ground, too, which was very uncomfortable for me, but I hung on, because I was afeared if I let go I'd never get on him again. I also knowed that if he ever shaken me loose I'd had to shoot him to keep him from stomping my guts out. So I stuck, though I'll admit that they is few sensations more onpleasant than having a hoss as big as Cap'n Kidd roll on you nine or ten times.

He tried to scrape me off agen the walls, too, but all he done was scrape off some hide and most of my pants, though it was when he lurched agen that outjut of rock that I got them ribs cracked, I reckon.

He looked like he was able to go on forever, and aimed to, but I hadn't never met nothing which could outlast me, and I stayed with him, even after I started bleeding at the nose and mouth and ears, and got blind, and then all to onst he was standing stock still in the middle of the bowl, with his tongue hanging out about three foot, and his sweat-soaked sides heaving, and the sun was just setting over the mountains. He'd bucked nearly all afternoon!

But he was licked. I knowed it and he knowed it. I shaken the stars and sweat and blood out of my eyes and dismounted by the simple process of pulling my feet out of stirrups and falling off. I laid there for maybe a hour, and was most amazing sick, but so was Cap'n Kidd. When I was able to stand on my feet I taken the saddle and the hackamore off and he didn't kick me nor nothing. He jest made a half-hearted attempt to bite me but all he done was to bite the buckle offa my gunbelt. They was a little spring back in the cleft where the bowl narrered in the cliff, and plenty of grass, so I figgered he'd be all right when he was able to stop blowing and panting long enough to eat and drink.

I made a fire outside the bowl and cooked me what was left of the b'ar meat, and then I lay down on the ground and slept till sunup.

When I riz up and see how late it was, I jumped up and run

and looked over the wall, and there was Cap'n Kidd mowing the grass down as ca'm as you please. He give me a mean look, but didn't say nothing. I was so eager to see if he was going to let me ride him without no more foolishness that I didn't stop for breakfast, nor to fix the buckle onto my gunbelt. I left it hanging on a spruce limb, and clumb into the bowl. Cap'n Kidd laid back his ears but didn't do nothing as I approached outside of making a swipe at me with his left hoof. I dodged and give him a good hearty kick in the belly and he grunted and doubled up, and I clapped the saddle on him. He showed his teeth at that, but he let me cinch it up, and put on the hackamore, and when I got on him he didn't pitch but about ten jumps and make but one snap at my laig.

Well, I was plumb tickled as you can imagine. I clumb down and opened the gap in the wall and led him out, and when he found he was outside the bowl he bolted and dragged me for a hundred yards before I managed to get the rope around a tree. After I tied him up though, he didn't try to burst loose.

I started back towards the tree where I left my gunbelt when I heard hosses running, and the next thing I knowed Donovan and his five men busted into the open and pulled up with their mouths wide open. Cap'n Kidd snorted warlike when he seen 'em, but didn't cut up no other way.

"Blast my soul!" says Donovan. "Can I believe my eyes? If there ain't Cap'n Kidd hisself, saddled and tied to that tree! Did *you* do that?"

"Yeah," I said.

He looked me over and said: "I believe it. You looked like you been through a sausage-grinder. Air you still alive?"

"My ribs is kind of sore," I said.

"——!" says Donovan. "To think that a blame half-naked hill-billy should do what the best hossmen of the West has attempted in vain! I don't aim to stand for it! I knows my rights! That there is my hoss by rights! I've trailed him nigh a thousand miles, and combed this cussed plateau in a circle. He's my hoss!"

"He ain't, nuther," I says. "He come from the Humbolts original, jest like me. You said so yoreself. Anyway, I caught him and broke him, and he's mine."

"He's right, Bill," one of the men says to Donovan.

"You shet up!" roared Donovan. "What Wild Bill Donovan wants, he gits!"

I reched for my gun and then remembered in despair that it

was hanging on a limb a hundred yards away. Donovan covered me with the sawed-off shotgun he jerked out of his saddle-holster as he swung down.

"Stand where you be," he advised me. "I ought to shoot you for not comin' and tellin' me when you seen the hoss, but after all you've saved me the trouble of breakin' him in."

"So yo're a hoss-thief!" I said wrathfully.

"You be kerrful what you calls me!" he roared. "I ain't no hoss thief. We gambles for that hoss. Set down!"

I sot and he sot on his heels in front of me, with his sawed-off still covering me. If it'd been a pistol I would of took it away from him and shoved the barrel down his throat. But I was quite young in them days and bashful about shotguns. The others squatted around us, and Donovan says: "Smoky, haul out yore deck— the special one. Smoky deals, hillbilly, and the high hand wins the hoss."

"I'm puttin' up my hoss, it looks like," I says fiercely. "What *you* puttin' up?"

"My Stetson hat!" says he. "Haw! haw! haw!"

"Haw! haw! haw!" chortles the other hoss-thieves.

Smoky started dealing and I said: "Hey! Yo're dealin' Donovan's hand offa the bottom of the deck!"

"Shet up!" roared Donovan, poking me in the belly with his shotgun. "You be keerful how you slings them insults around! This here is a fair and square game, and I just happen to be lucky. Can you beat four aces?"

"How you know you got four aces?" I says fiercely. "You ain't looked at yore hand yet."

"Oh," says he, and picked it up and spread it out on the grass, and they was four aces and a king. "By golly!" he says. "I shore called that shot right!"

"Remarkable foresight!" I said bitterly, throwing down my hand which was a three, five and seven of hearts, a ten of clubs and a jack of diamonds.

"Then I wins!" gloated Donovan, jumping up. I riz too, quick and sudden, but Donovan had me covered with that cussed shotgun.

"Git on that hoss and ride him over to our camp, Red," says Donovan, to a big red-haired *hombre* which was shorter than him but jest about as big. "See if he's properly broke. I wants to keep my eye on this hillbilly myself."

So Red went over to Cap'n Kidd which stood there saying nothing, and my heart sunk right down to the tops of my spiked shoes. Red ontied him and clumb on him and Cap'n Kidd didn't so much as snap at him. Red says: "Git goin', cuss you!" Cap'n Kidd turnt his head and looked at Red and then he opened his mouth like a alligator and started laughing. I never seen a hoss laugh before, but now I know what they mean by a hoss-laugh. Cap'n Kidd didn't neigh nor nicker. He jest laughed. He laughed till the acorns come rattling down outa the trees and the echoes rolled through the cliffs like thunder. And then he reched his head around and grabbed Red's laig and dragged him out of the saddle, and held him upside down with the guns and things spilling out of his scabbards and pockets, and Red yelling blue murder. Cap'n Kidd shaken him till he looked like a rag and swung him around his head three or four times, and then let go and throwed him clean through a alder thicket.

Them fellers all stood gaping, and Donovan had forgot about me, so I grabbed the shotgun away from him and hit him under the ear with my left fist and he bit the dust. I then swung the gun on the others and roared: "Onbuckle them gunbelts, cuss ye!" They was bashfuller about the buckshot at close range than I was. They didn't argy. Them four gunbelts was on the grass before I stopped yelling.

"All right," I said. "Now go catch Cap'n Kidd."

Because he had gone over to where their hosses was tied and was chawing and kicking the tar out of them and they was hollering something fierce.

"He'll kill us!" squalled the men.

"Well, what of it!" I snarled. "Gwan!"

So they made a desperate foray onto Cap'n Kidd and the way he kicked 'em in the belly and bit the seat out of their britches was beautiful to behold. But whilst he was stomping them I come up and grabbed his hackamore and when he seen who it was he stopped fighting, so I tied him to a tree away from the other hosses. Then I throwed Donovan's shotgun onto the men and made 'em get up and come over to where Donovan was laying, and they was a bruised and battered gang. The way they taken on you'd of thought somebody had mistreated 'em.

I made 'em take Donovan's gunbelt offa him and about that time he come to and sot up, muttering something about a tree falling on him.

"Don't you remember me?" I says. "I'm Breckinridge Elkins."

"It all comes back," he muttered. "We gambled for Cap'n Kidd."

"Yeah," I says, "and you won, so now we gambles for him

again. You sot the stakes before. This time I sets 'em. I matches these here britches I got on agen Cap'n Kidd, and yore saddle, bridle, gunbelt, pistol, pants, shirt, boots, spurs and Stetson."

"Robbery!" he bellered. "Yo're a cussed bandit!"

"Shet up," I says, poking him in the midruff with his shotgun. "Squat! The rest of you, too."

"Ain't you goin' to let us do somethin' for Red?" they said. Red was laying on the other side of the thicket Cap'n Kidd had throwed him through, groaning loud and fervent.

"Let him lay for a spell," I says. "If he's dyin' they ain't nothin' we can do for him, and if he ain't, he'll keep till this game's over. Deal, Smoky, and deal from the top of the deck this time."

So Smoky dealed in fear and trembling, and I says to Donovan: "What you got?"

"A royal flush of diamonds, by God!" he says. "You cain't beat that!"

"A royal flush of hearts'll beat it, won't it, Smoky?" I says, and Smoky says: "Yuh-yuh-yeah! Yeah! Oh, yeah!"

"Well," I said, "I ain't looked at my hand yet, but I bet that's jest what I got. What you think?" I says, p'inting the shotgun at Donovan's upper teeth. "Don't you reckon I've got a royal flush in hearts?"

"It wouldn't surprise me a bit," says Donovan, turning pale.

"Then everybody's satisfied and they ain't no use in me showin' my hand," I says, throwing the cards back into the pack. "Shed them duds!"

He shed 'em without a word, and I let 'em take up Red, which had seven busted ribs, a dislocated arm and a busted laig, and they kinda folded him acrost his saddle and tied him in place. Then they pulled out without saying a word or looking back. They all looked purty wilted, and Donovan particularly looked very pecooliar in the blanket he had wropped around his middle. If he'd had a feather in his hair he'd of made a lovely Piute, as I told him. But he didn't seem to appreciate the remark. Some men just naturally ain't got no sense of humour.

They headed east, and as soon as they was out of sight, I put the saddle and bridle I'd won onto Cap'n Kidd and getting the bit in his mouth was about like rassling a mountain tornado. But I done it, and then I put on the riggins I'd won. The boots was too small and the shirt fit a mite too snug in the shoulders, but I sure felt elegant nevertheless, and stalked up and down admiring myself and wishing Glory McGraw could see me then.

I cached my old saddle, belt and pistol in a holler tree, aiming to send my younger brother Bill back after 'em. He could have 'em, along with Alexander. I was going back to Bear Creek in style, by golly!

With a joyful whoop I swung onto Cap'n Kidd, headed him west and tickled his flanks with my spurs—them trappers in the mountains which later reported having seen a blue streak travelling westwardly so fast they didn't have time to tell what it was, and was laughed at and accused of being drunk, was did a injustice. What they seen was me and Cap'n Kidd going to Bear Creek. He run fifty miles before he even pulled up for breath.

I ain't going to tell how long it took Cap'n Kidd to cover the distance to Bear Creek. Nobody wouldn't believe me. But as I come up the trail a few miles from my home cabin, I heard a hoss galloping and Glory McGraw bust into view. She looked pale and scairt, and when she seen me she give a kind of a holler and pulled up her hoss so quick it went back onto its haunches.

"Breckinridge!" she gasped. "I jest heard from yore folks that yore mule come home without you, and I was just startin' out to look for—oh!" says she, noticing my hoss and elegant riggings for the first time. She kind of froze up, and said stiffly: "Well, *Mister* Elkins, I see yo're back home again."

"And you sees me rigged up in store-bought clothes and ridin' the best hoss in the Humbolts, too, I reckon," I said. "I hope you'll excuse me, *Miss* McGraw. I'm callin' on Ellen Reynolds as soon as I've let my folks know I'm home safe. Good day!"

"Don't let me detain you!" she flared, but after I'd rode on past she hollered: "Breckinridge Elkins, I hate you!"

"I know that," I said bitterly; "they warn't no use in tellin' me again——"

But she was gone, riding lickety-split off through the woods towards her home-cabin and I rode on for mine, thinking to myself what curious critters gals was anyway.

CHAPTER IV

Guns of the Mountains

Things run purty smooth for maybe a month after I got back to Bear Creek. Folks come from miles around to see Cap'n Kidd and hear me tell about licking Wild Bill Donovan, and them fancy clothes sure had a pleasing effeck on Ellen Reynolds. The only flies in the 'intment was Joel Braxton's brother Jim, Ellen's old man, and my Uncle Garfield Elkins; but of him anon as the French says.

Old Man Braxton didn't like me much, but I had learnt my lesson in dealing with Old Man McGraw. I taken no foolishness offa him, and Ellen warn't nigh as sensitive about it as Glory had been. But I warn't sure about Jim Braxton. I discouraged him from calling on Ellen, and I done it purty vi'lent, but I warn't sure he warn't sneaking around and sparking her on the sly, and I couldn't tell just what she thought about him. But I was making progress, when the third fly fell into the 'intment.

Pap's Uncle Garfield Elkins come up from Texas to visit us.

That was bad enough by itself, but between Grizzly Run and Chawed Ear the stage got held up by some masked bandits, and Uncle Garfield, never being able to forget that he was a gun-fighting fool thirty or forty years ago, pulled his old cap-and-ball instead of reching for the clouds like he was advised to. For some reason, instead of blowing out his light, they merely busted him over the head with a .45 barrel, and when he come to he was rattling on his way towards Chawed Ear with the other passengers, minus his money and watch.

It was his watch what caused the trouble. That there timepiece had been his grandpap's, back in Kentucky, and Uncle Garfield

42

sot more store by it than he did all his kin folks.

When he arriv onto Bear Creek he imejitly let into howling his woes to the stars like a wolf with the belly-ache. And from then on we heered nothing but that watch. I'd saw it and thunk very little of it. It was big as my fist, and wound up with a key which Uncle Garfield was always losing and looking for. But it was solid gold, and he called it a hairloom, whatever them things is. And he nigh driv the family crazy.

"A passle of big hulks like you-all settin' around and lettin' a old man git robbed of all his property," he would say bitterly. "When *I* was a young buck, if'n *my* uncle had been abused that way, I'd of took the trail and never slept nor et till I brung back his watch and the sculp of the skunk which hived it. Men now days——" And so on and so on, till I felt like drownding the old jassack in a barrel of corn licker.

Finally pap says to me, combing his beard with his fingers; "Breckinridge," says he, "I've endured Uncle Garfield's belly-achin' all I aim to. I wants you to go look for his cussed watch, and don't come back without it."

"How'm I goin' to know where to look?" I protested. "The feller which got it may be in Californy or Mexico by now."

"I realizes the difficulties," says pap. "But warn't you eager for farin's which would make you a name in the world?"

"They is times for everything," I said. "Right now I'm interested in sparkin' a gal, which I ain't willin' to leave for no wild goose chase."

"Well," says pap, "I've done made up our mind. If Uncle Garfield knows somebody is out lookin' for his cussed time-piece, maybe he'll give the rest of us some peace. You git goin', and if you cain't find that watch, don't come back till after Uncle Garfield has went home."

"How long does he aim to stay?" I demanded.

"Well," says pap, "Uncle Garfield's visits generally last a year, at least."

At this I bust into earnest profanity.

I says: "I got to stay away from home a *year?* Dang it, Pap, Jim Braxton'll steal Ellen Reynolds away from me whilst I'm gone. I been courtin' that gal till I'm ready to fall dead. I done licked her old man three times, and now, jest when I got her goin', you tells me I got to up and leave her for a year with that dern Jim Braxton to have no competition with."

"You got to choose between Ellen Reynolds and yore own

flesh and blood," says pap. "I'm derned if I'll listen to Uncle Garfield's squawks any longer. You make yore own choice—but if you don't choose to do what I asks you to, I'll fill yore hide with buckshot every time I see you from now on."

Well, the result was that I was presently riding morosely away from home and Ellen Reynolds, and in the general direction of where Uncle Garfield's blasted watch might possibly be.

I rode by the Braxton cabin with the intention of dropping Jim a warning about his actions whilst I was gone, but I didn't see his saddle on the corral fence, so I knowed he warn't there. So I issued a general defiance to the family by slinging a .45 slug through the winder which knocked a corn cob pipe outa old man Braxton's mouth. That soothed me a little, but I knowed very well that Jim would make a bee-line for the Reynolds cabin the second I was out of sight. I could just see him gorging on Ellen's b'ar meat and honey, and bragging on hisself. I hoped Ellen would notice the difference between a loud-mouthed boaster like him, and a quiet, modest young man like me, which never bragged, though admittedly the biggest man and the best fighter in the Humbolts.

I hoped to meet Jim somewhere in the woods as I rode down the trail, because I was intending to do something to kinda impede his courting whilst I was gone, like breaking his laig or something, but luck wasn't with me.

I headed in the general direction of Chawed Ear, and a few days later seen me riding in gloomy grandeur through a country quite some distance from Ellen Reynolds. Nobody'd been able to tell me anything in Chawed Ear, so I thought I might as well comb the country between there and Grizzly Run. Probably wouldn't never find them dern bandits anyway.

Pap always said my curiosity would be the ruination of me some day, but I never could listen to guns popping up in the mountains without wanting to find out who was killing who. So that morning, when I heard the rifles talking off amongst the trees, I turned Cap'n Kidd aside and left the trail and rode in the direction of the noise.

A dim path wound up through the big boulders and bushes, and the shooting kept getting louder. Purty soon I come out into a glade, and just as I did, bam! somebody let go at me from the bresh and a .45-70 slug cut both my bridle reins nearly in half. I instantly returned the shot with my .45, getting jest a glimpse of something in the bresh, and a man let out a squall and jumped out into the open, wringing his hands. My bullet had hit the lock of his Winchester and mighty nigh jarred his hands offa him.

"Cease that ungodly noise," I said sternly, p'inting my .45 at his bay-winder, "and explain how come you waylays innercent travellers."

He quit working his fingers and moaning, and he said: "I thought you was Joel Cairn, the outlaw. Yo're about his size."

"Well, I ain't," I said. "I'm Breckinridge Elkins, from Bear Creek. I was jest ridin' over to find out what all the shootin' was about."

The guns was banging in the trees behind the feller, and somebody yelled what was the matter.

"Ain't nothin' the matter," he hollered back. "Just a misunderstandin'." And he says to me: "I'm glad to see you, Elkins. We need a man like you. I'm Sheriff Dick Hopkins, from Grizzly Run."

"Where at's yore star?" I inquired.

"I lost it in the bresh," he said. "Me and my deputies have been chasin' Tarantula Bixby and his gang for a day and a night, and we got 'em cornered over there in a old deserted cabin in a holler. The boys is shootin' at 'em now. I heered you comin' up the trail and snuck over to see who it was. Just as I said, I thought you was Cairn. Come on with me. You can help us."

"I ain't no deperty," I said. "I got nothin' against Tranchler Bixby."

"Well, you want to uphold the law, don't you?" he said.

"Naw," I said.

"Well, gee whiz!" he wailed. "If you ain't a hell of a citizen! The country's goin' to the dogs. What chance has a honest man got?"

"Aw, shet up," I said. "I'll go over and see the fun, anyhow."

So he picked up his gun, and I tied Cap'n Kidd, and follered the sheriff through the trees till we come to some rocks, and there was four men laying behind them rocks and shooting down into a hollow. The hill sloped away mighty steep into a small basin that was jest like a bowl, with a rim of slopes all around. In the middle of this bowl they was a cabin and puffs of smoke was coming from the cracks between the logs.

The men behind the rocks looked at me in surprise, and one of 'em said: "What the hell?"

The sheriff scowled at them and said, "Boys, this here is Breck Elkins. I done already told him about us bein' a posse from Grizzly Run, and about how we got Tarantula Bixby and two of his cutthroats trapped in that there cabin."

One of the deputies burst into a loud guffaw and Hopkins glared at him and said: "What *you* laughin' about, you spotted hyener?"

"I swallered my terbaccer and that allus gives me the hyster-icals," mumbled the deputy, looking the other way.

"Hold up yore right hand, Elkins," requested Hopkins, so I done so, wondering what for, and he said: "Does you swear to tell the truth, the whole truth and nothing but the truth, e pluribus unum, anno dominecker, to wit in status quo?"

"What the hell are you talkin' about?" I demanded.

"Them which God has j'ined asunder let no man put together," said Hopkins. "Whatever you say will be used agen you and the Lord have mercy on yore soul. That means yo're a deputy. I just swore you in."

"Go set on a prickly pear," I snorted disgustedly. "Go catch yore own thieves. And don't look at me like that. I might bend a gun over yore skull."

"But Elkins," pleaded Hopkins, "with yore help we can catch them rats easy. All you got to do is lay up here behind this big rock and shoot at the cabin and keep 'em occupied till we can sneak around and rush 'em from the rear. See, the bresh comes down purty close to the foot of the slope on the other side, and gives us cover. We can do it easy, with somebody keepin' their attention over here. I'll give us part of the reward."

"I don't want no derned blood-money," I said, backing away, "And besides—*ow!*"

I'd absent-mindedly backed out from behind the big rock where I'd been standing, and a .30-30 slug burned its way acrost the seat of my britches.

"Dern them murderers!" I bellered, seeing red. "Gimme a rifle! I'll learn 'em to shoot a man behind his back! Gwan, and git 'em from behind whilst I attracts their attention with a serenade of hot lead!"

"Good boy!" says Hopkins. "You'll git plenty for this!"

It sounded like somebody was snicking to theirselves as they snuck away, but I give no heed. I squinted cautiously around the big boulder and begun sniping at the cabin. All I could see to shoot at was the puffs of smoke which marked the cracks they was shooting through, but from the cussing and yelling which begun to float up from the shack, I must of throwed some lead mighty close to them.

They kept shooting back, and the bullets splashed and buzzed on the rocks, and I kept looking at the further slope for some sign of Sheriff Hopkins and the posse. But all I heard was a sound of hosses galloping away towards the west. I wondered who it was, and I kept expecting the posse to rush down the oppersite slope and take them desperadoes in the rear, and whilst I was craning my neck around a corner of the boulder—whang! A bullet smashed into the rock a few inches from my face and a sliver of stone taken a notch out of my ear. I don't know of nothing that makes me madder'n getting shot in the ear.

I seen red and didn't even shoot back. A ordinary rifle was too paltry to satisfy me. Suddenly I realized that the big boulder in front of me was jest poised on the slope, its underside partly embedded in the earth. I throwed down my rifle and bent my knees and spread my arms and gripped it.

I shook the sweat and blood outa my eyes, and bellered so them in the hollow could hear me: "I'm givin' you-all a chance to surrender! Come out with yore hands up!"

They give loud and sarcastic jeers, and I yelled: "All right, you ring-tailed jackasses! If you gits squashed like a pancake, it's yore own fault. *Here she comes!*"

And I heaved with all I had. The veins stood out onto my temples, and my feet sunk into the ground, but the earth bulged and cracked all around the big rock, rivulets of dirt began to trickle down, and the big boulder groaned, give way and lurched over.

A dumbfounded yell riz from the cabin. I lept behind a bush, but the outlaws was too surprised to shoot at me. That enormous boulder was tumbling down the hill, crushing bushes flat and gathering speed as it rolled. And the cabin was right in its path.

Wild yells bust the air, the door was throwed vi'lently open, and a man hove into view. Jest as he started out of the door I let bam at him and he howled and ducked back jest like anybody will when a .45-90 slug knocks their hat off. The next instant that thundering boulder hit the cabin. Smash! It knocked it sidewise like a ten pin and caved in the wall, and the whole structure collapsed in a cloud of dust and bark and splinters.

I run down the slope, and from the yells which issued from under the ruins, I knowed they warn't all kilt.

"Does you-all surrender?" I roared.

"Yes, dern it!" they squalled. "Git us out from under this landslide!"

"Throw out yore guns," I ordered.

"How in hell can we throw anything?" they hollered wrathfully. "We're pinned down by a ton of rocks and boards and we're bein' squoze to death. Help, murder!"

"Aw, shet up," I said. "You all don't hear *me* carryin' on in no such hysterical way, does you?"

Well, they moaned and complained, and I sot to work dragging the ruins offa them, which warn't no great task. Purty soon I seen a booted laig and I laid hold of it and dragged out the critter it was fastened to, and he looked more done up than what my brother Buckner did that time he rassled a mountain lion for a bet. I taken his pistol out of his belt, and laid him down on the ground and got the others out. They was three, altogether, and I taken their arms and laid 'em out in a row.

Their clothes was nearly tore off, and they was bruised and scratched and had splinters in their hair, but they warn't hurt permanent. They sot up and felt of theirselves, and one of 'em said: "This here's the first earthquake I ever seen in this country."

"'Twarn't no earthquake," said another'n. "It was a avalanche."

"Lissen here, Joe Partland," said the first 'n, grinding his teeth. "I says it was a earthquake, and I ain't the man to be called a liar——"

"Oh, you ain't hey?" says the other'n, bristling up. "Well, lemme tell you somethin', Frank Jackson——"

"This ain't no time for sech argyments," I admonished 'em sternly. "As for that there rock, I rolled that at you-all myself."

They gaped at me, and one of 'em says: "Who are you?" he says, mopping the blood offa his ear.

"Never mind that," I says. "You see this here Winchester? Well, you-all set still and rest yorselves. Soon as the sheriff gits here I'm goin' to hand you over to him."

His mouth fell open. "Sheriff?" he said, dumb-like. "What sheriff?"

"Dick Hopkins, from Grizzly Run," I said.

"Why, you darn fool!" he screamed, scrambling up.

"Set down!" I roared, shoving my rifle barrel at him, and he sank back, all white and shaking. He couldn't hardly talk.

"Lissen to me!" he gasped. "*I'm* Dick Hopkins! *I'm* sheriff of Grizzly Run! These men are my deputies."

"Yeah?" I said sarcastically. "And who was the fellers shootin' at you from the bresh?"

"Tarantula Bixby and his gang," he says. "We was follerin' 'em when they jumped us, and bein' outnumbered and surprised, we taken cover in that old hut. They robbed the Grizzly Run bank day before yesterday. And now they'll be gittin' further away every minute! Oh, Judas J. Iscariot! Of all the dumb, bone-headed jackasses——"

"Heh! heh! heh!" I said cynically. "You must think I ain't got no sense. If yo're the sheriff, where at's yore star?"

"It was on my suspenders," he said despairingly. "When you hauled me out by the laig my suspenders caught on somethin' and tore off. If you'll lemme look amongst them rooins——"

"You set still," I commanded. "You cain't fool me. Yo're Tranchler Bixby yoreself. Sheriff Hopkins told me so. Him and the posse'll be here directly. Set still and shet up."

We stayed there, and the feller which claimed to be the sheriff moaned and pulled his hair and shed a few tears, and the other fellers tried to convince me they was deputies till I got tired of their gab and told 'em to shet up or I'd bend my Winchester over their heads. I wondered why Hopkins and them didn't come, and I begun to get nervous, and all to onst the feller which said he was the sheriff give a yell that startled me so I jumped and nearly shot him. He had something in his hand and was waving it around.

"See here?" he hollered so loud his voice cracked. "I found it! It must of fell down into my shirt when my suspenders busted! Look at it, you derned mountain grizzly!"

I looked and my flesh crawled. It was a shiny silver star.

"Hopkins said he lost his'n," I said weakly. "Maybe you found it in the bresh."

"You know better!" he bellered. "Yo're one of Bixby's men. You was left here to hold us whilst Tarantula and the rest made their gitaway. You'll git ninety years for this!"

I turned cold all over as I remembered them hosses I heard galloping. I'd been fooled! This *was* the sheriff! That potbellied thug which shot at me had been Bixby hisself! And whilst I held up the real sheriff and his posse, them outlaws was riding out of the country! I was the prize sucker.

"You better gimme that gun and surrender," opined Hopkins. "Maybe if you do they won't hang you."

"Set still!" I snarled. "I'm the biggest fool that ever straddled a mustang, but even idjits has their feelin's. Pap said never resist a officer, but this here is a special case. You ain't goin' to put me behind no bars, jest because I made a mistake. I'm goin' up that there slope, but I'll be watchin' you. I've throwed yore guns over there in the bresh. If anybody makes a move towards 'em, I'll shove a harp right into his hand."

They set up a chant of hate as I backed away, but they sot still. I went up the slope backwards till I hit the rim, and then I turned and ducked into the bresh and run. I heard 'em cussing something awful down in the hollow, but I didn't pause. I come to where I'd left Cap'n Kidd and forked him and pulled out, being thankful them outlaws had been in too big a hurry to steal him. But I doubt if he'd a-let 'em. I throwed away the rifle they give me and headed west.

I aimed to cross Thunder River at Ghost Canyon, and head into the wild mountain region beyond there. I figgered I could dodge a posse indefinite onst I got there. I let Cap'n Kidd out into a long lope, cussing my reins which had been notched deep by Bixby's bullet. I didn't have time to fix 'em, and Cap'n Kidd was a iron-jawed outlaw.

He was sweating plenty when I finally hove in sight of the place I was heading for. As I topped the canyon's crest before I dipped down to the crossing, I looked back. They was a high notch in the hills a few miles behind me, and as I looked three hossmen was etched in that notch, lined agen the sky behind 'em. I cussed free and fervent. Why hadn't I had sense enough to know Hopkins and his men was bound to have hosses tied somewheres near? They got their mounts and follered me, figgering I'd aim for the country beyond Thunder River. It was about the only place I could go.

Not wanting no running fight with no sheriff's posse, I raced recklessly down the sloping canyon wall, busted out of the bushes— and stopped short. Thunder River was on the rampage—bank-full in the narrow channel and boiling and foaming. Been a cloud-bust somewhere away up on the head, and the hoss warn't never foaled which could swum it. Not even Cap'n Kidd, though he snorted warlike and was game to try it.

They wasn't but one thing to do, and I done it, I wheeled Cap'n Kidd and headed up the canyon. Five miles up the river they was another crossing, with a bridge—if it hadn't been washed away. Like as not it had been, with the luck I was having. A nice pickle Uncle Garfield's cussed watch had got me in, I reflected bitterly. Jest when I was all sot to squelch Glory McGraw onst and for all by marrying Ellen Reynolds, here I was throwed into circumstances which made me a fugitive from justice. I could just imagine Glory laughing at me, and it nigh locoed me.

I was so absorbed in these thoughts I paid little attention to my imejit surroundings, but all of a sudden I heard a noise ahead, above the river and the thunder of Cap'n Kidd's hoofs on the rocky canyon floor. We was approaching a bend in the gorge where a low ridge run out from the canyon wall, and beyond that ridge I heard guns banging. I heaved back on the reins—and both of 'em snapped in two!

Cap'n Kidd instantly clamped his teeth on the bit and bolted, like he always does when he gits the chance. He headed straight for the bushes at the end of the ridge, and I leaned forward and tried to get hold of the bit rings with my fingers. But all I done was swerve him from his course. Instead of follering the canyon bed on around the end of the ridge, he went right over the rise, which sloped on that side. It didn't slope on t'other side; it fell away abrupt. I had a fleeting glimpse of five men crouching amongst the bushes on the canyon floor with guns in their hands. They looked up—and Cap'n Kidd braced his laigs and slid to a halt at the lip of the blow bluff, and simultaneous bogged his head and throwed me heels over head down amongst 'em.

My boot heel landed on somebody's head, and the spur knocked him cold and blame near sculped him. That partly bust my fall, and it was further cushioned by another feller which I lit on in a setting position, and which taken no further interest in the proceedings. But the other three fell on me with loud brutal yells, and I reched for my .45 and found to my humiliation that it had fell out of my scabbard when I was throwed.

So I riz up with a rock in my hand and bounced it offa the head of a feller which was fixing to shoot me, and he dropped his pistol and fell on top of it. At this juncture one of the survivors put a buffalo gun to his shoulder and sighted, then evidently fearing he would hit his companion which was carving at me on the other side with his bowie knife, he reversed it and run in swinging it like a club.

The man with the knife got in a slash across my ribs and I then hit him on the chin which was how his jawbone got broke in four places. Meanwhile the other'n swung at me with his rifle, but missed my head and broke the stock off across my shoulder. Irritated at his persistency in trying to brain me with the barrel, I laid hands on him and throwed him head-on agen the bluff, which is when he got his fractured skull and concussion of the brain, I reckon.

I then shaken the sweat outa my eyes, and glaring down, rekernized the remains as Bixby and his gang. I might have knew they'd head for the wild country across the river, same as me. Only place they could go.

Just then, however, a clump of bushes parted, nigh the river bank, and a big black-bearded man riz up from behind a dead hoss. He had a sixshooter in his hand and he approached me cautiously.

"Who're you?" he demanded suspiciously. "Whar'd you come from?"

"I'm Breckinridge Elkins," I answered, wringing the blood outa my shirt. "What is this here business, anyway?"

"I was settin' here peaceable waitin' for the river to go down so I could cross," he says, "when up rode these yeggs and started shootin'. I'm a honest citizen——"

"Yo're a liar," I said with my usual diplomacy. "Yo're Joel Cairn, the wust outlaw in these hills. I seen yore picher in the post office at Chawed Ear."

With that he p'inted his .45 at me and his beard bristled like the whiskers of a old timber wolf.

"So you know me, hey?" he said. "Well, what you goin' to do about it, hey? Want to colleck the reward money, hey?"

"Naw, I don't," I says. "I'm a outlaw myself, now. I just run foul of the law account of these skunks. They's a posse right behind me."

"They is?" he snarled. "Why'nt you say so? Here, le's catch these fellers' hosses and light out. Cheap skates! They claims I double-crossed 'em in the matter of a stage-coach hold-up we pulled together recent. I been avoidin' 'em 'cause I'm a peaceful man by nater, but they rode onto me onexpected awhile ago. They shot down my hoss first crack; we been tradin' lead for more'n a hour, without doin' much damage, but they'd got me eventually, I reckon. Come on. We'll pull out together."

"No, we won't," I said. "I'm a outlaw by force of circumstances, but I ain't no murderin' bandit."

"Purty particular of yore comperny, ain'tcha?" he sneered. "Well, anyway, help me catch me a hoss. Yore's is still up thar on that bluff. The day's still young——"

He pulled out a big gold watch and looked at it; it was one which wound with a key.

I jumped like I was shot. "Where'd you git that watch?" I hollered.

He jerked up his head kinda startled, and said: "My grandpap gimme it. Why?"

"You're a liar!" I bellered. "You taken that off'n my Uncle Garfield. *Gimme that watch!*"

"Air you crazy?" he yelled, going white under his whiskers. I plunged for him, seeing red, and he let bang! and I got it in the left thigh. Before he could shoot again I was on top of him and knocked the gun up. It banged but the bullet went singing up over the bluff and Cap'n Kidd squealed with rage and started changing ends. The pistol flew outa Cairn's hand and he hit me vi'lently on the nose which made me see stars. So I hit him in the belly and he grunted and doubled up; and come up with a knife out of his boot which he cut me acrost the boozum with, also in the arm and shoulder and kicked me in the groin. So I swung him clear of the ground and throwed him down headfirst and jumped on him with both boots. And that settled his hash.

I picked up the watch where it had fell, and staggered over to the cliff, spurting blood at every step like a stuck hawg.

"At last my search is at a end!" I panted. "I can go back to Ellen Reynolds whot patiently awaits the return of her hero——"

It was at this instant that Cap'n Kidd, which had been stung by Cairn's wild shot and was trying to buck off his saddle, bucked hisself off the bluff. He fell on me. . . .

The first thing I heard was bells ringing, and then they turned to hosses galloping. I sot up and wiped off the blood which was running into my eyes from where Cap'n Kidd's left hind shoe had split my sculp. And I seen Sheriff Hopkins, Jackson and Partland come tearing around the ridge. I tried to get up and run, but my right laig wouldn't work. I reched for my gun and it still wasn't there. I was trapped.

"Look there!" yelled Hopkins, plumb wild-eyed. "That's Bixby on the ground—and all his gang! And ye gods, there's Joel Cairn! What is this, anyway? It looks like a battle-field! What's that settin' there? He's so bloody I cain't rekernize him!"

"It's the hillbilly!" yelped Jackson. "Don't move or I'll shoot 'cha!"

"I already been shot," I snarled. "Gwan—do yore wust. Fate is agen me."

They dismounted and stared in awe.

"Count the dead, boys," said Hopkins in a still, small voice.

"Aw," said Partland, "ain't none of 'em dead, but they'll never be the same men again. Look! Bixby's comin' to! Who done this, Bixby?"

Bixby cast a wabbly eye about till he spied me, and then he moaned and shrivelled up. "He tried to sculp me!" he wailed. "He ain't human!"

They all looked at me, and all taken their hats off.

"Elkins," says Hopkins in a tone of reverence, "I see it all now. They fooled you into thinkin' they was the posse and we was the outlaws, didn't they? And when you realized the truth, you hunted ''em down, didn't you? And cleaned 'em out single-handed, and Joel Cairn, too, didn't you?"

"Well," I said groggily, "the truth is———"

"We understand," Hopkins soothed. "You mountain men is all modest. Hey, boys, tie up them outlaws whilst I look at Elkins' wounds."

"If you'll catch my hoss," I said, "I got to be ridin' back———"

"Gee whiz, man!" he said, "you ain't in no shape to ride a hoss! Do you know you got five busted ribs and a fractured arm, and one laig broke and a bullet in the other'n, to say nothin' of bein' slashed to ribbons? We'll rig up a litter for you. What's that you got in yore good hand?"

I suddenly remembered Uncle Garfield's watch which I'd kept clutched in a death grip. I stared at what I held in my hand; and I fell back with a low moan. All I had in my hand was a bunch of busted metal and broken wheels and springs, bent and smashed plumb beyond recognition.

"Grab him!" yelled Hopkins. "He's fainted!"

"Plant me under a pine tree, boys," I murmured weakly. "Just kyarve onto my tombstone: 'He fit a good fight but Fate dealt him the joker.'"

A few days later a melancholy procession wound its way up the trail to Bear Creek. I was being toted on a litter. I told 'em I wanted to see Ellen Reynolds before I died, and to show Uncle Garfield the rooins of the Watch so he'd know I done my duty as I seen it.

When we'd got to within a few miles of my home cabin, who should meet us but Jim Braxton, which tried to conceal his pleasure when I told him in a weak voice that I was a dying man. He was all dressed up in new buckskins and his exuberance was plumb disgustful to a man in my condition.

"Too bad," says he. "Too bad, Breckinridge. I hoped to meet you, but not like this, of course. Yore pap told me to tell you about yore Uncle Garfield's watch if I seen you. He thought I might run into you on my way to Chawed Ear to git a licence———"

"Hey?" I said, pricking up my ears.

"Yeah, me and Ellen Reynolds is goin' to git married," he says. "Well, as I started to say, seems like one of them bandits which robbed the stage was a feller whose dad was a friend of yore Uncle Garfield's back in Texas. He rekernized the name in the watch and sent it back, and it got here the day after you left———"

They say it was jealousy which made me rise up on my litter

and fracture Jim Braxton's jaw-bone. I denies that. I stoops to no sech petty practices. What impelled me was family conventions. I couldn't hit Uncle Garfield; I had to hit somebody; and Jim Braxton jest happened to be the only man in rech.

CHAPTER V

A Gent From Bear Creek

"You," says my sister Ouachita, p'inting a accusing finger at me, "oughta be shot for the way you treat Glory McGraw!"

"Don't mention that gal's name to me," I says bitterly. "I don't want to hear nothin' about her. Don't talk to me about her—why you think I ain't treated her right?"

"Well," says Ouachita, "after they brung you back from Chawed Ear lookin' like you'd been through a sorghum mill, Glory come right over when she heered you was hurt. And what did you do when she come through the door?"

"I didn't do nothin'," I says. "What'd I do?"

"You turnt over towards the wall," says Ouachita, "and you says, says you: 'Git that woman outa here; she's come to t'ant me in my helpless condition!'"

"Well, she did!" I said fiercely.

"She didn't!" says Ouachita. "When she heered you say them words, she turnt pale, and she turnt around and walked outa the cabin with her head up in the air, not sayin' a word. And she ain't been back since."

"Well, I don't want her to," I says. "She come over here jest to gloat on my misery."

"I don't believe no sech," says Ouachita. "First thing she says, was: 'Is Breckinridge hurt bad?' And she didn't say it in no gloatin' way. She come over here to help you, I bet, and you talked to her like that! You ought to be ashamed."

"You mind yore own business," I advised her, and got up and got outa the cabin to get some peace and quiet.

I went towards the creek aiming to do a little fishing. My laig had knit proper and quick, and that had been the only thing which had kept me laid up. On my way to the creek I got to thinking over what Ouachita had said, and I thought, well, maybe I was a mite hasty. Maybe Glory did repent of her treatment of me when I was laying wounded. Maybe I ought not to of spoke so bitterly.

I thought, it's no more'n my neighbourly duty to go over and thank Glory for coming over to see me, and tell her I didn't mean what I said. I'd tell her I was delirious and thought it was Ellen Reynolds. After all, I was a man with a great, big, generous, forgiving heart, and if forgiving Glory McGraw was going to brighten her life, why, I warn't one to begrudge it. So I headed for the McGraw cabin—a trail I hadn't took since the day I shot up Mister Wilkinson.

I went afoot because I wanted to give my laig plenty of exercise now it was healed. And I hadn't gone more'n half way when I met the gal I was looking for. She was riding her bay mare, and we met face to face right spang in the middle of the trail. I taken off my Stetson and says: "Howdy, Glory. You warn't by any chance headin' for my cabin?"

"And why should I be headin' for yore cabin, Mister Elkins?" she said as stiff and cold as a frozen bowie knife.

"Well," I said, kinda abashed, "well—uh—that is, Glory, I jest want to thank you for droppin' in to see about me when I was laid up, and——"

"I didn't," she snapped. "I jest come to borrer some salt. I didn't even know you'd been hurt."

"What you want to talk like that for, Glory?" I protested. "I didn't aim to hurt yore feelin's. Fact is, I war delirious, and thought you was somebody else—"

"Ellen Reynolds, maybe?" says she sneeringly. "Or was she already there, holdin' yore hand? Oh, no! I'd plumb forgot! She was gittin' married to Jim Braxton about that time! Too bad, Breckinridge! But cheer up! Ellen's got a little sister which'll be growed up in a few years. Maybe you can git her—if some Braxton don't beat you to her."

"To hell with the Braxtons and the Reynolds too!" I roared, seeing red again. "And you can go along with 'em, far's I'm consarned! I was right! Ouachita's a fool, sayin' you was sorry for me. You jest come over there to gloat over me when I was laid up!"

"I didn't!" she says, in a changed voice.

"You did, too!" I says bitterly. "You go yore way and I'll go

mine. You think I cain't git me no woman, just because you and
Ellen Reynolds turned me down. Well, you-all ain't the only
women they is! I ain't goin' to marry no gal on Bear Creek! I'm
goin' to git me a town-gal!"

"A town-gal wouldn't look at a hillbilly like you!" she sneered.

"Oh, is that so?" I bellered, convulsively jerking some saplings
up by the roots in my agitation. "Well, lemme tell you somethin',
Miss McGraw, I'm pullin' out right now, this very day, for the
settlements, where purty gals is thick as flies in watermelon time,
and I aim to bring back the purtiest one of the whole kaboodle!
You wait and see!"

And I went storming away from there so blind mad that I fell
into the creek before I knowed it, and made a most amazing splash.
I thought I heard Glory call me to come back, jest before I fell,
but I was so mad I didn't pay no attention. I'd had about all the
badgering I could stand for one day. I clumb out on t'other side,
dripping like a musk-rat, and headed for the tall timber. I could
hear her laughing behind me, and she must of been kinda hysterical, because it sounded like she was crying instead of laughing,
but I didn't stop to see. All I wanted was to put plenty of distance
between me and Glory McGraw, and I headed for home as fast
as I could laig it.

It was my fullest intention to saddle Cap'n Kidd and pull out
for Chawed Ear or somewheres as quick as I could. I meant what
I said about getting me a town-gal. But right then I was fogging
head-on into the cussedest mix-up I'd ever saw, up to that time,
and didn't know it. I didn't even get a inkling of it when I almost
stumbled over a couple of figures locked in mortal combat on the
bank of the creek.

I was surprised when I seen who it was. The folks on Bear
Creek ain't exactly what you'd call peaceable by nature, but Erath
Elkins and his brother-in-law Joel Gordon had always got along
well together, even when they was full of corn juice. But there
they was, so tangled up they couldn't use their bowies to no
advantage, and their cussin' was scandalous to hear.

Remonstrances being useless, I kicked their knives out of their
hands and throwed 'em bodily into the creek. That broke their
holds and they come swarming out with blood-thirsty shrieks and
dripping whiskers, and attacked me. Seeing they was too blind
mad to have any sense, I bashed their heads together till they was
too dizzy to do anything but holler.

"Is this any way for relatives to ack?" I ast disgustedly.

"Lemme at him!" howled Joel, gnashing his teeth whilst blood streamed down his whiskers. "He's broke three of my fangs and I'll have his life!"

"Stand aside, Breckinridge!" raved Erath. "No man can chaw a ear offa me and live to tell the tale!"

"Aw, shet up," I snorted. "Ca'm down, before I sees is yore fool heads harder'n this." I brandished a large fist under their noses and they subsided sulkily. "What's all this about?" I demanded.

"I jest discovered my brother-in-law is a thief," said Joel bitterly. At that Erath give a howl and a vi'lent plunge to get at his relative, but I kind of pushed him backwards, and he fell over a willer stump.

"The facks is, Breckinridge," says Joel, "me and this here polecat found a buckskin poke full of gold nuggets in a holler oak over on Apache Ridge yesterday, right nigh the place whar yore brother Garfield fit them seven wildcats last year. We didn't know whether somebody in these parts had jest hid it thar for safekeepin', or whether some old prospector had left it thar a long time ago and maybe got sculped by the Injuns and never come back to git it. We agreed to leave it alone for a month, and if it was still thar when we come back, we'd feel purty shore that the original owner was dead, and we'd split the gold between us. Well, last night I got to worryin' lest somebody'd find it which warn't as honest as me, so this mornin' I thought I better go see if it was still thar . . ."

At this p'int Erath laughed bitterly.

Joel glared at him ominously and continued: "Well, no sooner I hove in sight of the holler tree than this skunk let go at me from the bresh with a rifle-gun——"

"That's a lie!" yelped Erath. "It war jest the other way around!"

"Not bein' armed, Breckinridge," Joel said with dignity, "and realizin' that this coyote was tryin' to murder me so he could claim all the gold, I laigged it for home and my weppin's. And presently I sighted him sprintin' through the bresh after me."

Erath begun to foam slightly at the mouth. "I warn't chasin' you!" he howled. "I war goin' home after my rifle-gun."

"What's yore story, Erath?" I inquired.

"Last night I drempt somebody had stole the gold," he answered sullenly. "This mornin' I went to see if it was safe. Jest as I got to the tree, this murderer begun shootin' at me with a Winchester. I run for my life, and by some chance I finally run right into him. Likely he thought he'd hived me and was comin' for the sculp."

"Did either one of you see t'other'n shoot at you?" I ast.

"How could I, with him hid in the bresh?" snapped Joel. "But who else could it been?"

"I didn't have to see him," growled Erath. "I felt the wind of his lead."

"But each one of you says he didn't have no rifle," I said.

"He's a cussed liar," they accused simultaneous, and would have fell onto each other tooth and nail if they could have got past my bulk. "I'm convinced they'd been a mistake," I said. "Git home and cool off."

"Yo're too big for me to lick, Breckinridge," said Erath. "But I warn you, if you cain't prove to me that it warn't Joel which tried to murder me, I ain't goin' to rest nor sleep nor eat till I've nailed his mangy sculp to the highest pine on Apache Ridge."

"That goes for me, too," says Joel, grinding his teeth. "I'm declarin' truce till to-morrer mornin'. If Breckinridge cain't show me by then that you didn't shoot at me, either my wife or yore'n'll be a widder before midnight."

So saying they stalked off in oppersite directions, whilst I stared helplessly after 'em, slightly dazed at the responsibility which had been dumped onto me. That's the drawback of being the biggest man in yore settlement. All the relatives piles their trouble onto you. Here it was up to me to stop what looked like the beginnings of a regular family feud which was bound to reduce the population awful. I couldn't go sparking me no town-gal with all this hell brewing.

The more I thought of the gold them idjits had found, the more I felt like I ought to go and take a look at it myself, so I went back to the corral and saddled Cap'n Kidd and lit out for Apache Ridge. From the remarks they'd let fall whilst cussing each other, I had a purty good idee where the holler oak was at, and sure enough I found it without much trouble. I tied Cap'n Kidd and clumb up onto the trunk till I reched the holler. And then as I was craning my neck to look in, I heard a voice say: "Another dern thief!"

I looked around and seen Uncle Jeppard Grimes p'inting a gun at me.

"Bear Creek is goin' to hell" says Uncle Jeppard. "First it was Erath and Joel, and now it's you. I aim to throw a bullet through yore hind laig jest to teach you a little honesty. Hold still whilst I draws my bead."

With that he started sighting along the barrel of his Winchester, and I says: "You better save yore lead for that Injun over there."

Him being a old Injun fighter he jest naturally jerked his head around quick, and I pulled my .45 and shot the rifle out of his hands. I jumped down and put my foot on it, and he pulled a knife out of his leggin', and I taken it away from him and shaken him till he was so addled when I let him go he run in a circle and fell down cussing something terrible.

"Is everybody on Bear Creek gone crazy?" I demanded. "Cain't a man look into a holler tree without gittin' assassinated?"

"You was after my gold!" swore Uncle Jeppard.

"So it's yore gold, hey?" I said. "Well, a holler tree ain't no bank."

"I know it," he growled, combing the pine-needles out of his whiskers. "When I come here early this mornin' to see if it was safe, like I frequent does, I seen right off somebody'd been handlin' it. Whilst I was meditatin' over this, I seen Joel Gordon sneakin' towards the tree. I fired a shot acrost his bows in warnin' and he run off. But a few minutes later here comes Erath Elkins slitherin' through the pines. I was mad by this time, so I combed his whiskers with a chunk of lead and *he* high-tailed it. And now, by golly, here you come——"

"You shet up!" I roared. "Don't you accuse me of wantin' yore blame gold. I jest wanted to see if it was safe, and so did Joel and Erath. If them men was thieves, they'd have took it when they found it yesterday. Where'd you git it, anyway?"

"I panned it, up in the hills," he said sullenly. "I ain't had time to take it to Chawed Ear and git it changed into cash money. I figgered this here tree was as good a place as any. But I done put it elsewhar now."

"Well," I said, "you got to go tell Erath and Joel it war you which shot at 'em, so they won't kill each other. They'll be mad at you, but I'll restrain 'em, with a hickery club, if necessary."

"All right," he said. "I'm sorry I misjedged you, Breckinridge. Jest to show I trusts you, I'll show you whar I hid it after I taken it outa the tree."

He led me through the trees till he come to a big rock jutting out from the side of a cliff, and p'inted at a smaller rock wedged beneath it.

"I pulled out that there rock," he said, "and dug a hole and stuck the poke in. Look!"

He heaved the rock out and bent down. And then he went straight up in the air with a yell that made me jump and pull my gun with cold sweat busting out all over me.

"What's the matter?" I demanded. "Air you snakebit!"

"Yeah, by human snakes!" he hollered. *"It's gone!* I been robbed!"

I looked and seen the impressions the wrinkles in the buckskin poke had made in the soft earth. But there warn't nothing there now.

Uncle Jeppard was doing a scalp dance with a gun in one hand and a bowie knife in the other'n. "I'll fringe my leggin's with their mangy sculps! I'll pickle their hearts in a barr'l of brine! I'll feed their gizzards to my houn' dawgs!" he yelled.

"Whose gizzards?" I inquired.

"Whose, you idjit?" he howled. "Joe Gordon and Erath Elkins, dern it! They didn't run off. They snuck back and seen me move the gold! War-paint and rattlesnakes! I've kilt better men than them for less'n half that much!"

"Aw," I said, "t'ain't possible they stole yore gold——"

"Then whar is it?" he demanded bitterly. "Who else knowed about it?"

"Look here!" I said, p'inting to a belt of soft loam nigh the rocks. "There's a hoss's tracks."

"Well, what of it?" he demanded. "Maybe they had hosses tied in the bresh."

"Aw, no," I said. "Look how the calks is sot. They ain't no hosses on Bear Creek shod like that. These is the tracks of a stranger—I bet the feller I seen ride past my cabin jest about daybreak. A black-whiskered man with one ear missin'. That hard ground by the big rock don't show where he got off and stomped around, but the man which rode this hoss stole yore gold, I'll bet my guns."

"I ain't convinced," says Uncle Jeppard. "I'm goin' home and ile my rifle-gun, and then I'm goin' to go over and kill Joel and Erath."

"Now you lissen," I said forcibly, taking hold of the front of his buckskin shirt and h'isting him off the ground by way of emphasis, "I know what a stubborn old jassack you are, Uncle Jeppard, but this time you got to listen to reason, or I'll forgit myself to the extent of kickin' the seat out of yore britches. I'm goin' to foller this feller and take yore gold away from him, because I know it war him that stole it. And don't you dare to kill nobody till I git back."

"I'll give you till to-morrer mornin'," he compromised. "I won't pull a trigger till then. But," said Uncle Jeppard waxing poetical, "if my gold ain't in my hands by the time the mornin' sun h'ists itself over the shinin' peaks of the Jackass Mountains, the buzzards will rassle their hash on the carcasses of Joel Gordon and Erath Elkins."

I went away from there . . . mounted Cap'n Kidd and headed

west on the stranger's trail. A hell of a chance *I* had to go sparking a town-gal, with my lunatickal relatives thirsting for each other's gore.

It was still tolerably early in the morning, and one of them long summer days ahead of me. They warn't a hoss in the Humbolts which could equal Cap'n Kidd for endurance. I've rode him a hundred miles between sun-down and sun-up. But the hoss the stranger was riding must have been some chunk of hoss-meat hisself, and of course he had a long start of me. The day wore on, and still I hadn't come up with my man. I'd covered a lot of distance and was getting into country I warn't familiar with, but I didn't have no trouble follering his trail, and finally, late in the evening, I come out on a narrer dusty path where the calk-marks of his hoss's shoes was very plain.

The sun sunk lower and my hopes dwindled. Even if I got the thief and got the gold, it'd be a awful push to get back to Bear Creek in time to prevent mayhem. But I urged on Cap'n Kidd, and presently we come out into a road, and the tracks I was follering merged with a lot of others. I went on, expecting to come to some settlement, and wondering jest where I was.

Jest at sun-down I rounded a bend in the road and seen something hanging to a tree, and it was a man. They was another man in the act of pinning something to the corpse's shirt, and when he heard me he wheeled and jerked his gun—the man, I mean, not the corpse. He was a mean looking cuss, but he warn't Black Whiskers. Seeing I made no hostile motion, he put up his gun and grinned.

"That feller's still kickin'?" I said.

"We just strung him up," he said. "The other boys has rode back to town, but I stayed to put this warnin' on his buzzum. Can you read?"

"No," I said.

"Well," says he, "this here paper says: 'Warnin' to all outlaws and specially them on Grizzly Mountain—Keep away from Wampum.'"

"How far's Wampum from here?" I ast.

"Half a mile down the road," he said. "I'm Al Jackson, one of Bill Ormond's deputies. We aim to clean up Wampum. This is one of them outlaws which has denned up on Grizzly Mountain."

Before I could say anything more, I heard somebody breathing quick and gaspy, and they was a patter of bare feet in the bresh, and a kid gal about fourteen years old bust into the road.

"You've killed Uncle Joab!" she shrieked. "You murderers! A

boy told me they was fixin' to hang him! I run as fast as I could——"

"Git away from that corpse!" roared Jackson, hitting at her with his quirt.

"You stop that!" I ordered. "Don't you hit that young 'un."

"Oh, please, Mister!" she wept, wringing her hands. "You ain't one of Ormond's men. Please help me! He ain't dead—I seen him move!"

Waiting for no more I spurred alongside the body and drawed my knife.

"Don't you cut that rope!" squawked the deputy, jerking his gun. So I hit him under the jaw and knocked him out of his saddle and into the bresh beside the road where he lay groaning. I then cut the rope and eased the hanged man down onto my saddle and got the noose offa his neck. He was purple in the face and his eyes was closed and his tongue lolled out, but he still had some life in him. Evidently they didn't drop him, but jest hauled him up to strangle to death.

I laid him on the ground and worked over him till some of his life begun to come back to him, but I knowed he ought to have medical attention, so I said: "Where's the nearest doctor?"

"Doc Richards in Wampum," whimpered the kid. "But if we take him there Ormond'll git him again. Won't you please take him home?"

"Where you-all live?" I inquired.

"We been livin' in a cabin on Grizzly Mountain every since Ormond run us out of Wampum," she whimpered.

"Well," I said, "I'm goin' to put yore uncle onto Cap'n Kidd and you can set behind the saddle and help hold him on, and tell me which way to go."

I done this and Cap'n Kidd didn't like it none, but after I busted him between the ears with the butt of my sixshooter he subsided and come along sulkily as I led him. As we went I seen that deputy Jackson drag hisself out of the bresh and go limping down the road holding onto his jaw.

I was losing a awful lot of time, but I couldn't leave this feller to die, even if he was a outlaw, because probably the little gal didn't have nobody else to take care of her but him.

It was well after dark when we come up a narrer trail that wound up a thickly timbered mountain side, and purty soon somebody in a thicket ahead of us hollered: "Halt whar yoo be or I'll shoot!"

"Don't shoot, Jim!" called the gal. "This is Betty, and we're bringin' Uncle Joab home."

A tall hard-looking young feller stepped out into the open, p'inting his Winchester at me. He cussed when he seen our load.

"He ain't dead," I said. "But we oughta git him to his cabin."

So Jim led the way through the thickets till we come into a clearing where they was a cabin and a woman come running out and screamed like a catamount when she seen Joab. Me and Jim lifted him off and toted him in and laid him on a bunk, and the women begun to work over him, and I went out to my hoss, because I was in a hurry to get gone. Jim follered me.

"This is the kind of stuff we've been havin' ever since Ormond come to Wampum," he says bitterly. "We been livin' up here like rats, afeared to stir in the open. I warned Joab agen slippin' down into the village to-day, but he was sot on it, and wouldn't let none of the boys go with him. Said he'd sneak in and git what he wanted and sneak out again."

"Well," I says, "what's yore business ain't none of mine. But this here life is hard lines on the women and chillern."

"You must be a friend of Joab's," he said. "He sent a man east some days ago, but we was afraid one of Ormond's men trailed him and killed him. But maybe he got through. Air you the man Joab sent for?"

"Meanin' am I some gunman come in to clean up the town?" I snorted. "Naw, I ain't. I never seen this feller Joab before."

"Well," says Jim, "cutting him down like you done has already got you in bad with Ormond. Whyn't you help us run them fellers out of the country? They's still a good many of us in these hills, even if we have been run out of Wampum. This hangin' is the last straw. I'll round up the boys to-night, and we'll have a show-down with Ormond's men. We're out-numbered, and we been licked bad onst before, but we'll try it again. Why don't you throw in with us?"

"Lissen," I says, climbing into the saddle, "jest because I cut down a outlaw ain't no sign I'm ready to be one myself. I done it jest because I couldn't stand to see the little gal take on so. Anyway, I'm looking for a feller with black whiskers and one ear missin' which rides a roan with a big Lazy-A brand."

Jim fell back from me and lifted his rifle. "You better ride on, then," he said sombrely. "I'm obleeged to you for what you've did—but a friend of Wolf Ashley cain't be no friend of our'n."

I give him a snort of defiance and rode off down the mountains and headed for Wampum, because it was reasonable to suppose that maybe I'd find Black Whiskers there.

Wampum warn't much of a town, but they was one big saloon and gambling hall where sounds of hilarity was coming from, and not many people on the streets and them which was mostly went in a hurry. I stopped one of them and ast him where a doctor lived, and he p'inted out a house where he said Doc Richards lived, so I rode up to the door and hollered, and somebody inside said: "What do you want? I got you covered."

"Air you Doc Richards?" I said, and he said: "Yes, keep your hands away from your belt or I'll salivate you."

"This is a nice, friendly town!" I snorted. "I ain't figgerin' on doin' you no harm. They's a man up in the hills which needs yore attention."

At that the door opened and a man with red whiskers and a shotgun stuck his head out and said: "Who do you mean?"

"They call him Joab," I said. "He's on Grizzly Mountain."

"Hmmmmm!" said Doc Richards, looking at me very sharp where I sot Cap'n Kidd in the starlight. "I set a man's jaw tonight, and he had a good deal to say about a certain party who cut down a man that was hanged. If you happen to be that party, my advice to you is to hit the trail before Ormond catches you."

"I'm hungry and thirsty and I'm lookin' for a man," I said. "I aim to leave Wampum when I'm good and ready."

"I never argue with a man as big as you," said Doc Richards. "I'll ride to Grizzly Mountain as quick as I can get my horse saddled. If I never see you alive again, which is very probable, I'll always remember you as the biggest man I ever saw, and the biggest fool. Good night!"

I thought the folks in Wampum is the queerest acting I ever seen. I taken Cap'n Kidd to the barn which served as a livery stable and seen that he was properly fixed in a stall to hisself, as far away from the other hosses as I could get him, because I knowed if he got to 'em he'd chaw the ears off 'em. The barn didn't look strong enough to hold him, but I told the livery stable man to keep him occupied with fodder, and to run for me if he got rambunctious. Then I went into the big saloon which was called the Golden Eagle. I was low in my spirits because I seemed to have lost Black Whiskers' trail entirely, and even if I found him in Wampum, which I hoped, I never could make it back to Bear Creek by sun-up. But I hoped to recover that derned gold yet, and get back in time to save a few lives, anyway.

They was a lot of tough looking fellers in the Golden Eagle

drinking and gambling and talking loud and cussing, and they all stopped their noise as I come in, and looked at me very fishy. But I give 'em no heed and went up to the bar, and purty soon they kinda forgot about me, and the racket started up again.

Whilst I was drinking me a few fingers of whisky, somebody shouldered up to me and said: "Hey!" I turnt around and seen a big, broad-built man with a black beard and blood-shot eyes and a pot-belly and two guns on.

I says: "Well?"

"Who air you?" he demanded.

"Who air you?" I come back at him.

"I'm Bill Ormond, sheriff of Wampum," he says. "That's who!" And he showed me a star onto his shirt.

"Oh," I says. "Well, I'm Breckinridge Elkins, from Bear Creek."

I noticed a kind of quiet come over the place, and fellers was laying down their glasses and their billiard sticks, and hitching up their belts and kinda gathering around me. Ormond scowled and combed his beard with his fingers, and rocked on his heels and said: "I got to 'rest you!"

I sot down my glass quick and he jumped back and hollered: "Don't you dast pull no gun on the law!" And they was a kind of movement amongst the men around me.

"What you arrestin' me for?" I demanded. "I ain't busted no law."

"You assaulted one of my deperties," he said, and then I seen that feller Jackson standing behind the sheriff with his jaw all bandaged up. He couldn't work his chin to talk. All he could do was p'int his finger at me and shake his fists.

"You likewise cut down a outlaw we had just hunged," says Ormond. "Yo're under arrest!"

"But I'm lookin' for a man!" I protested. "I ain't got time to be arrested!"

"You should of thunk about that when you busted the law," opined Ormond. "Gimme yore gun and come along peaceable."

A dozen men had their hands on their guns, but it warn't that which made me give in. Pap had always told me not to resist no officer of the law. It was kind of instinctive for me to hand over my gun to this feller with the star on his shirt. Somehow it didn't seem right, but I was kind of bewildered and my thoughts was addled. I ain't one of these fast thinking sharps. So I jest done what pap always told me to do.

Ormond taken me down the street a-ways, with a whole bunch of men follering us, and stopped at a log building with barred winders which was next to a board shack. A man come out of this shack with a big bunch of keys, and Ormond said he was the jailer. So they put me in the log jail and Ormond went off with everybody but the jailer, who sot down on the step outside his shack and rolled hisself a cigaret.

They warn't no light in the jail, but I found the bunk and tried to lay down on it, but it warn't built for a man six and a half foot tall. I sot down on it and at last realized what a infernal mess I was in. Here I ought to be hunting Black Whiskers and getting the gold to take back to Bear Creek and save the lives of a swarm of my kin-folks, but instead of that I was in jail, and no way of getting out without killing a officer of the law. With daybreak Joel and Erath would be at each others' throats, and Uncle Jeppard would be gunning for both of 'em. It was too much to hope that the other relatives would let them three fight it out amongst their-selves. I never seen sech a clan for buttin into each others' business. The guns would be talking all up and down Bear Creek, and the population would be decreasing with every volley. I thunk about it till I got dizzy and then the jailer stuck his head up to the winder and said if I'd give him five dollars he'd go get me something to eat.

I had five dollars I won in a poker game a few days before and I give it to him, and he went off and was gone quite a spell, and at last he come back and give me a ham sandwich. I ast him was that all he could get for five dollars, and he said grub was awful high in Wampum. I et the sandwich with one bite, and he said if I'd give him some more money he'd get me another sandwich. But I didn't have no more and told him so.

"What!" he said, breathing licker fumes in my face through the winder bars. "No money? And you expect us to feed you for nothin'?" So he cussed me, and went off, and purty soon the sheriff come and looked in at me, and said: "What's this I hear about you not havin' no money?"

"I ain't got none left," I said, and he cussed something fierce.

"How you expeck to pay yore fine?" he demanded. "You think you can lay up in our jail and eat us out of house and home? What kind of a critter are you, anyway?"

Just then the jailer chipped in and said somebody told him I had a hoss down at the livery stable.

"Good," said the sheriff. "We'll sell his hoss for his fine."

"You won't neither," I says, beginning to get mad. "You try to sell Cap'n Kidd, and I'll forgit what pap told me about law-officers, and take you plumb apart."

I riz up and glared at him through the winder, and he fell back and put his hand on his gun. But jest about that time I seen a man going into the Golden Eagle which was in easy sight of the jail, and lit up so the light streamed out into the street. I give a yell that made Ormond jump about a foot. It was Black Whiskers!

"Arrest that man, Sheriff!" I hollered. "He's a thief!"

Ormond whirled and looked, and then he said: "Air you plumb crazy? That's Wolf Ashley, my deperty."

"I don't give a dern," I said. "He stole a poke of gold from my Uncle Jeppard Grimes up in the Humbolts, and I've trailed him clean from Bear Creek. Do yore duty and arrest him."

"You shet up!" roared Ormond. "You cain't tell me my business! I ain't goin' to arrest my best gunman—my star deperty, I mean. What you mean tryin' to start trouble this way? One more yap outa you and I'll throw a chunk of lead through you."

And he turned around and stalked off muttering: "Poke of gold, huh? Holdin' out on me, is he? I'll see about that!"

I sot down and held my head in bewilderment. What kind of a sheriff was this which wouldn't arrest a derned thief? My thoughts run in circles till my wits was addled. The jailer had gone off and I wondered if he had went to see Cap'n Kidd. I wondered what was going on back on Bear Creek, and I shivered to think what would bust loose at daybreak. And here I was in jail, with them fellers fixing to sell my hoss, whilst that dern thief swaggered around at large. I looked helplessly outa the winder.

It was getting late, but the Golden Eagle was going full blast. I could hear the music blaring away, and the fellers yipping and shooting their pistols in the air, and their boot heels stomping on the board walk. I felt like busting down and bawling, and then I begun to get mad. I get mad slow, generally, and before I was plumb mad, I heard a noise at the winder.

I seen a pale face staring in at me, and a couple of small white hands on the bars.

"Mister!" a voice whispered. "Oh, Mister!"

I stepped over and looked out and it was the kid gal Betty.

"What you doin' here, gal?" I ast.

"Doc Richards said you was in Wampum," she whispered. "He said he was afraid Ormond would do for you because you helped us, so I slipped away on his hoss and rode here as hard as I could. Jim was out tryin' to round up the boys for a last stand, and Aunt Rachel and the other women was busy with Uncle Joab. They wasn't nobody but me to come, but I had to! You saved Uncle Joab, and I don't care if Jim does say yo're a outlaw because yo're a friend of Wolf Ashley. Oh, I wish't I wasn't jest a gal! I wish't I could shoot a gun, so's I could kill Bill Ormond!"

"That ain't no way for a gal to talk," I says. "Leave the killin' to the men. But I appreciates you goin' to all this trouble. I got some kid sisters myself—in fact I got seven or eight as near as I remember. Don't you worry none about me. Lots of men gits throwed in jail."

"But that ain't it!" she wept, wringing her hands. "I listened outside the winder of the back room in the Golden Eagle and heard Ormond and Ashley talkin' about you. I dunno what you wanted with Ashley when you ast Jim about him, but he ain't yo're friend. Ormond accused him of stealin' a poke of gold and holdin' out on him, and Ashley said it was a lie. Then Ormond said you told him about it, and he said he'd give Ashley till midnight to perjuice that gold, and if he didn't Wampum would be too small for both of 'em.

"Then he went out to the bar, and I heered Ashley talkin' to a pal of his'n, and Ashley said he'd have to raise some gold somehow, or Ormond would have him killed, but that he was goin' to fix *you*, Mister, for lyin' about him. Mister, Ashley and his bunch air over in the back of the Golden Eagle right now plottin' to bust into jail before daylight and hang you!"

"Aw," I says, "the sheriff wouldn't let 'em do that."

"But Ormond ain't the sheriff!" she cried. "Him and his gun-men come into Wampum and killed all the people that tried to oppose him, or run 'em up into the hills. They got us penned up there like rats, nigh starvin' and afeared to come to town. Uncle Joab come into Wampum this mornin' to git some salt, and you seen what they done to him. *He's* the real sheriff. Ormond is jest a bloody outlaw. Him and his gang is usin' Wampum for a hang-out whilst they rob and steal and kill all over the country."

"Then that's what yore friend Jim meant," I said slowly. "And me, like a dumb damn' fool, I thought him and Joab and the rest of you-all was jest outlaws, like that fake deperty said."

"Ormond took Uncle Joab's badge and called hisself the sheriff to fool strangers," she whimpered. "What honest people is left in Wampum air afeared to say anything. Him and his gunmen air rulin' this whole part of the country. Uncle Joab sent a man east to git us some help in the settlements on Buffalo River, but none never come, and from what I overheard to-night, I believe Wolf Ashley follered him and killed him over east of the Humbolts somewheres. What air we goin' to do?" she sobbed.

"Git on Doc Richards' hoss and ride for Grizzly Mountain," I said. "When you git there, tell the Doc to light a shuck for Wampum, because there's goin' to be plenty of work for him time he gits here."

"But what about you?" she cried. "I cain't go off and leave you to git hanged!"

"Don't worry about me, gal," I said. "I'm Breckinridge Elkins of the Humbolt Mountains, and I'm preparin' for to shake my mane! Hustle!"

I reckon something about me convinced her, because she glided away into the shadders, whimpering, and presently I heard the clack of hoss's hoofs dwindling in the distance. I then riz and laid hold of the winder bars and tore 'em out by the roots. Then I sunk my fingers into the sill log and tore it out, and three or four more along with it, and the wall give way and the roof fell down on me, but I shaken aside the rooins and heaved up out of the wreckage like a b'ar out of a deadfall.

About this time the jailer come running up, and when he seen what I had did he was so surprised he forgot to shoot with his pistol. So I taken it away from him and knocked down the door of his shack with him and left him laying in its rooins.

I then strode up the street towards the Golden Eagle and here come a feller galloping down the street, and who should it be but that derned fake deputy, Jackson. He couldn't holler with his bandaged jaw, but when he seen me he jerked loose his lariat and piled it around my neck, and sot spurs to his cayuse aiming for to drag me to death. But I seen he had his rope tied fast to his horn, Texas style, so I laid hold onto it with both hands and braced my laigs, and when the hoss got to the end of the rope, the girths busted and the hoss went out from under the saddle, and Jackson come down on his head in the street and laid still.

I throwed the rope off my neck and went onto the Golden Eagle with the jailer's .45 in my scabbard. I looked in and seen the same crowd there, and Ormond r'ared back at the bar with his belly stuck out, roaring and bragging.

I stepped in and hollered: "Look this way, Bill Ormond, and pull iron, you dirty thief!"

He wheeled, paled, and went for his gun, and I slammed six bullets into him before he could hit the floor. I then throwed the empty gun at the dazed crowd and give one deafening roar and tore into 'em like a mountain cyclone. They begun to holler and surge onto me and I throwed 'em and knocked 'em right and left like ten pins. Some was knocked over the bar and some under the tables and some I knocked down stacks of beer kegs with. I ripped

the roulette wheel loose and mowed down a whole row of 'em
with it, and I throwed a billiard table through the mirror behind
the bar jest for good measure. Three or four fellers got pinned
under it and yelled bloody murder.

Meanwhile they was hacking at me with bowies and hitting me
with chairs and brass knuckles and trying to shoot me, but all they
done with their guns was shoot each other because they was so
many they got in each other's way, and the other things just made
me madder. I laid hands on as many as I could hug at onst, and
the thud of their heads banging together was music to me. I also
done good work heaving 'em head-on agen the walls, and I further
slammed several of 'em heartily agen the floor and busted all the
tables with their carcasses. In the melee the whole bar collapsed,
and the shelves behind the bar fell down when I slang a feller into
'em, and bottles rained all over the floor. One of the lamps also
fell off the ceiling which was beginning to crack and cave in, and
everybody begun to yell: "Fire!" and run out through the doors
and jump out the winders.

In a second I was alone in the blazing building except for them
which was past running. I'd started for a door myself when I seen
a buckskin pouch on the floor along with a lot of other belongings
which had fell out of men's pockets as they will when the men
gets swung by the feet and smashed agen the wall.

I picked it up and jerked the tie-string, and a trickle of gold
dust spilt into my hand. I begun to look on the floor for Ashley,
but he warn't there. But he was watching me from outside, because
I looked and seen him jest as he let bam at me with a .45 from
the back room which warn't on fire much yet. I plunged after him,
ignoring his next slug which took me in the shoulder, and then I
grabbed him and taken the gun away from him. He pulled a bowie
and tried to stab me in the groin, but only sliced my thigh, so I
throwed him the full length of the room and he hit the wall so
hard his head went through the boards.

Meantime the main part of the saloon was burning so I couldn't
go out that way. I started to go out the back door of the room I
was in, but got a glimpse of some fellers which was crouching
jest outside the door waiting to shoot me as I come out. So I
knocked out a section of the wall on another side of the room,
and about that time the roof fell in so loud them fellers didn't hear
me coming, so I fell on 'em from the rear and beat their heads
together till the blood ran out of their ears, and stomped 'em and
taken their shotguns away from 'em.

Then I was aware that people was shooting at me in the light of the burning saloons, and I seen that a bunch was ganged up on the other side of the street, so I begun to loose my shotguns into the thick of them, and they broke and run yelling blue murder.

And as they went out one side of the town, another gang rushed in from the other, yelling and shooting, and I snapped a empty shell at 'em before one yelled: "Don't shoot, Elkins! We're friends!" And I seen it was Jim and Doc Richards, and a lot of other fellers I hadn't never seen before then.

They went tearing after Ormond's gang, whooping and yelling, and the way them outlaws took to the tall timber was a caution. They warn't no fight left in 'em at all.

Jim pulled up, and looked at the wreckage of the jail, and the remnants of the Golden Eagle, and he shook his head like he couldn't believe it.

"We was on our way to make a last effort to take the town back from that gang," says he. "Betty met us as we come down the trail and told you was a friend and a honest man. We hoped to git here in time to save you from gittin'. hanged." Again he shaken his head with a kind of bewildered look. Then he says "Oh, say, I'd forgot. On the way here we run onto a man on the road who said he was lookin' for you. Not knowin' who he was, we roped him and brung him along with us. Bring the prisoner, boys!"

They brung him, tied to his saddle, and it was Jack Gordon, Joel's youngest brother and the fastest gunslinger on Bear Creek.

"What you doin' houndin' me?" I demanded bitterly. "Has the feud begun already and has Joel sot you on *my* trail? Well, I got what I come after, and I'm headin' back for Bear Creek. I cain't git there by daylight, but maybe I'll git there in time to keep everybody from gittin' kilt. Here's Uncle Jeppard's cussed gold!" And I waved the poke in front of him.

"But that cain't be it!" says he. "I been trailin' you all the way from Bear Creek, tryin' to catch you and tell you the gold had been found! Uncle Jeppard and Joel and Erath got together and everything was explained and is all right. Where'd you git that gold!"

"I dunno whether Ashley's pals got it together so he could give it to Ormond and not git kilt for holdin' out on his boss, or what," I says. "But I know the owner ain't got no more use for it now, and probably stole it in the first place. I'm givin' this gold to Betty," I says. "She shore deserves a reward. And giving it to her makes me feel like maybe *some* good come outa this wild goose chase, after all."

Jim looked around at the ruins of the outlaw hangout, and murmured something I didn't catch. I says to Jack: "You said Uncle Jeppard's gold was found. Where was it, anyway?"

"Well," said Jack, "little General William Harrison Grimes, Joash Grimes's youngest boy, he seen his grandpap put the gold under the rock, and he got it out to play with it. He was usin' the nuggets for slugs in his nigger-shooter," Jack said, "and it's plumb cute the way he pops a rattlesnake with 'em. What did you say?"

"Nothin'," I said between my teeth. "Nothin' that'd be fit to repeat, anyway."

"Well," he said, "if you've had yore fun, I reckon yo're ready to start back to Bear Creek with me."

"I reckon I ain't," I said. "I'm goin' to 'tend to my own private affairs for a change. I told Glory McGraw early this mornin' I was goin' to git me a town-gal, and by golly, I meant it. Gwan on back to Bear Creek, and if you see Glory, tell her I'm headin' for Chawed Ear where the purty gals is as thick as honey bees around a apple tree."

CHAPTER VI

The Feud Buster

I pulled out of Wampum before sun-up. The folks wanted me to stay and be a deputy sheriff, but I taken a good look at the female population and seen that the only single woman in town was a Piute squaw. So I headed acrost the mountains for Chawed Ear, swinging wide to avoid coming anywheres nigh to the Humbolts. I didn't want to chance running into Glory McGraw before I had me a town-gal.

But I didn't get to Chawed Ear nigh as soon as I'd figgered to. As I passed through the hills along the head-waters of Mustang River, I run into a camp of cowpunchers from the Triple L which was up there rounding up strays. The foreman needed some hands, and I happened to think maybe I'd cut a better figger before the Chawed Ear belles if'n I had some money in my pocket, so I taken on with them. After he seen me and Cap'n Kidd do one day's work the foreman 'lowed that they warn't no use in hiring the six or seven other men he aimed; he said I filled the bill perfect.

So I worked with 'em three weeks, and then collected my pay and pulled for Chawed Ear.

I was all primed for the purty settlement-gals, little suspected the jamboree I was riding into blind, the echoes of which ain't yet quite circulating through the mountain country. And that reminds me to remark that I'm sick and tired of the slanders which has been noised abroad about that there affair, and if they don't stop, I'll liable to lose my temper, and anybody in the Humbolts can tell you when I loses my temper the effect on the population is wuss'n fire, earthquake and cyclone.

First-off, it's a lie that I rode a hundred miles to mix into a feud which wasn't none of my business. I never heard of the Warren-Barlow war before I come into the Mezquital country. I hear tell the Barlows is talking about suing me for destroying their property. Well, they ought to build their cabins solider if they don't want 'em tore down. And they're all liars when they says the Warrens hired me to exterminate 'em at five dollars a sculp. I don't believe even a Warren would pay five dollars for one of their mangy sculps. Anyway, I don't fight for hire for nobody, And the Warrens needn't belly-ache about me turnin' on 'em and trying to massacre the entire clan. All I wanted to do was kind of disable 'em so they couldn't interfere with my business. And my business, from first to last, was defending the family honour. If I had to wipe up the earth with a couple of feuding clans whilst so doing, I cain't help it. Folks which is particular of their hides ought to stay out of the way of tornadoes, wild bulls, devastating torrents and a insulted Elkins.

This is the way it was: I was dry and hot and thirsty when I hit Chawed Ear, so I went into a saloon and had me a few drinks. Then I was going out and start looking for a gal, when I spied a friendly game of kyards going on between a hoss-thief and three train-robbers, and I decided I'd set in for a hand or so. And whilst we was playing, who should come in but Uncle Jeppard Grimes. I should of knew my day was spoilt the minute he hove in sight. Dern near all the calamities which takes place in southern Nevada can be traced back to that old lobo. He's got a ingrown diposition and a natural talent for pestering his feller man. Specially his relatives.

He didn't say a word about that wild goose chase I went on to get back the gold I thought Wolf Ashley had stole from him. He come over and scowled down on me like I was the missing lynx or something, and purty soon, jest as I was all sot to make a killing, he says: "How can you set there so free and keerless, with four aces into yore hand, when yore family name is bein' besmirched?"

I flang down my hand in annoyance, and said: "Now look what you done! What you mean blattin' out information of sech a private nature? What you talkin' about, anyhow?"

"Well," he says, "durin' the time you been away from home rolsterin' and wastin' yore substance in riotous livin'——"

"I been punchin' cows!" I said fiercely. "And before that I was chasing a man to git back the gold I thought he'd stole from you! I ain't squandered nothin' nowheres. Shet up and tell me whatever yo're a-talkin' about."

"Well," says he, "whilst you been gone young Dick Blanton of Grizzly Run has been courtin' yore sister Elinor, and the family's been expectin' 'em to set the day, any time now. But now I hear he's been braggin' all over Grizzly Run about how he done jilted her. Air you goin' to set there and let yore sister become the laughin' stock of the country? When I was a young man——"

"When you was a young man Dan'l Boone warn't whelped yet!" I bellered, so mad I included him and everybody else in my irritation. They ain't nothing upsets me like injustice done to some of my close kin. "Git out of my way! I'm headin' for Grizzly Run—what *you* grinnin' at, you spotted hyener?" This last was addressed to the hoss-thief in which I seemed to detect signs of amusement.

"I warn't grinnin'," he said.

"So I'm a liar, I reckon!" I said, impulsively shattering a demi-john over his head, and he fell under the table hollering bloody murder, and all the fellers drinking at the bar abandoned their licker and stampeded for the street hollering: "Take cover, boys! Breckinridge Elkins is on the rampage!"

So I kicked all the slats out of the bar to relieve my feelings, and stormed out of the saloon and forked Cap'n Kidd. Even he seen it was no time to take liberties with me; he didn't pitch but seven jumps, and then he settled down to a dead run, and we headed for Grizzly Run.

Everything kind of floated in a red haze all the way, but them folks which claims I tried to murder 'em in cold blood on the road between Chawed Ear and Grizzly Run is jest narrer-minded and super-sensitive. The reason I shot off everybody's hats that I met was jest to kind of ca'm my nerves, because I was afeared if I didn't cool off some by the time I hit Grizzly Run I might hurt somebody. I'm that mild-mannered and retiring by nature that I wouldn't willing hurt man, beast, nor Injun unless maddened beyond all endurance.

That's why I acted with so much self-possession and dignity when I got to Grizzly Run and entered the saloon where Dick Blanton generally hung out.

"Where's Dick Blanton?" I demanded, and everybody must of been nervous, because when I boomed out they all jumped and looked around, and the bartender dropped a glass and turned pale.

"Well," I hollered, beginning to lose patience. "Where is the coyote?"

"G—gimme time, will ya?" stuttered the bar-keep. "I—I—uh—he—uh——"

"Evadin' the question, hey?" I said, kicking the foot-rail loose. "Friend of his'n, hey? Tryin' to pertect him, hey?" I was so overcome by this perfidy that I lunged for him and he ducked down behind the bar and I crashed into it bodily with all my lungs and weight, and it collapsed on top of him, and all the customers run out of the saloon hollering: "Help, murder, Elkins is killin' the bar-tender!"

That individual stuck his head up from amongst the rooins of the bar and begged: "For God's sake, lemme alone! Blanton headed south for the Mezquital Mountains yesterday."

I throwed down the chair I was fixing to bust all the ceiling lamps with, and run out and jumped on Cap'n Kidd and headed south, whilst behind me folks emerged from their cyclone cellars and sent a rider up in the hills to tell the sheriff and his deputies they could come on back now.

I knowed where the Mezquitals was, though I hadn't never been there. I crossed the Californy line about sundown, and shortly after dark I seen Mezquital Peak looming ahead of me. Having ca'med down somewhat, I decided to stop and rest Cap'n Kidd. He warn't tired, because that hoss has got alligator blood in his veins, but I knowed I might have to trail Blanton clean to The Angels, and they warn't no use in running Cap'n Kidd's laigs off on the first lap of the chase.

It warn't a very thick settled country I'd come into, very mountainous and thick timbered, but purty soon I come to a cabin beside the trail and I pulled up and hollered: "Hello!"

The candle inside was instantly blowed out, and somebody pushed a rifle barrel through the winder and bawled: "Who be you?"

"I'm Breckinridge Elkins from Bear Creek, Nevada," I said. "I'd like to stay all night, and git some feed for my hoss."

"Stand still," warned the voice. "We can see you agen the stars, and they's four rifle-guns a-kiverin' you."

"Well, make up yore minds," I said, because I could hear 'em discussin' me. I reckon they thought they was whispering. One of 'em said: "Aw, he cain't be a Barlow. Ain't none of 'em that big." T'other'n said: "Well, maybe he's a derned gun-fighter they've sent for to help 'em. Old Jack's nephew's been up in Nevady."

"Le's let him in," says a third. "We can mighty quick tell what he is."

So one of 'em come out and 'lowed it would be all right for me to stay the night, and he showed me a corral to put Cap'n Kidd in, and hauled out some hay for him.

"We got to be keerful," he said. "We got lots of enemies in these hills."

We went into the cabin, and they lit the candle again, and sot some corn pone and sow-belly and beans on the table and a jug of corn licker. They was four men, and they said their names was Wareen—George, Ezra, Elisha, and Joshua, and they was brothers. I'd always heard tell the Mezquital country was famed for big men, but these fellers warn't so big—not much over six foot high apiece. On Bear Creek they'd been considered kind of puny and undersized, so to speak.

They warn't very talkative. Mostly they sot with their rifles acrost their knees and looked at me without no expression onto their faces, but that didn't stop me from eating a hearty supper, and would of et a lot more only the grub give out; and I hoped they had more licker somewheres else because I was purty dry. When I turned up the jug to take a snort it was brim-full, but before I'd more'n dampened my gullet the dern thing was plumb empty.

When I got through I went over and sot down on a raw-hide bottomed chair in front of the fireplace where they warn't no fire because it was summer time, and they said: "What's yore business, stranger?"

"Well," I said, not knowing I was going to get the surprise of my life, "I'm lookin' for a feller named Dick Blanton——"

By golly, the words warn't clean out of my mouth when they was four men onto my neck like catamounts!

"He's a spy!" they hollered. "He's a cussed Barlow! Shoot him! Stab him! Hit him on the head!"

All of which they was endeavouring to do with such passion they was getting in each other's way, and it was only his over-eagerness which caused George to miss me with his bowie and sink it into the table instead, but Joshua busted a chair over my head and Elisha would of shot me if I hadn't jerked back my head so he jest singed my eyebrows. This lack of hospitality so irritated me that I riz up amongst 'em like a b'ar with a pack of wolves hanging onto him, and commenced committing mayhem on my hosts, because I seen right off they was critters which couldn't be persuaded to respect a guest no other way.

Well, the dust of battle hadn't settled, the casualities was groaning all over the place, and I was jest relighting the candle when I heard a hoss galloping up the trail from the south. I wheeled and drawed my guns as it stopped before the cabin. But I didn't shoot, because the next instant they was a bare-footed gal standing in the

door. When she seen the rooins she let out a screech like a catamount.

"You've kilt 'em!" she screamed. "You murderer!"

"Aw, I ain't, neither," I said. "They ain't hurt much—jest a
few cracked ribs and dislocated shoulders and busted laigs and
sech-like trifles. Joshua's ear'll grow back on all right, if you take
a few stitches into it."

"You cussed Barlow!" she squalled, jumping up and down with
the hysthericals. "I'll kill you! You damned Barlow!"

"I ain't no Barlow, dern it," I said. "I'm Breckinridge Elkins,
of Bear Creek. I ain't never even heard of no Barlows."

At that George stopped his groaning long enough to snarl: "If
you ain't a friend of the Barlows, how come you askin' for Dick
Blanton? He's one of 'em."

"He jilted my sister!" I roared. "I aim to drag him back and
make him marry her."

"Well, it was all a mistake," groaned George. "But the damage
is done now."

"It's wuss'n you think," said the gal fiercely. "The Warrens
has all forted theirselves over at pap's cabin, and they sent me to
git you boys. We got to make a stand. The Barlows is gatherin'
over to Jake Barlow's cabin, and they aims to make a foray onto
us to-night. We was outnumbered to begin with, and now here's
our best fightin' men laid out! Our goose is cooked plumb to hell!"

"Lift me onto my hoss," moaned George. "I cain't walk, but
I can still shoot." He tried to rise up, and fell back cussing and
groaning.

"You got to help us!" said the gal desperately, turning to me.
"You done laid out our four best fightin' men, and you owes it
to us. It's yore duty! Anyway, you says Dick Blanton's yore
enemy—well, he's Jake Barlow's nephew, and he come back here
to help 'em clean out us Warrens. He's over to Jake's cabin right
now. My brother Bill snuck over and spied on 'em, and he says
every fightin' man of the clan is gatherin' there. All we can do is
hold the fort, and you got to come help us hold it? Yo're nigh as
big as all four of these boys put together."

Well, I figgered I owed the Warrens something, so, after setting
some bones and bandaging some wounds and abrasions of which
they was a goodly lot, I saddled Cap'n Kidd and we sot out.

As we rode along she said: "That there is the biggest, wildest,
meanest-lookin' critter I ever seen. Is he actually a hoss, or some
kind of a varmint?"

"He's a hoss," I said. "But he's got painter's blood and a shark's disposition. What's this feud about?"

"I dunno," she said. "It's been goin' on so long everybody's done forgot what started it. Somebody accused somebody else of stealin' a cow, I think. What's the difference?"

"They ain't none," I assured her. "If folks wants to have feuds it's their own business."

We was follering a winding path, and purty soon we heard dogs barking and about that time the gal turned aside and got off her hoss, and showed me a pen hid in the bresh. It was full of hosses.

"We keep our mounts here so's the Barlows ain't so likely to find 'em and run 'em off," she said, and she turnt her hoss into the pen, and I put Cap'n Kidd in, but I tied him over in one corner by hisself—otherwise he would of started fighting all the other hosses and kicked the fence down.

Then we went on along the path and the dogs barked louder and purty soon we come to a big two-story cabin which had heavy board-shutters over the winders. They was jest a dim streak of candle light come through the cracks. It was dark, because the moon hadn't come up. We stopped in the shadders of the trees, and the gal whistled like a whippoorwill three times, and somebody answered from up on the roof. A door opened a crack in a room which didn't have no light at all, and somebody said: "That you, Elizerbeth? Air the boys with you?"

"It's me," says she, starting towards the door. "But the boys ain't with me."

Then all to onst he throwed open the door and hollered: "Run, gal! They's a grizzly b'ar standin' up on his hind laigs right behind you!"

"Aw, that ain't no b'ar," says she. "That there's Breckinridge Elkins, from up in Nevady. He's goin' to help us fight the Barlows."

We went on into a room where they was a candle on the table, and they was nine or ten men there and thirty-odd women and chillern. They all looked kinda pale and scairt, and the men was loaded down with pistols and Winchesters.

They all looked at me kind of dumb-like, and the old man kept staring at me like he warn't any too sure he hadn't let a grizzly in the house, after all. He mumbled something about making a natural mistake, in the dark, and turnt to the gal, and demanded: "Whar's the boys I sent you after?"

And she says: "This gent mussed 'em up so's they ain't fitten for to fight. Now, don't git rambunctious, Pap. It war jest a honest mistake all around. He's our friend, and he's gunnin' for Dick Blanton."

"Ha! Dick Blanton!" snarled one of the men, lifting his Winchester. "Jest lemme line my sights on him! I'll cook his goose!"

"You won't neither," I said. "He's got to go back to Bear Creek and marry my sister Elinor.... Well," I says, "what's the campaign?"

"I don't figger they'll git here till well after midnight," said Old Man Warren. "All we can do is wait for 'em."

"You means you all sets here and waits till they comes and lays siege?" I says.

"What else?" says he. "Lissen here, young man, don't start tellin' me how to conduck a feud. I growed up in this here'n. It war in full swing when I was born, and I done spent my whole life carryin' it on."

"That's jest it," I snorted. "You lets these dern wars drag on for generations. Up in the Humbolts we bring sech things to a quick conclusion. Mighty nigh everybody up there come from Texas, original, and we fights our feuds Texas style, which is short and sweet—a feud which lasts ten years in Texas is a humdinger. We winds 'em up quick and in style. Where-at is this here cabin where the Barlows is gatherin'?"

"'Bout three mile over the ridge," says a young feller they called Bill.

"How many is they?" I ast.

"I counted seventeen," says he.

"Jest a fair-sized mouthful for a Elkins," I said. "Bill, you guide me to that there cabin. The rest of you can come or stay, it don't make no difference to me."

Well, they started jawing with each other then. Some was for going and some for staying. Some wanted to go with me, and try to take the Barlows by surprise, but the others said it couldn't be done—they'd git ambushed theirselves, and the only sensible thing to be did was to stay forted and wait for the Barlows to come. They given me no more heed—jest sot there and augered.

But that was all right with me. Right in the middle of the dispute, when it looked like maybe the Warrens would get to fighting among theirselves and finish each other before the Barlows could get there, I lit out with the boy Bill, which seemed to have considerable sense for a Warren.

He got him a hoss out of the hidden corral, and I got Cap'n

Kidd, which was a good thing. He'd somehow got a mule by the neck, and the critter was almost at its last gasp when I rescued it. Then me and Bill lit out.

We follered winding paths over thick-timbered mountain-sides till at last we come to a clearing and they was a cabin there, with light and profanity pouring out of the winders. We'd been hearing the last mentioned for half a mile before we sighted the cabin.

We left our hosses back in the woods a ways, and snuck up on foot and stopped amongst the trees back of the cabin.

"They're in there tankin' up on corn licker to whet their appertites for Warren blood!" whispered Bill, all in a shiver. "Lissen to 'em! Them fellers ain't hardly human! What you goin' to do? They got a man standin' guard out in front of the door at the other end of the cabin. You see they ain't no doors nor winders at the back. They's winders on each side, but if we try to rush it from the front or either side, they'll see us and fill us full of lead before we could git in a shot. Look! The moon's comin' up. They'll be startin' on their raid before long."

I'll admit that cabin looked like it was going to be harder to storm than I'd figgered. I hadn't had no idee in mind when I sot out for the place. All I wanted was to get in amongst them Barlows—I does my best fighting at close quarters. But at the moment I couldn't think of no way that wouldn't get me shot up. Of course I could jest rush the cabin, but the thought of seventeen Winchesters blazing away at me from close range was a little stiff even for me, though I was game to try it, if they warn't no other way.

Whilst I was studying over the matter, all to onst the hosses tied out in front of the cabin snorted, and back up in the hills something went *Oooaaaw-w-w!* And a idee hit me.

"Git back in the woods and wait for me," I told Bill, as I headed for the thicket where we'd left the hosses.

I rode up in the hills towards where the howl had come from, and purty soon I lit and throwed Cap'n Kidd's reins over his head, and walked on into the deep bresh, from time to time giving a long squall like a cougar. They ain't a catamount in the world can tell the difference when a Bear Creek man imitates one. After a while one answered, from a ledge jest a few hundred feet away.

I went to the ledge and clumb up on it, and there was a small cave behind it, and a big mountain lion in there. He give a grunt of surprise when he seen I was a human, and made a swipe at me, but I give him a bat on the head with my fist, and whilst he was still dizzy I grabbed him by the scruff of the neck and hauled him out of the cave and lugged him down to where I left my hoss.

Cap'n Kidd snorted when he seen the cougar and wanted to kick his brains out, but I give him a good kick in the stummick hisself, which is the only kind of reasoning Cap'n Kidd understands, and got on him and headed for the Barlow hangout.

I can think of a lot more pleasant jobs than totin' a full-growed mountain lion down a thick-timbered mountain-side on the back of a iron-jawed outlaw at midnight. I had the cat by the back of the neck with one hand, so hard he couldn't squall, and I held him out at arm's length as far from me and the hoss as I could, but every now and then he'd twist around so he could claw Cap'n Kidd with his hind laigs, and when this would happen Cap'n Kidd would squall with rage and start bucking all over the place. Sometimes he would buck the derned cougar onto me, and pulling him loose from my hide was wuss'n pulling cockle-burrs out of a cow's tail.

But presently I arriv close behind the cabin. I whistled like a whippoorwill for Bill, but he didn't answer and warn't nowheres to be seen, so I decided he'd got scairt and pulled out for home. But that was all right with me. I'd come to fight the Barlows, and I aimed to fight 'em, with or without assistance. Bill would jest of been in the way.

I got off in the trees back of the cabin and throwed the reins over Cap'n Kidd's head, and went up to the back of the cabin on foot, walking soft and easy. The moon was well up, by now, and what wind they was, was blowing towards me, which pleased me, because I didn't want the hosses tied out in front to scent the cat and start cutting up before I was ready.

The fellers inside was still cussing and talking loud as I approached one of the winders on the side, and one hollered out: "Come on! Le's git started! I craves Warren gore!" And about that time I give the cougar a heave and throwed him through the winder.

He let out a awful squall as he hit, and the fellers in the cabin hollered louder'n he did. Instantly a most awful bustle broke loose in there and of all the whooping and bellering and shooting I ever heard, and the lion squalling amongst it all, and clothes and hides tearing so you could hear it all over the clearing, and the hosses busting loose and tearing out through the bresh.

As soon as I hove the cat I run around to the door and a man was standing there with his mouth open, too surprised at the racket to do anything. So I taken his rifle away from him and broke the stock off on his head, and stood there at the door with the barrel intending to brain them Barlows as they run out. I was plumb certain they *would* run out, because I have noticed the average man is funny that way, and hates to be shet up in a cabin with a mad cougar as bad as the cougar would hate to be shet up in a cabin with a infuriated settler of Bear Creek.

But them scoundrels fooled me. 'Pears like they had a secret door in the back wall, and whilst I was waiting for them to storm out through the front door and get their skulls cracked, they knocked the secret door open and went piling out that way.

By the time I realized what was happening and run around to the other end of the cabin, they was all out and streaking for the trees, yelling blue murder, with their clothes all tore to shreds and them bleeding like stuck hawgs.

That there catamount sure improved the shining hours whilst he was corralled with them Barlows. He come out after 'em with his mouth full of the seats of their britches, and when he seen me he give a kind of despairing yelp and taken out up the mountain with his tail betwixt his laigs like the devil was after him with a red-hot branding iron.

I taken after the Barlows, sot on scuttling at least a few of 'em, and I was on the p'int of letting bam at 'em with my six-shooters as they run, when, jest as they reched the trees, all the Warren men riz out of the bresh and fell on 'em with piercing howls.

That fray was kind of pecooliar. I don't remember a single shot being fired. The Barlows had all dropped their guns in their flight, and the Warrens seemed bent on wiping out their wrongs with their bare fists and gun butts. For a few seconds they was a hell of a scramble—men cussing and howling and bellering, and rifle-stocks cracking over heads, and the bresh crashing underfoot, and then before I could get into it, the Barlows broke every which-way and took out through the woods like jack-rabbits squalling Jedgment Day.

Old Man Warren come prancing out of the bresh waving his Winchester and his beard flying in the moonlight and he hollered: "The sins of the wicked shall return onto 'em! Elkins, we have hit a powerful lick for righteousness this here night!"

"Where'd you all come from?" I ast. "I thought you was still back in yore cabin chawin' the rag."

"Well," he says, "after you pulled out we decided to trail along and see how you come out with whatever you planned. As we come through the woods expectin' to git ambushed every second, we met Bill here who told us he believed you had a idee of circumventin' them devils, though he didn't know what it war. So we come and hid ourselves at the aidge of the trees to see what'd happen. I see we been too timid in our dealin's with these heathens. We been lettin' 'em force the fightin' too long. You was right. A good offence is the best defence.

"We didn't kill any of the varmints, wuss luck, but we give 'em a prime lickin'. Hey, look there!" he hollered. "The boys has caught one of the critters! Lug him into the cabin, boys!"

They done so, and by the time me and the old man got there, they had the candles lit, and a rope around the Barlow's neck and one end throwed on a rafter.

That cabin was a sight, all littered with broke guns and splintered chairs and tables, and pieces of clothes and strips of hide. It looked jest about like a cabin ought to look where they has jest been a fight between seventeen polecats and a mountain lion. It was a dirt floor, and some of the poles which helped hold up the roof was splintered, so most of the weight was resting on a big post in the centre of the hut.

All the Warrens was crowding around their prisoner, and when I looked over their heads and seen the feller's pale face in the light of the candle I give a yell: "Dick Blanton!"

"So it is!" said Old Man Warren, rubbing his hands with glee. "So it is! Well, young feller, you got any last words to orate?"

"Naw," said Blanton sullenly. "But if it hadn't been for that derned lion spilin' our plans we'd of had you derned Warrens like so much pork. I never heard of a cougar jumpin' through a winder before."

"That there cougar didn't jump," I said, shouldering through the mob. "He was hev. I done the heavin'."

His mouth fell open and he looked at me like he'd saw the ghost of Sitting Bull. "Breckinridge Elkins!" says he. "I'm cooked now, for sure!"

"I'll say you air!" gritted the feller who'd yearned to shoot Blanton earlier in the night. "What we waitin' for? Le's string him up."

"Hold on," I said. "You all cain't hang him. I'm goin' to take him back to Bear Creek."

"You ain't neither," says Old Man Warren. "We're much obleeged to you for the help you've give us tonight, but this here is the first chance we've had to hang a Barlow in fifteen year, and we aims to make the most of it. String him, boys!"

"Stop!" I roared, stepping for'ard.

In a second I was covered by seven rifles, whilst three men laid hold of the rope and started to heave Blanton's feet off the floor. Them seven Winchesters didn't stop me. I'd of taken them guns away and wiped up the floor with them ongrateful mavericks, but I was afeared Blanton might get hit in the wild shooting that was certain to accompany it.

What I wanted to do was something which would put 'em all horse-de-combat, as the French say, without getting Blanton killed. So I laid hold on the centrepost and before they knowed what I was doing, I tore it loose and broke it off, and the roof caved in and the walls fell inwards on the roof.

In a second they warn't no cabin at all—jest a pile of timber with the Warrens all underneath and screaming blue murder. Of course I jest braced my laigs and when the roof fell my head busted a hole through it, and the logs of the falling walls hit my shoulders and glanced off, so when the dust settled I was standing waist-deep amongst the rooins and nothing but a few scratches to show for it.

The howls that riz from beneath the rooins was blood-curdling, but I knowed nobody was hurt permanent because if they was they wouldn't be able to howl like that. But I expect some of 'em would of been hurt if my head and shoulders hadn't kind of broke the fall of the roof and wall-logs.

I located Blanton by his voice, and pulled pieces of roof board and logs off him until I come onto his laig, and I pulled him out by it and laid him on the ground to get his wind back, because a beam had fell acrost his stummick and when he tried to holler he made the funniest noise I ever heard.

I then kind of rooted around amongst the debris and hauled Old Man Warren out, and he seemed kind of dazed and kept talking about earthquakes.

"You better git to work extricatin' yore misguided kin from under them logs," I told him sternly. "After that there display of ingratitude I got no sympathy for you. In fact, if I was a short-tempered man I'd feel inclined to vi'lence. But bein' the soul of kindness and generosity, I controls my emotions and merely remarks that if I *wasn't* mild-mannered as a lamb, I'd hand you a boot in the pants—like this!"

I showed him how I meant.

"Owww!" wails he, sailing through the air and sticking his nose to the hilt in the dirt.

"I'll have the law on you, you derned murderer!" he wept, shaking his fists at me, and as I departed with my captive I could hear him chanting a hymn of hate as he pulled logs off of his bellering relatives.

Blanton was trying to say something, but I told him I warn't in no mood for perlite conversation and the less he said the less likely I was to lose my temper and tie his neck into a knot around a blackjack. I was thinking how the last time I seen Glory McGraw I told her I was faring forth to find me a town-gal, and now instead of bringing a wife back to Bear Creek, I was bringing back a brother-in-law. My relatives, I reflected bitterly, was sure playing hell with my matrimonial plans. Looked like I warn't never going to get started on my own affairs.

Cap'n Kidd made the hundred miles from the Mezquital Mountains to Bear Creek by noon the next day, carrying double, and never stopping to eat, sleep, nor drink. Them that don't believe that kindly keep their mouths shet. I have already licked nineteen men for acting like they didn't believe it.

I stalked into the cabin and throwed Dick Blanton down onto the floor before Elinor which looked at him and me like she thought I was crazy.

"What you finds attractive about this coyote," I said bitterly, "is beyond the grasp of my dust-coated brain. But here he is, and you can marry him right away."

She said: "Air you drunk or sun-struck? Marry that good-for-nothin', whisky-swiggin', kyard-shootin' loafer? Why, it ain't been a week since I run him out of the house with a broom-handle."

"Then he didn't jilt you?" I gasped.

"Him jilt me?" she said. "I jilted him!"

I turned to Dick Blanton more in sorrer than in anger.

"Why," said I, "did you boast all over Grizzly Run about jiltin' Elinor Elkins?"

"I didn't want folks to know she turned me down," he said sullenly. "Us Blantons is proud. The only reason I ever thought about marryin' her was I was ready to settle down on the farm pap gave me, and I wanted to marry me a Elkins gal, so I wouldn't have to go to the expense of hirin' a couple of hands and buyin' a span of mules, and——"

They ain't no use in Dick Blanton threatening to have the law onto me. He got off light to what he'd have got if pap and my brothers hadn't all been off hunting. They've got terrible tempers. But I was always too soft-hearted for my own good. In spite of Dick Blanton's insults I held my temper. I didn't do nothing to him at all, except escort him with dignity for five or six miles down the Chawed Ear trail, kicking him in the seat of his britches.

CHAPTER VII

The Road to Bear Creek

As I come back up the trail after escorting Dick Blanton down it, I got nervous as I approached the p'int where the path that run from the McGraw cabin come out onto it. If they was anybody in the world right then I didn't want to meet, it was Glory McGraw. I got past and hove a sigh of relief, and jest as I done so, I heard a hoss, and looked back and she was riding out of the path.

I taken to the bresh and to my rage she spurred her hoss and come after me. She was on a fast cayuse, but I thought if I keep my lead I'd be all right, because soon I'd be in the dense thickets where she couldn't come a-hossback. I speeded up, because I'd had about all of her rawhiding I could endure. And then, as I was looking back over my shoulder, I run right smack into a low-hanging oak limb and nearly knocked my brains out. When things stopped spinning around me, I was setting on the ground, and Glory McGraw was setting on her hoss looking down at me.

"Why, Breckinridge," she says mockingly. "Air you scairt of me? What you want to run from me for?"

"I warn't runnin' from you," I growled, glaring up at her. "I didn't even know you was anywheres around. I seen one of pap's steers sneakin' off in the bresh, and I was tryin' to head him. Now you done scairt him away!"

I riz and breshed the dust offa my clothes with my hat, and she says: "I been hearin' a lot about you, Breckinridge. Seems like yo're gittin' to be quite a famous man."

"Hmmmm!" I says, suspicious.

"But where, Breckinridge," she cooed, leaning over the saddle horn towards me, "where is that there purty town-gal you was goin' to bring back to Bear Creek as yore blushin' bride?"

"We ain't sot the day yet," I muttered, looking off.

"Is she purty, Breckinridge?" she pursued.

"Purty as a pitcher," I says. "They ain't a gal on Bear Creek can hold a candle to her."

"Where's she live?" ast Glory.

"War Paint," I said, that being the first town that come into my mind.

"What's her name, Breckinridge?" ast Glory, and I couldn't think of a gal's name if I'd knowed I was going to be shot.

I stammered and floundered, and whilst I was trying my damndest to think of *some* name to give her, she bust into laughter.

"What a lover *you* be!" says she. "Cain't even remember the name of the gal yo're goin' to marry—you *air* goin' to marry her, ain't you, Breckinridge?"

"Yes, I am!" I roared. "I *have* got a gal in War Paint! I'm goin' to see her right now, soon as I can git back to my corral and saddle my hoss! What d'you think of *that,* Miss Smarty?"

"I think yo're the biggest liar on Bear Creek!" says she, with a mocking laugh, and reined around and rode off whilst I stood in helpless rage. "Give my regards to yore War Paint sweetheart, Breckinridge!" she called back over her shoulder—"Soon as you remember what her name is!"

I didn't say nothing. I was past talking. I was too full of wishing that Glory McGraw was a man for jest about five minutes. She was clean out of sight before I could even see straight, much less talk or think reasonable. I give a maddened roar and ripped a limb off a tree as big as a man's laig and started thrashing down the bresh all around, whilst chawing the bark offa all the trees I could rech, and by the time I had cooled off a little that thicket looked like a cyclone had hit it. But I felt a little better and I headed for home on the run, cussing a blue streak and the bobcats and painters taken to the high ridges as I come.

I made for the corral, and as I come out into the clearing I heard a beller like a mad bull up at the cabin, and seen my brothers Buckner and Garfield and John and Bill run out of the cabin and take to the woods, so I figgered pap must be having a touch of the rheumatiz. It makes him remarkable peevish. But I went on and saddled Cap'n Kidd. I was determined to make good on what I told Glory. I didn't have no gal in War Paint, but by golly, I aimed to, and this time I warn't to be turnt aside. I was heading for War Paint, and I was going to get me a gal if I had to lick the entire town.

Well, jest as I was leading Cap'n Kidd outa the corral, my sister Brazoria come to the door of the cabin and hollered: "Oh, Breckinridge! Come up to the shack! Pap wants you!"

"——!" I says. "What the hell now?"

I went up to the cabin and tied Cap'n Kidd and went in. At first glance I seen pap had past the peevish stage and was having a remorseful spell. Rheumatism effects him that way. But the remorse is always for something that happened a long time ago. He didn't seem a bit regretful for having busted a ox-yoke over brother Garfield's head that morning.

He was laying on his b'ar-skin with a jug of corn licker at his elbow, and he says: "Breckinridge, the sins of my youth is ridin' my conscience heavy. When I was a young man I was free and keerless in my habits, as numerous tombstones on the boundless prairies testifies. I sometimes wonders if I warn't a trifle hasty in shootin' some of the gents which disagreed with my principles. Maybe I should of controlled my passion and jest chawed their ears off.

"Take Uncle Esau Grimes, for instance." And then pap hove a sigh like a bull, and said: "I ain't seen Uncle Esau for many years. Me and him parted with harsh words and gun-smoke. I've often wondered if he still holds a grudge agen me for plantin' that charge of buckshot in his hind laig."

"What about Uncle Esau?" I said.

Pap perjuiced a letter and said: "He was brung to my mind by this here letter which Jim Braxton fotched me from War Paint. It's from my sister Elizabeth, back in Devilville, Arizona, whar Uncle Esau lives. She says Uncle Esau is on his way to Californy, and is due to pass through War Paint about the tenth—that's tomorrer. She don't know whether he intends turnin' off to see me or not, but suggests that I meet him at War Paint, and make peace with him."

"Well?" I demanded, because from the way pap combed his beard with his fingers and eyed me, I knowed he was aiming to call on me to do something for him.

"Well," said pap, taking a long swig out of the jug, "I want you to meet the stage to-morrer morning' at War Paint, and invite Uncle Esau to come up here and visit us. Don't take no for a answer. Uncle Esau is as cranky as hell, and a pecooliar old duck, but I think he'll like you. Specially if you keep yore mouth shet and don't expose yore ignorance."

"Well," I said, "for onst the job you've sot for me falls in with my own plans. I was just fixin' to light out for War Paint. But how'm I goin' to know Uncle Esau? I ain't never seen him."

"He ain't a big man," said pap. "Last time I seen him he had a right smart growth of red whiskers. You bring him home regardless. Don't pay no attention to his belly-achin'. He's awful suspicious because he's got lots of enemies. He burnt plenty of powder in his younger days, all the way from Texas to Californy. He war mixed up in more feuds and range-wars than any man I ever knowed. He's supposed to have considerable money hid away somewheres, but that ain't got nothin' to do with us. I wouldn't take his blasted money as a gift. All I want to do is talk to him, and git his forgiveness for fillin' his hide with buckshot in a moment of youthful passion.

"If he don't forgive me," says pap, taking another pull at his jug, "I'll bend my .45 over his stubborn old skull. Git goin'."

So I hit out acrost the mountains, and the next morning found me eating breakfast at the aidge of War Paint, with a old hunter and trapper by the name of old Bill Polk which was camped there temporary.

War Paint was a new town which had sprung up out of nothing on account of a gold rush right recent, and old Bill was very bitter.

"A hell of a come-off this is!" he snorted. "Clutterin' up the scenery and scarin' the animals off with their fool houses and claims. Last year I shot deer right whar that saloon yonder stands now," he said, glaring at me like it was my fault.

I said nothing but chawed my venison which we was cooking over his fire, and he said: "No good'll come of it, you mark my word. These mountains won't be fit to live in. These camps draws scum like a dead hoss draws buzzards. The outlaws is already ridin' in from Arizona and Utah and Californy, besides the native ones. Grizzly Hawkins and his thieves is hidin' up in the hills, and no tellin' how many more'll come in. I'm glad they cotched Badger Chisom and his gang after they robbed that bank at Gunstock. That's one gang which won't bedevil us, becaze they're in jail. If somebody'd jest kill Grizzly Hawkins, now——"

"Who's that gal?" I ejaculated suddenly, forgetting to eat in my excitement.

"Who? Whar?" says old Bill, looking around. "Oh, that gal jest goin' by the Golden Queen restaurant? Aw, that's Dolly Rixby, the belle of the town."

"She's awful purty," I says.

"*You* never seen a purtier," says he.

"I have, too," I says absent-mindedly. "Glory McGraw——"

Then I kind of woke up to what I was saying and flang my breakfast into the fire in disgust. "Sure, she's the purtiest gal I ever seen!" I snorted. "Ain't a gal in the Humbolts can hold a candle to her. What you say her name was? Dolly Rixby? A right purty name, too."

"You needn't start castin' sheep's eyes at her," he opined. "They's a dozen young bucks sparkin' her already. I think Blink Wiltshaw's the favourite to put his brand onto her, though. She wouldn't look at a hillbilly like you."

"I might remove the competition," I suggested.

"You better not try no Bear Creek rough-stuff in War Paint," says he. "The town's jest reekin' with law and order. Why, I actually hear they ups and puts you in jail if you shoots a man within the city limits."

I was scandalized. Later I found out that was jest a slander started by the citizens of Chawed Ear which was jealous of War Paint, but at the time I was so upsot by this information I was almost afeared to go into town for fear I'd get arrested.

"Where's Miss Rixby goin' with that bucket?" I ast him.

"She's takin' a bucket of beer to her old man which is workin' a claim up the creek," says old Bill.

"Well, lissen," I says. "You git over there behind that thicket, and when she comes by, make a noise like a Injun."

"What kind of damfoolishness is this?" he demanded. "You want me to stampede the whole camp?"

"Don't make a loud noise," I said. "Jest make it loud enough for her to hear."

"Air you crazy?" he ast.

"No, dern it!" I said fiercely, because she was coming along stepping purty fast. "Git in there and do like I say. I'll rush up from the other side and pertend to rescue her from the Injuns and that'll make her like me. Gwan!"

"I mistrusts yo're a blasted fool," he grumbled. "But I'll do it." He snuck into the thicket which she'd have to pass on the other side, and I circled around so she wouldn't see me till I was ready to rush out and save her from being sculped. Well, I warn't hardly in position when I heard a kind of mild war-whoop, and it sounded jest like a Blackfoot, only not so loud. But imejitly there come the crack of a pistol and another yell which warn't subdued like the first. It was lusty and energetic. I run towards the thicket, but before I could get into the open trail, old Bill come piling out of the back side of the clump with his hands to the seat of his britches.

"You planned this a-purpose, you snake in the grass!" he yelped. "Git outa my way!"

"Why, Bill," I says. "What happened?"

"I bet you knowed she had a derringer in her stockin'," he snarled as he run past me. "It's all yore fault! When I whooped, she pulled it and shot into the bresh! Don't speak to me! I'm lucky to be alive. I'll git even with you for this if it takes a hundred years!"

He headed on into the deep bresh, and I run around the thicket and seen Dolly Rixby peering into it with her gun smoking in her hand. She looked up as I come onto the trail, and I taken off my hat and said, perlite: "Howdy, miss; can I be of no assistance to you?"

"I jest shot a Injun," she said. "I heard him holler. You might go in there and git the sculp, if you don't mind. I'd like to have it for a soovenir."

"I'll be glad to, miss," I says heartily. "I'll likewise cure and tan it for you myself."

"Oh, thank you!" she says, dimpling when she smiled. "It's a pleasure to meet a real gent like you."

"The pleasure is all mine," I assured her, and went into the bresh and stomped around a little, and then come out and says: "I'm awful sorry, miss, but the critter ain't nowheres to be found. You must of jest winged him. If you want me to I'll take his trail and foller it till I catch up with him, though."

"Oh, I wouldn't think of puttin' you to no sech trouble," she says much to my relief, because I was jest thinking that if she did demand a sculp, the only thing I could do would be to catch old Bill and sculp him, and I'd hate awful bad to have to do that.

But she looked me over with admiration in her eyes, and said: "I'm Dolly Rixby. Who're you?"

"I knowed you the minute I seen you," I says. "The fame of yore beauty has reched clean into the Humbolts. I'm Breckinridge Elkins."

Her eyes kind of sparkled, and she said: "I've heard of you, too! You broke Cap'n Kidd, and it was you that cleaned up Wampum!"

"Yes, 'm," I says, and jest then I seen the stage coach fogging it down the road from the east, and I says: "Say, I got to meet that there stage, but I'd like to call on you at yore convenience."

"Well," she says, "I'll be back at the cabin in about a hour. What's the matter with then? I live about ten rods north of The Red Rooster gamblin' hall."

"I'll be there," I promised, and she gimme a dimply smile and went on down the trail with her old man's bucket of beer, and I hustled back to where I left Cap'n Kidd. My head was in a whirl, and my heart was pounding. And here, thinks I, is where I show Glory McGraw what kind of stuff a Elkins is made of. Jest wait till I ride back to Bear Creek with Dolly Rixby as my bride!

I rode into War Paint just as the stage pulled up at the stand, which was also the post office and a saloon. They was three passengers, and they warn't none of 'em tenderfeet. Two was big hard-looking fellers, and t'other 'n was a wiry oldish kind of a bird with red whiskers, so I knowed right off it was Uncle Esau Grimes. They was going into the saloon as I dismounted, the big men first, and the older feller follering 'em. Thinks I, I'll start him on his way to Bear Creek, and then I'll come back and start sparking Dolly Rixby.

I touched him on the shoulder, and he whirled most amazing quick with a gun in his hand, and he looked at me very suspicious, and said: "What you want?"

"I'm Breckinridge Elkins," I said. "I want you to come with me. I recognized you as soon as I seen you——"

I then got a awful surprise, but not as sudden as it would have been if pap hadn't warned me that Uncle Esau was pecooliar. He hollered: "Bill! Jim! Help!" And swung his six-shooter agen my head with all his might.

The other two fellers whirled and their hands streaked for their guns, so I knocked Uncle Esau flat to keep him from getting hit by a stray slug, and shot one of 'em through the shoulder before he could unlimber his artillery. T'other'n grazed my neck with a bullet, so I perforated him in the arm and the hind laig and he fell down acrost the other'n. I was careful not to shoot 'em in no vital parts, because I seen they was friends of Uncle Esau; but when guns is being drawn it ain't no time to argy or explain.

Men was hollering and running out of saloons, and I stooped and started to lift Uncle Esau, who was kind of groggy because he'd hit his head agen a hitching post. He was crawling around on his all-fours cussing something terrible, and trying to find his gun which he'd dropped. When I laid hold onto him he commenced biting and kicking and hollering, and I said: "Don't ack like that, Uncle Esau. Here comes a lot of fellers, and the sheriff may be here any minute and 'rest me for shootin' them idjits. We got to git goin'. Pap's waitin' for you, up on Bear Creek."

But he jest fit that much harder and hollered that much louder, so I scooped him up bodily and jumped onto Cap'n Kidd and throwed Uncle Esau face down acrost the saddle-bow, and headed for the hills. A lot of men yelled at me to stop, and some of 'em started shooting at me, but I give no heed.

I give Cap'n Kidd the rein and we went tearing down the road and around the first bend, and I didn't even take time to change Uncle Esau's position, because I didn't want to get arrested. A fat chance I had of keeping my date with Dolly Rixby. I wonder if anybody ever had sech cussed relatives as me.

Jest before we reched the p'int where the Bear Creek trail runs into the road, I seen a man on the road ahead of me, and he must have heard the shooting and Uncle Esau yelling because he whirled his hoss and blocked the road. He was a wiry old cuss with grey whiskers.

"Where you goin' with that man?" he yelled as I approached at a thundering gait.

"None of yore business," I retorted. "Git outa my way."

"Help! Help!" hollered Uncle Esau. "I'm bein' kidnapped and murdered!"

"Drop that man, you derned outlaw!" roared the stranger, suiting his actions to his words.

Him and me drawed simultaneous, but my shot was a split-second quicker'n his'n. His slug fanned my ear, but his hat flew off and he pitched out of his saddle like he'd been hit with a hammer. I seen a streak of red along his temple as I thundered past him.

"Let that larn you not to interfere in family affairs!" I roared, and turned up the trail that switched off the road and up into the mountains.

"Don't never yell like that," I said irritably to Uncle Esau. "You like to got me shot. That feller thought I was a criminal."

I didn't catch what he said, but I looked back and down over the slopes and shoulders, and seen men boiling out of town full tilt, and the sun glinted on six-shooters and rifles, so I urged on Cap'n Kidd and we covered the next few miles at a fast clip.

Uncle Esau kept trying to talk, but he was bouncing up and down so all I could understand was his cuss words, which was free and fervent. At last he gasped: "For God's sake lemme git off this cussed saddle-horn; it's rubbin' a hole in my belly."

So I pulled up and seen no sign of my pursuers, so I said: "All right, you can ride in the saddle and I'll set on behind. I was goin' to hire you a hoss at the livery stable, but we had to leave so quick they warn't no time."

"Where you takin' me?" he demanded.

"To Bear Creek," I said. "Where you think?"

"I don't wanta go to Bear Creek," he said fiercely. "I *ain't* goin' to Bear Creek."

"You are, too," I said. "Pap said not to take no for a answer. I'm goin' to slide over behind the saddle, and you can set in it."

So I pulled my feet outa the stirrups and moved over the cantle, and he slid into the seat—and the first thing I knowed he had a knife out of his boot and was trying to kyarve my gizzard.

Now I likes to humour my relatives, but they is a limit to everything. I taken the knife away from him, but in the struggle, me being handicapped by not wanting to hurt him, I lost hold of the reins and Cap'n Kidd bolted and run for several miles through the pines and bresh. What with me trying to grab the reins and keep Uncle Esau from killing me at the same time, and neither one of us in the stirrups, finally we both fell off, and if I hadn't managed to catch hold of the bridle as I went off, we'd had a long walk ahead of us.

I got Cap'n Kidd stopped, after being drug for about seventy-five yards, and then I went back to where Uncle Esau was laying on the ground trying to get his wind back, because I had kind of fell on him.

"Is that any way to ack, tryin' to stick a knife in a man which is doin' his best to make you comfortable?" I said reproachfully. All he done was gasp, so I said: "Well, pap told me you was a cranky old duck, so I reckon the only thing to do is to jest not notice yore pecooliarities."

I looked around to get my bearings, because Cap'n Kidd had got away off the trail. We was west of it, in very wild country, but I seen a cabin off through the trees, and I said: "We'll go over there and see can I buy or hire a hoss for you to ride. That'll be more convenient for both of us."

I h'isted him back into the saddle, and he said kind of dizzily: "This here's a free country. I don't have to go to Bear Creek if'n I don't want to."

"Well," I said severely, "you oughta want to, after all the trouble I've went to, comin' and invitin' you, and passin' up a date with the purtiest gal in War Paint on account of you. Set still now. I'm settin' on behind but I'm holdin' the reins."

"I'll have yore life for this," he promised blood-thirstily, but I ignored it, because pap had said Uncle Esau was pecooliar.

Purty soon we hove up to the cabin I'd glimpsed through the trees. Nobody was in sight, but I seen a hoss tied to a tree in front of the cabin. I rode up to the door and knocked, but nobody answered. But I seen smoke coming out of the chimney, so I decided I'd go in.

I dismounted and lifted Uncle Esau off, because I seen from the gleam in his eye that he was intending to run off on Cap'n Kidd if I give him half a chance. I got a firm grip onto his collar, because I was determined that he was going to visit us up on Bear Creek if I had to tote him on my shoulder all the way, and I went into the cabin with him.

They warn't nobody in there, though a big pot of beans was simmering over some coals in the fireplace, and I seen some rifles in racks on the wall and a belt with two pistols hanging on a peg.

Then I heard somebody walking behind the cabin, and the back door opened and there stood a big, black-whiskered man with a bucket of water in his hand and a astonished glare on his face. He didn't have no guns on.

"Who the hell are you?" he demanded, but Uncle Esau give a kind of gurgle, and said: "Grizzly Hawkins!"

The big man jumped and glared at Uncle Esau, and then his black whiskers bristled in a ferocious grin, and he said: "Oh, it's you, is it? Who'd of thunk I'd ever meet you *here?*"

"Grizzly Hawkins, hey?" I said, realizing that I'd stumbled onto the hideout of the wust outlaw in them mountains. "So you-all know each other?"

"I'll say we do!" rumbled Hawkins, looking at Uncle Esau like a wolf looks at a fat yearling.

"I'd heard you was from Arizona," I said, being naturally tactful. "Looks to me like they's enough cow-thieves in these hills already without outsiders buttin' in. But yore morals ain't none of my business. I want to buy or hire or borrer a hoss for this here gent to ride."

"Oh, no, you ain't!" said Grizzly. "You think I'm goin' to let a fortune slip through my fingers like that? Tell you what I'll do, though: I'll split with you. My gang had business over towards Chawed Ear this mornin', but they're due back soon. Me and you will work him over before they gits back, and we'll nab all the loot ourselves."

"What you mean?" I ast. "My uncle and me is on our way to Bear Creek——"

"Aw, don't ack innercent with me!" he snorted disgustedly. "Uncle! Hell! You think I'm a plumb fool? Cain't I see he's yore prisoner, the way you got him by the neck? Think I don't know what yo're up to? Be reasonable. Two can work this job better'n one. I know lots of ways to make a man talk. I betcha if we kinda massage his hinder parts with a red-hot brandin' iron he'll tell us quick enough where the money is hid."

Uncle Esau turnt pale under his whiskers, and I said indignantly: "Why, you low-lifed polecat! You got the crust to pertend to think I'm kidnappin' my own uncle for his dough? I got a good mind to shoot you."

"So yo're greedy, hey?" he snarled, showing his teeth. "Want all the loot yoreself, hey? I'll show you!" And quick as a cat he swung that water bucket over his head and let it go at me. I ducked and it hit Uncle Esau in the head and stretched him out all drenched with water, and Hawkins give a roar and dived for a .45-90 on the wall. He wheeled with it and I shot it out of his hands. He then come for me wildeyed with a bowie out of his boot, and my next cartridge snapped, and he was on top of me before I could cock my gun again.

I dropped it and grappled with him, and we fit all over the cabin and every now and then we would tromple on Uncle Esau which was trying to crawl towards the door, and the way he would holler was pitiful to hear.

Hawkins lost his knife in the melee, but he was as big as me, and a bear-cat at rough-and-tumble. We would stand up and whale away with both fists, and then clinch and roll around the floor, biting and gouging and slugging, and onst we rolled clean over Uncle Esau and kind of flattened him out like a pancake.

Finally Hawkins got hold of the table which he lifted like it was a board and splintered over my head, and this made me mad, so I grabbed the pot off the fire and hit him in the head with it, and about a gallon of red-hot beans went down his back and he fell into a corner so hard he jolted the shelves loose from the logs, and all the guns fell off the walls.

He come up with a gun in his hand, but his eyes was so full of blood and hot beans that he missed me the first shot, and before he could shoot again I hit him on the chin so hard it fractured his jaw bone and sprained both his ankles and laid him out cold.

Then I looked around for Uncle Esau, and he was gone and the front door was open. I rushed out of the cabin and there he was jest climbing aboard Cap'n Kidd. I hollered for him to wait, but he kicked Cap'n Kidd in the ribs and went tearing off through the trees. Only he didn't head north back towards War Paint. He was p'inted south-east, in the general direction of Hideout Mountain. I grabbed my gun up off the floor and lit out after him, though I didn't have much hope of catching him. Grizzly's cayuse was a good hoss, but he couldn't hold a candle to Cap'n Kidd.

I wouldn't have caught him, neither, if it hadn't been for Cap'n Kidd's determination not to be rode by nobody but me. Uncle Esau was a crack hossman to stay on as long as he did.

But finally Cap'n Kidd got tired of sech foolishness, and about the time he crossed the trail we'd been follerin' when he first bolted, he bogged his head and started busting hisself in tow, with his snoot rubbing the grass and his heels scraping the clouds offa the sky.

I could see mountain peaks between Uncle Esau and the saddle, and when Cap'n Kidd start sunfishing it looked like the wrath of Jedgment Day, but somehow Uncle Esau managed to stay with him till Cap'n Kidd plumb left the earth like he aimed to aviate from then on, and Uncle Esau left the saddle with a shriek of despair and sailed head-on into a blackjack thicket.

Cap'n Kidd give a snort of contempt and trotted off to a patch of grass and started grazing, and I dismounted and went and ontangled Uncle Esau from amongst the branches. His clothes was tore and he was scratched so he looked like he'd been fighting with a drove of wildcats, and he left a right smart bunch of whiskers amongst the bresh.

But he was full of pizen and hostility.

"I understand this here treatment," he said bitterly, like he blamed me for Cap'n Kidd pitching him into the thicket, "but you'll never git a penny. Nobody but me knows whar the dough is, and you can pull my toe nails out by the roots before I tells you."

"I know you got money hid away," I said, deeply offended, "but I don't want it."

He snorted skeptical and said sarcastic: "Then what're you draggin' me over these cussed hills for?"

"'Cause pap wants to see you," I said. "But they ain't no use in askin' me a lot of fool questions. Pap said for me to keep my mouth shet."

I looked around for Grizzly's hoss, and seen he had wandered off. He sure hadn't been trained proper.

"Now I got to go look for him," I said disgustedly. "Will you stay here till I git back?"

"Sure," he said. "Sure. Go on and look for the hoss. I'll wait here."

But I give him a searching look, and shook my head.

"I don't want to seem like I mistrusts you," I said, "but I see a gleam in yore eye which makes me believe that you intends to run off the minute my back's turned. I hate to do this, but I got to bring you safe to Bear Creek; so I'll just kinda hawg-tie you with my lariat till I git back."

Well, he put up a awful holler, but I was firm, and when I rode off on Cap'n Kidd I was satisfied that he couldn't untie them knots by hisself. I left him laying in the grass beside the trail, and his language was painful to listen to.

That derned hoss had wandered farther'n I thought. He'd moved north along the trail for a short way, and then turned off and headed in a westerly direction, and after a while I heard hosses galloping somewheres behind me, and I got nervous, thinking what if Hawkins's gang had got back to their hangout and he'd told 'em about us, and sent 'em after us, to capture pore Uncle Esau and torture him to make him tell where his savings was hid. I wished I'd had sense enough to shove Uncle Esau back in the thicket so he wouldn't be seen by anybody riding along the trail, and I'd just decided to let the hoss go and turn back, when I seen him grazing amongst the trees ahead of me.

I caught him and headed back for the trail, aiming to hit it a short piece north of where I'd left Uncle Esau, and before I got in sight of it, I heard hosses and saddles creaking ahead of me.

I pulled up on the crest of a slope, and looked down onto the trail, and there I seen a gang of men riding north, and they had Uncle Esau amongst 'em. Two of the men was ridin' double, and they had him on a hoss in the middle of 'em. They'd took the ropes off'n him, but he didn't look happy. Instantly I realized that my premonishuns was correct. The Hawkins gang had follered us, and now pore Uncle Esau was in their clutches.

I let go of Hawkins's hoss and reched for my gun, but I didn't dare fire for fear of hitting Uncle Esau, they was clustered so clost about him. I reched up and tore a limb off a oak tree as big as my arm, and I charged down the slope yelling: "I'll save you, Uncle Esau!"

I come so sudden and onexpected them fellers didn't have time to do nothing but holler before I hit 'em. Cap'n Kidd ploughed through their hosses like a avalanche through saplings, and he was going so hard I couldn't check him in time to keep him from knocking Uncle Esau's hoss sprawling. Uncle Esau hit the turf with a shriek.

All around me men was yelling and surging and pulling guns and I riz in my stirrups and laid about me right and left, and pieces of bark and oak leaves and blood flew in showers and in a second the ground was littered with writhing figgers, and the hollering and cussing was awful to hear. Knives was flashing and pistols was banging, but them outlaws' eyes was too full of bark and stars and blood for them to aim, and right in the middle of the brawl, when the guns was roaring and hosses was neighing and men yelling and my oak-limb going crack! crack! crack! on their skulls; down from the north swooped *another* gang, howling like hyeners!

"There he is!" one of 'em yelled. "I see him crawlin' around under them hosses! After him, boys! We got as much right to his dough as anybody!"

The next minute they'd dashed in amongst us and embraced the members of the other gang and started hammering 'em over the heads with their pistols, and in a second there was the damndest three-cornered war you ever seen, men fighting on the ground and on the hosses, all mixed and tangled up, two gangs trying to exterminate each other, and me whaling hell out of both of 'em.

Meanwhile Uncle Esau was on the ground under us, yelling bloody murder and being stepped on by the hosses, but finally I cleared me a space with a devastating sweep of my club, and leaned down and scooped him up with one hand and hung him over my saddle horn and started battering my way clear.

But a big feller which was one of the second gang come charging through the melee yelling like a Injun, with blood running down his face from a cut in his scalp. He snapped a empty ca'tridge at me, and then leaned out from his saddle and grabbed Uncle Esau by the foot.

"Leggo!" he howled. "He's my meat!"

"Release Uncle Esau before I does you a injury!" I roared, trying to jerk Uncle Esau loose, but the outlaw hung on, and Uncle Esau squalled like a catamount in a wolf-trap. So I lifted what was left of my club and splintered it over the outlaw's head, and he give up the ghost with a gurgle. I then wheeled Cap'n Kidd and rode off like the wind. Them fellers was too busy fighting each other to notice my flight. Somebody did let bam at me with a Winchester, but all it done was to nick Uncle Esau's ear.

The sounds of carnage faded out behind us as I headed south along the trail. Uncle Esau was belly-aching about something. I never seen sech a cuss for finding fault, but I felt they was no time to be lost, so I didn't slow up for some miles. Then I pulled Cap'n Kidd down and said: "What did you say, Uncle Esau?"

"I'm a broken man!" he gasped. "Take my secret, and lemme go back to the posse. All I want now is a good, safe prison term."

"What posse?" I ast, thinking he must be drunk, though I couldn't figger where he could of got any booze.

"The posse you took me away from," he said. "Anything's

better'n bein' dragged through these hellish mountains by a homicidal maneyack."

"Posse?" I gasped wildly. "But who was the second gang?"

"Grizzly Hawkins's outlaws," he said, and added bitterly: "Even they'd be preferable to what I been goin' through. I give up. I know when I'm licked. The dough's hid in a holler oak three miles west of Gunstock."

I didn't pay no attention to his remarks, because my head was in a whirl. A posse! Of course; the sheriff and his men had follered us from War Paint, along the Bear Creek trail, and finding Uncle Esau tied up, had thought he'd been kidnapped by a outlaw instead of merely being invited to visit his relatives. Probably he was too cussed ornery to tell 'em any different. I hadn't rescued him from no bandits; I'd took him away from a posse which thought *they* was rescuing him.

Meanwhile Uncle Esau was clamouring: "Well, why'n't you lemme go? I've told you whar the dough is. What else you want?"

"You got to go on to Bear Creek with me—" I begun; and Uncle Esau give a shriek and went into a kind of convulsion, and the first thing I knowed he'd twisted around and jerked my gun out of its scabbard and let bam! right in my face so close it singed my hair. I grabbed his wrist and Cap'n Kidd bolted like he always does whenever he gets the chance.

"They's a limit to everything!" I roared. "A hell of a relative you be, you old maneyack!"

We was tearing over slopes and ridges at breakneck speed and fighting all over Cap'n Kidd's back—me to get the gun away from him, and him to commit murder. "If you warn't kin to me, Uncle Esau," I said wrathfully, "I'd plumb lose my temper!"

"What you keep callin' me that fool name for?" he yelled, frothing at the mouth. "What you want to add insult to injury——" Cap'n Kidd swerved sudden and Uncle Esau tumbled over his neck. I had him by the shirt and tried to hold him on, but the shirt tore. He hit the ground on his head and Cap'n Kidd run right over him. I pulled up as quick as I could and hove a sigh of relief to see how close to home I was.

"We're nearly there, Uncle Esau," I said, but he made no comment. He was out cold.

A short time later I rode up to the cabin with my eccentric relative slung over my saddle-bow, and I taken him off and stalked into where pap was laying on his b'ar-skin, and slung my burden down on the floor in disgust. "Well, here he is," I said.

Pap stared and said: "Who's this?"

"When you wipe the blood off," I said, "you'll find it's yore Uncle Esau Grimes. And," I added bitterly, "the next time you wants to invite him to visit us, you can do it yoreself. A more ungrateful cuss I never seen. Pecooliar ain't no name for him; he's as crazy as a locoed jackass."

"But *that* ain't Uncle Esau!" said pap.

"What you mean?" I said irritably. "I know most of his clothes is tore off, and his face is kinda scratched and skint and stomped outa shape, but you can see his whiskers is red, in spite of the blood."

"Red whiskers turn grey, in time," said a voice, and I wheeled and pulled my gun as a man loomed in the door.

It was the grey-whiskered old feller I'd traded shots with on the edge of War Paint. He didn't go for his gun, but stood twisting his moustache and glaring at me like I was a curiosity or something.

"Uncle Esau!" said pap.

"What?" I hollered. "Air *you* Uncle Esau?"

"Certainly I am!" he snapped.

"But you warn't on the stage-coach——" I begun.

"Stage-coach!" he snorted, taking pap's jug and beginning to pour licker down the man on the floor. "Them things is for wimmen and children. I travel hoss-back. I spent last night in War Paint, and aimed to ride on up to Bear Creek this mornin'. In fact, Bill," he addressed pap, "I was on the way here when this young maneyack creased me." He indicated a bandage on his head.

"You mean Breckinridge shot you?" ejaculated pap.

"It seems to run in the family," grunted Uncle Esau.

"But who's this?" I hollered wildly, pointing at the man I'd thought was Uncle Esau, and who was jest coming to.

"I'm Badger Chisom," he said, grabbing the jug with both hands. "I demands to be pertected from this lunatick and turned over to the sheriff."

"Him and Bill Reynolds and Jim Hopkins robbed a bank over at Gunstock three weeks ago," said Uncle Esau; the real one, I mean. "A posse captured them, but they'd hid the loot somewhere and wouldn't say where. They escaped several days ago, and not only the sheriffs was lookin' for 'em, but all the outlaw gangs too, to find out where they'd hid their plunder. It was a awful big haul. They must of figgered that escapin' out of the country by stage-coach would be the last thing folks would expect 'em to do, and they warn't known around War Paint.

"But I recognized Billy Reynolds when I went back to War Paint to have my head dressed, after you shot me, Breckinridge.

The doctor was patchin' him and Hopkins up, too. I knowed Reynolds back in Arizona. The sheriff and a posse lit out after you, and I follered 'em when I'd got my head fixed. 'Course, I didn't know who you was. I come up while the posse was fightin' with the Hawkins gang, and with my help we corralled the whole bunch. Then I took up yore trail again. Purty good day's work, wipin' out two of the wust gangs in the West. One of Hawkins's men said Grizzly was laid up in his cabin, and the posse was going to drop by for him."

"What you goin' to do about me?" clamoured Chisom.

"Well," said pap, "we'll bandage you up good, and then I'll let Breckinridge here take you back to War Paint—hey, what's the matter wih him?"

Badger Chisom had fainted.

CHAPTER VIII

The Scalp Hunter

My return to War Paint with Badger Chisom was plumb uneventful. He was awful nervous all the way and every time I spoke to him he jumped and ducked like he expected to be shot at, and he hove a distinct sigh of relief when the sheriff taken charge of him. He said something like, "Safe at last, thank God!" and seemed in a sweat to get into a good, strong cell. Criminals is pecooliar people.

Well, to my surprise I found that I had become a kind of personage in War Paint account of shooting Chisom's pards and bringing him in. It warn't a narrer-minded town at all, like the folks over to Chawed Ear had led me to believe. Things was free and easy, big gambling games running all the time, bars open all day and all night, and pistols popping every hour of the day. They had a sheriff but he was a sensible man which didn't interfere with the business of honest citizens. He 'lowed it was his job to see that the town warn't overrun by thieving, murdering outlaws, not to go butting into folks' affairs. He told me that if I had occasion to shoot another gent he'd take it as a personal favour if I'd be careful not to hit no innercent bystander by mistake, and when I said I would, he said I was a credit to the community, and we had a drink.

I was about half scairt to go see Dolly Rixby, but I screwed up my courage by thinking of what Glory McGraw would say if I didn't get me a gal soon, and called on her. She warn't as peeved as I thought, though she did say: "Well, yo're a mite late, ain't you? About two days, I believe! But better late than never, I reckon."

She was broad-minded enough to understand my position, and

we got along fine. Well, we did after I persuaded them young bucks which was mooning around her that I wasn't going to stand for no claim-jumping. I had to be kind of subtle about this, because it always made Dolly mad for me to disable any of her admirers. She liked me, but she also seemed to like a lot of other fellers, especially young Blink Wiltshaw, which was a good-looking young miner. Sometimes I wondered whether Dolly's interest in me was really for myself, or on account of the glory which was reflected onto her by me calling on her regular. Because by this time I'd made quite a name for myself around over the country, jest like I told Glory McGraw I would. But it didn't make much difference to me, as long as Dolly let me spark her, and I figgered that in a little time more I'd have her roped and hawg-tied and branded, and I drempt of the day when I'd take her back to Bear Creek and interjuice her to everybody as my wife. I plumb gloated over how Glory McGraw'd look then, and got to feeling kind of sorry for her, and decided I wouldn't rub it in on her too raw. I'd jest be dignified and tolerant, as become a man of my importance.

And then my money give out. Things had run remarkable smooth since I come back to War Paint, and my luck had suited it. The first night I was there I sot into a poker game in The Rebel Captain saloon with ten dollars and run it up to five hundred before I riz—more money than I'd ever knowed they was in the world. I had a remarkable run of luck at gambling for maybe three weeks, and lived high, wide and handsome, and spent money on Dolly right and left. Then my streak broke, and the first thing I knowed, I was busted.

Well, it taken money to live in a fast-stepping town like War Paint, and go with a gal like Dolly Rixby, so I cast about for something to do to get me some dough. About the time I was about ready to start working somebody's claim for day-wages, I got wind of a big jamboree which was going to be staged in Yavapai, a cowcountry town about a hundred miles north of War Paint. They was going to be hoss-races and roping and bull-dogging and I seen where it was a good chance to pick up me some easy prize money. I knowed, of course, that all them young bucks which I'd cut out could be counted on to start shining up to Dolly the minute my back was turnt, but I didn't look for no serious competition from them, and Blink Wiltshaw had pulled out for Teton Gulch a week before. I figgered he'd decided I was too much for him.

So I went and told Dolly that I was heading for Yavapai, and urged her not to pine away in my absence, because I'd be back before many days with plenty of dough. She 'lowed she could bear up under it till I got back, so I kissed her heartily, and sallied forth into the starlit evening where I got a onpleasant surprise. I run into Blink Wiltshaw jest coming up onto the stoop. I was so overcome by irritation that I started to sweep the street with him, when Dolly come out and stopped me and made us shake hands. Blink swore that he was going back to Teton Gulch next morning, and had jest stopped by to say hello, so I was mollified and pulled out for Yavapai without no more delay.

Well, a couple of days later I pulled into Yavapai, which was plumb full of wild cowboys and drunk Injuns, and everybody was full of licker and rambunctiousness, so it taken 'em a whole day to get things into shape enough and everybody sober enough to get the races started. I started entering Cap'n Kidd in every race that was run, me riding him, of course, and he won the first three races, one after another, and everybody cussed something terrible, and then the jedges said they'd have to bar me from entering any more races. So I said all right I will now lick the jedges and they turnt pale and gimme fifty dollars to agree not to run Cap'n Kidd in any more of their races.

What with that, and the prizes, and betting on Cap'n Kidd myself, I had about a thousand dollars, so I decided I wouldn't stay for the roping and bull-dogging contests next day, but would hustle back to War Paint. I'd been gone three days and was beginning to worry about them young bucks which was sweet on Dolly. I warn't scairt of 'em, but they warn't no use givin' 'em too much chance.

But I thought I'd have a little hand of poker before I pulled out, and that was a mistake. My luck warn't holding. When I ariz at midnight I had exactly five dollars in my pants. But I thinks, to hell with it; I ain't going to stay away from Dolly no longer. Blink Wiltshaw might not have went back to Teton Gulch after all. They is plenty of dough in the world, but not many gals like Dolly.

So I headed back for War Paint without waiting for morning. After all, I was five bucks to the good, and by playing clost to my shirt I might run them up to several hundred, when I got back amongst men whose style of play I knowed.

About the middle of the next morning I run head-on into a snag on the path of progress in the shape of Tunk Willoughby.

And right here lemme say that I'm sick and tired of these lies which is being circulated about me terrorizing the town of Grizzly

Claw. They is always more'n one side to anything. These folks which is going around telling about me knocking the mayor of Grizzly Claw down a flight of steps with a kitchen stove ain't yet added that the mayor was trying to blast me with a sawed-off shotgun. If I was a hot-headed man like some I know, I could easy lose my temper over them there slanders, but being shy and retiring by nature, I keeps my dignity and merely remarks that these gossipers is blamed liars which I'll kick the ears off of if I catch 'em.

I didn't have no intention whatever of going to Grizzly Claw, in the first place. It lay away off my road.

But as I passed the place where the trail from Grizzly Claw comes into the road that runs from War Paint to Yavapai, I seen Tunk Willoughby setting on a log in the fork of the trails. I knowed him at War Paint. Tunk ain't got no more sense'n the law allows anyway, and now he looked plumb discouraged. He had a mangled ear, a couple of black eyes, and a lump onto his head so big his hat wouldn't fit. From time to time he spit out a tooth.

I pulled up Cap'n Kidd and said: "What kind of a brawl have you been into?"

"I been to Grizzly Claw," he said, jest like that explained it. But I didn't get the drift, because I hadn't never been to Grizzly Claw.

"That's the meanest town in these mountains," he says. "They ain't got no real law there, but they got a feller which claims to be a officer, and if you so much as spit, he says you busted a law and has got to pay a fine. If you puts up a holler, the citizens comes to his assistance. You see what happened to me. I never found out jest what law I was supposed to have broke," Tunk said, "but it must of been one they was particular fond of. I give 'em a good fight as long as they confined theirselves to rocks and gun butts, but when they interjuiced fence rails and wagon-tongues into the fray, I give up the ghost."

"What you go there for, anyhow?" I ast.

"Well," he said, mopping off some dried blood, "I was lookin' for you. Three days ago I met yore cousin Jack Gordon, and he told me somethin' to tell you."

Him showing no signs of going on, I says: "Well, what was it?"

"I cain't remember," he said. "That lammin' they give me in Grizzly Claw has plumb addled my brains. Jack told me to tell you to keep a sharp look-out for somebody, but I cain't remember who, or why. But somebody had did somethin' awful to somebody on Bear Creek—seems like it was yore Uncle Jeppard Grimes."

"But what did you go to Grizzly Claw for?" I demanded. "I warn't there."

"I dunno," he said. "Seems like the feller which Jack wanted you to git was from Grizzly Claw, or was supposed to go there, or somethin'."

"A great help you be!" I said in disgust. "Here somebody has went and wronged one of my kinfolks, maybe, and you forgits the details. Try to remember the name of the feller, anyway. If I knew who he was, I could lay him out, and then find out what he done later on. Think, cain't you?"

"Did you ever have a wagon-tongue busted over yore head?" he said. "I tell you, it's jest right recent that I remembered my own name. It was all I could do to rekernize you jest now. If you'll come back in a couple of days, maybe by then I'll remember what all Jack told me."

I give a snort of disgust and turned off the road and headed up the trail for Grizzly Claw. I thought maybe I could learn something there. Anyway, it was up to me to try. Us Bear Creek folks may fight amongst ourselves, but we stands for no stranger to impose on any one of us. Uncle Jeppard was about as old as the Humbolt Mountains, and he'd fit Injuns for a living in his younger days. He was still a tough old knot. Anybody that could do him a wrong and get away with it, sure wasn't no ordinary man, so it warn't no wonder that word had been sent out for me to get on his trail. And now I hadn't no idee who to look for, or why, jest because of Tunk Willoughby's weak skull. I despise these here egg-headed weaklings.

I arrove in Grizzly Claw late in the afternoon and went first to the wagon-yard and seen that Cap'n Kidd was put in a good stall and fed proper, and warned the feller there to keep away from him if he didn't want his brains kicked out. Cap'n Kidd has got a disposition like a shark and he don't like strangers. There was only five other hosses in the wagon-yard, besides me and Cap'n Kidd—a pinto, a bay, a piebald, and a couple of pack-hosses.

I then went back into the business part of the village, which was one dusty street with stores and saloons on each side, and I didn't pay much attention to the town, because I was trying to figger out how I could go about trying to find out what I wanted to know, and couldn't think of no questions to ask nobody about nothing.

Well, I was approaching a saloon called the Apache Queen, and was looking at the ground in meditation, when I seen a silver dollar laying in the dust clost to a hitching rack. I immejitly stooped down and picked it up, not noticing how clost it was to the hind laigs of a mean-looking mule. When I stooped over he hauled off and kicked me in the head. Then he let out a awful bray and commenced jumping around holding up his hind hoof, and some men come running out of the saloon, and one of 'em hollered: "He's tryin' to kill my mule! Call the law!"

Quite a crowd gathered and the feller which owned the mule hollered like a catamount. He was a mean-looking cuss with mournful whiskers and a cock-eye. He yelled like somebody was stabbing him, and I couldn't get in a word aidge-ways. Then a feller with a long skinny neck and two guns come up and said: "I'm the sheriff. What's goin' on here? Who is this giant? What's he did?"

The whiskered cuss hollered: "He kicked hisself in the head with my mule and crippled the pore critter for life! I demands my rights! He's got to pay me three hundred and fifty dollars for my mule!"

"Aw, heck," I said, "that mule ain't hurt none; his laig's jest kinda numbed. Anyway, I ain't got but six bucks, and whoever gits them will take 'em offa my dead corpse." I then hitched my six-shooters for'ards, and the crowd kinda fell away.

"I demands that you 'rest him!" howled Drooping-whiskers. "He tried to 'ssassinate my mule!"

"You ain't got no star," I told the feller which said he was the law. "You ain't goin' to arrest me."

"Does you dast resist arrest?" he says, fidgeting with his belt.

"Who said anything about resistin' arrest?" I retorted. "All I aim to do is see how far yore neck will stretch before it breaks."

"Don't you dast lay hands onto a officer of the law!" he squawked, backing away in a hurry.

I was tired of talking, and thirsty, so I merely give a snort and turned away through the crowd towards a saloon pushing 'em right and left out of my way. I seen 'em gang up in the street behind me, talking low and mean, but I give no heed.

They warn't nobody in the saloon except the barman and a gangling cowpuncher which had draped hisself over the bar. I ordered whisky, and when I had drunk a few fingers of the rottenest muck I believe I ever tasted, I give it up in disgust and throwed the dollar on the bar which I found, and was starting out when the bartender hollered: "Hey!"

I turned around and said courteously: "Don't you yell at me like that, you bat-eared buzzard! What you want?"

"This here dollar ain't no good!" says he, banging it on the bar.

"Well, neither is yore whisky!" I snarled, because I was getting mad. "So that makes us even!"

I am a long-suffering man, but it looked like everybody in Grizzly Claw was out to gyp the stranger in their midst.

"You cain't run no blazer over me!" he hollered. "You gimme a real dollar, or else——"

He ducked down behind the bar and come up with a shotgun so I taken it away from him and bent the barrel double acrost my knee and throwed it after him as he run out the back door hollering help, murder.

The cowpuncher had picked up the dollar and bit on it, and then he looked at me very sharp, and said: "Where did you get this?"

"I found it, if it's any of yore derned business," I snapped, and strode out of the door, and the minute I hit the street somebody let *bam!* at me from behind a rain-barrel acrost the street and shot my hat off. So I slammed a bullet back through the barrel and the feller hollered and fell out in the open yelling blue murder. It was the feller which called hisself the sheriff and he was drilled through the hind laig. I noticed a lot of heads sticking up over winder sills and around doors, so I roared: "Let that be a warnin' to you Grizzly Claw coyotes! I'm Breckinridge Elkins from Bear Creek up in the Humbolts, and I shoot better in my sleep than most men does wide awake!"

I then lent emphasis to my remarks by punctuating a few sign-boards and knocking out a few winder panes and everybody hollered and ducked. So I shoved my guns back in their scabbards and went into a restaurant. The citizens come out from their hiding-places and carried off my victim, and he made more noise over a broke laig than I thought was possible for a grown man.

They was some folks in the restaurant but they stampeded out the back door as I come in at the front, all except the cook which tried to take refuge somewheres else.

"Come outa there and fry me some bacon!" I commanded, kicking a few slats out of the counter to add p'int to my request. It disgusts me to see a grown man trying to hide under a stove. I am a very patient and mild-mannered human, but Grizzly Claw was getting under my hide. So the cook come out and fried me a mess of bacon and ham and aigs and pertaters and sourdough bread and beans and coffee, and I et three cans of cling peaches. Nobody come into the restaurant whilst I was eating but I thought I heard somebody sneaking around outside.

When I got through I ast the feller how much, and he told me, and I planked down the cash, and he commenced to bite it. This lack of faith in his feller humans so enraged me that I drawed my bowie knife and said: "They is a limit to any man's patience! You jest dast to say that coin's phoney and I'll slice off yore whiskers plumb at the roots!"

I brandished my bowie under his nose, and he hollered and stampeded back into the stove and upsot it and fell over it, and the coals went down the back of his shirt, so he riz up and run for the creek yelling bloody murder. And that's how the story got started that I tried to burn a cook alive, Injun-style, because he fried my bacon too crisp. Matter of fact, I kept his shack from catching fire and burning down, because I stomped out the coals before they done no more than burn a big hole through the floor, and I throwed the stove out the back door.

It ain't my fault if the mayor of Grizzly Claw was sneaking up the back steps with a shotgun jest at that moment. Anyway, I hear he was able to walk with a couple of crutches after a few months.

I emerged suddenly from the front door, hearing a suspicious noise, and I seen a feller crouching clost to a side winder peeking through a hole in the wall. It was the cowboy I seen in the Apache Queen. He whirled when I come out, but I had him covered.

"Air you spyin' on me?" I demanded. "'Cause if you air——"

"No, no!" he says in a hurry. "I was jest leanin' up agen that wall restin'."

"You Grizzly Claw folks is all crazy," I said disgustedly, and looked around to see if anybody else tried to shoot me, but they warn't nobody in sight, which was suspicious, but I give no heed. It was dark by that time so I went to the wagon-yard, and they warn't nobody there. I reckon the man which run it was off somewheres drunk, because that seemed to be the main occupation of most of them Grizzly Claw devils.

The only place for folks to sleep was a kind of double log-cabin. That is, it had two rooms, but they warn't no door between 'em; and in each room they wasn't nothing but a fireplace and a bunk, and jest one outside door. I seen Cap'n Kidd was fixed for the night, and then I went into the cabin and brought in my saddle and bridle and saddle blanket because I didn't trust the people thereabouts. I taken off my boots and hat and hung 'em on the wall, and hung my guns and bowie on the end of the bunk, and then spread my saddle-blanket on the bunk and laid down glumly.

I dunno why they don't build them dern things for ordinary sized humans. A man six and a half foot tall like me can't never find one comfortable for him. You'd think nobody but pigmies ever expected to use one. I laid there and was disgusted at the bunk, and at myself too, because I hadn't learnt who it was done something to Uncle Jeppard, or what he done. It looked like I'd have to go clean to Bear Creek to find out, and then maybe have to come clean back to Grizzly Claw again to get the critter. By that time Dolly Rixby would be plumb wore out of patience with me, and I wouldn't blame her none.

Well, as I lay there contemplating, I heard a man come into the wagon-yard, and purty soon I heard him come towards the cabin, but I thought nothing of it. Then the door begun to open, and I riz up with a gun in each hand and said: "Who's there? Make yoreself knowed before I blasts you down!"

Whoever it was mumbled some excuse about being on the wrong side, and the door closed. But the voice sounded kind of familiar, and the feller didn't go into the other room. I heard his footsteps sneaking off, and I riz and went to the door, and looked over towards the row of stalls. So purty soon a man led the pinto out of his stall, and swung aboard him and rode off. It was purty dark, but if us folks on Bear Creek didn't have eyes like a hawk, we'd never live to get grown. I seen it was the cowboy I'd seen in the Apache Queen and outside the restaurant. Onst he got clear of the wagon-yard, he slapped in the spurs and went racing through the village like they was a red war-party on his trail. I could hear the beat of his hoss's hoofs fading south down the rocky trail after he was out of sight.

I knowed he must of follered me to the wagon-yard, but I couldn't make no sense out of it, so I went and laid down on the bunk again. I was jest about to go to sleep when I was woke by the sounds of somebody coming into the other room of the cabin, and I heard somebody strike a match. The bunk was built agen the partition wall, so they was only a few feet from me, though with the log wall betwixt us.

They was two of them, from the sounds of their talking.

"I tell you," one of them was saying, "I don't like his looks. I don't believe he's what he pertends to be. We better take no chances, and clear out. After all, we cain't stay here forever. These people air beginning to get suspicious, and if they find out for shore, they'll be demandin' a cut in the profits, to pertect us. The stuff's all packed and ready to jump at a second's notice. Let's run for it to-night. It's a wonder nobody ain't never stumbled onto that hide-out before now."

"Aw," said the other'n, "these Grizzly Claw yaps don't do nothin' but swill licker and gamble and think up swindles to work on sech strangers as is unlucky enough to wander in here. They don't never go into the hills south-west of the village whar our cave is. Most of 'em don't even know there's a path past that big rock to the west."

"Well, Bill," said t'other'n, "we've done purty well, countin' that job up in the Bear Creek country."

At that I was wide awake and listening with both ears.

Bill laughed. "That was kind of funny, warn't it, Jim?" says he.

"You ain't never told me the particulars," says Jim. "Did you have any trouble?"

"Well," said Bill. "Twarn't to say easy. That old Jeppard Grimes was a hard old nut. If all Injun fighters was like him, I feel plumb sorry for the Injuns."

"If any of them Bear Creek devils ever catches you——" begun Jim.

Bill laughed again.

"Them hillbillies never strays more'n ten miles from Bear Creek," says he. "I had the sculp and was gone before they knowed what was up. I've collected bounties for wolves and b'ars, but that's the first time I ever got money for a human sculp!"

A icy chill run down my spine. Now I knowed what had happened to pore old Uncle Jeppard! Scalped! After all the Injun sculps he'd lifted! And them coldblooded murderers could set there and talk about it like it was the ears of a coyote or a rabbit!

"I told him he'd had the use of that there sculp long enough," Bill was saying. "A old cuss like him——"

I waited for no more. Everything was red around me. I didn't stop for my boots, guns nor nothing. I was too crazy mad even to know sech things existed. I riz up from that bunk and put my head down and rammed that partition wall like a bull going through a rail fence.

The dried mud poured out of the chinks and some of the logs give way, and a howl went up from the other side.

"What's that?" hollered one, and t'other'n yelled: "Look out! It's a b'ar!"

I drawed back and rammed the wall again. It caved inwards and I crashed headlong through it in a shower of dry mud and splinters, and somebody shot at me and missed. They was a lighted lantern setting on a handhewn table, and two men about six feet tall each that hollered and let *bam* at me with their sixshooters. But they was too dumbfounded to shoot straight. I gathered 'em to my bosom and we went backwards over the table, taking it and the lantern with us, and you ought to of heard them critters howl when the burning ile splashed down their necks.

It was a dirt floor so nothing caught on fire, and we was fighting in the dark, and they was hollering: "Help! Murder! We are bein' 'sassinated! Ow! Release go my ear!" And then one of 'em got his boot heel wedged in my mouth, and whilst I was twisting it out with one hand, the other'n tore out of his shirt which I was gripping with t'other hand, and run out the door. I had hold of the other feller's foot and commenced trying to twist it off, when he wrenched his laig outa the boot, and took it on the run. When I started to foller him I fell over the table in the dark and got all tangled up in it.

I broke off a laig for a club and rushed to the door, and jest as I got to it a whole mob of folks come surging into the wagon-yard with torches and guns and dogs and a rope, and they hollered: "There he is, the murderer, the outlaw, the counterfeiter, the house-burner, the mule-killer!"

I seen the man that owned the mule, and the restaurant feller, and the bar-keep, and a lot of others. They come roaring and bellering up to the door, hollering: "Hang him! Hang him! String up the murderer!" And they begun shooting at me, so I fell amongst 'em with my table-laig and laid right and left till it busted. They was packed so clost together I laid out three or four at a lick, and they hollered something awful. The torches was all knocked down and trompled out except them which was held by fellers which danced around on the aidge of the mill, hollering: "Lay hold on him! Don't be scairt of the big hillbilly! Shoot him! Knife him! Knock him in the head!" The dogs having more sense than the men, they all run off except one big mongrel that looked like a wolf, and he bit the mob often'ern he did me.

They was a lot of wild shooting and men hollering: "Oh, I'm shot! I'm kilt! I'm dyin'!" and some of them bullets burnt my hide they come so clost, and the flashes singed my eyelashes, and somebody broke a knife agen my belt buckle. Then I seen the torches was all gone except one, and my club was broke, so I bust right through the mob, swinging right and left with my fists and stomping on them that tried to drag me down. I got clear of everybody except the man with the torch who was so excited he was jumping up and down trying to shoot me without cocking his gun. That blame dog was snapping at my heels, so I swung him by the tail and hit the man over the head with him. They went down in a heap and the torch went out, and the dog clamped onto the feller's ear, and he let out a squall like a steam-whistle.

They was milling in the dark behind me, and I run straight to Cap'n Kidd's stall and jumped on him bareback with nothing but a hackamore on him. Jest as the mob located where I went, we come storming out of the stall like a hurricane and knocked some of 'em galleywest and run over some more, and headed for the gate. Somebody shet the gate but Cap'n Kidd took it in his stride, and we was gone into the darkness before they knowed what hit 'em.

Cap'n Kidd decided then was a good time to run away, like he usually does, so he taken to the hills and run through bushes and clumps of trees trying to scrape me off. When I finally pulled him up we was maybe a mile south of the village, with Cap'n Kidd no bridle nor saddle nor blanket, and me with no guns, knife, boots nor hat. And what was wuss, them devils which sculped Uncle Jeppard had got away from me, and I didn't know where to look for 'em.

I sot meditating whether to go back and fight the whole town of Grizzly Claw for my boots and guns, or what to do, when all to onst I remembered what Bill and Jim had said about a cave and a path running to it. I thought I bet them fellers will go back and get their hosses and pull out, jest like they was planning, and they had stuff in the cave, so that's the place to look for 'em. I hoped they hadn't already got the stuff, whatever it was, and gone.

I knowed where that rock was, because I'd saw it when I come into town that afternoon—a big rock that jutted up above the trees about a mile to the west of Grizzly Claw. So I started out through the bresh, and before long I seen it looming up agen the stars, and I made straight for it. Sure enough, they was a narrer trail winding around the base and leading off to the south-west. I follered it, and when I'd went nearly a mile, I come to a steep mountain-side, all clustered with bresh.

When I seen that I slipped off and led Cap'n Kid off the trail and tied him back amongst the trees. Then I crope up to the cave which was purty well masked with bushes. I listened, but everything was dark and still, but all to onst, away down the trail, I heard a burst of shots, and what sounded like hosses running. Then everything was still again, and I quick ducked into the cave, and struck a match.

They was a narrer entrance that broadened out after a few feet, and the cave run straight like a tunnel for maybe thirty steps, about fifteen foot wide, and then it made a bend. After that it widened out and got purty big—about fifty feet wide, and I couldn't tell how far back into the mountain it run. To the left the wall was very broken and notched with ledges, mighty nigh like stair-steps, and when the match went out, away up above me I seen some stars which meant that they was a cleft in the wall or roof away up on the mountain somewheres.

Before the match went out, I seen a lot of junk over in a corner covered up with a tarpaulin, and when I was fixing to strike another match I heard men coming up the trail outside. So I quick clumb up the broken wall and laid on a ledge about ten feet up and listened.

From the sounds as they arriv at the cave mouth, I knowed it was two men on foot, running hard and panting loud. They rushed into the cave and made the turn, and I heard 'em fumbling around. Then a light flared up and I seen a lantern being lit and hung up on a spur of rock.

In the light I seen them two murderers, Bill and Jim, and they looked plumb dilapidated. Bill didn't have no shirt on and the other'n was wearing jest one boot and limped. Bill didn't have no gun and his belt neither, and both was mauled and bruised, and scratched, too, like they'd been running through briars.

"Look here," said Jim, holding his head which had a welt on it which was likely made by my fist. "I ain't sartain in my mind as to jest what all *has* happened. Somebody must of hit me with a club some time tonight, and things is happened too fast for my addled wits. Seems like we been fightin' and runnin' all night. Listen, *was* we settin' in the wagon-yard shack talkin' peaceable, and *did* a grizzly b'ar bust through the wall and nigh slaughter us?"

"That's plumb correct," said Bill. "Only it warn't no b'ar. It was some kind of a human critter—maybe a escaped maneyack. We ought to of stopped for hosses——"

"I warn't thinkin' 'bout no hosses," broke in Jim. "When I found myself outside that shack my only thought was to kiver ground, and I done my best, considerin' that I'd lost a boot, and that critter had nigh onhinged my hind laig. I'd lost you in the dark, so I made for the cave knowin' you'd come there eventual, if you was still alive, and it seemed like I was forever gittin' through the woods, crippled like I was. I hadn't no more'n hit the path when you come up it on the run."

"Well," says Bill, "as I went over the wagon-yard wall a lot of people come whoopin' through the gate, and I thought they was after us, but it must of been the feller we fit, because as I run I seen him layin' into 'em right and left. After I'd got over my panic, I went back after our hosses, but I run right into a gang of men on hossback, and one of 'em was that derned feller which passed hisself off as a cowboy. I didn't need no more. I taken out through the woods as hard as I could pelt, and they hollered, 'There he goes!' and hot-foot after me."

"And was them the fellers I shot at back down the trail?" ast Jim.

"Yeah," says Bill. "I thought I'd shooken 'em off, but jest as I seen you on the path, I heard hosses comin' behind us, so I hollered to let 'em have it, and you did."

"Well, I didn't know who it was," said Jim. "I tell you, my head's buzzin' like a circle-saw."

"Well," said Bill, "we stopped 'em and scattered 'em. I dunno if you hit anybody in the dark, but they'll be mighty keerful about comin' up the trail. Let's clear out."

"On foot?" says Jim. "And me with jest one boot?"

"How else?" says Bill. "We'll have to hoof it till we can steal us some cayuses. We'll have to leave all this stuff here. We don't dare go back to Grizzly Claw after our hosses. I *told* that derned cowboy would do to watch. He ain't no cowpoke at all. He's a blame detective."

"What's that?" broke in Jim.

"Hosses' hoofs!" exclaimed Bill, turning pale. "Here, blow out that lantern! We'll climb the ledges and git out through the cleft, and take out over the mountain whar they cain't foller with hosses, and then——"

It was at that instant that I launched myself offa the ledge on top of 'em. I landed with all my two hundred and ninety pounds square on Jim's shoulders and when he hit the ground under me he kind of spread out like a toad when you tromp on him. Bill give a scream of astonishment and tore off a hunk of rock about the size of a man's head and lammed me over the ear with it as I riz. This irritated me, so I taken him by the neck, and also taken away a knife which he was trying to hamstring me with, and begun sweeping the floor with his carcass.

Presently I paused and kneeling on him, I strangled him till his tongue lolled out, whilst hammering his head fervently agen the rocky floor.

"You murderin' devil!" I gritted betwixt my teeth. "Before I varnishes this here rock with yore brains, tell me why you taken my Uncle Jeppard's sculp!"

"Let up!" he gurgled, being purple in the face where he warn't bloody. "They was a dude travellin' through the country and collectin' souvenirs, and he heard about that sculp and wanted it. He hired me to go git it for him."

I was so shocked at that cold-bloodedness that I forgot what I was doing and choked Bill nigh to death before I remembered to ease up on him.

"Who was he?" I demanded. "Who is the skunk which hires old men murdered so's he can colleck their sculps? My God, these Eastern dudes is wuss'n Apaches! Hurry up and tell me, so I can finish killin' you."

But he was unconscious; I'd squoze his neck too hard. I riz up and looked around for some water or whisky or something to bring him to so he could tell who hired him to sculp Uncle Jeppard, before I twisted his head off, which was my earnest intention of doing, when somebody said, "Han's up!"

I whirled and there at the crook of the cave stood that there cowboy which had spied on me in Grizzly Claw, and ten other men. They all had their Winchesters p'inted at me, and the cowboy had a star on his buzum.

"Don't move!" he said. "I'm a Federal detective, and I'm arrestin' you for manufactorin' counterfeit money!"

"What you mean?" I snarled, backing up to the wall.

"You know," he said, kicking the tarpaulin off the junk in the corner. "Look here, men! All the stamps and dyes he used to make phoney coins and bills! All packed up, ready to light out. I been hangin' around Grizzly Claw for days knowin' that whoever was passin' this stuff made his, or their headquarters here somewheres. To-day I spotted that dollar you give the barkeep, and I went *pronto* for my men which was camped back in the hills a few miles. I thought you was settled in the wagon-yard for the night, but it seems you give us the slip. Put the cuffs on him, men!"

"No, you don't!" I snarled, bounding back. "Not till I've finished these devils on the floor—and maybe not then! I dunno what yo're talkin' about, but——"

"Here's a couple of corpses!" hollered one of the men. "He's kilt a couple of fellers!"

One of them stooped over Bill, but he had recovered his senses, and now he riz up on his elbows and give a howl. "Save me!" he bellered. "I confesses! I'm a counterfeiter, and so is Jim there on the floor! We surrenders, and you got to pertect us!"

"Yo're the counterfeiters?" ejaculated the detective, took aback as it were. "Why, I was follerin' this giant! I seen him pass fake money myself. We got to the wagon-yard awhile after he'd run off, but we seen him duck in the woods not far from there, and we been chasin' him. He shot at us down the trail while ago——"

"That was us," said Bill. "It was me you was chasin'. If he was passin' fake stuff, he musta found it somewheres. I tell you, we're the men you're after, and you got to pertect us! I demands to be put in the strongest jail in this state, which even this here devil cain't bust into!"

"And he ain't no counterfeiter?" said the detective.

"He ain't nothin' but a man-eater," said Bill. "Arrest us and take us outa his rech."

"No!" I roared, clean beside myself. "They belongs to me! They sculped my uncle! Give 'em knives or guns or somethin', and let us fight it out."

"Cain't do that," said the detective. "They're Federal prisoners. If you got any charge agen 'em, they'll have to be indicted in the proper form."

His men hauled 'em up and handcuffed 'em and started to lead 'em out.

"Blast yore cussed souls!" I raved. "You low-down, mangy, egg-suckin coyotes! Does you mean to perteck a couple of dirty sculpers? I'll——"

I started for 'em and they all p'inted their Winchesters at me.

"Keep back!" said the detective. "I'm grateful for you leadin' us into this den, and layin' out these criminals for us, but I don't hanker after no battle in a cave with a human grizzly like you."

Well, what could I do? If I'd had my guns, or even my knife, I'd of took a chance with the whole eleven men, officers or not, but even I can't fight eleven .45-90's with my bare hands. I stood speechless with rage whilst they filed out, and then I went for Cap'n Kidd in a kind of a daze. I felt wuss'n a hoss-thief. Them fellers would be put in the pen safe out of my rech, and Uncle Jeppard's sculp was unavenged! It was awful. I felt like bawling.

Time I got my hoss back onto the trail, the posse with their prisoners was out of sight and hearing. I seen the only thing to do was to go back to Grizzly Claw and get my outfit, and then foller 'em and try to take their prisoners away from 'em some way.

Well, the wagon-yard was dark and still. The wounded had

been carried away to have their injuries bandaged, and from the groaning that was still coming from the shacks and cabins along the street, the casualties had been plenteous. The citizens of Grizzly Claw must have been shook up something terrible, because they hadn't even stole my guns and saddle and things yet; everything was in the cabin jest like I'd left 'em.

I put on my boots, hat and belt, saddled and bridled Cap'n Kidd and sot out on the road I knowed the posse had took. But they had a long start on me, and when daylight come I hadn't overtook 'em, though I knowed they couldn't be far ahead of me. But I did meet somebody else. It was Tunk Willoughby riding up the trail, and when he seen me he grinned all over his battered features.

"Hey, Breck!" he hailed me. "After you left I sot on that there log and thunk, and thunk, and I finally remembered what Jack Gordon told me, and I started out to find you again and tell you. It was this: he said to keep a close lookout for a feller from Grizzly Claw named Bill Croghan, because he'd gypped yore Uncle Jeppard in a deal."

"What?" I said.

"Yeah," said Tunk. "He bought somethin' from Jeppard and paid him in counterfeit money. Jeppard didn't know it was phoney till after the feller had got plumb away," said Tunk, "and bein' as he was too busy kyorin' some b'ar meat to go after him, he sent word for you to git him."

"But the sculp——" I said wildly.

"Oh," said Tunk, "that was what Jeppard sold the feller. It was the sculp Jeppard taken offa old Yeller Eagle, the Comanche warchief forty years ago, and been keepin' for a souvenear. Seems like a Eastern dude heard about it and wanted to buy it, but this Croghan feller must of kept the money he give him to git it with, and give Jeppard phoney cash. So you see everything's all right, even if I did forgit a little, and no harm did——"

And that's why Tunk Willoughby is going around saying I'm a homicidal maneyack, and run him five miles down a mountain and tried to kill him—which is a exaggeration, of course. I wouldn't of kilt him if I could of caught him—which I couldn't when he taken to the thick bresh. I would merely of raised a few knots on his head and tied his hind laigs in a bow-knot around his fool neck, and did a few other little things that might of improved his memory.

CHAPTER IX

Cupid From Bear Creek

When I reined my hoss towards War Paint again, I didn't go back the way I'd come. I was so far off my route that I kno_ed it would be nearer to go through the mountains by the w^ of Teton Gulch than it would be to go clean back to the Yavapai—War Paint road. So I headed out.

I aimed to pass right through Teton Gulch without stopping, because I was in a hurry to get back to War Paint and Dolly Rixby, but my thirst got the best of me, and I stopped in the camp. It was one of them new mining towns that springs up over night like mushrooms. I was drinking me a dram at the bar of the Yaller Dawg Saloon and Hotel, when the barkeep says, after studying me a spell, he says: "You must be Breckinridge Elkins, of Bear Creek."

I give the matter due consideration, and 'lowed as how I was.

"How come you knowed me?" I inquired suspiciously, because I hadn't never been in Teton Gulch before, and he says: "Well, I've heard tell of Breckinridge Elkins, and when I seen you, I figgered you must be him, because I don't see how they can be two men in the world that big. By the way, there's a friend of yore'n upstairs—Blink Wiltshaw, from War Paint. I've heered him brag about knowin' you personal. He's upstairs now, fourth door from the stair-head, on the left."

So Blink had come back to Teton, after all. Well, that suited me fine, so I thought I'd go up and pass the time of day with him, and find out if he had any news from War Paint, which I'd been gone from for about a week. A lot of things can happen in a week in a fastmoving town like War Paint.

123

I went upstairs and knocked on the door, and bam! went a gun inside and a .45 slug ripped through the door and taken a nick out of my off-ear. Getting shot in the ear always did irritate me, so without waiting for no more exhibitions of hospitality, I give voice to my displeasure in a deafening beller and knocked the door off'n its hinges and busted into the room over its rooins.

For a second I didn't see nobody, but then I heard a kind of gurgle going on, and happened to remember that the door seemed kind of squshy underfoot when I tromped over it, so I knowed that whoever was in the room had got pinned under the door when I knocked it down.

So I reched under it and got him by the collar and hauled him out, and sure enough it was Blink Wiltshaw. He was limp as a lariat, and glassy-eyed and pale, and was still trying to shoot me with his six-shooter when I taken it away from him.

"What the hell's the matter with you?" I demanded sternly, dangling him by the collar with one hand, whilst shaking him till his teeth rattled. "Didn't Dolly make us shake hands? What you mean by tryin' to 'sasserinate me through a hotel door?"

"Lemme down, Breck," he gasped. "I didn't know it was you. I thought it was Rattlesnake Harrison comin' after my gold."

So I sot him down. He grabbed a jug of licker and taken him a swig, and his hand shook so he spilt half of it down his neck.

"Well?" I demanded. "Ain't you goin' to offer me a snort, dern it?"

"Excuse me, Breckinridge," he apolergized. "I'm so derned jumpy I dunno what I'm doin'. You see them buckskin pokes?" says he, p'inting at some bags on the bed. "Them is plumb full of nuggets. I got a claim up the Gulch, and the day I got back from War Paint I hit a regular bonanza. But it ain't doin' me no good."

"What you mean?" I ast.

"The mountains around Teton is full of outlaws," says he. "They robs and murders every man which makes a strike. The stage-coach has been stuck up so often nobody sends their dust out on it no more. When a man makes a pile he sneaks out through the mountains at night, with his gold on pack-mules. I aimed to do that last night. But them outlaws has got spies all over the camp, and I know they got me spotted. Rattlesnake Harrison's their chief, and he's a ring-tailed he-devil. I been squattin' over this here gold with my pistol in fear and tremblin', expectin' 'em to come right into camp after me. I'm dern nigh loco!"

And he shivered and cussed kind of whimpery, and taken an-

other dram, and cocked his pistol and sot there shaking like he'd
saw a ghost or two.

"You got to help me, Breckinridge," he said desperately. *"You*
take this here gold out for me, willya? The outlaws don't know
you. You could hit the old Injun path south of the camp and foller
it to Hell-Wind Pass. The Chawed Ear-Wahpeton stage goes there
about sun-down. You could put the gold on the state there, and
they'd take it on to Wahpeton. Harrison wouldn't never think of
holdin' it up *after* it left Hell-Wind. They always holds it up this
side of the Pass."

"What I want to risk my neck for you for?" I demanded bitterly,
memories of Dolly Rixby rising up before me. "If you ain't got
the guts to tote out yore own gold——"

"'Tain't altogether the gold, Breck," says he. "I'm tryin' to
git married, and——"

"Married?" says I. "Here? In Teton Gulch? To a gal in Teton
Gulch?"

"Married to a gal in Teton Gulch," he avowed. "I was aimin'
to git hitched to-morrer, but they ain't a preacher or a justice of
the peace in camp to tie the knot. But her uncle the Reverant
Rembrandt Brockton is a circuit rider, and he's due to pass through
Hell-Wind Pass on his way to Wahpeton today. I was aimin' to
sneak out last night, hide in the hills till the stage come through,
and then put the gold on it and bring Brother Rembrandt back with
me. But yesterday I learnt Harrison's spies was watchin' me, and
I'm scairt to go. Now Brother Rembrandt will go on to Wahpeton,
not knowin' he's needed here, and no tellin' when I'll be able to
git married——"

"Hold on," I said hurriedly, doing some quick thinking. I didn't
want this here wedding to fall through. The more Blink was married
to some gal in Teton, the less he could marry Dolly Rixby.

"Blink," I said, grasping his hand warmly, "never let it be said
that a Elkins ever turned down a friend in distress. I'll take yore
gold to Hell-Wind Pass and bring back Brother Rembrandt."

Blink fell onto my neck and wept with joy. "I'll never forgit
this, Breckinridge," says he, "and I bet you won't neither! My
hoss and pack-mule are in the stables behind the saloon."

"I don't need no pack-mule," I says. "Cap'n Kidd can pack
the dust easy."

Cap'n Kidd was getting fed out in the corral next to the hotel.
I went out there and got my saddle-bags, which is a lot bigger'n
most saddle-bags, because all my plunder has to be made to fit
my size. They're made outa three-ply elkskin, stitched with raw-

hide thongs, and a wildcat couldn't claw his way out of 'em.

I noticed quite a bunch of men standing around the corral looking at Cap'n Kidd, but thunk nothing of it, because he is a hoss which naturally attracks attention. But whilst I was getting my saddle-bags, a long lanky cuss with long yaller whiskers come up and said, says he: "Is that yore hoss in the corral?"

I says: "If he ain't he ain't nobody's."

"Well, he looks a whole lot like a hoss that was stole off my ranch six months ago," he said, and I seen ten or fifteen hard-looking *hombres* gathering around me. I laid down my saddle-bags sudden-like and reched for my guns, when it occurred to me that if I had a fight there I might get arrested and it would interfere with me bringing Brother Rembrandt in for the wedding.

"If that there is yore hoss," I said, "you ought to be able to lead him out of that there corral."

"Shore I can," he says with a oath. "And what's more, I aim'ta."

"That's right, Jake," says another feller. "Stand up for yore rights. Us boys is right behind you."

"Go ahead," I says. "If he's yore hoss, prove it. Go git him!"

He looked at me suspiciously, but he taken up a rope and clumb the fence and started towards Cap'n Kidd which was chawing on a block of hay in the middle of the corral. Cap'n Kidd throwed up his head and laid back his ears and showed his teeth, and Jake stopped sudden and turned pale.

"I—I don't believe that there *is* my hoss, after all!" says he.

"Put that lasso on him!" I roared, pulling my right-hand gun. "You say he's yore'n; I say he's mine. One of us is a liar and a hoss-thief and I aim to prove which. Gwan, before I festoons yore system with lead polkadots!"

He looked at me and he looked at Cap'n Kidd, and he turned bright green all over. He looked again at my .45 which I now had cocked and p'inted at his long neck, which his adam's apple was going up and down like a monkey on a pole, and he begun to aidge towards Cap'n Kidd again, holding the rope behind him and sticking out one hand.

"Whoa, boy," he says, kind of shudderingly. "Whoa—good old feller—nice hossie—whoa, boy—*ow!*"

He let out a awful howl as Cap'n Kidd made a snap and bit a chunk out of his hide. He turned to run but Cap'n Kidd wheeled and let fly both heels which catched Jake in the seat of the britches, and his shriek of despair was horrible to hear as he went head-first through the corral-fence into a hoss trough on the other side. From this he ariz dripping water, blood and profanity, and he shook a quivering fist at me and croaked: "You derned murderer! I'll have yore life for this!"

"I don't hold no conversation with hoss-thieves," I snorted, and picked up my saddle-bags and stalked through the crowd which give back in a hurry and take care to cuss under their breath when I tromped on their fool toes.

I taken the saddle-bags up to Blink's room, and told him about Jake, thinking he'd be amoosed, but he got a case of the aggers again, and said: "That was one of Harrison's men! He aimed to take yore hoss. It's a old trick, and honest folks don't dare interfere. Now they got you spotted! What'll you do?"

"Time, tide and a Elkins waits for no man!" I snorted, dumping the gold into the saddle-bags. "If that yaller-whiskered coyote wants any trouble, he can git a bellyfull! Don't worry, yore gold will be safe in my saddle-bags. It's as good as in the Wahpeton stage right now. And by midnight I'll be back with Brother Rembrandt Brockton to hitch you up with his niece."

"Don't yell so loud," begged Blink. "The cussed camp's full of spies. Some of 'em may be downstairs right now, lissenin'."

"I warn't speakin' above a whisper," I said indignantly.

"That bull's beller may pass for a whisper on Bear Creek," says he, wipin' off the sweat, "but I bet they can hear it from one end of the Gulch to the other'n, at least."

It's a pitable sight to see a man with a case of the scairts. I shook hands with him and left him pouring red licker down his gullet like it was water, and I swung the saddle-bags over my shoulder and went downstairs, and the barkeep leaned over the bar and whispered to me: "Look out for Jake Roman! He was in here a minute ago, lookin' for trouble. He pulled out jest before you come down, but he won't be forgittin' what yore hoss done to him."

"Not when he tries to set down, he won't," I agreed, and went out to the corral, and they was a crowd of men watching Cap'n Kidd eat his hay, and one of 'em seen me and hollered: "Hey, boys, here comes the giant! He's goin' to saddle that man-eatin' monster! Hey, Bill! Tell the boys at the bar."

And here come a whole passel of fellers running out of all the saloons, and they lined the corral fence solid, and started laying bets whether I'd get the saddle onto Cap'n Kidd, or get my brains kicked out. I thought miners must all be crazy. They ought've knowed I was able to saddle my own hoss.

Well, I saddled him and throwed on the saddle-bags and clumb aboard, and he pitched about ten jumps like he always does when

I first fork him—'twarn't nothing, but them miners hollered like
wild Injuns. And when he accidentally bucked hisself and me
through the fence and knocked down a section of it along with
fifteen men which was setting on the top rail, the way they howled
you'd of thought something terrible had happened. Me and Cap'n
Kidd don't bother about gates. We usually makes our own through
whatever happens to be in front of us. But them miners is a weakly
breed. As I rode out of town I seen the crowd dipping nine or ten
of 'em into a hoss-trough to bring 'em to, on account of Cap'n
Kidd having accidentally tromped on 'em.

Well, I rode out of the Gulch and up the ravine to the south
and come out into the high-timbered country, and hit the old Injun
trail Blink had told me about. It warn't travelled much. I didn't
meet nobody after I left the Gulch. I figgered to hit Hell-Wind
Pass at least a hour before sun-down which would give me plenty
of time. Blink said the stage passed through there about sun-down.
I'd have to bring back Brother Rembrandt on Cap'n Kidd, I reckoned, but that there hoss can carry double and still out-run and
out-last any other hoss in the State of Nevada. I figgered on getting
back to Teton about midnight or maybe a little later.

After I'd went several miles I come to Apache Canyon, which
was a deep, narrer gorge, with a river at the bottom which went
roaring and foaming along betwixt rock walls a hundred and fifty
feet high. The old trail hit the rim at a place where the canyon
warn't only about seventy foot wide, and somebody had felled
a whopping big pine tree on one side so it fell across and made a
foot-bridge, where a man could walk acrost. They'd onst been a
gold strike in Apache Canyon, and a big camp there, but now it
was plumb abandoned and nobody lives anywheres near it.

I turned east and follered the rim for about half a mile. Here
I come into a old wagon road which was jest about growed up
with saplings now, but it run down into a ravine into the bed of
the canyon, and they was a bridge acrost the river which had been
built during the days of the gold rush. Most of it had done been
washed away by head-rises, but a man could still ride a hoss acrost
what was left. So I done so, and rode up a ravine on the other
side, and come out on high ground again.

I'd rode a few hundred yards past the mouth of the ravine when
somebody said: "Hey!" and I wheeled with both guns in my hands.
Out of the bresh sa'ntered a tall gent in a long frock tail coat and
broad-brimmed hat.

"Who air you and what the hell you mean by hollerin' 'Hey!'

at me?" I demanded courteously, p'inting my guns at him. A Elkins is always perlite.

"I am the Reverant Rembrandt Brockton, my good man," says he. "I am on my way to Teton Gulch to unite my niece and a young man of that camp in the bonds of holy matrimony."

"The he——you don't say!" I says. "Afoot?"

"I alit from the stage-coach at—ah—Hades-Wind Pass," says he. "Some very agreeable cowboys happened to be awaiting the stage there, and they offered to escort me to Teton."

"How come you knowed yore niece was wantin' to be united in acrimony?" I ast.

"The cowpersons informed me that such was the case," says he.

"Where-at are they now?" I next inquore.

"The mount with which they supplied me went lame a little while ago," says he. "They left me here while they went to procure another from a nearby ranch-house."

"I dunno who'd have a ranch anywheres around near here," I muttered. "They ain't got much sense leavin' you here by yore high lonesome."

"You mean to imply there is danger?" says he, blinking mildly at me.

"These here mountains is lousy with outlaws which would as soon kyarve a preacher's gullet as anybody's," I said, and then thought of something else. "Hey!" I says. "I thought the stage didn't come through the Pass till sun-down?"

"Such was the case," says he. "But the schedule has been altered."

"Heck!" I says. "I was aimin' to put this here gold on it which my saddle-bags is full of. Now I'll have to take it back to Teton with me. Well, I'll bring it out to-morrer and catch the stage then. Brother Rembrandt, I'm Breckinridge Elkins of Bear Creek, and I come out here to meet you and escort you back to the Gulch, so's you can unite yore niece and Blink Wiltshaw in the holy bounds of alimony. Come on. We'll ride double."

"But I must await my cowboy friends!" he said. "Ah, here they come now!"

I looked over to the east, and seen about fifteen men ride into sight and move towards us. One was leading a hoss without no saddle onto it.

"Ah, my good friends!" beamed Brother Rembrandt. "They have procured a mount for me, even as they promised."

He hauled a saddle out of the bresh, and says: "Would you please saddle my horse for me when they get here? I should be delighted tó hold your rifle while you did so."

I started to hand him my Winchester, when the snap of a twig under a hoss's hoof made me whirl quick. A feller had jest rode out of a thicket about a hundred yards south of me, and he was raising a Winchester to his shoulder. I recognized him instantly. If us Bear Creek folks didn't have eyes like a hawk, we'd never live to get growed. It was Jake Roman!

Our Winchesters banged together. His lead fanned my ear and mine knocked him end-ways out of his saddle.

"Cowboys, hell!" I roared. "Them's Harrison's outlaws! I'll save you, Brother Rembrandt!"

I swooped him up with one arm and gouged Cap'n Kidd with the spurs and he went from there like a thunderbolt with its tail on fire. Them outlaws come on with wild yells. I ain't in the habit of running from people, but I was afeared they might do the Reverant harm if it come to a close fight, and if he stopped a chunk of lead, Blink might not get to marry his niece, and might get disgusted and go back to War Paint and start sparking Dolly Rixby again.

I was heading for the canyon, aiming to make a stand in the ravine if I had to, and them outlaws was killing their hosses trying to get to the bend of the trail ahead of me, and cut me off. Cap'n Kidd was running with his belly to the ground, but I'll admit Brother Rembrandt warn't helping me much. He was laying acrost my saddle with his arms and laigs waving wildly because I hadn't had time to set him comfortable, and when the horn jobbed him in the belly he uttered some words I wouldn't of expected to hear spoke by a minister of the gospel.

Guns begun to crack and lead hummed past us, and Brother Rembrandt twisted his head around and screamed: "Stop that — shootin', you——sons of——! You'll hit me!"

I thought it was kind of selfish from Brother Rembrandt not to mention me, too, but I said: "'Tain't no use to remonstrate with them skunks, Reverant. They ain't got no respeck for a preacher even."

But to my amazement, the shooting did stop, though them bandits yelled louder'n ever and flogged their cayuses harder. But about that time I seen they had me cut off from the lower canyon crossing, so I wrenched Cap'n Kidd into the old Injun track and headed straight for the canyon rim as hard as he could hammer, with the bresh lashing and snapping around us, and slapping Brother Rembrandt in the face when it whipped back. Them outlaws yelled and wheeled in behind us, but Cap'n Kidd drawed away from them with every stride, and the canyon rim loomed jest ahead of us.

"Pull up, you jack-eared son of Baliol!" howled Brother Rembrandt. "You'll go over the edge!"

"Be at ease, Reverant," I reassured him. "We're goin' over the log."

"Lord have mercy on my soul!" he squalled, and shet his eyes and grabbed a stirrup leather with both hands, and then Cap'n Kidd went over that log like thunder rolling on Jedgment Day.

I doubt if they is another hoss west of the Pecos, or east of it either, which would bolt out onto a log foot-bridge acrost a canyon a hundred and fifty foot deep like that, but they ain't nothing in this world Cap'n Kidd's scairt of except maybe me. He didn't slacken his speed none. He streaked acrost that log like it was a quarter-track, with the bark and splinters flying from under his hoofs, and if one foot had slipped a inch, it would of been Sally bar the door. But he didn't slip, and we was over and on the other side almost before you could catch yore breath.

"You can open yore eyes now, Brother Rembrandt," I said kindly, but he didn't say nothing. He'd fainted. I shaken him to wake him up, and in a flash he come to and give a shriek and grabbed my laig like a b'ar trap. I reckon he thought we was still on the log. I was trying to pry him loose when Cap'n Kidd chose that moment to run under a low-hanging oak tree limb. That's his idee of a joke. That there hoss has got a great sense of humour.

I looked up jest in time to see the limb coming, but not in time to dodge it. It was as big around as my thigh, and it took me smack acrost the wish-bone. We was going full-speed, and something had to give way. It was the girths—both 'em. Cap'n Kidd went out from under me, and me and Brother Rembrandt and the saddle hit the ground together.

I jumped up but Brother Rembrandt laid there going: "Wug wug wug!" like water running out of a busted jug. And then I seen them cussed outlaws had dismounted off of their hosses and was coming acrost the bridge single file on foot, with their Winchesters in their hands.

I didn't waste no time shooting them misguided idjits. I run to the end of the foot-bridge, ignoring the slugs they slung at me. It was purty pore shooting, because they warn't shore of their footing, and didn't aim good. So I only got one bullet in the hind laig and was creased three or four other unimportant places—not enough to bother about.

I bent my knees and got hold of the end of the tree and heaved up with it, and them outlaws hollered and fell along it like ten pins, and dropped their Winchesters and grabbed holt of the log. I given it a shake and shook some of 'em off like persimmons off a limb after a frost, and then I swung the butt around clear of the rim and let go, and it went down end over end into the river a hundred and fifty feet below, with a dozen men still hanging onto it and yelling blue murder.

A regular geyser of water splashed up when they hit, and the last I seen of 'em they was all swirling down the river together in a thrashing tangle of arms and laigs and heads.

I remembered Brother Rembrandt and run back to where he'd fell, but he was already on his feet. He was kind of pale and wild-eyed and his laigs kept bending under him, but he had hold of the saddle-bags, and was trying to drag 'em into a thicket, mumbling kind of dizzily to hisself.

"It's all right now, Brother Rembrandt," I said kindly. "Them outlaws is all horse-de-combat now, as the French say. Blink's gold is safe."

"——!" says Brother Rembrandt, pulling two guns from under his coat tails, and if I hadn't grabbed him, he would of ondoubtedly shot me. We rassled around and I protested: "Hold on, Brother Rembrandt! I ain't no outlaw. I'm yore friend, Breckinridge Elkins. Don't you remember?"

His only reply was a promise to eat my heart without no seasoning, and he then sunk his teeth into my ear and started to chaw it off, whilst gouging for my eyes with both thumbs, and spurring me severely in the hind laigs. I seen he was out of his head from fright and the fall he got, so I said sorrerfully: "Brother Rembrandt, I hates to do this. It hurts me more'n it does you, but we cain't waste time like this. Blink is waitin' to git married." And with a sigh I busted him over the head with the butt of my six-shooter, and he fell over and twitched a few times and then lay limp.

"Pore Brother Rembrandt," I sighed sadly. "All I hope is I ain't addled yore brains so's you've forgot the weddin' ceremony."

So as not to have no more trouble with him when, and if, he come to, I tied his arms and laigs with pieces of my lariat, and taken his weppins which was most surprising arms for a circuit rider. His pistols had the triggers out of 'em, and they was three notches on the butt of one, and four on t'other'n. Moreover he had a bowie knife in his boot, and a deck of marked kyards and a pair of loaded dice in his hip-pocket. But that warn't none of my business.

About the time I finished tying him up, Cap'n Kidd come back to see if he'd kilt me or jest crippled me for life. To show him I could take a joke too, I give him a kick in the belly, and when he could get his breath again, and ondouble hisself, I throwed the saddle on him. I spliced the girths with the rest of my lariat, and put Brother Rembrandt in the saddle and clumb on behind and we headed for Teton Gulch.

After a hour or so Brother Rembrandt come to and says kind of dizzily: "Was anybody saved from the typhoon?"

"Yo're all right, Brother Rembrandt," I assured him. "I'm takin' you to Teton Gulch."

"I remember," he muttered. "It all comes back to me. Damn Jake Roman! I thought it was a good idea, but it seems I was mistaken. I thought we had an ordinary human being to deal with. I know when I'm licked. I'll give you a thousand dollars to let me go."

"Take it easy, Brother Rembrandt," I soothed, seeing he was still delirious. "We'll be to Teton in no time."

"I don't want to go to Teton!" he hollered.

"You got to," I told him. "You got to unite yore niece and Blink Wiltshaw in the holy bums of parsimony."

"To hell with Blink Wiltshaw and my——niece!" he yelled.

"You ought to be ashamed usin' sech langwidge, and you a minister of the gospel," I reproved him sternly. His reply would of curled a Piute's hair.

I was so scandalized I made no reply. I was jest fixing to until him, so's he could ride more comfortable, but I thought if he was that crazy, I better not. So I give no heed to his ravings which growed more and more unbearable as we progressed. In all my born days I never seen sech a preacher.

It was sure a relief to me to sight Teton at last. It was night when we rode down the ravine into the Gulch, and the dance halls and saloons were going full blast. I rode up behind the Yaller Dawg Saloon and hauled Brother Rembrandt off with me and sot him onto his feet, and he said, kind of despairingly: "For the last time, listen to reason. I've got fifty thousand dollars cached up in the hills. I'll give you every cent if you'll untie me."

"I don't want no money," I said. "All I want is for you to marry yore niece and Blink Wiltshaw. I'll untie you then."

"All right," he said. "All right! But untie me now!"

I was jest fixing to do it, when the bar-keep come out with a lantern, and he shone it on our faces and said in a startled tone: "Who the hell is that with you, Elkins?"

"You wouldn't never suspect if from his langwidge," I says, "but it's the Reverant Rembrandt Brockton."

"Are you crazy?" says the bar-keep. "That's Rattlesnake Harrison!"

"I give up," said my prisoner. "I'm Harrison. I'm licked. Lock me up somewhere away from this lunatic!"

I was standing in a kind of daze, with my mouth open, but now I woke up and bellered: *"What?* Yo're Harrison? I see it all now! Jake Roman overheard me talkin' to Blink Wiltshaw, and rode off and fixed it with you to fool me like you done, so's to git Blink's gold! That's why you wanted to hold my Winchester whilst I saddled yore cayuse."

"How'd you ever guess it?" he sneered. "We ought to have shot you from ambush like I wanted to, but Jake wanted to catch you alive and torture you to death account of your horse bitin' him. The fool must have lost his head at the last minute and decided to shoot you after all. If you hadn't recognized him we'd had you surrounded and stuck up before you knew what was happening."

"But now the real preacher's gone on to Wahpeton!" I hollered. "I got to foller him and bring him back——"

"Why, he's here," said one of the men which was gathering around us. "He come in with his niece a hour ago on the stage from War Paint."

"War Paint?" I howled, hit in the belly by a premonishun. I run into the saloon, where they was a lot of people, and there was Blink and a gal holding hands in front of a old man with a long white beard, and he had a book in his hand, and t'other'n lifted in the air. He was saying: "—And I now pernounces you-all man and wife. Them which God has j'ined togither let no snake-hunter put asunder."

"Dolly!" I yelled. Both of 'em jumped about four foot and whirled, and Dolly jumped in front of Blink and spread her arms like she was shoo-ing chickens.

"Don't you tech him, Breckinridge!" she hollered. "I jest married him and I don't aim for no Humbolt grizzly to spile him!"

"But I don't *sabe* all this—" I said dizzily, nervously fumbling with my guns which is a habit of mine when upsot.

Everybody in the wedding party started ducking out of line, and Blink said hurriedly: "It's this way, Breck. When I made my pile so onexpectedly quick, I sent for Dolly to come and marry me, like she'd promised that night, jest after you pulled out for Yavapai. I *was* aimin' to take my gold out to-day, like I told you, so me and Dolly could go to San Francisco on our honeymoon, but I learn't Harrison's gang was watchin' me, jest like I told you. I wanted to git my gold out, and I wanted to git you out of the way before Dolly and her uncle got here on the War Paint stage, so I told you that there lie about Brother Rembrandt bein' on the Wahpeton stage. It was the only lie."

"You said you was marryin' a gal in Teton," I accused fiercely.

"Well," says he, "I did marry her in Teton. You know, Breck, all's fair in love and war."

"Now, now, boys," says Brother Rembrandt—the real one, I mean. "The gal's married, yore rivalry is over, and they's no use holdin' grudges. Shake hands and be friends."

"All right," I said heavily. No man can't say I ain't a good loser. I was cut deep, but I concealed my busted heart.

Leastways I concealed it all I was able to. Them folks which says I crippled Blink Wiltshaw with malice aforethought is liars which I'll sweep the road with when I catches 'em. I didn't aim to break his cussed arm when we shaken hands. It was jest the convulsive start I give when I suddenly thought of what Glory McGraw would say when she heard about this mess. And they ain't no use in folks saying that what imejitly follered was done in revenge for Dolly busting me in the head with that cuspidor. When I thought of the rawhiding I'd likely get from Glory McGraw I kind of lost my head and stampeded like a loco bull. When something got in my way I removed it without stopping to see what it was. How was I to know it was Dolly's Uncle Rembrandt which I absent-mindedly throwed through a winder. And as for them fellers which claims they was knocked down and trompled on, they ought to of got outa my way, dern 'em.

As I headed down the trail on Cap'n Kidd I wondered if I ever really loved Dolly, after all, because I was less upsot over her marrying another feller than I was about what Glory McGraw would say.

CHAPTER X

The Haunted Mountain

They say when a critter is mortally wounded he generally heads for his den, so maybe that's why I headed for Bear Creek when I rode out of Teton Gulch that night; I'd had about as much civilization as I could stand for awhile.

But the closer I got to Bear Creek the more I thought about Glory McGraw and I bust into profuse sweat every time I thought about what she'd say to me, because I'd sent her word by one of the Braxton boys that I aimed to bring Dolly Rixby to Bear Creek as Miz Breckinridge Elkins.

I thought about this so much that when I cut the Chawed Ear road I turned aside and headed up it. I'd met a feller a few miles back which told me about a rodeo which was going to take place at Chawed Ear, so I thought it was a good way to pick up some easy money whilst avoiding Glory at the same time. But I forgot I had to pass by the cabin of one of my relatives.

The reason I detests tarantulas, stinging lizards, and hydro-phobia skunks is because they reminds me so much of Aunt Lavaca Grimes, which my Uncle Jacob Grimes married in a absent-minded moment, when he was old enough to know better.

That there woman's voice plumb puts my teeth on aidge, and it has the same effect on Cap'n Kidd, which don't otherwise shy at nothing less'n a cyclone. So when she stuck her head out of her cabin as I was riding by and yelled: "Breck*in*ri-i-idge!" Cap'n Kidd jumped like he was shot, and then tried to buck me off.

"Stop tormentin' that pore animal and come here," commanded Aunt Lavaca, whilst I was fighting for my life agen Cap'n Kidd's spine-twisting sun-fishing. "Always showin' off! I never see such a inconsiderate, worthless, no-good——"

She kept on yapping away till I had wore him down and reined up alongside the cabin-stoop, and said: "What you want, Aunt Lavaca?"

She give me a scornful snort, and put her hands onto her hips and glared at me like I was something she didn't like the smell of.

"I want you to go git yore Uncle Jacob and bring him home," she said at last. "He's off on one of his idjiotic prospectin' sprees again. He snuck out before daylight with the bay mare and a pack mule—I wisht I'd woke up and caught him. I'd of fixed him! If you hustle you can catch him this side of Haunted Mountain Gap. You bring him back if you have to lasso him and tie him to his saddle. Old fool! Off huntin' gold when they's work to be did in the alfalfa fields. Says he ain't no farmer. Huh! I 'low I'll make a farmer outa him yet. You git goin'."

"But I ain't got time to go chasin' Uncle Jacob all over Haunted Mountain," I protested. "I'm headin' for the rodeo over to Chawed Ear. I'm goin' to win me a prize bull-doggin' some steers——"

"Bull-doggin'!" she snapped. "A fine ockerpashun! Gwan, you worthless loafer! I ain't goin' to stand here all day argyin' with a big ninny like you be. Of all the good-for-nothin', triflin', lunk-headed——"

When Aunt Lavaca starts in like that you might as well travel. She can talk steady for three days and nights without repeating herself, with her voice getting louder and shriller all the time till it nigh splits a body's ear drums. She was still yelling at me as I rode up the trail towards Haunted Mountain Gap, and I could hear her long after I couldn't see her no more.

Pore Uncle Jacob! He never had much luck prospecting, but trailing around with a jackass is a lot better'n listening to Aunt Lavaca. A jackass's voice is mild and soothing alongside of her'n.

Some hours later I was climbing the long rise that led up to the gap and I realized I had overtook the old coot when something went *ping!* up on the slope, and my hat flew off. I quick reined Cap'n Kidd behind a clump of bresh, and looked up towards the Gap, and seen a pack-mule's rear end sticking out of a cluster of boulders.

"You quit that shootin' at me, Uncle Jacob!" I roared.

"You stay whar you be," his voice come back rambunctious and warlike. "I know Lavacky sent you after me, but I ain't goin' home. I'm onto somethin' big at last, and I don't aim to be interfered with."

"What you mean?" I demanded.

"Keep back or I'll ventilate you," he promised. "I'm goin' after the Lost Haunted Mine."

"You been huntin' that thing for fifty years," I snorted.

"This time I finds it," he says. "I bought a map off'n a drunk Mexican down to Perdition. One of his ancestors was a Injun which helped pile up the rocks to hide the mouth of the cave whar it is."

"Why didn't he go find it and git the gold?" I ast.

"He's scairt of ghosts," said Uncle Jacob. "All Mexes is awful superstitious. This 'un'd ruther set and drink, anyhow. They's millions in gold in that there mine. I'll shoot you before I'll go home. Now will you go on back peaceable, or will you throw in with me? I might need you, in case the pack-mule plays out."

"I'll come with you," I said, impressed. "Maybe you have got somethin', at that. Put up yore Winchester. I'm comin'."

He emerged from his rocks, a skinny, leathery old cuss, and he said: "What about Lavacky? If you don't come back with me, she'll foller us herself, she's that strong-minded."

"You can write, cain't you, Uncle Jacob?" I said, and he said, "Yeah, I always carries me a pencil-stub in my saddle-bags. Why?"

"We'll write her a note," I said. "Joe Hopkins always comes down through the Gap onst a week on his way to Chawed Ear. He's due through here to-day. We'll stick the note on a tree, where he'll see it and take it to her."

So I tore a piece of wrapping paper off'n a can of tomatoes Uncle Jacob had in his pack, and he got out his pencil stub, and writ as I told him, as follers:

"Dear Ant Lavaca: I am takin uncle Jacob way up in the mountains dont try to foler us it wont do no good gold is what Im after. Breckinridge."

We folded it and I told Uncle Jacob to write on the outside:

"Dere Joe: pleeze take this here note to Mis Lavaca Grimes on the Chawed Ear rode."

It was lucky Joe knowed how to read. I made Uncle Jacob read me what he had writ to be sure he had got it right. Education is a good thing in its place, but it never taken the place of common hoss-sense.

But he had got it right for a wonder, so I stuck the note on a spruce limb, and me and Uncle Jacob sot out for higher ranges. He started telling me all about the Lost Haunted Mine again, like he'd already did about forty times before. Seems like they was onst a old prospector which stumbled onto a cave about sixty years before then, which the walls was solid gold and nuggets all over the floor till a body couldn't walk, as big as mushmelons. But the Injuns jumped him and run him out and he got lost and nearly starved in the desert, and went crazy. When he come to a settlement and finally got his mind back, he tried to lead a party back to it, but never could find it. Uncle Jacob said the Injuns had took rocks and bresh and hid the mouth of the cave so nobody could tell it was there. I ast him how he knowed the Injuns done that, and he said it was common knowledge. He said any fool oughta know that's jest what they done.

"This here mine," says Uncle Jacob, "is located in a hidden valley which lies away up amongst the high ranges. I ain't never seen it, and I thought I'd explored these mountains plenty. Ain't nobody more familiar with 'em than me, except old Joshua Braxton. But it stands to reason that the cave is awful hard to find, or somebody'd already found it. Accordin' to this here map, that lost valley must lie jest beyond Wildcat Canyon. Ain't many white men know whar that is, even. We're headin' there."

We had left the Gap far behind us, and was moving along the slanting side of a sharp-angled crag whilst he was talking. As we passed it we seen two figgers with hosses emerge from the other side, heading in the same direction we was, so our trails converged. Uncle Jacob glared and reched for his Winchester.

"Who's that?" he snarled.

"The big 'un's Bill Glanton," I said. "I never seen t'other'n."

"And nobody else, outside of a freak show," growled Uncle Jacob.

The other feller was a funny-looking little maverick, with laced boots and a cork sun-helmet and big spectacles. He sot his hoss like he thought it was a rocking-chair, and held his reins like he was trying to fish with 'em. Glanton hailed us. He was from Texas, original, and was rough in his speech and free with his weppins, but me and him had always got along together very well.

"Where you-all goin'?" demanded Uncle Jacob.

"I am Professor Van Brock, of New York," said the tenderfoot, whilst Bill was getting rid of his terbaccer wad. "I have employed Mr. Glanton, here, to guide me up into the mountains. I am on the track of a tribe of aborigines, which according to fairly well substantiated rumour, have inhabited the haunted Mountains since time immemorial."

"Lissen here, you four-eyed runt," said Uncle Jacob in wrath, "air you givin' me the hoss-laugh?"

"I assure you that equine levity is the furthest thing from my thoughts," says Van Brock. "Whilst touring the country in the interests of science, I heard the rumours to which I have referred. In a village possessing the singular appellation of Chawed Ear, I met an aged prospector who told me that he had seen one of the aborigines, clad in the skin of a wild animal and armed with a bludgeon. The wild man, he said, emitted a most peculiar and piercing cry when sighted, and fled into the recesses of the hills. I am confident that it is some survivor of a pre-Indian race, and I am determined to investigate."

"They ain't no sech critter in these hills," snorted Uncle Jacob. "I've roamed all over 'em for fifty year, and I ain't seen no wild man."

"Well," says Glanton, "they's *somethin'* onnatural up there, because I been hearin' some funny yarns myself. I never thought I'd be huntin' wild men," he says, "but since that hash-slinger in Perdition turned me down to elope with a travellin' salesman, I welcomes the chance to lose myself in the mountains and forgit the perfidy of women-kind. What you-all doin' up here? Prospectin'?" he said, glancing at the tools on the mule.

"Not in earnest," said Uncle Jacob hurriedly. "We're jest whilin' away our time. They ain't no gold in these mountains."

"Folks say the Lost Haunted Mine is up here somewheres," said Glanton.

"A pack of lies," snorted Uncle Jacob, busting into a sweat. "Ain't no sech mine. Well, Breckinridge, le's be shovin'. Got to make Antelope Peak before sundown."

"I thought we was goin' to Wildcat Canyon," I says, and he give me a awful glare, and said: "Yes, Breckinridge, that's right, Antelope Peak, jest like you said. So long, gents."

"So long," says Glanton.

So we turned off the trail almost at right angles to our course, me follering Uncle Jacob bewilderedly. When we was out of sight of the others, he reined around again.

"When Nature give you the body of a giant, Breckinridge," he said, "she plumb forgot to give you any brains to go along with yore muscles. You want everybody to know what we're lookin' for, and whar?"

"Aw," I said, "them fellers is jest lookin' for wild men."

"Wild men!" he snorted. "They don't have to go no further'n Chawed Ear on payday night to find more wild men than they could handle. I ain't swallerin' no sech tripe. Gold is what they're after, I tell you. I seen Glanton talkin' to that Mex in Perdition the day I bought that map from him. I believe they either got wind of that mine, or know I got that map, or both."

"What you goin' to do?" I ast him.

"Head for Wildcat Canyon by another trail," he said.

So we done so and arriv there after night, him not willing to stop till we got there. It was deep, with big high cliffs cut with ravines and gulches here and there, and very wild in appearance. We didn't descend into the canyon that night, but camped on a plateau above it. Uncle Jacob 'lowed we'd begin exploring next morning. He said they was lots of caves in the canyon, and he'd been in all of 'em. He said he hadn't never found nothing except b'ars and painters and rattlesnakes, but he believed one of them caves went on through into another hidden canyon, and that was where the gold was at.

Next morning I was awoke by Uncle Jacob shaking me, and his whiskers was curling with rage.

"What's the matter?" I demanded, setting up and pulling my guns.

"They're here!" he squalled. "Dawgone it, I suspected 'em all the time! Git up, you big lunk! Don't set there gawpin' with a gun in each hand like a idjit! They're here, I tell you!"

"Who's here?" I ast.

"That dern tenderfoot and his cussed Texas gunfighter," snarled Uncle Jacob. "I was up jest at daylight, and purty soon I seen a wisp of smoke curlin' up from behind a big rock t'other side of the flat. I snuck over there, and there was Glanton fryin' bacon, and Van Brock was pertendin' to be lookin' at some flowers with a magnifyin' glass—the blame fake. He ain't no perfessor. I bet he's a derned crook They're follerin' us. They aim to murder us and take my map."

"Aw, Glanton wouldn't do that," I said, and Uncle Jacob said: "You shet up! A man will do anything whar gold's consarned. Dang it all, git up and do somethin'! Air you goin' to set there, you big lummox, and let us git murdered in our sleep?"

That's the trouble of being the biggest man in yore clan; the rest of the family always dumps all the onpleasant jobs onto yore shoulders. I pulled on my boots and headed across the flat with Uncle Jacob's war-songs ringing in my ears, and I didn't notice whether he was bringing up the rear with his Winchester or not.

They was a scattering of trees on the flat, and about halfway acrost a figger emerged from amongst it and headed my direction with fire in his eyes. It was Glanton.

"So, you big mountain grizzly," he greeted me rambunctiously, "you was goin' to Antelope Peak, hey? Kinda got off the road, didn't you? Oh, we're on to you, we air!"

"What you mean?" I demanded. He was acting like he was the one which oughta feel righteously indignant instead of me.

"You know what I mean!" he says, frothing slightly at the mouth. "I didn't believe it when Van Brock first said he suspicioned you, even though you *hombres* did act funny yesterday when he met you on the trail. But this mornin' when I glimpsed yore fool Uncle Jacob spyin' on our camp, and then seen him sneakin' off through the bresh, I knowed Van Brock was right. Yo're after what we're after, and you-all resorts to dirty, onderhanded tactics. Does you deny yo're after the same thing we air?"

"Naw, I don't," I said. "Uncle Jacob's got more right to it than you-all has. And when you says we uses onderhanded tricks, yo're a liar."

"That settles it!" gnashed he. "Go for yore gun!"

"I don't want to perforate you," I growled.

"I ain't hankerin' to conclude yore mortal career," he admitted. "But Haunted Mountain ain't big enough for both of us. Take off yore guns, and I'll maul the livin' daylights out you, big as you be."

I unbuckled my gun-belt, and hung it on a limb, and he laid off his'n, and hit me in the stummick and on the ear and in the nose, and then he busted me in the jaw and knocked out a tooth. This made me mad, so I taken him by the neck and throwed him agen the ground so hard it jolted all the wind outa him. I then sot on him and started banging his head agen a convenient boulder, and his cussing was terrible to hear.

"If you-all had acted like white men," I gritted, "we'd of *give* you a share in that there mine."

"What the hell air you talkin' about?" he gurgled, trying to haul his bowie out of his boot which I had my knee on.

"The Lost Haunted Mine, what you think?" I snarled, getting a fresh grip on his ears.

"Hold on!" he protested. "You mean you-all air jest lookin' for gold? Is that on the level?"

I was so astonished I quit hammering his skull agen the rock.

"Why, what else?" I demanded. "Ain't you-all follerin' us to steal Uncle Jacob's map which shows where at the mine is hid?"

"Git offa me!" he snorted disgustfully, taking advantage of my surprise to push me off. "Hell!" says he, starting to knock the dust offa his britches. "I might of knowed that tenderfoot was woolgatherin'. After we seen you-all yesterday, and he heard you mention Wildcat Canyon, he told me he believed you was follerin' us. He said that yarn about prospectin' was jest a blind. He said he believed you was workin' for a rival scientific society to git ahead of us and capture that there wild man yoreselves."

"What?" I said. "You mean that wild man yarn is straight goods?"

"Far as we're consarned," said Bill. "Prospectors is been tellin' some onusual stories about Wildcat Canyon. Well, I laughed at him at first, but he kept on usin' so many .45 calibre words that he got me to believin' it might be so. 'Cause, after all, here was me guidin' a tenderfoot on the trail of a wild man, and they warn't no reason to think that you and Jacob Grimes was any more sensible than me.

"Then, this mornin' when I seen Jacob peekin' at me from the bresh, I decided Van Brock must be right. You-all hadn't never went to Antelope Peak. The more I thought it over, the more sartain I was that you was follerin' us to steal our wild man, so I started over to have a show-down."

"Well," I said, "we're reched a understandin'. You don't want our mine, and we sure don't want yore wild man. They's plenty of them amongst my relatives on Bear Creek. Le's git Van Brock and lug him over to our camp and explain things to him and my weak-minded uncle."

"All right," said Glanton, buckling on his guns. "Hey, what's that?"

From down in the canyon come a yell: "Help! Aid! Assistance!"

"It's Van Brock!" yelped Glanton. "He's wandered down into the canyon by hisself! Come on!"

Right nigh their camp they was a ravine leading down to the floor of the canyon. We pelted down that at full speed and emerged nigh the wall of the cliffs. They was the black mouth of a cave showing nearby, in a kind of cleft, and jest outside this cleft Van Brock was staggering around, yowling like a hound-dawg with his tail caught in the door.

His cork helmet was laying on the ground all bashed outa shape, and his specs was lying nigh it. He had a knot on his head as big as a turnip and he was doing a kind of ghost-dance or something all over the place.

He couldn't see very good without his specs, 'cause when he sighted us he give a shriek and started legging it up the canyon, seeming to think we was more enemies. Not wanting to indulge in no sprinting in that heat, Bill shot a heel offa his boot, and that brung him down squalling blue murder.

"Help!" he shrieked. "Mr. Glanton! Help! I am being attacked! Help!"

"Aw, shet up," snorted Bill. "I'm Glanton. Yo're all right. Give him his specs, Breck. Now, what's the matter?"

He put 'em on, gasping for breath, and staggered up, wild-eyed, and p'inted at the cave, and hollered: "The wild man! I saw him, as I descended into the canyon on a private exploring expedition! A giant with a panther's skin about his waist, and a club in his hand. When I sought to apprehend him he dealt me a murderous blow with the bludgeon and fled into that cavern. He should be arrested!"

I looked into the cave. It was too dark to see anything except for a hoot-owl.

"He must of saw *somethin'*, Breck," said Glanton, hitching his gun-harness. "Somethin' shore cracked him on the conk. I've been hearin' some queer tales about this canyon, myself. Maybe I better sling some lead in there——"

"No, no, no!" broke in Van Brock. "We must capture him alive!"

"What's goin' on here?" said a voice, and we turned to see Uncle Jacob approaching with his Winchester in his hands.

"Everything's all right, Uncle Jacob," I said. "They don't want yore mine. They're after the wild man, like they said, and we got him cornered in that there cave."

"All right, huh?" he snorted. "I reckon you thinks it's all right for you to waste yore time with sech dern foolishness when you oughta be helpin' me look for my mine. A big help you be!"

"Where was you whilst I was argyin' with Bill here?" I demanded.

"I knowed you could handle the situation, so I started explorin' the canyon," he said. "Come on, we got work to do."

"But the wild man!" cried Van Brock. "Your nephew would be invaluable in securing the specimen. Think of science! Think of progress! Think of——"

"Think of a striped skunk!" snorted Uncle Jacob. "Breckinridge, air you comin'?"

"Aw, shet up," I said disgustedly. "You both make me tired. I'm goin' in there and run that wild man out, and Bill, you shoot him in the hind-laig as he comes out, so's we can catch him and tie him up."

"But you left yore guns hangin' onto that limb up on the plateau," objected Glanton.

"I don't need 'em," I said. "Didn't you hear Van Brock say we was to catch him alive? If I started shootin' in the dark I might rooin him."

"All right," says Bill, cocking his six-shooters. "Go ahead. I figger yo're a match for any wild man that ever come down the pike."

So I went into the cleft and entered the cave and it was dark as all get-out. I groped my way along and discovered the main tunnel split in two, so I taken the biggest one. It seemed to get dark the further I went, and purty soon I bumped into something big and hairy and it went "Wump!" and grabbed me.

Thinks I, it's the wild man, and he's on the war path. So I waded into him and he waded into me, and we tumbled around on the rocky floor in the dark, biting and mauling and tearing. Bear Creek is famed far and wide for its ring-tailed scrappers, and I don't have to repeat I'm the fightin'est of 'em all, but that cussed wild man sure give me my hands full. He was the biggest, hairiest critter I ever laid hands on, and he had more teeth and talons than I thought a human could possibly have. He chawed me with vigour and enthusiasm, and he walzed up and down my frame free and hearty, and swept the floor with me till I was groggy.

For a while I thought I was going to give up the ghost, and I thought with despair of how humiliated my relatives on Bear Creek would be to hear their champeen battler had been clawed to death by a wild man in a cave.

This thought maddened me so I redoubled my onslaughts, and the socks I give him ought to of laid out any man, wild or tame, to say nothing of the pile-driver kicks in his belly, and butting him with my head so he gasped. I got what felt like a ear in my mouth and commenced chawing on it, and presently, what with this and other mayhem I committed on him, he give a most inhuman squall and bust away and went lickety-split for the outside world.

I riz up and staggered after him, hearing a wild chorus of yells break forth, but no shots. I bust out into the open, bloody all over, and my clothes hanging in tatters.

"Where is he?" I hollered. "Did you let him git away?"

"Who?" said Glanton, coming out from behind a boulder, whilst

Van Brock and Uncle Jacob dropped down out of a tree nearby.

"The wild man, damn it!" I roared.

"We ain't seen no wild man," said Glanton.

"Well, what was that thing I jest run outa the cave?" I hollered.

"That was a grizzly b'ar," said Glanton.

"Yeah," sneered Uncle Jacob, "and that was Van Brock's 'wild man'! And now, Breckinridge, if yo're through playin', we'll—"

"No, no!" hollered Van Brock, jumping up and down. "It was indubitably a human being which smote me and fled into the cavern. Not a bear! It is still in there somewhere, unless there is another exit to the cavern."

"Well, he ain't in there now," said Uncle Jacob, peering into the mouth of the cave. "Not even a wild man would run into a grizzly's cave, or if he did, he wouldn't stay long—ooomp!"

A rock come whizzing out of the cave and hit Uncle Jacob in the belly, and he doubled up on the ground.

"Aha!" I roared, knocking up Glanton's ready six-shooter. "I know! They's two tunnels in there. He's in that smaller cave. I went into the wrong one! Stay here, you-all, and gimme room! This time I gits him!"

With that I rushed into the cave mouth again, disregarding some more rocks which emerged, and plunged into the smaller opening. It was dark as pitch, but I seemed to be running along a narrer tunnel, and ahead of me I heard bare feet pattering on the rock. I follered 'em at full lope, and presently seen a faint hint of light. The next minute I rounded a turn and come out into a wide place, which was lit by a shaft of light coming in through a cleft in the wall, some yards up. In the light I seen a fantastic figger climbing up on a ledge, trying to rech that cleft.

"Come down offa that!" I thundered, and give a leap and grabbed the ledge by one hand and hung on, and reched for his laigs with t'other hand. He give a squall as I grabbed his ankle and splintered his club over my head. The force of the lick broke off the lip of the rock ledge I was holding on to, and we crashed to the floor together, because I didn't let loose of him. Fortunately, I hit the rock floor headfirst which broke my fall and kept me from fracturing any of my important limbs, and his head hit my jaw, which rendered him unconscious.

I riz up and picked up my limp captive and carried him out into the daylight where the others was waiting. I dumped him on the ground and they stared at him like they couldn't believe it. He was a ga'nt old cuss with whiskers about a foot long and matted hair, and he had a mountain lion's hide tied around his waist.

"A white man!" enthused Van Brock, dancing up and down. "An unmistakable Caucasian! This is stupendous! A pre-historic survivor of a pre-Indian epoch! What an aid to anthropology! A wild man! A veritable wild man!"

"Wild man, hell!" snorted Uncle Jacob. "That there's old Joshua Braxton, which was trying to marry that old maid school-teacher down at Chawed Ear all last winter."

"*I* was tryin' to marry her!" said Joshua bitterly, setting up suddenly and glaring at all of us. "That there is good, that there is! And me all the time fightin' for my life agen it. Her and all her relations was tryin' to marry *her* to me. They made my life a curse. They was finally all set to kidnap me and marry me by force. That's why I come away off up here, and put on this rig to scare folks away. All I crave is peace and quiet and no dern women."

Van Brock begun to cry because they warn't no wild man, and Uncle Jacob said: "Well, now that this dern foolishness is settled, maybe I can git to somethin' important. Joshua, you know these mountains even better'n I do. I want ya to help me find the Lost Haunted Mine."

"There ain't no sech mine," said Joshua. "That old prospector imagined all that stuff whilst he was wanderin' around over the desert crazy."

"But I got a map I bought from a Mexican in Perdition!" hollered Uncle Jacob.

"Lemme see that map," said Glanton. "Why, hell," he said, "that there is a fake. I seen that Mexican drawin' it, and he said he was goin' to try to sell it to some old jassack for the price of a drunk."

Uncle Jacob sot down on a rock and pulled his whiskers. "My dreams is bust. I'm goin' to go home to my wife," he said weakly.

"You must be desperate if it's come to that," said old Joshua acidly. "You better stay up here. If they ain't no gold, they ain't no women to torment a body, neither."

"Women is a snare and a delusion," agreed Glanton. "Van Brock can go back with these fellers. I'm stayin' with Joshua."

"You all oughta be ashamed talkin' about women that way," I reproached 'em. "I've suffered from the fickleness of certain women more'n either of you snake-hunters, but I ain't let it sour me on the sex. What," I says, waxing oratorical, "in this lousy and troubled world of six-shooters and centipedes, what, I asts you all, can compare to women's gentle sweetness——"

"There the scoundrel is!" screeched a familiar voice like a rusty buzzsaw. "Don't let him git away! Shoot him if he tries to run!"

We turned sudden. We'd been argying so loud amongst ourselves we hadn't noticed a gang of folks coming down the ravine. There was Aunt Lavaca and the sheriff of Chawed Ear with ten men, and they all p'inted sawed-off shotguns at me.

"Don't git rough, Elkins," warned the sheriff nervously. "They're loaded with buckshot and ten-penny nails. I knows yore repertation and I takes no chances. I arrests you for the kidnappin' of Jacob Grimes."

"Air you plumb crazy?" I demanded.

"Kidnappin'!" hollered Aunt Lavaca, waving a piece of paper. "Abductin' yore pore old uncle! Aimin' to hold him for ransom! It's all writ down over yore name right here on this here paper! Sayin' yo're takin' Jacob away off into the mountains—warnin' me not to try to foller! Same as threatenin' me! I never heered of sech doin's! Soon as that good-for-nothin' Joe Hopkins brung me that there imperdent letter, I went right after the sheriff. . . . Joshua Braxton, what *air* you doin' in them ondecent togs? My land, I dunno what we're comin' to! Well, sheriff, what you standin' there for like a ninny? Why'n't you put some handcuffs and chains and shackles onto him? Air you scairt of the big lunkhead?"

"Aw, heck," I said. "This is all a mistake. I warn't threatenin' nobody in that there letter——"

"Then where's Jacob?" she demanded. "Perjuice him imejitly, or——"

"He ducked into the cave," said Glanton.

I stuck my head in and roared: "Uncle Jacob! You come outa there and explain before I come in after you!"

He snuck out looking meek and down-trodden, and I says: "You tell these idjits that I ain't no kidnapper."

"That's right," he said. "I brung him along with me."

"Hell!" said the sheriff disgustedly. "Have we come all this way on a wild goose chase? I should of knew better'n to lissen to a woman——"

"You shet yore fool mouth!" squalled Aunt Lavaca. "A fine sheriff you be. Anyway—what was Breckinridge doin' up here with you, Jacob?"

"He was helpin' me look for a mine, Lavacky," he said.

"*Helpin'* you?" she screeched. "Why, I sont him to fetch you back! Breckinridge Elkins, I'll tell yore pap about this, you big, lazy, good-for-nothin', low-down, ornery——"

"AW, SHET UP!" I roared, exasperated beyond endurance. I seldom lets my voice go its full blast. Echoes rolled through the canyon like thunder, the trees shook and pine cones fell like hail, and rocks tumbled down the mountain sides. Aunt Lavaca staggered backwards with a outraged squall.

"Jacob!" she hollered. "Air you goin' to 'low that ruffian to use that there tone of voice to me? I demands that you frail the livin' daylights outa the scoundrel right now!"

"Now, now, Lavacky," he started soothing her, and she give him a clip under the ear that changed ends with him, and the sheriff and his posse and Van Brock took out up the ravine like the devil was after 'em.

Glanton bit hisself off a chaw of terbaccer and says to me, he says: "Well, what was you fixin' to say about women's gentle sweetness?"

"Nothin'," I snarled. "Come on, let's git goin'. I yearns to find a more quiet and secluded spot than this here'n. I'm stayin' with Joshua and you and the grizzly."

CHAPTER XI

Educate or Bust

Me and Bill Glanton and Joshua Braxton stood on the canyon rim and listened to the orations of Aunt Lavaca Grimes fading in the distance as she herded Uncle Jacob for the home range.

"There," says Joshua sourly, "goes the most henpecked pore critter in the Humbolts. For sech I has only pity and contempt. He's that scairt of a woman he don't dast call his soul his own."

"And what air we, I'd like to know?" says Glanton, slamming his hat down on the ground. "What right has we to criticize Jacob, when it's on account of women that we're hidin' in these cussed mountains? Yo're here, Joshua, because yo're scairt of that old maid school-teacher. Breck's here because a gal in War Paint give him the gate. And I'm here sourin' my life because a hash-slinger done me wrong!"

"I'm tellin' you gents," says Bill, "no woman is goin' to rooin my life! Lookin' at Jacob Grimes has teached me a lesson. I ain't goin' to eat my heart out up here in the mountains in the company of a soured old hermit and a love-lorn human grizzly. I'm goin' to War Paint, and bust the bank at the Yaller Dawg's Tail gamblin' hall, and then I'm goin' to head for San Francisco and a high-heeled old time! The bright lights calls me, gents, and I heeds the summons! You-all better take heart and return to yore respective corrals."

"Not me," I says. "If I go back to Bear Creek without no gal, Glory McGraw will rawhide the life outa me."

"As for me returnin' to Chawed Ear," snarls old Joshua, "whilst that old she-mudhen is anywhere in the vicinity, I haunts the wilds and solitudes, if it takes all the rest of my life. You 'tend to yore own business, Bill Glanton."

"Oh, I forgot to tell you," says Bill. "So dern many things is been happenin' I ain't had time to tell you. But that old maid school-teacher ain't to Chawed Ear no more. She pulled out for Arizona three weeks ago."

"That's news!" says Joshua, straightening up and throwing away his busted club. "Now I can return and take my place among men—Hold on!" says he, reching for his club again. "Likely they'll be gittin' some other old harridan to take her place! That new-fangled schoolhouse they got at Chawed Ear is a curse and a blight. We'll never be rid of female school-shooters. I better stay up here, after all."

"Don't worry," says Bill. "I seen a pitcher of the gal that's comin' to take Miss Stark's place, and I can assure you right now, that a gal as young and purty as her wouldn't never try to sot her brand on no old buzzard like you."

I come alive suddenly.

"Young and purty, you says?" I says.

"As a pitcher," he says. "First time I ever knowed a school-teacher could be less'n forty and have a face that didn't look like the beginnin's of a long drouth. She's due into Chawed Ear to-morrer, on the stage from the East, and the whole town's goin' to turn out to welcome her. The mayor aims to make a speech, if he's sober enough, and they've got together a band to play."

"Damn foolishness!" snorted Joshua. "I don't take no stock in eddication."

"I dunno," I said. "They's times when I wish I could read and write."

"What would you read outside of the labels on whisky bottles?" snorted old Joshua.

"Everybody ought to know how," I said defiantly. "We ain't never had no school on Bear Creek."

"Funny how a purty face changes a man's views," says Bill. "I remember onst Miss Stark ast you how you folks up on Bear Creek would like for her to come up there and teach yore chillern, and you taken one look at her face, and told her that it was agen the principles of Bear Creek to have their peaceful innercence invaded by the corruptin' influences of education, and the folks was all banded together to resist sech corruption."

I ignored him and says: "It's my duty to Bear Creek to pervide culture for the risin' generation. We ain't never had a school, but by golly, we're goin' to, if I have to lick every old moss-back in the Humbolts. I'll build the cabin for the schoolhouse myself."

"And where'll you git a teacher?" ast old Joshua. "This gal that's comin' to teach at Chawed Ear is the only one in the country. Chawed Ear ain't goin' to let you have her."

"Chawed Ear is, too," I says. "If they won't give her up peaceful, I resorts to vi'lence. Bear Creek is goin' to have education and culture, if I have to wade ankle-deep in gore to pervide it. Come on, le's go! I'm r'arin' to start the ball for arts and letters. Air you all with me?"

"Till hell freezes!" acclaimed Bill. "My shattered nerves needs a little excitement, and I can always count on you to pervide sech. How about it, Joshua?"

"Yo're both crazy," growls old Joshua. "But I've lived up here eatin' nuts and wearin' a painter-hide till I ain't shore of my own sanity. Anyway, I know the only way to disagree successfully with Elkins is to kill him, and I got strong doubts of bein' able to do that, even if I wanted to. Lead on! I'll do anything in reason to keep eddication out of Chawed Ear. 'Tain't only my own feelin's in regard to school-teachers. It's the principle of the thing."

"Git yore clothes then," I said, "and le's hustle."

"This painter hide is all I got," he said.

"You cain't go down into the settlements in that garb," I says.

"I can and will," says he. "I look about as civilized as you do, with yore clothes all tore to rags account of that b'ar. I got a hoss down in that canyon. I'll git him."

So Joshua got his hoss, and Glanton got his'n, and I got Cap'n Kidd, and then the trouble started. Cap'n Kidd evidently thought Joshua was some kind of a varmint, because every time Joshua come near him he taken in after him and run him up a tree. And every time Joshua tried to come down, Cap'n Kidd busted loose from me and run him back up again.

I didn't get no help from Bill; all he done was laugh like a spotted hyener, till Cap'n Kidd got irritated at them guffaws and kicked him in the belly and knocked him clean through a clump of spruces. Time I got him ontangled he looked about as disreputable as what I did, because his clothes was tore most off of him. We couldn't find his hat, neither, so I tore up what was left of my shirt and he tied the pieces around his head like a Apache. We was sure a wild-looking bunch.

But I was so disgusted thinking about how much time we was wasting while all the time Bear Creek was wallering in ignorance, so the next time Cap'n Kidd went for Joshua I took and busted him betwixt the ears with my six-shooter, and that had some effect on him.

So we sot out, with Joshua on a ga'nt old nag he rode bareback with a hackamore, and a club he toted not having no gun. I had Bill to ride betwixt him and me, so's to keep that painter hide as far from Cap'n Kidd as possible, but every time the wind shifted and blowed the smell to him, Cap'n Kidd reched over and taken a bite at Joshua, and sometimes he bit Bill's hoss instead, and sometimes he bit Bill, and the langwidge Bill directed at that pore dumb animal was shocking to hear.

But between rounds, as you might say, we progressed down the trail, and early the next morning we come out onto the Chawed-Ear Road, some miles west of Chawed Ear. And there we met our first human—a feller on a pinto mare, and when he seen us he gave a awful squall and took out down the road towards Chawed Ear like the devil had him by the seat of the britches.

"Le's catch him and find out if the teacher's got there yet!" I hollered, and we taken out after him, yelling for him to wait a minute, but he spurred his hoss that much harder, and before we'd gone any piece, hardly, Joshua's fool hoss jostled agen Cap'n Kidd, which smelt that painter skin and got his bit betwixt his teeth and run Joshua and his hoss three miles through the bresh before I could stop him. Glanton follered us, and of course, time we got back to the road, the feller on the pinto mare was out of sight long ago.

So we headed for Chawed Ear, but everybody that lived along the road had run into their cabins and bolted the doors, and they shot at us through their winders as we rode by. Glanton said irritably, after having his off-ear nicked by a buffalo rifle, he says: "Dern it, they must know we aim to steal their school-teacher."

"Aw, they couldn't know that," I said. "I bet they is a war on between Chawed Ear and War Paint."

"Well, what they shootin' at *me* for then?" demanded old Joshua. "I don't hang out at War Paint like you fellers. I'm a Chawed Ear man myself."

"I doubt if they rekernizes you with all them whiskers and that rig you got on," I said. "Anyway—what's that?"

Ahead of us, away down the road, we seen a cloud of dust, and here come a gang of men on hosses, waving their guns and yelling.

"Well, whatever the reason is," says Glanton, "we better not stop to find out! Them gents is out for blood!"

"Pull into the bresh," says I. "I'm goin' to Chawed Ear today in spite of hell, high water, and all the gunmen they can raise!"

So we taken to the bresh, leaving a trail a blind man could of follered, but we couldn't help it, and they lit into the bresh after us, about forty or fifty of 'em, but we dodged and circled and taken short cuts old Joshua knowed about, and when we emerged into the town of Chawed Ear, our pursuers warn't nowhere in sight. They warn't nobody in sight in the town, neither. All the doors was closed and the shutters up on the cabins and saloons and stores and every thing. It was pecooliar.

As we rode into the clearing somebody let bam at us with a shotgun from the nearest cabin, and the load combed old Joshua's whiskers. This made me mad, and I rode at the cabin and pulled my foot out'n the stirrup and kicked the door in, and while I was doing this, the feller inside hollered and jumped out the winder, and Glanton grabbed him by the neck and taken his gun away from him. It was Esau Barlow, one of the Chawed Ear's confirmed citizens.

"What the hell does you Chawed Ear buzzards mean by this here hostility?" roared Bill.

"Is that you, Glanton?" gasped Barlow, blinking his eyes.

"Yes, it's me!" bellered Bill wrathfully. "Do I look like a Injun?"

"Yes—ow! I mean, I didn't know you in that there turban," says Barlow. "Am I dreamin', or is that Joshua Braxton and Breckinridge Elkins?"

"Shore it's us!" snorted Joshua. "Who you think?"

"Well," says Esau, rubbing his neck, "I didn't know!" He stole a glance at Joshua's painter-hide and he batted his eyes again, and kind of shaken his head like he warn't sure of hisself, even then.

"Where is everybody?" Joshua demanded.

"Well," says Esau, "a little while ago Dick Lynch rode into town with his hoss all of a lather, and swore he'd jest out-run the wildest war-party that ever come down from the hills!

"'Boys,' says Dick, 'they ain't neither Injuns nor white men! They're them cussed wild men that New York perfessor was talkin' about! One of 'em's big as a grizzly b'ar, with no shirt on, and he's ridin' a hoss bigger'n a bull moose. One of the others is as ragged and ugly as him, but not so big, and wearin' a Apache head-dress. T'other'n's got nothin' on but a painter's hide, and a club, and his hair and whiskers falls to his shoulders! When they seen me,' says Dick, 'they sot up the awfullest yells I ever heard and come for me like so many wild Injuns. I fogged it for town,' says Dick, 'warnin' everybody along the road to fort theirselves in their cabins.'

"Well," says Esau, "when he says that, sech men as was left in town got their hosses and guns—except me which cain't ride account of a risin' I got in a vital spot—and they taken out up the road to meet the war-party before it got into town."

"Well, of all the cussed fools!" I snorted. "Lissen, whereat's the new school-teacher?"

"She ain't arriv yet," says he. "She's due on the next stage, and the mayor and the band rode out to meet her at the Yaller Creek crossin' and escort her into town in honour. They pulled out before Dick Lynch brung news of the war-party."

"Well, come on!" I says to my warriors. "I aims to meet that stage too!"

So we pulled out and fogged it down the road, and purty soon we heard music blaring ahead of us, and men yipping and shooting off their pistols like they does when they're celebrating, so we jedged the stage had already arriv.

"What you goin' to do now?" ast Glanton, and about that time a noise bust out behind us, and I looked back and seen that gang of Chawed Ear maniacs which had been chasing us dusting down the road after us, waving their Winchesters. I seen it warn't no use to try to stop and argy with 'em. They'd fill us full of lead before we could get clost enough to make 'em hear what we was saying. So I hollered: "Come on! If they git her into town they'll fort theirselves agen us, and we'll never git her! We'll have to take her by force! Foller me!"

So we swept down the road and around the bend, and there was the stage coach coming up the road with the mayor riding alongside with his hat in his hand, and a whisky bottle sticking out of each saddle-bag and his hip pocket. He was orating at the top of his voice to make hisself heard above the racket the band was making. They was blowing horns of every kind, and banging drums, and twanging on Jews harps, and the hosses was skittish and shying and jumping. But we heard the mayor say: "—And so we welcomes you, Miss Devon, to our peaceful little community, where life runs smooth and tranquil, and men's souls is overflowing with milk and honey——" And jest then we stormed around the bend and come tearing down on 'em with the mob right behind us yelling and cussing and shooting free and fervent.

The next minute they was the damndest mix-up you ever seen, what with the hosses bucking their riders off, and men yelling and cussing, and the hosses hitched to the stage running away and knocking the mayor off his hoss. We hit 'em like a cyclone and they shot at us and hit us over the head with their derned music horns, and right in the middle of the fray the mob behind us rounded the bend and piled up amongst us before they could check theirselves, and everybody was so confused they started fighting everybody else. Old Joshua was laying right and left with his club, and Glanton was beating the band over their heads with his six-shooter, and I was trompling everybody in my rush for the stage.

Because the fool hosses had whirled around and started in the general direction of the Atlantic ocean, and neither the driver nor the shotgun guard could stop 'em. But Cap'n Kidd overtook it in maybe a dozen strides, and I left the saddle in a flying leap and landed on it. The guard tried to shoot me with his shotgun so I throwed it into a alder clump and he didn't let go of it quick enough so he went along with it.

I then grabbed the reins out of the driver's hands and swung them fool hosses around, and the stage kind of revolved on one wheel for a dizzy instant and then settled down again and we headed back up the road lickety-split and in an instant was right amongst the melee that was going on around Bill and Joshua.

About that time I realized that the driver was trying to stab me with a butcher knife, so I kind of tossed him off the stage, and there ain't no sense in him going around saying he's going to have me arrested account of him landing headfirst in the bass horn so it take seven men to pull his head out of it. He ought to watch where he falls, when he gets throwed off a stage going at a high run.

I feels, moreover, that the mayor is prone to carry petty grudges, or he wouldn't be belly-aching about me accidentally running over him with all four wheels. And it ain't my fault he was stepped on by Cap'n Kidd, neither. Cap'n Kidd was jest follering the stage, because he knowed I was on it. And it naturally irritates any well-trained hoss to stumble over somebody, and that's why Cap'n Kidd chawed the mayor's ear.

As for them fellers which happened to get knocked down and run over by the stage, I didn't have nothing personal agen 'em. I was jest rescuing Joshua and Bill which I seen was outnumbered about twenty to one. I was doing them idjits a favour, if they only knowed it, because in about another minute Bill would of started using the front ends of his six-shooters instead of the butts, and the fight would of turnt into a massacre. Glanton has got a awful temper.

Him and Joshua had laid out a remarkable number of the enemy, but the battle was going agen 'em when I arriv on the field of carnage. As the stage crashed through the mob I reched down and got Joshua by the neck and pulled him out from under about fifteen men which was beating him to death with their gun butts and pulling out his whiskers, and I slung him up on top of the other luggage. About that time we was rushing past the melee which Bill was the center of, and I reched down and snared him as we went by, but three of the men which had hold of him wouldn't let go, so I hauled all four of 'em up into the stage. I then handled the team with one hand whilst with the other'n I pulled them idjits loose from Bill like pulling ticks off a cow's hide, and throwed 'em at the mob which was chasing us.

Men and hosses piled up in a stack on the road which was further complicated by Cap'n Kidd's actions as he come busting along after the stage, and by the time we sighted Chawed Ear again, our enemies was far behind us down the road.

We busted right through Chawed Ear in a fog of dust, and the women and chillern which had ventured out of their cabins, squalled and run back in again, though they warn't in no danger at all. But Chawed Ear folks is pecooliar that way.

When we was out of sight of Chawed Ear on the road to War Paint I give the lines to Bill and swung down on the side of the stage and stuck my head in.

They was one of the purtiest gals I ever seen in there, all huddled up in a corner as pale as she could be, and looking so scairt I thought she was going to faint, which I'd heard Eastern gals had a habit of doing.

"Oh, spare me!" she begged, clasping her hands in front of her. "Please don't scalp me! I cannot speak your language, but if you can understand English, please have mercy on me——"

"Be at ease, Miss Devon," I reassured her. "I ain't no Injun, nor wild man neither. I'm a white man, and so is my friends here. We wouldn't none of us hurt a flea. We're that refined and tender-hearted you wouldn't believe it——" About that time a wheel hit a stump and the stage jumped into the air and I bit my tongue, and roared in some irritation: "Bill, you——son of a——polecat! Stop them hosses before I comes up there and breaks yore—— neck!"

"Try it and see what you git, you beefheaded lummox!" he retorted, but he pulled the hosses to a stop, and I taken off my hat and opened the stage door. Bill and Joshua clumb down and peered over my shoulder.

"Miss Devon," I says, "I begs yore pardon for this here informal welcome. But you sees before you a man whose heart bleeds for the benighted state of his native community. I'm Breckinridge Elkins from Bear Creek, where hearts is pure and motives is noble, but education is weak.

"You sees before you," I says, "a man which has growed up in ignorance. I cain't neither read nor write my own name. Joshua here, in the painter-skin, he cain't neither, and neither can Bill——"

"That's a lie," says Bill. "I can read and—ooomp!" Because I'd kind of stuck my elbow in his stummick. I didn't want Bill Glanton to spile the effeck of my speech.

"They is some excuse for men like us," I says. "When we was cubs schools was unknown in these mountains, and keepin' a sculpin' knife from betwixt yore skull and yore hair was more important than makin' marks onto a slate.

"But times has changed. I sees the young 'uns of my home range growin' up in the same ignorance as me," I said, "and my heart bleeds for 'em. They is no sech excuse for them as they was for me. The Injuns has went, mostly, and a age of culture is due to be ushered in.

"Miss Devon," I says, "will you please come up to Bear Creek and be our school-teacher?"

"Why," says she, bewilderedly, "I came West expecting to teach school at a place called Chawed Ear, but I haven't signed any contract——"

"How much was them snake-hunters goin' to pay you?" I ast.

"Ninety dollars a month," says she.

"We pays you a hundred on Bear Creek," I says. "Board and lodgin' free."

"But what will the people of Chawed Ear say?" she said.

"Nothin'!" I says heartily. "I done arranged that. They got the interests of Bear Creek so much at heart, that they wouldn't think of interferin' with any arrangements I make. You couldn't drag 'em up to Bear Creek with a team of oxen!"

"It seems all very strange and irregular," says she, "but I sup-pose——"

So I says: "Good! Fine! Great! Then it's all settled. Le's go!"

"Where?" she ast, grabbing hold of the stage as I clumb into the seat.

"To War Paint, first," I says, "where I gits me some new clothes and a good gentle hoss for you to ride—because nothin' on wheels can git over the Bear Creek road—and then we heads for home! Git up, hosses! Culture is on her way to the Humbolts!"

Well, a few days later me and the school-teacher was riding sedately up the trail to Bear Creek, with a pack-mule carrying her plunder, and you never seen nothing so elegant—store-bought clothes and a hat with a feather into it, and slippers and everything. She rode in a side-saddle I bought for her—the first that ever come into the Humbolts. She was sure purty. My heart beat in wild enthusiasm for education ever time I looked at her.

I swung off the main trail so's to pass by the spring in the creek where Glory McGraw filled her pail every morning and evening. It was jest about time for her to be there, and sure enough she was. She straightened when she heard the hosses, and started to say something, and then her eyes got wide as she seen my elegant companion, and her purty red mouth stayed open. I pulled up my hoss and taken off my hat with a perlite sweep I learnt from a gambler in War Paint, and I says: "Miss Devon, lemme interjuice you to Miss Glory McGraw, the datter of one of Bear Creek's leadin' citizens. Miss McGraw, this here is Miss Margaret Devon, from Boston, Massachusetts, which is goin' to teach school here."

"How do you do?" says Miss Margaret, but Glory didn't say nothing. She jest stood there, staring, and the pail fell outa her hand and splashed into the creek.

"Allow me to pick up yore pail," I said, and started to lean down from my saddle to get it, but she started like she was stung, and said, in a voice which sounded kind of strained and onnatural: "Don't tech it! Don't tech nothin' I own! Git away from me!"

"What a beautiful girl!" says Miss Margaret as we rode on. "But how peculiarly she acted!"

But I said nothing, because I was telling myself, well, I reckon I showed Glory McGraw something this time. I reckon she sees now that I warn't lying when I said I'd bring a peach back to Bear Creek with me. But somehow I warn't enjoying my triumph nigh as much as I'd thought I would.

CHAPTER XII

War on Bear Creek

Pap dug the nineteenth buckshot out of my shoulder and said: "Pigs is more disturbin' to the peace of a community than scandal, divorce, and corn-licker put together. And," says pap, pausing to strop his bowie on my sculp where the hair was all burnt off, "when the pig is a razor-back hawg, and is mixed up with a lady school-teacher, a English tenderfoot, and a passle of blood-thirsty relatives, the result is appallin' for a peaceable man to behold. Hold still till Buckner gits yore ear sewed back on."

Pap was right. I warn't to blame for nothing that happened. Breaking Joe Gordon's laig was a mistake, and Erath Elkins is a liar when he says I caved in them five ribs of his'n on purpose. If Uncle Jeppard Grimes had been tending to his own business, he wouldn't have got the seat of his britches filled with bird-shot, and I don't figger it was my fault that cousin Bill Kirby's cabin got burned down. And I don't take no blame for Jim Gordon's ear which Jack Grimes shot off, neither. I figger everybody was more to blame than I was, and I stand ready to wipe up the road with anybody which disagrees with me.

But I'm getting ahead of myself. Lemme go back to the days when culture first reared its head amongst the simple inhabitants of Bear Creek.

Jest like I said, I was determined that education should be committed on the rising generation, and I gathered the folks in a clearing too far away for Miss Devon to be stampeded by the noise of argyment and persuasion, and I sot forth my views. Opinions differed vi'lently like they always does on Bear Creek, but when the dust settled and the smoke drifted away, it was found that a

160

substantial majority of folks agreed to see things my way. Some was awful sot agen it, and said no good would come of book larning, but after I had swept the clearing with six or seven of them, they allowed it might be a good thing after all, and agreed to let Miss Margaret take a whack at uplifting the young 'uns.

Then they ast me how much money I'd promised her, and when I said a hundred a month they sot up a howl that they wasn't that much hard money seen on Bear Creek in a year's time. But I settled that. I said each family would contribute whatever they was able—coonskins, honey, b'ar hides, cornlicker, or what not, and I'd pack the load into War Paint each month and turn it into cash money. I added that I'd be more'n glad to call around each month to make sure nobody failed to contribute.

Then we argyed over where to build the cabin for the school-house, and I wanted to build it between pap's cabin and the corral, but he riz up and said he'd be dadgasted he'd have a school-house anywhere nigh his dwelling-house, with a passle of yelling kids scaring off all the eatable varmints. He said if it was built within a mile of his cabin it would be because they was somebody on Bear Creek which had a quicker trigger finger and a better shooting eye than what he did. So after some argyment in the course of which five of Bear Creek's leading citizens was knocked stiff, we decided to build the school-house over nigh the settlement on Apache Mountain. That was the thickest populated spot on Bear Creek anyway. And Cousin Bill Kirby agreed to board her for his part of contributing to her wages.

Well, it would of suited me better to had the school-house built close to my home-cabin, and have Miss Margaret board with us, but I was purty well satisfied, because this way I could see her any time I wanted to. I done this every day, and she looked purtier every time I seen her. The weeks went by, and everything was going fine. I was calling on Miss Margaret every day, and she was learning me how to read and write, though it was a mighty slow process. But I was progressing a little in my education, and a whole lot—I thought—in my love affair, when peace and· romance hit a snag in the shape of a razorback pig named Daniel Webster.

It begun when that there tenderfoot come riding up the trail from War Paint with Tunk Willoughby. Tunk ain't got no more sense than the law allows, but he sure showed good jedgment that time, because having delivered his charge to his destination, he didn't tarry. He merely handed me a note, and p'inted dumbly at the tenderfoot, whilst holding his hat reverently in his hand meanwhile.

"What you mean by that there gesture?" I ast him rather irritably, and he said: "I doffs my sombrero in respect to the departed. Bringin' a specimen like that onto Bear Creek is jest like heavin' a jackrabbit to a pack of starvin' loboes."

He hove a sigh and shook his head, and put his hat back on. "Rassle a cat in pieces," he said.

"What the hell air you talkin' about?" I demanded.

"That's Latin," he said. "It means rest in peace."

And with that he dusted it down the trail and left me alone with the tenderfoot which all the time was setting his cayuse and looking at me like I was a curiosity or something.

I called for my sister Ouachita to come read that there note for me, because she'd learnt how from Miss Margaret, so she did, and it run as follows:

Dere Breckinridge:
    This will interjuice Mr. J. Pembroke Pemberton a English sportsman which I met in Frisco recent. He was disapinted because he hadnt found no adventures in America and was fixing to go to Aferker to shoot liuns and elerfants but I perswaded him to come with me because I knowed he would find more hell on Bear Creek in a week than he would find in a yere in Aferker or any other place. But the very day we hit War Paint I run into a old ackwaintance from Texas I will not speak no harm of the ded but I wish the son of a buzzard had shot me somewheres besides in my left laig which already had three slugs in it which I never could get cut out. Anyway I am lade up and not able to come on to Bear Creek with J. Pembroke Pemberton. I am dependin' on you to show him some good bear huntin' and other excitement and pertect him from yore relatives I know what a awful responsibility I am puttin on you but I am askin this as yore friend,
                                William Harrison Glanton, Esqy.

I looked J. Pembroke over. He was a medium-sized young feller and looked kinda soft in spots. He had yaller hair and very pink cheeks like a gal; and he had on whip-cord britches and tan riding boots which was the first I ever seen. And he had on a funny kinda coat with pockets and a belt which he called a shooting jacket, and a big hat like a mushroom made outa cork with a red ribbon around it. And he had a packhoss loaded with all kinds of plunder, and five or six different kinds of shotguns and rifles.

"So yo're J. Pembroke," I says, and he says: "Oh, rahther! And you, no doubt, are the person Mr. Glanton described to me as Breckinridge Elkins?"

"Yeah," I said. "Light and come in. We got b'ar meat and honey for supper."

"I say," he says, climbing down. "Pardon me for being a bit personal, old chap, but may I ask if your—ah—magnitude of bodily stature is not a bit unique?"

"I dunno," I says, not having the slightest idea what he was talking about. "I always votes a straight Democratic ticket, myself."

He started to say something else, but jest then pap and my brothers John and Bill and Jim and Buckner and Garfield come to the door to see what the noise was about, and he turned pale and said faintly: "I beg your pardon; giants seem to be the rule in these parts."

"Pap says men ain't what they was when he was in his prime," I said, "but we manage to git by."

Well, J. Pembroke laid into them b'ar steaks with a hearty will, and when I told him we'd go after b'ar next day, he ast me how many days travel it'd take till we got to the ba'r country.

"Heck!" I says. "You don't have to travel to git b'ar in these parts. If you forgit to bolt yore door at night yo're liable to find a grizzly sharin' yore bunk before mornin'. This here'n we're eatin' was catched by my sister Elinor there whilst tryin' to rob the pigpen out behind the cabin last night."

"My word!" he says, looking at her pecooliarly. "And may I ask, Miss Elkins, what calibre of firearm you used?"

"I knocked him in the head with a wagon spoke," she said, and he shook his head to hisself and muttered: "Extraordinary!"

J. Pembroke slept in my bunk and I taken the floor that night; and we was up at daylight and ready to start after the b'ar. Whilst J. Pembroke was fussing over his guns, pap come out and pulled his whiskers and shook his head and said: "That there is a perlite young man, but I'm afeared he ain't as hale as he oughta be. I jest give him a pull at my jug, and he didn't gulp but one good snort and like to choked to death."

"Well," I said, buckling the cinches on Cap'n Kidd, "I've done learnt not to jedge outsiders by the way they takes their licker on Bear Creek. It takes a Bear Creek man to swig Bear Creek corn juice."

"I hopes for the best," sighed pap. "But it's a dismal sight to see a young man which cain't stand up to his licker. Whar you takin' him?"

"Over towards Apache Mountain," I said. "Erath seen a exter big grizzly over there day before yesterday."

"Hmmmmm!" says pap. "By a pecooliar coincidence the school-house is over on the side of Apache Mountain, ain't it, Breckin-ridge?"

"Maybe it is and maybe it ain't," I replied with dignerty, and rode off with J. Pembroke ignoring pap's sourcastic comment which he hollered after me: "Maybe they is a connection betwixt book-larnin' and b'ar-huntin', but who am I to say?"

J. Pembroke was a purty good rider, but he used a funnylooking saddle without no horn nor cantle, and he had the derndest gun I ever seen. It was a double-barrel rifle, and he said it was a elerfant-gun. It was big enough to knock a hill down. He was surprised I didn't tote no rifle and ast me what would I do if we met a b'ar. I told him I was depending on him to shoot it, but I said if it was necessary for me to go into action, my six-shooters was plenty.

"My word!" says he. "You mean to say you can bring down a grizzly with a shot from a pistol?"

"Not always," I said. "Sometimes I have to bust him over the head with the barrel to finish him."

He didn't say nothing for a long time after that.

Well, we rode over on the lower slopes of Apache Mountain, and tied the hosses in a holler and went through the bresh on foot. That was a good place for b'ars, because they come there very frequently looking for Uncle Jeppard Grimes' pigs which runs loose all over the lower slopes of the mountain.

But jest like it always is when yo're looking for something special, we didn't see a cussed b'ar.

The middle of the evening found us around on the side of the mountain where they is a settlement of Kirbys and Grimeses and Gordons. Half a dozen families has their cabins within a mile or so of each other, and I dunno what in hell they want to crowd up together that way for, it would plumb smother me, but pap says they was always pecooliar that way.

We warn't in sight of the settlement, but the school-house warn't far off, and I said to J. Pembroke: "You wait here a spell, and maybe a b'ar will come by. Miss Margaret Devon is teachin' me how to read and write, and it's time for my lesson."

I left J. Pembroke setting on a log hugging his elerfant-gun, and I strode through the bresh and come out at the upper end of the run which the settlement was at the other'n, and school had jest turned out and the chillern was going home, and Miss Margaret was waiting for me in the log school-house.

She was setting at her hand-made desk as I come in, ducking my head aso as not to bump it agen the top of the door and perlitely taking off my Stetson. She looked kinda tired and discouraged, and I said: "Has the young'uns been raisin' any hell to-day, Miss Margaret?"

"Oh, no," she said. "They're very polite—in fact I've noticed that Bear Creek people are always polite when they're not killing each other. I've finally gotten used to the boys wearing their pistols and bowie knives to school. But somehow it seems so futile. This is all so terribly different from everything to which I've always been accustomed. I get discouraged and feel like giving it up."

"You'll git used to it," I consoled her. "It'll be a lot different onst yo're married to some honest reliable young man."

She give me a startled look and said: "Married to someone here on Bear Creek?"

"Shore," I said, involuntarily expanding my chest. "Everybody is jest wonderin' when you'll set the day. But le's git at my readin' lesson. I done learnt the words you writ out for me yesterday."

But she warn't listenin', and she said: "Do you have any idea of why Mr. Joel Grimes and Mr. Esau Gordon quit calling on me? Until a few days ago one or the other was at Mr. Kirby's cabin where I board almost every night."

"Now don't you worry none about them," I soothed her. "Joel'll be about on crutches before the week's out, and Esau can already walk without bein' helped. I always handles my relatives as easy as possible."

"You fought with them?" she exclaimed.

"I jest convinced 'em you didn't want to be bothered with 'em," I reassured her. "I'm easy-goin', but I don't like competition."

"Competition!" Her eyes flared wide open and she looked at me like she hadn't never seen me before. "Do you mean that you—that I—that——"

"Well," I said modestly, "everybody on Bear Creek is jest wonderin' when yo're goin' to set the day for us to git hitched. You see gals don't generally stay single very long in these parts—hey, what's the matter?"

Because she was getting paler and paler like she'd et something which didn't agree with her.

"Nothing," she said faintly. "You—you mean people are expecting me to marry you?"

"Sure," I said.

She muttered something that sounded like "My God!" and licked her lips with her tongue and looked at me like she was about ready to faint. Well, it ain't every gal which has a chance to get hitched to Breckinridge Elkins, so I didn't blame her for being excited.

"You've been very kind to me, Breckinridge," she said feebly. "But I—this is so sudden—so unexpected—I never thought—I never *dreamed*——"

"I don't want to rush you," I said. "Take yore time. Next week will be soon enough. Anyway, I got to build us a cabin, and——"

Bang! went a gun, too loud for a Winchester.

"Elkins!" It was J. Pembroke yelling for me up the slope. "Elkins! Hurry!"

"Who's that?" she exclaimed, jumping to her feet like she was working on a spring.

"Aw," I said in disgust, "it's a fool tenderfoot Bill Glanton wished on me. I reckon a b'ar is got him by the neck. I'll go see."

"I'll go with you!" she said, but from the way J. Pembroke was yelling I figgered I better not waste no time getting to him, so I couldn't wait for her, and she was some piece behind me when I mounted the lap of the slope and met him running out from amongst the trees. He was gibbering with excitement.

"I winged it!" he squawked. "I'm sure I winged the blighter! But it ran in among the underbrush and I dared not follow it, for the beast is most vicious when wounded. A friend of mine once wounded one in South Africa, and——"

"A b'ar?" I ast.

"No, no!" he said. "A wild boar! The most vicious brute I have ever seen! It ran into that brush there!"

"Aw, they ain't no wild boars in the Humbolts," I snorted. "You wait here, I'll go see jest what you did shoot."

I seen some splashes of blood on the grass, so I knowed he'd shot *something*. Well, I hadn't gone more'n a few hundred feet and was jest out of sight of J. Pembroke when I run into Uncle Jeppard Grimes.

Uncle Jeppard was one of the first white men to come into the Humbolts, in case I ain't mentioned that before, and he wears fringed buckskins and moccasins jest like he done fifty years ago. He had a bowie knife in one hand and he waved something in the other'n like a flag of revolt, and he was frothing at the mouth.

"The derned murderer!" he shrieked. "You see this? That's the proper tail of Dan'l Webster, the finest derned razorback boar which ever trod the Humbolts! That danged tenderfoot of yore'n tried to 'sassernate him! Shot his tail off, right spang up to the hilt! I'll show him he cain't muterlate my animals like this! I'll have his heart's blood!"

And he done a war-dance waving that pig-tail and his bowie and cussing in American and Spanish and Apache Injun all at onst.

"You ca'm down, Uncle Jeppard," I said sternly. "He ain't got no sense, and he thought Daniel Webster was a wild boar like they have in Aferker and England and them foreign places. He didn't mean no harm."

"No harm," said Uncle Jeppard fiercely. "And Dan'l Webster with no more tail onto him than a jackrabbit!"

"Well," I said, "here's a five dollar gold piece to pay for the dern hawg's tail, and you let J. Pembroke alone!"

"Gold cain't satisfy honour," he said bitterly, but nevertheless grabbing the coin like a starving Kiowa grabbing a beefsteak. "I'll let this here outrage pass for the time. But I'll be watchin' that maneyack to see that he don't muterlate no more of my prize livestock."

And so saying he went off muttering in his beard.

I went back to where I left J. Pembroke, and there he was talking to Miss Margaret which had jest come up. She had more colour in her face than I'd saw recent.

"Fancy meeting a girl like you here!" J. Pembroke was saying.

"No more surprising than meeting a man like you!" says she with a kind of fluttery laugh.

"Oh, a sportsman wanders into all sorts of out-of-the-way places," says he, and seeing they hadn't noticed me coming up, I says: "Well, J. Pembroke, I didn't find yore wild boar, but I met the owner."

He looked at me kinda blank, and said vaguely: "Wild boar? *What* wild boar?"

"That'un you shot the tail off of with that there fool elerfant gun," I said. "Lissen: next time you see a hawg-critter you remember there ain't no wild boars in the Humbolts. They is critters called haverleeners in South Texas, but they ain't even none of them in Nevada. So next time you see a hawg, jest reflect that it's merely one of Uncle Jeppard Grimes' razorbacks and refrain from shootin' at it."

"Oh, quite!" he agreed absently, and started talking to Miss Margaret again.

So I picked up the elerfant gun which he'd absent-mindedly

laid down, and said: "Well, it's gittin' late. Let's go. We won't go back to pap's cabin to-night, J. Pembroke. We'll stay at Uncle Saul Garfield's cabin on t'other side of the Apache Mountain settlement."

Like I said, them cabins was awful clost together. Uncle Saul's cabin was below the settlement, but it warnt much over three hundred yards from cousin Bill Kirby's cabin where Miss Margaret boarded. The other cabins was on t'other side of Bill's, mostly, strung out up the run and up and down the slopes.

I told J. Pembroke and Miss Margaret to walk on down to the settlement whilst I went back and got the hosses.

They'd got to the settlement time I catched up with 'em, and Miss Margaret had gone into the Kirby cabin, and I seen a light spring up in her room. She had one of them newfangled ile lamps she brung with her, the only one on Bear Creek. Taller candles and pine chunks was good enough for us folks. And she'd hanged rag things over the winders which she called curtains. You never seen nothing like it. I tell you she was that elegant you wouldn't believe it.

We walked on towards Uncle Saul's, me leading the hosses, and after a while J. Pembroke says: "A wonderful creature!"

"You mean Dan'l Webster?" I ast.

"No!" he said. "No, no! I mean Miss Devon."

"She sure is," I said. "She'll make me a fine wife."

He whirled like I'd stabbed him and his face looked pale in the dusk.

"You?" he said. "*You* a fine wife?"

"Well," I said bashfully, "she ain't sot the day yet, but I've sure sot my heart on that gal."

"Oh!" he says. "*Oh!*" says he, like he had the toothache. Then he said kinda hesitatingly: "Suppose—er, just suppose, you know! Suppose a rival for her affections should appear? What would you do?"

"You mean if some dirty, low-down son of a mangy skunk was to try to steal my gal?" I said, whirling so sudden he staggered backwards.

"*Steal my gal?*" I roared, seeing red at the mere thought. "Why, I'd—I'd——"

Words failing me I grabbed a big sapling and tore it up by the roots and broke it acrost my knee and throwed the pieces clean through a rail fence on the other side of the road.

"That there is a faint idee!" I said, panting with passion.

"That gives me a very vivid conception," he said faintly, and

he said nothing more till we reched the cabin and seen Uncle Saul
Garfield standing in the light of the door combing his black beard
with his fingers.

Next morning J. Pembroke seemed like he'd kinda lost interest
in b'ars. He said all that walking he done over the slopes of Apache
Mountain had made his laig muscles sore. I never heard of sech
a thing, but nothing that gets the matter with these tenderfeet
surprises me much, they is sech a effemernate race, so I ast him
would he like to go fishing down the run and he said all right.

But we hadn't been fishing more'n a hour when he said he
believed he'd go back to Uncle Saul's cabin and take him a nap,
and he insisted on going alone, so I stayed where I was and catched
me a nice string of trout.

I went back to the cabin about noon, and ast Uncle Saul if J.
Pembroke had got his nap out.

"Why, heck," said Uncle Saul, "I ain't seen him since you and
him started down the run this mornin'. Wait a minute—yonder
he comes from the other direction."

Well, J. Pembroke didn't say where he'd been all morning,
and I didn't ast him, because a tenderfoot don't generally have no
reason for anything he does.

We et the trout I catched, and after dinner he perked up a right
smart and got his shotgun and said he'd like to hunt some wild
turkeys. I never heard of anybody hunting anything as big as a
turkey with a shotgun, but I didn't say nothing, because tenderfeet
is like that.

So we headed up the slopes of Apache Mountain, and I stopped
by the school-house to tell Miss Margaret I probably wouldn't get
back in time to take my reading and writing lesson, and she said:
"You know, until I met your friend, Mr. Pembroke, I didn't realize
what a difference there was between men like him, and—well,
like the men on Bear Creek."

"I know," I said. "But don't hold it agen him. He means well.
He jest ain't got no sense. Everybody cain't be smart like me. As
a special favour to me, Miss Margaret, I'd like for you to be exter
nice to the poor sap, because he's a friend of my friend Bill Glanton
down to War Paint."

"I will, Breckinridge," she replied heartily, and I thanked her
and went away with my big manly heart pounding in my gigantic
bosom.

Me and J. Pembroke headed into the heavy timber, and we
hadn't went far till I was convinced that somebody was follering
us. I kept hearing twigs snapping, and onst I thought I seen a

shadowy figger duck behind a bush. But when I run back there, it was gone, and no track to show in the pine needles. That sort of thing would of made me nervous, anywheres else, because they is a goodly number of people which would like to get a clean shot at my back from the bresh, but I knowed none of them dast come after me in my own territory. If anybody was trailing us it was bound to be one of my relatives and to save my neck I couldn't think of no reason why any one of 'em would be gunning for me.

But I got tired of it, and left J. Pembroke in a small glade whilst I snuck back to do some shaddering of my own. I aimed to cast a big circle around the clearing and see could I find out who it was, but I'd hardly got out of sight of J. Pembroke when I heard a gun bang.

I turned to run back and here come J. Pembroke yelling: "I got him! I got him! I winged the bally aborigine!"

He had his head down as he busted through the bresh and he run into me in his excitement and hit me in the belly with his head so hard he bounced back like a rubber ball and landed in a bush with his riding boots brandishing wildly in the air.

"Assist me, Breckinridge!" he shrieked. "Extricate me! They will be hot on our trail!"

"Who?" I demanded, hauling him out by the hind laig and setting him on his feet.

"The Indians!" he hollered, jumping up and down and waving his smoking shotgun frantically. "The bally redskins! I shot one of them! I saw it sneaking through the bushes! I saw his legs! I knew it was an Indian instantly because he had on moccasins instead of boots! Listen! That's him now!"

"A Injun couldn't cuss like that," I said. "You've shot Uncle Jeppard Grimes!"

Telling him to stay there, I run through the bresh guided by the maddened howls which riz horribly on the air, and busting through some bushes I seen Uncle Jeppard rolling on the ground with both hands clasped to the rear bosom of his buckskin britches which was smoking freely. His langwidge was awful to hear.

"Air you in misery, Uncle Jeppard?" I inquired solicitously. This evoked another ear-splitting squall.

"I'm writhin' in my death-throes," he says in horrible accents, "and you stands there and mocks my mortal agony! My own blood-kin!" he says "——!" says Uncle Jeppard with passion.

"Aw," I said, "that there bird-shot wouldn't hurt a flea. It cain't be very deep under yore thick old hide. Lie on yore belly, Uncle

Jeppard," I says, stropping my bowie on my boot, "and I'll dig out them shot for you."

"Don't tech me!" he said fiercely, painfully climbing onto his feet. "Where's my rifle-gun? Gimme it! Now then, I demands that you bring that Bristish murderer here where I can git a clean lam at him! The Grimes honour is besmirched and my new britches is rooint. Nothin' but blood can wipe out the stain on the family honour!"

"Well," I said, "you didn't have no business sneakin' around after us thataway——"

Here Uncle Jeppard give tongue to loud and painful shrieks.

"Why shouldn't I?" he howled. "Ain't a man got no right to perteck his own property? I war follerin' him to see that he didn't shoot no more tails offa my hawgs. And now he shoots me in the same place! He's a fiend in human form—a monster which stalks ravelin' through these hills bustin' for the blood of the innercent!"

"Aw, J. Pembroke thought you was a Injun," I said.

"He thought Dan'l Webster was a wild wart-hawg," gibbered Uncle Jeppard. "He thought I was Geronimo. I reckon he'll massacre the entire population of Bear Creek under a misapprehension, and you'll uphold and defend him! When the cabins of yore kinfolks is smoulderin' ashes, smothered in the blood of yore own relations, I hope you'll be satisfied—bringin' a foreign assassin into a peaceful community!"

Here Uncle Jeppard's emotions choked him, and he chawed his whiskers and then yanked out the five-dollar gold piece I give him for Daniel Webster's tail, and throwed it at me.

"Take back yore filthy lucre," he said bitterly. "The day of retribution is nigh onto hand, Breckinridge Elkins, and the Lord of battles shall jedge betwixt them which turns agen their kinsfolks in their extremerties!"

"In their which?" I ast, but he merely snarled and went limping off through the trees, calling back over his shoulder: "They is still men on Bear Creek which will see jestice did for the aged and helpless. I'll git that English murderer if it's the last thing I do, and you'll be sorry you stood up for him, you big lunkhead!"

I went back to where J. Pembroke was waiting bewilderedly, and evidently still expecting a tribe of Injuns to bust out of the bresh and sculp him, and I said in disgust: "Let's go home. Tomorrer I'll take you so far away from Bear Creek you can shoot in any direction without hittin' a prize razorback or a antiquated gunman with a ingrown disposition. When Uncle Jeppard Grimes gits mad enough to throw away money, it's time to ile the Winchesters and strap yore scabbard-ends to yore laigs."

"Legs?" he said mistily. "But what about the Indians?"

"They warn't no Injun, gol-dern it!" I howled. "They ain't been none on Bear Creek for four or five year. They—aw, hell! What the hell! Come on. It's gittin' late. Next time you see somethin' you don't understand, ast me before you shoot it. And remember, the more ferocious and woolly it looks, the more likely it is to be a leadin' citizen of Bear Creek."

It was dark when we approached Uncle Saul's cabin, and J. Pembroke glanced back up the road, towards the settlement, and said: "My word, is it a political rally? Look! A torchlight parade!"

I looked, and said: "Quick! Git into the cabin and stay there!"

He turned pale, but said: "If there is danger, I insist on——"

"Insist all you dern please," I said, "but git in that house and stay there. I'll handle this. Uncle Saul, see he gits in there."

Uncle Saul is a man of few words. He taken a firm grip onto his pipe stem and he grabbed J. Pembroke by the neck and the seat of the britches and throwed him bodily into the cabin, and shet the door and sot down on the stoop.

"They ain't no use in you gittin' mixed up in this, Uncle Saul," I said.

"You got yore faults, Breckinridge," he grunted. "You ain't got much sense, but yo're my favourite sister's son—and I ain't forgot that lame mule Jeppard traded me for a sound animal back in '69. Let 'em come!"

They come all right, and surged up in front of the cabin— Jeppard's boys Jack and Buck and Esau and Joash and Polk County. And Erath Elkins, and a mob of Gordons and Buckners and Polks, all more or less kin to me, except Joel Braxton who wasn't kin to none of us, but didn't like me because he was sweet on Miss Margaret. But Uncle Jeppard warn't with 'em. Some had torches and Polk County Grimes had a rope with a noose in it.

"Where at air you-all goin' with that there lariat?" I ast them sternly, planting my enormous bulk in their path.

"Perjuice the scoundrel!" commanded Polk County, waving his rope around his head. "Bring out the foreign invader which shoots hawgs and defenceless old men from the bresh!"

"What you aim to do?" I inquired.

"We aim to hang him!" they replied with hearty enthusiasm.

Uncle Saul knocked the ashes out of his pipe and stood up and stretched his arms which looked like knotted oak limbs, and he grinned in his black beard like a old timber wolf, and he says:

"Whar is dear cousin Jeppard to speak for hisself?"

"Uncle Jeppard was havin' the shot picked outa his hide when we left," says Jim Gordon. "He'll be along directly. Breckinridge, we don't want no trouble with you, but we aims to have that Englishman."

"Well," I snorted, "you-all cain't. Bill Glanton is trustin' me to return him whole of body and limb, and——"

"What you want to waste time in argyment for, Breckinridge?" Uncle Saul reproved mildly. "Don't you know it's a plumb waste of time to try to reason with the off-spring of a lame-mule trader?"

"What would you sejest, old man?" sneeringly remarked Polk County.

Uncle Saul beamed on him benevolently, and said gently: "I'd try moral suasion—like this!" And he hit Polk County under the jaw and knocked him clean acrost the yard into a rain barrel amongst the rooins of which he reposed till he was rescued and revived some hours later.

But they was no stopping Uncle Saul onst he took the warpath. No sooner had he disposed of Polk County than he jumped seven foot in the air, cracked his heels together three times, give the rebel yell and come down with his arms around the necks of Esau Grimes and Joel Braxton, and started mopping up the cabin yard with 'em.

That started the fight, and they is no scrap in the world where mayhem is committed as free and fervent as in one of these here family rukuses.

Polk County had hardly crashed into the rain-barrel when Jack Grimes stuck a pistol in my face. I slapped it aside jest as he fired and the bullet missed me and taken a ear offa Jim Gordon. I was scairt Jack would hurt somebody if he kept on shooting reckless that way, so I kinda rapped him with my left fist and how was I to know it would dislocate his jaw? But Jim Gordon seemed to think I was to blame about his ear, because he give a maddened howl and jerked up his shotgun and let bam with both barrels. I ducked jest in time to keep from getting my head blowed off, and catched most of the double charge in my shoulder, whilst the rest hived in the seat of Steve Kirby's britches. Being shot that way by a relative was irritating, but I controlled my temper and merely taken the gun away from Jim and splintered the stock over his head.

In the meantime Joel Gordon and Buck Grimes had grabbed one of my laigs apiece and was trying to rassle me to the earth, and Joash Grimes was trying to hold down my right arm, and cousin Pecos Buckner was beating me over the head from behind with a axe-handle, and Erath Elkins was coming at me from the front with a bowie knife. I reched down and got Buck Grimes by the neck with my left hand, and I swung my right and hit Erath with it, but I had to lift Joash clean off his feet and swing him around with the lick, because he wouldn't let go, so I only knocked Erath through the rail fence which was around Uncle Saul's garden.

About this time I found my left laig was free and discovered that Buck Grimes was unconscious, so I let go of his neck and begun to kick around with my left laig, and it ain't my fault if the spur got tangled up in Uncle Jonathan Polk's whiskers and jerked most of 'em out by the roots. I shaken Joash off and taken the axe-handle away from Pecos because I seen he was going to hurt somebody if he kept on swinging it around so reckless, and I dunno why he blames me because his skull got fractured when he hit that tree. He oughta look where he falls when he gets throwed acrost a cabin yard. And if Joel Gordon hadn't been so stubborn trying to gouge me he wouldn't of got his laig broke neither.

I was handicapped by not wanting to kill any of my kinfolks, but they was so mad they all wanted to kill me, so in spite of my carefulness the casualties was increasing at a rate which would of discouraged anybody but Bear Creek folks. But they are the stubbornest people in the world. Three or four had got me around the laigs again, refusing to be convinced that I couldn't be throwed that way, and Erath Elkins, having pulled hisself out of the rooins of the fence, come charging back with his bowie.

By this time I seen I'd have to use vi'lence in spite of myself, so I grabbed Erath Elkins and squoze him with a grizzly-hug and that was when he got them five ribs caved in, and he ain't spoke to me since. I never seen sech a cuss for taking offence over trifles.

For a matter fact, if he hadn't been wrought up, he'd of realized how kindly and kindredly I felt towards him, even in the heat of battle. If I had dropped him underfoot he might of got fatally tromped on, for I was kicking folks right and left. So I carefully throwed Erath out of range of the melee, and he's a liar when he says I aimed him at Ozark Grimes' pitchfork; I didn't even see the cussed implement.

It was at this moment that somebody swung at me with a axe and ripped a ear offa my head, and I begun to lose my temper. Four or five other relatives was kicking and hitting and biting me all at onst, and they is a limit even to my timid manners and mild nature. I voiced my displeasure with a beller of wrath that shook the leaves offa the trees, and lashed out with both fists, and my misguided relatives fell all over the yard like persimmons after a frost. I grabbed Joash Grimes by the ankles and began to knock them ill-advised idjits in the head with him, and the way he hollered you'd of thought somebody was man-handling him. The yard was beginning to look like a battle-field when the cabin door opened and a deluge of b'iling water descended on us.

I got about a gallon down my neck, but paid very little attention to it, however the others ceased hostilities and started rolling on the ground and hollering and cussing, and Uncle Saul riz up from amongst the rooins of Esau Grimes and Joel Braxton, and bellered: "Woman! Whar air you at?"

Aunt Zavalla Garfield was standing in the doorway with a kettle in her hand, and she said: "Will you idjits stop fightin'? The Englishman's gone. He run out the back door when the fightin' started, and saddled his nag and pulled out. Now will you born fools stop, or will I give you another surge? Land save us! What's that light?"

Somebody was yelling off towards the settlement, and I was aware of a pecooliar glow which didn't come from sech torches as was still burning. And here come Medina Kirby, one of Bill's gals, yelping like a Comanche.

"Our cabin's burnin'!" she squalled. "A stray bullet went through the winder and busted Miss Margaret's ile lamp!"

With a yell of dismay I abandoned the fray and headed for Bill's cabin, follered by everybody which was able to foller me. They had been several wild shots fired during the melee and one of 'em must have hived in Miss Margaret's winder. The Kirbys had dragged most of their belongings into the yard and some was toting water from the creek, but the whole cabin was in a blaze by now.

"Where's Miss Margaret?" I roared.

"She must be still in there," shrilled Miz Kirby. "A beam fell and wedged her door so we couldn't open it, and——"

I grabbed a blanket one of the gals had rescued and plunged it into the rain barrel and run for Miss Margaret's room. They wasn't but one door in it, which led into the main part of the cabin, and was jammed like they said, and I knowed I couldn't never get my shoulders through either winder, so I jest put down my head and rammed the wall full force and knocked four or five logs outa place and made a hole big enough to go through.

The room was so full of smoke I was nigh blinded but I made

out a figger fumbling at the winder on the other side. A flaming
beam fell outa the roof and broke acrost my head with a loud
report and about a bucketful of coals rolled down the back of my
neck, but I paid no heed.

I charged through the smoke, nearly fracturing my shin on a
bedstead or something, and enveloped the figger on the wet blanket
and swept it up in my arms. It kicked wildly and fought and though
its voice was muffled in the blanket I catched some words I never
would of thought Miss Margaret would use, but I figgered she
was hysterical. She seemed to be wearing spurs, too, because I
felt 'em every time she kicked.

By this time the room was a perfect blaze and the roof was
falling in and we'd both been roasted if I'd tried to get back to
the hole I'd knocked in the oppersite wall. So I lowered my head
and butted my way through the near wall, getting all my eyebrows
and hair burnt off in the process, and come staggering through the
rooins with my precious burden and fell into the arms of my
relatives which was thronged outside.

"I've saved her!" I panted. "Pull off the blanket! Yo're safe,
Miss Margaret!"

"——!" said Miss Margaret.

Uncle Saul groped under the blanket and said: "By golly, if
this is the school-teacher she's growed a remarkable set of whiskers
since I seen her last!"

He yanked off the blanket—to reveal the bewhiskered coun-
tenance of Uncle Jeppard Grimes!

"Hell's fire!" I bellered. "What *you* doin' here?"

"I was comin' to jine the lynchin', you blame fool!" he snarled.
"I seen Bill's cabin was afire so I clum in through the back winder
to save Miss Margaret. She was gone, but they was a note she'd
left. I was fixin' to climb out the winder when you grabbed me,
you cussed maneyack!"

"Gimme that note!" I bellered, grabbing it. "Medina! Come
here and read it for me."

That note run:

Dear Breckinridge,
    I am sorry, but I can't stay on Bear Creek any longer. It
was tough enough anyway, but being expected to marry you
was the last straw. You've been very kind to me, but it would
be too much like marrying a grizzly bear. Please forgive me.
I am eloping with J. Pembroke Pemberton. We're going out
the back window to avoid any trouble, and ride away on his

horse. Give my love to the children. We are going to Europe on our honeymoon.

With Love,
Margaret Devon.

"Now what you got to say?" sneered Uncle Jeppard.

"Where's my hoss?" I yelled, going temporarily insane. "I'll foller 'em! They cain't do me this way! I'll have his sculp if I have to foller 'em to Europe or to hell! Git outa my way!"

Uncle Saul grabbed me as I plunged through the crowd.

"Now, now, Breckinridge," he expostulated, trying to brace his laigs as he hung on and was dragged down the road. "You cain't do nothin' to him. She done this of her own free will. She made her choice, and——"

"Release go of me!" I roared, jerking loose. "I'm ridin' on their trail, and the man don't live which can stop me! Life won't be worth livin' when Glory McGraw hears about this, and I aim to take it out on that Britisher's hide! Hell hath no fury like a Elkins scorned! Git outa my way!"

CHAPTER XIII

When Bear Creek Came to Chawed Ear

I dunno how far I rode that night before the red haze cleared out from around me so's I could even see where I was. I knowed I was follering the trail to War Paint, but that was about all. I knowed Miss Margaret and J. Pembroke would head for War Paint, and I knowed Cap'n Kidd would run 'em down before they could get there, no matter how much start they had. And I must of rode for hours before I come to my senses.

It was like waking up from a bad dream. I pulled up on the crest of a rise and looked ahead of me where the trail dipped down into the holler and up over the next ridge. It was jest getting daylight and everything looked kinda grey and still. I looked down in the trail and seen the hoof prints of J. Pembroke's hoss fresh in the dust, and knowed they couldn't be more'n three or four miles ahead of me. I could run 'em down within the next hour.

But thinks I, what the hell? Am I plumb locoed? The gal's got a right to marry whoever she wants to, and if she's idjit enough to choose him instead of me, why, 'tain't for me to stand in her way. I wouldn't hurt a hair onto her head; yet here I been aiming to hurt her the wust way I could, by shooting down her man right before her eyes. I felt so ashamed of myself I wanted to cuss — and so sorry for myself I wanted to bawl.

"Go with my blessin'," I said bitterly, shaking my fist in the direction where they'd went, and then I reined Cap'n Kidd around and headed for Bear Creek. I warn't aiming to stay there and endure Glory McGraw's rawhiding, but I had to get me some clothes. Mine was burnt to rags, and I didn't have no hat, and the buckshot in my shoulder was stinging me now and then.

A mile or so on the back-trail I crossed the road that runs from Cougar Paw to Grizzly Run, and I was hungry and thirsty so I turnt up it to the tavern which had been built recent on the crossing at Mustang Creek.

The sun warn't up when I pulled at the hitch-rack and clumb off and went in. The bar-tender give a holler and fell backwards into a tub of water and empty beer bottles, and started yelling for help, and I seen a man come to one of the doors which opened into the bar, and look at me. They was something familiar about him, but I couldn't place him for the instant.

"Shet up and git outa that tub," I told the bar-keep petulantly. "It's me, and I want a drink."

"Excuse me, Breckinridge," says he, hauling hisself onto his feet. "I rekernize you now, but I'm a nervous man, and you got no idee what a start you gimme when you come through that door jest now, with yore hair and eye-lashes all burnt off, and most of yore clothes, and yore hide all black with soot. What the hell——"

"Cease them personal remarks and gimme some whisky," I snarled, being in no mood for airy repartee. "Likewise wake up the cook and tell him to fry me some ham and aigs."

So he sot the bottle onto the bar and stuck his head into the kitchen and hollered: "Break out a fresh ham and start bustin' aigs. Breckinridge Elkins craves fodder!"

When he come back I said: "Who was that lookin' through that door there while ago?"

"Oh, that?" says he. "Why, that was a man nigh as famous as what you be—Wild Bill Donovan. You-all ever met?"

"I'll say we has," I grunted, pouring me a drink. "He tried to take Cap'n Kidd away from me when I was a ignorant kid. I was forced to whup him with my bare fists before he'd listen to reason."

"He's the only man I ever seen which was as big as you," said the bar-keep. "And at that he ain't quite as thick in the chest and arms as you be. I'll call him in and you-all can chin about old times."

"Save yore breath," I growled. "The thing I craves to do about chins with that coyote is to bust his'n with a pistol butt."

This seemed to kinda intimidate the bartender. He got behind the bar and started shining beer mugs whilst I et my breakfast in gloomy grandeur, halting only long enough to yell for somebody to feed Cap'n Kidd. Three or four menials went out to do it, and being afeared to try to lead Cap'n Kidd to the trough, they filled it and carried it to him, so only one of them got kicked in the belly. It's awful hard for the average man to dodge Cap'n Kidd.

Well, I finished my breakfast whilst they was dipping the stable-hand in a hoss-trough to bring him to, and I said to the bar-keep: "I ain't got no money to pay for what me and Cap'n Kidd et, but I'll be headin' for War Paint late this evenin' or to-night, and when I git the money I'll send it to you. I'm broke right now, but I ain't goin' to be broke long."

"All right," he said, eyeing my scorched skull in morbid fascination. "You got no idee how pecoolier you look, Breckinridge, with that there bald dome——"

"Shet up!" I roared wrathfully. A Elkins is sensitive about his personal appearance. "This here is merely a temporary inconvenience which I cain't help. Lemme hear no more about it. I'll shoot the next son of a polecat which calls attention to my singed condition!"

I then tied a bandanner around my head and got on Cap'n Kidd and pulled for home.

I arriv at pap's cabin about the middle of the afternoon and my family rallied around to remove the buckshot from my hide and repair other damages which had been did.

Maw made each one of my brothers lend me a garment, and she let 'em out to fit me.

"Though how much good it'll do you," said she, "I don't know. I never seen any man so hard on his clothes as you be, in my life. If it ain't fire it's bowie knives, and if it ain't bowie knives, it's buckshot."

"Boys will be boys, maw," soothed pap. "Breckinridge is jest full of life and high spirits, ain't you, Breckinridge?"

"From the whiff I got of his breath," snorted Elinor, "I'd say they is no doubt about the spirits."

"Right now I'm full of gloom and vain regrets," I says bitterly. "Culture is a flop on Bear Creek, and my confidence has been betrayed. I have tooken a sarpent with a British accent to my bosom and been bit. I stands knee-deep in the rooins of education and romance. Bear Creek lapses back into ignorance and barbarism and corn-licker, and I licks the wounds of unrequited love like a old wolf after a tussle with a pack of hound dawgs."

"What you goin' to do?" ast pap, impressed.

"I'm headin' for War Paint," I said gloomily. "I ain't goin' to stay here and have the life rawhided outa me by Glory McGraw. It's a wonder to me she ain't been over already to gloat over my misery."

"You ain't got no money," says pap.

"I'll git me some," I said. "And I ain't particular how. I'm going now. I ain't goin' to wait for Glory McGraw to descend onto me with her derned sourcasm."

So I headed for War Paint as soon as I could wash the soot off of me. I had a Stetson I borrowed from Garfield and I jammed it down around my ears so my bald condition warn't evident, because I was awful sensitive about it.

Sundown found me some miles from the place where the trail crossed the Cougar Paw—Grizzly Run road, and jest before the sun dipped I was hailed by a pecooliar-looking gent.

He was tall and gangling—tall as me, but didn't weigh within a hundred pounds as much. His hands hung about three foot out of his sleeves, and his neck with a big adam's apple riz out of his collar like a crane's, and he had on a plug hat instead of a Stetson, and a long-tailed coat. He moreover sot his hoss like it was a see-saw, and his stirrups was so short his bony knees come up almost level with his shoulders. He wore his pants laigs down over his boots, and altogether he was the funniest-looking human I ever seen. Cap'n Kidd give a disgusted snort when he seen him and wanted to kick his bony old sorrel nag in the belly, but I wouldn't let him.

"Air you," said this apparition, p'inting a accusing finger at me, "air you Breckinridge Elkins, the bearcat of the Humbolts?"

"I'm Breckinridge Elkins," I replied suspiciously.

"I dedooced as much," he says ominously. "I have come a long ways to meet you, Elkins! They can be only one sun in the sky; my roarin' grizzly from the high ranges! They can be only one champeen in the State of Nevada! I'm him!"

"Oh, be you?" I says, scenting battle afar. "Well, I feels the same way about one sun and one champeen! You look a mite skinny and gantlin' to be makin' sech big talk, but far be it from me to deny you a tussle after you've come so far to git in. Light down from yore hoss whilst I mangles yore frame with a free and joyful spirit! They is nothin' I'll enjoy more'n uprootin' a few acres of junipers with yore carcass and festoonin' the crags with yore innards."

"You mistakes my meanin', my bloodthirsty friend," says he. "I warn't referrin' to mortal combat. Far as I'm consarned, yo're supreme in that line. Nay, nay, B. Elkins, esquire! Reserve yore personal ferocity for the b'ars and knife-fighters of yore native mountains. I challenges you in another department entirely!

"Look, well, my bowie-wieldin' orang-outang of the high peaks!

Fame is shakin' her mane. I am Jugbelly Judkins, and my talent is gusslin'. From the live-oak grown coasts of the Gulf to the sun-baked buttes of Montana," says he oratorical, "I ain't yet met the gent I couldn't drink under the table betwixt sun-down and sun-up. I have met the most celebrated topers of plain and mountain, and they have all went down in inglorious and rum-soaked defeat. Afar off I heard men speak of you, praisin' not only yore genius in alterin' the features of yore feller man, but also laudin' yore capacity for corn-licker. So I have come to cast the ga'ntlet at yore feet, as it were."

"Oh," I says, "you wants a drinkin' match."

"'Wants' is a weak word, my murderous friend," says he. "I demands it."

"Well, come on," I said. "Le's head for War Paint then. They'll be plenty of gents there willin' to lay heavy bets——"

"To hell with filthy lucre!" snorted Jugbelly. "My mountainous friend, I am an artist. I cares nothin' for money. My reputation is what I upholds."

"Well, then," I said, "they's a tavern on Mustang Creek——"

"Let it rot," says he. "I scorns these vulgar displays in low inns and cheap taverns, my enormous friend. I supplies the sinews of war myself. Foller me!"

So he turnt his hoss off the trail, and I follered him through the bresh for maybe a mile, till he come to a small cave in a bluff with dense thickets all around. He reched into the cave and hauled out a gallon jug of licker.

"I hid a goodly supply of the cup that cheers in that cave," says he. "This is a good secluded spot where nobody never comes. We won't be interrupted here, my brawny but feeble-minded gorilla of the high ridges!"

"But what're we bettin'?" I demanded. "I ain't got no money. I was goin' down to War Paint and git me a job workin' somebody's claim for day-wages till I got me a stake and built it up playin' poker, but——"

"You wouldn't consider wagerin' that there gigantic hoss you rides?" says he, eyeing me very sharp.

"Never in the world," I says with a oath.

"Very well," says he. "Let the bets go. We battles for honour and glory alone! Let the carnage commence!"

So we started. First he'd take a gulp, and then me, and the jug was empty about the fourth gulp I taken, so he dragged out an-other'n, and we emptied it, and he hauled out another. They didn't seem to be no limit to his supply. He must of brought it there on a whole train of pack mules. I never seen a man drink like that skinny cuss. I watched the liquor careful, but he lowered it every time he taken a swig, so I knowed he warn't jest pertending. His belly expanded enormous as we went along and he looked very funny, with his skinny frame, and that there enormous belly bulging out his shirt till the buttons flew off of his coat.

I ain't goin' to tell you how much we drunk, because you wouldn't believe me. But by midnight the glade was covered with empty jugs and Jugbelly's arms was so tired lifting 'em he couldn't hardly move. But the moon and the glade and everything was dancing around and around to me, and he warn't even staggering. He looked kind of pale and wan, and onst he says, in a awed voice: "I wouldn't of believed it if I hadn't saw it myself!" But he kept on drinking and so did I, because I couldn't believe a skinny maverick like that could lick me, and his belly kept getting bigger and bigger till I was scairt it was going to bust, and things kept spinning around me faster than ever.

After awhile I heard him muttering to hisself, away off: "This is the last jug, and if it don't fix him, nothin' will. By God, he ain't human."

That didn't make no sense to me, but he passed me the jug and said: "Air you capable, my gulf-bellied friend?"

"Gimme that jug!" I muttered, bracing my laigs and getting a firm hold of myself. I taken a big gulp—and then I didn't know nothing.

When I woke up the sun was high above the trees. Cap'n Kidd was cropping grass nearby, but Jugbelly was gone. So was his hoss and all the empty jugs. There warn't no sign to show he'd ever been there, only the taste in my mouth which I cain't describe because I am a gent and there is words no gent will stoop to use. I felt like kicking myself in the pants. I was ashamed something terrible at being beat by that skinny mutt. It was the first time I'd ever drunk enough to lay me out. I don't believe in a man making a hawg out of hisself, even in a good cause.

I saddled Cap'n Kidd and pulled out for War Paint, and stopped a few rods away and drunk five or six gallons of water at a spring, and felt a lot better. I started on again, but before I come to the trail, I heard somebody bawling and pulled up, and there sot a feller on a stump, crying like his heart would bust.

"What's the trouble?" I ast, and he blinked the tears out of his eyes and looked up mournful and melancholy. He was a scrawny cuss with over-sized whiskers.

"You beholds in me," says he sobfully, "a critter tossed on the crooel tides of fate. Destiny has dealt my hand from the bottom of the deck. Whoa is me!" says he, and wept bitterly.

"Buck up," I said. "Things might well be wuss. Dammit," I said, waxing irritable, "stop that blubberin' and tell me what's the matter. I'm Breckinridge Elkins. Maybe I can help you."

He swallered some sobs, and said: "You air a man of kind impulses and a noble heart. My name is Japhet Jalatin. In my youth I made a enemy of a wealthy, powerful and unscrupulous man. He framed me and sent me to the pen for somethin' I never done. I busted free and under a assumed name, I come West. By hard workin' I accumulated a tidy sum which I aimed to send to my sorrowing wife and baby datters. But datters. But jest last night I learnt that I had been rekernized and the bloodhounds of the law was on my trail. I have got to skip to Mexico. My loved ones won't never git the dough.

"Oh," says he, "if they was only some one I could trust to leave it with till I could write 'em a letter and tell 'em where it was so they could send a trusted man after it! But I trust nobody. The man I left it with might tell where he got it, and then the bloodhounds of the law would be onto my trail again, houndin' me day and night."

He looked at me desperate, and says: "Young man, you got a kind and honest face. Won't *you* take this here money and hold it for my wife, till she can come after it?"

"Yeah, I'll do that," I said. He jumped up and run to his hoss which was tied nearby, and hauled out a buckskin poke, and shoved it into my hands.

"Keep it till my wife comes for it," says he. "And promise me you won't breathe a word of how you got it, except to her!"

"A Elkins never broke his word in his life," I said. "Wild hosses couldn't drag it outa me."

"Bless you, young man!" he cries, and grabbed my hand with both of his'n and pumped it up and down like a pump-handle, and then jumped on his hoss and fogged. I thought they is some curious people in the world, as I stuffed the poke in my saddle-bags and headed for War Paint again.

I thought I'd turn off to the Mustang Creek tavern and eat me some breakfast, but I hadn't much more'n hit the trail I'd been follerin' when I met Jugbelly, then I heard hosses behind me, and somebody hollered: "Stop, in the name of the law!"

I turnt around and seen a gang of men riding towards me, from the direction of Bear Creek, and there was the sheriff leading 'em, and right beside him was pap and Uncle John Garfield and Uncle

Bill Buckner and Uncle Bearfield Gordon. A tenderfoot onst called them four men the patriarchs of Bear Creek. I dunno what he meant, but they generally decides argyments which has got beyond the public control, as you might say. Behind them and the sheriff come about thirty more men, most of which I rekernized as citizens of Chawed Ear, and therefore definitely not my friends. Also, to my surprise, I rekernized Wild Bill Donovan amongst 'em, with his thick black hair falling down to his shoulders. They was four other hard-looking strangers which rode clost beside him.

All the Chawed Ear men had sawed-off shotguns and that surprised me, because that made it look like maybe they was coming to arrest me, and I haven't done nothing, except steal their school-teacher, several weeks before, and if they'd meant to arrest me for that, they'd of tried it before now.

"There he is!" yelped the sheriff, p'inting at me. "Han's up!"

"Don't be a damn' fool!" roared pap, knocking his shotgun out of his hands as he started to raise it. "You want to git you and yore cussed posse slaughtered? Come here, Breckinridge," he said, and I rode up to them, some bewildered. I could see pap was worried. He scowled and tugged at his beard. My uncles didn't have no more expression onto their faces than so many red Injuns.

"What the hell's all this about?" I ast.

"Take off yore hat," ordered the sheriff.

"Look here, you long-legged son of a mangy skunk," I said heatedly, "if yo're tryin' to rawhide me, lemme tell you right now——"

"'Tain't a joke," growled pap. "Take off yore sombrero."

I done so bewilderedly, and instantly four men in the gang started hollering: "That's him! That's the man! He had on a mask, but when he taken his hat off, we seen the hair was all off his head! That's shore him!"

"Elkins," said the sheriff, "I arrests you for the robbery of the Chawed Ear stage!"

I convulsively went for my guns. It was jest a instinctive move which I done without knowing it, but the sheriff hollered and ducked, and the possemen throwed up their guns, and pap spurred in between us.

"Put down them guns, everybody!" he roared, covering me with one six-shooter and the posse with the other'n. "First man that pulls a trigger, I'll salivate him!"

"I ain't aimin' to shoot nobody!" I bellered. "But what the hell is this all about?"

"As if he didn't know!" sneered one of the posse. "Tryin' to ack innercent! Heh heh heh—*gulp!*"

Pap riz in his stirrups and smashed him over the head with his right-hand six-shooter barrel, and he crumpled into the trail and laid there with the blood oozing out of his sculp.

"Anybody else feel humorous?" roared pap, sweeping the posse with a terrible eye. Evidently nobody did, so he turnt around and says to me, and I seen drops of perspiration standing on his face which warn't caused altogether by the heat. Says he: "Breckinridge, early last night the Chawed Ear stage was stuck up and robbed a few miles t'other side of Chawed Ear. The feller which done it not only taken the passengers' money and watches and things, and the mail sack, but he also shot the driver, old Jim Harrigan, jest out of pure cussedness. Old Jim's layin' over in Chawed Ear now with a bullet through his laig.

"These born fools thinks you done it! They was on Bear Creek before daylight—the first time a posse ever dared to come onto Bear Creek, and it was all me and yore uncles could do to keep the boys from massacrein' 'em. Bear Creek was sure wrought up. These mavericks," pap p'inted a finger of scorn at the four men which had claimed to identify me, "was on the stage. You know Ned Ashley, Chawed Ear's leadin' merchant. The others air strangers. They say their names is Hurley, Jackson and Slade. They claim to lost considerable money."

"We done that!" clamoured Jackson. "I had a buckskin poke crammed full of gold pieces the scoundrel taken. I tell you, that's the man which done it!" He p'inted at me, and pap turnt to Ned Ashley, and said: "Ned, what do you say?"

"Well, Bill," says Ashley reluctantly, "I hates to say it, but I don't see who else it could of been. The robber was Breckinridge's size, all right, and you know they ain't many men that big. He warn't ridin' Cap'n Kidd, of course; he was ridin' a big bay mare. He had on a mask, but as he rode off he taken off his hat, and we all seen his head in the moonlight. The hair was all off of it, jest like it is Breckinridge's. Not like he was naturally bald, but like it had been burnt off or shaved off recent."

"Well," says the sheriff, "unless he can prove a alibi I'll have to arrest him."

"Breckinridge," says pap, "whar was you last night?"

"I was layin' out in the woods drunk," I says.

I felt a aidge of doubt in the air.

"I didn't know you could drink enough to git drunk," says pap. "It ain't like you, anyway. What made you? Was it thinkin' about that gal?"

"Naw," I said. "I met a gent in a plug hat named Jugbelly Judkins and he challenged me to a drinkin' match."

"Did you win?" ast pap anxiously.

"Naw," I confessed in bitter shame. "I lost."

Pap muttered disgustedly in his beard, and the sheriff says: "Can you perduce this Judkins *hombre?*"

"I dunno where he went," I said. "He'd pulled out when I woke up."

"Very inconvenient, I says!" says Wild Bill Donovan, running his fingers lovingly through his long black locks, and spitting.

"Who ast you yore opinion?" I snarled bloodthirstily. "What you doin' in the Humbolts? Come back to try to git even for Cap'n Kidd?"

"I forgot that trifle long ago," says he. "I holds no petty grudge. I jest happened to be ridin' the road this side of Chawed Ear when the posse come by and I come with 'em jest to see the fun."

"You'll see more fun than you can tote home if you fool with me," I promised.

"Enough of this," snorted pap. "Breckinridge, even I got to admit yore alibi sounds kind of fishy. A critter named Jugbelly with a plug hat! It sounds plumb crazy. Still and all, we'll look for this cussed maverick, and if we find him and he establishes whar you was last night, why——"

"He put my gold in his saddle-bags!" clamoured Jackson. "I seen him! That's the same saddle! Look in them bags and I bet you'll find it!"

"Go ahead and look," I invited, and the sheriff went up to Cap'n Kidd very gingerly, whilst I restrained Cap'n Kidd from kicking his brains out. He run his hand in the bags and I'll never forget the look on pap's face when the sheriff hauled out that buckskin poke Japhet Jalatin had give me. I'd forgot all about it.

"How you explain *this?*" exclaimed the sheriff. I said nothing. A Elkins never busts his word, not even if he hangs for it.

"It's mine!" hollered Jackson. "You'll find my initials worked onto it! J. J., for Judah Jackson."

"There they air," announced the sheriff. "J. J. That's for Judah Jackson, all right."

"They don't stand for that!" I roared. "They stand for——" Then I stopped. I couldn't tell him they stood for Japhet Jalatin without breaking my word and giving away Japhet's secret.

"'Tain't his'n," I growled. "I didn't steal it from nobody."

"Then where'd you git it?" demanded the sheriff.

"None of yore business," I said sullenly.

Pap spurred forwards, and I seen beads of sweat on his face.

"Well, say somethin', damn it!" he roared. "Don't jest set there! No Elkins was ever accused of thievin' before, but if you done it, say so! I demands that you tells me whar you got that gold! If you didn't take it off 'n the stage, why don't you say so?"

"I cain't tell you," I muttered.

"Hell's fire!" bellered pap. "Then you must of robbed that stage! What a black shame onto Bear Creek this here is! But these town-folks ain't goin' to haul you off to their cussed jail, even if you did turn thief! Jest come out plain and tell me you done it, and we'll lick the whole cussed posse if necessary!"

I seen my uncles behind him drawing in and cocking their Winchesters, but I was too dizzy with the way things was happening to think straight about anything.

"I never robbed the cussed stage!" I roared. "I cain't tell you where I got that gold—but I didn't rob the gol-derned stage."

"So yo're a liar as well as a thief!" says pap, drawing back from me like I was a reptile. "To think it should come to this! From this day onwards," he says, shaking his fist in my face, "you ain't no son of mine! I disowns you! When they lets you out of the pen, don't you come sneakin' back to Bear Creek! Us folks there is rough and ready; we kyarves and shoots each other free and frequent; but no Bear Creek man ever yet stole nor lied. I could forgive the thievin', maybe, maybe even the shootin' of pore old Jim Harrigan. But I cain't forgive a lie. Come on, boys."

And him and my uncles turnt around and rode back up the trail towards Bear Creek with their eyes straight ahead of 'em and their backs straight as ramrods. I glared after 'em wildly, feeling like the world was falling to pieces. It war the first time in my life I'd ever knowed Bear Creek folks to turn their backs on a Bear Creek man.

"Well, come along," said the sheriff, and started to hand the poke to Jackson, when I come alive. I warn't going to let Japhet Jalatin's wife spend the rest of her life in poverty if I could help it. I made one swoop and grabbed the poke out of his hand and simultaneous drove in the spurs. Cap'n Kidd made one mighty lunge and knocked Jackson and his hoss sprawling and went over them and into the bresh whilst them fool posse-men was fumbling with their guns. They was a lot of cussing and yelling behind me and some shooting, but we was out of sight of them in a instant, and I went crashing on till I hit a creek I knowed was there. I jumped off and grabbed a big rock which was in the bed of the creek, with about three foot of water around it—jest the top stuck out above the water. I grabbed it and lifted it, and stuck the poke down under it, and let the rock back down again. It was safe there. Nobody'd ever suspect it was hid there, and it was a cinch nobody was going to be lifting the rock jest for fun and find the gold accidental. It weighted about as much as the average mule.

Cap'n Kidd bolted off through the woods as the posse come crashing through the bresh, yelling like Injuns, and they throwed down their shotguns on me as I clumb up the bank, dripping wet.

"Catch that hoss!" yelled the sheriff. "The gold's in the saddle-bags!"

"You'll never catch that hoss," opined Wild Bill Donovan. "I know him of old."

"Maybe Elkins is got the gold on him!" hollered Jackson. "Search him!"

I didn't make no resistance as the sheriff taken my guns and snapped a exter heavy pair of hand-cuffs onto my wrists. I was still kind of numb from having pap and my uncles walk out on me like that. All I'd been able to think of up to then was to hide the gold, and when that was hid my brain wouldn't work no further.

"Elkins ain't got it on him!" snarled the sheriff, after slapping my pockets. "Go after that hoss! Shoot him if you cain't catch him."

"No use for that," I says. "It ain't in the saddle-bags. I hid it where you won't never find it."

"Look in all the holler trees!" says Jackson, and added viciously: "We might *make* him talk."

"Shet up," said the sheriff. "Anything *you* could do to him would jest make him mad. He's actin' tame and gentle now. But he's got a broodin' gleam in his eye. Le's git him in jail before he gits a change of heart and starts remodellin' the landscape with the posse's carcasses."

"I'm a broken man," I says mournfully. "My own clan has went back on me, and I got no friends. Take me to jail if you wanta! All places is dreary for a man whose kin has disown him."

So we went to Chawed Ear.

One of the fellers who was riding a big strong hoss lemme have his'n, and the posse closed around me with their shotguns p'inting at me, and we headed out.

It was after dark when we got to Chawed Ear, but everybody was out in the streets to see the posse bring me in. They warn't no friendly faces in that crowd. I'd been very onpopular in Chawed Ear ever since I stole their school-teacher. I looked for old Joshua Braxton, but somebody said he was off on a prospecting trip.

They stopped at a log-hut clost to the jail, and some men was jest getting through working onto it.

"That there," says the sheriff, "is yore private jail. We built it special for you. As soon as word come last night that you'd robbed the stage, I set fifteen men buildin' that jail, and they're jest now gittin' through."

Well, I didn't think anybody could build anything in a night and a day which could hold me, but I didn't have no thought of trying to break out. I didn't have the heart. All I could think of was the way pap and my uncles had rode off and left me disowned and arrested.

I went in like he told me, and sot down on the bunk, and heard 'em barring the door on the outside. They was fellers holding torches outside, and the light come in at the winder so I could see it was a good strong jail. They was jest one room, with a door towards the town and a winder in the other side. It had a floor made out of logs, and the roof and walls was made out of heavy logs, and they was a big log at each corner sot in concrete, which was something new in them mountains, and the concrete wasn't dry yet. The bars in the winder was thick as a man's wrist, and drove clean through the sill and lintel logs and the ends clinched, and chinks betwixt the logs was tamped in with concrete. The door was made outa sawed planks four inches thick and braced with iron, and the hinges was big iron pins working in heavy iron sockets, and they was a big lock onto the door and three big bars made outa logs sot in heavy iron brackets.

Everybody outside was jammed around the winder trying to look in at me, but I put my head in my hands and paid no attention to 'em. I was trying to think but everything kept going round and round. Then the sheriff chased everybody away except them he told off to stay there and guard the jail, and he put his head to the bars and said: "Elkins, it'll go easier with you, maybe, if you'll tell us where you hid that there gold."

"When I do," I said gloomily, "there'll be ice in hell thick enough for the devil to skate on."

"All right," he snapped. "If you want to be stubborn. You'll git twenty years for this, or I miss my guess."

"Gwan," I said, "and leave me to my misery. What's a prison term to a man which has jest been disowned by his own blood-kin?"

He pulled back from the winder and I heard him say to somebody: "It ain't no use. Them Bear Creek devils are the most uncivilized white men I ever seen in my life. You cain't do nothin'

with one of 'em. I'm goin' to send some men back to look for
the gold around that creek we found him climbin' out of. I got a
idee he hid it in a holler tree somewheres. He's that much like a
b'ar. Likely he hid it and then run and got in the creek jest to
throw us off the scent. Thought he'd make us think he hid it on
t'other side of the creek. I bet he hid it in a tree this side somewheres.

"I'm goin' to git some food and some sleep. I didn't git to bed
at all last night. You fellers watch him clost, and if folks git too
rambunctious around the jail, call me quick."

"Ain't nobody around the jail now," said a familiar voice.

"I know," says the sheriff. "They're back in town lickerin' up
at all the bars. But Elkins is got plenty of enemies here, and they
ain't no tellin' what might bust loose before mornin'."

I heard him leave, and then they was silence, except for some
men whispering off somewheres nearby but talking too low for
me to make out what they was saying. I could hear noises coming
from the town, snatches of singing, and a occasional yell, but no
pistol-shooting like they usually is. The jail was on the aidge of
town, and the winder looked in the other direction, acrost a narrer
clearing with thick woods bordering it.

Purty soon a man come and stuck his head up to the winder
and I seen by the starlight that it was Wild Bill Donovan.

"Well, Elkins," says he, "you think you've finally found a jail
which can hold you?"

"What you doin' hangin' around here?" I muttered.

He patted his shotgun and said: "Me and four of my friends
has been app'inted special guards. But I tell you what I'll do. I
hate to see a man down and out like you be, and booted out by
his own family and shore to do at least fifteen years in the pen.
You tell me where you hid that there gold, and give me Cap'n
Kidd, and I'll contrive to let you escape before mornin'. I got a
fast hoss hid out there in the thickets, right over yonder, see? You
can fork that hoss and be gone outa the country before the sheriff
could catch you. All you got to do is give me Cap'n Kidd, and
that gold. What you say?"

"I wouldn't give you Cap'n Kidd," I said, "not if they was
goin' to hang me."

"Well," he sneered, "'Tain't none too shore they ain't. They's
plenty of rope-law talk in town to-night. Folks are purty well
wrought up over you shootin' old Jim Harrigan."

"I didn't shoot him, damn yore soul!" I said.

"You'll have a hell of a time provin' it," says he, and turnt around and walked around towards the other end of the jail with his shotgun under his arm.

Well, I dunno how long I sot there with my head in my hands and jest suffered. Noises from the town seemed dim and far off. I didn't care if they come and lynched me before morning, I was that low-spirited. I would of bawled if I could of worked up enough energy, but I was too low for that even.

Then somebody says: "Breckinridge!" and I looked up and seen Glory McGraw looking in at the winder with the rising moon behind her.

"Go ahead and t'ant me," I said numbly. "Everything else has happened to me. You might as well, too."

"I ain't goin' to t'ant you!" she said fiercely. "I come here to help you, and I aim to, no matter what you says!"

"You better not let Donovan see you talkin' to me," I says.

"I done seen him," she said. "He didn't want to let me come to the winder, but I told him I'd go to the sheriff for permission if he didn't, so he said he'd let me talk ten minutes. Listen: did he offer to help you escape if you'd do somethin' for him?"

"Yeah," I said. "Why?"

She ground her teeth slightly.

"I thought so!" says she. "The dirty rat! I come through the woods, and snuck on foot the last few hundred feet to git a look at the jail before I come out in the open. They's a hoss tied out there in the thickets and a man hidin' behind a log right nigh it with a sawed-off shotgun. Donovan's always hated you, ever since you taken Cap'n Kidd away from him. He aimed to git you shot whilst tryin' to escape. When I seen that ambush I jest figgered on somethin' like that."

"How'd you git here?" I ast, seeing she seemed to really mean what she said about helping me.

"I follered the posse and yore kinfolks when they came down from Bear Creek," she said. "I kept to the bresh on my pony, and was within hearin' when they stopped you on the trail. After everybody had left I went and caught Cap'n Kidd, and——"

"*You* caught Cap'n Kidd!" I said in dumbfoundment.

"Certainly," says she. "Hosses has frequently got more sense than men. He'd come back to the creek where he'd saw you last and looked like he was plumb broken-hearted because he couldn't find you. I turnt the pony loose and started him home, and I come on to Chawed Ear on Cap'n Kidd."

"Well, I'm a saw-eared jackrabbit!" I said helplessly.

"Hosses knows who their friends is," says she. "Which is

more'n I can say for some men. Breckinridge, pull out of this!
Tear this blame jail apart and le's take to the hills! Cap'n Kidd's
waitin' out there behind that big clump of oaks. They'll never
catch you!"

"I ain't got the strength, Glory," I said helplessly. "My strength
has oozed out of me like licker out of a busted jug. What's the
use to bust jail, even if I could? I'm a marked man, and a broken
man. My own kin has throwed me down. I got no friends."

"You have, too!" she said fiercely. "*I* ain't throwed you down.
I'm standin' by you till hell freezes!"

"But folks thinks I'm a thief and a liar!" I says, about ready
to weep.

"What I care what they thinks?" says she. "If you *was* all them
things, I'd still stand by you! But you ain't, and I know it!"

For a second I couldn't see her because my sight got blurry,
but I groped and found her hand tense on the winder bar, and I
said: "Glory, I dunno what to say. I been a fool, and thought hard
things about you and——"

"Forgit it," says she. "Listen: if you won't bust out of here,
we got to prove to them fools that you didn't rob that stage. And
we got to do it quick, because them strangers Hurley and Jackson
and Slade air in town circulatin' around through the bars and stirrin'
them fool Chawed Ear folks up to lynchin' you. A mob's liable
to come bustin' out of town any minute. Won't you tell me where
you got that there gold they found in yore saddle-bags? *I* know
you never stole it, but if you was to tell me, it might help us."

I shaken my head helplessly.

"I cain't tell you," I said. "Not even you. I promised not to.
A Elkins cain't break his word."

"Ha!" says she. "Listen: did some stranger meet you and give
you that poke of gold to give to his starvin' wife and chillern, and
make you promise not to tell nobody where you got it, because
his life was in danger?"

"Why, how'd you know?" I exclaimed in amazement.

"So that *was* it!" she exclaimed, jumping up and down in her
excitement. "How'd I know? Because I know you, you big bone-
headed mush-hearted chump! Lissen: don't you see how they worked
you? This was a put-up job.

"Jugbelly got you off and made you drink so's you'd be outa
the way and couldn't prove no alibi. Then somebody that looked
like you robbed the stage and shot old man Harrigan in the laig
jest to make the crime wuss. Then this feller what's-his-name give
you the money so they'd find it onto you!"

"It looks sensible!" I said dizzily.

"It's bound to be!" says she. "Now all we got to do is find Jugbelly and the feller which give you the gold, and the bay mare the robber rode. But first we got to find a man which has got it in for you enough to frame you like that."

"That's a big order," I says. "Nevada's full of gents which would give their eye-teeth to do me a injury."

"A big man," she mused. "Big enough to be mistook for you, with his head shaved, and ridin' a big bay mare. Hmmmmm! a man which hates you enough to do anything to you, and is got sense enough to frame somethin' like this!"

And jest then Wild Bill Donovan come around the corner of the jail with his shotgun under his arm.

"You've talked to that jail-bird long enough, gal," he says. "You better pull out. The noise is gettin' louder all the time in town, and it wouldn't surprise me to see quite a bunch of folks comin' to the jail before long—with a necktie for yore friend there."

"And I bet you'll plumb risk yore life defendin' him," she sneered.

He laughed and taken off his sombrero and run his fingers through his thick black locks.

"I don't aim to git none of my valuable gore spilt over a stage-coach robber," says he. "But I like yore looks, gal. Why you want to waste yore time with a feller like that when they is a man like me around, I dunno! His head looks like a peeled onion! The hair won't never git no chance to grow out, neither, 'cause he's goin' to git strung up before it has time. Whyn't you pick out a handsome *hombre* like me, which has got a growth of hair as is hair?"

"He got his hair burnt off tryin' to save a human life," says she. "Somethin' that ain't been said of you, you big monkey!"

"Haw haw haw!" says he. "Ain't you got the spunk, though! That's the way I like gals."

"You might not like me so much," says she suddenly, "if I told you I'd found that big bay mare you rode last night!"

He started like he was shot and blurted out: "Yo're lyin'! Nobody could find her where I hid her——"

He checked hisself sudden, but Glory give a yelp.

"I thought so! It was you!" And before he could stop her she grabbed his black locks and yanked. And his sculp come off in her hands and left his head as bare as what mine was!

"A wig jest like I thought!" she shrieked. "You robbed that stage! You shaved yore head to look like Breckinridge——" He grabbed her and clapped his hand over her mouth, and yelped: "Joe! Tom! Buck!" And at the sight of Glory struggling in his grasp I snapped them handcuffs like they was rotten cords and laid hold of them winder bars and tore 'em out. The logs they was sot in split like kindling wood and I come smashing through that winder like a b'ar through a chicken coop. Donovan let go of Glory and grabbed up his shotgun to blow my head off, but she grabbed the barrel and throwed all her weight onto it, so he couldn't bring it to bear on me, and my feet hit the ground jest as three of his pals come surging around the corner of the jail.

They was so surprised to see me out, and going so fast they couldn't stop and they run right into me and I gathered 'em to my bosom and you ought to of heard the bones crack and snap. I jest hugged the three of 'em together onst and then throwed 'em in all direction like a b'ar ridding hisself of a pack of hounds. Two of 'em fractured their skulls agen the jail-house and t'other broke his laig on a stump.

Meanwhile Donovan had let loose of his shotgun and run for the woods and Glory scrambled up onto her feet with the shotgun and let bam at him, but he was so far away by that time all she done was sting his hide with the shot. But he hollered tremendous jest the same. I started to run after him, but Glory grabbed me.

"He's headed for that hoss I told you about!" she panted. "Git Cap'n Kidd! We'll have to be a-hoss-back if we catch him!"

Bang! went a shotgun in the thickets, and Donovan's maddened voice yelled: "Stop that, you cussed fool! This ain't Elkins! It's me! The game's up! We got to shift!"

"Lemme ride with you!" hollered another voice, which I reckoned was the feller Donovan had planted to shoot me if I agreed to try to escape. "My hoss is on the other side of the jail!"

"Git off, blast you!" snarled Donovan. "This hoss won't carry double!" Wham! I jedged he'd hit his pal over the head with his six-shooter. "I owe you that for fillin' my hide with buckshot, you blame fool!" Donovan roared as he went crashing off into the bresh.

By this time we'd reached the oaks Cap'n Kidd was tied behind, and I swung into the saddle and Glory jumped up behind me.

"I'm goin' with you!" says she. "Don't argy! Git goin'!"

I headed for the thickets Donovan had disappeared into, and jest inside of 'em we seen a feller sprawled on the ground with a shotgun in his hand and his sculp split open. Even in the midst of my righteous wrath I had a instant of ca'm and serene joy as I reflected that Donovan had got sprinkled with buckshot by the feller who evidently mistook him for me. The deeds of the wicked sure do return onto 'em.

Donovan had took straight out through the bresh, and left gaps in the bushes a blind man could foller. We could hear his hoss crashing through the timber ahead of us, and then purty soon the smashing stopped but we could hear the hoofs lickety-split on hard ground, so I knowed he'd come out into a path, and purty soon so did we. Moonlight hit down into it, but it was winding so we couldn't see very far ahead, but the hood-drumming warn't pulling away from us, and we knowed we was closing in onto him. He was riding a fast critter but I knowed Cap'n Kidd would run it off its fool laigs within the next mile.

Then we seen a small clearing ahead and a cabin in it with candle-light coming through the winders, and Donovan busted out of the trees and jumped off his hoss which bolted into the bresh. Donovan run to the door and yelled: "Lemme in, you damn' fools! The game's up and Elkins is right behind me!"

The door opened and he fell in onto his all-fours and yelled: "Shet the door and bolt it! I don't believe even he can bust it down!" And somebody else hollered: "Blow out the candles! There he is at the aidge of the trees!"

Guns began to crack and bullets whizzed past me, so I backed Cap'n Kidd back into cover and jumped off and picked up a big log which warn't rotten yet, and run out of the clearing and made towards the door. This surprised the men in the cabin, and only one man shot at me and he hit the log. The next instant I hit the door—or rather I hit the door with the log going full clip and the door splintered and ripped offa the hinges and crashed inwards, and three or four men got pinned under it and yelled bloody murder.

I lunged into the cabin over the rooins of the door and the candles was all out, but a little moonlight streamed in and showed me three or four vague figgers before me. They was all shooting at me but it was so dark in the cabin they couldn't see to aim good and only nicked me in a few unimportant places. So I went for them and got both arms full of human beings and started sweeping the floor with 'em. I felt several fellers underfoot because they hollered when I tromped on 'em, and every now and then I felt somebody's head with my foot and give it a good rousing kick. I didn't know who I had hold of because the cabin was so full of gunpowder smoke by this time that the moon didn't do much good. But none of the fellers was big enough to be Donovan, and them I stomped on didn't holler like him, so I started clearing house by heaving 'em one by one through the door, and each time I throwed one they was a resounding whack! outside that I couldn't figger out till I realized that Glory was standing outside with a club and knocking each one in the head as he come out.

Then the next thing I knowed the cabin was empty except for me and a figger which was dodging back and forth in front of me trying to get past me to the door. So I laid hands onto it and heaved it up over my head and started to throw it through the door when it hollered: "Quarter, my titanic friend, quarter! I surrenders and demands to be treated as a prisoner of war!"

"Jugbelly Judkins!" I says.

"The same," says he, "or what's left of him!"

"Come out here where I can talk to you!" I roared, and groped my way out of the door with him. As I emerged I got a awful lick over the head, and then Glory give a shriek like a stricken elk.

"Oh, Breckinridge!" she wailed. "I didn't know it war you!"

"Never mind!" I says, brandishing my victim before her. "I got my alerbi right here by the neck! *Jugbelly Judkins,"* I says sternly, clapping him onto his feet and waving a enormous fist under his snoot, "if you values yore immortal soul, speak up and tell where I was all last night!"

"Drinkin' licker with me a mile off the Bear Creek trail," gasps he, staring wildly about at the figgers which littered the ground in front of the cabin. "I confesses all! Lead me to the bastile! My sins has catched up with me. I'm a broken man. Yet I am but a tool in the hands of a master mind, same as these misguided sons of crime which lays there——"

"One of 'em's tryin' to crawl off," quoth Glory, fetching the aforesaid critter a clout on the back of the neck with her club. He fell on his belly and howled in a familiar voice.

I started vi'lently and bent over to look close at him.

"Japhet Jalatin!" I hollered. "You cussed thief, you lied to me about yore wife starvin'!"

"If he told you he had a wife it was a gross understatement," says Jugbelly. "He's got three that I know of, includin' a Piute squaw, a Mexican woman, and a Chinee gal in San Francisco. But to the best of my knowledge they're all fat and hearty."

"I have been took for a cleanin' proper," I roared, gnashing my teeth. "I've been played for a sucker! My trustin' nature has been tromped on! My faith in humanity is soured! Nothin' but blood can wipe out this here infamy!"

"Don't take it out on us," begged Japhet. "It war all Donovan's idee."

"Where's he?" I yelled, glaring around.

"Knowin' his nature as I does," said Judkins, working his jaw to see if it was broke in more'n one place, "I would sejest that he snuck out the back door whilst the fightin' was goin' on, and is now leggin' it for the corral he's got hid in the thicket behind the cabin, where he secreted the bay mare he rode the night he held up the stage coach."

Glory pulled a pistol out of one of 'em's belt which he'd never got a chance to use, and she says: "Go after him, Breck. I'll take care of these coyotes!"

I taken one look at the groaning rooins on the ground, and decided she could all right, so I whistled to Cap'n Kidd, and he come, for a wonder. I forked him and headed for the thicket behind the cabin and jest as I done so I seen Donovan streaking it out the other side on a big bay mare. The moon made everything as bright as day.

"Stop and fight like a man, you mangy polecat!" I thundered, but he made no reply except to shoot at me with his six-shooter, and seeing I ignored this, he spurred the mare which he was riding bareback and headed for the high hills.

She was a good mare, but she didn't have a chance agen Cap'n Kidd. We was only a few hundred feet behind and closing in fast when Donovan busted out onto a bare ridge which overlooked a valley. He looked back and seen I was going to ride him down within the next hundred yards, and he jumped offa the mare and taken cover behind a pine which stood by itself a short distance from the aidge of the bresh. They warn't no bushes around it, and to rech him I'd of had to cross a open space in the moonlight, and every time I come out of the bresh he shot at me. So I kept in the aidge of the bresh and unslung my lariat and roped the top of the pine, and sot Cap'n Kidd agen it with all his lungs and weight, and tore it up by the roots.

When it fell and left Donovan without no cover he run for the rim of the valley, but I jumped down and grabbed a rock about the size of a man's head and throwed it at him, and hit him jest above the knee on the hind laig. He hit the ground rolling and throwed away both of his six-shooters and hollered: "Don't shoot! I surrenders!"

I quiled my lariat and come up to where he was laying, and says: "Cease that there disgustin' bellyachin'. You don't hear *me* groanin' like that, do you?"

"Take me to a safe, comfortable jail," says he. "I'm a broken man. My soul is full of remorse and my hide is full of buckshot.

My laig is broke and my spirit is crushed. Where'd you git the cannon you shot me with?"

"'Twarn't no cannon," I said with dignity. "I throwed a rock at you."

"But the tree fell!" he says wildly. "Don't tell me you didn't do *that* with artillery!"

"I roped it and pulled it down," I said, and he give a loud groan and sunk back on the ground, and I said: "Pardon me if I seems to tie yore hands behind yore back and put you acrost Cap'n Kidd. Likely they'll set yore laig at Chawed Ear if you remember to remind 'em about it."

He said nothin' except to groan loud and lusty all the way back to the cabin, and when we got there Glory had tied all them scoundrels' hands behind 'em, and they'd all come to and was groaning in chorus. I found a corral near the house full of their hosses, so I saddled 'em and put them critters onto 'em, and tied their laigs to their stirrups. Then I tied the hosses head to tail, all except one I saved for Glory, and we headed for Chawed Ear.

"What you aimin' to do now, Breck?" she ast as we pulled out.

"I'm goin' to take these critters back to Chawed Ear," I said fiercely, "and make 'em make their spiel to the sheriff and the folks. But my triumph is dust and ashes into my mouth, when I think of the way my folks has did me."

There warn't nothing for her to say; she was a Bear Creek woman. She knowed how Bear Creek folks felt.

"This here night's work," I said bitterly, "has learnt me who my friends is—and ain't. If it warn't for you these thieves would be laughin' up their sleeves at me whilst I rotted in jail."

"I wouldn't never go back on you when you was in trouble, Breck," she says, and I says: "I know that now. I had you all wrong."

We was nearing the town with our groaning caravan strung out behind us, when through the trees ahead of us, we seen a blaze of torches in the clearing around the jail, and men on hosses, and a dark mass of humanity swaying back and forth. Glory pulled up.

"It's the mob, Breck!" says she, with a catch in her throat. "They'll never listen to you. They're crazy mad like mobs always is. They'll shoot you down before you can tell 'em anything. Wait——"

"I waits for nothin'," I said bitterly. "I takes these coyotes in and crams them down the mob's throat! I makes them cussed fools listen to my exoneration. And then I shakes the dust of the Humbolts offa my boots and heads for foreign parts. When a man's kin lets him down, it's time for him to travel."

"Look there!" exclaimed Glory.

We had come out of the trees, and we stopped short at the aidge of the clearing, in the shadder of some oaks.

The mob was there, all right, with torches and guns and ropes— backed up agen the jail with their faces as pale as dough and their knees plumb knocking together. And facing 'em, on hosses, with guns in their hands, I seen pap and every fighting man on Bear Creek! Some of 'em had torches, and they shone on the faces of more Elkinses, Garfields, Gordons, Kirbys, Grimeses, Buckners, and Polks than them Chawed Ear misfits ever seen together at one time. Some of them men hadn't never been that far away from Bear Creek before in their lives. But they was all there now. Bear Creek had sure come to Chawed Ear.

"Whar is he, you mangy coyotes?" roared pap, brandishing his rifle. "What you done with him? I war a fool and a dog, desertin' my own flesh and blood to you polecats! I don't care if he's a thief or a liar, or what! A Bear Creek man ain't made to rot in a blasted town-folks jail! I come after him and I aim to take him back, alive or dead! And if you've kilt him, I aim to burn Chawed Ear to the ground and kill every able-bodied man in her! *Whar is he, damn yore souls?"*

"I swear we don't know!" panted the sheriff, pale and shaking. "When I heard the mob was formin' I come as quick as I could, and got here by the time they did, but all we found was the jail winder tore out like you see, and three men layin' senseless here and another'n out there in the thicket. They was the guards, but they ain't come to yet to tell us what happened. We was jest startin' to look for Elkins when you come, and——"

"Don't look no farther!" I roared, riding into the torchlight. "Here I be!"

"Breckinridge!" says pap. "Whar you been? Who's that with you?"

"Some gents which has got a few words to say to the assemblage," I says, drawing my string of captives into the light of the torches. Everybody gaped at 'em, and I says: "I interjuices you to Mister Jugbelly Judkins. He's the slickest word-slingin' sharp I ever seen, so I reckon it oughta be him which does the spielin'. He ain't got on his plug-hat jest now, but he ain't gagged. Speak yore piece, Jugbelly."

"Honest confession is good for the soul," says he. "Lemme have the attention of the crowd, whilst I talks myself right into the penitentiary." You could of heard a pin drop when he commenced.

"Donovan had brooded a long time about failin' to take Cap'n Kidd away from Elkins," says he. "He laid his plans careful and long to git even with Elkins without no risk to hisself. This was a job which taken plenty of caution and preparation. He got a gang of versatile performers together—the cream of the illegal crop, if I do say so myself.

"Most of us kept hid in that cabin back up in the hills, from which Elkins recently routed us. From there he worked out over the whole country—Donovan, I mean. One mornin' he run into Elkins at the Mustang Creek tavern. He overheard Elkins say he was broke, also that he was goin' back to Bear Creek and was aimin' to return to War Paint late that evenin'. All this, and Elkins' singed sculp, give him a idee how to work what he'd been plannin'.

"He sent me to meet Elkins and git him drunk and keep him out in the hills all night. Then I was to disappear, so Elkins couldn't prove no alibi. Whilst we was drinkin' up there, Donovan went and robbed the stage. He had his head shaved so's to make him look like Elkins, of course, and he shot old Him Harrigan jest to inflame the citizens.

"Hurley and Jackson and Slade was his men. The gold Jackson had on him really belonged to Donovan. Donovan, as soon as he'd robbed the stage, he give the gold to Jalatin who lit out for the place where me and Elkins was boozin'. Then Donovan beat it for the cabin and hid the bay mare and put on his wig to hide his shaved head, and got on another hoss, and started sa'nterin' along the Cougar Paw—Grizzly Run road—knowin' a posse would soon be headin' for Bear Creek.

"Which it was, as soon as the stage got in. Hurley and Jackson and Slade swore they'd knowed Elkins in Yavapai, and rekernized him as the man which robbed the stage. Ashley and Harrigan warn't ready to say for sure, but thought the robber looked like him. But you Chawed Ear gents know about that—as soon as you heard about the robbery you started buildin' yore special jail, and sent a posse to Bear Creek, along with Ashley and them three fakes that claimed to of rekernized Elkins. On the way you met Donovan, jest like he planned, and he jined you.

"But meanwhile, all the time, me and Elkins was engaged in alcoholic combat, till he passed out, long after midnight. Then I taken the jugs and hid 'em, and pulled out for the cabin to hide till I could sneak outa the country. Jalatin got there jest as I was leavin', and he waited till Elkins sobered up the next mornin', and told him a sob story about havin' a wife in poverty, and give him the gold to give to her, and made him promise not to tell nobody where he got it. Donovan knowed the big grizzly wouldn't bust his word, if it was to save his neck even.

"Well, as you all know, the posse didn't find Elkins on Bear Creek. So they started out lookin' for him, with his pap and some of his uncles, and met him jest comin' out into the trail from the place where me and him had our famous boozin' bout. Imejitly Slade, Hurley and Jackson begun yellin' he was the man, and they was backed by Ashley which is a honest man but really thought Elkins was the robber, when he seen that nude skull. Donovan planned to git Elkins shot while attemptin' to escape. And the rest is now history—war-history, I might say."

"Well spoke, Jugbelly," I says, dumping Donovan off my hoss at the sheriff's feet. "That's the story, and you-all air stuck with it. My part of the game's done did, and I washes my hands of it."

"We done you a big injestice, Elkins," says the sheriff. "But how was we to know——"

"Forget it," I says, and then pap rode up. Us Bear Creek folks don't talk much, but we says plenty in a few words.

"I was wrong, Breckinridge," he says gruffly, and that said more'n most folks could mean in a long-winded speech. "For the first time in my life," he says, "I admits I made a mistake. But," says he, "the only fly in the 'intment is the fack that a Elkins was drunk off'n his feet by a specimen like that!" And he p'inted a accusing finger at Jugbelly Judkins.

"I alone have come through the adventure with credit," admitted Jugbelly modestly. "A triumph of mind over muscle, my law-shootin' friends!"

"Mind, hell!" says Jalatin viciously. "That coyote didn't drink none of that licker! He was a sleight-of-hand performer in a vaude-ville show when Donovan picked him up. He had a rubber stummick inside his shirt and he poured the licker into that. He couldn't outdrink Breckinridge Elkins if he was a whole corporation, the derned thief!"

"I admits the charge," sighed Jugbelly. "I bows my head in shame."

"Well," I says, "I've saw worse men than you, at that, and if they's anything I can do, you'll git off light, you derned wind-bag, you!"

"Thank you, my generous friend," says he, and pap reined his hoss around and said: "You comin' home, Breckinridge?"

"Go ahead," I said. "I'll come on with Glory."

So pap and the men of Bear Creek turnt and headed up the trail, riding single file, with their rifles gleaming in the flare of the torches, and nobody saying nothing, jest saddles creaking and hoofs clinking softly, like Bear Creek men generally ride.

And as they went the citizens of Chawed Ear hoved a loud sigh of relief, and grabbed Donovan and his gang with enthusiasm and lugged 'em off to the jail—the one I hadn't busted, I mean.

"And that," said Glory, throwing her club away, "is that. You ain't goin' off to foreign parts now, be you, Breckinridge?"

"Naw," I said. "My misguided relatives has redeemed theirselves."

We stood there a minute looking at each other, and she said: "You—you ain't got nothin' to say to me, Breckinridge?"

"Why, sure I has," I responded. "I'm mighty much obliged for what you done."

"Is that all?" she ast, gritting her teeth slightly.

"What else you want me to say?" I ast, puzzled. "Ain't I jest thanked you? They was a time when I would of said more, and likely made you mad, Glory, but knowin' how you feel towards me, I——"

"——!" says Glory, and before I knowed what she was up to, she grabbed up a rock the size of a watermelon and busted it over my head. I was so tooken by surprise I stumbled backwards and fell sprawling and as I looked up at her, a great light bust onto me.

"She loves me!" I exclaimed.

"I been wonderin' how long it was goin' to take you to find out!" says she.

"But what made you treat me like you done?" I demanded presently. "I thought you plumb hated me!"

"You ought to of knowed better," says she, snuggling in my arms. "You made me mad that time you licked pap and them fool brothers of mine. I didn't mean most of them things I said. But you got mad and said some things which made me madder, and after that I was too proud to act any way but like I done. I never loved nobody but you, but I wouldn't admit it as long as you was at the top of the ladder, struttin' around with money in yore pocket, and goin' with purty gals, and everybody eager to be friends with you. I was lovin' you then so's it nearly busted me, but I wouldn't let on. I wouldn't humble myself to no blamed man! But you seen how quick I come to you when you needed a friend, you big lunkhead!"

"Then I'm glad all this happened," I says. "It made me see things straight. I never loved no other gal but you. I was jest tryin' to forgit you and make you jealous when I was goin' with them other gals. I thought I'd lost you, and was jest tryin' to git the next best. I know that now, and I admits it. I never seen a gal which could come within a hundred miles of you in looks and nerve and everything."

"I'm glad you've come to yore senses, Breckinridge," says she.

I swung up on Cap'n Kidd and lifted her up before me, and the sky was jest getting pink and the birds was beginning to cut loose as we started up the road towards Bear Creek.

PART TWO:

The Pride of Bear Creek

The Riot at Cougar Paw

I was out in the blacksmith shop by the corral beating out some shoes for Cap'n Kidd, when my brother John come sa'ntering in. He'd been away for a few weeks up in the Cougar Paw country, and he'd evidently done well, whatever he'd been doing, because he was in a first class humor with hisself, and plumb spilling over with high spirits and conceit. When he feels prime like that he wants to rawhide everybody he meets, especially me. John thinks he's a wit, but I figger he's just half right.

"Air you slavin' over a hot forge for that mangy, flea-bit hunk of buzzard-meat again?" he greeted me. "That broom-tail ain't wuth the iron you wastes on his splayed-out hooves!"

He knows the easiest way to git under my hide is to poke fun at Cap'n Kidd. But I reflected it was jest envy on his part, and resisted my natural impulse to bend the tongs over his head. I taken the white-hot iron out of the forge and put it on the anvil and started beating it into shape with the sixteen pound sledge I always uses. I got no use for the toys which most blacksmiths uses for hammers.

"If you ain't got nothin' better to do than criticize a animal which is a damn sight better hoss than you'll ever be a man," I said with dignerty, between licks, "I calls yore attention to a door right behind you which nobody ain't usin' at the moment."

He bust into loud rude laughter and said: "You call that thing a hoss-shoe? It's big enough for a snow plow! Here, long as yo're in the business, see can you fit a shoe for that!"

He sot his foot up on the anvil and I give it a good slam with the hammer. John let out a awful holler and begun hopping around over the shop and cussing fit to curl yore hair. I kept on hammering my iron.

Jest then pap stuck his head in the door and beamed on us, and said: "You boys won't never grow up! Always playin' yore childish games, and sportin' in yore innercent frolics!"

"He's busted my toe," said John bloodthirstily, "and I'll have his heart's blood if it's the last thing I do."

"Chips off the old block," beamed pap. "It takes me back to the time when, in the days of my childhood, I emptied a sawed-off shotgun into the seat of brother Joel's britches for tellin' our old man it was me which put that b'ar trap in his bunk."

"He'll rue the day," promised John, and hobbled off to the cabin with moans and profanity. A little later, from his yells, I gathered that he had persuaded maw or one of the gals to rub his toe with hoss-liniment. He could make more racket about nothing than any Elkins I ever knowed.

I went on and made the shoes and put 'em on Cap'n Kidd, which is a job about like roping and hawg-tying a mountain cyclone, and by the time I got through and went up to the cabin to eat, John seemed to have got over his mad spell. He was laying on his bunk with his foot up on it all bandaged up, and he says: "Breckinridge, they ain't no use in grown men holdin' a grudge. Let's fergit about it."

"Who's holdin' any grudge?" I ast, making sure he didn't have a bowie knife in his left hand. "I dunno why they should be so much racket over a trifle that didn't amount to nothin', nohow."

"Well," he said, "this here busted foot discommodes me a heap. I won't be able to ride for a day or so, and they is business up to Cougar Paw I ought to 'tend to."

"I thought you just come from there," I says.

"I did," he said, "but they is a man up there which has promised me somethin' which is due me, and now I ain't able to go collect. Whyn't you go collect for me, Breckinridge? You ought to, dern it, because it's yore fault I cain't ride. The man's name is Bill Santry, and he lives up in the mountains a few miles from Cougar Paw. You'll likely find him in Cougar Paw any day, though."

"What's this he promised you?" I ast.

"Just ask for Bill Santry," he said. "When you find him say to him: 'I'm John Elkins' brother, and you can give me what you promised him.'"

My family always imposes onto my good nature; generally I'd

rather go do what they want me to than to go to the trouble with arguing with 'em.

"Oh, all right," I said. "I ain't got nothin' to do right now."

"Thanks, Breckinridge," he said. "I knowed I could count on you."

So a couple of days later I was riding through the Cougar Range, which is very thick-timbered mountains, and rapidly approaching Cougar Paw. I hadn't never been there before, but I was follering a winding wagon-road which I knowed would eventually fetch me there.

The road wound around the shoulder of a mountain, and ahead of me I seen a narrer path opened into it, and just before I got there I heard a bull beller, and a gal screamed: "Help! Help! Old Man Kirby's bull's loose!"

They came a patter of feet, and behind 'em a smashing and crashing in the underbrush, and a gal run out of the path into the road, and a rampaging bull was right behind her with his head lowered to toss her. I reined Cap'n Kidd between her and him, and I knowed Cap'n Kidd would do the rest without no advice from me. He done so by wheeling and lamming his heels into that bull's ribs so hard he kicked the critter clean through a rail fence on the other side of the road. Cap'n Kidd hates bulls, and he's too big and strong for any of 'em. He would of then jumped on the critter and stomped him, but I restrained him, which made him mad, and whilst he was trying to buck me off, the bull on-tangled hisself and high-tailed it down the mountain, bawling like a scairt yearling.

When I had got Cap'n Kidd in hand I looked around and seen the gal looking at me very admiringly. I swept off my Stetson and bowed from my saddle and says: "Can I assist you any farther, m'am?"

She blushed purty as a pitcher and said: "I'm much obliged, stranger. That there critter nigh had his hooks into my hide. Whar you headin'? If you ain't in no hurry I'd admire to have you drop by the cabin and have a smack of b'ar meat and honey. We live up the path about a mile."

"They ain't nothin' I'd ruther do," I assured her. "But jest at the present I got business in Cougar Paw. How far is it from here?"

"'Bout five mile down the road," says she. "My name's Joan; what's yore'n?"

"Breckinridge Elkins, of Bear Creek," I said. "Say, I got to push on to Cougar Paw, but I'll be ridin' back this way tomorrer mornin' about sun-up. If you could—"

"I'll be waitin' right here for you," she said so promptly it made my head swim. No doubt about it; it was love at first sight. "I—I got store-bought shoes," she added shyly. "I'll be a-wearin' 'em when you come along."

"I'll be here if I have to wade through fire, flood and hostile Injuns," I assured her, and rode on down the wagon-trace with my manly heart swelling with pride in my bosom. They ain't many mountain men which can awake the fire of love in a gal's heart at first sight—a gal, likewise, which was as beautiful as that there gal, and rich enough to own store-bought shoes. As I told Cap'n Kidd, they was just somethin' about a Elkins.

It was about noon when I rode into Cougar Paw which was a tolerably small village sot up amongst the mountains, with a few cabins where folks lived, and a few more which was a grocery store and a jail and a saloon. Right behind the saloon was a good-sized cabin with a big sign onto it which said: Jonathan Middleton, Mayor of Cougar Paw.

They didn't seem to be nobody in sight, not even on the saloon porch, so I rode on to the corrals which served for a livery stable and wagon yard, and a man come out of the cabin nigh it, and took charge of Cap'n Kidd. He wanted to turn him in with a couple of mules which hadn't never been broke, but I knowed what Cap'n Kidd would do to them mules, so the feller give him a corral to hisself, and belly-ached jest because Cap'n Kidd playfully bit the seat out of his britches.

He ca'med down when I paid for the britches. I ast him where I could find Billy Santry, and he said likely he was up to the store.

So I went up to the store, and it was about like all them stores you see in them kind of towns—groceries, and drygoods, and grindstones, and harness and such-like stuff, and a wagon-tongue somebody had needed recent. They warn't but the one store in the town and it handled a little of everything. They was a sign onto it which said: General Store; Jonathan Middleton, Prop.

They was a bunch of fellers setting around on goods boxes and benches eating sody crackers and pickles out of a barrel, and they was a tolerable hard-looking gang. I said: "I'm lookin' for Bill Santry."

The biggest man in the store, which was setting on a bench, says: "You don't have to look no farther. I'm Bill Santry."

"Well," I says, "I'm Breckinridge Elkins, John Elkins' brother. You can give what you promised him."

"Ha!" he says with a snort like a hungry catamount, rising sudden. "They is nothin' which could give me more pleasure! Take it with my blessin'!" And so saying he picked up the wagon tongue and splintered it over my head.

It was so unexpected that I lost my footing and fell on my back, and Santry give a wolfish yell and jumped into my stummick with both feet, and the next thing I knowed nine or ten more fellers was jumping up and down on me with their boots.

Now I can take a joke as well as the next man, but it always did make me mad for a feller to twist a spur into my hair and try to tear the sculp off. Santry having did this, I throwed off them lunatics which was tryin' to tromp out my innards, and riz up amongst them with a outraged beller. I swept four or five of 'em into my arms and give 'em a grizzly-hug and when I let go all they was able to do was fall on the floor and squawk about their busted ribs.

I then turned onto the others which was assaulting me with pistols and bowie knives and the butt ends of quirts and other villainous weppins, and when I laid into 'em you should of heard 'em howl. Santry was trying to dismember my ribs with a butcher knife he'd got out of the pork barrel, so I picked up the pickle barrel and busted it over his head. He went to the floor under a avalanche of splintered staves and pickles and brine, and then I got hold of a grindstone and really started getting destructive. A grindstone is a good comforting implement to have hold of in a melee, but kind of clumsy. For instance when I hove it at a feller which was trying to cock a sawed-off shotgun, it missed him entirely and nigh squashed four or five men which was trying to shoot me from behind it. I settled the shotgun feller's hash with a box of canned beef, and then I got hold of a double-bitted axe, and the embattled citizens of Cougar Paw quit the field with blood-curdling howls of fear—them which was able to quit and howl.

I stumbled over the thickly-strewn casualties to the door, taking a few casual swipes at the shelves as I went past, and knocking all the cans off of them. Jest as I emerged into the street, with my axe lifted to chop down anybody which opposed me, a skinny lookin' human bobbed up in front of me and hollered: "Halt, in the name of the law!"

Paying no attention to the double-barreled shotgun he shoved in my face, I swung back my axe for a swipe, and accidentally hit the sign over the door and knocked it down on top of him. He let out a squall as he went down and let bam! with the shotgun right in my face so close it singed my eyebrows. I pulled the signboard off him so I could git a good belt at him with my axe, but he hollered: "I'm the sheriff! I demands that you surrenders to properly constupated authority!"

I then noticed that he had a star pinned onto one gallus, so I put down my axe and let him take my guns. I never resists a officer of the law—well, seldom ever, that is.

He p'inted his shotgun at me and says: "I fines you ten dollars for disturbin' the peace!"

About this time a lanky maverick with side-whiskers come prancing around the corner of the building, and he started throwing fits like a locoed steer.

"The scoundrel's rooint my store!" he howled. "He's got to pay me for the counters and winders he busted, and the shelves he knocked down, and the sign he rooint, and the pork-keg he busted over my clerk's head!"

"What you think he ought to pay, Mr. Middleton?" ast the sheriff.

"Five hundred dollars," said the mayor blood-thirstily.

"Five hundred hell!" I roared, stung to wrath. "This here whole dern town ain't wuth five hundred dollars. Anyway, I ain't got no money but fifty cents I owe to the feller that runs the wagon yard."

"Gimme the fifty cents," ordered the mayor. "I'll credit that onto yore bill."

"I'll credit my fist onto yore skull," I snarled, beginning to lose my temper, because the butcher knife Bill Santry had carved my ribs with had salt on the blade, and the salt got into the cuts and smarted. "I owes this fifty cents and I gives it to the man I owes it to."

"Throw him in jail!" raved Middleton. "We'll keep him there till we figures out a job of work for him to do to pay out his fine."

So the sheriff marched me down the street to the log cabin which they used for a jail, whilst Middleton went moaning around the rooins of his grocery store, paying no heed to the fellers which lay groaning on the floor. But I seen the rest of the citizens packing them out on stretchers to take 'em into the saloon to bring 'em to. The saloon had a sign: Square Deal Saloon; Jonathan Middleton, Prop. And I heard fellers cussin' Middleton because he made 'em pay for the licker they poured on the victims' cuts and bruises.

But they cussed under their breath. Middleton seemed to pack a lot of power in that there town.

Well, I laid down on the jail-house bunk as well as I could, because they always build them bunks for ordinary-sized men about six foot tall, and I wondered what in hell Bill Santry had hit me with that wagon tongue for. It didn't seem to make no sense.

I laid there and waited for the Sheriff to bring me my supper, but he didn't bring none, and purty soon I went to sleep and dreamed about Joan, with her store-bought shoes.

What woke me up was a awful racket in the direction of the saloon. I got up and looked out of the barred winder. Night had fell, but the cabins and the saloon was well lit up, but too far away for me to tell what was going on. But the noise was so familiar I thought for a minute I must be back on Bear Creek again, because men was yelling and cussing, and guns was banging, and a big voice roaring over the din. Once it sounded like somebody had got knocked through a door, and it made me right home-sick, it was so much like a dance on Bear Creek.

I pulled the bars out of the winder trying to see what was going on, but all I could see was what looked like men flying headfirst out of the saloon, and when they hit the ground and stopped rolling, they jumped up and run off in all directions, hollering like the Apaches was on their heels.

Purty soon I seen somebody running toward the jail as hard as he could leg it, and it was the sheriff. Most of his clothes was tore off, and he had blood on his face, and he was gasping and panting.

"We got a job for you, Elkins!" he panted. "A wild man from Texas jest hit town, and is terrorizin' the citizens! If you'll pertect us, and lay out this friend from the prairies, we'll remit yore fine! Listen at that!"

From the noise I jedged the aforesaid wild man had splintered the panels out of the bar.

"What started him on his rampage?" I ast.

"Aw, somebody said they made better chili con carne in Santa Fe than they did in El Paso," says the sheriff. "So this maneyack starts cleanin' up the town—"

"Well, I don't blame him," I said. "That was a dirty lie and a low-down slander. My folks all come from Texas, and if you Cougar Paw coyotes thinks you can slander the State and git away with it—"

"We don't think nothin'!" wailed the sheriff, wringing his hands and jumping like a startled deer everytime a crash resounded up the street. "We admits the Lone Star State is the cream of the West in all ways! Lissen, will you lick this homicidal lunatic for us? You got to, dern it. You got to work out yore fine, and—"

"Aw, all right," I said, kicking the door down before he could unlock it. "I'll do it. I cain't waste much time in this town. I got a engagement down the road tomorrer at sun-up."

The street was deserted, but heads was sticking out of every door and window. The sheriff stayed on my heels till I was a few feet from the saloon, and then he whispered: "Go to it, and make it a good job! If anybody can lick that grizzly in there, it's you!" He then ducked out of sight behind the nearest cabin after handing me my gun-belt.

I stalked into the saloon and seen a gigantic figger standing at the bar and just fixing to pour hisself a dram out of a demijohn. He had the place to hisself, but it warn't near as much of a wreck as I'd expected.

As I came in he wheeled with a snarl, as quick as a cat, and flashing out a gun. I drawed one of mine just as quick, and for a second we stood there, glaring at each other over the barrels.

"Breckinridge Elkins!" says he. "My own flesh and blood kin!"

"Cousin Bearfield Buckner!" I says, shoving my gun back in its scabbard. "I didn't even know you was in Nevada."

"I got a ramblin' foot," says he, holstering his shootin' iron. "Put 'er there, Cousin Breckinridge!"

"By golly, I'm glad to see you!" I said, shaking with him. Then I recollected. "Hey!" I says. "I got to lick you."

"What you mean?" he demanded.

"Aw," I says, "I got arrested, and ain't got no money to pay my fine, and I got to work it out. And lickin' you was the job they gimme."

"I ain't got no use for law," he said grumpily. "Still and all, if I had any dough, I'd pay yore fine for you."

"A Elkins don't accept no charity," I said slightly nettled. "We works for what we gits. I pays my fine by lickin' the hell out of you, Cousin Bearfield."

At this he lost his temper; he was always hot-headed that way. His black brows come down and his lips curled up away from his teeth and he clenched his fists which was about the size of mallets.

"What kind of kinfolks air you?" he scowled. "I don't mind a friendly fight between relatives, but yore intentions is mercenary and unworthy of a true Elkins. You put me in mind of the fact that yore old man had to leave Texas account of a hoss gittin' its head tangled in a lariat he was totin' in his absent-minded way."

"That there is a cussed lie," I said with heat. "Pap left Texas because he wouldn't take the Yankee oath after the Civil War, and you know it. Anyway," I added bitingly, "nobody can ever say a Elkins ever stole a chicken and roasted it in a chaparral thicket."

He started violently and turned pale.

"What you hintin' at, you son of Baliol?" he hollered.

"Yore iniquities ain't no family secret," I assured him bitterly. "Aunt Atascosa writ Uncle Jeppard Grimes about you stealin' that there Wyandotte hen off of Old Man Westfall's roost."

"Shet up!" he bellered, jumping up and down in his wrath, and clutching his six-shooters convulsively. "I war just a yearlin' when I lifted that there fowl and et it, and I was plumb famished, because a posse had been chasin' me six days. They was after me account of Joe Richardson happenin' to be in my way when I was emptyin' my buffalo rifle. Blast yore soul, I have shot better men than you for talkin' about chickens around me."

"Nevertheless," I said, "the fact remains that yo're the only one of the clan which ever swiped a chicken. No Elkins never stole no hen."

"No," he sneered, "they prefers hosses."

Jest then I noticed that a crowd had gathered timidly outside the doors and winders and was listening eagerly to this exchange of family scandals, so I said: "We've talked enough. The time for action has arriv. When I first seen you, Cousin Bearfield, the thought of committin' mayhem onto you was very distasteful. But after our recent conversation, I feels I can scramble yore homely features with a free and joyful spirit. Le's have a snort and then git down to business."

"Suits me," he agreed, hanging his gunbelt on the bar. "Here's a jug with about a gallon of red licker into it."

So we each taken a medium-sized snort, which of course emptied the jug, and then I hitched my belt and says: "Which does you desire first, Cousin Bearfield—a busted laig or a fractured skull?"

"Wait a minute," he requested as I approached him. "What's that on yore boot?"

I stooped over to see what it was, and he swung his laig and kicked me in the mouth as hard as he could and immediately busted into a guffaw of brutal mirth. Whilst he was thus employed I spit his boot out and butted him in the belly with a vi'lence which changed his haw-haw to a agonized grunt, and then we laid hands on each other and rolled back and forth acrost the floor, biting and gouging, and that was how the tables and chairs got busted. Mayor Middleton must of been watching through a winder because I heard him squall: "My Gawd, they're wreckin' my saloon! Sheriff, arrest 'em both."

And the sheriff hollered back: "I've took yore orders all I aim to, Jonathan Middleton! If you want to stop that double-cyclone git in there and do it yoreself!"

Presently we got tired scrambling around on the floor amongst the cuspidors, so we riz simultaneous and I splintered the roulette wheel with his carcass, and he hit me on the jaw so hard he knocked me clean through the bar and all the bottles fell off the shelves and showered around me, and the ceiling lamp come loose and spilled about a gallon of red hot ile down his neck.

Whilst he was employed with the ile I clumb up from among the debris of the bar and started my right fist in a swing from the floor, and after it traveled maybe nine feet it took Cousin Bearfield under the jaw, and he hit the oppersite wall so hard he knocked out a section and went clean through it, and that was when the roof fell in.

I started kicking and throwing the rooins off me, and then I was aware of Cousin Bearfield lifting logs and beams off of me, and in a minute I crawled out from under 'em."

"I could of got out all right," I said. "But jest the same I'm much obleeged to you."

"Blood's thicker'n water," he grunted, and hit me under the jaw and knocked me about seventeen feet backwards toward the mayor's cabin. He then rushed forward and started kicking me in the head, but I riz up in spite of his efforts.

"Git away from that cabin!" screamed the mayor, but it was too late. I hit Cousin Bearfield between the eyes and he crashed into the mayor's rock chimney and knocked the whole base loose with his head, and the chimney collapsed and the rocks come tumbling down on him.

But being a Texas Buckner, Bearfield riz out of the rooins. He not only riz, but he had a rock in his hand about the size of a watermelon and he busted it over my head. This infuriated me, because I seen he had no intention of fighting fair, so I tore a log out of the wall of the mayor's cabin and belted him over the ear with it, and Cousin Bearfield bit the dust. He didn't git up that time.

Whilst I was trying to git my breath back and shaking the sweat out of my eyes, all the citizens of Cougar Paw come out of their hiding places and the sheriff yelled: "You done a good job, Elkins! Yo're a free man!"

"He is like hell!" screamed Mayor Middleton, doing a kind of war-dance, whilst weeping and cussing together. "Look at my cabin! I'm a rooint man! Sheriff, arrest that man!"

"Which 'un?" inquired the sheriff.

"The feller from Texas," said Middleton bitterly. "He's unconscious, and it won't be no trouble to drag him to jail. Run the other'n out of town. I don't never want to see him no more."

"Hey!" I said indignantly. "You cain't arrest Cousin Bearfield. I ain't goin' to stand for it."

"Will you resist a officer of the law?" ast the sheriff, sticking his gallus out on his thumb.

"You represents the law whilst you wear yore badge?" I inquired.

"As long as I got that badge on," boasts he, "I am the law!"

"Well," I said, spitting on my hands, "you ain't got it on now. You done lost it somewhere in the shuffle tonight, and you ain't nothin' but a common citizen like me! Git ready, for I'm comin' head-on and wide-open!"

I whooped me a whoop.

He glanced down in a stunned sort of way at his empty gallus, and then he give a scream and took out up the street with most of the crowd streaming out behind him.

"Stop, you cowards!" screamed Mayor Middleton. "Come back here and arrest these scoundrels—"

"Aw, shet up," I said disgustedly, and give him a kind of push and how was I to know it would dislocate his shoulder blade. It was jest beginning to git light by now, but Cousin Bearfield wasn't showing no signs of consciousness, and I heard them Cougar Paw skunks yelling to each other back and forth from the cabins where they'd forted themselves and from what they said I knowed they figgered on opening up on us with their Winchesters as soon as it got light enough to shoot good.

Jest then I noticed a wagon standing down by the wagon-yard, so I picked up Cousin Bearfield and lugged him down there and throwed him into the wagon. Far be it from a Elkins to leave a senseless relative to the mercy of a Cougar Paw mob. I went into the corral where them two wild mules was and started putting harness onto 'em, and it warn't no child's play. They hadn't never been worked before, and they fell onto me with a free and hearty enthusiasm. Onst they had me down stomping on me, and the citizens of Cougar Paw made a kind of half-hearted sally. But I unlimbered my .45s and throwed a few slugs in their direction and they all hollered and run back into their cabins.

I finally had to stun them fool mules with a bat over the ear with my fist, and before they got their senses back, I had 'em harnessed to the wagon, and Cap'n Kidd and Cousin Bearfield's hoss tied to the rear end.

"He's stealin' our mules!" howled somebody, and taken a wild shot at me, as I headed down the street, standing up in the wagon and keeping them crazy critters straight by sheer strength of the lines.

"I ain't stealin' nothin'!" I roared as we thundered past the cabins where spurts of flame was already streaking out of the winders. "I'll send this here wagon and these mules back tomorrow!"

The citizens answered with bloodthirsty yells and a volley of lead, and with their benediction singing past my ears, I left Cougar Paw in a cloud of dust and profanity.

Them mules, after a vain effort to stop and kick loose from the harness, laid their bellies to the ground and went stampeding down that crooking mountain road like scairt jackrabbits. We went around each curve on one wheel, and sometimes we'd hit a stump that would throw the whole wagon several foot into the air, and that must of been what brung Cousin Bearfield to hisself. He was laying sprawled in the bed, and finally we taken a bump that throwed him in a somersault clean to the other end of the wagon.

He hit on his neck and riz up on his hands and knees and looked around dazedly at the trees and stumps which was flashin' past, and bellered: "What the hell's happenin'? Whar-at am I, anyway?"

"Yo're on yore way to Bear Creek, Cousin Bearfield!" I yelled, cracking my whip over them fool mules' backs. "Yippee ki-yi! This here is fun, ain't it, Cousin Bearfield?"

I was thinking of Joan waiting with her store-bought shoes for me down the road, and in spite of my cuts and bruises, I was rolling high and handsome.

"Slow up!" roared Cousin Bearfield, trying to stand up. But jest then we went crashing down a steep bank, and the wagon tilted, throwing Cousin Bearfield to the other end of the wagon where he rammed his head with great force against the front-gate. "!●¾$%¢*" says Cousin Bearfield. "Glug!" Because he had hit the creek bed going full speed and knocked all the water out of the channel, and about a hundred gallons splashed over into the wagon and nearly washed Cousin Bearfield out.

"If I ever git out of this alive," pronounced Cousin Bearfield, "I'll kill you if it's the last thing I do—"

But at that moment the mules stampeded up the bank on the other side and Cousin Bearfield was catapulted to the rear end of the wagon so hard he knocked out the end-gate with his head and nearly went out after it, only he just managed to grab hisself.

We went plunging along the road and the wagon hopped from stump to stump and sometimes it crashed through a thicket of bresh. Cap'n Kidd and the other hoss was thundering after us, and the mules was braying and I was whooping and Cousin Bearfield was cussin', and purty soon I looked back at him and hollered: "Hold on, Cousin Bearfield! I'm goin' to stop these critters. We're close to the place where my gal will be waitin' for me—"

"Look out, you blame fool!" screamed Cousin Bearfield, and then the mules left the road and went one on each side of a white oak tree, and the tongue splintered, and they run right out of the harness and kept high-tailing it, but the wagon piled up on that tree with a jolt that throwed me and Cousin Bearfield headfirst into a blackjack thicket.

Cousin Bearfield vowed and swore, when he got back home, that I picked this thicket special on account of the hornets' nest that was there, and drove into it plumb deliberate. Which same is a lie which I'll stuff down his gizzard next time I cut his sign. He claimed they was trained hornets which I educated not to sting me, but the fact was I had sense enough to lay there plumb quiet. Cousin Bearfield was fool enough to run.

Well, he knows by this time, I reckon, that the fastest man afoot can't noways match speed with a hornet. He taken out through the bresh and thickets, yelpin' and hollerin' and hoppin' most bodacious. He run in a circle, too, for in three minutes he come bellerin' back, gave one last hop and dove back into the thicket. By this time I figgered he'd wore the hornets out, so I came alive again.

I extricated myself first and locating Cousin Bearfield by his profanity, I laid hold onto his hind laig and pulled him out. He lost most of his clothes in the process, and his temper wasn't no better. He seemed to blame me for his misfortunes.

"Don't tech me," he said fiercely. "Leave me be. I'm as close to Bear Creek right now as I want to be. Whar's my hoss?"

The hosses had broke lose when the wagon piled up, but they hadn't gone far, because they was fighting each other in the middle of the road. Bearfield's hoss was almost as big and mean as Cap'n

Kidd. We separated 'em and Bearfield clumb aboard without a word.

"Where you goin', Cousin Bearfield?" I ast.

"As far away from you as I can," he said bitterly. "I've saw all the Elkinses I can stand for awhile. Doubtless yore intentions is good, but a man better git chawed by lions than rescued by a Elkins!"

And with a few more observations which highly shocked me, and which I won't repeat, he rode off at full speed, looking very pecooliar, because his pants was about all that hadn't been tore off of him, and he had scratches and bruises all over him.

I was sorry Cousin Bearfield was so sensitive, but I didn't waste no time brooding over his ingratitude. The sun was up and I knowed Joan would be waiting for me where the path come down into the road from the mountain.

Sure enough, when I come to the mouth of the trail, there she was, but she didn't have on her store-bought shoes, and she looked flustered and scairt.

"Breckinridge!" she hollered, running up to me before I could say a word. "Somethin' terrible's happened! My brother was in Cougar Paw last night, and a big bully beat him up somethin' awful! Some men are bringin' him home on a stretcher. One of 'em rode ahead to tell me!"

"How come I didn't pass 'em on the road?" I said, and she said: "They walked and taken a short cut through the hills. There they come now."

I seen some men come into the road a few hundred yards away and come toward us, lugging somebody on a stretcher like she said.

"Come on!" she says, tugging at my sleeve. "Git down off yore hoss and come with me. I want him to tell you who done it, so you can whup the scoundrel!"

"I got a idee, I know who done it," I said, climbing down. "But I'll make sure." I figgered it was one of Cousin Bearfield's victims.

"Why, look!" said Joan. "How funny the men are actin' since you started toward 'em. They've sot down the litter and they're runnin' off into the woods! Bill!" she shrilled as we drawed nigh. "Bill, air you hurt bad?"

"A busted laig and some broke ribs," groaned the victim on the litter, which also had his head so bandaged I didn't recognize him. Then he sot up with a howl. "What's that ruffian doin' with you?" he roared, and to my amazement I recognized Bill Santry.

"Why, he's a friend of our'n, Bill—" Joan begun, but he interrupted her loudly and profanely: "Friend, hell! He's John Elkins' brother, and furthermore he's the one which is responsible for the crippled and mutilated condition in which you now sees me!"

Joan said nothing. She turned and looked at me in a very pecooliar manner, and then dropped her eyes shyly to the ground.

"Now, Joan," I begun, when all at once I saw what she was looking for. One of the men had dropped a Winchester before he run off. Her first bullet knocked off my hat as I forked Cap'n Kidd, and her second, third and fourth missed me so close I felt their hot wind. Then Cap'n Kidd rounded a curve with his belly to the ground and my busted romance was left far behind me. . . .

A couple of days later a mass of heartaches and bruises which might of been recognized as Breckinridge Elkins, the pride of Bear Creek, rode slowly down the trail that led to the settlements on the aforesaid creek. And as I rode, it was my fortune to meet my brother John coming up the trail on foot.

"Where you been?" he greeted me hypocritically. "You look like you been rasslin' a pack of mountain lions."

I eased myself down from the saddle and said without heat: "John, jest what was it that Bill Santry promised you?"

"Oh," says John with a laugh, "I skinned him in a hoss-trade before I left Cougar Paw, and he promised if he ever met me, he'd give me the lickin' of my life. I'm glad you don't hold no hard feelin's, Breck. It was jest a joke, me sendin' you up there. You can take a joke, cain't you?"

"Sure," I said. "By the way, John, how's yore toe?"

"It's all right," says he.

"Lemme see," I insisted. "Set yore foot on that stump."

He done so and I give it a awful belt with the butt of my Winchester.

"That there is a receipt for yore joke," I grunted, as he danced around on one foot and wept and swore. And so saying I mounted and rode on in gloomy grandeur. A Elkins always pays his debts.

Pilgrims to the Pecos

That there wagon rolled up the trail and stopped in front of our cabin one morning, jest after sun-up. We all come out to see who it was, because strangers ain't common on Bear Creek—and not very often welcome, neither. They was a long, hungry-looking old coot driving, and four or five growed boys sticking their heads out.

"Good mornin', folks," said the old coot, taking off his hat. "My name is Joshua Richardson. I'm headin' a wagontrain of immigrants which is lookin' for a place to settle. The rest of 'em's camped three miles back down the trail. Everybody we met in these here Humbolt Mountings told us we'd hev to see Mister Roaring Bill Elkins about settlin' hereabouts. Be you him?"

"I'm Bill Elkins," says pap suspiciously.

"Well, Mister Elkins," says Old Man Richardson, wagging his chin whiskers, "we'd admire it powerful if you folks would let us people settled somewheres about."

"Hmmmm!" says pap, pulling his beard. "Whar you all from?"

"Kansas," says Old Man Richardson.

"Ouachita," says pap, "git my shotgun."

"Don't you do no sech thing, Ouachie," says maw. "Don't be stubborn, Willyum. The war's been over for years."

"That's what I say," hastily spoke up Old Man Richardson. "Let bygones be bygones, I says!"

"What," says pap ominously, "is yore honest opinion of General Sterlin' Price?"

"One of nature's noblemen!" declares Old Man Richardson earnestly.

222

"Hmmmm!" says pap. "You seem to have considerable tact and hoss-sense for a Red-laig. But they hain't no more room on Bear Creek fer no more settlers, even if they was Democrats. They's nine er ten families now within a rech of a hunnert square miles, and I don't believe in over-crowdin' a country."

"But we're plumb tuckered out!" wailed Old Man Richardson. "And nowheres to go! We hev been driv from pillar to post, by settlers which got here ahead of us and grabbed all the best land. They claims it whether they got any legal rights or not."

"Legal rights be damned," snorted pap. "Shotgun rights is what goes in this country. But I know jest the place fer you. It's ten er fifteen day's travel from here, in Arizony. It's called Bowie Knife Canyon, and hit's jest right fer farmin' people, which I jedge you all be."

"We be," says Old Man Richardson. "But how we goin' to git there?"

"My son Breckinridge will be plumb delighted to guide you there," says pap. "Won't you, Breckinridge?"

"No, I won't," I said. "Why the tarnation have I got to be picked on to ride herd on a passle of tenderfooted mavericks—"

"He'll git you there safe," says pap, ignoring my remarks. "He dotes on lendin' folks a helpin' hand, don't you, Breckinridge?"

Seeing the futility of argyment, I merely snarled and went to saddle Cap'n Kidd. I noticed Old Man Richardson and his boys looking at me in a very pecooliar manner all the time, and when I come out on Cap'n Kidd, him snorting and bucking and kicking the rails out of the corral like he always does, they turnt kind of pale and Old Man Richardson said: "I wouldn't want to impose on yore son, Mister Elkins. After all, we wasn't intendin' to go to that there canyon, in the first place—"

"I'm guidin' you to Bowie Knife Canyon!" I roared. "Maybe you warn't goin' there before I saddled my hoss, but you air now! C'm'on."

I then cut loose under the mules' feets with my .45s to kind of put some ginger in the critters, and they brayed and sot off down the trail jest hitting the high places with Old Man Richardson hanging onto the lines and bouncing all over the seat and his sons rolling in the wagonbed.

We come into camp full tilt, and some of the men grabbed their guns and the women hollered and jerked up their kids, and one feller was so excited he fell into a big pot of beans which was simmering over a fire and squalled out that the Injuns was trying to burn him alive.

Old Man Richardson had his feet braced again the front-gate, pulling back on the lines as hard as he could and yelling bloody murder, but the mules had the bits betwixt their teeth. So I rode to their heads and grabbed 'em by the bridles and throwed 'em back onto their haunches, and Old Man Richardson ought to of knew the stop would be sudden. T'warn't my fault he done a dive off of the seat and hit on the wagon-tongue on his head. And it warn't my fault neither that one of the mules kicked him and t'other'n bit him before I could ontangle him from amongst them. Mules is mean critters howsoever you take 'em.

Everybody hollered amazing, and he riz up and mopped the blood offa his face and waved his arms and hollered: "Ca'm down, everybody! This hain't nawthin' to git excited about. This gent is Mister Breckinridge Elkins, which has kindly agreed to guide us to a land of milk and honey down in Arizony."

They received the news without enthusiasm. They was about fifty of 'em, mostly women, chillern, and half-grown young 'uns. They warn't more'n a dozen fit fighting men in the train. They all looked like they'd been on the trail a long time. And they was all some kin to Old Man Richardson—sons and daughters, and grandchillern, and nieces and nephews, and their husbands and wives, and sech like. They was one real purty gal, the old man's youngest daughter Betty, who warn't married yet.

They'd jest et breakfast and was hitched up when we arrove, so we pulled out without no more delay. I rode along of Old Man Richardson's wagon, which went ahead with the others strung out behind, and he says to me: "If this here Bowie Knife Canyon is sech a remarkable place, why ain't it already been settled?"

"Aw, they was a settlement there," I said, "but the Apaches kilt some, and Mexican bandits kilt some, and about three years ago the survivors got to fightin' amongst theirselves and jest kind of kilt each other off."

He yanked his beard nervously and said: "I dunno! I dunno! Maybe we had ought to hunt a more peaceful spot than that there sounds like."

"You won't find no peaceful spots west of the Pecos," I assured him. "Say no more about it. I've made up our minds that Bowie Knife Canyon is the place for you all, and we're goin' there!"

"I wouldn't think of argyin' the p'int," he assured me hastily. "What towns does we pass on our way?"

"Jest one," I said. "War Smoke, right on the Arizona line. Tell yore folks to keep out of it. It's a hangout for every kind of a outlaw. I jedge yore boys ain't handy enough with weppins to mix in sech company."

"We don't want no trouble," says he. "I'll tell 'em."

So we rolled along, and the journey was purty uneventful except for the usual mishaps which generally happens to tenderfeet. But we progressed until we was within striking distance of the Arizona border. And there we hit a snag. The rear wagon bogged in a creek we had to cross a few miles north of the line. They'd been a head rise, and the wagons churned the mud so the last one stuck fast. It was getting on toward sun-down, and I told the others to go on and make camp a mile west of War Smoke, and me and the folks in the wagon would foller when we got it out.

But that warn't easy. It was mired clean to the hubs, and the mules was up to their bellies. We pried and heaved and hauled, and night was coming on, and finally I said: "If I could git them cussed mules out of my way, I might accomplish somethin'."

So we unhitched 'em from the wagon, but they was stuck too, and I had to wade out beside 'em and lift 'em out of the mud one by one and tote 'em to the bank. A mule is a helpless critter. But then, with them out of the way, I laid hold of the tongue and hauled the wagon out of the creek in short order. Them Kansas people sure did look surprised, I dunno why.

Time we'd scraped the mud offa the wagon and us, and hitched up the mule again, it was night, and so it was long after dark when we come up to the camp the rest of the train had made in the place I told 'em. Old Man Richardson come up to me looking worried, and he says: "Mister Elkins, some of the boys went into that there town in spite of what I told 'em."

"Don't worry," I says. "I'll go git 'em."

I clumb on Cap'n Kidd without stopping to eat supper, and rode over to War Smoke, and tied my hoss outside the only saloon they was there. It was a small town, and awful hard looking. As I went into the saloon I seen the four Richardson boys, and they was surrounded by a gang of cut-throats and outlaws. They was a Mexican there, too, a tall, slim cuss, with a thin black mustash, and gilt braid onto his jacket.

"So you theenk you settle in Bowie Knife Canyon, eh?" he says, and one of the boys said: "Well, that's what we was aimin' to do."

"I theenk not," he said, grinning like a cougar, and I seen his hands steal to the ivory-handled guns at his hips. "You never heard of Senor Gonzeles Zamora? No? Well, he is a beeg hombre in thees country, and he has use for thees canyon in hees business."

"Start the fireworks whenever yo're ready, Gomez," muttered a white desperado. "We're backin' yore play."

The Richardson boys didn't know what the deal was about, but they seen they was up agen real trouble, and they turnt pale and looked around like trapped critters, seeing nothing but hostile faces and hands gripping guns.

"Who tell you you could settle thees canyon?" ast Gomez. "Who bring you here? Somebody from Kansas? Yes? No?"

"No," I said, shouldering my way through the crowd. "My folks come from Texas. My granddaddy was at San Jacinto. You remember that?"

His hands fell away from his guns and his brown hide turnt ashy. The rest of them renegades give back, muttering: "Look out, boys! It's Breckinridge Elkins!"

They all suddenly found they had business at the bar, or playing cards, or something, and Gomez found hisself standing alone. He licked his lips and looked sick, but he tried to keep up his bluff.

"You maybe no like what I say about Senor Zamora?" says he. "But ees truth. If I tell him gringoes come to Bowie Knife Canyon, he get very mad!"

"Well, suppose you go tell him now," I said, and so as to give him a good start, I picked him up and throwed him through the nearest winder.

He picked hisself up and staggered away, streaming blood and Mex profanity, and them in the saloon maintained a kind of pallid silence. I hitched my guns forard, and said to the escaped convict which was tending bar, I says: "You don't want me to pay for that winder, do you?"

"Oh, no!" says he, polishing away with his rag at a spittoon he must of thought was a beer mug. "Oh, no, no, no, no! We needed that winder busted fer the ventilation!"

"Then everybody's satisfied," I suggested, and all the hoss-thieves and stage-coach bandits in the saloon give me a hearty agreement.

"That's fine," I says. "Peace is what I aim to have, if I have to lick every——in the joint to git it. You boys git back to the camp."

They was glad to do so, but I lingered at the bar, and bought a drink for a train-robber I'd knowed at Chawed Ear onst, and I said: "Jest who is this cussed Zamora that Mex was spielin' about?"

"I dunno," says he. "I never heard of him before."

"I wouldn't say you was lyin'," I said tolerantly. "Yo're jest sufferin' from loss of memory. Frequently cases like that is cured and their memory restored by a severe shock or jolt like a lick onto the head. Now then, if I was to take my sixshooter butt and drive yore head through that whiskey barrel with it, I bet it'd restore yore memory right sudden."

"Hold on!" says he in a hurry. "I just remembered that Zamora is the boss of a gang of Mexicans which claims Bowie Knife Canyon. He deals in hosses."

"You mean he steals hosses," I says, and he says: "I ain't argyn'. Anyway, the canyon is very convenient for his business, and if you dump them immigrants in his front yard, he'll be very much put out."

"He sure will," I agreed. "As quick as I can git my hands onto him."

I finished my drink and strode to the door and turnt suddenly with a gun in each hand. The nine or ten fellers which had drawed their guns aiming to shoot me in the back as I went through the door, they dropped their weppins and throwed up their hands and yelled: "Don't shoot!" So I jest shot the lights out, and then went out and got onto Cap'n Kidd whilst them idjits was hollering and falling over each other in the dark, and rode out of War Smoke, casually shattering a few winder lights along the street as I went.

When I got back to camp the boys had already got there, and the whole wagon train was holding their weppins and scairt most to death.

"I'm mighty relieved to see you back safe, Mister Elkins," says Old Man Richardson. "We heard the shootin' and was afeared them bullies had kilt you. Le's hitch up and pull out right now!"

Them tenderfoots is beyond my comprehension. They'd of all pulled out in the dark if I'd let 'em, and I believe most of 'em stayed awake all night, expecting to be butchered in their sleep. I didn't say nothing to them about Zamora. The boys hadn't understood what Gomez was talking about, and they warn't no use getting 'em worse scairt then what they generally was.

Well, we pulled out before daylight, because I aimed to rech the canyon without another stop. We kept rolling and got there purty late that night. It warn't really no canyon at all, but a whopping big valley, well timbered, and mighty good water and grass. It was a perfect place for a settlement, as I p'inted out, but tenderfoots is powerful pecooliar. I happened to pick our camp site that night on the spot where the Apaches wiped out a mule-train of Mexicans six years before, and it was too dark to see the bones scattered around till next morning. Old Man Richardson was using what he thought was a round rock for a piller, and when he woke up the next morning and found he'd been sleeping with his head onto a human skull he like to throwed a fit.

And when I wanted to stop for the noonday meal in that there grove where the settlers hanged them seven cattle-rustlers three years before, them folks got the willies when they seen some of the ropes still sticking onto the limbs, and wouldn't on no account eat their dinner there. You got no idee what pecooliar folks them immigrants is till you've saw some.

Well, we stopped a few miles further on, in another grove in the midst of a wide rolling country with plenty of trees and tall grass, and I didn't tell 'em that was where them outlaws murdered the three Grissom boys in their sleep. Old Man Richardson said it looked like as good a place as any to locate the settlement. But I told him we was going to look over the whole derned valley before we chosed a spot. He kind of wilted and said at least for God's sake let 'em rest a few days.

I never seen folks which tired out so easy, but I said all right, and we camped there that night. I hadn't saw no signs of Zamora's gang since we come into the valley, and thought likely they was all off stealing hosses somewhere. Not that it made any difference.

Early next morning Ned and Joe, the old man's boys, they wanted to look for deer, and I told 'em not to go more'n a mile from camp, and be keerful, and they said they would, and sot out to the south.

I went back of the camp a mile or so to the creek where Jim Dornley ambushed Tom Harrigan four years before, and taken me a swim. I stayed longer'n I intended to, it was sech a relief to get away from them helpless tenderfoots for a while, and when I rode back into camp, I seen Ned approaching with a stranger—a young white man, which carried hisself with an air of great importance.

"Hey, pap!" hollered young Ned as they dismounted. "Where's Mister Elkins? This feller says we can't stay in Bowie Knife Canyon!"

"Who're you?" I demanded, emerging from behind a wagon, and the stranger's eyes bugged out as he seen me.

"My name's George Warren," says he. "A wagon train of us just came into the valley from the east yesterday. We're from Illinois."

"And by what right does you order people outa this canyon?" I ast.

"We got the fightin'est man in the world guidin' us," says he. "I thought he was the biggest man in the world till I seen you. But he ain't to be fooled with. When he heard they was another train in the valley, he sent me to tell you to git. You better, too, if you got any sense!"

"We don't want no trouble!" quavered Old Man Richardson.

"You got a nerve!" I snorted, and I pulled George Warren's hat down so the brim come off and hung around his neck like a collar, and turnt him around and lifted him off the ground with a boot in the pants, and then throwed him bodily onto his hoss. "Go back and tell yore champeen that Bowie Knife Canyon belongs to us!" I roared, slinging a few bullets around his hoss's feet. "And we gives him one hour to hitch up and clear out!"

"I'll git even for this!" wept George Warren, as he streaked it for his home range. "You'll be sorry, you big polecat! Jest wait'll I tell Mister—" I couldn't catch what else he said.

"Now I bet he's mad," says Old Man Richardson. "We better go. After all—"

"Shet up!" I roared. "This here valley's our'n, and I intends to defend our rights to the last drop of yore blood! Hitch them mules and swing the wagons in a circle! Pile yore saddles and plunder betwixt the wheels. I got a idee you all fights better behind breastworks. Did you see their camp, Ned?"

"Naw," says he, "but George Warren said it lies about three miles east of our'n. Me and Joe got separated and I was swingin' east around the south end of that ridge over there, when I met this George Warren. He said he was out lookin' for a hoss before sun-up and seen our camp and went back and told their guide, and he sent him over to tell us to git out."

"I'm worried about Joe," said Old Man Richardson. "He ain't come back."

"I'll go look for him," I said. "I'll also scout their camp, and if the odds ain't more'n ten to one, we don't wait for 'em to attack. We goes over and wipes 'em out pronto. Then we hangs their fool sculps to our wagon bows as a warnin' to other sech scoundrels."

Old Man Richardson turnt pale and his knees knocked together, but I told him sternly to get to work swinging them wagons, and clumb onto Cap'n Kidd and lit out.

Reason I hadn't saw the smoke of the Illinois camp was on account of a thick-timbered ridge which lay east of our camp. I swung around the south end of that ridge and headed east, and I'd gone maybe a mile and a half when I seen a man riding toward me.

When he seen me he come lickety-split, and I could see the sun shining on his Winchester barrel. I cocked my .45-90 and rode toward him and we met in the middle of a open flat. And suddenly we both lowered our weppins and pulled up, breast to breast, glaring at each toher.

"Breckinridge Elkins!" says he.

"Cousin Bearfield Buckner!" says I. "Air you the man which sent that unlicked cub of a George Warren to bring me a defiance?"

"Who else?" he snarled. He always had a awful temper.

"Well," I says, "this here is our valley. You all got to move on."

"What you mean, move on?" he yelled. "I brung them pore critters all the way from Dodge City, Kansas, where I encountered 'em bein' tormented by some wuthless buffalo-hunters which is no longer in the land of the livin'. I've led 'em through fire, flood, hostile Injuns and white renegades. I promised to lead 'em into a land of milk and honey, and I been firm with 'em, even when they weakened theirselves. Even when they begged on bended knees to be allowed to go back to Illinois, I wouldn't hear of it, because, as I told 'em, I knowed what was best for 'em. I had this canyon in mind all the time. And now you tells me to move on!"

Cousin Bearfield rolled an eye and spit on his hand. I jest waited.

"What sort of a reply does you make to my request to go on and leave us in peace," he goes on. "George Warren come back to camp wearin' his hat brim around his neck and standin' up in the stirrups because he was too sore to set in the saddle. So I set 'em fortifyin' the camp whilst I went forth to reconnoiter. That word I sent you, I now repeats in person. Yo're my blood-kin, but principles come first!"

"Me, too," I said. "A Nevada Elkins' principles is as lofty as a Texas Buckner's any day. I whupped you a year ago in Cougar Paw—"

"That's a cussed lie!" gnashed he. "You taken a base advantage and lammed me with a oak log when I warn't expectin' it!"

"Be that as it may," says I, "—ignorin' the fack that you had jest beaned me with a rock the size of a water-bucket—the only way to settle this dispute is to fight it out like gents. But we got to determine what weppins to use. The matter's too deep for fists."

"I'd prefer butcher knives in a dark room," says he, "only they ain't no room. If we jest had a couple of sawed-off shotguns, or good double-bitted axes—I tell you, Breck, le's tie our left hands together and work on each other with our bowies."

"Naw," I says, "I got a better idee. We'll back our hosses together, and then ride for the oppersite sides of the flat. When we get there we'll wheel and charge back, shootin' at each other with our Winchesters. Time they're empty we'll be clost enough to use our pistols, and when we've emptied them we'll be clost enough to finish the fight with our bowies."

"Good idee!" agreed Bearfield. "You always was a brainy, cultured sort of a lobo, if you wasn't so damn' stubborn. Now, me, I'm reasonable. When I'm wrong, I admit it."

"You ain't never admitted it so far," says I.

"I ain't never been wrong yet!" he roared. "And I'll kyarve the gizzard of the buzzard which says I am! Come on! Le's git goin'."

So we started to gallop to the oppersite sides of the flat when I heard a voice hollering: "Mister Elkins! Mister Elkins!"

"Hold on!" I says. "That's Joe Richardson."

Next minute Joe come tearing out of the bresh from the south on a mustang I hadn't never seen before, with a Mexican saddle and bridle on. He didn't have no hat nor shirt, and his back was criss-crossed with bloody streaks. He likewise had a cut in his sculp which dribbled blood down his face.

"Mexicans!" he panted. "I got separated from Ned and rode further'n I should ought to had. About five miles down the canyon I run into a big gang of Mexicans—about thirty of 'em. One was that feller Gomez. Their leader was a big feller they called Zamora.

"They grabbed me and taken my hoss, and whupped me with their quirts. Zamora said they was goin' to wipe out every white man in the canyon. He said his scouts had brung him news of our camp, and another'n east of our'n, and he aimed to destroy both of 'em at one sweep. Then they all got onto their hosses and headed north, except one man which I believe they left there to kill me before he follered 'em. He hit me with his sixshooter and knocked me down, and then put up his gun and started to cut my throat with his knife. But I wasn't unconscious like he thought, and I grabbed his gun and knocked him down with it, and jumped on his hoss and lit out. As I made for camp I heard you and this gent talkin' loud to each other, and headed this way."

"Which camp was they goin' for first?" I demanded.

"I dunno," he said. "They talked most in Spanish I can't understand."

"The duel'll have to wait," I says. "I'm headin' for our camp."

"And me for mine," says Bearfield. "Lissen: le's decide it this way: one that scuppers the most Mex hoss-thieves wins and t'other'n takes his crowd and pulls out!"

"Bueno!" I says, and headed for camp.

The trees was dense. Them bandits could of passed either to the west or the east of us without us seeing 'em. I quickly left Joe, and about a quarter of a mile further on I heard a sudden burst of firing and screaming, and then silence. A little bit later I bust out of the trees into sight of the camp, and I cussed earnestly. Instead of being drawed up in a circle, with the men shooting from between the wheels and holding them bandits off like I expected, them derned wagons was strung out like they was heading back north. The hosses was cut loose from some of 'em, and mules was laying acrost the poles of the others, shot full of lead. Women was screaming and kids was squalling, and I seen young Jack Richardson laying face down in the ashes of the campfire with his head in a puddle of blood.

Old Man Richardson come limping toward me with tears running down his face. "Mexicans!" he blubbered. "They hit us like a harrycane jest a little while ago! They shot Jack down like he was a dog! Three or four of the other boys is got knife slashes er bullet marks or bruises from loaded quirt-ends! As they rode off they yelled they'd come back and kill us all!"

"Why'n't you throw them wagons around like I told you?" I roared.

"We didn't want no fightin'!" he bawled. "We decided to pull out of the valley and find some more peaceful place—"

"And now Jack's dead and yore stock's scattered!" I raged. "Jest because you didn't want to fight! What the hell you ever cross the Pecos for if you didn't aim to fight nobody? Set the boys to gatherin' sech stock as you got left—"

"But them Mexicans taken Betty!" he shrieked, tearing his scanty locks. "Most of 'em headed east, but six or seven grabbed Betty right out of the wagon and rode off south with her, drivin' the hosses they stole from us!"

"Well, git yore weppins and foller me!" I roared. "For Lord's sake forgit they is places where sheriffs and policemen pertecks you, and make up yore minds to fight! I'm going after Betty."

I headed south as hard as Cap'n Kidd could run. The reason I hadn't met them Mexicans as I rode back from the flat where I met Cousin Bearfield was because they swung around the north end of the ridge when they headed east. I hadn't gone far when I heard a sudden burst of firing, off to the east, and figgered they'd hit the Illinois camp. But I reckoned Bearfield had got there ahead of 'em. Still, it didn't seem like the shooting was far enough off to be at the other camp. But I didn't have no time to study it.

Them gal-thieves had a big start, but it didn't do no good. I hadn't rode over three miles till I heard the stolen hosses running ahead of me, and in a minute I bust out into a open flat and seen six Mexicans driving them critters at full speed, and one of 'em was holdin' Betty on the saddle in front of him. It was that blasted Gomez.

I come swooping down onto 'em, with a six-shooter in my right hand and a bowie knife in my left. Cap'n Kidd needed no guiding. He'd smelt blood and fire and he come like a hurricane on Jedgement Day, with his name flying and his hoofs burning the grass.

The Mexicans seen I'd ride 'em down before they could get acrost the flat and they turnt to meet me, shooting as they come. But Mexicans always was rotten shots. As we come together I let bam three times with my .45, and: "Three!" says I.

One of 'em rode at me from the side and clubbed his rifle and hit at my head, but I ducked and made one swipe with my bowie. "Four!" says I. Then the others turnt and high-tailed it, letting the stolen hosses run where they wanted to. One of 'em headed south, but I was crowding Gomez so clost he whirled around and lit a shuck west.

"Keep back or I keel the girl!" he howled, lifting a knife, but I shot it out of his hand, and he give a yowl and let go of her and she fell off into the high grass. He kept fogging it.

I pulled up to see if Betty was hurt, but she warn't—jest scairt. The grass cushioned her fall. I seen her pap and sech of the boys as was able to ride was all comin' at a high run, so I left her to 'em and taken in after Gomez again. Purty soon he looked back and seen me overhauling him, so he reched for his Winchester which he'd evidently jest thought of using, when about that time his hoss stepped into a prairie dog hole and throwed him over his head. Gomez never twitched after he hit the ground. I turnt around and rode back, cussing disgustedly, because a Elkins is ever truthful, and I couldn't honestly count Gomez in my record.

But I thought I'd scuttle that coyote that run south, so I headed in that direction. I hadn't gone far when I heard a lot of hosses running somewheres ahead of me and to the east, and then presently I bust out of the trees and come onto a flat which run to the mouth of a narrer gorge opening into the main canyon.

On the left wall of this gorge-mouth they was a ledge about

fifty foot up, and they was a log cabin on that ledge with loop-holes in the walls. The only way up onto the ledge was a log ladder, and about twenty Mexicans was running their hosses toward it acrost the flat. Jest as I reched the aidge of the bushes, they got to the foot of the wall and jumped off their hosses and run up that ladder like monkeys, letting their hosses run any ways. I seen a big feller with gold ornaments on his sombrero which I figgered was Zamora, but before I could unlimber my Winchester they was all in the cabin and slammed the door.

The next minute Cousin Bearfield busted out of the trees a few hundred yards east of where I was and started recklessly acrost the flat. Imejitely all them Mexicans started shooting at him, and he grudgingly retired into the bresh again, with terrible language. I yelled, and rode toward him, keeping to the trees.

"How many you got?" he bellered as soon as he seen me.

"Four," I says, and he grinned like a timber wolf and says: "I got five! I was ridin' for my camp when I heard the shootin' behind me, and so I knowed it was yore camp they hit first. I turnt around to go back and help you out—"

"When did I ever ast you for any help?" I bristled, but he said: "But purty soon I seen a gang of Mexicans comin' around the north end of the ridge, so I taken cover and shot five of 'em out of their saddles. They must of knowed it was me, because they high-tailed it."

"How could they know that, you conceited jackass?" I snorted. "They run off because they probably thought a whole gang had ambushed 'em."

Old Man Richardson and his boys had rode up whilst we was talking, and now he broke in with some heat, and said: "That hain't the question! The p'int is we got 'em hemmed up on that ledge for the time bein', and can git away before they come down and massacre us."

"What you talkin' about?" I roared. "They're the ones which is in need of gittin' away. If any massacrein' is did around here, we does it!"

"It's flyin' in the face of Providence!" he bleated, but I told him sternly to shet up, and Bearfield says: "Send somebody over to my camp to bring my warriors," so I told Ned to go and he pulled out.

Then me and Bearfield studied the situation, setting our hosses in the open whilst bullets from the cabin whistled all around us, and the Richardsons hid in the bresh and begged us to be keerful.

"That ledge is sheer on all sides," says Bearfield. "Nobody couldn't climb down onto it from the cliff. And anybody tryin' to climb that ladder in the teeth of twenty Winchesters would be plum crazy."

But I says, "Look, Bearfield, how the ledge overhangs about ten foot to the left of that ladder. A man could stand at the foot of the bluff there and them coyotes couldn't see to shoot him."

"And," says Bearfield, "he could sling his rope up over that spur of rock at the rim, and they couldn't shoot it off. Only way to git to it would be to come out of the cabin and rech down and cut it with a knife. Door opens toward the ladder, and they ain't no door in the wall on that side. A man could climb right up onto the ledge before they knowed it—if they didn't shoot him through the loopholes as he come over the rim."

"You stay here and shoot 'em when they tries to cut the rope," I says.

"You go to hell!" he roared. "I see through yore hellish plot. You aims to git up there and kill all them Mexes before I has a chance at 'em. You thinks you'll outwit me! By golly, I got my rights, and—"

"Aw, shet up," I says disgustedly. "We'll both go." I hollered to Old Man Richardson: "You all lay low in the bresh and shoot at every Mex which comes outa the cabin."

"What you goin' to do now?" he hollered. "Don't be rash—"

But me and Bearfield was already headed for the ledge at a dead run.

This move surprised the Mexicans, because they knowed we couldn't figger to ride our hosses up that ladder. Being surprized they shot wild and all they done was graze my sculp and nick Bearfield's ear. Then, jest as they begun to get their range and started trimming us clost, we swerved aside and thundered in under the overhanging rock.

We clumb off and tied our hosses well apart, otherwise they'd of started fighting each other. The Mexicans above us was yelling most amazing but they couldn't even see us, much less shoot us. I whirled my lariat, which is plenty longer and stronger than the average lasso, and roped the spur of the rock which jutted up jest below the rim.

"I'll go up first," says I, and Bearfield showed his teeth and drawed his bowie knife.

"You won't neither!" says he. "We'll cut kyards! High man wins!"

So we squatted, and Old Man Richardson yelled from the trees:

"For God's sake, what are you doin' now? They're fixin' to roll rocks down onto you!"

"You tend to yore own business," I advised him, and shuffled the cards which Bearfield hauled out of his britches. As it turned out, the Mexes had a supply of boulders in the cabin. They just opened the door and rolled 'em toward the rim. But they shot off the ledge and hit beyond us.

Bearfield cut, and yelped: "A ace! You cain't beat that!"

"I can equal it," I says, and drawed a ace of diamonds.

"I wins!" he clamored. "Hearts beats diamonds!"

"That rule don't apply here," I says. "It war a draw, and—"

"Why, you—!" says Bearfield, leaning for'ard to grab the deck, and jest then a rock about the size of a bushel basket come bounding over the ledge and hit a projection which turnt its course, so instead of shooting over us, it fell straight down and hit Bearfield smack between the ears.

It stunned him for a instant, and I jumped up and started climbing the rope, ignoring more rocks which come thundering down. I was about half-way up when Bearfield come to, and he riz with a beller of rage. "Why, you dirty, double-crossin' so-and-so!" says he, and started throwing rocks at me.

They was a awful racket, the Mexicans howling, and guns banging, and Bearfield cussing, and Old Man Richardson wailing: "They're crazy, I tell you! They're both crazy as mudhens! I think everybody west of the Pecos must be maneyacks!"

Bearfield grabbed the rope and started climbing up behind me, and about that time one of the Mexicans run to cut the rope. But for onst my idiotic follerers was on the job. He run into about seven bullets that hit him all to onst, and fell down jest above the spur where the loop was caught onto.

So when I reched my arm over the rim to pull myself up they couldn't see me on account of the body. But jest as I was pulling myself up, they let go a boulder at random and it bounded along and bounced over the dead Mexican and hit me right smack in the face. It was about as big as a pumpkin.

I give a infuriated beller and swarmed up onto the ledge and it surprized 'em so that most of them missed me clean. I only got one slug through the arm. Before they had time to shoot again I made a jump to the wall and flattened myself between the loopholes, and grabbed the rifle barrels they poked through the loopholes and bent 'em and ruint 'em. Bearfield was coming up the rope right behind me, so I grabbed hold of the logs and tore that whole side of the wall out, and the roof fell in and the other walls come apart.

In an instant all you could see was logs falling and rolling and Mexicans busting out into the open. Some got pinned by the falling logs and some was shot by my embattled Kansans and Bearfield's Illinois warriors which had jest come up, and some fell offa the ledge and broke their fool necks.

One of 'em run agen me and tried to stab me so I throwed him after them which had already fell off the ledge, and hollered: "Five for me, Bearfield!"

"————!" says Bearfield, arriving onto the scene with blood in his eye and his bowie in his hand. Seeing which a big Mexican made for him with a butcher knife, which was pore jedgment on his part, and in about the flick of a mustang's tail Bearfield had a sixth man to his credit.

This made me mad. I seen some of the Mexicans was climbing down the ladder, so I run after 'em, and one turnt around and missed me so close with a shotgun he burnt my eyebrows. I taken it away from him and hit him over the head with it, and yelled: "Six for me, too, Cousin Bearfield!"

"Lookout!" he yelled. "Zamora's gittin' away!"

I seen Zamora had tied a rope to the back side of the ledge and was sliding down it. He dropped the last ten feet and run for a corral which was full of hosses back up the gorge, behind the ledge.

We seen the other Mexicans was all laid out or running off up the valley, persued by our immigrants, so I went down the ladder and Bearfield slid down my rope. Zamora's rope wouldn't of held our weight. We grabbed our hosses and lit out up the gorge, around a bend of which Zamora was jest disappearing.

He had a fast hoss and a long start, but I'd of overtook him within the first mile, only Cap'n Kidd kept trying to stop and fight Bearfield's hoss, which was about as big and mean as he was. After we'd run about five miles, and come out of the gorge onto a high plateau, I got far enough ahead of Bearfield so Cap'n Kidd forgot about his hoss, and then he settled down to business and run Zamora's hoss right off his laigs.

They was a steep slope on one side of us, and a five hundred drop on the other, and Zamora seen his hoss was winded, so he jumped off and started up the slope on foot. Me and Bearfield jumped off, too, and run after him. Each one of us got him by a laig as he was climbing up a ledge.

"Leggo my prisoner!" roared Bearfield.

"He's my meat," I snarled. "This makes me seven! I wins!"

"You lie!" bellered Bearfield, jerking Zamora away from me and hitting me over the head with him. This made me mad so I grabbed Zamora and throwed him in Bearfield's face. His spurs jabbed Bearfield in the belly, and my cousin give a maddened beller and fell on me fist and tush, and in the battle which follered we forgot all about Zamora till we heard a man scream. He'd snuck away and tried to mount Cap'n Kidd. We stopped fighting and looked around jest in time to see Cap'n Kidd kick him in the belly and knock him clean over the aidge of the cliff.

"Well," says Bearfield disgustedly, "that decides nothin', and our score is a draw."

"It was my hoss which done it," I said. "It oughta count for me."

"Over my corpse it will!" roared Bearfield. "But look here, it's nearly night. Le's git back to the camps before my follerers start cuttin' yore Kansans' throats. Whatever fight is to be fought to decide who owns the canyon, it's betwixt you and me, not them."

"All right," I said. "If my Kansas boys ain't already kilt all yore idjits, we'll fight this out somewhere where we got better light and more room. But I jest expect to find your Illinoisans writhin' in their gore."

"Don't worry about them," He snarled. "They're wild as painters when they smell gore. I only hope they ain't kilt all yore Kansas mavericks."

So we pulled for the valley. When we got there it was dark, and as we rode outa the gorge, we seen fires going on the flat, and folks dancing around 'em and fiddles was goin' at a great rate.

"What the hell is this?" bellered Bearfield, and then Old Man Richardson come up to us, overflowing with good spirits. "Glad to see you gents!" he says. "This is a great night! Jack warn't kilt, after all. Jest creased. We come out of that great fight whole and sound—"

"But what you doin'?" roared Bearfield. "What's my people doin' here?"

"Oh," says Old Man Richardson, "we got together after you gents left and agreed that the valley was big enough for both parties, so we decided to jine together into one settlement, and we're celebratin'. Them Illinois people is fine folks. They're as peace-lovin' as we are."

"Blood-thirsty painters!" I sneers to Cousin Bearfield.

"I ain't no bigger liar'n you air," he says, more in sorrer than in anger. "Come on. They ain't nothin' more we can do. We air swamped in a mess of pacifism. The race is degeneratin'. Le's head for Bear Creek. This atmosphere of brotherly love is more'n I can stand."

We set our hosses there a minnit and watched them pilgrims dance and listened to 'em singing. I squints across at Cousin Bearfield's face and doggoned if it don't look almost human in the firelight. He hauls out his plug of tobaccer and offers me first chaw. Then we headed yonderly, riding stirrup to stirrup.

Must of been ten miles before Cap'n Kidd retches over and bites Cousin Bearfield's hoss on the neck. Bearfield's hoss bites back, and by accident Cap'n Kidd kicks Cousin Bearfield on the ankle. He lets out a howl and thumps me over the head, and I hit him, and then we gits our arms around each other and roll in the bresh in a tangle.

We fit fer two hours, I reckon, and we'd been fighting yet if we hadn't scrambled under Cap'n Kidd's hoofs where he was feeding. He kicked Cousin Bearfield one way and me the other.

I got up after a while and went hunting for my hat. The bresh crackled, and in the moonlight I could see Cousin Bearfield on his hands and knees. "Whar air ye, Cousin Breckinridge?" says he. "Air you all right?"

Well, mebbe my clothes was tore more'n his was and a lip split and a rib or two busted, but I could still see, which was more'n he could say with both eyes swole that way. "Shore I'm all right," I says. "How air you, Cousin Bearfield?"

He let out a groan and tried to git up. He made 'er on the second heave and stood there swaying.

"Why, I'm fine," he says. "Plumb fine. I feel a whole lot better, Breck. I was afraid fer a minnit back there, whilst we was ridin' along, that that daggone brotherly love would turn out to be catchin'."

High Horse Rampage

I got a letter from Aunt Saragosa Grimes the other day which said.

Dear Breckinridge:

I believe time is softenin' yore Cousin Bearfield Buckner's feelings toward you. He was over here to supper the other night jest after he shot the three Evans boys, and he was in the best humor I seen him in since he got back from Colorado. So I jest kind of casually mentioned you and he didn't turn near as purple as he used to every time he heered yore name mentioned. He jest kind of got a little green around the years, and that might of been on account of him chokin' on the b'ar meat he was eatin'. And all he said was he was going to beat yore brains out with a post oak maul if he ever ketched up with you, which is the mildest remark he's made about you since he got back to Texas. I believe he's practically give up the idea of sculpin' you alive and leavin' you on a prairie for the buzzards with both laigs broke like he used to swear was his sole ambition. I believe in a year or so it would be safe for you to meet dear Cousin Bearfield, and if you do have to shoot him, I hope you'll be broadminded and shoot him in some place which ain't vital because after all you know it was yore fault to begin with. We air all well and nothin's happened to speak of except Joe Allison got a arm broke argyin' politics with Cousin Bearfield. Hopin' you air the same, I begs to remane,
Yore lovin' Ant Saragosa.

It's heartening to know a man's kin is thinking kindly of him and forgetting pretty grudges. But I can see that Bearfield is been misrepresenting things and pizening Aunt Saragosa's mind agen

240

me, otherwise she wouldn't of made that there remark about it being my fault. All fair-minded men knows that what happened warn't my fault—that is all except Bearfield, and he's naturally prejudiced, because most of it happened to him.

I knowed Bearfield was somewheres in Colorado when I j'ined up with Old Man Brant Mulholland to make a cattle drive from the Pecos to the Platte, but that didn't have nothing to do with it. I expects to run into Bearfield almost any place where the licker is red and the shotguns is sawed-offs. He's a liar when he says I come into the High Horse Country a-purpose to wreck his life and ruin his career.

Everything I done to him was in kindliness and kindredly affection. But he ain't got no gratitude. When I think of the javelina meat I et and the bare-footed bandits I had to associate with whilst living in Old Mexico to avoid having to kill that wuthless critter, his present attitude embitters me.

I never had no notion of visiting High Horse in the first place. But we run out of grub a few miles north of there, so what does Old Man Mulholland do but rout me outa my blankets before daylight, and says, "I want you to take the chuck wagon to High Horse and buy some grub. Here's fifty bucks. If you spends a penny of that for anything but bacon, beans, flour, salt and coffee, I'll have yore life, big as you be."

"Why'n't you send the cook?" I demanded.

"He's layin' helpless in a chaparral thicket reekin' with the fumes of vaniller extract," says Old Man Mulholland. "Anyway, yo're responsible for this famine. But for yore inhuman appetite we'd of had enough grub to last the whole drive. Git goin'. Yo're the only man in the string I trust with money and I don't trust you no further'n I can heave a bull by the tail."

Us Elkinses is sensitive about sech remarks, but Old Man Mulholland was born with a conviction that everybody is out to swindle him, so I maintained a dignerfied silence outside of tellin' him to go to hell, and harnessed the mules to the chuck wagon and headed for Antioch. I led Cap'n Kidd behind the wagon because I knowed if I left him unguarded he'd kill every he-hoss in the camp before I got back.

Well, jest as I come to the forks where the trail to Gallego splits off of the High Horse road, I heard somebody behind me thumping a banjer and singing, "Oh, Nora he did build the Ark!" So I pulled up and purty soon around the bend come the derndest looking rig I'd saw since the circus come to War Paint.

It was a buggy all painted red, white and blue and drawed by a couple of wall-eyed pintos. And they was a feller in it with a long-tailed coat and a plug hat and fancy checked vest, and a cross-eyed negro playing a banjer, with a monkey settin' on his shoulder.

The white man taken off his plug hat and made me a bow, and says, "Greetings, my mastodonic friend! Can you inform me which of these roads leads to the fair city of High Horse?"

"That's leadin' south," I says. "T'other'n goes east to Gallego. Air you all part of a circus?"

"I resents the implication," says he. "In me you behold the greatest friend to humanity since the inventor of corn licker. I am Professor Horace J. Lattimer, inventor and sole distributor of that boon to suffering humanity, Lattimer's Lenitive Loco Elixir, good for man or beast!"

He then h'isted a jug out from under the seat and showed it to me and a young feller which had jest rode up along the road from Gallego.

"A sure cure," says he. "Have you a hoss which has nibbled the seductive locoweed? That huge brute you've got tied to the end-gate there looks remarkable wild in his eye, now—"

"He ain't loco," I says. "He's jest bloodthirsty."

"Then I bid you both a very good day, sirs," says he. "I must be on my way to allay the sufferings of mankind. I trust we shall meet in High Horse."

So he drove on, and I started to cluck to the mules, when the young feller from Gallego, which has been eyeing me very cose, he says, "Ain't you Breckinridge Elkins?"

When I says I was, he says with some bitterness, "That there perfessor don't have to go to High Horse to find locoed critters. They's a man in Gallego right now, crazy as a bedbug—yore own cousin, Bearfield Buckner!"

"What?" says I with a vi'lent start, because they hadn't been no insanity in the family before, only Bearfield's great-grand-uncle Esau who onst voted agen Hickory Jackson. But he recovered before the next election.

"It's the truth," says the young feller. "He's sufferin' from a hallucination that he's going to marry a gal over to High Horse by the name of Ann Wilkins. They ain't even no gal by that name there. He was havin' a fit in the saloon when I left, me not bearin' to look on the rooins of a onst noble character. I'm feared he'll do hisself a injury if he ain't restrained."

"Hell's fire!" I said in great agitation. "Is this the truth?"

"True as my name's Lem Campbell," he declared. "I thought bein' as how yo're a relation of his'n, if you could kinda git him out to my cabin a few miles south of Gallego, and keep him there a few days maybe he might git his mind back—"

"I'll do better'n that," I says, jumping out of the wagon and tying the mules. "Foller me," I says, forking Cap'n Kidd. The Perfessor's buggy was jest going out of sight around a bend, and I lit out after it. I was well ahead of Lem Campbell when I overtaken it. I pulled up beside it in a cloud of dust and demanded, "You say that stuff kyores man or beast?"

"Absolutely!" declared Lattimer.

"Well, turn around and head for Gallego," I said. "I got you a patient."

"But Gallego is but a small inland village," he demurs. "There is a railroad and many saloons at High Horse and—"

"With a human reason at stake you sets and maunders about railroads!" I roared, drawing a .45 and impulsively shooting a few buttons off of his coat. "I buys yore whole load of loco licker. Turn around and head for Gallego."

"I wouldn't think of arguing," says he, turning pale. "Meshak, don't you hear the gentleman? Get out from under that seat and turn these hosses around."

"Yes, suh!" says Meshak, and they swung around jest as Lem Campbell galloped up.

I hauled out the wad Old Man Mulholland gimme and says to him, "Take this dough on to High Horse and buy some grub and have it sent out to Old Man Mulholland's cow camp on the Little Yankton. I'm goin' to Gallego and I'll need the wagon to lug Cousin Bearfield in."

"I'll take the grub out myself," he declared, grabbing the wad. "I knowed I could depend on you as soon as I seen you."

So he told me how to get to his cabin, and then lit out for High Horse and I headed back up the trail. When I passed the buggy I hollered, "Foller me into Gallego. One of you drive the chuck wagon which is standin' at the forks. And don't try to shake me as soon as I git out of sight, neither!"

"I wouldn't think of such a thing," says Lattimer with a slight shudder. "Go ahead and fear not. We'll follow you as fast as we can."

So I dusted the trail for Gallego.

It warn't much of a town, with only jest one saloon, and as I rode in I heard a beller in the saloon and the door flew open and three or four fellows come sailing out on their heads and picked themselves up and tore out up the street.

"Yes," I says to myself, "Cousin Bearfield is in town, all right."

Gallego looked about like any town does when Bearfield is celebrating. The stores had their doors locked and the shutters up, nobody was on the streets, and off down across the flat I seen a man which I taken to be the sheriff spurring his hoss for the hills. I tied Cap'n Kidd to the hitch-rail and as I approached the saloon I nearly fell over a feller which was crawling around on his all-fours with a bartender's apron on and both eyes swelled shet.

"Don't shoot!" says he. "I give up!"

"What happened?" I ast.

"The last thing I remember is tellin' a feller named Buckner that the Democratic platform was silly," says he. "Then I think the roof must of fell in or somethin'. Surely one man couldn't of did all this to me."

"You don't know my cousin Bearfield," I assured him as I stepped over him and went through the door which was tore off its hinges. I'd begun to think that maybe Lem Campbell had exaggerated about Bearfield; he seemed to be acting in jest his ordinary normal manner. But a instant later I changed my mind.

Bearfield was standing at the bar in solitary grandeur, pouring hisself a drink, and he was wearing the damnedest-looking red, yaller, green and purple shirt ever I seen in my life.

"What," I demanded in horror, "is that thing you got on?"

"If yo're referrin' to my shirt," he retorted with irritation, "it's the classiest piece of goods I could find in Denver. I bought it special for my weddin'."

"It's true!" I moaned. "He's crazy as hell."

I knowed no sane man would wear a shirt like that.

"What's crazy about gittin' married?" he snarled, biting the neck off of a bottle and taking a big snort. "Folks does it every day."

I walked around him cautious, sizing him up and down, which seemed to exasperate him considerable.

"What the hell's the matter with you?" he roared, hitching his harness for'ard. "I got a good mind to—"

"Be ca'm, Cousin Bearfield," I soothed him. "Who's this gal you imagine yo're goin' to marry?"

"I don't imagine nothin' about it, you ignerant ape," he retorts cantankerously. "Her name's Ann Wilkins and she lives in High Horse. I'm ridin' over there right away and we gits hitched today."

I shaken my head mournful and said, "You must of inherited this from yore great-grand-uncle Esau. Pap's always said Esau's insanity might crop out in the Buckners again some time. But don't worry. Esau was kyored and voted a straight Democratic ticket the rest of his life. You can be kyored too, Bearfield, and I'm here to do it. Come with me, Bearfield," I says, getting a good rassling grip on his neck.

"Consarn it!" says Cousin Bearfield, and went into action.

We went to the floor together and started rolling in the general direction of the back door and every time he come up on top he'd bang my head agen the floor which soon became very irksome. However, about the tenth revolution I come up on top, and pried my thumb out of his teeth and said, "Bearfield, I don't want to have to use force with you, but—ulp!" That was account of him kicking me in the back of the neck.

My motives was of the loftiest, and they warn't no use in the saloon owner bellyaching the way he done afterwards. Was it my fault if Bearfield missed me with a five-gallon demijohn and busted the mirror behind the bar? Could I help it if Bearfield wrecked the billiard table when I knocked him through it? As for the stove which got busted, all I got to say is that self-preservation is the first law of nature. If I hadn't hit Bearfield with the stove he would of ondoubtedly scrambled my features with that busted beer mug he was trying to use like brass knuckles.

I've heard maniacs fight awful, but I dunno as Bearfield fit any different than usual. He hadn't forgot his old trick of hooking his spur in my neck whilst we was rolling around on the floor, and when he knocked me down with the roulette wheel and started jumping on me with both feet I thought for a minute I was going to weaken. But the shame of having a maniac in the family revived me and I throwed him off and riz and tore up a section of the brass foot-rail and wrapped it around his head. Cousin Bearfield dropped the bowie he'd jest drawed and collapsed.

I wiped the blood off of my face and discovered I could still see outa one eye. I pried the brass rail off of Cousin Bearfield's head and dragged him out onto the porch by a hind laig, jest as Perfessor Lattimer drove up in his buggy. Meshak was behind him in the chuck wagon with the monkey, and his eyes was as big and white as saucers.

"Where's the patient?" ast Lattimer, and I said, "This here's him! Throw me a rope outa that wagon. We takes him to Lem Campbell's cabin where we can dose him till he recovers his reason."

Quite a crowd gathered whilst I was tying him up, and I don't believe Cousin Bearfield had many friends in Gallego by the remarks they made. When I lifted his limp carcass up into the wagon one of 'em ast me if I was a lawman. And when I said I warn't, purty short, he says to the crowd, "Why, hell, then, boys, what's to keep us from payin' Buckner back for all the lickins he's give us? I tell you, it's our chance! He unconscious and tied up, and this here feller ain't no sheriff."

"Git a rope!" howled somebody. "We'll hang 'em."

They begun to surge for'ards, and Lattimer and Meshak was so scairt they couldn't hardly hold the lines. But I mounted my hoss and pulled my pistols and says, "Meshak, swing that chuck wagon and head south. Perfessor, you foller him. Hey, you, git away from them mules!"

One of the crowd had tried to grab their bridles and stop 'em, so I shot a heel off'n his boot and he fell down hollering bloody murder.

"Git outa the way!" I bellered, swinging my pistols on the crowd, and they give back in a hurry. "Git goin'," I says, firing some shots under the mules' feet to encourage 'em, and the chuck wagon went out of Gallego jumping and bouncing with Meshak holding onto the seat and hollering blue ruin, and the Perfessor come right behind it in his buggy. I follered the Perfessor, looking back to see nobody didn't shoot me in the back, because several men had drawed their pistols. But nobody fired till I was out of good pistol range. Then somebody let loose with a buffalo rifle, but he missed me by at least a foot, so I paid no attention to it, and we was soon out of sight of the town.

I was afeared Bearfield might come to and scare the mules with his bellering, but that brass rail must of been harder'n I thought. He was still unconscious when we pulled up to the cabin which stood in a little wooded cove amongst the hills a few miles south of Gallego. I told Meshak to onhitch the mules and turn 'em into the corral whilst I carried Bearfield into the cabin and laid him on a bunk. I told Lattimer to bring in all the elixir he had, and he brung ten gallons in one-gallon jugs. I give him all the money I had to pay for it.

Purty soon Bearfield come to and he raised his head and looked at Perfessor Lattimer settin' on the bunk opposite him in his long tailed coat and plug hat, cross-eyed Meshak and the monkey settin' beside him. Bearfield batted his eyes and says, "My God, I must be crazy. That can't be real!"

"Sure, yo're crazy, Cousin Bearfield," I soothed him. "But

don't worry. We're goin' to kyore you—"

Bearfield here interrupted me with a yell that turned Meshak the color of a fish's belly.

"Untie me, you son of Perdition!" he roared, heaving and flopping on the bunk like a python with the belly-ache, straining agen his ropes till the veins knotted blue on his temples. "I oughta be in High Horse right now gittin' married—"

"See there?" I sighed to Lattimer. "It's a sad case. We better start dosin' him right away. Git a drenchin' horn. What size dose do you give?"

"A quart at a shot for a hoss," he says doubtfully. "But—"

"We'll start out with that," I says. "We can increase the size of the dose if we need to."

Ignoring Bearfield's terrible remarks I was jest twisting the cork out of a jug when I heard somebody say, "What the hell air you doin' in my shack?"

I turned around and seen a bow-legged critter with drooping whiskers glaring at me kinda pop-eyed from the door.

"What you mean, yore shack?" I irritated at the interruption. "This shack belongs to a friend of mine which has lent it to us."

"Yo're drunk or crazy," says he, clutching at his whiskers convulsively. "Will you git out peaceable or does I have to git vi'lent?"

"Oh, a cussed claim-jumper, hey?" I snorted, taken his gun away from him when he drawed it. But he pulled a bowie so I throwed him out of the shack and shot into the dust around him a few times jest for warning.

"I'll git even with you, you big lummox!" he howled, as he ran for a scrawny looking sorrel he had tied to the fence. "I'll fix you yet," he promised blood-thirstily as he galloped off, shaking his fist at me.

"Who do you suppose he was?" wondered Lattimer, kinda shaky, and I says, "What the hell does it matter? Forgit the incident and help me give Cousin Bearfield his medicine."

That was easier said than did. Tied up as he was, it was all we could do to get that there elixir down him. I thought I never would get his jaws pried open, using the poker for a lever, but when he opened his mouth to cuss me, we jammed the horn in before he could close it. He left the marks of his teeth so deep on that horn it looked like it'd been in a b'ar-trap.

He kept on heaving and kicking till we'd poured a full dose down him and then he kinda stiffened out and his eyes went glassy.

When we taken the horn out of his jaws, they worked but didn't make no sound. But the Perfessor said hosses always acted like that when they'd had a good healthy shot of the remedy, so we left Meshak to watch him, and me and Lattimer went out and sot down on the stoop to rest and cool off.

"Why ain't Meshak onhitched yore buggy?" I ast.

"You mean you expect us to stay here over night?" says he, aghast.

"Over night, hell!" says I. "You stays till he's kyored, if it takes a year. You may have to make up some more medicine if this ain't enough."

"You mean to say we got to rassle with that maniac three times a day like we just did?" squawked Lattimer.

"Maybe he won't be so vi'lent when the remedy takes holt," I encouraged him. Lattimer looked like he was going to choke, but jest then inside the cabin sounds a yell that even made my hair stand up. Cousin Bearfield had found his voice again.

We jumped up and Meshak come out of the cabin so fast he knocked Lattimer out into the yard and fell over him. The monkey was right behind him streaking it like his tail was on fire.

"Oh, lawdy!" yelled Meshak, heading for the tall timber. "Dat crazy man am bustin' dem ropes like dey was twine. He gwine kill us all, sho!"

I run into the shack and seen Cousin Bearfield rolling around on the floor and cussing amazing, even for him. And to my horror I seen he'd busted some of the ropes so his left arm was free. I pounced on it, but for a few minutes all I was able to do was jest to hold onto it whilst he throwed me hither and thither around the room with freedom and abandon. At last I kind of wore him down and got his arm tied again jest as Lattimer run in and done a snake dance all over the floor.

"Meshak's gone," he howled. "He was so scared he run off with the monkey and my buggy and team. It's all your fault."

Being too winded to argy I jest heaved Bearfield up on the bunk and staggered over and sot down on the other'n, whilst the Perfessor pranced and whooped and swore I owed him for his buggy and team.

"Listen," I said when I'd got my wind back. "I spent all my money for that elixir, but when Bearfield recovers his reason he'll be so grateful he'll be glad to pay you hisself. Now forgit sech sordid trash as money and devote yore scientific knowledge to gittin' Bearfield sane."

"Sane!" howls Bearfield. "Is that what yo're doin'—tyin' me

up and pizenin' me? I've tasted some awful muck in my life, but I never drempt nothin' could taste as bad as that stuff you poured down me. It plumb paralyzes a man. Lemme loose, dammit."

"Will you be ca'm if I onties you?"

"I will," he promised heartily, "jest as soon as I've festooned the surroundin' forest with yore entrails!"

"Still vi'lent," I said sadly. "We better keep him tied, Perfessor."

"But I'm due to git married in High Horse right now!" Bearfield yelled, giving sech a convulsive heave that he throwed hisself clean offa the bunk. It was his own fault, and they warn't no use in him later blaming me because he hit his head on the floor and knocked hisself stiff.

"Well," I said, "at least we'll have a few minutes of peace and quiet around here. Help me lift him back on his bunk."

"What's that?" yelped the Perfessor, jumping convulsively as a rifle cracked out in the bresh and a bullet whined through the cabin.

"That's probably Droopin' Whiskers," I says, lifting Cousin Bearfield. "I thought I seen a Winchester on his saddle. Say, it's gittin' late. See if you cain't find some grub in the kitchen. I'm hungry."

Well, the Perfessor had an awful case of the willies, but we found some bacon and beans in the shack and cooked 'em and et 'em, and fed Bearfield, which had come to when he smelt the grub cooking. I don't think Lattimer enjoyed his meal much because every time a bullet hit the shack he jumped and choked on his grub. Drooping Whiskers was purty persistent, but he was so far back in the bresh he wasn't doing no damage. He was a rotten shot anyhow. All of his bullets was away too high, as I p'inted out to Lattimer, but the Perfessor warn't happy.

I didn't dare untie Bearfield to let him eat, so I made Lattimer set by him and feed him with a knife, and he was scairt and shook so he kept spilling hot beans down Bearfield's collar, and Bearfield's langwidge was awful to hear.

Time we got through it was long past dark, and Drooping Whiskers had quit shooting at us. As it later appeared, he'd run out of ammunition and gone to borrow some ca'tridges from a ranch house some miles away. Bearfield had quit cussing us, he jest laid there and glared at us with the most horrible expression I ever seen on a human being. It made Lattimer's hair stand up.

But Bearfield kept working at his ropes and I had to examine 'em every little while and now and then put some new ones on him. So I told Lattimer we better give him another dose, and when we finally got it down him, Lattimer staggered into the kitchen and collapsed under the table and I was as near wore out myself as a Elkins can get.

But I didn't dare sleep for fear Cousin Bearfield would get loose and kill me before I could wake up. I sot down on the other bunk and watched him and after a while he went to sleep and I could hear the Perfessor snoring out in the kitchen.

About midnight I lit a candle and Bearfield woke up and said, "Blast yore soul, you done woke me up out of the sweetest dream I ever had. I drempt I was fishin' for sharks off Mustang Island."

"What's sweet about that?" I ast.

"I was usin' you for bait," he said. "Hey, what you doin'?"

"It's time for yore dose," I said, and then the battle started. This time he got my thumb in his mouth and would ondoubtedly have chawed it off if I hadn't kind of stunned him with the iron skillet. Before he could recover hisself I had the elixir down him with the aid of Lattimer which had been woke up by the racket.

"How long is this going on?" Lattimer ast despairingly. "Ow!"

It was Drooping Whiskers again. This time he'd crawled up purty clost to the house and his first slug combed the Perfessor's hair.

"I'm a patient man but I've reached my limit," I snarled, blowing out the candle and grabbing a shotgun off the wall. "Stay here and watch Bearfield whilst I go out and hang Droopin' Whiskers' hide to the nearest tree."

I snuck out of the cabin on the opposite side from where the shot come from, and begun to sneak around in a circle through the bresh. The moon was coming up, and I knowed I could out-Injun Droopin Whiskers. Any Bear Creek man could. Sure enough, purty soon I slid around a clump of bushes and seen him bending over behind a thicket whilst he took aim at the cabin with a Winchester. So I emptied both barrels into the seat of his britches and he give a most amazing howl and jumped higher'n I ever seen a bowlegged feller jump, and dropped his Winchester and taken out up the trail toward the north.

I was determined to run him clean off the range this time, so I pursued him and shot at him every now and then, but the dern gun was loaded with bird-shot and all the shells I'd grabbed along with it was the same. I never seen a white man run like he did. I never got clost enough to do no real damage to him, and after I'd chased him a mile or so he turned off into the bresh, and I soon lost him.

Well, I made my way back to the road again, and was jest fixing to step out of the bresh and start down the road toward the cabin, when I heard hosses coming from the north. So I stayed behind a bush, and purty soon a gang of men come around the bend, walking their hosses, with the moonlight glinting on Winchesters in their hands.

"Easy now," says one. "The cabin ain't far down the road. We'll ease up and surroun it before they know what's happenin'."

"I wonder what the shootin' was we heered a while back?" says another'n kind of nervous.

"Maybe they was fightin' amongst theirselves," says yet another'n. "No matter. We'll rush in and settle the big feller's hash before he knows what's happenin'. Then we'll string Buckner up."

"What you reckon they kidnapped Buckner for?" some feller begun, but I waited for no more. I riz up from behind the bushes and the hosses snorted and reared.

"Hang a helpless man because he licked you in fair fight, hey?" I bellowed, and let go both barrels amongst 'em.

They was riding so clost-grouped I don't think I missed any of 'em. The way they hollered was disgusting to hear. The hosses was scairt at the flash and roar right in their faces and they wheeled and bolted, and the whole gang went thundering up the road a dern sight faster than they'd come. I sent a few shots after 'em with my pistols, but they didn't shoot back, and purty soon the weeping and wailing died away in the distance. A fine mob they turned out to be!

But I thought they might come back, so I sot down behind a bush where I could watch the road from Gallego. And the first thing I knowed I went to sleep in spite of myself.

When I woke up it was jest coming daylight. I jumped up and grabbed my guns, but nobody was in sight. I guess them Gallego gents had got a bellyful. So I headed for the cabin and when I got there the corral was empty and the chuck wagon gone!

I started on a run for the shack and then I seen a note stuck on the corral fence. I grabbed it. It said—

Dear Elkins:

This strain is too much for me. I'm getting white-haired sitting and watching this devil laying there glaring at me, and wondering all the time how soon he'll bust loose. I'm pulling out. I'm taking the chuck wagon and team in payment for my rig that Meshak ran off with. I'm leaving the elixir but I doubt

if it'll do Buckner any good. It's for locoed critters, not homicidal maniacs.

                              Respectfully yours
                              Horace J. Lattimer, Esquire

"Hell's fire," I said wrathfully, starting for the shack.

I dunno how long it had took Bearfield to wriggle out of his
ropes. Anyway he was laying for me behind the door with the iron
skillet and if the handle hand't broke off when he lammed me over
the head with it he might of did me a injury.

I dunno how I ever managed to throw him, because he fit like
a frothing maniac, and every time he managed to break loose from
me he grabbed a jug of Lattimer's Loco Elixir and busted it over
my head. By the time I managed to stun him with a table laig
he'd busted every jug on the place, the floor was swimming in
elixir, and my clothes was soaked in it whar they wasn't soaked
with blood.

I fell on him and tied him up again and then sot on a bunk and
tried to get my breath back and wondered what in hell to do.
Because here the elixir was all gone and I didn't have no way of
treating Bearfield and the Perfessor had run off with the chuck
wagon so I hadn't no way to get him back to civilization.

Then all at onst I heard a train whistle, away off to the west,
and remembered that the track passed through jest a few miles to
the south. I'd did all I could for Bearfield, only thing I could do
now was to get him back to his folks where they could take care
of him.

I run out and whistled for Cap'n Kidd and he busted out from
around the corner of the house where he'd been laying for me,
and tried to kick me in the belly before I could get ready for him,
but I warn't fooled. He's tried that trick too many times. I dodged
and give him a good bust in the nose, and then I throwed the bridle
and saddle on him, and brung Cousin Bearfield out and throwed
him acrost the saddle and headed south.

That must of been the road both Meshak and Lattimer taken
when they run off. It crossed the railroad track about three miles
from the shack. The train had been whistling for High Horse when
I first heard it. I got to the track before it come into sight. I flagged
it and it pulled up and the train crew jumped down and wanted to
know what the hell I was stopping them for.

"I got a man here which needs medical attention," I says. "It's
a case of temporary insanity. I'm sendin' him back to Texas."

"Hell," says they, "this train don't go nowheres near Texas."

"Well," I says, "you unload him at Dodge City. He's got plenty of friends there which will see that he gits took care of. I'll send word from High Horse to his folks in Texas tellin' 'em to go after him."

So they loaded Cousin Bearfield on, him being still unconscious, and I give the conductor his watch and chain and pistol to pay for his fare. Then I headed along the track for High Horse.

When I got to High Horse I tied Cap'n Kidd nigh the track and started for the depot when who should I run smack into but Old Man Mulholland who immejitly give a howl like a hungry timber wolf.

"Whar's the grub, you hoss-thief?" he yelled before I could say nothing.

"Why, didn't Lem Campbell bring it out to you?" I ast.

"I never seen a man by that name," he bellered. "Whar's my fifty bucks?"

"Heck," I says, "he looked honest."

"Who?" yowled Old Man Mulholland. "Who, you polecat?"

"Lem Campbell, the man I give the dough to for him to buy the grub," I says. "Oh, well, never mind. I'll work out the fifty."

The Old Man looked like he was fixing to choke. He gurgled, "Whar's my chuck wagon?"

"A feller stole it," I said. "But I'll work that out too."

"You won't work for me," foamed the Old Man, pulling a gun. "Yo're fired. And as for the dough and the wagon, I takes them out of yore hide here and now."

Well, I taken the gun away from him, of course, and tried to reason with him, but he jest hollered that much louder, and got his knife out and made a pass at me. Now it always did irritate me for somebody to stick a knife in me, so I taken it away from him and throwed him into a nearby hoss trough. It was one of these here V-shaped troughs which narrers together at the bottom, and somehow his fool head got wedged and he was about to drown.

Quite a crowd had gathered and they tried pulling him out by the hind laigs but his feet was waving around in the air so wild that every time anybody tried to grab him they got spurred in the face. So I went over to the trough and taken hold of the sides and tore it apart. He fell out and spit up maybe a gallon of water. And the first words he was able to say he accused me of trying to drownd him on purpose, which shows how much gratitude people has got.

But a man spoke up and said, "Hell, the big feller didn't do it on purpose. I was right here and I seen it all."

And another'n said, "I seen it as good as you did, and the big feller did try to drownd him, too!"

"Air you callin' me a liar?" said the first feller, reaching for his gun.

But jest then another man chipped in and said, "I dunno what the argyment's about, but I bet a dollar you're both wrong!"

And then some more fellers butted in and everybody started cussing and hollering till it nigh deefened me. Someone else reaches for a gun and I seen that as soon as one feller shoots another there is bound to be trouble so I started to gentle the first feller by hitting him over the head. The next thing I know someone hollers at me, "You big hyeener!" And tries to ruint me with a knife. Purty soon there is hitting and shooting all over the town. High Horse is sure on the rampage.

I jest had finished blunting my Colts on a varmint's haid when I thinks disgustedly, "Heck, Breckinridge, you came to this town on a mission of good will! You got business to do. You got yore poor family to think about."

I started to go on to the depot but I heard a familiar voice screech above the racket. "There he is, Sheriff! Arrest the dern' claim-jumper!"

I whirled around quick and there was Drooping Whiskers, a saddle blanket wropped around him like a Injun and walking purty spraddle-legged. He was p'inting at me and hollering like I'd did something to him.

Everybody else quieted down for a minute, and he hollered, "Arrest him, dern him. He throwed me out of my own cabin and ruint my best pants with my own shotgun. I been to Knife River and come back several days quicker'n I aimed to, and there this big hyener was in charge of my shack. He was too dern big for me to handle, so I come to High Horse after the sheriff—soon as I got three or four hundred bird-shot picked out of my hide."

"What you got to say about this?" ast the sheriff, kinda uncertain, like he warn't enjoying his job for some reason or other.

"Why, hell," I says disgustedly. "I throwed this varmint out of a cabin, sure, and later peppered his anatomy with bird shot. But I was in my rights. I was in a cabin which had been loaned me by a man named Lem Campbell—"

"Lem Campbell!" shrieked Drooping Whiskers, jumping up and down so hard he nigh lost the blanket he was wearing instead of britches. "That wuthless critter ain't got no cabin. He was workin' for me till I fired him jest before I started for Knife River, for bein' so triflin'."

"Hell's fire!" I says, shocked. "Ain't there no honesty any more? Shucks, stranger, it looks like the joke's on me."

At this Drooping Whiskers collapsed into the arms of his friends with a low moan, and the sheriff says to me uncomfortably, "Don't take this personal, but I'm afeared I'll have to arrest you, if you don't mind—"

Jest then a train whistled away off to the east, and somebody said, "What the hell, they ain't no train from the east this time of day!"

Then the depot agent run out of the depot waving his arms and yelling, "Git them cows off'n the track! I jest got a flash from Knife River, the train's comin' back. A maniac named Buckner busted loose and made the crew turn her around at the switch. Orders' gone down the line to open the track all the way. She's comin' uner full head of steam. Nobody knows where Buckner's takin' her. He's lookin' for some relative of his'n!"

There was a lot of noise comin' down that track and all of it warn't the noise that a steam-ingine makes by itself. No, thet noise was a different noise all right. That noise was right familiar to me. It struck a chord in my mind and made me wonder kinda what happened to them trainmen.

"Can that be Bearfield Buckner?" wondered a woman. "It sounds like him. Well, if it is, he's too late to git Ann Wilkins."

"What?" I yelled. "Is they a gal in this town named Ann Wilkins?"

"They was," she snickered. "She was to marry this Buckner man yesterday, but never showed up, and when her old beau, Lem Campbell, come along with fifty dollars he'd got some place, she up and married him and they lit out for San Francisco on their honeymoon—Why, what's the matter, young man? You look right green in the face. Maybe it's somethin' you et—"

It weren't nothin' I et. It was the thoughts I was thinkin'. Here I hed gone au' ruint Cousin Bearfield's whole future. And outa kindness. Thet's what busted me wide open. I had ruint Cousin Bearfield's future out of kindness. My motives had been of the loftiest, I hed tried to kyore an hombre what was loco from goin' locoer yet, and what was my reward? Jest thet moment I looks up and I seen a cloud of smoke a puffin' down the track and they is a roarin' like the roarin' of a herd of catamounts.

"Here she comes around the bend," yelled somebody. "She's burnin' up the track. Listen at that whistle. Jest bustin' it wide open."

But I was already astraddle of Cap'n Kidd and traveling. The man which says I'm scairt of Bearfield is a liar. A Elkins fears neither man, beast nor Buckner. But I seen that Lem Campbell had worked me into getting Bearfield out of his way, and if I waited till Bearfield got there, I'd have to kill him or get killed, and I didn't crave to do neither.

I headed south jest to save Cousin Bearfield's life, and I didn't stop till I was in Durango. Let me tell you the revolution I got mixed up in there was a plumb restful relief after my association with Cousin Bearfield.

The Apache Mountain War

Some day, maybe, when I'm old and gray in the whiskers, I'll have sense enough not to stop when I'm riding by Uncle Shadrach Polk's cabin, and Aunt Tascosa Polk hollers at me. Take the last time, for instance. I ought to of spurred Cap'n Kidd into a high run when she stuck her head out'n the winder and yelled: "Breckinridge! Oh, Breckinriddggge!"

But I reckon pap's right when he says Nater gimme so much muscle she didn't have no room left for brains. Anyway, I reined Cap'n Kidd around, ignoring his playful efforts to bite the muscle out of my left thigh, and I rode up to the stoop and taken off my coonskin-cap. I said: "Well, Aunt Tascosa, how air you all?"

"You may well ast how air we," she said bitterly. "How should a pore weak woman be farin' with a critter like Shadrach for a husband? It's a wonder I got a roof over my head, or so much as a barr'l of b'ar meat put up for the winter. The place is goin' to rack and rooin. Look at that there busted axe-handle, for a instance. Is a pore weak female like me got to endure sech abuse?"

"You don't mean to tell me Uncle Shadrach's been beatin' you with that axe-handle?" I says, scandalized.

"No," says this pore weak female. "I busted it over his head a week ago, and he's refused to mend it. It's licker is been Shadrach's rooin. When he's sober he's a passable figger of a man, as men go. But swiggin' blue rooin is brung him to shame an' degradation."

"He looks fat and sassy," I says.

"Beauty ain't only skin-deep," she scowls. "Shadrach's like

Dead Sea fruit—fair and fat-bellied to look on, but ready to dissolve in dust and whiskey fumes when prodded. Do you know whar he is right now?" And she glared at me so accusingly that Cap'n Kidd recoiled and turned pale.

"Naw," says I. "Whar?"

"He's over to the Apache Mountain settlement a-lappin' up licker," she snarled. "Just a-rootin' and a-wallerin' in sin and corn juice, riskin' his immortal soul and blowin' in the money he got off'n his coon hides. I had him locked in the corn crib, aimin' to plead with him and appeal to his better nater, but whilst I was out behind the corral cuttin' me a hickory club to do the appealin' with, he kicked the door loose and snuk out. I know whar he's headin'—to Joel Garfield's stillhouse, which is a abomination in the sight of the Lord and oughta be burnt to the ground and the ashes skwenched with the blood of the wicked. But I cain't stand here listenin' to yore gab. I got hominy to make. What you mean wastin' my time like this for? I got a good mind to tell yore pap on you. You light a shuck for Apache Mountain and bring Shadrach home."

"But—" I said.

"Don't you give me no argyments, you imperdent scoundrel!" she hollered. "I should think you'd be glad to help a pore, weak female critter 'stead of wastin' yore time gamblin' and fightin', in such dens of iniquity as War Paint. I want you to fix some way so's to disgust Shadrach with drink for the rest of his nateral life, and if you don't you'll hear from me, you good-for-nothin'—"

"All right!" I yelled. "All right! Anything for a little peace! I'll git him and bring him home, and make a teetotaler outa him if I have to strangle the old son of a—"

"How dast you use such langwidge in front of me?" she hollered. "Ain't you got no respect for a lady? I'll be ¾4%*¢●?—!'d if I know what the !%$●*¢ world's comin' to! Git outa here and don't show yore homely mug around here again unless you git Shadrach off of rum for good!"

Well, if Uncle Shadrach ever took a swig of rum in his life it was because they warn't no good red corn whiskey within reach, but I didn't try to argy with Aunt Tascosa. I lit out down the trail feeling like I'd been tied up to a Apache stake with the whole tribe sticking red-hot Spanish daggers into my hide. Aunt Tascosa affects a man that way. I heard Cap'n Kidd heave a sigh of relief plumb up from his belly, too, as we crossed a ridge and her distant voice was drowned out by the soothing noises of a couple of bobcats fighting with a timber wolf. I thought what ca'm and happy lives them simple critters lived, without no Aunt Tascosa.

I rode on, forgetting my own troubles in feeling sorry for pore Uncle Shadrach. They warn't a mean bone in his carcass. He was just as good-natered and hearty a critter as you'd ever meet even in the Humbolts. But his main object in life seemed to be to stow away all the corn juice they is in the world.

As I rode along I racked my brain for a plan to break Uncle Shadrach of this here habit. I like a dram myself, but in moderation, never more'n a gallon or so at a time, unless it's a special occasion. I don't believe in a man making a hawg out of hisself, and anyway I was sick and tired running Uncle Shadrack down and fetching him home from his sprees.

I thought so much about it on my way to Apache Mountain that I got so sleepy I seen I was gittin' into no state to ride Cap'n Kidd. He got to lookin' back at me now and then, and I knowed if he seen me dozin' in the saddle he'd try his derndest to break my neck. I was passin' Cousin Bill Gordon's barn about that time, so I thought I'd go in and take me a nap up in the hayloft, and maybe I'd dream about a way to make a water-drinker out of Uncle Shadrach or somethin'.

I tied Cap'n Kidd and started into the barn, and what should I see but Bill's three youngest boys engaged in daubing paint on Uncle Jeppard Grimes' favorite jackass, Joshua.

"What air you all a-doin' to Joshua?" I demanded, and they jumped back and looked guilty. Joshua was a critter which Uncle Jeppard used for a pack-mule when he went prospectin'. He got the urge maybe every three or four year, and between times Joshua just et and slept. He was the sleepin'est jackass I ever seen. He was snoozing now, whilst them young idjits was working on him.

I seen what they was at. Bill had loaned a feller some money which had a store down to War Paint, and the feller went broke, and give Bill a lot of stuff outa the store for pay. They was a lot of paint amongst it. Bill packed it home, though I dunno what he aimed to do with it, because all the houses in the Humbolts was log cabins which nobody ever painted, or if they did, they just white-washed 'em. But anyway, he had it all sorted in his barn, and his boys was smearing it on Joshua.

He was the derndest sight you ever seen. They'd painted a big stripe down his spine, like a Spanish mustang, only this stripe was green instead of black, and more stripes curving over his ribs and down under his belly, red, white and blue, and they'd painted his ears green.

"What you all mean by sech doin's?" I ast. "Uncle Jeppard'll plumb skin you all alive. He sets a lot of store by that there jack."

"Aw, it's just funnin'," they said. "He won't know who done it."

"You go scrub that paint off," I ordered 'em. "Joshua'll lick it off and git pizened."

"It won't hurt him," they assured me. "He got in here yesterday and et three cans of paint and a bucket of whitewash. That's what give us the idee. He kin eat anythin'. Eatin'est jack you ever seen."

"Heh, heh, heh!" snickered one of 'em. "He looks like a drunkard's dream!"

Instantly a idee hit me.

"Gimme that jackass!" I explained. "He's just what I need to kyore Uncle Shadrach Polk of drinkin' licker. One glimpse of that there jack in his present state and Uncle Shadrach'll think he's got the delerious trimmin's and git so scairt he'll swear off whiskey for life."

"If you aims to lead Joshua to Joel's stillhouse," they said, "you'll be all day gittin' there. You cain't hustle Joshua."

"I ain't goin' to lead him," I said. "You all hitch a couple of mules to yore pa's spring wagon. I'll leave Cap'n Kidd here till I git back."

"We'll put him the corral behind the barn," they says. "Them posts are set four foot deep in concrete and the fence is braced with railroad iron, so maybe it'll hold him till you git back, if you ain't gone too long."

When they got the mules hitched, I tied Joshua's laigs and laid him in the wagon bed, where he went to sleep, and I climbed onto the seat and lit out for Apache Mountain. I hadn't went far when I run over a rock and woke Joshua up and he started braying and kept it up till I stopped and give him a ear of corn to chew on. As I started off again I seen Dick Grimes' youngest gal peeping at me from the bresh, and when I called to her she run off. I hoped she hadn't heard Joshua braying. I knowed she couldn't see him, laying down in the wagon bed, but he had a very pecooliar bray and anybody in the Humbolts could recognize him by it. I hoped she didn't know I had Joshua, because she was the derndest tattletale in the Bear Creek country and Uncle Jeppard is such a crossgrained old cuss you can't explain nothing to him. He was born with the notion that the whole world was plottin' agen him.

It hadn't been much more'n good daylight when I rode past Uncle Shadrach's, and I'd pushed Cap'n Kidd purty brisk from there; the mules made good time, so it warn't noon yet when I come to Apache Mountain. As I approached the settlement, which was a number of cabins strung up and down a breshy run, I swung wide of the wagon-road and took to the trails, because I didn't want nobody to see me with Joshua. It was kind of tough going, because the trails was mostly footpaths and not wide enough for the wagon, and I had to stop and pull up saplings every few yards. I was scairt the noise would wake up Joshua and he'd start braying again, but that jackass could sleep through a bombardment, long as he warn't being jolted personal.

I was purty close to the settlement when I had to git out of the wagon and go ahead and break down some bresh so the wheels wouldn't foul, and when I laid hold of it, a couple of figgers jumped up on the other side. One was Cousin Buckner Kirby's gal Kit, and t'other'n was young Harry Braxton from the other side of the mountain, and no kin to none of us.

"Oh!" says Kit, kind of breathless.

"What you all doin' out here?" I scowled, fixing Harry with a eye which made him shiver and fuss with his gun-belt. "Air yore intentions honorable, Braxton?"

"I dunno what business it is of yore'n," said Kit bitterly.

"I makes it mine," I assured her. "If this young buck cain't come sparkin' you at a respectable place and hour, why, I figgers—"

"Yore remarks is ignorant and insultin'," says Harry, sweating profusely, but game. "I aims to make this here young lady my wife, if it warn't for the toughest prospective father-in-law ever blighted young love's sweet dream with a number twelve boot in the seat of the pants."

"To put it in words of one syllable so's even you can understand, Breckinridge," says Kit, "Harry wants to marry me, but pap is too derned mean and stubborn to let us. He don't like the Braxtons account of one of 'em skun him in a hoss-swap thirty years ago."

"I don't love 'em myself," I grunted. "But go on."

"Well," she says, "after pap had licked Harry out of the house five or six times, and dusted his britches with birdshot on another occasion, we kind of got the idee that he was prejudiced agen Harry. So we had to take this here method of seein' each other."

"Whyn't you all run off and git married anyway?" I ast.

Kit shivered. "We wouldn't dare try it. Pap might wake up and catch us, and he'd shoot Harry. I taken a big chance sneakin' out of here today. Ma and the kids are all over visitin' a few days with Aunt Ouachita, but pap wouldn't let me go for fear I'd meet

Harry over there. I snuck out here for a few minutes—pap thinks
I'm gatherin' greens for dinner—but if I don't hustle back he'll
come lookin' for me with a hickory gad."

"Aw, shucks," I said. "You all got to use yore brains like I
do. You leave it to me. I'll git yore old man out of the way for
the night, and give you a chance to skip."

"How'll you do that?" Kit ast skeptically.

"Never mind," I told her, not having the slightest idee how I
was going to do it. "I'll 'tend to that. You git yore things ready,
and you, Harry, you come along the road in a buckboard just about
moonrise, and Kit'll be waitin' for you. You all git hitched over
to War Paint. Buckner won't do nothin' after yo're hitched."

"Will you, shore enough?" says Harry, brightening up.

"Shore I will," I assured him. "Vamoose now, and git that
buckboard."

He hustled off, and I said to Kit: "Git in the wagon and ride
to the settlement with me. This time tomorrer you'll be a happy
married woman shore enough."

"I hope so," she said sad-like. "But I'm bettin' somethin' will
go wrong and pap'll catch us, and I'll eat my meals off the mantel-
board for the next week."

"Trust me," I assured her, as I helped her in the wagon.

She didn't seem much surprised when she looked down in the
bed and seen Joshua all tied up and painted and snoring his head
off. Humbolt folks expects me to do onusual things.

"You needn't look like you thought I was crazy," I says irritably. "That critter is for Uncle Shadrach Polk."

"If Uncle Shadrach sees that thing," says she, "he'll think he's
seein' worse'n snakes."

"That's what I aim for him to think," I says. "Who's he stayin'
with?"

"Us," says she.

"Hum!" I says. "That there complicates things a little. Whar-
at does he sleep?"

"Upstairs," she says.

"Well," I says, "he won't interfere with our elopement none.
You git outa here and go on home, and don't let yore pap suspect
nothin'."

"I'd be likely to, wouldn't I?" says she, and clumb down and
pulled out.

I'd stopped in a thicket at the aidge of the settlement, and I
could see the roof of Cousin Buckner's house from where I was.

I could also hear Cousin Buckner bellerin': "Kit! "Kit! Whar air you? I know you ain't in the garden. If I have to come huntin' you, I 'low I'll—"

"Aw, keep yore britches on," I heard Kit call. "I', a-comin'!"

I heard Cousin Buckner subside into grumblings and rumblings like a grizzly talking to hisself. I figgered he was out on the road which run past his house, but I couldn't see him and neither he couldn't see me, nor nobody could which might happen to be passin' along the road. I onhitched the mules and tied 'em where they could graze and git water, and I h'isted Joshua outa the wagon, and taken the ropes offa his laigs and tied him to a tree, and fed him and the mules with some corn I'd brung from Cousin Bill Gordon's. Then I went through the bresh till I come to Joel Garfield's stillhouse, which was maybe half a mile from there, up the run. I didn't meet nobody.

Joel was by hisself in the stillhouse, for a wonder, but he was making up for lack of trade by his own personal attention to his stock.

"Ain't Uncle Shadrach Polk nowhere around?" I ast, and Joel lowered a jug of white corn long enough to answer me.

"Naw," he says, "he ain't right now. He's likely still sleepin' off the souse he was on last night. He didn't leave here till after midnight," says Joel, with another pull at the jug, "and he was takin' all sides of the road to onst. He'll pull in about the middle of the afternoon and start in to fillin' his hide so full he can just barely stagger back to Buckner Kirby's house by midnight or past. I bet he has a fine old time navigatin' them stairs Buckner's got into his house. I'd be afeared to tackle 'em myself, even when I was sober. A pole ladder is all I want to get into a loft with, but Buckner always did have high-falutin' idees. Lately he's been arguin' with Uncle Shadrach to cut down on his drinkin'—specially when he's full hisself."

"Speakin' of Cousin Buckner," I says, "has he been around for his regular dram yet?"

"Not yet," says Joel. "H'll be in right after dinner, as usual."

"He wouldn't if he knowed what I knowed," I opined, because I'd thought up a way to git Cousin Buckner out of the way that night. "He'd be headin' for Wolf Canyon fast as he could spraddle. I just met Harry Braxton with a pack-mule headin' for there."

"You don't mean somebody's made a strike in Wolf Canyon?" says Joel, pricking up his ears.

"You never heard nothin' like it," I assured him. "Alder Gulch warn't nothin' to this."

"Hum!" says Joel, absent-mindedly pouring hisself a quart-size tin cup full of corn juice.

"I'm a Injun if it ain't!" I says, and dranken me a dram and went back to lay in the bresh and watch the Kirby house, I was well pleased with myself, because I knowed what a wolf Cousin Buckner was after gold. If anything could draw him away from home and his daughter, it would be news of a big strike. I was willing to bet my sixshooters against a prickly pear that as soon as Joel told him the news, he'd light out for Wolf Canyon. More especially as he'd think Harry Braxton was goin' there, too, and no chance of him sneakin' off with Kit whilst the old man was gone.

After a while I seen Cousin Buckner leave the house and go down the road toward the stillhouse, and purty soon Uncle Shadrach emerged and headed the same way. Purty well satisfied with myself, I went back to where I left Cousin Bill's wagon, and fried me five or six pounds of venison I'd brung along for provisions and et it, and drunk at the creek, and then laid down and slept for a few hours.

It was right at sundown when I woke up. I went on foot through the bresh till I come out behind Buckner's cow-pen and seen Kit milkin'. I ast her if anybody was in the house.

"Nobody but me," she said. "And I'm out here. I ain't seen neither pap nor Uncle Shadrach since they left right after dinner. Can it be yore scheme is actually workin' out?"

"Certainly," I says. "Uncle Shadrach'll be swillin' at Joel's stillhouse till past midnight, and yore pap is ondoubtedly on his way towards Wolf Canyon. You git through with yore chores, and git ready to skip. Don't have no light in yore room, though. It's just likely yore pap told off one of his relatives to lay in the bresh and watch the house—him bein' of a suspicious nater. We don't want to have no bloodshed. When I hear Harry's buckboard I'll come for you. And if you hear any pecooliar noises before he gits here, don't think nothin' of it. It'll jest be me luggin' Joshua upstairs."

"That critter'll bray fit to wake the dead," says she.

"He won't, neither," I said. "He'll go to sleep and keep his mouth shet. Uncle Shadrach won't suspect nothin' till he lights him a candle to go to bed by. Or if he's too drunk to light a candle, and just falls down on the bed in the dark, he'll wake up during the night some time to git him a drink of water. He's bound to see Joshua some time between midnight and mornin'. All I hope is the shock won't prove fatal. You go git ready to skip now."

I went back to the wagon and cooked me some more venison, also about a dozen aigs Kit had give me along with some corn pone and a gallon of buttermilk. I managed to make a light snack out of them morsels, and then, as soon as it was good and dark, I hitched up the mules and loaded Joshua into the wagon and went slow and easy down the road. I stopped behind the corral and tied the mules.

The house was dark and still. I toted Joshua into the house and carried him upstairs. I heard Kit moving around in her room, but they warn't nobody else in the house.

Cousin Buckner had regular stairs in his house like what they have in big towns like War Paint and the like. Most folks in the Bear Creek country just has a ladder going up through a trap-door, and some said they would be a jedgment onto Buckner account of him indulging in such vain and sinful luxury, but I got to admit that packing a jackass up a flight of stairs was a lot easier than what it would have been to lug him up a ladder.

Joshua didn't bray nor kick none. He didn't care what was happening to him so long as he didn't have to do no work personal. I onfastened his laigs and tied a rope around his neck and t'other end to the foot of Uncle Shadrach's bunk, and give him a hat I found on a peg to chaw on till he went to sleep, which I knowed he'd do pronto.

I then went downstairs and heard Kit fussing around in her room, but it warn't time for Harry so I went back out behind the corral and sot down and leaned my back agen the fence, and I reckon I must of gone to sleep. Just associatin' with Joshua give a man the habit. First thing I knowed I heard a buckboard rumbling over a bridge up the draw, and knowed it was Harry coming in fear and trembling to claim his bride. The moon warn't up yet but they was a glow above the trees on the eastern ridges.

I jumped up and ran quick and easy to Kit's winder—I can move light as a cougar in spite of my size—and I said: "Kit, air you ready?"

"I'm ready!" she whispered, all of a tremble. "Don't talk so loud!"

"They ain't nothin' to be scairt of," I soothed her, but lowered my voice just to humor her. "Yore pap is in Wolf Canyon by this time. Ain't nobody in the house but us. I been watchin' out by the corral."

Kit sniffed.

"Warn't that you I heard come into the house while ago?" she ast.

"You been dreamin'," I said. "Come on! That's Harry's buckboard comin' up the road."

"Lemme get just a few more things together!" she whispered, fumbling around in the dark. That's just like a woman. No matter how much time they has aforehand, they always has something to do at the last minute.

I waited by the winder and Harry druv on past the house a few rods and tied the hoss and come back, walking light and soft, and plenty pale in the starlight.

"Go on out the front door and meet him," I told her. "No, wait!"

Because all to onst Harrry had ducked back out of the road, and he jumped over the fence and come to the winder where I was. He was shaking like a leaf.

"Somebody comin' up the road afoot!" he says.

"It's pap!" gasped Kit. Her and Harry was shore scairt of the old man. They hadn't said a word above a whisper you could never of heard three yards away, and I was kinda suiting my voice to their'n.

"Aw, it cain't be!" I said. "He's in Wolf Canyon. That's Uncle Shadrach comin' home to sleep off his drunk, but he's back a lot earlier'n what I figgered he would be. He ain't important, but we don't want no delay. Here, Kit, gimme that bag. Now lemme lift you outa the winder. So! Now you all skin out. I'm goin' to climb this here tree whar I can see the fun. Git!"

They crope out the side-gate of the yards just as Uncle Shadrach come in at the front gate, and he never seen 'em because the house was between 'em. They went so soft and easy I thought if Cousin Buckner had been in the house he wouldn't have woke up. They was hustling down the road towards the buckboard as Uncle Shadrach was coming up on the porch and going into the hall. I could hear him climbing the stair. I could of seen him if they'd been a light in the house, because I could look into a winder in his room and one in the downstairs hall, too, from the tree where I was setting.

He got into his room about the time the young folks reached their buckboard, and I seen a light flare up as he struck a match. They warn't no hall upstairs. The stairs run right up to the door of his room. He stood in the doorway and lit a candle on a shelf by the door. I could see Joshua standing by the bunk with his head down, asleep, and I reckon the light must of woke him up, because he throwed up his head and gave a loud ringing bray. Uncle Shadrach turned and seen Joshua and he let out a shriek and fell backwards downstairs.

The candle light streamed down into the hall, and I got the shock of my life. Because as Uncle Shadrach went pitching down them steps, yelling bloody murder, they sounded a bull's roar below, and out of the room at the foot of the stair come prancing a huge figger waving a shotgun in one hand and pulling on his britches with the other'n. It was Cousin Buckner which I thought was safe in Wolf Canyon! That'd been him which Kit heard come in and go to bed a while before.

"What's goin' on here?" he roared. "What you doin', Shadrach?"

"Git outa my way!" screamed Uncle Shadrach. "I just seen the devil in the form of a zebray jackass! Lemme outa here!"

He busted out of the house, and jumped the fence and went up the road like a quarter-hoss, and Cousin Buckner run out behind him. The moon was just comin' up, and Kit and Harry was jest startin' down the road. When she seen her old man irrupt from the house, Kit screeched like a scairt catamount, and Buckner heard her. He whirled and seen the buckboard rattling down the road and he knowed what was happening. He give a beller and let bam at 'em with his shotgun, but it was too long a range.

"Whar's my hoss?" he roared, and started for the corral. I knowed if he got astraddle of that derned long-laigged bay gelding of his'n, he'd ride them pore infants down before they'd went ten miles. I jumped down out of the tree and yelled: "Hey, there, Cousin Buckner! Hey, Buck—"

He whirled and shot the tail offa my coonskin cap before he seen who it was.

"What you mean jumpin' down on me like that?" he roared. "What you doin' up that tree? Whar you come from?"

"Never mind that," I said. "You want to catch Harry Braxton before he gits away with yore gal, don't you? Don't stop to saddle a hoss. I got a light wagon hitched up behind the corral. We can run 'em down easy in that."

"Let's go!" he roared, and in no time at all we was off, him standing up in the bed and cussin' and wavin' his shotgun.

"I'll have his scalp!" he roared. "I'll pickle his heart and feed it to my houn' dawgs! Cain't you go no faster?"

Them dern mules was a lot faster than I'd thought. I didn't dare hold 'em back for fear Buckner would git suspicious, and the first thing I knowed he was overhauling the buckboard foot by foot. Harry's critters warn't much account, and Cousin Bill Gordon's mules was laying their bellies to the ground.

I dunno what Kit thought when she looked back and seen us tearing after 'em, but Harry must of thought I was betraying 'em, otherwise he wouldn't of opened up on me with his sixshooter. But all he done was to knock some splinters out of the wagon and nick my shoulder. The old man would of returned the fire with his shotgun but he was scairt he might hit Kit, and both vehicles was bounding and bouncing along too fast and furious for careful aimin'.

All to onst we come to a place where the road forked, and Kit and Harry taken the right-hand turn. I taken the left.

"Air you crazy, you blame fool?" roared Cousin Buckner. "Turn back and take the othe road!"

"I cain't!" I responded. "These mules is runnin' away!"

"Yo're a liar!" howled Cousin Buckner. "Quit pourin' leather into them mules, you blasted ¾$%¢&*●, and turn back! Turn back, cuss you!" With that he started hammering me in the head with the stock of his shotgun.

We was thundering along a road which run along the rim of a sloping bluff, and when Buckner's shotgun went off accidentally the mules really did git scairt and started running away, jest about the time I reached back to take the shotgun away from Cousin Buckner. Being beat in the head with the butt was getting awful monotonous, because he'd been doing nothing else for the past half mile.

I yanked the gun out of his hand and jest then the left hind wheel hit a stump and the hind end of the wagon went straight up in the air and the pole splintered. The mules run right out of the harness and me and the wagon and Cousin Buckner went over the bluff and down the slope in a whirling tangle of wheels and laigs and heads and profanity.

We brung up against a tree at the bottom, and I throwed the rooins off of me and riz, swearing fervently when I seen how much money I'd have to pay Cousin Bill Gordon for his wagon. But Cousin Buckner give me no time for meditation. He'd ontangled hisself from the hind wheel and was doing a war-dance in the moonlight and frothing at the mouth.

"You done that on purpose!" he raged. "You never aimed to ketch them wretches! You taken the wrong road on purpose! You turned us over on purpose! Now I'll never ketch the scoundrel which run away with my datter—the pore, dumb, trustin' *&¢%$¾●! innercent!"

"Be ca'm, Cousin Buckner," I advised. "He'll make her a good husband. They're well onto their way to War Paint and a happy married life. Best thing you can do is forgive 'em and give 'em yore blessin'."

"Well," he snarled, "you ain't neither my datter nor my son-in-law. Here's my blessin' to you!"

It was a pore return for all the trouble I'd taken for him to push me into a cactus bed and hit me with a rock the size of a water-melon. However, I taken into consideration that he was over-wrought and not hisself, so I ignored his incivility and made no retort whatever, outside of splintering a wagon spoke over his head.

I then clumb the bluff, making no reply to his impassioned and profane comments, and looked around for the mules. They hadn't run far. I seen 'em grazing down the road, and I started after 'em, when I heard horses galloping up the road toward the settlement, and around a turn in the road come Uncle Jeppard Grimes with his whiskers streaming in the moonlight, and nine or ten of his boys riding hard behind him.

"Thar he is!" he howled, impulsively discharging his sixshooter at me. "Thar's the fiend in human form! That's the kidnapper of helpless jackasses! Boys, do yore duty!"

They pulled up around me and started piling off their horses with blood in their eyes and weppins in their hands.

"Hold on!" I says. "If it's Joshua you fools are after—"

"He admits the crime!" howled Uncle Jeppard. "Is it Joshua, says you! You know dern well it is! We been combin' the hills for you, ever since my gran'-datter brought me the news! What you done with him, you scoundrel?"

"Aw," I said, "he's all right. I was jest goin' to—"

"He evades the question!" screamed Uncle Jeppard. "Git him, boys!"

"I tell you he's all right!" I roared, but they give me no chance to explain. Them Grimeses is all alike; you cain't tell 'em nothing. You got to knock it into their fool heads. They descended on me with fence rails and rocks and wagon spokes and loaded quirts and gun stocks in a way which would of tried the patience of a saint. I always try to be as patient with my erring relatives as I can be. I merely taken their weapons away from 'em and kind of pushed 'em back away from me, and if they'd looked where they fell Jim and Joe and Erath wouldn't of fell down that bluff and broke their arms and laigs and Bill wouldn't of fractured his skull agen that tree.

I handled 'em easy as babies, and kept my temper in spite of Uncle Jeppard dancing around on his hoss and yelling: "Lay into him, boys! Don't be scairt of the big grizzly! He cain't hurt us!" and shooting at me every time he thought he could shoot without hitting one of his own offspring. He did puncture two or three of 'em, and then blamed me for it, the old jackass.

Nobody could have acted with more restraint than I did when Dick Grimes broke the blade of his bowie knife off on my hip bone, and the seven fractured ribs I give his brother Jacob was a mild retaliation for chawing my ear like he done. But it was ill-advised impulse which prompted Esau Grimes to stab me in the seat of the britches with a pitchfork. There ain't nothing which sours the milk of human kindness in a man's veins any more'n getting pitchforked by a raging relative behind his back.

I give a beller which shook the acorns out of the oaks all up and down the run, and whirled on Esau so quick it jerked the pitchfork out of his hands and left it sticking in my hide. I retched back and pulled it out and wrapped the handle around Esau's neck, and then I taken him by the ankles and started remodeling the landscape with him. I mowed down a sapling thicket with him, and leveled a cactus bed with him, and swept the road with him, and when his brothers tried to rescue him, I beat 'em over the head with him till they was too groggy to do anything but run in circles.

Uncle Jeppard came spurring at me, trying to knock me down with his hoss and trample me, and Esau was so limp by this time he warn't much good for a club no more, so I whirled him around my head a few times and throwed him at Uncle Jeppard. Him and Uncle Jeppard and the hoss all went down in a heap together, and from the way Uncle Jeppard hollered you'd of thought somebody was trying to injure him. It was plumb disgusting.

Five or six of his boys recovered enough to surge onto me then, and I knocked 'em all down on top of him and Esau and the hoss, and the hoss was trying to git up, and kicking around right and left, and his hoofs was going bam, bam, bam on human heads, and Uncle Jeppard was hollering so loud I got to thinking maybe he was hurt or something. So I retched down in the heap and got him by the whiskers and pulled him out from under the hoss and four or five of his fool boys.

"Air you hurt, Uncle Jeppard?" I inquired.

"¾$%¢&●*!" responded Uncle Jeppard, rewarding my solic-
itude by trying to stab me with his bowie knife. This ingratitude
irritated me, and I tossed him from me fretfully, and as he was
pulling hisself out of the prickly pear bed whar he landed, he
suddenly gave a louder scream than ever. Something come ambling
up the road and I seen it was that fool jackass Joshua, which had
evidently et his rope and left the house looking for more grub. He
looked like a four-legged nightmare in the moonlight, but all Uncle
Jeppard noticed was the red paint on him.

"Halp! Murder!" howled Uncle Jeppard. "They've wounded
him mortally! He's bleedin' to death! Git a tourniquet, quick!"

With that they all deserted the fray, them which was able to
hobble, and run to grab Joshua and stanch his bleeding. But when
he seen all them Grimeses coming for him, Joshua got scairt and
took out through the bresh. They all pelted after him, and the last
thing I heard as they passed out of hearing was Uncle Jeppard
wailing: "Joshua! Stop, dern it! This here's yore friends! Pull up,
dang you! We wants to help you, you cussed fool!"

I turned to see what I could do for the casualties which lay
groaning in the road and at the foot of the bluff, but they said
unanamous they didn't want no help from a enemy—which they
meant me. They one and all promised to pickle my heart and eat
it as soon as they was able to git about on crutches, so I abandoned
my efforts and headed for the settlement.

The fighting had scairt the mules up the road a ways, but I
catched 'em and made a hackamore outa one of my galluses, and
rode one and led t'other'n, and lit out straight through the bresh
for Bear Creek. I'd had a belly-full of Apache Mountain. But I
swung past Joel's stillhouse to find out how come Cousin Buckner
didn't go to Wolf Canyon. When I got there the stillhouse was
dark and the door was shet, and they was a note on the door. I
could read a little by then, and I spelt it out. It said:

Gone to Wolf Canyon
Joel Garfield.

That selfish polecat hadn't told Cousin Buckner nor nobody
about the strike. He'd got hisself a pack-mule and lit out for Wolf
Canyon hisself. A hell of a relative he was, maybe doing pore
Cousin Buckner out of a fortune, for all he knew.

A mile from the settlement I met Jack Gordon comin' from a
dance on t'other side of the mountain, and he said he seen Uncle

Shadrach Polk fogging down the trail on a mule he was riding bare-back without no bridle, so I thought well, anyway my scheme for scairing him out of a taste for licker worked. Jack said Uncle Shadrach looked like he'd saw a herd of ha'nts.

It was about daylight when I stopped at Bill Gordon's ranch to leave him his mules. I paid him for his wagon and also for the damage Cap'n Kidd had did to his corral. Bill had to build a new one, and Cap'n Kidd had also run his prize stallion offa the ranch, and chawed the ears off a longhorn bull, and busted into the barn and gobbled up about ten dollars' worth of oats. When I lit out for Bear Creek agen I warn't feelin' in no benevolent mood, but, thinks I, it's worth it if it's made a water-swigger outa Uncle Shadrach.

It was well along toward noon when I pulled up at the door and called for Aunt Tascosa. Jedge my scandalized amazement when I was greeted by a deluge of b'iling water from the winder and Aunt Tascosa stuck her head out and says: "You buzzard in the form of a human bein'! How you got the brass to come bulgin' around here? If I warn't a lady I'd tell you jest what I thought of you, you ¾$%¢&●! Git, before I opens up on you with this here shotgun!"

"Why, Aunt Tascosa, what you talkin' about?" I ast, combing the hot water outa my hair with my fingers.

"You got the nerve to ast!" she sneered. "Didn't you promise me you'd kyore Shadrach of drinkin' rum? Didn't you, hey? Well, come in here and look at him! He arriv home about daylight on one of Buckner Kirby's mules and it about ready to drop, and he's been rasslin' ever since with a jug he had hid. I cain't git no sense out'n him."

I went in and Uncle Shadrach was settin' by the back door and he had hold of that there jug like a drownding man clutching a straw-sack.

"I'm surprised at you, Uncle Shadrach," I said. "What in the—"

"Shet the door, Breckinridge," he says. "They is more devils onto the earth than is dreamed of in our philosophy. I've had a narrer escape, Breckinridge! I let myself be beguiled by the arg-yments of Buckner Kirby, a son of Baliol which is without under-standin'. He's been rasslin' with me to give up licker. Well, yesterday I got so tired of his argyments I said I'd try it a while, just to have some peace. I never taken a drink all day yesterday, and Breckinridge, I give you my word when I started to go to bed last night I saw a red, white and blue jackass with green ears

standin' at the foot of my bunk, just as plain as I sees you now!
It war the water that done it, Breckinridge," he says, curling his
fist lovingly around the handle of the jug. "Water's a snare and a
delusion. I drunk water all day yesterday, and look what it done
to me! I don't never want to see no water no more, agen."

"Well," I says, losing all patience, "you're a-goin' to, by golly,
if I can heave you from here to that hoss-trough in the backyard."

I done it, and that's how come the rumor got started that I tried
to drown Uncle Shadrach Polk in a hoss-trough because he refused
to swear off licker. Aunt Tascosa was responsible for that there
slander, which was a pore way to repay me for all I'd did for her.
But people ain't got no gratitude.

Pistol Politics

Politics and book-learnin' is bad enough took separate; together
they're a blight and a curse. Take Yeller Dog for a instance, a
mining camp over in the Apache River country, where I was rash
enough to take up my abode in onst.

Yeller Dog was a decent camp till politics reared its head in
our midst and education come slithering after. The whiskey was
good and middling cheap. The poker and faro games was honest
if you watched the dealers clost. Three or four piddlin' fights a
night was the usual run, and a man hadn't been shot dead in more
than a week by my reckoning. Then, like my Aunt Tascosa Polk
would say, come the deluge.

It all began when Forty-Rod Harrigan moved his gambling
outfit over to Alderville and left our one frame building vacant,
and Gooseneck Wilkerson got the idee of turning it into a city
hall. Then he said we ought to have a mayor to go with it, and
announced hisself as candidate. Naturally Bull Hawkins, our other
leading citizen, come out agen him. The election was set for April
11. Gooseneck established his campaign headquarters in the Silver
Saddle saloon, and Bull taken up his'n in the Red Tomahawk on
t'other side of the street. First thing we knowed, Yeller Dog was
in the grip of politics.

The campaign got under way, and the casualties was mounting
daily as public interest became more and more fataly aroused, and
on the afternoon of the 9th Gooseneck come into his headquarters,
and says: "We got to make a sweepin' offensive, boys. Bull Hawkins is out-generalin' us. That shootin' match he put on for a prime
beef steer yesterday made a big hit with the common herd. He's

tryin' to convince Yeller Dog that if elected he'd pervide the camp with more high-class amusement than I could. Breck Elkins, will you pause in yore guzzlin' and lissen here a minute? As chief of this here political organization I demand yore attention!"

"I hear you," I says. "I was to the match, and they barred me on a tecknicality, otherwise I would have won the whole steer. It warn't so excitin', far as I could see. Only one man got shot."

"And he was one of my voters," scowled Gooseneck. "But we got to outshine Bull's efforts to seduce the mob. He's resortin' to low, onder-handed tactics by buyin' votes outright. I scorns sech measures—anyway, I've bought all I'm able to pay for. We got to put on a show which out-dazzles his dern' shootin' match."

"A rodeo, maybe," suggested Mule McGrath. "Or a good dog-fight."

"Naw, naw," says Gooseneck. "My show will be a symbol of progress and culture. We stages a spellin' match tomorrow night in the city hall. Next mornin' when the polls open the voters'll still be so dazzled by the grandeur of our entertainment they'll elect me by a vast majority."

"How many men in this here camp can spell good enough to git into a spellin' bee?" says I.

"I'm confident they's at least thirty-five men in this camp which can read and write," says Gooseneck. "That's plenty. But we got to find somebody to give out the words. It wouldn't look right for me—it'd be beneath my offishul dignity. Who's educated enough for the job?"

"I am!" says Jerry Brennon and Bill Garrison simultaneous. They then showed their teeth at each other. They warn't friends nohow.

"Cain't but one git the job," asserted Gooseneck. "I tests yore ability. Can either one of you spell Constantinople?"

"K-o-n-" began Garrison, and Brennon burst into a loud and mocking guffaw, and said something pointed about ignoramuses.

"You! ●¾$%¢&*!" says Garrison bloodthirstily.

"Gentlemen!" squawked Gooseneck—and then ducked as they both went for their guns.

They cleared leather about the same time. When the smoke oozed away Gooseneck crawled out from under the roulette table and cussed fervently.

"Two more reliable voters gone to glory!" he raged. "Breck-inridge, whyn't you stop 'em?"

"'T'warn't none of my business," says I, reching for another drink, because a stray bullet had knocked my glass outa my hand. "Hey!" I addressed the barkeep sternly. "I see you fixin' to chalk up that there spilt drink agen me. Charge it to Jerry Brennon. He spilt it."

"Dead men pays no bills," complained the bartender.

"Cease them petty squabbles!" snarled Gooseneck. "You argys over a glass of licker when I've jest lost two good votes! Drag 'em out, boys," he ordered the other members of the organization which was emerging from behind the bar and the whiskey barrels where they'd took refuge when the shooting started. "Damn!" says Gooseneck with bitterness. "This here is a deadly lick to my campaign! I not only loses two more votes, but them was the best educated men in camp, outside me. Now who we goin' to git to conduck the spellin' match?"

"Anybody which can read can do it," says Lobo Harrison, a hoss-thief with a mean face and a ingrown disposition. He'd go a mile out of his way jest to kick a dog. "Even Elkins there could do it."

"Yeah, if they was anything to read from," snorted Gooseneck. "But they ain't a line of writin' in camp except on whiskey bottles. We got to have a man with a lot of long words in his head. Breckinridge, dammit, jest because I told the barkeep to charge yore drinks onto campaign expenses ain't no reason for you to freeze onto that bar permanent. Ride over to Alderville and git us a educated man."

"How'll he know whether he's educated or not?" sneered Lobo, which seemed to dislike me passionately for some reason or another.

"Make him spell Constantinople," says Gooseneck.

"He cain't go over there," says Soapy Jackson. "The folks has threatened to lynch him for cripplin' their sheriff."

"I didn't cripple their fool sheriff," I says indignantly. "He crippled hisself fallin' through a wagon wheel when I give him a kind of a push with a rock. How you spell that there Constance Hopple word?"

Well, he spelt it thirty or forty times till I had it memorized, so I rode over to Alderville. When I rode into town the folks looked at me coldly and bunched up and whispered amongst theirselves, but I paid no attention to 'em. I never seen the deperty sheriff, unless that was him I seen climbing a white oak tree as I hove in sight. I went into the White Eagle saloon and drunk a dram, and says to the barkeep: "Who's the best educated man in Alderville?"

Says he: "Snake River Murgatroyd, which deals monte over to the Elite Amusement Palace." So I went over there and jest as I went through the door I happened to remember that Snake River had swore he was going to shoot me on sight next time he seen me, account of some trouble we'd had over a card game. But sech things is too trivial to bother about. I went up to where he was setting dealing monte, and I says: "Hey!"

"Place your bet," says he. Then he looked up and said: "You !●¾$%¢&*" and reched for his gun, but I got mine out first and shoved the muzzle under his nose.

"Spell Constantinople!" I tells him.

He turnt pale and said: "Are you crazy?"

"Spell it!" I roared, and he says: "C-o-n-s-t-a-n-t-i-n-o-p-l-e! What the hell?"

"Good," I said, throwing his gun over in the corner out of temptation's way. "We wants you to come over to Yeller Dog and give out words at a spellin' match."

Everybody in the place was holding their breath. Snake River moved his hands nervous-like and knocked a jack of diamonds off onto the floor. He stooped like he was going to pick it up, but instead he jerked a bowie out of his boot and tried to stab me in the belly. Well, much as I would of enjoyed shooting him, I knowed it would spile the spellin' match, so I merely taken the knife away from him, and held him upside down to shake out whatever other weppins he might have had, and he begun to holler: "Help! Murder! Elkins is killin' me!"

"It's a Yeller Dog plot!" somebody howled, and the next instant the air was full of beer mugs and cuspidors. Some of them spittoons was quite heavy, and when one missed me and went bong on Snake River's head, he curled up like a angleworm which has been tromped on.

"Lookit there!" they hollered, like it was my fault. "He's tryin' to kill Snake River! Git him, boys!"

They then fell on me with billiard sticks and chair laigs in a way which has made me suspicious of Alderville's hospitality ever since.

Argyment being useless, I tucked Snake River under my left arm and started knocking them fool critters right and left with my right fist, and I reckon that was how the bar got wrecked. I never seen a bar a man's head would go through easier'n that'n. So purty soon the survivors abandoned the fray and run out of the door hollering: "Help! Murder! Rise up, citizens! Yeller Dog is at our throats! Rise and defend yore homes and loved ones!"

You would have thought the Apaches was burning the town, the way folks was hollering and running for their guns and shooting at me, as I clumb aboard Cap'n Kidd and headed for Yeller Dog. I left the main road and headed through the bresh for a old trail I knowed about, because I seen a whole army of men getting on their hosses to lick out after me, and while I knowed they couldn't catch Cap'n Kidd, I was afeared they might hit Snake River with a stray bullet if they got within range. The bresh was purty thick and I reckon it was the branches slapping him in the face which brung him to, because all to onst he begun hollering blue murder.

"You ain't takin' me to Yeller Dog!" he yelled. "You're takin' me out in the hills to murder me! Help! Help!"

"Aw, shet up," I snorted. "This here's a short cut."

"You can't get across Apache River unless you follow the road to the bridge," says he.

"I can, too," I says. "We'll go acrost on the footbridge."

With that he give a scream of horror and a convulsive wrench tore hisself clean out of his shirt which I was holding onto. The next thing I knowed all I had in my hand was a empty shirt and he was on the ground and scuttling through the bushes. I taken in after him, but he was purty tricky dodging around stumps and trees, and I begun to believe I was going to have to shoot him in the hind laig to catch him, when he made the mistake of trying to climb a tree. I rode up onto him before he could get out of rech, and reched up and got him by the laig and pulled him down, and his langwidge was painful to hear.

It was his own fault he slipped outa my hand, he kicked so vi'lent. I didn't go to drop him on his head.

But jest as I was reching down for him, I heard hosses running, and looked up and here come that derned Alderville posse busting through the bresh right on me. I'd lost so much time chasing Snake River they'd catched up with me. So I scooped him up and hung him over my saddle horn, because he was out cold, and headed for Apache River. Cap'n Kidd drawed away from them hosses like they was hobbled, so they warn't scarcely in pistol range of us when we busted out on the east bank. The river was up, jest a-foaming and a-b'ling, and the footbridge warn't nothing only jest a log.

But Cap'n Kidd's sure-footed as a billy goat. We started acrost it, and everything went all right till we got about the middle of it, and then Snake River came to and seen the water booming along under us. He lost his head and begun to struggle and kick and holler, and his spurs scratched Cap'n Kidd's hide. That made

Cap'n Kidd mad, and he turnt his head and tried to bite my laig, because he always blames me for everything that happens, and lost his balance and fell off.

That would of been all right, too, because as we hit the water I got hold of Cap'n Kidd's tail with one hand, and Snake River's undershirt with the other'n, and Cap'n Kidd hit out for the west bank. They is very few streams he cain't swim, flood or not. But jest as we was nearly acrost the posse appeared on the hind bank and started shooting at me, and they was apparently in some doubt as to which head in the water was me, because some of 'em shot at Snake River, too, jest to make sure. He opened his mouth to holler at 'em, and got it full of water and dern near strangled.

Then all to onst somebody in the bresh on the west shore opened up with a Winchester, and one of the posse hollered: "Look out, boys! It's a trap! Elkins has led us into a ambush!"

They turnt around and high-tailed it for Alderville.

Well, what with the shooting and gullet full of water, Snake River was having a regular fit and he kicked and thrashed so he kicked hisself clean out of his undershirt, and jest as my feet hit bottom, he slipped out of my grip and went whirling off downstream.

I jumped out on land, ignoring the hearty kick Cap'n Kidd planted in my midriff, and grabbed my lariat off my saddle. Gooseneck Wilkerson come prancing outa the bresh, waving a Winchester and yelling: "Don't let him drownd, dang you! My whole campaign depends on that spellin' bee! Do somethin'!"

I run along the bank and made a throw and looped Snake River around the ears. It warn't a very good catch, but the best I could do under the circumstances, and skin will always grow back onto a man's ears.

I hauled him out of the river, and it was plumb ungrateful for him to accuse me later of dragging him over them sharp rocks on purpose. I like to know how he figgered I could rope him outa Apache River without skinning him up a little. He'd swallered so much water he was nigh at his last gasp. Gooseneck rolled him onto his belly and jumped up and down on his back with both feet to git the water out; Gooseneck said that was artifishul respiration, but from the way Snake River hollered I don't believe it done him much good.

Anyway, he choked up several gallons of water. When he was able to threaten our lives betwixt cusswords, Gooseneck says: "Git him on yore hoss and let's git started. Mine run off when the shootin' started. I jest suspected you'd be pursued by them dumb-wits and would take the short-cut. That's why I come to meet you. Come on. We got to get Snake River some medical attention. In his present state he ain't in no shape to conduck no spellin' match."

Snake River was too groggy to set in the saddle, so we hung him acrost it like a cow-hide over a fence, and started out, me leading Cap'n Kidd. It makes Cap'n Kidd very mad to have any-body but me on his back, so we hadn't went more'n a mile when he reched around and sot his teeth in the seat of Snake River's pants. Snake River had been groaning very weak and dismal and commanding us to stop and let him down so's he could utter his last words, but when Cap'n Kidd bit him he let out a remarkable strong yell and bust into langwidge unfit for a dying man.

"!●¾$%¢&*" quoth he passionately. "Why have I got to be butchered for a Yeller Dog holiday?"

We was reasoning with him, when Old Man Jake Hanson hove out of the bushes. Old Jake had a cabin a hundred yards back from the trail. He was about the width of a barn door, and his whiskers was marvelous to behold. "What's this ungodly noise about?" he demanded. "Who's gittin' murdered?"

"I am!" says Snake River fiercely. "I'm bein' sacrificed to the passions of the brutal mob!"

"You shet up," says Gooseneck severely. "Jake, this is the gent we've consented to let conduck the spellin' match."

"Well, well!" says Jake, interested. "A educated man, hey? Why, he don't look no different from us folks, if the blood war wiped offa him. Say, lissen, boys, bring him over to my cabin! I'll dress his wounds and feed him and take keer of him and git him to the city hall tomorrer night in time for the spellin' match. In the meantime he can teach my datter Salomey her letters."

"I refuse to tutor a dirty-faced cub—" began Snake River when he seen a face peeking eagerly at us from the trees. "Who's that?" he demanded.

"My datter Salomey," says Old Jake. "Nineteen her last birth-day and cain't neither read nor write. None of my folks ever could, far back as family history goes, but I wants her to git some ed-ucation."

"It's a human obligation," says Snake River. "I'll do it!"

So we left him at Jake's cabin, propped up on a bunk, with Salomey feeding him spoon-vittles and whiskey, and me and Goose-neck headed for Yeller Dog, which warn't hardly a mile from there.

Gooseneck says to me: "We won't say nothin' about Snake

River bein' at Jake's shack. Bull Hawkins is sweet on Salomey and he's so dern' jealous-minded it makes him mad for another man to even stop there to say hello to the folks. We don't want nothin' to interfere with our show."

"You ack like you got a lot of confidence in it," I says.

"I banks on it heavy," says he. "It's a symbol of civilization."

Well, jest as we come into town we met Mule McGrath with fire in his eye and corn-juice on his breath. "Gooseneck, lissen!" says he. "I jest got wind of a plot of Hawkins and Jack Clanton to git a lot of our voters so drunk election day that they won't be able to git to the polls. Le's call off the spellin' match and go over to the Red Tomahawk and clean out that rat-nest!"

"Naw," says Gooseneck, "we promised the mob a show, and we keeps our word. Don't worry; I'll think of a way to circumvent the heathen."

Mule headed back for the Silver Saddle, shaking his head, and Gooseneck sot down on the aidge of a hoss-trough and thunk deeply. I'd begun to think he'd drapped off to sleep, when he riz up and said: "Breckinridge, git hold of Soapy Jackson and tell him to sneak out of camp and stay hid till the mornin' of the eleventh. Then he's to ride in jest before the polls open and spread the news that they has been a big gold strike over in Wild Hoss Gulch. A lot of fellers will stampede for there without waitin' to vote. Meanwhile you will have circulated amongst the men you know air goin' to vote for me, and let'em know we air goin' to work this campaign strategy. With all my men in camp, and most of Bull's headin' for Wild Hoss Gulch, right and justice triumphs and I wins."

So I went and found Soapy and told him what Gooseneck said, and on the strength of it he imejitly headed for the Silver Saddle, and begun guzzling on campaign credit. I felt it was my duty to go along with him and see that he didn't get so full he forgot what he was supposed to do, and we was putting down the sixth dram apiece when in come Jack McDonald, Jim Leary, and Tarantula Allison, all Hawkins men. Soapy focused his wandering eyes on 'em, and says: "W-who's this here clutterin' up the scenery? Whyn't you mavericks stay over to the Red Tomahawk whar you belong?"

"It's a free country," asserted Jack McDonald. "What about this here derned spellin' match Gooseneck's braggin' about all over town?"

"Well, what about it?" I demanded, hitching my harness for'ard. The political foe don't live which can beard a Elkins in his lair.

"We demands to know who conducks it," stated Leary. "At

least half the men in camp eligible to compete is in our crowd. We demands fair play!"

"We're bringin' in a cultured gent from another town," I says coldly.

"Who?" demanded Allison.

"None of yore dang business!" trumpeted Soapy, which gets delusions of valor when he's full of licker. "As a champion of progress and civic pride I challenges the skunk-odored forces of corrupt politics, and—"

Bam! McDonald swung with a billiard ball and Soapy kissed the sawdust.

"Now look what you done," I says peevishly. "If you coyotes cain't ack like gents, you'll oblige me by gittin' to hell outa here."

"If you don't like our company suppose you tries to put us out!" they challenged.

So when I'd finished my drink I taken their weppins away from 'em and throwed 'em headfirst out the side door. How was I to know somebody had jest put up a new cast-iron hitching-rack out there? Their friends carried 'em over to the Red Tomahawk to sew up their sculps, and I went back into the Silver Saddle to see if Soapy had come to yet. Jest as I reched for the door he come weaving out, muttering in his whiskers and waving his sixshooter.

"Do you remember what all I told you?" I demanded.

"S-some of it!" he goggled, with his glassy eyes wobbling in all directions.

"Well, git goin' then," I urged, and helped him up onto his hoss. He left town at full speed, with both feet outa the stirrups and both arms around the hoss's neck.

"Drink is a curse and a delusion," I told the barkeep in disgust. "Look at that sickenin' example and take warnin'! Gimme a bottle of rye."

Well, Gooseneck done a good job of advertising the show. By the middle of the next afternoon men was pouring into town from claims all up and down the creek. Half an hour before the match was sot to begin the hall was full. The benches was moved back from the front part, leaving a space clear all the way acrost the hall. They had been a lot of argyment about who was to compete, and who was to choose sides, but when it was finally settled, as satisfactory as anything ever was settled in Yeller Dog, they was twenty men to compete, and Lobo Harrison and Jack Clanton was to choose up.

By a peculiar coincidence, half of that twenty men was Gooseneck's, and half was Bull's. So naturally Lobo chose his pals, and Clanton chose his'n.

"I don't like this," Gooseneck whispered to me. "I'd ruther they'd been mixed up. This is beginnin' to look like a contest between my gang and Bull's. If they win, it'll make me look cheap. Where the hell is Snake River?"

"I ain't seen him," I said. "You ought to of made 'em take off their guns."

"Shucks," says he. "What could possibly stir up trouble at sech a lady-like affair as a spellin' bee. Dang it, where is Snake River? Old Jake said he'd git him here on time."

"Hey, Gooseneck!" yelled Bull Hawkins from where he sot amongst his cohorts. "Whyn't you start the show?"

Bull was a big broad-shouldered hombre with black mustaches like a walrus. The crowd begun to holler and cuss and stomp their feet and this pleased Bull very much.

"Keep 'em amused," hissed Gooseneck. "I'll go look for Snake River."

He snuck out a side door and I riz up and addressed the throng. "Gents," I said, "be patient! They is a slight delay, but it won't be long. Meantime I'll be glad to entertain you all to the best of my ability. Would you like to hear me sing *Barbary Allen?*"

"No, by grab!" they answered in one beller.

"Well, yo're a-goin' to!" I roared, infuriated by this callous lack of the finer feelings. "I will now sing," I says, drawing my .45s, "and I blows the brains out of the first coyote which tries to interrupt me."

I then sung my song without interference, and when I was through I bowed and waited for the applause, but all I heard was Lobo Harrison saying: "Imagine what the pore wolves on Bear Creek has to put up with!"

This cut me to the quick, but before I could make a suitable reply, Gooseneck slid in, breathing heavy. "I can't find Snake River," he hissed. "But the barkeep gimme a book he found somewheres. Most of the leaves is tore out, but there's plenty left. I've marked some of the longest words, Breckinridge. You can read good enough to give 'em out. You got to! If we don't start the show right away, this mob'll wreck the place. Yo're the only man not in the match which can even read a little, outside of me and Bull. It wouldn't look right for me to do it, and I shore ain't goin' to let Bull run my show."

I knew I was licked.

"Aw, well, all right," I said. "I might of knew I'd be the goat. Gimme the book."

"Here it is," he said. "'The Adventures of a French Countess,' Be dern shore you don't give out no words except them I marked."

"Hey!" bawled Jack Clanton. "We're gettin' tired standin' up here. Open the ball."

"All right," I says. "We commences."

"Hey!" said Bull. "Nobody told us Elkins was goin' to conduck the ceremony. We was told a cultured gent from outa town was to do it."

"Well," I says irritably, "Bear Creek is my home range, and I reckon I'm as cultured as any snake-hunter here. If anybody think he's better qualified than me, step up whilst I stomp his ears off."

Nobody volunteered, so I says: "All right. I tosses a dollar to see who gits the first word." It fell for Harrison's gang, so I looked in the book at the first word marked, and it was a gal's name.

"Catherine," I says.

Nobody said nothin'.

"Catherine!" I roared, glaring at Lobo Harrison.

"What you lookin' at me for?" he demanded. "I don't know no gal by that name."

"!●¾$%¢*" I says with passion. "That's the word I give out. Spell it, dammit!"

"Oh," says he. "All right. K-a-t-h-a-r-i-n-n."

"That's wrong," I says.

"What you mean wrong?" he roared. "That's right!"

"'Tain't accordin' to the book," I said.

"Dang the book," says he. "I knows my rights and I ain't to be euchered by no ignorant grizzly from Bear Creek!"

"Who you callin' ignorant?" I demanded, stung. "Set down! You spelt it wrong."

"You lie!" he howled, and went for his gun. But I fired first.

When the smoke cleared away I seen everybody was on their feet preparing for the stampede, sech as warn't trying to crawl under the benches, so I said: "Sit down, everybody. They ain't nothin' to git excited about. The spellin' match continues—and I'll shoot the first scoundrel which tries to leave the hall before the entertainment's over."

Gooseneck hissed fiercely at me: "Dammit, be careful who you shoot, cain't'cha? That was another one of my voters."

"Drag him out!" I commanded, wiping off some blood where

a slug had notched my ear. "The spellin' match is ready to commence again."

They was a kind of tension in the air, men shuffling their feet and twisting their mustaches and hitching their gun-belts, but I give no heed. I now approached the other side, with my hand on my pistol, and says to Clanton: "Can you spell Catherine?"

"C-a-t-h-e-r-i-n-e!" says he.

"Right, by golly!" I says, consulting the book, and the audience cheered wildly and shot off their pistols into the roof.

"Hey!" says Bill Stark, on the other side. "That's wrong. Make him set down! It spells with a 'K'!"

"He spelt it jest like it is in the book," I says. "Look for yoreself."

"I don't give a damn!" he yelled, rudely knocking 'The French Countess' outa my hand. "It's a misprint! It spells with a 'K' or they'll be more blood on the floor! He spelt it wrong and if he don't set down I shoots him down!"

"I'm runnin' this show!" I bellered, beginning to get mad. "You got to shoot me before you shoots anybody else!"

"With pleasure!" snarled he, and went for his gun. . . . Well, I hit him on the jaw with my fist and he went to sleep amongst a wreckage of busted benches. Gooseneck jumped up with maddened shrieks.

"Dang yore soul, Breckinridge!" he squalled. "Quit cancelin' my votes! Who air you workin' for—me or Hawkins?"

"Haw! haw! haw!" bellered Hawkins. "Go on with the show! This is the funniest thing I ever seen!"

Wham! The door crashed open and in pranced Old Jake Hanson, waving a shotgun.

"Welcome to the festivities, Jake," I greeted him. "Where's—"

"You son of a skunk!" quoth he, and let go at me with both barrels. The shot scattered remarkable. I didn't get more'n five or six of 'em and the rest distributed freely amongst the crowd. You ought to of heard 'em holler—the folks, I mean, not the buckshot.

"What in tarnation air you doin'?" shrieked Gooseneck. "Where's Snake River?"

"Gone!" howled Old Jake. "Run off! Eloped with my datter!"

Bull Hawkins riz with a howl of anguish, convulsively clutching his whiskers.

"Salomey?" he bellered. "Eloped?"

"With a cussed gambolier they brung over from Alderville!" bleated Old Jake, doing a war-dance in his passion. "Elkins and Wilkerson persuaded me to take that snake into my boozum! In spite of my pleas and protests they forced him into my peaceful !¾$%¢* household, and he stole the pore, mutton-headed inner-cent's blasted heart with his cultured airs and his slick talk! They've run off to git married!"

"It's a political plot!" shrieked Hawkins, going for his gun. "Wilkerson done it a-purpose!"

I shot the gun out of his hand, but Jack Clanton crashed a bench down on Gooseneck's head and Gooseneck kissed the floor. Clanton came down on top of him, out cold, as Mule McGrath swung with a pistol butt, and the next instant somebody lammed Mule with a brick bat and he flopped down acrost Clanton. And then the fight was on. Them rival political factions jest kind of riz up and rolled together in a wave of profanity, gun-smoke and splintered benches.

I have always noticed that the best thing to do in sech cases is to keep yore temper, and that's what I did for some time, in spite of the efforts of nine or ten wild-eyed Hawkinites. I didn't even shoot one of 'em; I kept my head and battered their skulls with a joist I tore outa the floor, and when I knocked 'em down I didn't stomp 'em hardly any. But they kept coming, and Jack McDonald was obsessed with the notion that he could ride me to the floor by jumping up astraddle of my neck. So he done it, and having discovered his idee was a hallucination, he got a fistful of my hair with his left, and started beating me in the head with his pistol-barrel.

It was very annoying. Simultaneous, several other misfits got hold of my laigs, trying to rassle me down, and some son of Baliol stomped severely on my toe. I had bore my afflictions as patient as Job up to that time, but this perfidy maddened me.

I give a roar which loosened the shingles on the roof, and kicked the toe-stomper in the belly with sech fury that he curled up on the floor with a holler groan and taken no more interest in the proceedings. I likewise busted my timber on somebody's skull, and reched up and pulled Jack McDonald off my neck like pulling a tick off a bull's hide, and hev him through a convenient winder. He's a liar when he says I aimed him deliberate at that rain barrel. I didn't even know they was a rain barrel till I heard his head crash through the staves. I then shaken nine or ten idjits loose from my shoulders and shook the blood outa my eyes and perceived that Gooseneck's men was getting the worst of it, particularly including Gooseneck hisself. So I give another roar and prepared to wade through them fool Hawkinites like a b'ar through a pack of hound-dogs, when I discovered that some perfidious sidewinder had got my spur tangled in his whiskers.

I stooped to ontangle myself, jest as a charge of buckshot ripped through the air where my head had been a instant before. Three or four critters was rushing me with bowie knives, so I give a wrench and tore loose by main force. How could I help it if most of the whiskers come loose too? I grabbed me a bench to use for a club, and I mowed the whole first rank down with one swipe, and then as I drawed back for another lick, I heard somebody yelling above the melee.

"Gold!" he shrieked.

Everybody stopped like they was froze in their tracks. Even Bull Hawkins shook the blood outa his eyes and glared up from where he was kneeling on Gooseneck's wishbone with one hand in Gooseneck's hair and a bowie in the other'n. Everybody quit fighting everybody else, and looked at the door—and there was Soapy Jackson, a-reeling and a-weaving with a empty bottle in one hand, hollering.

"Big gold strike in Wild Hoss Gulch," he blats. "Biggest the West ever seen! Nuggets the size of osteridge 'aigs—gulp!"

He disappeared in a wave of frenzied humanity as Yeller Dog's population abandoned the fray and headed for the wide open spaces. Even Hawkins ceased his efforts to sculp Gooseneck alive and j'ined the stampede. They tore the whole front out of the city hall in their flight, and even them which had been knocked stiff come to at the howl of "Gold!" and staggered wildly after the mob, shrieking pitifully for their picks, shovels and jackasses. When the dust had settled and the thunder of boot-heels had faded in the distance, the only humans left in the city hall was me and Gooseneck and Soapy Jackson, which riz unsteadily with the prints of hobnails all over his homely face. They shore trompled him free and generous in their rush.

Gooseneck staggered up, glared wildly about him, and went into convulsions. At first he couldn't talk at all; he jest frothed at the mouth. When he found speech his langwidge was shocking.

"What you spring it this time of night for?" he howled. "Breck-inridge, I said tell him to bring the news in the mornin', not tonight!"

"I did tell him that," I says.

"Oh, so that was what I couldn't remember!" says Soapy. "That lick McDonald gimme so plumb addled my brains I knowed they was somethin' I forgot, but I couldn't remember what it was."

"Oh sole mio!" gibbered Gooseneck, or words to the effeck.

"Well, what you kickin' about?" I demanded peevishly, having jest discovered that somebody had stabbed me in the hind laig during the melee. My boot was full of blood, and they was brand new boots. "It worked, didn't it?" I says. "They're all headin' for Wild Hoss Gulch, includin' Hawkins hisself, and they cain't possibly git back afore day after tomorrer."

"Yeah!" raved Gooseneck. "They're all gone, includin' my gang! The damn camp's empty! How can I git elected with nobody here to hold the election, and nobody to vote?"

"Oh," I says. "That's right. I hadn't thunk of that."

He fixed me with a awful eye.

"Did you," says he in a blood-curdling voice, "did you tell my voters Soapy was goin' to enact a political strategy?"

"By golly!" I said. "You know it plumb slipped my mind! Ain't that a joke on me?"

"Git out of my life!" says Gooseneck, drawing his gun.

That was a genteel way for him to ack, trying to shoot me after all I'd did for him! I taken his gun away from him as gentle as I knowed how and it was his own fault he got his arm broké. But to hear him rave you would of thought he considered I was to blame for his misfortunes or something. I was so derned disgusted I clumb onto Cap'n Kidd and shaken the dust of that there camp offa my boots because I seen they was no gratitude in Yeller Dog.

I likewise seen I wasn't cut out for the skull-duggery of politics. I had me a notion one time that I'd make a hiyu sheriff but learn't my lesson. It's like my pap says, I reckon.

"All the law a man needs," says he, "is a gun tucked into his pants. And the main l'arnin' he needs is to know which end of that gun the bullet comes out of."

What's good enough for pap, gents, is good enough for me.

The Conquerin' Hero of the Humbolts

I was in Sundance enjoying myself a little after a long trail-drive up from the Cimarron, when I got a letter from Abednego Raxton which said as follers:

Dear Breckinridge:

That time I paid yore fine down in Tucson for breakin' the county clerk's laig you said you'd gimme a hand anytime I ever need help. Well Breckinridge I need yore assistance right now the rustlers is stealing me ragged it has got so I nail my bed-kivers to the bunk every night or they'd steal the blankets right offa me Breckinridge. Moreover a stumbling block on the path of progress by the name of Ted Bissett is running sheep on the range next to me this is more'n a man can endure Breckinridge. So I want you to come up here right away and help me find out who is stealing my stock and bust Ted Bissett's hed for him the low-minded scunk. Hoping you air the same I begs to remane as usual,

Your abused friend,
A. Raxton, Esq.

P.S.   That sap-headed misfit Johnny Willoughby which used to work for me down on Green River is sheriff here and he couldn't ketch flies if they was bogged down in merlasses.

Well, I didn't feel it was none of my business to mix into any row Abednego might be having with the sheepmen, so long as both sides fit fair, but rustlers was a different matter. A Elkins detests a thief. So I mounted Cap'n Kidd, after the usual battle, and headed for Lonesome Lizard, which was the nighest town to his ranch.

I found myself approaching this town a while before noon one blazing hot day, and as I crossed a right thick timbered creek, shrieks for aid and assistance suddenly bust the stillness. A hoss also neighed wildly, and Cap'n Kidd begun to snort and champ like he always does when they is a b'ar or a cougar in the vicinity. I got off and tied him, because if I was going to have to fight some critter like that, I didn't want him mixing into the scrap; he was jest as likely to kick me as the varmint. I then went on foot in the direction of the screams, which was growing more desperate every minute, and I presently come to a thicket with a big tree in the middle of it, and there they was. One of the purtiest gals I ever seen was roosting in the tree and screeching blue murder, and they was a cougar climbing up after her.

"Help!" she says wildly. "Shoot him!"

"I jest wish some of them tender-foots which calls theirselves naturalists could see this," I says, taking off my Stetson. A Elkins never forgets his manners. "Some of 'em has tried to tell me cougars never attacks human beings nor climbs trees, nor prowls in the daytime. I betcha this would make 'em realize they don't know it all. Jest like I said to that'n which I seen in War Paint, Nevada, last summer—"

"Will you stop talkin' and do somethin'?" she said fiercely. "Ow!"

Because he had reched up and made a pass at her foot with his left paw. I seen this had went far enough, so I told him sternly to come down, but all he done was look down at me and spit in a very insulting manner. So I reched up and got him by the tail and yanked him down, and whapped him agen the ground three or four times, and when I let go of him he run off a few yards, and looked back at me in a most pecooliar manner. Then he shaken his head like he couldn't believe it hisself, and lit a shuck as hard as he could peel it in the general direction of the North Pole.

"Why'n't you shoot him?" demanded the gal, leaning as far out as she could to watch him.

"Aw, he won't come back," I assured her. "Hey, look out! That limb's goin' to break—"

Which it did jest as I spoke and she come tumbling down with a shriek of despair. She still held onto the limb with a desperate grip, however, which is why it rapped me so severe on the head when I catched her.

"Oh!" says she, letting go of the limb and grabbing me. "Am I hurt?"

"I dunno," I says. "You better let me carry you to wherever you want to go."

"No," says she, gitting her breath back. "I'm all right. Lemme down."

So I done so, and she says: "I got a hoss tied over there behind that fir. I was ridin' home from Lonesome Lizard and stopped to poke a squirrel out of a holler tree. It warn't a squirrel, though. It was that dang lion. If you'll git my hoss for me, I'll be ridin' home. Pap's ranch is jest over that ridge to the west. I'm Margaret Brewster."

"I'm Breckinridge Elkins, of Bear Creek, Nevada," I says. "I'm headin' for Lonesome Lizard, but I'll be ridin' back this way before long. Can I call on you?"

"Well," she says, "I'm engaged to marry a feller, but it's conditional. I got a suspicion he's a spineless failure, and I told him flat if he didn't succeed at the job he's workin' on now, not to come back. I detests a failure. That's why I likes yore looks," says she, giving me a admiring glance. "A man which can rassle a mountain lion with his b'ar hands is worth any gal's time. I'll send you word at Lonesome Lizard; if my fiansay flops like it looks he's goin' to do, I'd admire to have you call."

"I'll be awaitin' yore message with eager heart and honest devotion," I says, and she blushed daintily and clumb on her hoss and pulled her freight. I watched her till she was clean out of sight, and then hove a sigh that shook the acorns out of the surrounding oaks, and wended my way back to Cap'n Kidd in a sort of rose-colored haze. I was so entranced I started to git onto Cap'n Kidd on the wrong end and never noticed till he kicked me vi'lently in the belly.

"Love, Cap'n Kidd," I says to him dreamily, batting him between the eyes with my pistol butt, "is youth's sweet dream."

But he made no response, outside of stomping on my corns; Cap'n Kidd has got very little sentiment.

So I mounted and pulled for Lonesome Lizard, which I arriv at maybe a hour later. I put Cap'n Kidd in the strongest livery stable I could find and seen he was fed and watered, and warned the stablehands not to antagonize him, and then I headed for the Red Warrior saloon. I needed a little refreshments before I started for Abednego's ranch.

I taken me a few drams and talked to the men which was foregathered there, being mainly cowmen. The sheepmen patronized the Bucking Ram, acrost the street. That was the first time I'd ever been in Montana, and them fellers warn't familiar with my repertation, as was showed by their manner.

Howthesomever, they was perlite enough, and after we'd downed a few fingers of corn scrapings, one of 'em ast me where I was from, proving they considered me a honest man with nothing to conceal. When I told 'em, one of 'em said: "By golly, they must grow big men in Nevada, if you're a sample. Yo're the biggest critter I ever seen in the shape of a human."

"I bet he's as stout as Big Jon," says one, and another'n says: "That cain't be. This gent is human, after all. Big Jon ain't."

I was jest fixing to ast'em who this Jon varmint was, when one of 'em cranes his neck toward the winder and says: "Speak of the devil and you gits a whiff of brimstone! Here comes Jon acrost the street now. He must of seen this gent comin' in, and is on his way to make his usual challenge. The sight of a man as big as him is like wavin' a red flag at a bull."

I looked out the winder and seen a critter about the size of a granary comin' acrost the street from the Bucking Ram, follered by a gang of men which looked like him, but not nigh as big.

"What kind of folks air they?" I ast with interest. "They ain't neither Mexicans nor Injuns, but they sure ain't white men, neither."

"Aw, they're Hunkies," says a little sawed-off cowman. "Ted Bissett brung 'em in here to herd sheep for him. That big 'un's Jon. He ain't got no sense, but you never seen sech a hunk of muscle in yore life."

"Where they from?" I ast. "Canader?"

"Naw," says he. "They come originally from a place called Yurrop. I dunno where it is, but I jedge it's somewhere's east of Chicago."

But I knowed them fellers never originated nowheres on this continent. They was rough-dressed and wild-looking, with knives in their belts, and they didn't look like no folks I'd ever saw before. They came into the barroom and the one called Jon bristled up to me very hostile with his little beady black eyes. He stuck out his chest about a foot and hit it with his fist which was about the size of a sledge hammer. It sounded like a man beating a bass drum.

"You strong man," says he. "I strong too. We rassle, eh?"

"Naw," I says. "I don't care nothin' about rasslin'."

He give a snort which blowed the foam off of every beer glass on the bar, and looked around till he seen a iron rod laying on the floor. It looked like the handle of a branding iron, and was purty thick. He grabbed this and bent it into a V, and throwed it down on the bar in front of me, and all the other Hunkies jabbered admiringly.

This childish display irritated me, but I controlled myself and drunk another finger of whiskey, and the bartender whispered to me: "Look out for him! He aims to prod you into a fight. He's nearly kilt nine or ten men with his b'ar hands. He's a mean 'un."

"Well," I says, tossing a dollar onto the bar and turning away, "I got more important things to do than rassle a outlandish foreigner in a barroom. I got to eat my dinner and git out to the Raxton ranch quick."

But at that moment Big Jon chose to open his bazoo. There are some folks which cain't never let well enough alone.

"'Fraid!" jeered he. "Yah, yah!"

The Hunkies all whooped and guffawed, and the cattlemen scowled.

"What you mean, afraid?" I gasped, more dumbfounded than mad. It'd been so long since anybody'd made a remark like that to me I was plumb flabbergasted. Then I remembered I was amongst strangers which didn't know my repertation, and I realized it was my duty to correct that there oversight before somebody got hurt on account of ignorance.

So I said, "All right, you dumb foreign muttonhead, I'll rassle you."

But as I went up to him, he doubled up his fist and hit me severely on the nose, and them Hunkies all bust into loud, rude laughter. That warn't wise. A man had better twist a striped thunderbolt's tail than hit a Elkins onexpected on the nose. I give a roar of irritation and grabbed Big Jon and started committing mayhem on him free and enthusiastic. I swept all the glasses and bottles off of the bar with him, and knocked down a hanging lamp with him, and fanned the floor with him till he was limp, and then I throwed him the full length of the barroom. His head went through the panels of the back door, and other Hunkies, which had stood petrified, stampeded into the street with howls of horror. So I taken the branding iron handle and straightened it out and bent it around his neck, and twisted the ends together in a knot, so he had to get a blacksmith to file it off after he come to, which was several hours later.

All them cowmen was staring at me with their eyes popped out of their heads, and seemed plumb incapable of speech, so I give a snort of disgust at the whole incerdent, and strode off to git my dinner. As I left I heard one feller, which was holding onto the bar like he was too weak to stand alone, say feebly to the dumbfounded bartender: "Gimme a drink, quick! I never thunk I'd live to see somethin' I couldn't believe when I was lookin' right smack at it."

I couldn't make no sense out of this, so I headed for the dining room of the Montana Hotel and Bar. But my hopes of peace and quiet was a illusion. I'd jest started on my fourth beefsteak when a big maverick in Star-top boots and store-bought clothes comes surging into the dining room and bellered: "Is your name Elkins?"

"Yes, it is," I says. "But I ain't deef. You don't have to yell."

"Well, what the hell do you mean by interferin' with my business?" he squalled, ignoring my reproof.

"I dunno what yo're talkin' about," I growled, emptying the sugar bowl into my coffee cup with some irritation. It looked like Lonesome Lizard was full of maneyacks which craved destruction. "Who air you, anyhow?"

"I'm Ted Bissett, that's who!" howled he, convulsively gesturing toward his six-shooter. "And I'm onto you! You're a damn' Nevada gunman old Abed' Raxton's brought up here to run me off the range! He's been braggin' about it all over town! And you starts your work by runnin' off my sheepherders!"

"What you mean, I run yore sheepherders off?" I demanded, amazed.

"They ran off after you maltreated Big Jon," he gnashed, with his face convulsed. "They're so scared of you they won't come back without double pay! You can't do this to me, you !●¾$%¢&*!"

The man don't live which can call me that name with impunity. I impulsively hit him in the face with my fried steak, and he give a impassioned shriek and pulled his gun. But some grease had got in his eyes, so all he done with his first shot was bust the syrup pitcher at my elbow, and before he could cock his gun again I shot him through the arm. He dropped his gun and grabbed the place with his other hand and made some remarks which ain't fitten for to repeat.

I yelled for another steak, and Bissett yelled for a doctor, and the manager yelled for the sheriff.

The last-named individual didn't git there till after the doctor and the steak had arrove and was setting Bissett's arm——the doctor, I mean, and not the steak, which a trembling waiting brung me. Quite a crowd had gathered by this time and was watching the doctor work with great interest, and offering advice which seemed to infuriate Bissett, jedging from his langwidge. He also discussed his busted arm with considerable passion, but the doctor warn't a bit worried. You never seen sech a cheerful gent. He was jovial and gay, no matter how loud Bissett yelled. You could tell right off he was a man which could take it.

But Bissett's friends was very mad, and Jack Campbell, his foreman, was muttering something about 'em taking the law into their own hands, when the sheriff come prancing in, waving a six-shooter and hollering: "Where is he? P'int out the scoundrel to me!"

"There he is!" everybody yelled, and ducked, like they expected gunplay, but I'd already recognized the sheriff, and when he seen me he recoiled and shoved his gun out of sight like it was red hot or something.

"Breckinridge Elkins!" says he. Then he stopped and studied a while, and then he told 'em to take Bissett out to the bar and pour some licker down him. When they'd went he sot down at the table, and says: "Breck, I want you to understand that they ain't nothin' personal about this, but I got to arrest you. It's agen the law to shoot a man inside of the city limits."

"I ain't got time to git arrested," I told him. "I got to git over to old Abed' Raxton's ranch."

"But lissen, Breck," argyed the sheriff—it was Johnny Willoughby, jest like old Abed' said—"What'll folks think if I don't jail you for shootin' a leadin' citizen? Election's comin' up and my hat's in the ring," says he, gulping my coffee.

"Bissett shot at me first," I said. "Whyn't you arrest him?"

"Well, he didn't hit you," says Johnny, absently cramming half a pie into his mouth and making a stab at my pertaters. "Anyway, he's got a busted arm and ain't able to go to jail jest now. Besides, I needs the sheepmen's votes."

"Aw, I don't like jails," I said irritably, and he begun to weep. "If you was a friend to me," sobs he, "you'd be glad to spend the night in jail to help me git re-elected. I'd do as much for you! The whole county's givin' me hell anyway, because I ain't been able to catch none of them cattle rustlers, and if I don't arrest you I won't have a Chinaman's chance at the polls. How can you do me like this, after the times we had together in the old days—"

"Aw, stop blubberin'," I says. "You can arrest me, if you want to. What's the fine?"

"I don't want to colleck no fine, Breck," says he, wiping his eyes on the oil-cloth table cover and filling his pockets with doughnuts. "I figgers a jail sentence will give me more prestige. I'll let you out first thing in the mornin'. You won't tear up the jail, will you, Breckinridge?"

I promised I wouldn't, and then he wants me to give up my guns, and I refuses.

"But good gosh, Breck," he pleaded. "It'd look awful funny for a prisoner to keep on his shootin' irons."

So I give 'em to him, jest to shet him up and then he wanted to put his handcuffs onto me, but they warn't big enough to fit my wrists. So he said if I'd lend him some money he could have the blacksmith to make me some laig-irons, but I refused profanely, so he said all right, it was jest a suggestion, and no offence intended, so we went down to the jail. The jailer was off sleeping off a drunk somewheres, but he'd left the key hanging on the door, so we went in. Purty soon along come Johnny's deperty, Bige Gantry, a long, loose-j'inted cuss with a dangerous eye, so Johnny sent him to the Red Warrior for a can of beer, and whilst he was gone Johnny bragged on him a heap.

"Why," says he, "Bige is the only man in the county which has ever got within shootin' distance of them dern' outlaws. He was by hisself, wuss luck. If I'd been along we'd of scuppered the whole gang."

I ast him if he had any idee who they was, and he said Bige believed they was a gang up from Wyoming. So I said well, then, in that case they got a hang-out in the hills somewheres, and ought to be easier to run down than men which scattered to their homes after each raid.

Bige got back with the beer about then, and Johnny told him that when I got out of jail he was going to depertize me and we'd all go after them outlaws together. So Bige said that was great, and looked me over purty sharp, and we sot down and started playing poker. Along about supper time the jailer come in, looking tolerable seedy, and Johnny made him cook us some supper. Whilst we was eating the jailer stuck his head into my cell and said: "A gent out there cravin' audience with Mister Elkins."

"Tell him the prisoner's busy," says Johnny.

"I done so," says the jailer, "and he says if you don't let him in purty dern quick, he's goin' to bust in and cut yore throat."

"That must be old Abed' Raxton," says Johnny. "Better let him in, Breck," says he, "I looks to you to pertect me if the old cuss gits mean."

So old Abed' come walzing into the jail with fire in his eye and corn licker on his breath. At the sight of me he let out a squall which was painful to hear.

"A hell of a help you be, you big lummox!" he hollered. "I sends for you to help me bust up a gang of rustlers and sheepherders, and the first thing you does is to git in jail!"

"T'warn't my fault," I says. "Them sheepherders started pickin' on me."

"Well," he snarls, "Whyn't you drill Bissett center when you was at it?"

"I come up here to shoot rustlers, not sheepherders," I says.

"What's the difference?" he snarled.

"Them sheepmen has probably got as much right on the range as you cowmen," I says.

"Cease sech outrageous blasphermy," says he, shocked. "You've bungled things so far, but they's one good thing—Bissett had to hire back his derned Hunkie herders at double wages. He don't no more mind spendin' money than he does spillin' his own blood, the cussed tightwad. Well, what's yore fine?"

"Ain't no fine," I said. "Johnny wants me to stay in jail a while."

At this old Abed' convulsively went for his gun and Johnny got behind me and hollered: "Don't you dast shoot a ossifer of the law!"

"It's a spite trick!" gibbered old Abed'. "He's been mad at me ever since I fired him off'n my payroll. After I kicked him off'n my ranch he run for sheriff, and the night of the election everybody was so drunk they voted for him by mistake, or for a joke, or somethin', and since he's been in office he's been lettin' the sheepmen steal me right out of house and home."

"That's a lie," says Johnny heatedly. "I've give you as much pertection as anybody else, you old buzzard! I jest ain't been able to run any of them critters down, that's all. But you wait! Bige is on their trail, and we'll have 'em behind the bars before the snow falls."

"Before the snow falls in Guatamala, maybe," snorted old Abed'. "All right, blast you, I'm goin', but I'll have Breckinridge outa here if I have to burn the cussed jail! A Raxton never forgits!" So he stalked out sulphurously, only turning back to snort: "Sheriff! Bah! Seven murders in the county unsolved since you come into office! You'll let the sheepmen murder us all in our beds! We ain't had a hangin' since you was elected!"

After he'd left, Johnny brooded a while, and finally says: "The old lobo's right about them murders, only he neglected to mention that four of 'em was sheepmen. I know it's cattlemen and sheepmen killin' each other, each side accusin' the other'n of rustlin' stock, but I cain't prove nothin'. A hangin' would see me solid with the voters." Here he eyed me hungrily, and ventured: "If somebody'd jest up and confess to some of them murders—"

"You needn't to look at me like that," I says. "I never kilt nobody in Montana."

"Well," he argyed, "nobody could prove you never done 'em, and after you was hanged—"

"Lissen here, you," I says with some passion, "I'm willin' to help a friend git elected all I can, but they's a limit!"

"Oh, well, all right," he sighed. "I didn't much figger you'd be willin', anyway; folks is so dern selfish these days. All they thinks about is theirselves. But lissen here: if I was to bust up a lynchin' mob it'd be nigh as good a boost for my campaign as a legal hangin'. I tell you what—tonight I'll have some of my friends put on masks and come and take you out and pretend like they was goin' to hang you. Then when they got the rope around yore neck I'll run out and shoot in the air and they'll run off and I'll git credit for upholdin' law and order. Folks always disapproves of mobs, unless they happens to be in 'em."

So I said all right, and he urged me to be careful and not hurt none of 'em, because they was all his friends and would be mine. I ast him would they bust the door down, and he said they warn't no use in damaging property like that; they could hold up the jailer and take the key off'n him. So he went off to fix things, and after a while Bige Gantry left and said he was on the trace of a clue to them cattle rustlers, and the jailer started drinking hair tonic mixed with tequila, and in about a hour he was stiffer'n a wet lariat.

Well, I laid down on the floor on a blanket to sleep, without taking my boots off, and about midnight a gang of men in masks come and they didn't have to hold up the jailer, because he was out cold. So they taken the key off'n him, and all the loose change and plug tobaccer out of his pockets too, and opened the door, and I ast: "Air you the gents which is goin' to hang me?" And they says: "We be!"

So I got up and ast them if they had any licker, and one of 'em gimme a good snort out of his hip flask, and I said: "All right, le's git it over with, so I can go back to sleep."

He was the only one which done any talking, and the rest didn't say a word. I figgered they was bashful. He said: "Le's tie yore hands behind you so's to make it look real," and I said all right, and they tied me with some rawhide thongs which I reckon would of held the average man all right.

So I went outside with 'em, and they was a oak tree right clost to the jail nigh some bushes. I figgered Johnny was hiding over behind them bushes.

They had a barrel for me to stand on, and I got onto it, and they throwed a rope over a big limb and put the noose around my neck, and the feller says: "Any last words?"

"Aw, hell," I says, "this is plumb silly. Ain't it about time for Johnny—"

At this moment they kicked the barrel out from under me.

Well, I was kind of surprised, but I tensed my neck muscles, and waited for Johnny to rush out and rescue me, but he didn't come, and the noose began to pinch the back of my neck, so I got disgusted and says: "Hey, lemme down!"

Then one of 'em which hadn't spoke before says: "By golly, I never heard a man talk after he'd been strung up before!"

I recognized that voice; it was Jack Campbell, Bissett's foreman! Well, I have got a quick mind, in spite of what my cousin Bearfield Buckner says, so I knowed right off something was fishy about this business. So I snapped the thongs on my wrist and reched up and caught hold of the rope I was hung with by both hands and broke it. Them scoundrels was so surprised they didn't think to shoot at me till the rope was already broke, and then the bullets all went over me as I fell. When they started shooting I knowed they meant me no good, and acted according.

I dropped right in the midst of 'em, and brung three to the ground with me, and during the few seconds it taken me to choke and batter them unconscious the others was scairt to fire for fear of hitting their friends, we was so tangled up. So they clustered around and started beating me over the head with their gun butts, and I riz up like a b'ar amongst a pack of hounds and grabbed four more of 'em and hugged 'em till their ribs cracked. Their masks came off during the process, revealing the faces of Bissett's friends; I'd saw 'em in the hotel.

Somebody prodded me in the hind laig with a bowie at that moment, which infuriated me, so I throwed them four amongst the crowd and hit out right and left, knocking over a man or so at each lick, till I seen a wagon spoke on the ground and stooped over to pick it up. When I done that somebody throwed a coat over my head and blinded me, and six or seven men then jumped onto my back. About this time I stumbled over some feller which had been knocked down, and fell onto my belly, and they all started jumping up and down on me enthusiastically. I reched around and grabbed one and dragged him around to where I could rech his left ear with my teeth. I would of taken it clean off at the first snap, only I had to bite through the coat which was over my head, but as it was I done a good job, jedging from his awful shrieks.

He put forth a supreme effort and tore away, taking the coat with him, and I shaken off the others and riz up in spite of their puny efforts, with the wagon spoke in my hand.

A wagon spoke is a good, comforting implement to have in a melee, and very demoralizing to the enemy. This'n busted all to pieces about the fourth or fifth lick, but that was enough. Them which was able to run had all took to their heels, leaving the battlefield strewed with moaning and cussing figgers.

Their remarks was shocking to hear, but I give 'em no heed. I headed for the sheriff's office, mad clean through. It was a few hundred yards east of the jail, and jest as I rounded the jail house, I run smack into a dim figger which come sneaking through the bresh making a curious clacking noise. It hit me with what appeared to be a iron bar, so I went to the ground with it and choked it and beat its head agen the ground, till the moon come out from behind a cloud and revealed the bewhiskered features of old Abednego Raxton!

"What the hell?" I demanded of the universe at large. "Is everybody in Montaner crazy? What air you doin' tryin' to murder me in my sleep?"

"I warn't, you jack-eared lunkhead," snarled he, when he could talk.

"Then what'd you hit me with that there pinch bar for?" I demanded.

"I didn't know it was you," says he, gitting up and dusting his britches. "I thought it was a grizzly b'ar when you riz up out of the dark. Did you bust out?"

"Naw, I never," I said. "I told you I was stayin' in jail to do Johnny a favor. And you know what that son of Baliol done? He framed it up with Bissett's friends to git me hung. Come on. I'm goin' over and interview the dern skunk right now."

So we went over to Johnny's office, and the door was unlocked and a candle burning, but he warn't in sight.

They was a small iron safe there which I figgered he had my guns locked up in, so I got a rock and busted it open, and sure enough there my shooting irons was. They was also a gallon of corn licker there, and me and Abed' was discussing whether or not we had the moral right to drink it, when I heard somebody remark in a muffled voice: "Whumpff! Gfuph! Oompg!"

So we looked around and I seen a pair of spurs sticking out

from under a camp cot over in the corner. I grabbed hold of the boots they was on, and pulled 'em out, and a human figger come with 'em. It was Johnny. He was tied hand and foot and gagged, and he had a lump onto his head about the size of a turkey aig.

I pulled off the gag, and the first thing he says was: "If you sons of Perdition drinks my private licker, I'll have yore hearts' blood!"

"You better do some explainin'," I says resentfully. "What you mean, siccin' Bissett's friends onto me?"

"I never done no sech!" says he heatedly. "Right after I left the jail I come to the office here, and was jest fixin' to git hold of my friends to frame the fake neck-tie party, when somebody come in at the door and hit me over the head. I thought it was Bige comin' in and didn't look around, and then whoever it was clouted me. I jest a while ago come to myself, and I was tied up like you see."

"If he's tellin' the truth," says old Abed'—"which he seems to be, much as I hates to admit it—it looks like some friend of Bissett overheard you all talkin' about this thing, follered Johnny over and put him out of the way for the time bein', and then raised a mob of his own, knowin' Breckinridge wouldn't put up any resistance, thinkin' they was friends. I told you—who's that?"

We all drawed our irons, and then put 'em up as Bige Gantry rushed in, holding onto the side of his head, which was all bloody.

"I jest had a bresh with the outlaws!" he hollered. "I been trailin' 'em all night! They waylaid me a while ago, three miles out of town! They nearly shot my ear off! But if I didn't wing one of 'em, I'm a Dutchman!"

"Round up a posse!" howled Johnny, grabbing a Winchester and cartridge belt. "Take us back to where you had the scrape, Bige—"

"Wait a minute," I says, grabbing Bige. "Lemme see that ear!" I jerked his hand away, disregarding the spur he stuck into my laig, and bellered: "Shot, hell! That ear was chawed, and I'm the man which done it! You was one of them illegitimates which tried to hang me!"

He then whipped out his gun, but I knocked it out of his hand and hit him on the jaw and knocked him through the door. I then follered him outside and taken away the bowie he drawed as he rose groggily, and throwed him back into the office, and went in and throwed him out again, and went out and throwed him back in again.

"How long is this goin' on?" he ast.

"Probably all night," I assured him. "The way I feel right now I can keep heavin' you in and out of this office from now till noon tomorrer."

"Hold up!" gurgled he. "I'm a hard nut but I know when I'm licked! I'll confess! I done it!"

"Done what?" I demanded.

"I hit Johnny on the head and tied him up!" he howled, grabbing wildly for the door jamb as he went past it. "I rigged the lynching party! I'm in with the rustlers!"

"Set him down!" hollered Abed', grabbing holt of my shirt. "Quick, Johnny! Help me hold Breckinridge before he kills a valurebull witness!"

But I shaken him off impatiently and sot Gantry onto his feet. He couldn't stand, so I helt him up by the collar and he gasped: "I lied about tradin' shots with the outlaws. I been foolin' Johnny all along. The rustlers ain't no Wyoming gang; they all live around here. Ted Bissett is the head chief of 'em—"

"Ted Bissett, hey?" whooped Abed', doing a war-dance and kicking my shins in his glee. "See there, you big lummox? What'd I tell you? What you think now, after showin' so dern much affexion for them cussed sheepmen? Jest shootin' Bissett in the arm, like he was yore brother, or somethin'! S'wonder you didn't invite him out to dinner. You ain't got the—"

"Aw, shet up!" I said fretfully. "Go on, Gantry."

"He ain't a legitimate sheepman," says he. "That's jest a blind, him runnin' sheep. Ain't no real sheepmen mixed up with him. His gang is jest the scrapin's of the country, and they hide out on his ranch when things gits hot. Other times they scatters and goes home. They're the ones which has been killin' honest sheepmen and cattlemen—tryin' to set the different factions agen each other, so as to make stealin' easier. The Hunkies ain't in on the deal. He jest brung 'em out to herd his sheep, because his own men wouldn't do it, and he was afeared if he hired local sheepherders, they'd ketch onto him. Naturally we wanted you outa the way, when we knowed you'd come up here to run down the rustlers, so tonight I seen my chance when Johnny started talkin' about stagin' that fake hangin'. I follered Johnny and tapped him on the head and tied him up and went and told Bissett about the business, and we got the boys together, and you know the rest. It was a peach of a frame-up, and it'd of worked, too, if we'd been dealin' with a human bein'. Lock me up. All I want right now is a good, quiet penitentiary where I'll be safe."

"Well," I said to Johnny, after he'd locked Gantry up, "all you got to do is ride over to Bissett's ranch and arrest him. He's laid up with his arm, and most of his men is crippled. You'll find a number of 'em over by the jail. This oughta elect you."

"It will!" says he, doing a war-dance in his glee. "I'm as good as elected right now! And I tell you, Breck, t'ain't the job alone I'm thinkin' about. I'd of lost my gal if I'd lost the race. But she's promised to marry me if I ketched them rustlers and got re-elected. And she won't go back on her word, neither!"

"Yeah?" I says with idle interest, thinking of my own true love. "What's her name?"

"Margaret Brewster!" says he.

"What?" I yelled, in a voice which knocked old Abed' over on his back like he'd been hit by a cyclone. Them which accuses me of vi'lent and onusual conduck don't consider how my emotions was stirred up by the knowledge that I had went through all them humiliating experiences jest to help a rival take my gal away from me. Throwing Johnny through the office winder and kicking the walls out of the building was jest a mild expression of the way I felt about the whole dern affair, and instead of feeling resentful, he ought to have been thankful I was able to restrain my natural feelings as well as I done.

A Ringtailed Tornado

I hear the citizens of War Whoop has organized theirselves into a committee of public safety which they says is to perfect the town agen me, Breckinridge Elkins. Sech doings as that irritates me. You'd think I was a public menace or somethin'.

I'm purty dern tired of their slanders. I didn't tear down their cussed jail; the buffalo-hunters done it. How could I when I was in it at the time.

As for the Silver Boot saloon and dance hall, it wouldn't of got shot up if the owner had showed any sense. It was Ace Middleton's own fault he got his hind laig busted in three places, and if the city marshal had been tending to his own business instead of persecuting a pore, helpless stranger, he wouldn't have got the seat of his britches fulled with buckshot.

Folks which says I went to War Whoop a-purpose to wreck the town, is liars. I never had no idea at first of going there at all. It's off the railroad and infested with tinhorn gamblers and buffalo-hunters and sech-like varmints, and no place for a trail-driver.

My visit to this lair of vice come about like this: I'd rode p'int on a herd of longhorns clean from the lower Pecos to Goshen, where the railroad was. And I stayed there after the trail-boss and the other boys headed south, to spark the belle of the town, Betty Wilkinson, which gal was as purty as a brand-new Bowie knife. She seemed to like me middling tolerable, but I had rivals, notably a snub-nosed Arizona waddy by the name of Bizz Ridgeway.

This varmint's persistence was so plumb aggravating that I come in on him suddenlike one morning in the back room of the Spanish Mustang, in Goshen, and I says:

"Lissen here, you sand-burr in the pants of progress, I'm a peaceable man, generous and retirin' to a fault. But I'm reachin' the limit of my endurance. Ain't they no gals in Arizona, that yuh got to come pesterin' mine? Whyn't yuh go on back home where you belong anyhow? I'm askin' yuh like a gent to keep away from

Betty Wilkinson before somethin' onpleasant is forced to happen to yuh."

He kind of r'ared up, and says: "I ain't the only gent which is sparkin' Betty. Why don't you make war-talk to Rudwell Shapley, Jr.?"

"He ain't nothin' but a puddin'-headed tenderfoot," I responded disdainfully. "I don't consider him in no serious light. A gal with as much sense as Betty wouldn't pay him no mind. But you got a slick tongue and might snake yore way ahead of me. So I'm tellin' you!"

He started to git up in a hurry, and I reched for my Bowie, but then he sunk back down in his chair and to my amazement he busted into tears.

"What in thunder's the matter with you?" I demanded, scratching my head.

"Woe is me!" moaned he. "Yuh're right, Breckinridge. I ain't got no business hangin' around Betty. But I didn't know she was yore gal. I ain't got no matrimonial intentions onto her. I'm jest kind of consolin' myself with her company, whilst bein' parted by crooel Fate from my own true love."

"Hey," I says, pricking up my years and uncocking my pistol. "You ain't in love with Betty? You got another gal?"

"A pitcher of divine beauty!" vowed he, wiping his eyes on my bandanner. "Gloria La Venner, which sings in the Silver Boot, over to War Whoop. We was to wed—"

Here his emotions overcome him and he sobbed loudly.

"But Fate interfered," he moaned. "I was banished from War Whoop, never to return. In a thoughtless moment I kind of pushed a bartender with a clawhammer, and he had a stroke of apperplexity or somethin' and died, and they blamed me. I was forced to flee without tellin' my true love where I was goin'.

"I ain't dared to go back because them folks over there is so prejudiced agen' me they threatens to arrest me on sight. My true love is eatin' her heart out, waitin' for me to come and claim her as my bride, whilst I lives here in exile!"

Bizz then wept bitterly on my shoulder till I throwed him off in some embarrassment.

"Whyn't yuh write her a letter, yuh dadblamed fool?" I ast.

"I can't write, nor read, neither," he said. "And I don't trust nobody to send word to her by. She's so beautiful, the critter I'd send would probably fall in love with her hisself, the lowdown polecat!" Suddenly he grabbed my hand with both of his'n, and said: "Breckinridge, you got a honest face, and I never did believe all they say about you, anyway. Whyn't you go and tell her?"

"I'll do better'n that if it'll keep you away from Betty," I says. "I'll bring this gal over here to Goshen."

"Yuh're a gent!" says he, wringing my hand. "I wouldn't entrust nobody else with sech a sacred mssion. Jest go to the Silver Boot and tell Ace Middleton you want to see Gloria La Venner."

"All right," I said. "I'll rent a buckboard to bring her back in."

"I'll be countin' the hours till yuh heaves over the horizon with my true love!" declaimed he, reaching for the whiskey-bottle.

So I hustled out, and who should I run into but that pore sapified shrimp of a Rudwell Shapley Joonyer in his monkey jacket and tight riding pants and varnished English boots. We like to had a collision as I barged through the swinging doors and he squeaked and staggered back and hollered: "Don't shoot!"

"Who said anything about shootin'?" I ast irritably, and he kind of got his color back and looked me over like I was a sideshow or something, like he always done.

"Your home," says he, "is a long way from here, is it not, Mr. Elkins?"

"Yeah," I said. "I'm from Bear Creek, Nevada."

"Indeed!" he says kind of hopefully. "I suppose you'll be returning soon?"

"Naw, I ain't," I says. "I'll probably stay here all fall."

"Oh!" says he dejectedly, and went off looking like somebody had kicked him in the pants. I wondered why he should git so down-in-the-mouth jest because I warn't goin' home. But them tenderfoots ain't got no sense and they ain't no use wasting time trying to figger out why they does things, because they don't generally know theirselves.

For instance, why should a object like Rudwell Shapley Jr. come to Goshen, I want to know? I ast him onct p'int blank and he says it was a primitive urge to see life in the raw, whatever that means. I thought maybe he was talking about grub, but the cook at the Laramie Restaurant said he takes his beefsteaks well done like the rest of us.

Well, anyway, I got onto my hoss Cap'n Kidd and pulled for War Whoop which laid some miles west of Goshen. I warn't wasting no time, because the quicker I acted, the quicker I'd have a clear field with Betty. Of course it would of been easier jest to shoot Bizz, but I didn't know how Betty'd take it. Women is funny that way.

I figgered to eat dinner at the Half-Way House, a drinkin'-place which stood on the prairie about half-way betwix Goshen and War Whoop, but as I approached it I met a most pecooliar-looking object heading east.

I presently recognized it as a cowboy name Tump Garrison, and he looked like he'd been through a sorghum mill. His hat brim was pulled loose from the crown and hung around his neck like a collar, his clothes hung in rags. His face was skint all over, and one ear showed signs of having been chawed on long and earnestly.

"Where was the tornado?" I ast, pulling up.

He give me a suspicious look out of the eye he could still see with.

"Oh, it's you Breckinridge," he says then. "My brains is so addled, I didn't recognize you at first. In fact," says he, tenderly caressing a lump on his head the size of a turkey aig, "it's jest a few minutes ago that I managed to remember my own name."

"What happened?" I ast with interest.

Garrison moves his arms as if to make certain that he's still got 'em.

"I ain't shore," says he, spitting out three or four loose tushes. "Leastways I ain't shore jest what happened after that there table laig was shattered over my head. Things is a little foggy after that. But up to that time my memory is flawless.

"Briefly, Breckinridge," says he, rising in his stirrups to rub his pants where they was the print of a boot heel, "I diskivered that I warn't welcome at the Half-Way House, and big as you be, I advises yuh to avoid it like yuh would the yaller j'indus."

"It's a public saloon," I says.

"It was," says he, working his right laig to see if it was still in j'int. "It was till Moose Harrison, the buffalo-hunter, arrove there to hold a private celebration of his own. He don't like cattle nor them which handles 'em. He told me so hisself, jest before he hit me with the bung-starter.

"He said he warn't aimin' to be pestered by no dern Texas cattle-pushers whilst he's enjoyin' a little relaxation. It was jest after issuin' this statement that he throwed me through the roulette wheel."

"You ain't from Texas," I said. "Yuh're from the Nations."

"That's what I told him whilst he was doin' a war-dance on my brisket," says Tump. "But he said he was too broadminded to bother with technicalities. Anyway, he says cowboys was the plague of the range, irregardless of where they come from."

"Oh, he did, did he?" I says irritably. "Well, I ain't huntin' trouble. I'm on a errand of mercy. But he better not shoot off his big mouth to me. I eats my dinner at the Half-Way House, regardless of all the buffler-hunters north of Cimarron."

"I'd give a dollar to see the fun," says Tump. "But my other eye is closin' fast and I got to git amongst friends."

So he pulled for Goshen and I rode on to the Half-Way House, where I seen a big bay hoss tied to the hitchrack. I watered Cap'n Kidd and went in. "Hssss!" the bartender says. "Git out as quick as yuh can! Moose Harrison's asleep in the back room!"

"I'm hongry," I responded, setting down at a table which stood nigh the bar. "Bring me a steak with pertaters and onions and a quart of coffee and a can of cling peaches. And whilst the stuff's cookin', gimme nine or ten bottles of beer to wash the dust out of my gullet."

"Lissen!" says the barkeep. "Reflect and consider. Yuh're young and life is sweet. Don't yuh know that Moose Harrison is pizen to anything that looks like a cowpuncher? When he's on a whiskey-tear, as at present, he's more painter than human. He's kilt more men than Gettysburg."

"Will yuh stop blattin' and bring me my rations?" I requested.

He shakes his head sad-like and says: "Well, all right. After all, it's yore hide. At least, try not to make no racket. He's swore to have the life blood of anybody which wakes him up."

I said I didn't want no trouble with nobody, and he tiptoed back to the kitchen and whispered my order to the cook, and then brung me nine or ten bottles of beer and slipped back behind the bar and watched me with morbid fascination.

I drunk the beer and whilst drinking I got to kind of brooding about Moose Harrison having the nerve to order everybody to keep quiet whilst he slept. But they're liars which claims I throwed the empty bottles at the door of the back room apurpose to wake Harrison up.

When the waiter brung my grub I wanted to clear the table to make room for it, so I jest kind of tossed the bottles aside, and could I help it if they all busted on the backroom door? Was it my fault that Harrison was sech a light sleeper?

But the bartender moaned and ducked down behind the bar, and the waiter run through the kitchen and follered the cook in a sprint acrost the prairie, and a most remarkable beller burst forth from the back room.

The next instant the door was tore off the hinges and an enormous human come bulging into the barroom. He wore buckskins, his whiskers bristled, and his eyes was red as a drunk Comanche's.

"What in tarnation?" remarked he in a voice which cracked the winder panes. "Does my gol-blasted eyes deceive me? Is that there a cussed cowpuncher settin' there wolfin' beefsteak as brash as if he was a hoomin' bein'?"

"You ride herd on them insults!" I roared, rising sudden, and his eyes kind of popped when he seen I was about three inches taller'n him. "I got as much right here as you have."

"Name yore weppins," blustered he. He had a butcher knife and two six-shooters in his belt.

"Name 'em yoreself," I snorted. "If you thinks yuh're sech a hell-whizzer at fist-and-skull, why, shuck yore weppin-belt and I'll claw yore ears off with my bare hands!"

At this, he glared at me and lets out a beller that shakes the buildin'.

"That suits me!" says he. "I'll festoon that bar with yore innards," and he takes hold of his belt like he was going to unbuckle it—then, quick as a flash, he whipped out a gun. But I was watching for that and my righthand .45 banged jest as his muzzle cleared leather.

The barkeep stuck his head up from behind the bar.

"Wow!" he says wild-eyed. "You beat Moose Harrison to the draw, and him with the aidge! I wouldn't of believed it was possible if I hadn't saw it! But his friends will ride yore trail for this!"

"Warn't it self-defence?" I demanded.

"A clear case," says he. "But that won't mean nothin' to them wild and wooly buffalo-skinners. You better git back to Goshen where yuh got friends."

"I got business in War Whoop," I says. "Dang it, my coffee's cold. Dispose of the carcass and heat it up, will yuh?"

So he drug Harrison out, cussing because he was so heavy, and claiming I ought to help him. But I told him it warn't my saloon, and I also refused to pay for a decanter which Harrison's wild shot had busted. He got mad and said he hoped the buffalo-hunters did hang me. But I told him they'd have to ketch me without my guns first, and I slept with them on.

Then I finished my dinner and pulled out for War Whoop.

It was about sundown when I got there, and I was purty hongry again. But I aimed to see Bizz's gal before I done anything else. So I put Cap'n Kidd in the livery stable and seen he had a big feed, and then I headed for the Silver Boot, which was the biggest j'int in town.

There was plenty hilarity going on, but I seen no cowboys.

The revelers was mostly gamblers, or buffalo-hunters, or soldiers, or freighters. War Whoop warn't popular with cattlemen. They warn't no buyers nor loading pens there, and for a pleasure it warn't nigh as good a town as Goshen, anyway.

I ast a barman where Ace Middleton was, and he p'inted out a big feller with a generous tummy decorated with a fancy vest and a gold watch chain about the size of a trace chain. He wore mighty handsome clothes and a diamond hoss-shoe stick pin and waxed mustache.

So I went up to him. He looked me over with very little favor.

"Oh, a cowpuncher, eh? Well, your money's as good as anybody's. Enjoy yourself, but don't get wild."

"I ain't aimin' to git wild," I says. "I want to see Gloria La Venner."

When I says that, he gives a convulsive start and choked on his cigar. Everybody nigh us stopped laughing and talking and turned to watch us.

"What did you say?" he gurgled, gagging up the cigar. "Did I honestly hear you asking to see Gloria La Venner?"

"Shore," I says. "I aim to take her back to Goshen to git married—"

"You !●¾$%*!" says he, and grabbed up a table, broke off a laig and hit me over the head with it. It was most unexpected and took me plumb off guard.

I hadn't no idee what he was busting the table up for, and I was too surprised to duck. If it hadn't been for my Stetson it might of cracked my head. As it was, it knocked me back into the crowd. Before I could git my balance, three or four bouncers grabbed me and jerked my pistol out of the scabbard.

"Throw him out!" roared Ace, acting like a wild man. He was plumb purple in the face. "Steal my girl, will he? Hold him while I bust him in the snoot!"

He then rushed up and hit me very severely in the nose, whilst them bouncers was holding my arms. Well, up to that time I hadn't made no resistance. I was too astonished. But this was going too far, even if Ace was loco, as it appeared.

Nobody warn't holding my laigs, so I kicked Ace in the stummick and he curled up on the floor with a strangled shriek. I then started spurring them bouncers in the laigs and they yelled and let go of me, and somebody hit me in the ear with a blackjack.

That made me mad, so I reched for my Bowie in my boot, but a big red-headed maverick kicked me in the face when I stooped down. That straightened me up, so I hit him on the jaw and he fell down acrost Ace which was holding his stummick and trying to yell for the city marshal.

Some low-minded scoundrel got a strangle holt around my neck from behind and started beating me on the head with a pair of brass knucks. I ducked and throwed him over my head. Then I kicked out backwards and knocked over a couple more. But a scar-faced thug with a bung starter got in a full-armed lick about that time, and I went to my knees feeling like my skull was dislocated.

Six or seven of them then throwed theirselves onto me with howls of joy, and I seen I'd have to use vi'lence in spite of myself. So I drawed my Bowie and started cutting my way through 'em. They couldn't of let go of me quicker if I'd been a cougar. They scattered every which-a-way, spattering blood and howling blue murder, and I riz r'aring and rampacious.

Somebody shot at me jest then, and I wheeled to locate him when a man run in at the door and p'inted a pistol at me. Before I could sling my knife through him, which was my earnest intention, he hollered:

"Drap yore deadly weppin! I'm the city marshal and yuh're under arrest!"

"What for?" I demanded. "I ain't done nothing."

"Nothing!" says Ace Middleton fiercely, as his menials lifted him onto his feet. "You've just sliced pieces out of five or six or our leading citizens! And there's my head bouncer, Red Croghan, out cold with a busted jaw. To say nothing of pushing my stomach through my spine. Ow! You must have mule blood in you, blast your soul!"

"Santry," he ordered the marshal, "he came in here drunk and raging and threatening, and started a fight for nothing. Do your duty! Arrest the cussed outlaw!"

Well, pap always tells me not to never resist no officer of the law, and anyway the marshal had my gun, and so many people was hollering and cussing and talking, it kind of confused me. When they's any thinking to be did, I like to have a quiet place to do it and plenty of time.

So the first thing I knowed Santry had handcuffs on me and he hauls me off down the street with a big crowd follering and making remarks which is supposed to be funny. They come to a log hut with bars on the back winder, take off the handcuffs, shove me in and lock the door. There I was in jail without even seeing Gloria La Venner. It was plumb disgustful.

The crowd all hustled back to the Silver Boot to watch them
fellers git sewed up which had fell afoul of my Bowie—all but
one fat cuss which said he was a guard. He sot down in front of
the jail with a double-barreled shotgun acrost his lap and went to
sleep.

Well, there warn't nothing in the jail but a bunk with a hoss
blanket on it, and a wooden bench. The bunk was too short for
me to sleep on with any comfort, being built for a six foot man,
so I sot down on it and waited for somebody to bring me some
grub.

So after a while the marshal come and looked in at the winder
and cussed me.

"It's a good thing for you," he says, "that yuh didn't kill none
of them fellers. As it is, maybe we won't hang yuh."

"Yuh won't have to hang me if yuh don't bring me some grub
purty soon," I said. "Are yuh goin' to let me starve in this dern
jail?"

"We don't encourage crime in our town by feedin' criminals,"
he says. "If yuh want grub, gimme the money to buy it with."

I told him I didn't have but five bucks and I thought I'd pay
my fine with that. He said five bucks wouldn't begin to pay my
fine, so I gave him the fivespot to buy grub with, and he took it
and went off.

I waited and waited, and he didn't come. I hollered to the
guard, but he kept on snoring. Then purty soon somebody said:
"Psst!" at the winder. I went over and looked out and they was a
woman standing behind the jail. The moon had come up over the
prairie as bright as day, and though she had a cloak with a hood
throwed over her, by what I could see of her face she was awful
purty.

"I'm Gloria La Venner," says she. "I'm risking my life coming
here, but I wanted to get a look at the man who was crazy enough
to tell Ace Middleton he wanted to see me."

"What's crazy about that?" I ast.

"Don't you know Ace has killed three men already for trying
to flirt with me?" says she. "Any man who can break Red Croghan's jaw like you did must be a grizzly bear—but it was sheer
madness to tell Ace you wanted to marry me."

"Aw, he never give me time to explain about that," I says. "It
warn't me which wants to marry yuh. But what business is it of
Middleton's? This here's a free country."

"That's what I thought till I started working for him," she says
bitterly. "He fell in love with me, and he's so insanely jealous he

won't let anybody even speak to me. He keeps me practically a prisoner and watches me like a hawk. I can't get away from him. Nobody in town dares to help me. The won't even rent me a horse at the livery stable.

"You see Ace owns most of the town, and lots of people are in debt to him. The rest are afraid of him. I guess I'll have to spend the rest of my life under his thumb," she says despairfully.

"Yuh won't, neither," I says. "As soon as I can git word to my friends in Goshen to send me a loan to pay my fine and git me out of this fool jail, I'll take yuh to Goshen where yore true love is pinin' for yuh."

"My true love?" says she, kind of startled-like. "What do you mean?"

"Bizz Ridgeway is in Goshen," I says. "He don't dare come after yuh hisself, so he sent me to fetch yuh."

She didn't say nothing for a spell, and then she spoke kind of breathless.

"All right, I must get back to the Silver Boot now, or Ace will miss me and start looking for me. I'll find Santry and pay your fine tonight. When he lets you out, come to the back door of the Silver Boot and wait in the alley. I'll come to you there as soon as I can slip away."

So I said all right, and she went away. The guard setting in front of the jail with his shotgun acrost his knees hadn't never woke up. But he did wake up about fifteen minutes after she left. A gang of men came up the street, whooping and cussing, and he jumped to his feet.

"Whoopee! Here comes Brant Hanson and a mob of them buffler-hunters, and they got a rope! They're headin' for the jail!"

"Who do yuh reckon they're after?" I inquired.

"They ain't nobody in jail but you," he suggested p'intedly. "And in about a minute they ain't goin' to be nobody nigh it but you and them. When Hanson and his bunch is in licker they don't care who they shoots!"

He then laid down his shotgun and lit out down a back alley as hard as he could go.

So about a dozen buffalo-hunters in buckskins and whiskers come surging up to the jail and kicked on the door. They couldn't get the door open so they went around behind the shack and looked in at the winder.

"It's him, all right," said one of 'em. "Let's shoot him through the winder."

But the others said, "Naw, let's do the job in proper order," and I ast them what they wanted.

"We aims to hang yuh!" they answered enthusiastically.

"You cain't do that," I says. "It's agin the law."

"You kilt Moose Harrison!" said the biggest one, which they called Hanson.

"Well, it was a even break, and he tried to git the drop on me," I says.

Then Hanson says: "Enough of sech quibblin'. We made up our mind to hang yuh, so let's don't hear no more argyments about it. Here," he says to his pals, "tie a rope to the bars and we'll jerk the whole winder out. It'll be easier'n bustin' down the door. And hustle up, because I'm in a hurry to git back to that poker game in the R'arin Buffalo."

So they tied a rope onto the bars and all laid onto it and heaved and grunted, and some of the bars come loose at one end. I picked up the bench aiming to bust their fool skulls with it as they clumb through the winder, but jest then another feller run up.

"Wait, boys," he hollered, "don't waste yore muscle. I jest seen Santry down at the Topeka Queen gamblin' with the money he taken off that dern cowboy, and he gimme the key to the door."

So they abandoned the winder and surged arount to the front of the jail, and I quick propped the bench agen the door, and run to the winder and tore out them bars which was already loose. I could hear 'em rattling at the door, and as I clumb through the winder one of 'em said: "The lock's turned but the door's stuck. Heave agin it."

So whilst they heaves I run around the jail and picks up the guard's shotgun where he'd dropped it when he run off. Jest then the bench inside give way and the door flew open, and all them fellers tried to crowd through. As a result they was all jammed in the door and cussin' something fierce.

"Quit crowdin'," yelled Hanson. "Holy catamount, he's gone! The jail's empty!"

I then up with my shotgun and give 'em both barrels in the seat of their britches, which was the handiest to aim at. They let out a most amazing squall and busted loose and fell headfirst into the jail. Some of 'em kept on going head-down like they'd started and hit the back wall so hard it knocked 'em stiff, and the others fell over 'em.

They was all tangled in a pile cussing and yelling to beat the devil, so I slammed the door and locked it and run around behind the jail house. Hanson was trying to climb out the winder, so I hit him over the head with my shotgun and he fell back inside and hollered.

"Halp! I'm mortally injured!"

"Shet up that unseemly clamor," I says sternly. "Ain't none of yuh hurt bad. Throw yore guns out the winder and lay down on the floor. Hustle, before I gives you another blast through the winder."

They didn't know the shotgun was empty, so they throwed their weppins out in a hurry and laid down, but they warn't quiet about it. They seemed to consider they'd been subjected to crooel and onusual treatment, and the birdshot in their sterns must a been a-stinging right smart, because the language they used was plumb painful to hear. I stuck a couple of their pistols in my belt.

"If one of you shows his head at that winder within a hour," I said, "he'll git it blowed off."

I then snuck back into the shadders and headed for the livery stable.

The livery stable man was reading a newspaper by a lantern. He looked surprised and said he thought I was in jail. I ignored this remark, and told him to hitch me a fast hoss to a buckboard whilst I saddled Cap'n Kidd.

"Wait a minute!" says he. "I hear tell yuh told Ace Middleton yuh aimed to elope with Gloria La Venner. Yuh takin' this rig for her?"

"Yes, I am," I says.

"Well I'm a friend of Middleton's," he says, "and I won't rent yuh no rig under the circumstances."

"Then git outa my way," I said. "I'll hitch the hoss up myself."

He then drawed a Bowie so I clinched with him, and as we was rasseling around he sort of knocked his head again a singletree I happen to have in my hand at the time and collapses with a low gurgle. So I tied him up and rolled him under a oats bin. I also rolled out a buckboard and hitched the best-looking harness hoss I could find to it, but them folks is liars which is going around saying I stole that there outfit. It was sent back later.

I saddles my hoss and tied him on behind the buckboard and got in and started for the Silver Boot, wondering how long it would take them fool buffalo-hunters to find out I was jest bluffing, and warn't lying out behind the jail to shoot 'em as they climb out.

I turned into the alley which run behind the Silver Boot and then tied the hosses and went up to the back door and peeked in.

Gloria was there. She grabbed me and I could feel her trembling.

"I thought you'd never come!" she whispered. "It'll be time for my singing act again in just a few minutes. I've been waiting here ever since I paid Santry your fine. What kept you so long. He left the Silver Boot as soon as I gave him the money."

"He never turned me out, the low-down skunk," I muttered. "Some—er—friends got me out. Come on, git in the buckboard."

I helped her up and gave her the lines.

"I got a debt to settle before I leave town," I said. "You go on and wait for me at that clump of cottonwoods east of town. I'll be on purty soon."

So she pulled out in a hurry and I got onto Cap'n Kidd. I rode him around to the front of the Silver Boot, tied him to the hitchrack and dismounted. The Silver Boot was crowded. I could see Ace strutting around chawing a big black cigar, and joking and slapping folks on the back.

Everybody was having such a hilarious time nobody noticed me as I stood in the doorway. So I pulled the buffalo-hunters' .45's, and let it bam at the mirror behind the bar. The barman yelped and ducked the flying glass, and everybody whirled and gaped, and Ace jerked his cigar out of his mouth and bawled:

"It's that dern cowpuncher again! Get him!"

But them bouncers had seen my guns, and they was shying away, all except the scar-faced thug which had hit me with the bung-starter. He whipped a gun from under his vest. So I shot him through the right shoulder, and he fell over behind the monte table.

I begun to spray the crowd with hot lead free and generous and they stampeded every which-a-way. Some went through the winder, glass and all, and some went out the side doors, and some busted down the back door in their flight.

I likewise riddled the mirror behind the bar and shot down some of the hanging lamps and busted most of the bottles on the shelves.

Ace ducked behind a stack of beer kaigs and opened fire on me, but he showed pore judgement in not noticing he was right under a hanging lamp. I shot it off the ceiling and it fell down on his head, and you ought to of heard him holler when the burning ile run down his wuthless neck.

He come prancing into the open, wiping his neck with one hand and trying to shoot me with the gun he had in the other hand, and I drilled him through the hind laig. He fell down and bellered like a bull with its tail cotched in a fence gate.

"You dern murderer!" says he passionately. "I'll have yore life for this!"

"Shet up!" I snarled. "I'm jest payin' yuh back for all the pain and humiliation I suffered in this den of iniquity."

At this moment a bartender riz up from behind a billiard table with a sawed-off shotgun, but I shot it out of his hands before he could cock it, and he fell over backwards hollering: "Spare my life!" Jest then somebody yelled: "Halt, in the name of the law!" and I looked around and it was that tinhorn marshal named Santry with a gun in his hand.

"I arrests you again!" he bawled. "Lay down yore weppins!"

"I'll lay yore carcase down," I responded. "Yuh ain't fitten for to be no law-officer. Yuh gambled away the five dollars I give yuh for grub, and yuh took the fine-money Miss La Venner give yuh, and didn't turn me out, and yuh give the key to that mob which wanted to hang me. You ain't no law. Yuh're a dern outlaw yoreself. Now yuh got a gun in yore hand same as me. Either start shootin' or throw it down!"

"Wait," he hollered, "Don't shoot!" and throwed it down and h'isted his hands. I seen he had my knife and pistol stuck in his belt, so I took them off of him, and tossed the .45's I'd been using onto the billiard table and said, "Give these back to the buffalo-hunters."

But jest then he whipped out a .38 he was wearing under his arm, and shot at me and knocked my hat off. Then he turned and run around the end of the bar, all bent over to git his head below it. So I grabbed the bartender's shotgun and let bam with both barrels jest as his rear end was going out of sight.

He shrieked blue ruin and started having a fit behind the bar. So I throwed the shotgun through the roulette wheel and stalked forth, leaving Ace and the bouncer and the marshall wailing and wallering on the floor. It was plumb disgustful the way they wept and cussed over their trifling injuries.

I come out on the street so sudden that them cusses which was hiding behind the hoss trough to shoot me as I come out, was took by surprize and only grazed me in a few places. So I throwed a few slugs amongst 'em and they took to their heels.

I got on Cap'n Kidd and headed east down the street, ignoring the shots fired at me from the alley and winders. That is, I ignored 'em except to shoot back at 'em as I run, and I reckon that's how the mayor got the lobe of his ear shot off. I thought I heard somebody holler when I answered a shot fired at me from behind the mayor's board fence.

Well, when I got to the clump of cottonwoods there warn't no sign of Gloria, the hoss, or the buckboard, but there was a note stuck up on a tree which I grabbed and read by the light of the moon.

It said:

Dear Cowboy:

    Your friend must have been kidding you. I never even knew anybody named Bizz Ridgeway. But I'm taking this chance of getting away from Ace. I'm heading for Trevano Springs, and I'll send back the buckboard from there. Thank you for everything.

                           Gloria La Venner

I got to Goshen about sunup, having loped all the way. Bizz Ridgeway was at the bar of the Spanish Mustang, and when he seen me he turned pale and dived for the winder, but I grabbed him.

"What you mean by tellin' me that lie about you and Gloria La Venner?" I demanded wrathfully. "Was you tryin' to git me kilt?"

"Well," says he, "to tell the truth, Breckinridge, I was. All's fair in love or war, yuh know. I wanted to git yuh out of the way so I'd have a clear field with Betty Wilkinson, and I knowed about Ace Middleton and Gloria, and figgered he'd do the job if I sent yuh over there. But yuh needn't git mad. It didn't do me no good. Betty's already married."

"What?" I yelled.

He ducked instinctively.

"Yeah!" he says. "He took advantage of yore absence to pop the question, and she accepted him, and they're on their way to Kansas City for their honeymoon. He never had the nerve to ast her when you was in town, for fear yuh'd shoot him. They're goin' to live in the East because he's too scairt of you to come back."

"Who?" I screamed, foaming slightly at the mouth.

"Rudwell Shapley Jr.," says he. "It's all yore fault—"

It was at this moment that I dislocated Bizz Ridgeway's hind laig. I likewise defies the criticism which has been directed at this perfectly natural action. A Elkins with a busted heart is no man to trifle with.

PART THREE:

Mayhem on Bear Creek

"No Cowherders Wanted"

I hear a gang of buffalo hunters got together recently in a saloon in Dodge City to discuss ways and means of keeping their sculps onto their heads whilst collecting pelts, and purty soon one of 'em riz and said, "You mavericks make me sick. For the last hour you been chawin' wind about the soldiers tryin' to keep us north of the Cimarron, and belly-achin' about the Comanches, Kiowas and Apaches which yearns for our hair. You've took up all that time jawin' about sech triflin' hazards, and plannin' steps to take agen 'em, but you ain't makin' no efforts whatsoever to pertect yore-selves agen the biggest menace they is to the entire buffalo-huntin' clan—which is Breckinridge Elkins!"

That jest shows how easy prejudiced folks is. You'd think I had a grudge agen buffalo hunters, the way they takes to the bresh whenever they sees me coming. And the way they misrepresents what happened at Cordova is plumb disgustful. To hear 'em talk you'd think I was th only man there which committed any vi'l-ence.

If that's so, I'd like to know how all them bullet holes got in the Diamond Bar saloon which I was usin' for a fort. Who throwed the mayor through that board fence? Who sot fire to Joe Emerson's store, jest to smoke me out? Who started the row in the first place by sticking up insulting signs in publick places? They ain't no use in them fellers tryin' to ack innercent. Any unbiased man which was there, and survived to tell the tale, knows I acted all the way through with as much dignerty as a man can ack which is being shot at by forty or fifty wild-eyed buffalo skinners.

321

I had never even saw a buffalo hunter before, because it was
the first time I'd ever been that far East. I was takin' a pasear into
New Mexico with a cowpoke by the name of Glaze Bannack which
I'd met in Arizona. I stopped in Albuquerque, and he went on,
heading for Dodge City. Well, I warn't in Albuquerque as long
as I'd aimed to be, account of goin' broke quicker'n I expected.
I had jest one dollar left after payin' for having three fellers sewed
up which had somehow got afoul of my bowie knife after critter-
sizin' the Democratic party. I ain't the man to leave my opponents
on the publick charge.

Well, I pulled out of town and headed for the cow camps on
the Pecos, aimin' to git me a job. But I hadn't went far till I met
a waddy ridin' in, and he taken a good look at me and Cap'n
Kidd, and says: "You must be him. Wouldn't no other man fit the
description he gimme."

"Who?" I said.

"Glaze Bannack," says he. "He gimme a letter to give to Breckinridge Elkins."

So I says, "Well, all right, gimme it." So he did, and it read
as follers:

Dere Breckinridge:
    I am in jail in Panther Springs for nothin all I done was
kind of push the deperty sheriff with a little piece of scrap iron
could I help it if he fell down and fraktured his skull Breckinridge. But they say I got to pay $Ten dolars fine and I have
not got no sech money Breckinridge. But old man Garnett over .
on Buck Creek owes me ten bucks so you colleck from him
and come and pay me out of this hen-coop. The food is terrible
Breckinridge. Hustle.

                            Yore misjedged friend,
                            Glaze Bannack, Eskwire.

Glaze never could stay out of trouble, not being tactful like
me, but he was a purty good sort of hombre. So I headed for Buck
Creek and collected the money off of Old Man Garnett, which
was somewhat reluctant to give up the dough. In fact he bit me
severely in the hind laig whilst I was setting on him prying his
fingers loose from that there ten spot, and when I rode off down
the road with the dinero, he run into his shack and got his buffalo
gun and shot at me till I was clean out of sight.

But I ignored his lack of hospitality. I knowed he was too dizzy
to shoot straight account of him having accidentally banged his

head on a fence post which I happened to have in my hand whilst we was rassling.

I left him waving his gun and howling damnation and destruction, and I was well on the road for Panther Springs before I discovered to my disgust that my shirt was a complete rooin. I considered going back and demanding that Old Man Garnett buy me a new one, account of him being the one which tore it. But he was sech a onreasonable old cuss I decided agen it and rode on to Panther Springs, arriving there shortly after noon.

The first critter I seen was the purtiest gal I saw in a coon's age. She come out of a store and stopped to talk to a young cowpuncher she called Curly. I reined Cap'n Kidd around behind a corn crib so she wouldn't see me in my scarecrow condition. After a while she went on down the street and went into a cabin with a fence around it and a front porch, which showed her folks was wealthy, and I come out from behind the crib and says to the young buck which was smirking after her and combing his hair with the other hand, I says: "Who is that there gal? The one you was jest talkin' to."

"Judith Granger," says he. "Her folks lives over to Sheba, but her old man brung her over here account of all the fellers out there was about to cut each other's throats over her. He's makin' her stay a spell with her Aunt Henrietta, which is a war-hoss if I ever seen one. The boys is so scairt of her they don't dast try to spark Judith. Except me. I persuaded the old mudhen to let me call on Judith and I'm goin' over there for supper."

"That's what you think," I says gently. "Fact is, though, Miss Granger has got a date with me."

"She didn't tell me—" he begun scowling.

"She don't know it herself, yet," I says. "But I'll tell her you was sorry you couldn't show up."

"Why, you—" he says bloodthirsty like, and started for his gun, when a feller who'd been watchin' us from the store door, he hollered: "By golly, if it ain't Breckinridge Elkins!"

"Breckinridge Elkins?" gasped Curly, and he dropped his gun and keeled over with a low gurgle.

"Has he got a weak heart?" I ast the feller which had recognized me, and he saw, "Aw, he jest fainted when he realized how clost he come to throwin' a gun on the terror of the Humbolts. Drag him over to the hoss trough, boys, and throw some water on him. Breckinridge, I owns that grocery store there, and yore paw knows me right well. As a special favor to me will you refrain from killin' anybody in my store?"

So I said all right, and then I remembered my shirt was tore too bad to call on a young lady in. I generally has 'em made to order, but they warn't time for that if I was going to eat supper with Miss Judith, so I went into the general store and bought me one. I dunno why they don't make shirts big enough to fit reasonable sized men like me. You'd think nobody but midgets wore shirts. The biggest one in the store warn't only eighteen in the collar, but I didn't figger on buttoning the collar anyway. If I'd tried to button it would of strangled me.

So I give the feller five dollars and put it on. It fit purty clost, but I believed I could wear it if I didn't have to expand my chest or something. Of course, I had to use some of Glaze's dough to pay for it with but I didn't reckon he'd mind considerin' all the trouble I was going to gittin' him out of jail.

I rode down the alley behind the jail and come to a barred winder and said, "Hey!"

Glaze looked out, kinda peaked, like his grub warn't settin' well with him, but he brightened up and says, "Hurray! I been on aidge expectin' you. Go on around to the front door, Breck, and pay them coyotes the ten spot, and let's go. The grub I been gittin' here would turn a lobo's stummick!"

"Well," I says, "I ain't exactly got the ten bucks, Glaze. I had to have a shirt, because mine got tore, so—"

He give a yelp like a stricken elk and grabbed the bars convulsively.

"Air you crazy?" he hollered. "You squanders my money on linens and fine raiment whilst I languishes in a prison dungeon?"

"Be ca'm," I advised. "I still got five bucks of yore'n, and one of mine. All I got to do is step down to a gamblin' hall and build it up."

"Build it up!" says he fiercely. "Lissen, blast your hide! Does you know what I've had for breakfast, dinner and supper ever since I was throwed in here? Beans! Beans! Beans!"

Here he was so overcome by emotion that he choked on the word. "And they ain't even first-class beans, neither," he said bitterly, when he could talk again. "They're full of grit and wormholes, and I think the Mex cook washes his feet in the pot he cooks 'em in."

"Well," I says, "sech cleanliness is to be encouraged, because I never heard of one before which washed his feet in anything. Don't worry. I'll git in a poker game and win enough to pay yore fine and plenty over."

"Well, git at it," he begged. "Git me out before supper time.

I wants a steak with ernyuns so bad I can smell it."

So I headed for the Golden Steer saloon.

They warn't many men in there jest then, but they was a poker game going on, and when I told 'em I craved to set in they looked me over and made room for me. They was a black-whiskered cuss which said he was from Cordova which was dealing, and the first thing I noticed was he was dealing his own hand off of the bottom of the deck. The others didn't seem to see it, but us Bear Creek folks has got eyes like hawks, otherwise we'd never live to git grown.

So I says, "I dunno what the rules is in these parts, but where I come from we almost always deals off of the top of the deck."

"Air you accusin' me of cheatin'?" he demanded passionately, fumbling for his weppins and in his agitation dropping three or four extra aces out of his sleeves.

"I wouldn't think of sech a thing," I says. "Probably them marked kyards I see stickin' out of yore boot-tops is merely soov-ernears."

For some reason this seemed to infuriate him to the p'int of drawing a bowie knife, so I hit him over the head with a brass cuspidor and he fell under the table with a holler groan.

Some fellers run in and looked at his boots sticking out from under the table, and one of 'em said, "Hey! I'm the Justice of the Peace. You can't do that. This is a orderly town."

And another'n said, "I'm the sheriff. If you cain't keep the peace I'll have to arrest you!"

This was too much even for a mild-mannered man like me.

"Shet yore fool heads!" I roared, brandishing my fists. "I come here to pay Glaze Bannack's fine, and git him outa jail, peaceable and orderly, and I'm tryin' to raise the dough like a ¾$%&*! gentleman! But by golly, if you hyenas pushes me beyond en-durance, I'll tear down the cussed jail and snake him out without payin' no blasted fine."

The J. P. turned white. He says to the sheriff: "Let him alone! I've already bought these here new boots on credit on the strength of them ten bucks we gits from Bannack."

"But—" says the sheriff dubiously, and the J. P. hissed fiercely, "Shet up, you blame fool. I jest now reckernized him. That's Breckinridge Elkins!"

The sheriff turnt pale and swallered his adam's apple and says feebly, "Excuse me—I—uh—I ain't feelin' so good. I guess it's somethin' I et. I think I better ride over to the next county and git me some pills."

But I don't think he was very sick from the way he run after he got outside the saloon. If they had been a jackrabbit ahead of him he would of trompled the gizzard out of it.

Well, they taken the black whiskered gent out from under the table and started pouring water on him, and I seen it was now about supper time so I went over to the cabin where Judith lived.

I was met at the door by a iron-jawed female about the size of a ordinary barn, which give me a suspicious look and says, "Well, what's *you* want?"

"I'm lookin' for yore sister, Miss Judith," I says, taking off my Stetson perlitely.

"What you mean, my sister?" says she with a scowl, but a much milder tone. "I'm her aunt."

"You don't mean to tell me!" I says, looking plumb astonished. "Why, when I first seen you, I thought you was her herself, and couldn't figger out how nobody but a twin sister could have sech a resemblance. Well, I can see right off that youth and beauty is a family characteristic."

"Go 'long with you, you young scoundrel," says she, smirking, and giving me a nudge with her elbow which would have busted anybody's ribs but mine. "You cain't soft-soap me—come in! I'll call Judith. What's yore name?"

"Breckinridge Elkins, ma'am," I says.

"So!" says she, looking at me with new interest. "I've heard tell of you. But you got a lot more sense than they give you credit for. Oh, Judith!" she called, and the winders rattled when she let her voice go. "You got company."

Judith come in, lookin' purtier than ever, and when she seen me she batted her eyes and recoiled vi'lently.

"Who—who's that?" she demanded wildly.

"Mister Breckinridge Elkins of Bear Creek, Nevader," says her aunt. "The only young man I've met in this whole dern town which has got any sense. Well, come on in and set. Supper's on the table. We was jest waitin' for Curly Jacobs," she says to me, "but if the varmint cain't git here on time, he can go hongry."

"He cain't come," I says. "He sent word by me he's sorry."

"Well, I ain't," snorted Judith's aunt. "I give him permission to call jest because I figgered even a bodacious flirt like Judith wouldn't cotton to sech a sapsucker, but—"

"Aunt Henrietta!" protested Judith, blushing.

"I cain't abide the sigh of sech weaklin's," says Aunt Henrietta, settling herself carefully into a rawhide-bottomed chair which groaned under her weight. "Drag up that bench, Breckinridge. It's the only thing in the house which has a chance of holdin' yore weight outside of the sofie in the front room. Don't angry with me, Judith! I says Curly Jacobs ain't no fit man for a gal like you. Didn't I see him strain his fool back tryin' to lift that there barrel of salt I wanted fotched to the smoke house? I finally had to tote it myself. What makes young men so blame spindlin' these days?"

"Pap blames the Republican party," I says.

"Haw! Haw! Haw!" says she in a guffaw which shook the doors on their hinges and scairt the cat into convulsions. "Young man, you got a great sense of humor. Ain't he, Judith?" says she, cracking a beef bone betwixt her teeth like it was a pecan.

Judith says yes kind of pallid, and all during the meal she eyed me kind of nervous like she was expecting me to go into a war-dance or somethin'. Well, when we was through, and Aunt Hen-rietta had et enough to keep a tribe of Sioux through a hard winter, she riz up and says, "Now clear out of here whilst I washes the dishes."

"But I must help with 'em," says Judith.

Aunt Henrietta snorted. "What makes you so eager to work all of a sudden? You want yore guest to think you ain't eager for his company? Git out of here."

So she went, but I paused to say kind of doubtful to Aunt Henrietta, "I ain't shore Judith likes me much."

"Don't pay no attention to her whims," says Aunt Henrietta, picking up the water barrel to fill her dish pan. "She's a flirtatious minx. I've took a likin' to you, and if I decide yo're the right man for her, yo're as good as hitched. Nobody couldn't never do nothin' with her but me, but she's learnt who her boss is—after havin' to eat her meals off of the mantel-board a few times. Gwan in and court her and don't be backward!"

So I went on in the front room, and Judith seemed to kind of warm up to me, and ast me a lot of questions about Nevada, and finally she says she's heard me spoke of as a fighting man and hoped I ain't had no trouble in Panther Springs.

I told her no, only I had to hit one black whiskered thug from Cordova over the head with a cuspidor.

At that she jumped up like she'd sot on a pin.

"That was my uncle Jabez Granger!" she hollered. "How dast how you, you big bully! You ought to be ashamed, a great big man like you pickin' on a little feller like him which don't weigh a ounce over two hundred and fifteen pounds!"

"Aw, shucks," I said contritely. "I'm sorry, Judith."

"Jest as I was beginnin' to like you," she mourned. "Now he'll write to pap and prejudice him agen you. You jest got to go and find him and apologize to him and make friends with him."

"Aw, heck," I said.

But she wouldn't listen to nothin' else, so I went out and clumb onto Cap'n Kidd and went back to the Golden Steer, and when I come in everybody crawled under the tables.

"What's the matter with you all?" I says fretfully. "I'm looking for Jabez Granger."

"He's left for Cordova," says the barkeep, sticking his head up from behind the bar.

Well, they warn't nothing to do but foller him, so I rode by the jail and Glaze was at the window looking out eagerly.

"Air you ready to pay me out?" he asks.

"Be patient, Glaze," I says. "I ain't got the dough yet, but I'll git it somehow as soon as I git back from Cordova."

"What?" he shrieked.

"Be ca'm like me," I advised. "You don't see *me* gittin' all het up, do you? I got to go catch Judith Granger's Uncle Jabez and apolergize to the old illegitimate for bustin' his conk with a spitoon. I'll be back tomorrer or the next day at the most."

Well, his langwidge was scandalous, considering all the trouble I was going to jest to git him out of jail, but I refused to take offense. I headed back for the Granger cabin and Judith was on the front porch.

I didn't see Aunt Henrietta; she was back in the kitchen washing dishes and singing: "They've laid Jesse James in his grave!" in a voice which loosened the shingles on the roof. So I told Judith where I was going and ast her to take some pies and cakes and things to the jail for Glaze, account of the beans was rooinin' his stummick, and she said she would. So I pulled up stakes for Cordova.

It laid quite a ways to the east, and I figgered to catch up with Uncle Jabez before he got there, but he had a long start and was on a mighty good hoss, I reckon. Anyway, Cap'n Kidd got one of his hell-fire streaks and insisted on stopping every few miles to buck all over the landscape, till I finally got sick of his mu-leishness and busted him over the head with my pistol butt. By this time we'd lost so much time that I never overtaken Uncle Jabez at all and it was gittin' daylight before I come in sight of Cordova.

Well, about sun-up I come onto a old feller and his wife in a ramshackle wagon drawed by a couple of skinny mules with a hound dawg. One wheel had run off into a sink hole and the mules was so pore and good-for-nothin' they couldn't pull it out, so I got off and laid hold on the wagon, and the old man said, "Wait a minute, young feller, whilst me and the old lady gits out to lighten the load."

"What for?" I ast. "Set still."

So I h'isted the wheel out, but if it had been stuck any tighter I might of had to use both hands.

"By golly!" says the old man. "I'd of swore nobody but Breckinridge Elkins could do that!"

"Well, I'm him," I says, and they both looked at me with reverence, and I ast 'em was they going to Panther Springs.

"We aim to," says the old woman, kind of hopeless. "One place is as good as another'n to old people which has been robbed out of their life's savin's."

"You all been robbed?" I ast, shocked.

"Well," says the old man, "I ain't in the habit of burdenin' strangers with my woes, but as a matter of fact, we has. My name's Hopkins. I had a ranch down on the Pecos till the drouth wiped me out and we moved to Panther Springs with what little we saved from the wreck. In a ill-advised moment I started speculatin' on buffler-hides. I put in all my cash buyin' a load over on the Llano Estacado which I aimed to freight to Santa Fe and sell at a fat profit—I happen to know they're fetchin' a higher price there jest now than they air at Dodge City—and last night the whole blame cargo disappeared into thin air, as it were.

"We was stoppin' at Cordova for the night, and the old lady was sleepin' in the hotel and I was camped at the aidge of town with the wagon, and sometime durin' the night somebody snuck up and hit me over the head. When I come to this mornin' hides, wagon and team was all gone, and no trace. When I told the city marshal he jest laughed in my face and ast me how I'd expect him to track down a load of buffalo hides in a town which was full of 'em. Dang him! They was packed and corded neat with my old brand, which was the Circle A, marked onto 'em in red paint.

"Joe Emerson, which owns the saloon and most all the town, taken a mortgage on our little shack in Panther Springs and loaned me enough money to buy this measly team and wagon. If we can git back to Panther Springs maybe I can git enough freightin' to do so we can kind of live, anyway."

"Well," I said, much moved by the story, "I'm goin' to Cordova, and I'll see if I cain't find yore hides."

"Thankee kindly, Breckinridge," says he. "But I got a idee them hides is already far on their way to Dodge City. Well, I hopes you has better luck in Cordova than we did."

So they driv on west and I rode east, and got to Cordova about a hour after sun-up. As I come into the aidge of town I seen a sign-board about the size of a door stuck up which says on it, in big letters, "No cowherders allowed in Cordova."

"What the hell does that mean?" I demanded wrathfully of a feller which had stopped by it to light him a cigaret. And he says, "Jest what it says! Cordova's full of buffler hunters in for a spree and they don't like cowboys. Big as you be, I'd advise you to light a shuck for some where else. Bull Croghan put that sign up, and you ought to seen what happened to the last puncher which ignored it!"

"¾$%&*¢!" I says in a voice which shook the beans out of the mesquite trees for miles around. And so saying I pulled up the sign and headed for main street with it in my hand. I am as peaceful and mildmannered a critter as you could hope to meet, but even with me a man can go too damned far. This here's a free country and no derned hairy-necked buffalo skinner can draw boundary lines for us cowpunchers and git away with it—not whilst I can pull a trigger.

They was very few people on the street and sech as was looked at me surprized-like.

"Where the hell is them fool buffalo hunters?" I roared, and a feller says, "They're all gone to the race track east of town to race horses, except Bull Croghan, which is takin' hisself a dram in the Diamond Bar."

So I lit and stalked in the Diamond Bar with my spurs ajingling and my disposition gitting thornier every second. They was a big hairy critter in buckskins and moccasins standing at the bar drinking whiskey and talking to the bar-keep and a flashy-dressed gent with slick hair and a diamond hoss-shoe stickpin. They all turned and gaped at me, and the buffalo hunter reched down for his belt where he was wearin' the longest knife I ever seen.

"Who air you?" he gasped.

"A cowman!" I roared, brandishing the sign. "Air you Bull Croghan?"

"Yes," says he. "What about it?"

So I busted the sign-board over his head and he fell onto the floor yellin' bloody murder and trying to draw his knife. The board was splintered, but the stake it had been fastened to was a purty good-sized post, so I took and beat him over the head with it till the bartender tried to shoot me with a sawed-off shotgun.

I grabbed the barrel and the charge jest busted a shelf-load of whiskey bottles and I throwed the shotgun through a nearby winder. As I neglected to git the bartender loose from it first, it appears he went along with it. Anyway, he picked hisself up off of the ground, bleeding freely, and headed east down the street shrieking, "Help! Murder! A cowboy is killin' Croghan and Emerson!"

Which was a lie, because Croghan had crawled out the front door on his all-fours whilst I was tending to the bar-keep, and if Emerson had showed any jedgment he wouldn't of got his sculp laid open to the bone. How did I know he was jest tryin' to hide behind the bar? I thot he was goin' for a gun he had hid back there. As soon as I realized the truth I dropped what was left of the bungstarter and commenced pourin' water on Emerson, and purty soon he sot up and looked around wildeyed with blood and water dripping off of his head.

"What happened?" he gurgled.

"Nothin' to git excited about," I assured him, knocking the neck off of a bottle of whiskey. "I'm lookin' for a gent named Jabez Granger."

It was at this moment that the city marshal opened fire on me through the back door. He grazed my neck with his first slug and would probably of hit me with the next if I hadn't shot the gun out of his hand. He then run off down the alley. I pursued him and catched him when he looked back over his shoulder and hit a garbage can.

"I'm a officer of the law!" he howled, tryin' to git his neck out from under my foot so as he could draw his bowie. "Don't you dast assault no officer of the law."

"I ain't," I snarled, kicking the knife out of his hand, and kind of casually swiping my spur acrost his whiskers. "But a officer which lets a old man git robbed of his buffalo hides and then laughs in his face ain't deservin' to be no officer. Gimme that badge! I demotes you to a private citizen!"

I then hung him onto a nearby hen-roost by the seat of his britches and went back up the alley, ignoring his impassioned profanity. I didn't go in at the back door of the saloon, because I figgered Joe Emerson might be layin' to shoot me as I come in. So I went around the saloon to the front and run smack onto a mob of buffalo hunters which had evidently been summoned from the race track by the barkeep. They had Bull Croghan at the hoss-trough and was trying to wash the blood off of him, and they was all yellin' and cussin' so loud they didn't see me at first.

"Air we to be defied in our own lair by a ¾$%&*¢! cowsheperd?" howled Croghan. "Scatter and comb the town for him! He's hidin' down some back alley, like as not. We'll hang him in front of the Diamond Bar and stick his sculp onto a pole as a warnin' to all his breed! Jest lemme lay eyes onto him agen—"

"Well, all you got to do is turn around," I says. And they all whirled so quick they dropped Croghan into the hoss-trough. They gaped at me with their mouths open for a second. Croghan riz out of the water snortin' and splutterin', and yelled, "Well, what you waitin' on? Grab him!"

It was in trying to obey his instructions that three of 'em got their skulls fractured, and whilst the others was stumblin' and fallin' over 'em, I back into the saloon and pulled my sixshooters and issued a defiance to the world at large and buffalo hunters in particular.

They run for cover behind hitch racks and troughs and porches and fences, and a feller in a plug hat comes out and says, "Gentlemen! Le's don't have no bloodshed within the city limits! As mayor of this fair city, I—"

It was at this instant that Croghan picked him up and throwed him through a board fence into a cabbage patch where he lay till somebody revived him a few hours later.

The hunters then all started shootin' at me with .50 caliber Sharps' buffalo rifles. Emerson, which was hidin' behind a Schlitz sign-board, hollered something amazing account of the holes which was being knocked in the roof and walls. The big sign in front was shot to splinters, and the mirror behind the bar was riddled, and all the bottles on the shelves and the hanging lamps was busted. It's plumb astonishing the damage a bushel or so of them big slugs can do to a saloon.

They went right through the walls. If I hadn't kept moving all the time I'd of been shot to rags, and I did git several bullets through my clothes and three or four grazed some hide off. But even so I had the aidge, because they couldn't see me only for glimpses now and then through the winders and was shooting more or less blind because I had 'em all spotted and slung lead so far and clost they didn't dast show theirselves long enough to take good aim.

But my ca'tridges begun to run short so I made a sally out into the alley jest as one of 'em was trying to sneak in at the back door. I hear tell he is very bitter toward me about his teeth, but I like to know how he expects to git kicked in the mouth without losing some fangs.

So I jumped over his writhing carcase and run down the alley, winging three or four as I went and collectin' a pistol ball in my

hind laig. They was hidin' behind board fences on each side of
the alley but them boards wouldn't stop a .45 slug. They all shot
at me, but they misjedged my speed. I move a lot faster than most
folks expect.

Anyway, I was out of the alley before they could git their wits
back. And as I went past the hitch rack where Cap'n Kidd was
champin' and snortin' to git into the fight, I grabbed my Winchester
.45–90 off of the saddle, and run acrost the street. The hunters
which was still shootin' at the front of the Diamond Bar seen me
and that's when I got my spurs shot off, but I ducked into Emerson's General Store whilst the clerks all run shrieking out the back
way.

As for that misguided hunter which tried to confiscate Cap'n
Kidd, I ain't to blame for what happened to him. They're going
around now sayin' I trained Cap'n Kidd special to jump onto a
buffalo hunter with all four feet after kicking him through a corral
fence. That's a lie. I didn't have to train him. He thot of it hisself.
The idjit which tried to take him ought to be thankful he was able
to walk with crutches inside of ten months.

Well, I was now on the same side of the street as the hunters
was, so as soon as I started shootin' at 'em from the store winders
they run acrost the street and taken refuge in a dance hall right
acrost from the store and started shootin' back at me, and Joe
Emerson hollered louder'n ever, because he owned the dance hall
too. All the citizens of the town had bolted into the hills long ago,
and left us to fight it out.

Well, I piled sides of pork and barrels of pickles and bolts of
calico in the winders, and shot over 'em, and I built my barricades
so solid even them buffalo guns couldn't shoot through 'em. They
was plenty of Colt and Winchester ammunition in the store, and
whiskey, so I knowed I could hold the fort indefinite.

Them hunters could tell they warn't doin' no damage, so purty
soon I heard Croghan bellerin', "Go git that cannon the soldiers
loaned the folks to fight the Apaches with. It's over behind the
city hall. Bring it in at the back door. We'll blast him out of his
fort, by golly!"

"You'll ruin my store!" screamed Emerson.

"I'll rooin' yore face if you don't shet up," opined Croghan.
"Gwan!"

Well, they kept on shootin' and so did I, and I must of him
some of 'em, jedging from the blood-curdlin' yells that went up
from time to time. Then a most remarkable racket of cussin' busted
out, and from the remarks passed, I gathered that they'd brung

the cannon and somehow got it stuck in the back door of the dance hall. The shootin' kind of died down whilst they rassled with it and in the lull I heard me a noise out behind the store.

They warn't no winders in the back, which is why they hadn't shot at me from that direction. I snuck back and looked through a crack in the door and I seen a feller in the dry gully which run along behind the store, and he had a can of kerosine and some matches and was settin' the store on fire.

I jest started to shoot when I recognized Judith Granger's Uncle Jabez. I laid down my Winchester and opened the door soft and easy and pounced out on him, but he let out a squawk and dodged and run down the gully. The shootin' acrost the street broke out agen, but I give no heed, because I warn't goin' to let him git away from me agen. I run him down the gully about a hundred yards and catched him, and taken his pistol away from him, but he got hold of a rock which he hammered me on the head with till I nigh lost patience with him.

But I didn't want to injure him account of Judith, so I merely kicked him in the belly and then throwed him before he could git his breath back, and sot on him, and says, "Blast yore hide, I apolergizes for lammin' you with that there cuspidor. Does you accept my apolergy, you pot-bellied hoss-thief?"

"Never!" says he rampacious. "A Granger never forgits!"

So I taken him by the ears and beats his head agen a rock till he gasps. "Let up! I accepts yore apolergy, you ¾$%&*¢!"

"All right," I says, arising and dusting my hands, "and if you ever goes back on yore word, I'll hang yore mangy hide to the—"

It was at that moment that Emerson's General Store blew up with a ear-splitting bang.

"What the hell?" shrieked Uncle Jabez, staggering, as the air was filled with fragments of groceries and pieces of flying timber.

"Aw," I said disgustedly, "I reckon a stray bullet hit a barrel of gunpowder. I aimed to move them barrels out of the line of fire, but kind of forgot about it—"

But Uncle Jabez had bit the dust. I hear tell he claims I hit him onexpected with a wagon pole. I didn't do no sech thing. It was a section of the porch roof which fell on him, and if he'd been watching, and ducked like I did, it wouldn't of hit him.

I clumb out of the gully and found myself opposite from the Diamond Bar. Bull Croghan and the hunters was pouring out of the dance hall whooping and yellin', and Joe Emerson was tearin' his hair and howlin' like a timber wolf with the belly ache because his store was blowed up and his saloon was shot all to pieces.

But nobody paid no attention to him. They went surging acrost the street and nobody seen me when I crossed it from the other side and went into the alley behind the saloon. I run on down it till I got to the dance hall, and sure enough the cannon was stuck in the back door. It warn't wide enough for the wheels to git through.

I heard Croghan roaring acrost the street, "Poke into the debray, boys! Elkins' remains must be here somewheres, unless he was plumb dissolved! That—"

Crash!

They was a splinterin' of planks, and somebody yelled, "Hey! Croghan's fell into a well or somethin'!"

I heard Joe Emerson shriek, "Dammit, stay away from there! Don't—"

I tore away a section of the wall and got the cannon loose and run it up to the front door of the dance hall and looked out. Them hunters was all ganged up with their backs to the dance hall, all bent over whilst they was apparently trying to pull Croghart out of some hole he'd fell into headfirst. His cussin' sounded kinda muffled. Joe Emerson was having a fit at the aidge of the crowd.

Well, they'd loaded that there cannon with nails and spikes and lead slugs and carpet tacks and sech like, but I put in a double handful of beer bottle caps jest for good measure, and touched her off. It made a noise like a thunder clap and the recoil knocked me about seventeen foot, but you should of heard the yell them hunters let out when that hurreycane of scrap iron hit 'em in the seat of the britches. It was amazing!

To my disgust, though, it didn't kill none of 'em. Seems like the charge was too heavy for the powder, so all it done was knock 'em off their feet and tear the britches off 'em. However, it swept the ground clean of 'em like a broom, and left 'em all standing on their necks in the gully behind where the store had been, except Croghan whose feet I still perceived sticking up out of the ruins.

Before they could recover their wits, if they ever had any, I run acrost the street and started beatin' 'em over the head with a pillar I tore off of the saloon porch. Some sech as was able ariz and fled howling into the desert. I hear tell some of 'em didn't stop till they got to Dodge City, having run right through a Kiowa war-party and scairt them pore Injuns till they turnt white.

Well, I laid holt of Croghan's laigs and hauled him out of the place he had fell into, which seemed to be a kind of cellar which had been under the floor of the store. Croghan's conversation didn't noways make sense, and every time I let go of him he fell on his neck.

So I abandoned him in disgust and looked down into the cellar to see what was in it that Emerson should of took so much to keep it hid. Well, it was plumb full of buffalo hides, all corded into neat bundles! At that Emerson started to run, but I grabbed him, and reached down with the other hand and hauled a bundle out. It was marked with a red Circle A brand.

"So!" I says to Emerson, impulsively busting him in the snout. "You stole old man Hopkins' hides yoreself! Perjuice that mortgage! Where's the old man's wagon and team?"

"I got 'em hid in my livery stable," he moaned.

"Go hitch 'em up and bring 'em here," I says. "And if you tries to run off, I'll track you down and sculp you alive!"

I went and got Cap'n Kidd and watered him. When I got back, Emerson came up with the wagon and team, so I told him to load on them hides.

"I'm a ruined man!" sniveled he. "I ain't able to load no hides."

"The exercize'll do you good," I assured him, kicking the seat loose from his pants, so he give a harassed howl and went to work. About this time Croghan sot up and gaped at me weirdly.

"It all comes back to me!" he gurgled. "We was going to run Breckinridge Elkins out of town!"

He then fell back and went into shrieks of hysterical laughter which was most hair-raising to hear.

"The wagon's loaded," panted Joe Emerson. "Take it and git out and be quick!"

"Well, let this be a lesson to you," I says, ignoring his hostile attitude. "Honesty's always the best policy!"

I then hit him over the head with a wagon spoke and clucked to the hosses and we headed for Panther Springs.

Old man Hopkins' mules had give out half way to Panther Springs. Him and the old lady was camped there when I drove up. I never seen folks so happy in my life as they was when I handed the team, wagon, hides and mortgage over to 'em. They both cried and the old lady kissed me, and the old man hugged me, and I thot I'd plumb die of embarrassment before I could git away. But I did, finally, and headed for Panther Springs again, because I still had to raise the dough to git Glaze out of jail.

I got there about sun-up and headed straight for Judith's cabin to tell her I'd made friends with Uncle Jabez. Aunt Henrietta was cleaning a carpet on the front porch and looking mad. When I come up she stared at me and said, "Good land, Breckinridge, what happened to you?"

"Aw, nothin'," I says. "Jest a argyment with them fool buffalo hunters over to Cordova. They'd cleaned a old gent and his old lady of their buffalo hides, to say nothin' of their hosses and wagon. So I rid on to see what I could do about it. Them hairy-necked hunters didn't believe me when I said I wanted them hides, so I had to persuade 'em a leetle. O'ny thing is they is sayin' now that I was to blame fer the hull affair. I apolergized to Judith's uncle, too. Had to chase him from here to Cordova. Where's Judith?"

"Gone!" she says, stabbing her broom at the floor so vicious she broke the handle off. "When she taken them pies and cakes to yore fool friend down to the jail house, she taken a shine to him at first sight. So she borrored the money from me to pay his fine—said she wanted a new dress to look nice in for you, the deceitful hussy! If I'd knowed what she wanted it for she wouldn't of got it—she'd of got somethin' acrost my knee! But she paid him out of the jug, and — "

"And what happened then?" I says wildly.

"She left me a note," snarled Aunt Henrietta, giving the carpet a whack that tore it into six pieces. "She said anyway she was afeared if she didn't marry him I'd make her marry you. She must of sent you off on that wild goose chase a purpose. Then she met him, and—well, they snuck out and got married and air now on their way to Denver for their honeymoon — Hey, what's the matter, Breckinridge? Air you sick?"

"I be," I gurgled. "The ingratitude of mankind cuts me to the gizzard! After all I'd did for Glaze Bannack! Well, by golly, this is a lesson to me! I bet I don't never work my fingers to the quick gittin' another ranny out of jail!"

Mayhem and Taxes

They is some disadvantage in being a healthy young man with wolfish inclinations and a educated trigger-finger. Folks is always dumping jobs onto me which is too hefty for them to throw and hawg-tie theirselves. Take that time down in Arizona, for instance.

I was headin' back for Bear Creek, having had business down in Mexico with a gent which was rumored to of said that my Uncle Saul Garfield was a horse-thief. I trailed that there vile slanderer from the Humbolts in southern Nevada to a town way down in Durango and finally catched up with him and made him take it back, and sign a paper sayin' he was a liar and a polecat. I was now heading back to Bear Creek to show the document to folks as a proof that the honor of the family had been vindicated with a pistol butt. Us folks on Bear Creek is proud. We allows nobody to defame honesty, of which we're plenty proud. Nobody can say we ever taken so much as a spur offen even a stranger which we happened to shoot.

Well, early one morning on my way back I pulled into San Jose, which is a little desert town mighty nigh in sight of the Border, and being awful thirsty I went into a saloon and drunk three or four gallons of beer. Whilst I was swiggin' my beer quite a gathering of folks come and stared at me like I was a curiosity or something, and I heard somebody on the outside holler: "Hey, Bill, come over here! They's the biggest man you ever seen lappin' up licker over here!"

Such attentions used to embarrass me when I was younger, but I soon got used to being gawked at when I was out away from my home cabin on Bear Creek. Up there I ain't so conspicuous because all the men in the Humbolts is fair sized, but other places I go seems like folks think a man as big as me is a miracle or somethin'.

So I paid no attention to 'em till a cow-poke in a yaller neck-cloth come up and taken off his hat respectful and says: "Excuse me, stranger; I don't want to seem too inquisitive nor nothin', but ain't you Breckinridge Elkins?"

I give the matter due consideration and 'lowed as how I was, and he says: "A gent acrost the street told me to find out, and if you was Breckinridge Elkins of Bear Creek, to ast you to come over and see him."

"Why cain't he come over here?" I demanded.

"He cain't walk," says the cowpunch. "He's got a misery in the hind laig."

"Does he wanta fight or to pow-wow?" I next ast, being cautious by nature, in spite of what folks says about me.

"Oh, he's a friend of yore'n," the waddy assured me. "His name's Johnny Bixby. He said he knowed you up in War Paint, Nevady."

I finished my beer and said I'd go see Johnny. I remembered him, all right: a little sawed-off feller which could talk yore left ear off. I always liked Johnny, even though he wore socks and store-bought shirts—regular dude. But he was born way back East in Kansas or Oklahoma or some place, so I didn't hold his effete ways agen him.

"What's Johnny doin' here?" I ast.

"Oh," says the puncher, "he's deperty under Bill Jackson, sheriff of Chisom County, and he aims to run for sheriff hisself next election. That's his office acrost the street. And that's Johnny groanin'. He's got the misery somethin' turrible."

He was doing a right smart job of groanin', all right. I could hear him clean acrost the street. The office was just a one-room shack with new boards and no paint on 'em. We stomped through the dust of the street and past the hitching rack where four or five cayuses was tied, and come to the office door which was wide open, of course. I could see a figger reclining in a chair with one foot h'isted onto a empty goods box and the foot was all wound up with bandages. It was Johnny all right, and his groans reverberated amongst the rafters overhead.

"Here's your friend, Johnny," said the cowpuncher, sticking his head through the door, and Johnny said firmly: "Thank'ee, McBride. Come in, Breckinridge—come in! It'll be good to see a old pal before I lets go all holts and slides into the Great Beyond!"

So I went into the office and McBride went off and I figgered he must think a lot of Johnny and be weeping about him, because he had one hand over his mouth and t'other over his stummick and was making peculiar noises. I'd a swore he was laughing only I couldn't see nothin' to laugh about.

I bumped my head as I went through the door—it's dern strange why folks can't build their cussed doors high enough for a ordinary-sized man to get through without braining hisself—but I kept my temper and said: "Hello, Johnny. Who shot you?"

"T'aint lead pizenin'," he moaned. "It's gout."

"What's that?" I inquired.

"A misery in the toe," he explained. "Us Bixbys is subject to sech attacks. Ow!" says he earnestly. "Ow! Ow! *Owww!*"

He had a letter in his hand, and it seemed to me like when he looked at that letter he groaned louder and more fervently than ever. It always disgusted me to hear a grown man carrying on like that, but I figgered gout was some kind of a ailment which folks born back East was subject to, so I didn't say nothin' but sot down on another chair and waited for him to get through pitying hisself.

Presently he says, very bitterly: "I'm in a jamb, Breck. Fate has conspired agen me. Fickle Fortune and a gouty toe has delivered me into the hands of my enemies, notably Bill Jackson, sheriff of Chisom County."

"I thought you was his deperty," I said.

"I am," says he. "But I aims high. My ambition is unfettered. She soars to the stars. Whole hawg or none, is my motter. I aims to run agen Jackson for sheriff, and he knows it. So he seeks to undermine my repertation. And Fate gives him the chance to deal me the joker with a kick like a mule's hind laig tied onto it."

He waved the letter at me.

"Look here!" he said. "My orders from the sheriff's office to go collect taxes over in Smokeville. He knowed I was so laid up I can't fork a bronk. He aims to use my infirmerty agen me. If I don't git them taxes in, he'll use that there fack agen me in the campaign. He'll accuse me of fraud and graft—well, he'll accuse me of that, anyhow, but he can't prove nothin'—uh, well, if I don't git that tax money in to the county treasurer I'll be rooint."

"What do you care if yo're goin' to die of that there gout anyway?" I ast.

"It ain't always fatal," says he. "I may pull through. Anyway, it's my duty as a deperty."

"Why don't you send somebody to do it for you?" I says.

"I can't trust nobody," he said dolefully. "I'm afeard they'd double-cross me and sell me out to Jackson. They'd side-track the

dough and I'd sit accused of pocketin' it. Hey, wait!" he says
suddenly, and p'inted his finger at me. "Whyn't *you* go and colleck
them taxes?" says he. "Yo're the only man in San Jose I can trust."

"I don't believe in taxes," I said. "We ain't never paid no taxes
on Bear Creek, and we don't aim to."

"You folks up there take keer of yourselves," he said. "You
ain't dependent onto the government nor nobody for nothin'. You
shoots, raises or weaves everythin' you eats, wears or drinks. You
even makes yore own licker and gun-powder, and from the Bear
Creek licker I've drank, I jedges you uses the same recipe for both
of them articles. But down here things is different. Folks owes
the government taxes and oughta pay, but they won't do it 'less'n
somebody rides out and gits it. But heck, Breck, it wouldn't be
no trouble. Just ride over to Smokeville, which is about ten miles
west of here, and colleck the taxes and bring the money back."

"I don't hold with it," I growled. "My granddaddy fit the
Britishers at King's Mountain jest on account of this here blame
tax business, and I considers it's a derned imposure on honest
people."

"But lissen, Breckinridge," he begged. "They got to pay it
anyhow, and somebody's got to colleck it. If I don't git it, I'm
rooint, and yo're the only man I can trust. Think of the old days
in Nevader! Think of the time we stood back to back and fit off
that sheriff's posse in Chawed Ear—"

"That's a lie," I said, suddenly recollecting it. "You run off
and left me to polish off them derned snake-hunters by myself."

"Will you hold onto a petty grudge at a time like this, Breckinridge?" he wailed. "Here I am at my last gasp! With tears in my
eyes and licker on my breath, I implores you—colleck them taxes
for me!"

"Oh, all right," I grunted. "I'll do it. Stop belly-achin'. How
much I got to colleck?"

"Great!" he enthused and stopped groanin' all to onst. "I hereby
app'ints you tax collector of the south district of Chisom County.
That's yore authority. I figger a dollar a head for every grown
man and grown woman oughta be about right. When you hit a
man with considerable property you better tack on a few dollars
for that. Take Smokeville today; you ought not to take more'n a
few days. When you get back you can take Alvaro if yo're still
ali—I mean if we don't have a sandstorm or nothin'. You better
start right away."

Well, I was shortly riding out of San Jose on Cap'n Kidd,
heading west and reflecting that my kinfolks on Bear Creek would

hang their heads in shame did they know I'd sunk low enough to go collecting taxes. I ain't forgot what they done to the only tax collector which ever come up in the Humbolts. That was the time folks wrote from all over the state and urged the governor to send the army up on Bear Creek. And he might of, too, only he didn't have but about a thousand men and he knowed that wasn't enough.

I hadn't much got outa sight of town when I met a wagon all piled up with a stove and chairs and sech like belongings, and a old cuss and his wife setting on the seat smokin' cob pipes and lookin' like they'd gone sour on the world in general.

I pulled up alongside of 'em and said: "Does you all live here in Chisom County?"

The old man taken his pipe out of his mouth and looked at me.

"We did," he said. "But we ain't." And he put the pipe back.

"Well," I said, "I'm the tax collector, but if you all are movin' outa the county, I don't reckon you owes the guvnment no taxes."

He laughed bitterly, and says: "Well, I ain't yet reached the p'int whar I pays cash money for the privilege of bein' shot. Yes, I'm movin', all right. I don't aim to pull the lines on these mules agen till I'm so far away from Chisom County that was all the jackasses in the county to start brayin', I couldn't hear 'em."

The old woman was staring at me very morbid-like, and she says: "Pore boy! Tax collector! Ain't thet a ¾$%¢&*●! shame! And him thet big!"

"Yeah!" snorted the old man. "They couldn't miss him if they wanted to! Git along there, mules!"

And the wagon went rumbling on down the road. I thinks them is very pecooliar acting people. Maybe they're sheep herders or somethin' else equally locoed. So I rode on and passed through a very rugged country and come out on a broad strip of desert and flats, and I met a leathery old cuss ridin' hossback and he p'inted a Winchester at me and says: "Come ye in peace or in war?"

"That depends," I said. "I come collectin' taxes."

He lowered the gun and said: "Huh! Did Johnny Bixby send you?" And when I said he did, he said he 'lowed that was so. And he said: "I don't own no property but this here horse and this here rifle. And I ain't goin' to pay no taxes on them."

I told him: "I don't reckon the guvment wants to tax a man's natural equipment. Leastways, I ain't aimin' to."

"Do you know Navajo Barlow?" he ast.

"Who's he?" I inquired.

"The boss of Smokeville," he said. "The man which you'll have to deal with."

"Johnny never said nothin' about him," I said, and he says: "No, I bet he never. He ain't the man to stomp his own snakes. Well, I'm headin' for San Jose. Thar's the road to Smokeville and God have mercy on yore soul."

He taken off his hat very solemn and held it in his hand as he rode off down the trail.

I thought these folks must all be locoed. I rode on and purty soon I come to a shack in the middle of a mesquite flat; everything looked wore out and busted down and the feller setting on the stoop looked the same way. His shirt and overalls was ragged and patched, and his hat had a hole in it, and his toes was excaping from his shoes. A woman was standing in the door behind him and a flock of kids was looking out the winders and they was as delapidated as him.

He give me a kind of dumb, haunting look, and I said: "I'm the tax collector. You all owes the guvment a dollar a head."

"I ain't got no money," he says hopeless-like. "I ain't got nothin'."

"Hell's fire!" I says. "I ain't gittin' nowheres this way. I *got* to colleck some taxes from somebody!"

"Well," he says with a sign, "I ain't a man to cheat the guvment. There's a rooster we was savin' to cook for the kid next Christmas. You can have that. That's all we got, 'cept these clothes on our backs, and they're mostly patches."

"This looks like good grazin' land," I said. "I'd of thot folks to these parts'd do right well."

"You won't find many people any better off'n us," he asserted.

"How come they're so porely?" I inquired.

"It's Navajo Barlow's fault!" said the woman fiercely.

The man turned pale and said: "Shet up!" but she said, kinda wild and desperate: "I won't shet up! If this feller is a guvment man he oughta know how Navajo Barlow and his thugs is runnin' south Chisom County. He's a derned outlaw! He runs Smokeville and the sheriff and his deperties are skeered to come over and interfere. You must be a stranger or a derned fool to come over here collectin' taxes. Last time a tax collector come to Smokeville they stamped Barlow's brand onto his hind end with a red hot iron and rode him outa town astraddle of a mesquite rail.

"Barlow's boss of this end of the county, and he's got the desperatest gun-men workin' for him—Jim Hopkins, and Bill Ridley, and Jack McBane, and I don't know who all. Smokeville's his headquarters and nobody there dast open their mouth agen him. He's stole cattle and horses till everybody's bankrupt. He steals cattle in Mexico and makes us buy 'em; and then steals 'em back and sells 'em to the Mexican agen. And every time any of us gets a little money, we got to give it to him to keep from gettin' shot and burned out. You won't get no tax-money in these parts."

"I bet I do," I said. "I reckon I'll go on to Smokeville."

So I rode on to Smokeville, and it wasn't much of a town. A few hard-looking hombres lounging along the street, with their gun-scabbards tied down give me very suspicious looks, but most of the folks, which I jedged was the honest citizens, looked downtrodden and went about their business in a hurry and didn't say much.

I picked out the outlaws as quick as I seen 'em; I can spot their brand a mile away. They warn't as many of 'em as I figgered, but I decided most of 'em was out stealin' cows.

I went into the biggest saloon they was, and it was a fine one alright, with a big bar and a gilded mirror behind it, and gambling tables, only it was too early in the day for anybody to be in there gambling.

The only men in there was the bar-tender, a big, tough-lookin' egg with cauliflower ears; and another big feller with a diamond horse-shoe stick-pin and a fancy vest and some big sparkling rings on his fingers. He come up to me and said:

"Who are you, and what do you want? I'm Navajo Barlow."

"I'm Breckinridge Elkins," I said. "I'm collectin' taxes."

"That's all right," says he, "so long as you don't try to collect none from me."

"Tax collector!" says the bar-keep. "Haw, haw, haw!"

"How many grown people is they in and around Smokeville?" I says.

"Oh, about seven hundred," says he.

"Well," I says, "gimme seven hundred dollars and we'll call it even."

His mouth flew wide open and his eyes bulged.

"What—what—" he gurgled. "Are you crazy?"

"I'm collectin' taxes," I says. "You've made paupers outa everybody in south Chisom. Now by golly you can pay their taxes."

"By God!" he says softly. "I believe you actually mean that!" And he went for his gun.

Well, I was afeared if he started shooting at me some of the bullets might go through the winders and hit some innocent bystanders, so I taken his gun away from him and put it outa action by bending the barrel over his head, and he fell under a table yelling bloody murder and bleeding like a stuck hawg. I had forgot about the bartender and he called my attention to him by hitting me over the head from behind with the bungstarter, which was bad for him, because at this piece of treachery, I come very near losin' my temper, and if I had, it would of been bad for him.

But I controlled my emotions and taken the bar-tender and throwed him through the gilded mirror, and about that time more of Barlow's warriors arrived through the door in answer to their chief's howls, and I took 'em as they come. Some I throwed through the winders and some I wiped the floor with and I tore down all the roulette wheels and busted 'em and kicked all the slats outa the bar and throwed the pool tables through the winders and pulled my guns and shot all the bottles offa the shelves and busted the lamps hanging from the ceiling, and Barlow riz from the debris and hollered: "For God's sake, let up! I'm rooint! I'll pay them cussed taxes!"

"Seven hundred dollars for the adult population," I says, screwing a smoking gun-muzzle into his ear to encourage him. "And you also owes a property tax, bein' as yo're the only man in Smokeville which owns anything."

"How much?" he demanded, grinding his teeth as he looked about him at the ruins.

"Three hundred dollars," I decided, and he let out a howl like a catamount.

"Oh, all right," I says. "If you thinks that's too much, I notice you owns a restaurant acrost the street. I think I'll go over there and do some more assessment."

"Hold on!" he begged. "I'll pay—you've did about all the assessin' the town can stand. Wait'll I open my safe, and I'll pay the taxes."

When he handed 'em over, he said: "Gimme a receipt."

"What's that?" I said.

"Somethin' that'll show you been paid," he said, so I said, "All right. Here's yore receipt." And I hit him under the jaw and knocked him about seventeen feet through a winder in a rain-barrel, and his maddened howls was rising to the skies as I rode outa Smokeville.

Evil Deeds at Red Cougar

I been accused of prejudice agen the town of Red Cougar, on account of my habit of avoiding it if I have to ride fifty miles outen my way to keep from goin' through there. I denies the slander. It ain't no more prejudiced for me to ride around Red Cougar than it is for a lobo to keep his paw out of a jump-trap. My experiences in that there lair of iniquity is painful to recall. I was a stranger and took in. I was a sheep for the fleecing, and if some of the fleecers got their fingers catched in the shears, it was their own fault. If I shuns Red Cougar like a plague, that makes it mutual, because the inhabitants of Red Cougar shuns me with equal enthusiasm, even to the p'int of deserting their wagons and taking to the bresh if they happens to meet me on the road.

I warn't intending to go there in the first place. I been punching cows over in Utah and was heading for Bear Creek, with the fifty bucks a draw poker game had left me outa my wages.

When I seen a trail branchin' offa the main road I knowed it turnt off to Red Cougar, but it didn't make no impression on me.

But I hadn't gone far past it when I heard a hoss running, and the next thing it busted around a bend in the road with foam flyin' from the bit rings. They was a gal on it, lookin' back over her shoulder down the road. Jest as she rounded the turn her hoss stumbled and went to its knees, throwing her over its head.

I was offa Cap'n Kidd in a instant and catched her hoss before it could run off. I helped her up, and she grabbed holt of me and hollered: "Don't let 'em get me!"

"Who?" I said, taking off my hat with one hand and drawing a .45 with the other'n.

"A gang of desperadoes!" she panted. "They've chased me for

five miles! Oh, please don't let 'em get me!"

"They'll tech you only over my dead carcass," I assured her.

She gimme a look which made my heart turn somersets. She had black curly hair and big innercent gray eyes, and she was the purtiest gal I'd saw in a coon's age.

"Oh, thank you!" she panted gratefully. "I knowed you was a gent the minute I laid eyes onto you. Will you help me up onto my hoss?"

"You shore you ain't hurt none?" I ast, and she said she warn't, so I helped her up, and she gathered up her reins and looked back down the road very nervous. "Don't let 'em foller me!" she begged. "I'm goin' on."

"You don't need to do that," I says. "Wait till I exterminates them scoundrels, and I'll escort you home."

But she started convulsively as the distant pound of hoof reched us, and said: "Oh, I dast not! They mustn't even see me again!"

"But I want to," I said. "Where you live?"

"Red Cougar," says she. "My name's Sue Pritchart. If you happen up that way, drop in."

"I'll be there!" I promised, and she flashed me a dazzling smile and loped on down the road and outa sight up the Red Cougar trail.

So I set to work. I uses a rope wove outa buffalo hide, a right smart longer and thicker and stronger'n the average riata because a man my size has got to have a rope to match. I tied said lariat acrost the road about three foot off the ground.

Then I backed Cap'n Kidd into the bushes, and purty soon six men swept around the bend. The first hoss fell over my rope and the others fallen over him, and the way they piled up in the road was beautiful to behold. Before you could bat yore eye they was a most amazing tangle of kicking hosses and cussing men. I chose that instant to ride out of the bresh and throw my pistols down on 'em.

"Cease that scandalous langwidge and rise with yore hands up!" I requested, and they done so, but not cheerfully. Some had been kicked right severe by the hosses, and one had pitched over his cayuse's neck and lit on his head, and his conversation warn't noways sensible.

"What's the meanin' of this here holdup?" demanded a tall maverick with long yaller whiskers.

"Shet up!" I told him sternly. "Men which chases a he'pless gal like a pack of Injuns ain't fittin' for to talk to a decent man."

"Oh, so that's it!" says he. "Well, lemme tell yuh—"

"I said shet up!" I roared, emphasizing my request by shooting the left tip offa his mustash. "I don't aim to powwow with no dern women-chasin' coyotes! In my country we'd decorate a live oak with yore carcasses!"

"But you don't—" began one of the others, but Yaller Whiskers profanely told him to shet up.

"Don't yuh see he's one of Ridgeway's men?" snarled he. "He's got the drop on us, but our turn'll come. Till it does, save your breath!"

"That's good advice," I says. "Onbuckle yore gun-belts and hang 'em on yore saddle-horns, and keep yore hands away from them guns whilst you does it. I'd plumb welcome a excuse to salivate the whole mob of you."

So they done it, and then I fired a few shots under the hosses' feet and stampeded 'em, and they run off down the road the direction they'd come from. Yaller Whiskers and his pals cussed something terrible.

"Better save yore wind," I advised 'em. "You likely got a good long walk ahead of you before you catches yore cayuses."

"I'll have yore heart's blood for this," raved Yaller Whiskers. "I'll have your sculp if I have to trail yuh from here to Jedgment Day! Yuh don't know who yo're monkeyin' with."

"And I don't care!" I snorted. "Vamoose!"

They taken out down the road after their hosses, and I shot around their feet a few times to kinda speed 'em on their way. They disappeared down the road in a faint blue haze of profanity, and I turnt around and headed for Red Cougar.

I hoped to catch up with Miss Pritchart before she got to Red Cougar, but she had too good a start and was going at too fast a gait. My heart pounded at the thought of her and my corns began to ache. It shore was love at first sight.

Well, I'd follered the trail for maybe three miles when I heard guns banging ahead of me. A little bit later I came to where the trail forked and I didn't know which'n led to Red Cougar. Whilst I was setting there wondering which branch to take, I heard hosses running agen, and purty soon a couple of men hove in sight, spurring hard and bending low like they was expectin' to be shot from behind. When they approached me I seen they had badges onto their vests, and bullet holes in their hats.

"Which is the road to Red Cougar?" I ast perlitely.

"That'n," says the older feller, p'inting back the way they'd come. "But if yo're aimin' to go there I advises yuh to reflect deeply on the matter. Ponder, young man, ponder and meditate! Life is sweet, after all!"

"What do you mean?" I ast. "Who're you all chasin'?"

"Chasin' hell!" says he, polishing his sheriff's badge with his sleeve. "We're bein' chased! Buck Ridgeway's in town!"

"Never heard of him," I says.

"Well," says the sheriff, "Buck don't like strangers no more'n he does law-officers. And yuh see how well he likes them!"

"This here's a free country!" I snorted. "When I stays outa town on account of this here Ridgeway or anybody else they'll be ice in hell thick enough for the devil to skate on. I'm goin' to visit a young lady—Miss Sue Pritchart. Can you tell me where she lives?"

They looked at me very pecooliar, and the sheriff says: "Oh, in that case—well, she lives in the last cabin north of the general store, on the lefthand side of the street."

"Le's git goin'," urged his deperty nervously. "They may foller us!"

They started spurring again, and as they rode off, I heard the deperty say: "Reckon he's one of 'em?" And the sheriff said: "If he ain't he's the biggest damn fool that ever lived, to come sparkin' Sue Pritchart—" Then they rode outa hearin'. I wondered who they was talking about, but soon forgot it as I rode on into Red Cougar.

I come in on the south end of the town, and it was about like all them little mountain villages. One straggling street, hound dogs sleeping in the dust of the wagon ruts, and a general store and a couple of saloons.

I seen some hosses tied at the hitching rack outside the biggest saloon which said "Mac's Bar" on to it, but I didn't see nobody on the streets, although noises of hilarity was coming outa the saloon. I was thirsty and dusty, and I decided I better have me a drink and spruce up some before I called on Miss Prichart. So I watered Cap'n Kidd at the trough, and tied him to a tree (if I'd tied him to the hitch rack he'd of kicked the tar outa the other horses) and went into the saloon. They warn't nobody in there but a old coot with gray whiskers tending bar, and the noise was all coming from another room. From the racket I jedged they was a bowling alley in there and the gents was bowling.

I beat the dust outa my pants with my hat and called for whiskey. Whilst I was drinking it the feller said: "Friend of Buck Ridgeway's?"

"Never seen him in my life," says I, and he says: "Then you better git outa town fast as you can dust it. Him and his bunch ain't here—he pulled out jest a little while ago — but Jeff Middleton's in there, and Jeff's plenty bad."

I started to tell him I warn't studying Jeff Middleton, but jest then a lot of whooping bust out in the bowling alley like somebody had made a ten-strike or somethin', and here come six men bustin' into the bar shooping and yelling and slapping one of 'em on the back.

"Decorate the mahogany, McVey!" they whooped. "Jeff's buyin'! He jest beat Tom Grissom here six straight games!"

They surged up to the bar and one of 'em tried to jostle me aside, but as nobody ain't been able to do that successful since I got my full growth, all he done was sprain his elbow. This seemed to irritate him because he turnt around and said heatedly: "What the hell you think yo're doin'?"

"I'm drinkin' me a glass of corn squeezin's," I replied coldly, and they all turnt around and looked at me, and they moved back from the bar and hitched at their pistol-belts. They was a hard looking gang, and the feller they called Middleton was the hardest looking one of 'em.

"Who're you and where'd you come from?" he demanded.

"None of yore damn business," I replied with a touch of old Southern curtesy.

He showed his teeth at this and fumbled at his gun-belt.

"Air you tryin' to start somethin'?" he demanded, and I seen McVey hide behind a stack of beer kaigs.

"I ain't in the habit of startin' trouble," I told him. "All I does is end it. I'm in here drinkin' me a quiet dram when you coyotes comes surgin' in hollerin' like you was the first critter which ever hit a pin."

"So you depreciates my talents, hey?" he squalled like he was stung to the quick. "Maybe you think you could beat me, hey?"

"I ain't yet seen the man which could hold a candle to my game," I replied with usual modesty.

"All right!" he yelled, grinding his teeth. "Come into the alley, and I'll show you some action, you big mountain grizzly!"

"Hold on!" says McVey, sticking his head up from behind the kaigs. "Be keerful, Jeff! I believe that's—"

"I don't keer who he is!" raved Middleton. "He has give me a mortal insult! Come on you, if you got the nerve!"

"You be careful with them insults!" I roared menacingly, striding into the alley. "I ain't the man to be bulldozed."

I was looking back over my shoulder when I shoved the door open with my palm and I probably pushed harder'n I intended to and that's why I tore the door offa the hinges. They all looked kinda startled, and McVey give a despairing squeak, but I went on into the alley and picked up a bowl ball with one hand, which I brandished in defiance.

"Here's fifty bucks!" I says, waving the greenbacks. "We puts up fifty each and rolls for five dollars a game. That suit you?"

I couldn't understand what he said, because he jest made a noise like a wolf grabbing a beefsteak, but he snatched up a bull dog, and perjuiced ten five-dollar bills, so I jedged it was agreeable with him.

But he had a awful temper, and the longer we played, the madder he got, and when I had beat him five straight games and taken twenty-five outa his fifty, the veins stood out purple onto his temples.

"It's yore roll," I says, and he throwed his bowl ball down and yelled: "Blast yore soul, I don't like yore style! I'm through and I'm takin' down my stake! You gits no more of my money, damn you!"

"Why, you cheap-heeled piker!" I roared. "I thought you was a sport, even if you was a hossthief, but—"

"Don't you call me a hoss-thief!" he screamed.

"Well, cow-thief then," I says. "If yo're so dern particular—"

It was at this instant that he lost his head to the p'int of pulling a pistol and firing at me p'int-blank. He would of ondoubtedly shot me, too, if I hadn't hit him in the head with my bowl ball jest as he fired. His bullet went into the ceiling and his friends begun to display their disapproval by throwing pins and bulldogs at me. This irritated me almost beyond control, but I kept my temper and taken a couple of 'em by the neck and beat their heads together till they was limp. The matter would of ended there, without any vi'lence, but the other three insisted on taking the thing serious. And I defy any man to remain tranquil when three hoss-thieves are kyarving at him with bowies and beating him over the head with ten-pins.

But I didn't intend to bust the big ceiling lamp; I jest hit it by accident with the chair which I knocked one of my enermies stiff with. And it warn't my fault if one of 'm got blood all over the alley. All I done was break his nose and knock out seven teeth with my fist. How'd I know he was going to fall in the alley and bleed on it. As for that section of wall which got knocked out, all I can say is it's a derned flimsy wall which can be wrecked by throwing a man through it. I thought I'd throwed him through a winder until I looked closer and seen it was a hole he busted through the wall. And can I help it if them scalawags blowed holes in the roof till it looked like a sieve?

It wasn't my fault, nohow. But when the dust settled and I looked around me to see if I'd made a clean sweep, I was jest in time to grab the shotgun which old man McVey was trying to shoot me through the barroom door with.

"You oughta be ashamed," I reproved. "A man of yore age and venerable whiskers tryin' to shoot a defenseless stranger in the back."

"But my bowlin' alley's wrecked!" he wept, tearing the aforesaid whiskers. "I'm a rooint man! I sunk my wad in it—and now look at it!"

"Aw, well," I says, "it warn't my fault, but I cain't see a honest man suffer. Here's seventy-five dollars, all I got."

"'Tain't enough," says he, nevertheless making a grab for the dough like a kingfisher diving after a pollywog. "'Tain't near enough."

"I'll colleck the rest from them coyotes," I says.

"Don't do it!" he shuddered. "They'd kill me after you left!"

"I wanta do the right thing," I says. "I'll work out the rest of it."

He looked at me right sharp then, and says, "Come into the bar."

But I seen three of 'em was comin' to, so I hauled me up and told 'em sternly to tote their friends out to the hoss trough and bring 'em to. They done so, kinda wabbling on their feet. They acted like they was still addled in the brains, and McVey said it looked to him like Middleton was out for the day, but I told him it was quite common for a man to be like that which has jest had a fifteen-pound ball split in two over his head.

Then I went into the bar with McVey and he poured out the drinks.

"Air you in earnest about workin' out that debt?" says he.

"Sure," I said. "I always pays my debts, by fair means or foul."

"Ain't you Breckinridge Elkins?" says he, and when I says I was, he says: "I thought I rekernized you when them fools was badgerin' you. Look out for 'em. That ain't all of 'em. The whole gang rode into town a hour or so ago and run the sheriff and his deperty out, but Buck didn't stay long. He seen his gal, and then he pulled out for the hills agen with four men. They's a couple more besides them you fit hangin' around somewheres. I dunno where."

"Outlaws?" I said, and he said: "Shore. But the local law-force ain't strong enough to deal with 'em, and anyway, most of the folks in town is in cahoots with 'em, and warns 'em if officers from outside come after 'em. They hang out in the hills ordinary, but they come into Red Cougar regular. But never mind them. I was jest puttin' you on yore guard."

"This is what I want you to do. A month ago I was comin' back to Red Cougar with a tidy fortune in gold dust I'd panned back up in the hills, when I was held up and robbed. It warn't one of Ridgeway's men; it was Three-Fingers Clements, a old lone wolf and the wust killer in these parts. He lives by hisself up in the hills and nobody knows where.

"But I jest learnt by accident. He sent a message by a sheep-herder and the sheepherder got drunk in my saloon and talked. I learnt he's still got my gold, and aims to sneak out with it as soon as he's j'ined by a gang of desperados from Tomahawk. It was them the sheepherder was takin' the message to. I cain't git no help from the sheriff; these outlaw's has got him plumb buf-faloed. I want you to ride up in the hills and git my gold. Of course, if yo're scairt of him—"

"Who said I was scairt of him or anybody else?" I demanded irritably. "Tell me how to git to his hide-out and I'm on my way."

McVey's eyes kinda gleamed, and he says: "Good boy! Foller the trail that leads outa town to the northwest till you come to Diablo Canyon. Foller it till you come to the fifth branch gulch openin' into it on the right. Turn off the trail then and foller the gulch till you come to a big white oak nigh the left-hand wall. Climb up outa the gulch there and head due west up the slope. Purty soon you'll see a crag like a chimney stickin' out above a clump of spruces. At the foot of that crag they's a cave, and Clements is livin' there. And he's a tough old—"

"It's as good as did," I assured him, and had another drink, and went out and clumb aboard Cap'n Kidd and headed out of town.

But as I rode past the last cabin on the left, I suddenly remem-bered about Sue Pritchart, and I 'lowed Three Fingers could wait long enough for me to pay my respecks on her. Likely she was expecting me and getting nervous and impatient because I was so long coming. So I reined up to the stoop and hailed, and somebody looked at me through a winder. They also appeared to be a rifle muzzle trained on me, too, but who could blame folks for being cautious with them Ridgeway coyotes in town.

"Oh, it's you!" said a sweet female voice, and then the door opened wide and Sue Pritchart said: "Light and come in! Did you kill any of them rascals?"

"I'm too soft-hearted for my own good," I says apologetically. "I jest merely—only sent 'em down the road on foot. But I ain't got time to come in now. I'm on my way up in the mountains to see Three Fingers Clements. I aimed to stop on my way back, if it's agreeable with you."

"Three Fingers Clements?" says she in a pecooliar voice. "Do you know where he is?"

"McVey told me," I said. "He's got a poke of dust he stole from McVey. I'm goin' after it."

She said something under her breath which I must have misunderstood because I was sure Miss Pritchart wouldn't use the word it sounded like.

"Come in jest a minute," she begged. "You got plenty time. Come in and have a snort of corn juice. My folks is all visitin' and it gets mighty lonesome to a gal. Please come in!"

Well, I never could resist a purty gal, so I tied Cap'n Kidd to a stump that looked solid, and went in, and she brung out her old man's jug. It was tolerable licker. She said she never drunk none, personal.

We set and talked, and there wasn't a doubt we cottoned to each other right spang off. There is some that says that Breckinridge Elkins hain't got a lick of sense when it comes to wimminfolks—among these bein' my cousin, Bearfield Buckner — but I vow and declare that same is my only weakness, if any, and that likewise it is manly weakness.

This Sue Pritchart was plumb sensible I seen. She wasn't one of these flighty kind that a feller would have to court with a banjo or geetar. We talked around about bear-traps and what was the best length barrel on shotguns and similar subjects of like nature. I likewise told her one or two of my mild experiences and her eyes boogered as big as saucers. We finally got around to my latest encounter.

"Tell me some more about Three Fingers," she coaxed. "I didn't know anybody knowed his hide-out." So I told her what all McVey said, and she was a heap interested, and had me repeat the instructions how to get there two or three times. Then she ast me if I'd met any badmen in town and I told her I'd met six and they was now recovering on pallets in the back of the general store. She looked startled at this, and purty soon she ast me to excuse her because she heard one of the neighbor women calling her. I didn't hear nobody, but I said all right, and she went out of the back door, and I heard her whistle three times. I sot there and had another snort or so and reflected that the gal was ondoubtedly taken with me.

She was gone quite a spell, and finally I got up and looked out the back winder and seen her standing down by the corral talking to a couple of fellers. As I looked one of 'em got on a bobtailed roan and headed north at a high run, and t'other'n come on back to the cabin with Sue.

"This here's my cousin Jack Montgomery," says she. "He wants to go with you. He's jest a boy, and likes excitement."

He was about the hardest-looking boy I ever seen, and he seemed remarkable mature for his years, but I said: "All right. But we got to git goin'."

"Be careful, Breckinridge," she advised. "You, too, Jack."

"I won't hurt Three Fingers no more'n I got to," I promised her, and we went on our way yonderly, headed for the hideout.

We got to Diablo Canyon in about a hour, and went up it about three miles till we come to the gulch mouth McVey had described. All to onst Jack Montgomery pulled up and p'inted down at a pool we was passing in a holler of the rock, and hollered: "Look there! Gold dust scattered at the aidge of the water!"

"I don't see none," I says.

"Light," he urged, getting off his cayuse. "I see it! It's as thick as butter along the aidge!"

Well, I got down and bent over the pool but I couldn't see nothing and all to onst something hit me in the back of the head and knocked my hat off. I turnt around and seen Jack Montgomery holding the bent barrel of a Winchester carbine in his hands. The stock was busted off and pieces was laying on the ground. He looked awful surprized about something; his eyes was wild and his hair stood up.

"Air you sick?" I ast. "What you want to hit me for?"

"You ain't human!" he gasped, dropping the bent barrel and jerking out his pistol. I grabbed him and taken it away from him.

"What's the matter with you?" I demanded. "Air you locoed?"

For answer he run off down the canyon shrieking like a lost soul. I decided he must have went crazy like sheepherders do sometimes, so I pursued him and catched him. He fit and hollered like a painter.

"Stop that!" I told him sternly. "I'm yore friend. It's my duty to yore cousin to see that you don't come to no harm."

"Cousin, hell!" says he with frightful profanity. "She ain't no more my cousin than you be."

"Pore feller," I sighed, throwing him on his belly and reachin' for his lariat. "Yo're outa yore head and sufferin' from hallucernations. I knowed a sheepherder jest like you onst, only he thought he was Sittin' Bull."

"What you doin'?" he hollered, as I started tying him with his rope.

"Don't you worry," I soothed him. "I cain't let you go tearin' around over these mountains in yore condition. I'll fix you so's you'll be safe and comfortable till I git back from Three Fingers' cave. Then I'll take you to Red Cougar and we'll send you to some nice quiet insane asylum."

"Blast yore soul!" he shrieked. "I'm sane as you be! A damn' sight saner, because no man with a normal brain could ignore gittin' a rifle stock broke off over his skull like you done!"

Whereupon he tries to kick me between the eyes and otherwise give evidence of what I oncet heard a doctor call his derangement. It was a pitiful sight to see, especially since he was a cousin to Miss Sue Pritchart and would ondoubtedly be my cousin-in-law one of these days. He jerked and rassled and some of his words was downright shocking.

But I didn't pay no attention to his ravings. I always heard the way to get along with crazy people was to humor 'em. I was afeared if I left him laying on the ground the wolves might chaw him, so I tied him up in the crotch of a big tree where they couldn't rech him. I likewise tied his hoss by the pool where it could drink and graze.

"Lissen!" Jack begged as I clumb onto Cap'n Kidd. "I give up! Ontie me and I'll spill the beans! I'll tell you everything!"

"You jest take it easy," I soothed. "I'll be back soon."

"●¾$%¢&*!" says he, frothing slightly at the mouth.

With a sigh of pity I turnt up the gulch, and his langwidge till I was clean outa sight ain't to be repeated. A mile or so on I come to the white oak tree, and clumb outa the gulch and went up a long slope till I seen a jut of rock like a chimney rising above the trees. I slid offa Cap'n Kidd and drawed my pistols and snuck for'ard through the thick bresh till I seen the mouth of a cave ahead of me. And I also seen somethin' else, too.

A man was laying in front of it with his head in a pool of blood.

I rolled him over and he was still alive. His sculp was cut open, but the bone didn't seem to be caved in. He was a lanky old coot, with reddish gray whiskers, and he didn't have but three fingers onto his left hand. They was a pack tore up and scattered on the ground nigh him, but I reckon the pack mule had run off. They was also hosstracks leading west.

They was a spring nearby and I brung my hat full of water and sloshed it into his face, and tried to pour some into his mouth, but it warn't no go. When I throwed the water over him he kinda twitched and groaned, but when I tried to pour the water down his gullet he kinda instinctively clamped his jaws together like a bulldog.

Then I seen a jug settin' in the cave, so I brung it out and pulled out the cork. When it popped he opened his mouth convulsively and reched out his hand.

So I poured a pint or so down his gullet, and he opened his eyes and glared wildly around till he seen his busted pack, and then he clutched his whiskers and shrieked: "They got it! My poke of dust! I been hidin' up here for weeks, and jest when I was goin' to make a jump for it, they finds me!"

"Who?" I ast.

"Buck Ridgeway and his gang!" he squalled. "I was keerless. When I heard hosses I thought it was the men which was comin' to help me take my gold out. Next thing I knowed Ridgeway's bunch had run outa the bresh and was beatin' me over the head with their Colts. I'm a rooint man!"

"Hell's fire!" quoth I with passion. Them Ridgeways was beginnin' to get on my nerves. I left ole man Clements howling his woes to the skies like a timber wolf with the bellyache, and I forked Cap'n Kidd and headed west. They'd left a trail the youngest kid on Bear Creek could foller.

It led for five miles through as wild a country as I ever seen outside the Humbolts, and then I seen a cabin ahead, on a wide benchland and that backed agen a steep mountain slope. I could jest see the chimney through the tops of a dense thicket. It warn't long till sun-down and smoke was comin' outa the chimney.

I knowed it must be the Ridgeway hideout, so I went bustin' through the thicket in sech a hurry that I forgot they might have a man on the lookout. I'm powerful absent minded thataway. They was one all right, but I was coming so fast he missed me with his buffalo gun, and he didn't stop to reload but run into the cabin yellin': "Bar the door quick! Here comes the biggest man in the world on the biggest hoss in creation!"

They done so. When I emerged from amongst the trees they

opened up on me through the loopholes with sawed-off shotguns. If it'd been Winchesters I'd of ignored 'em, but even I'm a little bashful about buckshot at close range, when six men is shootin' at me all to onst. So I retired behind a big tree and begun to shoot back with my pistols, and the howls of them worthless critters when my bullets knocked splinters in their faces was music to my ears.

They was a corral some distance behind the cabin with six hosses in it. To my surprise I seen one of 'em was a bob-tailed roan the feller was riding which I seen talking with Sue Pritchart and Jack Montgomery, and I wondered if them blame outlaws had captured him.

But I warn't accomplishing much, shooting at them loopholes, and the sun dipped lower and I begun to get mad. I decided to rush the cabin anyway and to hell with their derned buckshot, and I dismounted and stumped my toe right severe on a rock. It always did madden me to stump my toe, and I uttered some loud and profane remarks, and I reckon them scoundrels must have thunk I'd stopped some lead, the way they whooped. But jest then I had a inspiration. A big thick smoke was pourin' outa the rock chimney, so I knowed they was a big fire on the fireplace where they was cooking supper, and I was sure they warn't but one door in the cabin. So I taken up the rock which was about the size of a ordinary pig and throwed it at the chimney.

Boys on Bear Creek is ashamed if they have to use more'n one rock on a squirrel in a hundred-foot tree acrost the creek, and I didn't miss. I hit her center and she buckled and come crashing down in a regular shower of rocks, and most of 'em fell down into the fireplace as I knowed by the way the sparks flew. I jedged that the coals was scattered all over the floor, and the chimney hole was blocked so the smoke couldn't get out that way. Anyway, the smoke begun to pour outa the winders and the Ridgewayers stopped shootin' and started hollerin'.

Somebody yelled: "The floor's on fire; throw that bucket of water on it!" And somebody else shrieked: "Wait, you damn' fool! That ain't water, it's whiskey!"

But he was too late; I heard the splash and then a most amazin' flame sprung up and licked outa the winders and the fellers hollered louder'n ever and yelled: "Lemme out! I got smoke in my eyes! I'm chokin' to death!"

I left the thicket and run to the door just as a man throwed it open and staggered out blind as a bat and cussin' and shootin' wild. I was afeared he'd hurt hisself if he kept tearing around like that, so I taken his shotgun away from him and bent the barrel over his head to kinda keep him quiet, and then I seen to my surprise that he was the feller which rode the bob-tailed roan. I thunk how surpized Sue'd be to know a friend of her'n was a cussed outlaw.

I then went into the cabin which was so full of smoke and gunpowder fumes a man couldn't hardly see nothin'. The walls and roof was on fire by now, and them idjits was tearin' around with their eyes full of smoke tryin' to find the door, and one of 'em run head-on into the wall and knocked hisself stiff. I throwed him outside, and got hold of another'n to lead him out, and he cut me acrost the boozum with his bowie. I was so stung by this ingratitude that when I tossed him out to safety I maybe throwed him further'n I aimed to, and it appears they was a stump which he hit his head on. But I couldn't help it being there.

I then turnt around and located the remaining three, which was fighting with each other evidently thinking they was fighting me. Jest as I started for 'em a big log fell outa the roof and knocked two of 'em groggy and sot their clothes on fire, and a regular sheet of flame sprung up and burnt off most of my hair, and whilst I was dazzled by it the surviving outlaw run past me out the door, leaving his smoking shirt in my hand.

Well, I dragged the other two out and stomped on 'em to put out the fire, and the way they hollered you'd of thought I was injurin' 'em instead of savin' their fool lives.

"Shet up and tell me where the gold is," I ordered, and one of 'em gurgled: "Ridgeway's got it!"

I ast which'n of 'em was him and they all swore they wasn't, and I remembered the feller which run outa the cabin. So I looked around and seen him jest leading a hoss outa the corral to ride off bareback.

"You stop!" I roared, letting my voice out full, which I seldom does. The acorns rattled down outa the trees, and the tall grass bent flat, and the hoss Ridgeway was fixin' to mount got scairt and jerked away from him and bolted, and the other horses knocked the corral gate down and stampeded. Three or four of 'em run over Ridgeway before he could git outa the way.

He jumped up and headed out acrost the flat on foot, wabbling some but goin' strong. I could of shot him easy but I was afeared he'd hid the gold somewheres, and if I kilt him he couldn't tell me where. So I run and got my lariat and taken out after him on foot, because I figgered he'd duck into the thick bresh to git away. But when he seen I was overhaulin' him he made for the mountain side and begun to climb a steep slope.

I follered him, but before he was much more'n half way up he taken refuge on a ledge behind a dead tree and started shootin' at me. I got behind a boulder about seventy-five foot below him, and ast him to surrender, like a gent, but his only reply was a direct slur on my ancestry and more bullets, one of which knocked off a sliver of rock which gouged my neck.

This annoyed me so much that I pulled my pistols and started shootin' back at him. But all I could hit was the tree, and the sun was goin' down and I was afeared if I didn't get him before dark he'd manage to sneak off. So I stood up, paying no attention to the slug he put in my shoulder, and swang my lariat. I always uses a ninety-foot rope; I got no use for them little bitsy pieces of string most punchers uses.

I throwed my noose and looped that tree, and sot my feet solid and heaved, and tore the dern tree up by the roots. But them roots went so deep most of the ledge come along with 'em, and that started a landslide. The first thing I knowed here come the tree and Ridgeway and several tons of loose rock and shale, gatherin' weight and speed as they come. It sounded like thunder rollin' down the mountain, and Ridgeway's screams was frightful to hear. I jumped out from behind the boulder intending to let the landslide split on me and grab him out as it went past me, but I stumbled and fell and that dern tree hit me behind the ear and the next thing I knowed I was traveling down the mountain with Ridgeway and the rest of the avalanche. It was very humiliatin'.

I was right glad at the time, I recollect, that Miss Sue Pritchart wasn't nowheres near to witness this catastrophe. It's hard for a man to keep his dignity, I found, when he's scottin' in a hell-slue of trees and bresh and rocks and dirt, and I become aware, too, that a snag had tore the seat outa my pants, which made me some despondent. This, I figgered, is what a man gets for losing his self-control. I recollected another time or two when I'd exposed myself to the consequences by exertin' my full strength, and I made me a couple of promises then and there.

It's all right for a single young feller to go hellin' around and let the chips fall where they may, but it's different with a man like me who was almost just the same as practically married. You got to look before you leap, was the way I reckoned it. A man's got to think of his wife and children.

We brung up at the foot of the slope in a heap of boulders and shale, and I throwed a few hundred pounds of busted rocks offa me and riz up and shaken the blood outa my eyes and looked around for Ridgeway.

I presently located a boot stickin' outa the heap, and I laid hold onto it and hauled him out and he looked remarkable like a skint rabbit. About all the clothes he had left onto him beside his boots was his belt, and I seen a fat buckskin poke stuck under it. So I dragged it out, and about that time he sot up groggy and looked around dizzy and moaned feeble: "Who the hell are you?"

"Breckinridge Elkins, of Bear Creek," I said.

"And with all the men they is in the State of Nevada," he says weakly, "I *had* to tangle with you. What you goin' to do?"

"I think I'll turn you and yore gang over to the sheriff," I says. "I don't hold much with law—we ain't never had none on Bear Creek—but sech coyotes as you all don't deserve no better."

"A hell of a right you got to talk about law!" he said fiercely. "After plottin' with Badger McVey to rob old man Clements! That's all I done!"

"What you mean?" I demanded. "Clements robbed that old coot McVey of this here dust—"

"Robbed hell!" says Ridgeway. "McVey is the crookedest cuss that ever lived, only he ain't got the guts to commit robbery hisself. Why, Clements is a honest miner, the old jackass, and he panned that there dust up in the hills. He's been hidin' for weeks, scairt to try to git outa the country, we was huntin' him to industrious."

"McVey put me up to committin' robbery?" I ejaculated, aghast.

"That's jest what he did!" declared Ridgeway, and I was so overcome by this perfidy that I was plumb paralyzed. Before I could recover, Ridgeway give a convulsive flop and rolled over into the bushes and was gone in a instant.

The next thing I knowed I heard hosses runnin' and I turnt in time to see a bunch of men ridin' up on me. Old man Clements was with 'em, and I rekernized the others as the fellers I stopped from chasin' Sue Pritchart on the road below Red Cougar.

I reched for a pistol, but Clements yelled: "Hold on! They're friends!" He then jumped off and grabbed the poke outa my limp hand and waved it at them triumphantly. "See that?" he hollered. "Didn't I tell you he was a friend? Didn't I tell you he come up here to bust up that gang? He got my gold back for me, jest like I said he would!" He then grabbed my hand and shaked it energetic, and says: "These is the men I sent to Tomahawk for, to help me git my gold out. They got to my cave jest a while after you left.

They're prejudiced agen you, but—"

"No, we ain't!" denied Yaller Whiskers, which I now seen was wearin' a deputy's badge. And he got off and shaken my hand heartily. "You didn't know we was special law-officers, and I reckon it did look bad, six men chasin' a woman. We thought you was a outlaw! We was purty mad at you when we finally caught our hosses and headed back. But I begun to wonder about you when we found them six disabled outlaws in the store at Red Cougar. Then when we got to Clements' cave, and found you'd befriended him, and had lit out on Ridgeway's trail, it looked still better for you, but I still thought maybe you was after that gold on yo're own account. But, of course, I see now I was all wrong, and I apolergizes. Where's Ridgeway?"

"He got away," I said.

"Never mind!" says Clements, pumping my hand agen. "Kirby here and his men has got Jeff Middleton and five more men in the jail at Red Cougar. McVey, the old hypocrite, taken to the hills when Kirby rode into town. And we got six more of Ridgeway's gang tied up over at Ridgeway's cabin—or where it was till you burnt it down. They're shore a battered mob! It musta been a awful fight! You look like you been through a tornado yoreself. Come on with us and our prisoners to Tomahawk. I buys you a new suit of clothes, and we celebrates!"

"I got to git a feller I left tied up in a tree down the gulch," I said. "Jack Montgomery. He's et loco weed or somethin'. He's crazy."

They laughed hearty, and Kirby says: "You got a great sense of humor, Elkins. We found him when we come up the gulch, and brung him on with us. He's tied up with the rest of 'em back there. You shore was slick, foolin' McVey into tellin' you where Clements was hidin', and foolin' that whole Ridgeway gang into thinkin' you aimed to rob Clements! Too bad you didn't know we was officers, so we could of worked together. But I gotta laugh when I think how McVey thought he was gyppin' you into stealin' for him, and all the time you was jest studyin' how to rescue Clements and bust up Ridgeway's gang! Haw! Haw! Haw!"

"But I didn't—" I began dizzily, because my head was swimming.

"You jest made on mistake," says Kirby, "and that was when you let slip where Clements was hidin'."

"But I never told nobody but Sue Pritchart!" I says wildly.

"Many a good man has been euchered by a woman," says Kirby tolerantly. "We got the whole yarn from Montgomery. The minute you told her, she snuck out and called in two of Ridgeway's men and sent one of 'em foggin' it to tell Buck where to find Clements, and she sent the other'n, which was Montgomery, to go along with you and lay you out before you could git there. She lit for the hills when we come into Red Cougar and I bet her and Ridgeway are streakin' it over the mountains together right now. But that ain't yore fault. You didn't know she was Buck's gal."

The perfidity of wimmen!

"Gimme my hoss," I said groggily. "I been scorched and shot and cut and fell on by a avalanche, and my honest love has been betrayed. You sees before you the singed, skint and blood-soaked result of female treachery. Fate has dealt me the joker. My heart is busted and the seat is tore outa my pants. Git outa the way. I'm ridin'."

"Where to?" they ast, awed.

"Anywhere," I bellers, "jest so it's far away from Red Cougar."

Sharp's Gun Serenade

I was heading for War Paint, jogging along easy and comfortable, when I seen a galoot coming up the trail in a cloud of dust, jest aburning the breeze. He didn't stop to pass the time of day, he went past me so fast Cap'n Kidd missed the snap he made at his hoss, which shows he was sure hightailin' it. I recognized him as Jack Sprague, a young waddy which worked on a spread not far from War Paint. His face was pale and sot in a look of desprut resolution, like a man which has jest bet his pants on a pair of deuces, and he had a rope in his hand though I couldn't see nothin' he might be aimin' to lasso. He went foggin' on up the trail into the mountains and I looked back to see if I could see the posse. Because about the only time a outlander ever heads for the high Humbolts is when he's about three jumps and a low whoop ahead of a necktie party.

I seen another cloud of dust, all right, but it warn't big enough for more'n one man, and purty soon I seen it was Bill Glanton of War Paint. But that was good enough reason for Sprague's haste, if Bill was on the prod. Glanton is from Texas, original, and whilst he is a sentimental cuss in repose he's a ring-tailed whizzer with star-spangled wheels when his feelings is ruffled. And his feelings is ruffled tolerable easy.

As soon as he seen me he yelled, "Where'd he go?"

"Who?" I says. Us Humbolt folks ain't overflowin' with casual information.

"Jack Sprague!" says he. "You must of saw him. Where'd he go?"

"He didn't say," I says.

Glanton ground his teeth slightly and says, "Don't start yore derned hillbilly stallin' with me! I ain't got time to waste the week or so it takes to git information out of a Humbolt Mountain varmint. I ain't chasin' that misguided idjit to do him injury. I'm pursooin' him to save his life! A gal in War Paint has jilted him and he's so broke up about it he's threatened to ride right over the mortal ridge. Us boys has been watchin' him and follerin' him around and takin' pistols and rat-pizen and the like away from him, but this mornin' he gives us the slip and taken to the hills. It was a waitress in the Bawlin' Heifer Restawrant which put me on his trail. He told her he was goin' up in the hills where he wouldn't be interfered with and hang hisself!"

"So that was why he had the rope," I says. "Well, it's his own business, ain't it?"

"No, it ain't," says Bill sternly. "When a man is in his state he ain't responsible and it's the duty of his friends to look after him. He'll thank us in the days to come. Anyway, he owes me six bucks and if he hangs hisself I'll never git paid. Come on, dang it! He'll lynch hisself whilst we stands here jawin'."

"Well, all right," I says. "After all, I got to think about the repertation of the Humbolts. They ain't never been a suicide committed up here before."

"Quite right," says Bill. "Nobody never got a chance to kill hisself up here, somebody else always done it for him."

But I ignored this slander and reined Cap'n Kidd around jest as he was fixin' to bite off Bill's hoss's ear. Jack had left the trail but he left sign a blind man could foller. He had a long start on us, but we both had better hosses than his'n and after awhile we come to where he'd tied his hoss amongst the bresh at the foot of Cougar Mountain. We tied our hosses too, and pushed through the bresh on foot, and right away we seen him. He was climbing up the slope toward a ledge which had a tree growing on it. One limb stuck out over the aidge and was jest right to make a swell gallows, as I told Bill.

But Bill was in a lather.

"He'll git to that ledge before we can ketch him!" says he. "What'll we do?"

"Shoot him in the laig," I suggested, but Bill says, "No, dern it! He'll bust hisself fallin' down the slope. And if we start after him he'll hustle up to that ledge and hang hisself before we can git to him. Look there, though—they's a thicket growin' up the slope west of the ledge. You circle around and crawl up through it whilst I git out in the open and attracts his attention. I'll try to keep him talkin' till you can git up there and grab him from behind."

So I ducked low in the bresh and ran around the foot of the slope till I come to the thicket. Jest before I div into the tangle I seen Jack had got to the ledge and was fastening his rope to the limb which stuck out over the aidge. Then I couldn't see him no more because that thicket was so dense and full of briars it was about like crawlin' through a pile of fighting bobcats. But as I wormed my way up through it I heard Bill yell, "Hey, Jack, don't do that, you dern fool!"

"Lemme alone!" Jack hollered. "Don't come no closter. This here is a free country! I got a right to hang myself if I wanta!"

"But it's a damfool thing to do," wailed Bill.

"My life is rooint!" asserted Jack. "My true love has been betrayed. I'm a wilted tumblebug—I mean tumble-weed—on the sands of Time! Destiny has slapped the Zero brand on my flank! I—"

I dunno what else he said because at that moment I stepped into something which let out a ear-splitting squall and attached itself vi'lently to my hind laig. That was jest my luck. With all the thickets they was in the Humbolts, a derned cougar had to be sleeping in that'n. And of course it had to be me which stepped on him.

Well, no cougar is a match for a Elkins in a stand-up fight, but the way to lick him (the cougar, I mean; they ain't *no* way to lick a Elkins) is to git yore lick in before he can clinch with you. But the bresh was so thick I didn't see him till he had holt of me and I was so stuck up with them derned briars I couldn't hardly move nohow. So before I had time to do anything about it he had sunk most of his tushes and claws into me and was reching for new holts as fast as he could rake. It was old Brigamer, too, the biggest, meanest and oldest cat in the Humbolts. Cougar Mountain is named for him and he's so dang tough he ain't even scairt of Cap'n Kidd, which is plumb pizen to all cat-animals.

Before I could git old Brigamer by the neck and haul him loose from me he had clawed my clothes all to pieces and likewise lacerated my hide free and generous. In fact he made me so mad that when I did git him loose I taken him by the tail and mowed down the bresh in a fifteen foot circle around me with him, till the hair wore off of his tail and it slipped out of my hands. Old Brigamer than laiggered it off down the mountain squallin' fit to bust yore ear-drums. He was the maddest cougar you ever seen, but not mad enough to renew the fray. He must of recognized me.

At that moment I heard Bill yelling for help up above me so I headed up the slope, swearin' loudly and bleedin' freely, and crashin' through them bushes like a wild bull. Evidently the time for stealth and silence was past. I busted into the open and seen Bill hopping around on the aidge of the ledge trying to git holt of Jack which was kicking like a grasshopper on the end of the rope, jest out of rech.

"Whyn't you sneak up soft and easy like I said?" howled Bill. "I was jest about to argy him out of the notion. He'd tied the rope around his neck and was standin' on the aidge, when that racket bust loose in the bresh and scairt him so bad he fell offa the ledge! Do somethin'!"

"Shoot the rope in two," I suggested, but Bill said, "No, you cussed fool! He'd fall down the cliff and break his neck!"

But I seen it warn't a very big tree so I went and got my arms around it and give it a heave and loosened the roots, and then kinda twisted it around so the limb that Jack was hung to was over the ledge now. I reckon I busted most of the roots in the process, jedging from the noise. Bill's eyes popped out when he seen that, and he reched up kind of dazed like and cut the rope with his bowie. Only he forgot to grab Jack before he cut it, and Jack hit the ledge witha resounding thud.

"I believe he's dead," says Bill despairingful. "I'll never git that six bucks. Look how purple he is."

"Aw," says I, biting me off a chew of terbacker, "all men which has been hung looks that way. I remember onst the Vigilantes hung Uncle Jeppard Grimes, and it taken us three hours to bring him to after we cut him down. Of course, he'd been hangin' about a hour before we found him."

"Shet up and help me revive him," snarled Bill, gitting the noose off of his neck. "You seleck the damndest times to converse about the sins of yore infernal relatives—look, he's comin' to!"

Because Jack had begun to gasp and kick around, so Bill brung out a bottle and poured a snort down his gullet, and pretty soon Jack sot up and felt of his neck. His jaw wagged but didn't make no sound.

Glanton now seemed to notice my disheveled condition for the first time. "What the hell happened to you?" he ast in amazement.

"Aw, I stepped on old Brigamer," I scowled.

"Well, whyn't you hang onto him?" he demanded. "Don't you know they's a big bounty on his pelt? We could of split the dough."

"I've had a bellyful of old Brigamer," I replied irritably. "I don't care if I never see him agen. Look what he done to my best britches! If you wants that bounty, you go after it yoreself."

"And let me alone!" onexpectedly spoke up Jack, eyeing us balefully. "I'll hang myself if I wants to."

"You won't neither," says Bill sternly. "Me and yore paw is old friends and I aim to save yore wuthless life if I have to kill you to do it."

"I defies you!" squawked Jack, making a sudden dive betwixt Bill's laigs and he would of got clean away if I hadn't snagged the seat of his britches with my spur. He then displayed startling ingratitude by hitting me with a rock and, whilst we was tying him up with the hanging rope, his langwidge was scandalous.

"Did you ever see sech a idjit?" demands Bill, setting on him and fanning hisself with his Stetson. "What we goin' to do with him? We cain't keep him tied up forever."

"We got to watch him clost till he gits out of the notion of killin' hisself," I says. "He can stay at our cabin for a spell."

"Ain't you got some sisters?" says Jack.

"A whole cabin-full," I says with feeling. "You cain't hardly walk without steppin' on one. Why?"

"I won't go," says he bitterly. "I don't never want to see no woman agen, not even a mountain-woman. I'm a embittered man. The honey of love has turnt to tranchler pizen. Leave me to the buzzards and cougars."

"I got it," says Bill. "We'll take him on a huntin' trip way up in the high Humbolts. They's some of that country I'd like to see myself. Reckon yo're the only white man which has ever been up there, Breck."

"Hey, look out!" I yelled as I glimpsed a furry hide through the bresh, and thinking it was old Brigamer coming back, I pulled my pistols and started shooting at it, when a familiar voice yelled wrathfully, "Cut that out, dern you!"

The next instant a pecooliar figure hove into view—a tall ga'nt old ranny with long hair and whiskers with a club in his hand and a painter hide tied around his middle. Sprague's eyes bugged out and he says: "Who in the name uh God's that?"

"Another victim of feminine wiles," I says. "That's old Joshua Braxton, of Chawed Ear, the oldest and the toughest batchelor in South Nevada. I jedge that Miss Stark, the old maid schoolteacher has renewed her matrimonical designs onto him. When she starts rollin' sheep's eyes at him he always dons that there garb and takes to the high sierras."

"It's the only way to perteck myself," snarled Joshua. "She'd marry me by force if I didn't resort to strategy. Not many folks comes up here and sech as does don't recognize me in this rig. What you varmints disturbin' my solitude for? Yore racket woke me up, over in my cave. When I seen old Brigamer high tailin' it for distant parts I figgered Elkins was on the mountain."

"We're here to save this young idjit from his own folly," says Bill. "You come up here because a woman wants to marry you. Jack comes up here to decorate a oak limb with his own carcass because one wouldn't marry him."

"Some men never knows their luck," says old Joshua enviously. "Now me, I yearns to return to Chawed Ear which I've been away from for a month. But whilst that old mudhen of a Miss Stark is there I haunts the wilderness if it takes the rest of my life."

"Well, be at ease, Josh," says Bill. "Miss Stark ain't there no more. She pulled out for Arizona three weeks ago."

"Halleloojah!" says Joshua, throwing away his club. "Now I can return and take my place among men—Hold on!" says he, reching for his club again, "likely they'll be gittin' some other old harridan to take her place. That new-fangled schoolhouse they got at Chawed Ear is a curse and a blight. We'll never be shet of husband-huntin' 'rithmetic shooters. I better stay up here after all."

"Don't worry," says Bill. "I seen a pitcher of the gal that's comin' from the East to take Miss Stark's place and I can assure you that a gal as young and purty as her wouldn't never try to slap her brand on no old buzzard like you."

"Young and purty?" I ast with sudden interest.

"As a racin' filly!" he declared. "First time I ever knowed a school-mar'm could be less'n forty and 'have a face that didn't look like the beginnin's of a long drouth. She's due into Chawed Ear on the evenin' stage, and the whole town turns out to welcome her. The mayor aims to make a speech if he's sober enough, and they've got a band to play."

"Damn foolishness!" snorted Joshua. "I don't take no stock in eddication."

"I dunno," says I. That was before I got educated. "They's times when I wisht I could read and write. We ain't never had no school on Bear Creek."

"What would you read outside of the labels onto whiskey bottles?" snorted old Joshua.

"Funny how a purty face changes a man's viewp'int," remarked Bill. "I remember onst Miss Stark ast you how you folks up on Bear Creek would like for her to come up there and teach yore chillern, and you taken one look at her face and told her it was agen the principles of Bear Creek to have their peaceful innercence invaded by the corruptin' influences of education. You said the folks was all banded together to resist sech corruption to the last drop of blood."

"It's my duty to Bear Creek to pervide culture for the risin' generation," says I, ignoring them slanderous remarks. "I feels the urge for knowledge a-heavin' and a-surgin' in my boozum. We're goin' to have a school on Bear Creek, by golly, if I have to lick every old mossback in the Humbolts. I'll build a cabin for the schoolhouse myself."

"Where'll you git a teacher?" ast Joshua. "Chawed Ear ain't goin' to let you have their'n."

"Chawed Ear is, too," I says. "If they won't give her up peaceful I resorts to force. Bear Creek is goin' to have culture if I have to wade fetlock deep in gore to pervide it. Le's go! I'm r'arin to open the ball for arts and letters. Air you-all with me?"

"No!" says Jack, plenty emphatic.

"What we goin' to do with him?" demands Glanton.

"Aw," I said, "we'll tie him up some place along the road and pick him up as we come back."

"All right," says Bill, ignorin' Jack's impassioned protests. "I jest as soon. My nerves is frayed ridin' herd on this young idjit and I needs a little excitement to quiet'em. You can always be counted on for *that*. Anyway, I'd like to see that there school-marm gal myself. How about you, Joshua?"

"Yo're both crazy," growls Joshua. "But I've lived on nuts and jackrabbits till I ain't shore of my own sanity. Anyways, I know the only way to disagree with Elkins is to kill him, and I got strong doubts of bein' able to do that. Lead on! I'll do anything within reason to help keep eddication out of Chawed Ear. T'ain't only my personal feelin's regardin' school-teachers. It's the principle of the thing."

"Git yore clothes and le's hustle then," I says.

"This painter hide is all I got," says he.

"You cain't go down into the settlements in that rig," I says.

"I can and will," says he. "I look as civilized as you do, with yore clothes all tore in rags account of old Brigamer. I got a hoss clost by. I'll git him if old Brigamer ain't already."

So Joshua went to git his hoss and me and Bill toted Jack down the slope to where our hosses was. His conversation was plentiful and heated, but we ignored it, and was jest tyin' him onto his hoss when Joshua arov with his critter. Then the trouble started. Cap'n Kidd evidently thought Joshua was some kind of a varmint because every time Joshua come nigh him he taken in after him and run him up a tree. And every time Joshua tried to come down, Cap'n Kidd busted loose from me and run him back up agen.

I didn't git no help from Bill. All he done was laugh like a spotted hyener till Cap'n Kidd got irritated at them guffaws and kicked him in the belly and knocked him clean through a clump of spruces. Time I got ontangled he looked about as disreputable as what I did because most of his clothes was tore off of him. We couldn't find his hat, neither, so I tore up what was left of my shirt and he tied the pieces around his head, like a Apache. Exceptin' Jack, we was sure a wild-lookin' bunch.

But I was disgusted thinking about how much time we was wasting whilst all the time Bear Creek was wallerin' in ignorance, so the next time Cap'n Kidd went for Joshua I took and busted him betwixt the ears with my sixshooter and that had some effect onto him.

So we sot out, with Jack tied onto his hoss and cussin' somethin' terrible, and Joshua on a ga'nt old nag he rode bareback with a hackamore. I had Bill to ride betwixt him and me so's to keep that painter hide as far away from Cap'n Kidd as possible, but every time the wind shifted and blowed the smell to him, Cap'n Kidd reched over and taken a bite at Joshua, and sometimes he bit Bill's hoss by accident, and sometimes he bit Bill, and the langwidge Bill directed at that pore animal was shocking to hear.

We was aimin' for the trail that runs down from Bear Creek into the Chawed Ear road, and we hit it a mile west of Bowie Knife Pass. We left Jack tied to a nice shady oak tree in the pass and told him we'd be back for him in a few hours, but some folks is never satisfied. 'Stead of bein' grateful for all the trouble we'd went to for him, he acted right nasty and called us some names I wouldn't of endured if he'd been in his right mind.

But we tied his hoss to the same tree and hustled down the trail and presently come out onto the War Paint-Chawed Ear Road, some miles west of Chawed Ear. And there we sighted our first human—a feller onto a pinto mare and when he seen us he give a shriek and took out down the road toward Chawed Ear like the devil had him by the britches.

"Le's ast him if the teacher's got there yet," I suggested, so we taken out after him, yellin' for him to wait a minute. But he jest spurred his hoss that much harder and before we'd gone any piece, Joshua's fool hoss jostled agen Cap'n Kidd, which smelt that painter skin and got the bit betwixt his teeth and run Joshua and his hoss three miles through the bresh before I could stop him.

Bill follered us, and of course, time we got back to the road, the feller on the pinto was out of sight.

So we headed for Chawed Ear but everybody that lived along the road had run into their cabins and bolted the doors, and they shot at us through the winders as we rode by. Bill said irritably, after having his off-ear nicked by a buffalo rifle, he says, "Dern it, they must know we aim to steal their schoolteacher."

"Aw, they couldn't know that," I says. "I bet they is a war on betwixt Chawed Ear and War Paint."

"Well, what they shootin' at *me* for, then?" demanded Joshua.

"How could they recognize you in that rig?" I ast. "What's that?"

Ahead of us, away down the road, we seen a cloud of dust, and here come a gang of men on hosses, waving guns and yelling.

"Well, whatever the reason is," says Bill, "we better not stop to find out! Them gents is out for blood, and," says he as the bullets begun to knock up the dust around us, "I jedge it's *our* blood!"

"Pull into the bresh," says I. "I goes to Chawed Ear in spite of hell, high water and all the gunmen they can raise."

So we taken to the bresh, and they lit in after us, about forty or fifty of 'em, but we dodged and circled and taken short cuts old Joshua knowed about, and when we emerged into the town of Chawed Ear, our pursewers warn't nowheres in sight. All the doors was closed and the shutters up on the cabins and saloons and stores and everything. It was pecooliar.

As we rode into the clearing somebody let bam at us with a shotgun from the nearest cabin, and the load combed Joshua's whiskers. This made me mad, so I rode at the cabin and pulled my foot out'n the stirrup and kicked the door in, and whilst I was doin' this, the feller inside hollered and jumped out the winder, and Bill grabbed him by the neck. It was Esau Barlow, one of Chawed Ear's confirmed citizens.

"What the hell's the matter with you buzzards?" roared Bill.

"Is that you, Glanton?" gasped Esau, blinking his eyes.

"A-course it's me!" roared Bill. "Do I look like a Injun?"

"Yes—*ow!* I mean, I didn't know you in that there turban," says Esau. "Am I dreamin' or is that Josh Braxton and Breck Elkins?"

"Shore it's us, snorted Joshua. "Who you think?"

"Well," says Esau, rubbing his neck and looking sidewise at Joshua's painter skin. "I didn't know!"

"Where is everybody?" Joshua demanded.

"Well," says Esau, "a little while ago Dick Lynch rode into town with his hoss all of a lather and swore he'd jest outrun the wildest war-party that ever come down from the hills!

"'Boys,' says Dick, 'they ain't neither Injuns nor white men! They're wild men, that's what! One of 'em's big as a grizzly b'ar, with no shirt on, and he's ridin' a hoss bigger'n a bull moose! One of the others is as ragged and ugly as him, but not so big, and wearin' a Apache head-dress. T'other'n's got nothin' on but a painter's hide and a club and his hair and whiskers falls to his shoulders. When they seen me,' says Dick, 'they sot up awful yells and come for me like a gang of man-eatin' cannibals. I fogged it for town,' says Dick, 'warnin' everybody along the road to fort theirselves in their cabins.'

"Well," says Esau, "when he says that, sech men as was left in town got their hosses and guns and they taken out up the road to meet the war-party before it got into town."

"Well, of all the fools!" I says. "Say, where's the new teacher?"

"The stage ain't arriv yet," says he. "The mayor and the band rode out to meet it at the Yaller Creek crossin' and escort her into town with fullest honors. They'd left before Dick brung news of the war-party."

"Come on!" I says to my warriors. "We likewise meets that stage!"

So we fogged it on through the town and down the road, and purty soon we heard music blaring ahead of us, and men yipping and shooting off their pistols like they does when they're celebrating, so we jedged they'd met the stage and was escorting it in.

"What you goin' to do now?" ast Bill, and about that time a noise bust out behind us and we looked back and seen that gang of Chawed Ear maneyacks which had been chasing us dusting down the road after us, waving their Winchesters. I knowed they warn't no use to try to explain to them that we warn't no war-party of cannibals. They'd salivate us before we could git clost enough to make 'em hear what we was saying. So I yelled: "Come on. If they git her into town they'll fort theirselves agen us. We takes her now! Foller me!"

So we swept down the road and around the bend and there was the stagecoach coming up the road with the mayor riding alongside with his hat in his hand and a whiskey bottle sticking out of each saddlebag and his hip pocket. He was orating at the top of his voice to make hisself heard above the racket the band was making. They was blowing horns and banging drums and twanging on Jews harps, and the hosses was skittish and shying and jumping. But we heard the mayor say, "—And so we welcomes you, Miss Devon, to our peaceful little community where life runs smooth and tranquil and men's souls is overflowin' with milk and honey—" And jest then we stormed around the bend and come tearing down on 'em with the mob right behind us yelling and cussing and shooting free and fervent.

The next minute they was the damndest mixup you ever seen, what with the hosses bucking their riders off, and the men yelling and cussing, and the hosses hitched to the stage running away and knocking the mayor off'n his hoss. We hit 'em like a cyclone and they shot at us and hit us over the head with their music corns, and right in the middle of the fray the mob behind us rounded the bend and piled up amongst us before they could check their hosses, and everybody was so confused they started fighting everybody else. Nobody knowed what it was all about but me and my warriors. But Chawed Ear's motto is: "When in doubt, shoot!"

So they laid into us and into each other free and hearty. And we was far from idle. Old Joshua was laying out his feller-townsmen right and left with his ellum club, saving Chawed Ear from education in spite of itself, and Glanton was beating the band over their heads with his sixshooter, and I was trompling folks in my rush for the stage.

The fool hosses had whirled around and started in the general direction of the Atlantic ocean, and the driver and the shotgun guard couldn't stop 'em. But Cap'n Kidd overtook it in maybe a dozen strides and I left the saddle in a flying leap and landed on it. The guard tried to shoot me with his shotgun so I throwed it into a alder clump and he didn't let go of it quick enough so he went along with it.

I then grabbed the ribbons out of the driver's hands and swung them fool hosses around on their hind laigs, and the stage kind of revolved on one wheel for a dizzy instant, and then settled down again and we headed back up the road licketysplit and in a instant was right amongst the fracas that was going on around Bill and Joshua.

About that time I noticed that the driver was trying to stab me with a butcher knife so I kind of tossed him off the stage and there ain't no sense in him going around threatening to have me arrested account of him landing headfirst in the bass horn so it taken seven men to pull him out. He ought to watch where he falls when he gits throwed off of a stage going at a high run.

I also feels that the mayor is prone to carry petty grudges or

he wouldn't be so bitter about me accidentally running over him
with all four wheels. And it ain't my fault he was stepped on by
Cap'n Kidd, neither. Cap'n Kidd was jest follerin' the stage because he knowed I was on it. And it naturally irritates him to
stumble over somebody and that's why he chawed the mayor's
ear.

As for them other fellers which happened to git knocked down
and run over by the stage, I didn't have nothin' personal agen 'em.
I was jest rescuing Joshua and Bill which was outnumbered about
twenty to one. I was doing them Chawed Ear idjits a favor, if they
only knowed it, because in about another minute Bill would of
started using the front ends of his sixshooters instead of the butts
and the fight would of turnt into a massacre. Bill has got a awful
temper.

Him and Joshua had did the enemy considerable damage but
the battle was going agen 'em when I arriv on the field of carnage.
As the stage crashed through the mob I reched down and got Joshua
by the neck and pulled him out from under about fifteen men
which was beating him to death with their gun butts and pulling
out his whiskers by the handfulls and I slung him up on top of
the other luggage. About that time we was rushing past the dogpile
which Bill was the center of and I reched down and snared him
as we went by, but three of the men which had holt of him wouldn't
let go, so I hauled all four of 'em up onto the stage. I then handled
the team with one hand and used the other'n to pull them idjits
loose from Bill like pulling ticks off'n a cow's hide, and then
throwed 'em at the mob which was chasing us.

Men and hosses piled up in a stack on the road which was
further messed up by Cap'n Kidd plowing through it as he come
busting along after the stage, and by the time we sighted Chawed
Ear agen, our enemies was far behind us, though still rambunctious.

We tore through Chawed Ear in a fog of dust and the women
and chillern which had ventured out of their shacks squalled, and
run back agen, though they warn't in no danger. But Chawed Ear
folks is pecooliar that way.

When we was out of sight of Chawed Ear I give the lines to
Bill and swung down on the side of the stage and stuck my head
in. They was one of the purtiest gals I ever seen in there, all
huddled up in a corner and looking so pale and scairt I was afraid
she was going to faint, which I'd heard Eastern gals has a habit
of doing.

"Oh, spare me!" she begged. "Please don't scalp me!"

"Be at ease, Miss Devon," I reassured her. "I ain't no Injun, nor no wild man neither. Neither is my friends here. We wouldn't none of us hurt a flea. We're that refined and soft-hearted you wouldn't believe it—" At that instant a wheel hit a stump and the stage jumped into the air and I bit my tongue and roared in some irritation, "Bill, you condemned son of a striped polecat, stop this stage before I comes up there and breaks yore cussed neck!"

"Try, you beef-headed lummox," he invites, but he pulled up the hosses and I taken off my hat and opened the door. Bill and Joshua clumb down and peered over my shoulder. Miss Devon looked tolerable sick. Maybe it was something she et.

"Miss Devon," I says, "I begs yore pardon for this here informal welcome. But you sees before you a man whose heart bleeds for the benighted state of his native community. I'm Breckinridge Elkins, of Bear Creek, where hearts is pure and motives is lofty, but culture is weak.

"You sees before you," says I, growing more enthusiastic about education the longer I looked at them big brown eyes of her'n. "A man which has growed up in ignorance. I cain't neither read nor write. Joshua here, in the painter skin, he cain't neither, and neither can Bill."

"That's a lie," says Bill. "I can read and—*oomp!*" I'd kind of stuck my elbow in his stummick. I didn't want him to spile the effeck of my speech. Miss Devon was gitting some of her color back.

"Miss Devon," I says, "will you please ma'm come up to Bear Creek and be our schoolteacher?"

"Why," says she bewilderedly, "I came West expecting to teach at Chawed Ear, but I haven't signed any contract, and—"

"How much was them snake-hunters goin' to pay you?" I ast.

"Ninety dollars a month," says she.

"We pays you a hundred," I says. "Board and lodgin' free."

"Hell's fire," says Bill. "They never was that much hard cash money on Bear Creek."

"We all donates coon hides and corn licker," I snapped. "I sells the stuff in War Paint and hands the dough to Miss Devon. Will you keep yore snout out of my business?"

"But what will the people of Chawed Ear say?" she wonders.

"Nothin'," I said heartily. "I'll tend to *them!*"

"It seems so strange and irregular," says she weakly. "I don't know."

"Then it's all settled!" I says. "Great! Le's go!"

"Where?" she gasped, grabbing holt of the stage as I clumb onto the seat.

"Bear Creek!" I says. "Varmints and hoss-thieves, hunt the bresh! Culture is on her way to Bear Creek!" And we went fogging it down the road as fast as the hosses could hump it. Onst I looked back at Miss Devon and seen her getting pale agen, so I yelled above the clatter of the wheels, "Don't be scairt, Miss Devon! Ain't nothin' goin' to hurt you. B. Elkins is on the job to perteck you, and I aim to be at yore side from now on!"

At this she said something I didn't understand. In fack, it sounded like a low moan. And then I heard Joshua say to Bill, hollerin' to make hisself heard, "Eddication my eye! the big chump's lookin' for a wife, that's what! Ten to one she gives him the mitten!"

"I takes that," bawled Bill, and I bellered, "Shet up that noise! Quit discussin' my private business so dern public! I—what's that?"

It sounded like firecrackers popping down the road where we come from. Bill yelled, "It's them Chawed Ear maneyacks! They're still on our trail, and they're gainin' on us!"

Cussing heartily, I poured leather into them fool hosses, and jest then we hit the mouth of the Bear Creek trail and I swung into it. They'd never been a wheel on that trail before, and the going was tolerable rough. It was all Bill and Joshua could do to keep from gitting throwed off, and they was seldom more'n one wheel on the ground at a time. Naturally the mob gained on us and when we roared up into Bowie Knife Pass they warn't more'n a quarter mile behind us, whooping bodacious.

I pulled up the hosses beside the tree where Jack Sprague was still tied up to. He gawped at Miss Devon and gawped back at him.

"Listen," I says, "here's a lady in distress which we're rescuin' from teachin' schol in Chawed Ear. A mob's right behind us. This ain't no time to think about yoreself. Will you postpone yore sooicide if I turns you loose, and git onto this stage and take the young lady up the trail whilst the rest of us turns back the mob?"

"I will!" says he with more enthusiasm than he'd showed since we stopped him from hanging hisself. So I cut him loose and he clumb onto the stage.

"Drive on to Kiowa Canyon," I told him as he picked up the lines. "Wait for us there. Don't be scairt, Miss Devon!" I'll soon be with you! B. Elkins never fails a lady fair!"

"Gup!" says Jack, and the stage went clattering and banging up the trail and me and Joshua and Bill taken cover amongst the big rocks that was on each side of the trail. The pass was jest a narrer gorge, and a lovely place for a ambush as I remarked.

Well, here they come howling up the steep slope yelling and spurring and shooting wild, and me and Bill give 'em a salute with our pistols. The charge halted plumb sudden. They knowed they was licked. They couldn't git at us because they couldn't climb the cliffs. So after firing a volley which damaged nothing but the atmosphere, they turnt around and high-tailed it back towards Chawed Ear.

"I hope that's a lesson to 'em," says I as I riz. "Come! I cain't wait to git culture started on Bear Creek!"

"You cain't wait to git to sparkin' that gal," snorted Joshua. But I ignored him and forked Cap'n Kidd and headed up the trail, and him and Bill follered, riding double on Jack Sprague's hoss.

"Why should I deny my honorable intentions?" I says presently. "Anybody can see Miss Devon is already learnin' to love me! If Jack had my attraction for the fair sex, he wouldn't be luggin' around a ruint life. Hey, where's the stage?" Because we'd reched Kiowa Canyon and they warn't no stage.

"Here's a note stuck on a tree," says Bill. "I'll read it—well, for Lord's sake!" he yelped, "Lissen to this:

Dere boys:

I've desided I ain't going to hang myself, and Miss Devon has desided she don't want to teach school at Bear Creek. Breck gives her the willies. She ain't altogether shore he's human. With me it's love at first site and she's scairt if she don't marry somebody Breck will marry her, and she says I'm the best looking prospeck she's saw so far. So we're heading for War Paint to git married.

                              Yores trooly, Jack Sprague.

"Aw, don't take it like that," says Bill as I give a maddened howl and impulsively commenced to rip up all the saplings in rech. "You saved his life and brung him happiness!"

"And what have I brung me?" I yelled, tearing the limbs off a oak in a effort to relieve my feelings. "Culture on Bear Creek is shot to hell and my honest love has been betrayed! Bill Glanton, the next ranny you chase up into the Humbolts to commit sooicide he don't have to worry about gittin' bumped off—I attends to it myself, personal!"

The Peaceful Pilgrim

Gettin shot at by strangers and relatives is too plumb common to
bother about, and I don't generally pay no attention to it. But it's
kind of irritating to git shot at by yore best friend, even when yo're
as mild and gentle-natured as what I am. But I reckon I better
explain. I'd been way up nigh the Oregon line, and was headin'
home when I happened to pass through the mining camp of Moose
Jaw, which was sot right in the middle of a passle of mountains
nigh as wild and big as the Humbolts. I was takin' me a drink at
the bar of the Lazy Elk Saloon and Hotel, when the bar-keep says,
after studying me a spell, he says: "You must be Breckinridge
Elkins, of Bear Creek."

I give the matter due consideration, and 'lowed as how I was.

"How come you knowed me?" I inquired suspiciously, because
I hadn't never been in Moose Jaw before, and he says: "Well, I've
often heard tell of Breckinridge Elkins, and when I seen you, I
figgered you must be him, because I don't see how they can be
two men in the world that big. By the way, they's a friend of
yore'n upstairs—Blaze Carson. He come up here from the southern
part of the state, and I've often heered him brag about knowin'
you personal. He's upstairs now, fourth door from the stair-head,
on the right."

Well, I remembered Blaze. He warn't a Bear Creek man; he
was from War Paint, but I didn't hold that agen him. He was kind
of addle-headed, but I don't expeck everybody to be smart like
me.

So I went upstairs and knocked on the door, and *bam!* went a

gun inside and a .45 slug ripped through the door and taken a nick
out of my ear. As I remarked before, it irritates me to be shot at
by a man which has no reason to shoot at me, and my patience
is quickly exhausted. So, without waiting for any more exhibitions
of hospitality, I give a exasperated beller and knocked the door
off its hinges and busted into the room over its rooins.

For a second I didn't see nobody, but then I heard a kind of
gurgle going on, and happened to remember that the door seemed
kind of squshy when I tromped over it, so I knowed that whichever
was in the room had got pinned under the door when I knocked
it down.

So I reched under it with one hand and got him by the collar
and hauled him out, and shore enough it was Blaze Carson. He
was limp as a rag and glassy-eyed, and pale, and wild-looking,
and was still vaguely trying to shoot me with his sixshooter when
I taken it away from him.

"What the hell is the matter with you?" I demanded sternly,
dangling him by the collar with one hand, whilst shaking him till
his teeth rattled. "Air you got deliritus trimmin's, or what, shootin'
at yore friends through the door?"

"Lemme down, Breck," he gasped. "I didn't know it was you.
I thought it was Lobo Ferguson comin' after my gold."

So I sot him down and he grabbed a jug of licker and poured
hisself a dram and his hand shaken so he spilled half of it down
his neck when he tried to drink.

"Well?" I demanded. "Ain't you goin' to offer me a snort, dern
it?"

"Excuse me, Breckinridge," he apologized. "I'm so dern jumpy
I dunno what I'm doin'. I been livin' in this here room for a week,
too scairt to stick my head out. You see them buckskin pokes?"
says he, p'inting at some bags on the bed. "Them is bustin' full
of nuggets. I been minin' up the Gulch for over a year now, and
I got myself a neat fortune in them bags. But it ain't doin' me no
good."

"What you mean?" I demanded.

"These mountains is full of outlaws," says he. "They robs and
murders every man which tries to take his gold out. The stagecoach
has been stuck up so often nobody sends their dust out onto it no
more. When a man makes his pile, he watches his chance and
sneaks out through the mountains at night, with his gold on pack-
mules. Sometimes he makes it and sometimes he don't. That's
what I aimed to do. But them outlaws has got spies all over the

camp. I know they got me spotted. I been afeared to make my break, and afeared if I didn't, they'd git impatient and come right into camp and cut my throat. That's what I thought when I heard you knock. Lobo Ferguson's the big chief of 'em. I been squattin' over this here gold with my pistol night and day, makin' the bar-keep bring my licker and grub up to me. I'm dern near loco!"

And he shaken like he had the aggers, and shivered and cussed kind of whimpery, and taken another dram, and cocked his pistol and sot there shakin' like he'd saw a ghost or two.

"How'd you go if you snuck out?" I demanded.

"Up the ravine south of the camp and hit the old Injun path that winds up through Scalp-lock Pass," says he. "Then I'd circle wide down to Wahpeton and grab the stagecoach there. I'm safe, onst I git to Wahpeton."

"I'll take yore gold out for you," I says.

"But them outlaws'll kill you!" says he.

"Naw, they won't," I says. "First place, they won't know I got the gold. Second place, I'll bust their heads if they start any-thing with me in the first place. Is this all the gold they is?" I ast.

"Ain't it enough?" says he. "My hoss and pack-mule is in the stables behind the saloon—"

"I don't need no pack-mule," I says. "Cap'n Kidd can pack that easy."

"And you, too?" he ast.

"You ought to know Cap'n Kidd well enough not to have to ast no sech dern fool question as that there," I said irritably. "Wait till I git my saddle-bags."

Cap'n Kidd was getting fed out in the corral next to the hotel. I went out there and got my saddle-bags, which is a lot bigger'n most, because my plunder has to be made to fit my size. They're made outa three-ply elkskin, stitched with rawhide thongs, and a wildcat couldn't claw his way out of 'em.

Well, I noticed quite a bunch of men standing around the corral looking at Cap'n Kidd, but thought nothing of it, because he is a hoss which naturally attracts attention.

But whilst I was getting my saddle-bags, a long lanky cuss with long yaller whiskers come up and said: "Is that yore hoss in the corral?"

"If he ain't he ain't nobody's," I said.

"Well, he looks a lot like a hoss that was stole off my ranch six months ago," he said, and I seen ten or fifteen hardlooking hombres gatherin' around us. I laid down my saddle-bags suddenlike and started to pull my guns, when it occurred to me that if I had a fight there, I might git arrested and it would interfere with me taking out Blaze's gold.

"If that there is yore hoss," I said, "you ought to be able to lead him out of that there corral."

"Shore I can," he says with a oath. "And what's more, I aim to."

"That's the stuff, Bill," somebody says. "Don't let the big hill-billy tromple on yore rights!"

But I noticed some men in the crowd looked like they didn't like it, but was scairt to say anything.

"All right," I says to Bill, "here's a lariat. Climb over that fence and go and put it on that hoss, and he's yore'n."

He looked at me suspiciously, but he taken the rope and clumb the fence and started towards Cap'n Kidd which was chawing on a block of hay in the middle of the corral, and Cap'n Kidd throwed up his head and laid back his ears and showed his teeth. Bill stopped sudden and turned pale, and said: "I—I don't believe that there *is* my hoss, after all!"

"Put that lariat on him!" I roared, pulling my right-hand gun. "You say he's yore'n; I say he's mine. One of us is a liar and a hoss-thief, and I aim to prove which'n it is! Gwan, before I venti-lates yore yaller system with hot lead!"

He looked at me and he looked at Cap'n Kidd, and he turned bright green all over. He looked agen at my .45 which I now had cocked and p'inted at his long neck, which his Adam's apple was going up and down like a monkey on a pole, and he begun to aidge towards Cap'n Kidd again, holding the rope behind him and sticking out one hand.

"Whoa, boy," he says kind of shudderingly. "Whoa—good old feller—whoa, boy—*ow!*"

He let out a awful howl as Cap'n Kidd made a snap and bit a chunk out of his hide. He turned to run but Cap'n Kidd wheeled and let fly both heels which caught Bill in the seat of the britches, and his shriek of despair was horrible to hear as he went head-first through the corral fence into a hoss-trough on the other side. From this he ariz dripping water, blood and profanity. He shook a quivering fist at me and croaked: "You derned murderer! I'll have yore life for this!"

"I don't hold no conversation with hoss-thieves," I snorted, and picked up my saddle bags and stalked through the crowd which give back in a hurry on each side to let me through. And I noticed when I tromped on some fellers' toes, they done their cussing under their breath, and pertended to be choking on their terbaccer when I glared back at 'em. Folks oughta keep their derned hoofs out of the way if they don't want to be stepped on.

I taken the saddle-bags up to Blaze's room, and told him about Bill, thinking he'd be amoosed, but he got a case of aggers agen, and said: "That was one of Ferguson's men! He meant to take yore hoss. It's a old trick, and honest folks don't dare interfere. Now they got you spotted! You better wait till night, at least."

"Time, tide and a Elkins waits for no man!" I snorted, dumping the gold into the saddle-bags. "If that yaller-whiskered coyote wants any trouble, he can git a bellyfull. Tomorrer you git on the stagecoach and hit for Wahpeton. If I ain't there, wait for me. I ought to pull in a day or so after you git there, anyway. And don't worry about yore gold. It'll be plumb safe in my saddle-bags."

"Don't yell so loud," begged Blaze. "The derned camp's full of spies, and some of 'em may be downstairs."

"I warn't speakin' above a whisper," I said indignantly.

"That bull's beller may pass for a whisper on Bear Creek," says he, wiping off the perspiration, "but I bet they can hear it from one end of the Gulch to the other, at least."

It's a pitable sight to see a man with a case of the scairts; I shaken hands with him and left him pouring red licker down his gullet like so much water, and I swung the saddle-bags over my shoulder and went downstairs, and the bar-keep leaned over the bar and whispered to me: "Look out for Bill Price! He was in here a minute ago, lookin' for trouble. He pulled out just before you come down, but he won't be forgettin' what yore hoss done to him!"

"Not when he tries to sit down, he won't!" I agreed, and went on out to the corral, and they was a crowd of men watching Cap'n Kidd eat his hay, and one of 'em seen me and hollered: "Hey, boys, here comes the giant! He's goin' to saddle that man-eatin' monster! Hey, Tom! Tell the boys at the bar!"

And here come a whole passle of fellers running out of all the saloons, and they lined the corral fence solid, and started laying bets whether I'd git the saddle on Cap'n Kidd, or git my brains kicked out. I thought miners must all be crazy; they ought to knowed I rode into camp on him and was able to saddle my own hoss.

Well, I saddled him, and throwed on the saddle-bags, and clumb aboard, and he pitched about ten jumps like he always does when I first fork him—t'wan't nothing, but them miners hollered like wild Injuns. And when he accidentally bucked hisself and me through the fence and knocked down a section of it along with about fifteen men which was setting on the top-rail, the way they howled you'd of thought something terrible had happened. Me and Cap'n Kidd don't generally bother about gates. We usually makes our own through whatever happens to be in front of us. But them miners is a weakly breed, because as I rode out of the town I seen the crowd dipping four or five of 'em into a hoss-trough to bring 'em to, on account of Cap'n Kidd having accidentally stepped on 'em.

This trivial occurrence seemed to excite everybody so much nobody noticed me as I rode off, which suited me fine, because I am a modest man, shy and retiring by nature, which don't crave no publicity. I didn't see no sign of the feller they called Bill Price.

Well, I rode out of the Gulch and up the ravine to the south, and come out into the high-timbered country, and was casting around for the old Injun trail Blaze had told me about, when somebody said: "Hey!" I wheeled with both guns in my hands, and a long, lean, black-whiskered old cuss rode out of the bresh towards me.

"Who are you and what the hell you mean by hollerin' 'Hey!' at me?" I demanded. A Elkins is always perlite.

"Air you the man with the man-eatin' stallion?" he ast, and I says: "I dunno what yo're talkin' about. This here hoss is Cap'n Kidd, which I catched down in the Humbolt country, and a milder-mannered critter never kicked the brains out of a mountain lion."

"He's the biggest hoss I ever see," he said. "Looks fast, though."

"Fast?" says I, with the pride a Elkins always takes in his hoss-flesh. "Cap'n Kidd can outrun anything in this State, and carry me, and you, and all this here gold in these saddle-bags whilst doing it." Then I shaken my head in disgust, because I hadn't meant to mention the gold, but I couldn't see what harm it would do.

"Well," he said, "you've made a enemy of Bill Price, one of Lobo Ferguson's gunmen, and as pizenous a critter as ever wore boot-leather. He come by here a few minutes ago, frothin' at the mouth, and swearin' to have yore heart's blood. He's headin' up into the mountains to round up forty or fifty of his gang and take yore sculp."

"Well, what about it?" I inquired, not impressed. Somebody is always wanting my life, and forty or fifty outlaws ain't no odds to a Elkin.

"They'll waylay you," he predicted. "Yo're a fine, upstandin' young man, which deserves a better fate'n to git dry-gulched by a passle of low-down bandit varmints. I'm jest headin' for my cabin up in the hills. It's a right smart piece off the trail. Whyn't you come along with me and lay low till they've give up the search? They won't find you there."

"I ain't in the habit of hidin' from my enemies," I begun, when suddenly I remembered that there gold in my saddle-bags. It was my duty to git it to Wahpeton. If I was to tangle with Ferguson's gang, they was just a slim chance that they might down me, shooting from the bresh, and run off with pore Blaze's hard-earned dough. It was hard to do, but I decided I'd avoid a battle till after I'd give Blaze his gold safe and sound. Then, I was determined, I'd come back and frail the daylights outa Lobo Ferguson for forcing me into this here humiliating position.

"Lead on!" I says. "Lead me to yore hermitage in the wildwood, out of the reach of the maddenin' crowd and Lobo Ferguson's bullets. But I imposes a sacred trust of secrecy onto you. Let the world never know that Breckinridge Elkins, the pride of Bear Creek, took to kiver to dodge a mangy passle of minin' country road-agents."

"My lips is sealed," says he. "Yore fatal secret is safe with Polecat Rixby. Foller me."

He led me through the bresh till we hit the old Injun trail, which warn't more'n a trace through the hills, and we pushed hard all the rest of the day, not seeing anybody coming or going.

"They'll be lookin' for you in Moose Jaw," said the Polecat. "When they don't find you, they'll comb the hills. But they'll never find my cabin, even if they knowed you was hidin' there, which they don't."

Close to sun-down we turned off the trail onto a still dimmer trace that led east, and wound amongst crags and boulders till a snake would of broke his back tryin' to foller it, and just before it got good and dark we come to a log-bridge acrost a deep, narrer canyon. They was a river at the bottom of that there canyon, which was awful swift, and went roaring and foaming along betwixt rock walls and hundred feet high. But at one place the canyon wasn't only about seventy foot wide, and they'd felled a whopping big pine tree on one side so it fell acrost and made a bridge, and the top side was trimmed down flat so a hoss could walk acrost, though the average hoss wouldn't like it very much. Polecat's hoss was used to it, but he was scairt jest the same. But they ain't nothin' between Kingdom Come and Powder River that Cap'n Kidd's scairt of, except maybe me, and he walzed acrost that there tree like he was on a quartertrack.

The path wound through a lot of bresh on the other side, and so did we, and after awhile we come to a cabin built nigh the foot of a big cliff. It was on a kind of thick-timbered shelf, and the land fell away in a gradual slope to a breshy run, and they was a clear spring nigh the aidge of the bresh. It was a good place for a cabin.

They was a stone corral built up agen the foot of the cliff, and it looked to be a dern sight bigger'n Polecat oughta need for his one saddle hoss and the three pack hosses which was in there, but I have done learnt that there ain't no accounting for the way folks builds things. Polecat told me to turn Cap'n Kidd loose in the corral, but I knowed if I done that they would be one dead saddle hoss and three dead pack hosses in there before midnight, so I turned him loose to graze, knowing he wouldn't go far. Cap'n Kidd likes me too much to run off and leave me, regardless of the fact that he frequently tries to kill me.

By this time it was night, and Polecat said come in and he'd fix up a snack of supper. So we went in and he lit a candle and made coffee and fried bacon and sot out some beans and corn pone, and he taken a good look at me settin' there at the table all ready to fall to, and he fried up a lot more bacon and sot out more beans. He hadn't talked much all day, and now he was about as talkative as a clam with the lockjaw. He was jumpy, too, and nervous, and I decided he was scairt Lobo Ferguson might find him after all, and do vi'lence to him for hiding me. It's a dreary sight to see a grown man scairt of something. Being scairt must be some kind of disease; I cain't figger it out no other way.

I was watching Polecat, even if I didn't seem to, because that's a habit us Bear Creek folks gits into; if we didn't watch each other awful close, we'd never live to git grown. So when he poured a lot of white-looking powder into my coffee out of a box on the shelf, he didn't think I seen him, but I did, and I noticed he didn't put none in his'n. But I didn't say nothing, because it ain't perlite to criticize a man's cooking when yo're his guest; if Polecat had some new-fangled way of making coffee t'warn't for me to object.

He sot the grub on the table and sot down opposite me, with his head down, and looking at me kinda furtive-like from under his brows, and I laid into the grub and et hearty.

"Yore coffee'll git cold," he said presently, and I remembered it, and emptied the cup at one gulp, and it was the best coffee I ever drunk.

"Ha!" says I, smacking my lips. "You ain't much shakes of a man to look at, Polecat, but you shore can b'ile coffee! Gimme another cup! What's the matter; you ain't eatin' hardly anything?"

"I ain't a very hearty eater," he mumbled. "You—you want some more coffee?"

So I drunk six more cups, but they didn't taste near as good as the first, and I knowed it was because he didn't put none of that white stuff in 'em, but I didn't say nothing because it wouldn't have been perlite.

After I'd cleaned up everything in sight. I said I'd help him wash the pans and things, but he said, kind of funny-like: "Let 'em go. I—we can do that—tomorrer. How—how do you feel?"

"I feel fine," I said. "You can make coffee nigh as good as I can. Le's sit down out on the stoop. I hate to be inside walls any more'n I have to."

He follered me out and we sot down and I got to telling him about the Bear Creek country, because I was kind of homesick; but he didn't talk at all, just sot there staring at me in a most pecooliar manner. Finally I got sleep and said I believed I'd go to bed, so he got a candle and showed me where I was to sleep. The cabin had two rooms, and my bunk was in the back room. They wasn't any outside door to that room, just the door in the partition, but they was a winder in the back wall.

I throwed my saddle-bags under the bunk, and leaned my Winchester agen the wall, and sot down on the bunk and started pulling off my boots, and Polecat stood in the door looking at me, with the candle in his hand, and a very strange expression on his face.

"You feel good?" he says. "You—you ain't got no belly-ache nor nothin'?"

"Hell, no!" I says heartily. "What I want to have a belly-ache for? I never had one of them things in my life, only onst when my brother Buckner shot me in the belly with a buffalo gun. Us Elkinses is healthy."

He shaken his head and muttered something in his beard, and backed out of the room, closing the door behind him. But the light didn't go out in the next room. I could see it shining through the crack of the door. It struck me that Polecat was acting kind of queer, and I begun to wonder if he was crazy or something. So I riz up in my bare feet and snuck over to the door, and looked through the crack.

Polecat was standing by the table with his back to me, and he had that box he'd got the white stuff out of, and he was turning it around in his hand, and shaking his head and muttering to hisself.

"I didn't make no mistake," he mumbled. "This is the right stuff, all right. I put dern near a handful in his coffee. That oughta been enough for a elephant. I don't understand it. I wouldn't believe it if I hadn't saw it myself."

Well, I couldn't make no sense out of it, and purty soon he sot the box back on the shelf behind some pans and things, and snuck out the door. But he didn't take his rifle, and he left his pistol belt hanging on a peg nigh the door. What he took with him was the fire-tongs off of the hearth. I decided he must be a little locoed from living by hisself, and I went back to bed and went to sleep.

It was some hours later when I woke up and sot up with my guns in my hands, and demanded: "Who's that? Speak up before I drills you."

"Don't shoot," says the voice of Polecat Rixby, emanating from the shadowy figger hovering nigh my bunk. "It's just me. I just wanted to see if you wanted a blanket. It gits cold up here in these mountains before mornin'."

"When it gits colder'n fifteen below zero," I says, "I generally throws a saddle-blanket over me. This here's summer-time. G'wan back to bed and lemme git some sleep."

I could of swore he had one of my boots in his hand when I first woke up, but he didn't have it when he went out. I went back to sleep and I slept so sound it seemed like I hadn't more'n laid back till daylight was oozing through the winder.

I got up and pulled on my boots and went into the other room, and coffee was b'iling, and bacon was frying onto a skillet, but Polecat warn't in there. I laughed when I seen he'd just sot one place on the table. He'd lived by hisself so much he'd plumb forgot he had company for breakfast. I went over to the shelf where he'd got the white stuff he put in my coffee, and retched back and pulled out the box. It had some letters onto it, and while I couldn't read very good then, I knowed the alphabet, and was considered a highly-educated man on Bear Creek. I spelled them letters out and they went "A-r-s-e-n-i-c." It didn't mean nothing to me, so I decided it was some foreign word for a new-fangled coffee flavor. I decided the reason Polecat didn't put none in his coffee was because he didn't have enough for both of us, and wanted to be perlite to his guest. But they was quite a bit of stuff left in the box. I heard him coming back just then, so I put it back on the shelf and went over by the table.

He come through the door with a arm-load of wood, and when he seen me he turned pale under his whiskers and let go the wood and it fell onto the floor. Some good-sized chunks bounced off of his feet but he didn't seem to notice it.

"What the heck's the matter with you?" I demanded. "Yo're as jumpy as Blaze Carson."

He stood there licking his lips for a minute, and then he says faintly: "It's my nerves. I've lived up here so long by myself I kind of forgot I had company. I apolergizes."

"Aw, hell, don't apolergize," I said. "Just fry some more bacon."

So he done it, and pretty soon we sot down and et, and the coffee was purty sorry that morning.

"How long you reckon I ought to hide out here?" I ast, and he said: "You better stay here today and tomorrer. Then you can pull out, travelin' southwest, and hit the old Injun trail again just this side of Scalplock Pass. Did—did you shake out yore boots this mornin'?"

"Naw," I said. "Why?"

"Well," he says, "they's a awful lot of varmints around here, and sometimes they crawls into the cabin. I've found Santa Fes and stingin' lizards in my boots some mornin's."

"I didn't look," I says, drinking my fifth cup of coffee, "but now you mention it, I believe they must be a flea in my left boot. I been feelin' a kind of ticklin'."

So I pulled the boot off, and retched in my hand and pulled it out, and it warn't a flea at all, but a tarantula as big as your fist. I squshed it betwixt my thumb and forefinger and throwed it out the door, and Polecat looked at me kind of wildlike and said: "Did—did it bite you?"

"It's been nibblin' on my toe for the past half hour or so," I said, "but I thought it was just a flea."

"But my God!" he wailed. "Them things is pizen! I've seen men die from bein' bit by 'em!"

"You mean to tell me men in these parts is so puny they suffers when a tranchler bites 'em?" I says. "I never heard of nothin' so derned effeminate! Pass the bacon."

He done so in a kind of pale silence, and after I had mopped up all the grease out of my plate with the last of the corn pone, I ast: "What does a-r-s-e-n-i-c spell?"

He was jest taking a swig of coffee and he strangled and sprayed it all over the table and fell backwards off his stool and would probably have choked to death if I hadn't pounded him in the back.

"Don't you know what arsenic is?" he gurgled when he could talk, and he was shaking like he had the aggers.

"Never heard of it," I said, and he hove a shuddering sigh and said: "It's a Egyptian word which means sugar."

"Oh," I said, and he went over and sot down and held his head in his hands like he was sick at the stummick. He shore was a queer-acting old codger.

Well, I seen the fire needed some wood, so I went out and got a armload and started back into the cabin, and jest as I sot a foot on the stoop *bam!* went a Winchester inside the cabin, and a .45-70 slug hit me a glancing lick on the side of the head and ricocheted off down towards the run.

"What the hell you doin'?" I roared angrily, and Polecat's pale face appeared at the door, and he said: "Excuse me, Elkins! I war jest cleanin' my rifle-gun and it went off accidental!"

"Well, be careful," I advised, shaking the blood off, "Glancin' bullets is dangerous. It might of hit Cap'n Kidd."

"Don't you want to give yore hoss some corn?" he says. "They's plenty out there in that shed nigh the corral."

I thought that was a good idee, so I got a sack and dumped in about a bushel, because Cap'n Kidd is as hearty a eater as what I am, and I went down the run looking for him, and found him mowing down the high grass like a reaping machine, and he neighed with joy at the sight of the corn. Whilst he was gorging I went down the trail a ways to see if they was any outlaws sneaking up it, but I didn't see no signs of none.

It was about noon when I got back to the cabin, and Polecat warn't nowheres in sight, so I decided I'd cook dinner. I fried up a lot of bacon and fixed some bread and beans and potaters, and b'iled a whopping big pot of coffee, and whilst it was b'iling I emptied all the Gypshun sugar they was in the box into it, and taken a good swig, and it was fine. I thought foreigners ain't got much sense, but they shore know how to make sugar.

I was putting the things on the table when Polecat came in looking kind of pale and wayworn, but he perked up when he seen the grub, and sot down and started to eat with a better appertite than he'd been showing. I was jest finishing my first cup of coffee when he taken a swig of his'n, and he spit it out on the floor and said: "What in hell's the matter with this here coffee?"

Now, despite the fact that I am timid and gentle as a lamb by nature, they is one thing I will not endure, and that is for anybody to criticize my cooking. I am the best coffee-maker in Nevada, and I've crippled more'n one man for disagreeing with me. So I said sternly: "There ain't nothin' the matter with that there coffee."

"Well," he said, "I cain't drink it." And he started to pour it out.

At that I was overcome by culinary pride.

"Stop that!" I roared, jerking out one of my .45's. "They is a limit to every man's patience, and this here's mine! Even if I am yore guest, you cain't sneer at my coffee! Sech is a deadly insult, and not to be put up with by any man of spirit and self-respect! You drink that there coffee and display a proper amount of admiration for it, by golly!

"Yore lack of good taste cuts me to the marrer of my soul," I continued bitterly, as he lifted the cup to his lips in fear and trembling. "After I'd done gone to all the trouble of makin' that coffee specially good, and even flavorin' it with all the white stuff they was in that box on the shelf!"

At that he screeched: "Murder!" and fell offa his stool backwards, spitting coffee in every direction. He jumped up and bolted for the door, but I grabbed him, and he pulled a bowie out of his boot and tried to stab me, all the time yowling like a catamount. Irritated at this display of bad manners, I taken the knife away from him and slammed him back down on the stool so hard it broke off all three of the laigs, and he rolled on the floor again, letting out ear-splitting screams.

By this time I was beginning to lose my temper, so I pulled him up and sot him down on the bench I'd been sitting on, and shoved the coffee pot under his nose with one hand and my .45 with the other.

"This is the wust insult I ever had offered to me," I growled blood-thirstily. "So you'd do murder before you'd drink my coffee, hey? Well, you empty that there pot before you put her down, and you smack yore lips over it, too, or I'll—"

"It's murder!" he howled, twisting his head away from the pot. "I ain't ready to die! I got too many sins a-stainin' my soul! I'll confess! I'll tell everything! I'm one of Ferguson's men! This here is the hideout where they keeps the hosses they steals, only they ain't none here now. Bill Price was in the Lazy Elk Bar and heard you talkin' to Blaze Carson about totin' out his gold for him. Bill figgered it would take the whole gang to down you, so he lit out for 'em, and told me to try to git you up to my cabin if I could work it, and send up a smoke signal when I did, so the gang would come and murder you and take the gold.

"But when I got you up here, I decided to kill you myself and skip out with the gold, whilst the gang was waitin' for my signal. You was too big for me to tackle with a knife or a gun, so I put pizen in yore coffee, and when that didn't work I catched a tranchler last night with the tongs and dropped it into yore boot. This mornin' I got desperate and tried to shoot you. Don't make me drink that pizen coffee. I'm a broken man. I don't believe mortal weppin's can kill you. Yo're a jedgment sent onto me because of my evil ways. If you'll spare my life, I swear I'll go straight from now on!"

"What I care how you go, you back-whiskered old sarpent?" I snarled. "My faith in humanity has been give a awful lick. You mean to tell me that there arsenic stuff is pizen?"

"It's considered shore death to ordinary human beings," says he.

"Well, I'll be derned!" I says. "I never tasted nothin' I liked better. "Say!" I says, hit by another thought, "when you was out of the cabin awhile ago, did you by any chance build that there signal smoke?"

"I done so," he admitted. "Up on top of the cliff. Ferguson and his gang is undoubtedly on their way here now."

"Which way will they come?" I ast.

"Along the trail from the west," says he. "Like we come."

"All right," I says, snatching up my Winchester, and the saddlebags in the other hand. "I'll ambush 'em on this side of the gorge. I'm takin' the gold along with me in case yore natural instincts overcomes you to the extent of lightin' a shuck with it whilst I'm massacreein' them idjits."

I run out and whistled for Cap'n Kidd and jumped onto him bare-back and went lickety-split through the bresh till I come to the canyon. And by golly, just as I jumped off of Cap'n Kidd and run through the bushes to the edge of the gorge, out of the bresh on the other side come ten men on horses, with Winchesters in their hands, riding hard. I reckoned the tall, lean, black-whiskered devil leading was Ferguson; I recognized Bill Price right behind him.

They couldn't see me for the bushes, and I drawed a bead on Ferguson and pulled the trigger. And the hammer just clicked. Three times I worked the lever and jerked the trigger, and every time the derned gun snapped. By that time them outlaws had reached the bridge and strung out on it singlefile, Ferguson in the lead. In another minute they'd be acrost, and my chance of ambushing 'em would be plumb sp'iled.

I throwed down my Winchester and busted out of the bresh and they seen me and started yelling, and Ferguson started shooting at me, but the others didn't dare shoot for fear of hitting him, and some of the hosses started rearing, and the men was fighting to keep 'em from falling offa the bridge, but the whole passle come surging on. But I got to the end of the bridge in about three jumps, paying no attention to the three slugs Ferguson throwed into various parts of my anatomy. I bent my knees and got hold of the end of the tree and heaved up with it. It was such a big tree and had so many hosses and men on it even I couldn't lift it very high, but that was enough. I braced my laigs and swung the end around clear of the rim and let go and it went end over end a hundred feet down into the canyon, taking all them outlaws and their hosses along with it, them a-yelling and squalling like the devil. A regular geyer of water splashed up when they hit, and the last I seen of 'em they was all swirling down the river together in a thrashing tangle of arms and laigs and heads and manes.

Whilst I stood looking after 'em, Polecat Rixby bust out of the bresh behind me, and he give a wild look, and shaken his head weakly, and then he said: "I forgot to tell you—I taken the powder out of the ca'tridges in yore Winchester this mornin' whilst you was gone."

"This is a hell of a time to be tellin' me about it," I says. "But it don't make no difference now."

"I suppose it's too trivial to mention," says he, "but it looks to me like you been shot in the hind laig and the hip and the shoulder."

"It's quite likely," I agreed. "And if you really want to make yoreself useful, you might take this bowie and help me to dig the lead out. Then I'm headin' for Wahpeton. Blaze'll be waitin' for his gold, and I want to git me some of that there arsenic stuff. It makes coffee taste better'n skunk ile or rattlesnake pizen."

While Smoke Rolled

"The War of 1812 might have had a very different ending if Sir Wilmot Pembroke had succeeded in his efforts to organize the Western Indians into one vast confederacy to hurl against the American frontier; just why he *did* fail is as great a mystery as is the nature of the accident which forced his companions to carry him back to Canada on a stretcher."

Wilkinson's *History of the Northwest.*

Mister Wn. Wilkinson,
Chicago, Illinoy.

Dear Sir:
The schoolmarm down to Coon Creek was reading the above passage to me out of yore history book which you writ. It ain't no mystery. It's all explained in this here letter which I'm sending you which has been sticking in the family Bible along with the birth records for years. It was writ by my grandpop. Please send it back when you've read it, and oblige,

Yores respeckfully,
Breckinridge Elkins, Esquire.

Aboard the keelboat *Pirut Queen*
On the Missoury,
September, 1814

Mister Peter Elkins,
Nashville, Tennessee,
Dear Sir:
Well, pap, I hope you air satisfied, perswading me to stay out here on the Missoury and skin bufflers and fight musketeers, whilst everybody else in the family is having big doings and enjoying

theirselves. When I think about Bill and John and Joel marching around with Gen'ral Hickory Jackson, and wearing them gorgeous unerforms, and fighting in all them fine battles yore having back there I could dang near bawl. I ain't going to be put on no more jest because I'm the youngest. Soon's I git back to Saint Louis I'm going to throw up my job and head for Tennessee, and the Missoury Fur Company can go to hell. I ain't going to spend all my life working for a living whilsts my wuthless brothers has all the fun, by golly, I ain't. And if you tries to oppress me any more, I'll go and enlist up North and git to be a Yankee; you can see from this how desprut I be, so you better consider.

Anyway, I jest been through a experience up beyond Owl River which has soured me on the whole dern fur trade. I reckon you'll say what the hell has he been doing up the river this time of year, there ain't no furs up there in the summer. Well, it was all on account of Big Nose, the Minnetaree chief, and I git sick at my stummick right now every time I see a Minnetaree.

You know the way the gument takes Injun chiefs East and shows 'em the cities and forts and armies and things. The idea being that the chief will git so scairt when he sees how strong the white man is, that when he gits home he won't never go on the war-path no more. So he comes home and tells the tribe about what he seen, and they accuse him of being a liar and say he's been bought off by the white folks; so he gits mad and goes out and sculps the first white man he meets jest to demonstrate his independence. But it's a good theery, anyway.

So they taken Big Nose to Memphis and would of took him all the way to Washington, only they was scairt they'd run into a battle somewheres on the way and the cannon would scare Big Nose into a decline. So they brung him back to Saint Charles and left him for the company to git him back to his village on Knife River. So Joshua Humphrey, one of the clerks, he put a crew of twenty men and our hunters onto the *Pirut Queen*, and loaded Big Nose on, and we started. The other three hunters was all American too, and the boatmen was Frenchies from down the Mississippi.

I wisht you could of saw Big Nose. He had on a plug hat they give him, and a blue swaller-tailed coat with brass buttons, and a big red sash and broadcloth britches—only he'd cut the seat out of 'em like a Injun always does; and the boots they give him hurt his flat feet, so he wore 'em tied around his neck. He was the most pecooliar-looking critter I ever laid eyes onto, and I shuddered to think what'd happen when the Sioux first ketched sight of him.

Big Nose shuddered too, and more'n I did, because the Sioux hated him anyhow, and the Tetons had swore to kiver a drum with his hide.

But all the way up the Lower River he was like a hawg in clover, because the Omahas and Osages and Iowas would come down to the bank and look at him, clap their hands over their open mouths to show how astonished and admireful they was. He strutted and swelled all over the boat. But the further away from the Platte we got the more his feathers drooped; and one day a Injun rode up on the bluffs and looked at us as we went past, and he was a Sioux. Big Nose had a chill and we had to revive him with about a quart of company rum, and it plumb broke my heart to see all that good licker going to waste down his gullet. When Big Nose come to, he shed his white man's duds and got into his regular outfit—which was mostly a big red blanket that looked like a prairie fire by sunset. I told Joshua he better throw the blanket overboard, because it was knowed all up and down the river, and any Sioux would recognize it at a glance. But Joshua said if we threw it overboard we'd have to throw Big Nose overboard too, because he thought it was big medicine. Anyway, he said, they warn't no use trying to keep the Sioux from knowing we was taking Big Nose home. They knowed it already and would take him away from us if they could. Joshua said he aimed to use diplomacy to save Big Nose's sculp. I didn't like the sound of that, because I notice when somebody I'm working for uses diplomacy it generally means I got to risk my neck and he gits the credit. Jest like you, pap, when you git to working and figgering, like you say, the way it always comes around you do the figgering and I do the working.

The further north we got, the closter Big Nose stayed in the cabin which ain't big enough to swing a cat in; but Big Nose didn't want to swing no cat, and every time he come on deck he seen swarms of Sioux all over the bluffs jest fixing for to descent on him. Joshua said it was hallucernations, but I said it would be delirium trimmin's purty soon if that jug warn't took away from him.

We made purty good time, ten to twenty miles a day, except when we had winds agen us, or had to haul the boat along on the cordelle—which is a big line that the Frenchies gits out and pulls on, in case you don't know. Towing a twenty-ton keelboat in water up to yore neck ain't no joke.

Every day we expected trouble with the Sioux, but we got past the mouth of the Owl River all right, and Joshua said he guessed the Sioux knowed better'n to try any monkey business with *him*. And that very day a Yankton on a piebald hoss hailed us from the bluffs, and told us they was a hundred Tetons laying in ambush for us amongst the willers along the next p'int of land. We'd have to go around it on the cordelle; and whilst the boatmen was tugging and hauling in water up to their waists, the Sioux aimed to jump us. The Yankton said the Tetons didn't have nothing personal agen us white men, and warn't aiming to do us no harm—outside of mebbe cutting our throats for a joke—but you oughta herd what he said they was going to do to Big Nose. It war plumb scandalous.

Big Nose ducked down into the cabin and started having another chill; and the Frenchies got scairt and would of turnt the boat around and headed for Saint Charles if we'd let 'em. Us hunters wanted Joshua to put us ashore and let us circle the p'int from inland and come onto the Sioux from behind. We could do a sight of damage to 'em before they knowed we was onto 'em. But Joshua said not even four American hunters could lick a hundred Sioux, and he furthermore said shet up and let him think. So he sot down on a kag and thunk for a spell, and then he says to me: "Ain't Fat Bear's village out acrost yonder about five mile?"

I said yes, and he said: "Well look, you put on Big Nose's blanket and git on the Yankton's hoss and head for the village. The Sioux'll think we've throwed Big Nose out to root for hisself; and whilst they're chasin' you the boat can git away up the river with Big Nose."

"I don't suppose it matters what happens to *me!*" I says bitterly.

"Oh," says he, "Fat Bear is yore friend and wunst you git in his village he won't let the Sioux git you. You'll have a good start before they can see you, on account of the bluffs there, and you ought to be able to beat 'em into the village."

"I suppose it ain't occurred to you at all that they'll shoot arrers at me all the way," I says with some heat.

"You know a Sioux cain't shoot as good from a runnin' hoss as a Comanche can," he reassured me. "You jest keep three or four hundred yards ahead of 'em, and I bet they won't hit you hardly any at all."

"Well, why don't *you* do it, then?" I demanded.

At this Joshua bust into tears. "To think that you should turn agen me after all I've did for you!" he wept—though what he ever done for me outside of trying to skin me out of my wages I dunno. "After I taken you off'n a Natchez raft and persuaded the company to give you a job at a princely salary, you does this to me! A body'd think you didn't give a dern about my personal safety! My pore old grandpa used to say: 'Bewar' of a Southerner like you would a hawk! He'll eat yore vittles and drink yore licker and then stick you with a butcher knife jest to see you kick!" When I thinks—"

"Aw, hesh up," I says in disgust. "I'll play Injun for you. I'll put on the blanket and stick feathers in my hair, but I'll be derned if I'll cut the seat outa my britches."

"It'd make it look realer," he argued, wiping his eyes on the fringe of my hunting shirt.

"Shet up!" I yelled with passion. "They is a limit to everything!"

"Oh, well, all right," says he, "if you got to be temperamental. You'll have the blanket on over yore pants, anyway."

So we went into the cabin to git the blanket, and would you believe me, that derned Injun didn't want to lemme have it, even when his fool life was at stake. He thought it was a medicine blanket, and the average Injun would ruther lose his life than his medicine. In fack, he give us a tussle for it, and they is no telling how long it would of went on if he hadn't accidentally banged his head agen a empty rum bottle I happened to have in my hand at the time. It war plumb disgusting. He also bit me severely in the hind laig, whilst I was setting on him and pulling the feathers out of his hair—which jest goes to show how much gratitude a Injun has got. But Joshua said the company had contracted to deliver him to Hidatsa, and we was going to do it if we had to kill him.

Joshua give the Yankton a hatchet and a blanket, and three shoots of powder for his hoss—which was a awful price—but the Yankton knowed we had to have it and gouged us for all it was wuth. So I put on the red blanket, and stuck the feathers in my hair, and got on the hoss, and started up a gully for the top of the bluffs.

Joshua yelled: "If you git to the village, stay there till we come back down the river. We'll pick you up then. I'd be doin' this myself, but it wouldn't be right for me to leave the boat. T'wouldn't be fair to the company money to replace it, and—"

"Aw, go to hell!" I begged, and kicked the piebald in the ribs and headed for Fat Bear's village.

When I got up on the bluffs, I could see the p'int; and the Sioux seen me and was fooled jest like Joshua said, because they come b'iling out of the willers and piled onto their ponies and lit out after me. Their hosses was better'n mine, jest as I suspected, but I had a good start; and I was still ahead of 'em when we topped a low ridge and got within sight of Fat Bear's village—which was, so far as I know, the only Arikara village south of Grand River.

I kept expectin' a arrer in my back because they was within range now, and their howls was enough to freeze a mortal's blood; but purty soon I realized that they aimed to take me alive. They thought I was Big Nose, and they detested him so thorough a arrer through the back was too good for him. So I believed I had a good chance of making it after all, because I seen the piebald was going to last longer'n the Tetons thought he would.

I warn't far from the village now, and I seen that the tops of the lodges was kivered with Injuns watching the race. Then a trade-musket cracked, and the ball whistled so clost it stang my ear, and all to wunst I remembered that Fat Bear didn't like Big Nose no better'n the Sioux did. I could see him up on his lodge taking aim at me agen, and the Sioux was right behind me. I was in a hell of a pickle. If I taken the blanket off and let him see who I was, the Sioux would see I warn't Big Nose, too, and fill me full of arrers; and if I kept the blanket on he'd keep on shooting at me with his cussed gun.

Well, I'd ruther be shot at by one Arikara than a hundred Sioux, so all I could do was hope he'd miss. And he did, too; that is he missed me, but his slug taken a notch out of the piebald's ear, and the critter r'ared up and throwed me over his head; he didn't have no saddle nor bridle, jest a hackamore. The Sioux howled with glee and their chief, old Bitin' Hoss, he was ahead of the others, he rode in and grabbed me by the neck as I riz.

I'd lost my rifle in the fall, but I hit Bitin' Hoss betwixt the eyes with my fist so hard I knocked him off'n his hoss and I bet he rolled fifteen foot before he stopped. I grabbed for his hoss, but the critter bolted, so I shucked that blanket and pulled for the village on foot. The Sioux was so surprised to see Big Nose turn into a white man they forgot to shoot at me till I had run more'n a hundred yards; and then when they did let drive, all the arrers missed but one. It hit me right where you kicked Old Man Montgomery last winter and I will have their heart's blood for it if it's the last thing I do. You jest wait; the Sioux nation will regret shooting a Elkins behind his back. They come for me lickety-split but I had too good a start; they warn't a hoss in Dakota could of ketched me under a quarter of a mile.

The Arikaras was surprised too, and some of 'em fell off their *tipis* and nearly broke their necks. They was too stunned to open the gate to the stockade, so I opened it myself—hit it with my

shoulder and knocked it clean off'n the rawhide hinges and fell
inside on top of it. The Sioux was almost on top of me, with their
arrers drawed back, but now they sot their hosses back onto their
haunches and held their fire. If they'd come in after me it would
of meant a fight with the Arikaras. I half expected 'em to come
in anyways, because the Sioux ain't no ways scairt of the Arikaras,
but in a minute I seen why they didn't.

Fat Bear had come down off of his lodge, and I riz up and
says: *"Hao!"*

"Hao!" says he, but he didn't say it very enthusiastic. He's a
fat-bellied Injun with a broad good-natured face; and outside of
being the biggest thief on the Missouri, he's a good friend of the
white men—especially me, because I wunst taken him away from
the Cheyennes which was going to burn him alive.

Then I seen about a hundred strange braves in the crowd, and
they was Crows. I recognized their chief, old Spotted Hawk, and
I knowed why the Sioux didn't come in after me in spite of the
Arikaras. That was why Fat Bear was a chief, too. A long time
ago he made friends with Spotted Hawk, and when the Sioux or
anybody crowded him to clost, the Crows would come in and help
him. Them Crows air scrappers and no mistake.

"This is plumb gaudy!" I says. "Git yore braves together and
us and the Crows will go out and run them fool Tetons clean into
the Missouri, by golly."

"No, no, no!" says he. He's hung around the trading posts till
he can talk English nigh as good as me. "There's a truce between
us! Big powwow tonight!"

Well, the Sioux knowed by now how they'd been fooled; but
they also knowed the *Pirut Queen* would be past the p'int and
outa their reach before they could git back to the river; so they
camped outside, and Bitin' Hoss hollered over the stockade: "There
is bad flesh in my brother's village! Send it forth that we may
cleanse it with fire!"

Fat Bear bust into a sweat and says: "That means they want to
burn you! Why did you *have* to come here, jest at this time?"

"Well," I says in a huff, "air you goin' to hand me over to
'em?"

"Never!" says he, wiping his brow with a bandanner he stole
from the guvment trading post below the Kansas. "But I'd rather
a devil had come through that gate than a Big Knife!" That's what
them critters calls a American. "We and the Crows and Sioux
have a big council on tonight, and—"

Jest then a man in a gilded cock hat and a red coat come through the crowd, with a couple of French Canadian trappers and a pack of Soc Injuns from the Upper Mississippi. He had a sword on him and he stepped as proud as a turkey gobbler in the fall.

"What is this bloody American doing here?" says he, and I says: "Who the hell air you?" And he says: "Sir Wilmot Pembroke, agent of Indian affairs in North America for his Royal Majesty King George, that's who!"

"Well, step out from the crowd, you lobster-backed varmint," says I, stropping my knife on my leggin', "and I'll decorate a sculp-pole with yore innards—and that goes for them two Hudson Bay skunks, too!"

"No!" says Fat Bear, grabbing my arm. "There is a truce! No blood must be spilled in my village! Come into my lodge."

"The truce doesn't extend beyond the stockade," says Sir Wilmot. "Would you care to step outside with me?"

"So yore Teton friends could fill me with arrers?" I sneered. "I ain't as big a fool as I looks."

"No, that wouldn't be possible," agreed he, and I was so overcame with rage all I could do was gasp. Another instant and I would of had my knife in his guts, truce or no truce, but Fat Bear grabbed me and got me into his *tipi*. He had me set on a pile of buffler hides and one of his squaws brung me a pot of meat; but I was too mad to be hungry, so I only et four or five pounds of buffler liver.

Fat Bear sot down his trade musket, which he had stole from a Hudson Bay Company trapper, and said: "The council tonight is to decide whether or not the Arikaras shall take the warpath against the Big Knives. This Red-Coat, Sir Wilmot, says the Big White Chief over the water is whipping the Big White Father of the Big Knives, who lives in the village called Washington."

I was so stunned by this news I couldn't say nothing. We hadn't had no chance to git news about the war since we started up the river.

"Sir Wilmot wants the Sioux, Crows and Arikaras to join him in striking the American settlements down the river," says Fat Bear. "The Crows believe the Big Knives are losing the war, and they're wavering. If they go with the Sioux, I must go too; otherwise the Sioux will burn my village. I can not exist without the aid of the Crows. The Red-Coat has a Soc medicine, who will go into a medicine lodge tonight and talk with the Great Spirit. It is big medicine, such was never seen before on any village on the Missouri. The medicine man will tell the Crows and the Arikaras to go with the Sioux."

"You mean this Englishman aims to lead a war-party down the river?" I says, plumb horrified.

"Clear to Saint Louis!" says Fat Bear. "He will wipe out *all* the Americans on the river!"

"He won't neither," says I with great passion, rising and drawing my knife. "I'll go over to his lodge right now and cut his gizzard out!"

But Fat Bear grabbed me and hollered: "If you spill blood, no one will ever dare recognize a truce again! I cannot let you kill the Red-Coat!"

"But he's plannin' to kill everybody on the river, dern it!" I yelled. "What'm I goin' to do?"

"You must get up in council and persuade the warriors not to go on the war-path," says he.

"Good gosh," I says, "I can't make no speech."

"The Red-Coat has a serpent's tongue," says Fat Bear, shaking his head. "If he had presents to give the chiefs, his cause would be as good as won. But his boat upset as he came along the river, and all his goods were lost. If you had presents to give to Spotted Hawk and Biting Horse—"

"You know I ain't got no presents!" I roared, nigh out of my head. "What the hell am I goin' to do?"

"I dunno," says he, despairful. "Some white men pray when they're in a pickle."

"I'll do it!" I says. "Git outa my way!" So I kneeled down on a stack of buffler robes, and I'd got as far as: *"Now I lay me down to sleep—"* when my knee nudged something under the hides that felt familiar. I reched down and yanked it out—and sure enough, it was a keg!

"Where'd you git this?" I yelped.

"I stole it out of the company's storehouse the last time I was in Saint Louis," he confessed, "but—"

"But nothin'!" exulted I. "I dunno how come you ain't drunk it all up before now, but it's my *wampum!* I ain't goin' to try to out-talk that lobster-back tonight. Soon's the council's open, I'll git up kind of casual and say that the Red-Coat has got a empty bag of talk for 'em, with nothin' to go with it, but the Big White Father at Washington has sent 'em a present. Then I'll drag out the keg. T'ain't much to divide up amongst so many, but the chiefs what counts, and they's enough licker to git *them* too drunk to know what Sir Wilmot and the medicine man says."

"They know you didn't bring anything into the village with you," he says.

"So much the better," I says. "I'll tell 'em it's *wakan* and I can perjuice whiskey out of the air."

"They'll want you to perjuice some more," says he.

"I'll tell 'em a evil spirit, in the shape of a skunk with a red coat on, is interferin' with my magic powers," I says, gitting brainier every minute. "That'll make 'em mad at Sir Wilmot. Anyway, they won't care where the licker come from. A few snorts and the Sioux will probably remember all the gredges they got agen the Socs and run 'em outa camp."

"You'll get us all killed," says Fat Bear, mopping his brow. "But about that keg, I want to tell you—"

"You shet up about that keg," I says sternly. "It warn't yore keg in the first place. The fate of a nation is at stake, and you tries to quibble about a keg of licker! Git some stiffenin' into yore laigs; what we does tonight may decide who owns this continent. If we puts it over it'll be a big gain for the Americans."

"And what'll the Indians get out of it?" he ast.

"Don't change the subjeck," I says. "I see they've stacked buffler hides out at the council circle for the chiefs and guests to get on—and by the way, you be dern sure you gives me a higher stack to get on than Sir Wilmot gits. When nobody ain't lookin', you hide this keg clost to where I'm to set. If I had to send to yore lodge to git it, it'd take time and look fishy, too."

"Well," he begun reluctantly, but I flourished a fist under his nose and said with passion: "Dang it, do like I says! One more blat outa you and I busts the truce and yore snoot simultaneous!"

So he spread his hands kinda helpless, and said something about all white men being crazy, and anyway he reckoned he'd lived as long as the Great Spirit aimed for him to. But I give no heed, because I have not got no patience with them Injun superstitions. I started out of his lodge and dang near fell over one of them French trappers which they called Ondrey; t'other'n was named Franswaw.

"What the hell you doin' here?" I demanded, but he merely give me nasty look and snuck off. I started for the lodge where the Crows was, and the next man I met was old Shingis. I dunno what his real name is, we always calls him old Shingis; I think he's a Iowa or something. He's so old he's done forgot where he was born, and so ornery he jest lives around with first one tribe and then another till they git tired of him and kick him out.

He ast for some tobacker and I give him a pipe-full, and then he squinted his eye at me and said: "The Red-Coat did not have to bring a man from the Mississippi to talk with Waukontonka.

They say Shingis is *heyoka*. They say he is a friend of the Unktehi, the Evil Spirits."

Well, nobody never said that but him, but that's the way Injuns brag on themselves; so I told him everybody knowed he was *wakan*, and went on to the lodge where the Crows was. Spotted Hawk ast me if it was the Red-Coats had burnt Washington; and I told him not to believe everything a Red-Coat told him. Then I said: "Where's this Red-Coat's presents?"

Spotted Hawk made a wry face because that was a p'int which stuck in his mind, too, but he said: "The boat upset and the river took the gifts meant for the chiefs."

"Then that means that the Unktehi air mad at him," I says. "His medicine's weak. Will you foller a man which his medicine is weak?"

"We will listen to what he has to say in council," says Spotted Hawk, kind of uncertain, because a Injun is scairt of having anything to do with a man whose medicine is weak.

It was gitting dark by this time, and when I come out of the lodge I met Sir Wilmot, and he says: "Trying to traduce the Crows, eh? I'll have the pleasure of watching my Sioux friends roast you yet! Wait till Striped Thunder talks to them from the medicine lodge tonight."

"He who laughs last is a stitch in time," I replied with dignerty, so tickled inside about the way I was going to put it over him I was reconciled to not cutting his throat. I then went on, ignoring his loud, rude laughter. *Jest wait*, thunk I, *jest wait! Brains always wins in the end.*

I passed by the place where the buffler hides had been piled in a circle, in front of a small *tipi* made out of white buffler skins. Nobody come nigh that place till the powwow opened, because it was *wakan*, as the Sioux say, meaning magic. But all of a sudden I seen old Shingis scooting through the *tipis* clostest to the circle, making a arful face. He grabbed a water bucket made out of a buffler's stummick, and drunk about a gallon, then he shook his fists and talked to hisself energetic. I said: "Is my red brother's heart pained?"

"¾$%&●!" says old Shingis. "There is a man of black heart in this village! Let him beware! Shingis is the friend of the Unktehi!"

Then he lit out like a man with a purpose, and I went on to Fat Bear's lodge. He was squatting on his robes looking at hisself in a mirrer he stole from the Northwest Fur Company three seasons ago.

"What you doin'?" I ast, reching into the meat pot.

"Trying to imagine how I'll look after I'm scalped," says he. "For the last time, that keg—"

"Air you tryin' to bring that subjeck up agen?" I says, rising in wrath; and jest then a brave come to the door to say that everybody was ready to go set in council.

"See?" whispers Fat Bear to me. "I'm not even boss in my own village when Spotted Hawk and Biting Horse are here! *They* give the orders!"

We went to the powwow circle, which they had to hold outside because they warn't a lodge big enough to hold all of 'em. The Arikaras sot on one side, the Crows on the other and the Sioux on the other. I sot beside Fat Bear, and Sir Wilmot and his Socs and Frenchmen sot opposite us. The medicine man sot cross-legged, with a heavy wolf-robe over his shoulders—though it was hot enough to fry a aig, even after the sun had went down. But that's the way a *keyoka* man does. If it'd been snowing, likely he'd of went naked. The women and chillern got up on top of the lodges to watch us, and I whispered and ast Fat Bear where the keg was. He said under the robes right behind me. He then started humming his death-song under his breath.

I begun feeling for it, but before I found it, Sir Wilmot riz and said: "I will not worry my red brothers with empty words! Let the Big Knives sing like mosquitos in the ears of the people! The Master of Life shall speak through the lips of Striped Thunder. As for me, I bring no words, but a present to make your hearts glad!"

And I'm a Choctaw if he didn't rech down under a pile of robes and drag out Fat Bear's keg! I like to keeled over and I hear Fat Bear grunt like he'd been kicked in the belly. I seen Ondrey leering at me, and I instantly knowed he'd overheard us talking and had stole it out from amongst the hides after Fat Bear put it there for me. The way the brave's eyes glistened I knowed the Red-Coats had won, and I was licked.

Well, I war so knocked all of a heap, all I could think of was to out with my knife and git as many as I could before they got me. I aimed to git Sir Wilmot, anyway; they warn't enough men in the world to keep me from gutting him before I died. A Elkins on his last rampage is wuss'n a cornered painter. You remember great-uncle Esau Bearfield. When the Creeks finally downed him, they warn't enough of 'em left alive in that war party to sculp him, and *he* was eighty-seven.

I reched for my knife, but jest then Sir Wilmot says: "Presently the milk of the Red-Coats will make the hearts of the warriors sing. But now is the time for the manifestations of the Great Spirit, whom the Sioux call Waukontonka, and other tribes other names, but he is the Master of Life for all. Let him speak through the lips of Striped Thunder."

So I thought I'd wait till everybody was watching the medicine lodge before I made my break. Striped Thunder went into the lodge and closed the flap, and the Socs lit fires in front of it and started dancing back and forth in front of 'em singing:

> "Oh, Master of Life, enter the
> white skin lodge!
>
> Possess him who sits within!
> Speak through his mouth!"

I ain't going to mention what they throwed on the fires, but they smoked something fierce so you couldn't even see the lodge, and the Socs dancing back and forth looked like black ghosts. Then all to wunst they sounded a yell inside the lodge and a commotion begun like men fighting. The Injuns looked like they was about ready to rise up and go yonder in a hurry, but Sir Wilmot said: "Do not fear! The messenger of the Master of Life contends with the Unktehi for possession of the medicine man's body! Soon the good spirit will prevail and we will open the lodge and hear the words of Waukontonka!"

Well, hell, I knowed Striped Thunder wouldn't say nothing but jest what Sir Wilmot had told him to say; but them fool Injuns would believe they was gitting the straight goods from the Great Spirit hisself.

Things got quiet in the lodge and the smoke died down, and Sir Wilmot says: "Thy children await, O Waukontonka." He opened the door, and I'm a Dutchman if they was anything in that lodge but a striped polecat!

He waltzed out with his tail h'isted over his back and them Injuns let out one arful yell and fell over backwards; and then they riz up and stampeded—Crows, Arikaras, Sioux, Socs and all, howling: "The Unktehi have prevailed! They have turned Striped Thunder into an evil beast!"

They didn't stop to open the gate. The Sioux clumb the stockade and the Crows busted right through it. I seen old Biting Hoss and Spotted Hawk leading the stampede, and I knowed the great Western Injun Confederation was busted all to hell. The women and

chillern was right behind the braves, and in sight of fifteen seconds
the only Injun in sight was Fat Bear.

Sir Wilmot jest stood there like he'd been putrified into rock,
but Franswaw he run around behind the lodge and let out a squall.
"Somebody's slit the back wall!" he howled. "Here's Striped Thunder
der lying behind the lodge with a knot on his head the size of a
egg! Somebody crawled in and knocked him senseless and dragged
him out while the smoke rolled!" _

"The same man left the skunk!" frothed Sir Wilmot. "You
Yankee dog, you're responsible for this!"

"Who you callin' a Yankee?" I roared, whupping out my knife.

"Remember the truce!" squalled Fat Bear, but Sir Wilmot was
too crazy mad to remember anything. I parried his sword with my
knife as he lunged, and grabbed his arm, and I reckon that was
when he got his elber dislocated. Anyway he give a maddened
yell and tried to draw a pistol with his good hand; so I hit him in
the mouth with my fist, and that's when he lost them seven teeth
he's so bitter about. Whilst he was still addled, I taken his pistol
away from him and throwed him over the stockade. I got a idee
his fractured skull was caused by him hitting his head on a stump
outside. Meanwhile Ondrey and Franswaw was hacking at me with
their knives, so I taken 'em by their necks and beat their fool
heads together till they was limp, and then I throwed 'em over the
stockade after Sir Wilmot.

"And I reckon that settles that!" I panted. "I dunno how this
all come about, but you can call up yore women and chillern and
tell 'em they're now citizens of the United States, by golly!"

I then picked up the keg, because I was hot and thirsty, but
Fat Bear says: "Wait! Don't drink that! I—"

"Shet up!" I roared. "After all I've did for the nation tonight,
I deserve a dram! Shame on you to begredge a old friend—"

I taken a big gulp—and then I give a maddened beller and
throwed that keg as far as I could heave it, and run for water. I
drunk about three gallons, and when I could breathe again I got
a club and started after Far Bear, who clumb up on top of a lodge.

"Come down!" I requested with passion. "Come down whilst
I beats yore brains out! Whyn't you tell me what was in that keg?"

"I tried to," says he, "but you wouldn't lissen. I thought it was
whiskey when I stole it, or I wouldn't have taken it. I talked to
Shingis while you were hunting the water bucket, jest now. It was
him that put the skunk in the medicine lodge. He saw Ondrey hide
the keg on Sir Wilmot's side of the council circle; he sneaked a

drink out of it, and that's why he did what he did. It was for revenge. The onreasonable old buzzard thought Sir Wilmot was tryin' to pizen him."

So that's the way it was. Anyway, I'm quitting my job as soon as I git back to Saint Louis. It's bad enuff when folks gits to hifaluting to use candles, and has got to have oil lamps in a trading post. But I'll be derned if I'll work for a outfit which puts the whale-oil for their lamps in the same kind of kegs they puts their whiskey. Your respeckful son,

Boone Elkins.

A Elkins Never Surrenders

Pop was cussin' so loud I could hear him clear down to Sandy Crossing when I rode up to the cabin on my way back from Chawed Ear. He was layin' on a b'ar skin in the middle of the floor, with his jug of white corn nigh his elbow and a letter in his hand which my sister Ouachita must have read to him. He would look at the letter, taken a swig of corn, and then cuss somethin' terrible.

"Of all the times to have a feud," he said feercely. "They couldn't of waited till I was done with my rheumatiz. Not them! The selfishness of my relatives is a thorn in my hide. Breckinridge, you light out for Uncle Joel's ranch, right now."

"You mean Uncle Joel Garfield in Arizona?" I ast.

"Who else, you idjit?" roars pap. "The Garfield's is havin' trouble, and whilst they ain't ast for no help, I ain't one to stand by and let my kinfolks be imposed on. Uncle Joel was always too blame' peaceable for his own good. You git down thar to Arizona and taken charge, and don't lissen to no talk about truces or comprimizes. With a Elkins," says pap, h'istin his jug, "it's war to the bloody end! Git goin'!"

I left Cap'n Kidd in the corral that I built for him—nothin' else would hold him—and then made the trek to Perdition to catch the stage. The stage-stand was likewise a saloon, and some of the boys got to bettin' me I couldn't swill down a quart of red licker without to taken the bottle outa my mouth or stoppin' for breath. Every time I downed a quart, I winned a dollar and the loser had to pay for the whiskey.

I had a pocket full of silver when somebody hollered: "The

409

stage is fixin' to pull out!" so I clamb aboard amidst a lot of yellin' and pistol shots. The driver cracked his whup, and I was off to Arizona where I defends the family honor.

I was onnatural sleepy for some reason—mebbe 'cause I don't cotton to stagecoach ridin'—and have only a faint rekolection of the trip. A couple of times we stopped to change hosses, and once some men was talkin'. I heared one of 'em say: "My God, is that a *man* you got in there? If it be, it's the biggest hombre I ever seen."

When I finally waked up it was late afternoon and we was bowlin' along in a country plumb new to me. I hadn't never been in Arizona before. The driver stuck in his head and says: "Say, where do you want to go, anyhow?"

"Arizona," says I, and he says: "We *been* in Arizony since sun-up. Where 'bouts in Arizony?"

Well, I thunk and thunk, and I couldn't remember, and finally I says: "What towns you got around here?"

"We jest a while ago passed through Rifle River," replies he.

"Well," I says, "I want to git off at the town whar the Garfields lives. You oughta know whar that is. They's a big family of 'em."

"Oh," he says, "that's the next town, Sawtooth. They lives on a ranch 'bout a mile outa town."

"Who is these folks they been havin' trouble with?" I ast.

"The Clantons," he said. "Old man Clanton sued old man Garfield 'bout some land, and winned the suit and got a right smart chunk of money."

"The jedge was crooked," I said promptly.

"Well, I don't know . . ." he begun.

I seen right off what if he was any sample, the whole countryside was prejudiced agen the Garfields, and at the thought of this injustice, I swole with rage. "I said the jedge was crooked!" I roared, movin' for'ard a little, and he turned pale and said: "Y-yes, yes! Yo're right. I can see now, I spoke without thinkin'."

Purty soon we pulled into Sawtooth, and the drive p'inted with his whup and says with pride: "That thar is the new court house."

"What's that big iron tube on wheels settin' near to it?" I ast, and he says: "That's a cannon the folks borrowed from Fort Polk in case the Apaches tries to raid the town."

Jest then we pulled up at the stage-stand, and he p'inted at a old gent with droopin' whiskers which was leanin' up agen a hitchin'-rail, and says: "There's old man Garfield now; he always meets the stage."

He warn't as old lookin' as I thought he'd be, and he warn't near as big as pap. We hadn't never seen each other, but I walked over and grabbed his hand and shaked it. He looked surprized and made some funny noises in his whiskers.

"I'm yore grand-nephew Breckinridge Elkins, Uncle Joel," I informed him, and folks all up and down the street turns to look. I got a voice which carries. "I'm here to see that justice is did."

"G-glad to meetcha, Breckinridge," he says in a kinda dazed voice. I seen right off, pap was right. Uncle Joel warn't much like us Bear Creek folks.

"Fear no more, Uncle Joel," I says, slapping him on the neck. "I takes charge right now."

"Takes charge?" he sorta gurgled, straightening hisself up agen.

"Sure," I said. "Tell me, Uncle Joel," gettin' down to business—us Elkinses don't believe in procrastinatin', whar-at is them cussed Clantons?"

"Why," he said, p'intin' at a feller which was settin' on the aidge of a hoss trough acrost the street, "thar is one of 'em."

"Now, by nature I am as peaceable and mild an hombre as you can find, and it takes a powerful heep to irritate me. But family feuds is different and, as pap says, they is reason for war to the bloody end. Nevertheless, I keeps my temper and stalks acrost the street to whar this feller is sittin'.

He seen me comin' and gets up quick-like.

"Air you a Clanton?" I ast.

"Yes, I am," he replies belligeruntly. "What about it?"

"Well, I'm Breckinridge Elkins and I'm here to pertect my kinfolk," I begun, in a right civil fashun considerin' the injury done my kin.

"Well, I'm John Clanton and I never heared of you," he says irritated, and without further palaver he hits me on the ear and kicks me in both laigs, but I holds my temper and busts him one on the jaw and he flies over the hoss trough and comes to rest on his neck in the gutter with his laigs stuck up in the air agen a hitchin'-rack.

Uncle Joel let out a yelp, and I turned around jest in time to see a feller come runnin' up behind me.

"I'm the sheriff," he hollers, flashing a star. "I arrests you and charges you with breakin' the peace!"

I starts to submit meekly because pap always told me to respeck the law, when I remembers this is a affair of family honor, and the sheriff sides with the Clantons. So I taken away his guns so he wouldn't hurt hisself, meanwhile heavin' his carcass into a hoss trough.

"Considerin' you is a minion of the Clanton family," I declares, "I deals with you as with any wuthless coyote."

The last words come out in a roar that rattled all the winders on the street, since I was now beginnin' to git riled. I pulled my guns and shot up some signboards and winder lights to emphasize my p'int. Everybody run for their life except Uncle Joel which hid under a watering trough.

I figgered they wouldn't recognize me down here so I proclaims myself loudly: "I'm Breckinridge Elkins of Bear Creek, Nevada, and I'm takin' charge of the Garfield clan." Nobody answers, so I says: "Step out and declare yoreselves, you Sawtooth varmints! Them which ain't for me is agen me!" Then, struck by a sudden thot, I ast, "Whar's the deperty?"

Still nobody answered, so I run into the saloon and seen a feller down behind the bar tryin' to swaller a badge. I reched over and grabbed him by the slack of his shirt and heaved him over the bar onto the floor.

"So!" I raged, haulin' him back by the ear, "You tries to make a fool outa me by destroyin' the evidence! I'll have yore sculp—" But he had fainted, so I slung him fretfully into a corner and strode forth, and all them heads which was peekin' around the corners ducked back.

Uncle Joel was jest climbing into a buckboard and I run and give a leap and landed beside him, and the buckboard swayed, and the horses squealed, and we lit out.

"Whar you live, Uncle Joel?" I yelled.

"Over yonder," he said, moistening his lips and p'inting to the roof of a house we could jest see about a mile away acrost some alfalfa fields and rolling pastures.

"Well, we ain't makin' no speed at all," says I. "Gimme them lines," and I grabbed the lines give a yell that made them mustangs jump straight up in the air. Then they lit out down the pike, jest touchin' the high places.

Uncle Joel didn't act like he was enjoyin' the ride much. He held onto the buckboard and hollered every time we turned a corner on one wheel, and everybody we passed taken to the fields and hollered. "What in hell's the matter?" I ast. Then I shot some of them fellers' hats off to make Uncle Joel feel better, but he didn't.

As we approached the ranch house I seen no use stoppin' to open the gate because I knowed we was goin' fast enough to knock it down anyhow, and we did and a piece of it hit Uncle Joel in the head and he hollered somethin' fearful. As we busted into the ranch yard it become apparunt to me that the critters was runnin' away, so I wheeled 'em short, and a wheel come off the buckboard.

I would of stopped 'em anyway, only the lines broke, and the mustangs run on and hung theirselves up on a tree, and an old lady and four gals and three boys come runnin' out of the house and the old lady says: "Land sakes, what's happenin'?"

Then they all begun to holler because Uncle Joel was out cold, and the old lady squalled: "He's kilt! Git some water! Git some water!"

I dunno what good they thot water would do him if he *was* kilt, but I seen a hoss trough with about thirty or forty gallons in it, and I went and picked it up and brung it back, and they all stared like they hadn't never seen nobody carryin' a hoss trough around before. So I emptied it on Uncle Joel and he sot up convulsively and snorted and said, "What the hell, are you tryin' to drown me?"

"Who's this, pa?" ast the old lady uneasily, whilst the young folks stared at me like a man my size was somethin' onusual.

"He says he's my nephyew," says Uncle Joel, wipin' his face with a unsteady hand. "He 'lows he's here to help us agen the Clantons."

"But I thought that trouble was settled," says the old lady. "They won the case, and—"

"Trouble ain't never settled till the Elkinses and their kinfolk wins," I says fiercely. "The war's just commencin'. What's these young'uns' names?"

I was as disapp'inted in them as I was with Uncle Joel. That branch of the family sure didn't run to size like us Bear Creek folks. Them boys was full grown men, but not one of 'em was much over six feet.

"That's Bill, Jim and Joe," he said, designatin' 'em. "The gals—"

"Never mind the gals," I said. "All the women folks is got to be took to a place of safety. Joe, go unhang them mustangs and turn 'em out in the pasture. Bill, you hitch a couple of gentle hosses to that thar wagon and take yore maw and sisters to Sawtooth. They can stay there till the war's over."

The old lady looked bewildured at Uncle Joel, and he waggled his head helpless, and says: "You better do what he says. He seems to have took charge—and gosh knows, *I* ain't goin' to argy with him."

"Jim," I says, "git on a hoss and tie a piece of white cloth to a ramrod and ride over and tell them Clantons to send their women-folks into Sawtooth. We don't want to risk hurtin' no women."

"I ain't got no white rag," he said kinda dizzily, so I taken a sheet offa the clothes line and teared part of it off for him, and the old woman hollered: "My best sheet!" Women is always on-reasonable that way.

We could see the roof of the Clanton's ranch house, a big two-story house about a mile south, over the low, rolling ridges. Uncle Joel said they was seven of the men folks.

"Bill," I said, going down into my pockets, "buy up all the ammernishun they is in Sawtooth. This war may last a long time, and anyway, we don't want to leave none for the Clantons to git."

"I never seen the like," said the old lady dazedly, but her and the gals got into the wagun, and Bill started to town with 'em, and Jim lit out on a hoss wavin' his white flag, and I put Uncle Joel and Joe to helpin' me prepare for a siege.

We filled everything we could find with water, and I started them to buildin' shutters for the winders, whilst I cleaned and iled all the guns on the place. Some of 'em didn't look like they'd been fired since the Civil War.

Purty soon Jim come back and said the Clantons seemed con-siderable agitated. The oldest boy, John, he said, had been brung home with a dislocated jaw, and the women folk had heeded the warnin' sent 'em and lit out for Sawtooth.

"Good!" I says. "Now we can go over and slaughter the rest of the family with easy consciences. They ain't no use to delay hostilities no longer. Joe, you ride over to the Clantons and take a shot at the old man to let 'em know the ball's done opened."

Joe looked kinda sick, but after starin' mutely at Uncle Joel, which turned pale under his whiskers and said nothin', he clumb on his horse and pulled out.

"Yore boys, Uncle Joel," I said, reching for the ile can again, "disapp'ints me. They ain't got the proper ambition for blood and mayhem like'n they oughta. I never expected to see anybody kin to the Elkinses," I said, "which wasn't achin' for a fight twenty-four hours outa the day. I thot you Arizona Garfields was bear-cats. I'm plumb disapp'inted. What's this?"

"It's a Mexican *escopeta*," says Uncle Joel faintly. "Don't fool with it. It goes off onexpected."

It was a muzzle-loading shotgun with a big bell mouth and loaded with three or four handfuls of buckshot. I brightened up at the sight of it, and begun to git it in working order, when Joe come back looking dejected. The seat was missin' out'n his britches.

"I done like you instructed," said he. "I snuck up behind the corral and took a shot at old man Clanton, but I missed him, and they sot their bulldog on me."

"What!" I raged. "So they refuses to fight like civilized men, but descends to low, vile tactics. Have we got a dog?" I asked, smit by a sudden thought.

"Naw," they said.

"Well," I said, "you and Jim go git that bulldog and bring him over here. We needs a dog to bark when somebody tries to sneak up on the house at night."

"We'll git shot!" they protested.

"Naw, you won't, not if you work it right," I said. "Toll the dog away from the house without showin' yoreselves."

So they sot out with a beef bone and a fish net, and they were hardly out of sight when Bill pulled in and said Sawtooth was in considerable turmoil, and folks was talkin' about comin' over in a mob and lynchin' me. Uncle Joel said sarcastic that a mob would be fine, on top of our trouble with the Clantons, but I give no heed, because strangers is always tryin' to lynch me in their ignorance.

I packed in the ammernishun what Bill had brung back, and amongst the cartridges there was several bags of loose powder. I looked at it, and I looked at that thar *excopeta,* and I was smit by a idee that fetched a yell from me which caused Uncle Joel to jump clean through a nearby winder.

Purty soon Jim and Joe come back with the dog wrapped up in the fish net, and most of their clothes and hide tore offa them. They said the Clantons had barricaded theirselves in the ranch house and had shot at 'em from long range whilst they was struggling with the bulldog, but had evidently thot it was a plot to lure 'em into the open, and wouldn't come out.

That was jest what I wanted.

It was sundown by that time, and as soon as it got good and dark, I tied the bulldog in the yard and told Uncle Joel and Jim to lock all the doors and lay on the roofs with their rifles to guard the house. And I told Bill and Joe to go over and lay on the ridge above the Clanton ranch house and wait till I come. I then hitched a couple of the strongest mules to the wagon and lit out for Sawtooth. Folks went to bed early there, such as wasn't gathered in the saloon. I met nobody till I come to the court house.

I drove up near the cannon and got off and was fixin' to load it on to the wagon, when a figger hove outa the darkness which I later learned was the jedge. He didn't do nothin', only he said: "What are you doin'?"

"I'm borrowin' this here cannon," I said, and I bent and h'isted it on my back and started for the wagon with it. The jedge put his hands to his head and staggered back and said: "My God, the licker's got me! I'm sufferin' from the hallucinations!"

I places the cannon in the wagon and pulls out, thinkin' that them Sawtooth people was very pecooliar.

I didn't head for Uncle Joel's ranch. I aimed towards the Clanton place, and jest before I swung offa the road onta their land, I stopped and loaded the cannon with the ammernishun I had brung along in a bushel basket. She was a big, fine cannon, and I loaded her with several pecks of black powder, and about a quart of rifle bullets, and a gallon of buckshot, and some plough shares, and old bolts and nuts, and ten penny nails, and carpet tacks, and fence staples, and stove lids, and door knobs, and a trace chain.

I took down some fences and drove up close to the house where I stopped the wagon and hitched the hosses jest below the ridge what Bill and Joe was watchin'.

"Has any of them scoundrels come out?" I ast.

They said no, the lights was all out and they was evidently all asleep, except mebbe somebody left on watch.

"Good!" I said. "I want 'em all in one bunch. You boys hightail it for home, and wait there for me."

"What you aimin' to do?" they ast.

"I aim to settle this feud with one lick," I said, heavin' the cannon outa the wagon. "I'm goin' to blow the entire Clanton family to Kingdom Come."

They turned pale and their knees knocked together, and they pulled out in a hurry. I h'isted the cannon onto my back and snuck down the ridge past the corral and clumb a rail fence, and sot her down a hundred yards or so from the ranch house.

Nobody stirred. If anybody was on guard, he'd felled asleep. I didn't know which was the bedrooms, but I figgered the charge I had in the gun would sweep the whole lower part of the house anyway.

I set her, aimed her, and struck a match on my britches and touched it to the vent-hole.

Bam!

The night was split with a blinding burst of flame. They was a explosion that shook the ground, and the charge crashed through the ranch house like a tornado. Through the swirling cloud of smoke I seen that the blast had ripped a hole clean through the house you could of driven a herd of steers through, and the building begun to buckle and sag.

But simultaneous ariz a deafening clamor of yells, and men in night shirts fell outa the upstairs winders like rats out of a haystack. They scattered in every direction shrieking bloody murder, and I realized that all them slimy Clantons had been sleeping *upstairs*. I hadn't kilt a damned one!

And besides, I'd forgot about the recoil, and it had knocked me through the rail fence, and by the time I'd ontangled myself, they'd all disappeared in the bresh, so I didn't even get to shoot any of 'em as they run. Well, I was so derned disapp'inted I sot right down there and lamented loudly and bitterly.

Then I got mad and run into the bresh lookin' for my enemies, but didn't find nobody. They was still running, evidently, and I didn't know the country well enough to hunt 'em down in the dark. So finally I come back in disgust.

The barrel of the cannon was split in three or four places, and I seen I couldn't use it no more, so I thought I better take it back to Sawtooth. But the mules had broke loose and run off, so I had to pack it all the way on my shoulders, and it was jest getting daylight when I sot it down by the court house.

I then headed for the saloon, thirsty and disgruntled. I hates for my grand idees to fall flat because folks ain't got sense enough to stay whar they're supposed to. Early as it was, everybody was milling around in the streets and talkin' about the explosion. One of the Clantons had run through the town without stoppin', and yelled the news as he run, but didn't know hisself jest what had happened. Some of the folks said it was a bolt of lightning, and some said a earthquake, and some said a tornado.

They didn't even notice me as I come into the saloon. All the noise got on my nerves, so presently I roared: "Shet up! If you wanta know what wrecked the Clanton's house—I done it!"

Everybody stampeded for the door hollerin', "Run for your lives, he's back agen!" After a while, I pulled out for Uncle Joel's on foot. When I got there, Uncle Joel had a buckskin bag in one hand and a note in the other which he was reading, and he said: "Breckinridge, I guess the war's over. Old man Clanton's sent back the money he won offa me, and wants to call it quits. He says when we rings earthquakes and tornadoes in on him, he knows when he's licked."

"So he thinks he can buy us off, hey?" I gnashed, feelin' my honor'd been violated. "You send that money right back and tell him the Elkins clan ain't to be bribed."

"I ain't a-goin' to do it!" howled Uncle Joel, showin' fire for the first time as he clutched the filthy lucre to his boozum.

"You air too!" I roared. "No Elkins never sold their honor for gold! Nothin' but blood can wipe out a wrong to a Elkins!" I bellered, striding up and down and drawing both guns as is a habit of mine when excited. "When a Elkins declares war, it's always to a finish! We puts up our weppins only when our last enemy is stretched in their gore!"

The boys had all took refuge under the house, and Uncle Joel seemed to be thinkin' deeply. He said: "I guess yo're right, Breckinridge. I'll write a letter of defiance and send it along with the money to old man Clanton right now."

"Now yo're talkin' with proper spirut!" I approved, shootin' a few winder lights outa the house to ca'm my nerves. "Whilst yo're doin' that I'll be showin' the boys some things about knife throwin'."

Purty soon Uncle Joel come out with a note and the money, and he turned pale when he seen we was usin' his best hat for a target for our knives, but he said nothing. He give Bill the money and the note and I got one of Uncle Joel's white shirts and nailed it to a bean pole for a flag of truce, and Bill sot off.

I got restless purty soon, because it ain't in the nature of a Elkins to sot around waitin' to be attacked. We does the attacking. But the Clantons had scattered and I didn't know whar to look for 'em, and they warn't nothin' to do but wait till they come to us.

I warn't satisfied with the shutters and made the boys taken 'em down and make 'em all over agen, and I kept movin' the bulldog around trying to find the most strategic place for him, and every time Uncle Joel would come onto him onexpected and get bit, he hollered in a way that was plumb disgustin'. His langwidge was somethin' terrible to hear.

Bill was gone a awful long time. I decided the Clantons had violated the flag of truce, and was about to go look for him, when he rode in, pale and excited. He said he give the money and note to the Clantons, and he said he'd discovered whar they was hidin'. He said they was camped in a canyon a few miles south of there, and was aimin' to attack us jest before daylight. Bill said we could sneak up on 'em when night fell, and slaughter 'em all.

I was jubilunt and pleased that he was beginnin' to show some real Garfield spirut at last, so we laid our plans.

Me and Uncle Joel was to sneak down the canyon and attack

'em from the rear, whilst the boys took 'em on the flank. Bill said they was a narrer neck in the canyon jest below whar the Clantons was camped, and him and the other boys would get on the cliffs abouve this neck, and as the Clantons run down it, the boys was to light torches and throw 'em down in the gorge and shoot the Clantons by the light of 'em.

Well, that raised my spirits wonderful, and I was more pleased when Uncle Joel wanted to clean my guns for me. I give 'em to him, and sent the boys off to watch the roads in case the Clantons changed their minds and attacked by daylight. I give the bulldog a big feed of raw beef soaked in whiskey and gunpowder to keep up his fighting spirut, and after he'd broke a tooth off tryin' to bite me, we got to be good friends.

Then I loaded the *escopeta* with a big charge of powder and buckshot and nails, and a few hunks of rock salt for good measure. It wouldn't carry far, but ought to do plenty damage at close range.

I was awful restless and eager for night to come so we could to wipe out all the Clantons, and finally it come and we started. I was ready long before the others, and strapped the *escopeta* to my saddle without sayin' nothing about it because I knowed Uncle Joel was scairt of it.

When we got to the canyon, above whar the Clantons was camped, we split. We all tied our hosses in a thicket, and the boys went along the rim, on foot, to git over the neck below the camp.

Me and Uncle Joel went down into the canyon, and it was so dark we couldn't see nothing except the crests on each side jutting up against the stars. Uncle Joel couldn't even see that I had the *escopeta* slung onto my back. We give the boys plenty of time to git in place, and then we started down the canyon, feelin' our way in the dark.

Uncle Joel made enough noise to wake up a army. I finally made him take of'n his boots, but every time he'd step on a sharp rock he'd moan and cuss, till I told him he was goin' to get us all murdered.

About that time we hit a smooth trail, and he said he'd sneak ahead and see if the Clantons was asleep, and if they was, he'd yap like a coyote. I didn't want to let him, but he insisted, so I stopped and he snuck away in the dark, and after awhile I heard a coyote yelp.

I groped through a narrer gorge and come out into a wider space, and all to onst somebody jerked a blanket off a lantern and blinded me, and a lariat fell around my shoulders, what pinned my arms to my sides. Simultaneous there ariz a wild yell and a wave of dark figgers come surging onto me. I give a roar and broke that lariat like it was a cotton string and grabbed the *escopeta* and let go point-blank. The blast raked the whole gang, and men went down like ten-pins, hollerin' and screechin'. Somebody squawked: "You old fool, I thought you said his guns was empty!" And somebody else howled: "He's got that cussed cannon agen! Grab him before he can reload it!" And then me and the mob was locked in mortal combat, them which was able to lock.

I could hear Uncle Joel yellin' blue murder somewhere, and I didn't draw my pistols because I was afeared I might hit him, because the lantern was smashed and we was fighting in the dark. I waded through that mob with my bare hands, knocking down three and four with every lick, and I gathered as many as I could in my arms and bear-hugged 'em till their ribs caved in, and some I threwed head-on against the cliffs and some I swept the canyon floor with till they was limp.

They was a lot more'n any seven men. The floor was covered with carcasses I kept stumblin' over, and the whole canyon seemed to be full of active humans ragin' for my gore. I thot mebbe the whole country had come to help the Clantons against my helpless relatives, and this favoritism so enraged me I redoubled my efforts and the howls of the stricken ascended to the star-flecked Arizona skies.

Men was shootin' at me in the dark and hitting each other, and trying to pull my legs out from under me and gettin' stomped on, and carvin' each other with their bowies thunking it was me, and finally I found the biggest man in the crowd, to jedge from the heft of him, and I taken him by the ankles and whirled him around my head like a flail and mowed down them idjits in swaths and rows.

So they begun to holler, "Help, murder!" and all stampeded off down the canyon as hard as they could pelt, them which was able to pelt. I throwed my human bludgeon after them, and struck a match to count the dead. The canyon floor was littered with groaning figgers, but I'd evidently put a heavier charge in the *escopeta* than the powder could carry, because them buckshot and nails and things never kilt nobody, though they mussed 'em up considerable.

I found Uncle Joel by follerin' his bellerin'. He was laying onto his stummick, and his howls was frightful to hear. Seems like he'd stopped most of that there rock salt with the seat of his britches.

"Whyn't you tell me you had that cussed blunderbuss?" he demanded feercely. "Lemme lone. I'm dyin', and I wanta die in peace."

I was afeared the Clantons would come back, so I picked him up and packed him to his hoss. I yelled for the boys, but they never answered, so I knowed the Clantons had kilt them, and there were nothin' for us to do but head for the ranch house and make a last stand. Uncle Joel had to lay acrost the saddle onto his belly, and he groaned and wept, and after awhile he got to cussing, and he cussed somethin' horrible.

"Yo're the last of the Garfields, Uncle Joel," I said with emotion. "But don't worry. Yore sons will be avenged. I'll stand by you to the end."

They was no signs of persuit when we got to the ranch house. I left Uncle Joel tryin' to gouge some of the salt outa his hide, and nailed up the shutters and brought in the bulldog and all the rain barrels full of water I could find.

"I'll do the fightin' when they come, Uncle Joel," I said. "You watch when they set the house on fire, and pour water onto it."

He didn't say nothin'. He seemed kinda stunned. Well, I thought, anybody would, getting all his boys wiped out that way. But feuds is like that.

It was jest getting good daylight when I looked out of a upstairs winder, and exclaimed: "Here they come! And by God, they got the army along with 'em!"

I seen the Clantons at the head of the bunch, and with 'em was the sheriff and his deperty, and forty or fifty men, and from their bruised and battered appearance, I jedged they was some of the men what had fought in the canyon. With them was a whole company of cavalrymen from the fort, and three or four hundred people taggin' after 'em, to see the fun, I reckon.

I drawed a bead on old man Clanton for a long shot with my right-hand .45, and when I pulled the trigger everybody ducked and yelled, but he didn't drop, and from the kick of the recoil, I knowed they wasn't no bullet in the cartridge. I begun to frantically throw out the shells, and by golly, both guns was loaded with *blanks!* Jest then I seen Bill, Jim and Joe out in the crowd with the Clantons.

"I demands that you surrender!" roared the sheriff.

"Keep back or I ventilates you!" I roared back, grabbing a Winchester. I turned feercely on Uncle Joel.

"*You* loaded my guns with blanks whilst pertendin' to clean 'em!" I accused. "Air you crazy? And what's yore boys doin' out there?"

At this he kinda flew to pieces.

"Yes, I pulled the bullets outa yore cartridges!" he hollered wildly. "And I went ahead to warn the posse you was comin', you blame' maneyack! When I sent that money back to old man Clanton yesterday, I writ him in that note to rig up some plan with Bill to capture you, and to git the sheriff and a posse, and I'd lead you into their trap."

I glared at him plumb paralyzed.

"*I* didn't wanta fight the Clantons!" he shrieked. "You dragged us into this blame' mess! Yo're a menace to society! Now you lemme outa here!"

"That I should live to hear it!" I said numbly. "To buy a shameful peace you betrays yore nephew like a lamb to the wolves! But won't do. I come here all the way from Nevada to uphold the family honor, and I upholds it in spite of you!"

He sunk down with a low moan, and I heard old man Clanton squalling outside: "Go in and git him, dern it! He wrecked my house and stole my building and mauled my sons nigh to death!"

The sheriff yelled: "Elkins, if you don't come out with yore hands up, we're goin' to storm the house!"

"Come on with yore storm!" I bellered. "It'll run into the damndest mountain cyclone you Arizona sidewinders ever seen!"

I shot off his hat to emphasize my remarks, and some folks started to shootin' at the house.

The captain of the soldiers held up his hand and hollered to me: "Elkins, I'm comin' to talk to you. Don't shoot!"

He rode up under the winder and frowned up at me, and said: "My man, you can't defy the United States army!"

"I ain't yore man!" I bellered. "I'm Breckinridge Elkins, the fightin'est critter what ever come down from the Humbolt Mountains! I can rassle a grizzly, swing a mountain lion by the tail, and give a rattler the first bite! Open the ball whenever yo're ready, you brass-buttoned, tenderfooted maverick! I'll spile them blue-bellied uniforms wuss'n my pap did at Bull Run!"

He turned purple and gasped and sputtered, and jest then a old cuss with grey whiskers come through the crowd and hollered: "I'm the postmaster at Sawtooth. I got a special letter for Breckinridge Elkins."

He sailed her up through the winder and I grabbed her. Then he turned around and very ca'mly rode through the crowd and left. I opened it and read:

Dear Breckinridge:

I been hearin' about you. What in hell are you doin' over there at Sawtooth? Them folks ain't no kin of ourn. They spell it Guarfele. Come on over here whar you belong.

Yore affeckshunate unkle,
Joel Garfield, Rifle River, Arizona.

P.S. We have done run the family we was feudin' with clean out of the country, but come on anyway; I want to see you and so does all the folks.

I stared dizzily at the figger moaning on the floor.

"You ain't the Joel Garfield what come here from Guadalupe County, Texas, in '69?" I gasped.

"Naw, I ain't!" he said feercely. "I'm Joseph L. Guarfele, and I come out here from Kansas, only ten years ago!"

At that I went berserk.

"So you takes advantage of my ignorance!" I raved, hurling his Winchester through a pane of the door in my emotion. "You inveigles me into fightin' yore battles! You grey-whiskered old sarpent, I oughta shoot you for imposin' on a innocent stranger!"

At this he become hysterical and begun to shriek with frightful laughter. I turned from him with a snort of righteous contempt, and yelled down to the captain: "You told me to come out—all right! Here I come!"

I then catapulted myself through the winder and fell astraddle of the captain's hoss, behind the saddle. The critter gasped and went to its knees, but instantly sprung up and bolted. I had the captain around the waist and the soldiers was afeared to shoot at me for fear of hitting him, and I went through that cavalry like a thunderbolt. The general population scattered shrieking as they seen me comin', and in a instant I was through and fogging it acrost the hills.

Them folks which says I stole the captain's hoss is liars. I sent it back later. And it is also a lie that I throwed the captain into a cactus bed when I was out of range of his soldiers. I didn't throw him nowheres. I jest warn't lookin' whar I dropped him, and he oughta have looked whar he fell. All I wanted was to get as far away from Sawtooth and them slimy Guarfeles as I could. They ain't nothin' I hates more'n ingratitude.

CONAN